THE FLORIDA EDITION
OF THE WORKS OF LAURENCE STERNE

Tristram Shandy: The Notes

Laurence Sterne

THE LIFE AND OPINIONS
OF
TRISTRAM SHANDY, GENTLEMAN

Volume III: The Notes

by Melvyn New
with Richard A. Davies and W. G. Day

A University of Florida Book
UNIVERSITY PRESSES OF FLORIDA
Gainesville

The editors are pleased to acknowledge those members of the Advisory Board of the Florida Edition who gave their generous assistance to the production of this volume: Arthur H. Cash, State University College, New Paltz; John M. Stedmond, Queens University; and Ian Watt, Stanford University.

We would also like to thank the National Endowment for the Humanities for its Research Fellowship for Melvyn New in 1980–81; and the Canada Council for its Leave Fellowship for Richard A. Davies in 1976–77 and summer research grants in 1972 and 1975.

Material from *Tristram Shandy*, edited by James Aiken Work (New York: Odyssey Press, 1940), has been quoted with the permission of the Bobbs-Merrill Company, Indianapolis.

University Presses of Florida, the agency of the State of Florida's university system for the publication of scholarly and creative works, operates under the policies adopted by the Board of Regents. Its offices are located at 15 NW 15th Street, Gainesville, Florida 32603.

Library of Congress Cataloging in Publication Data
(Revised for volume III)

Sterne, Laurence, 1713–1768.
  The life and opinions of Tristram Shandy, gentleman.

  (The Florida edition of the works of Laurence
Sterne; v. 1–)
  "A University of Florida book."
  Includes bibliographical references.
  Contents: v. 1–2. Text—v. 3. Notes / by Melvyn New
with Richard A. Davies and W.G. Day.
  I. New, Melvyn. II. New, Joan. III. Title.
IV. Series: Sterne, Laurence, 1713–1768. Works.
1978; v. 1, etc.
PR3710.F78   823'.6   [823'.6]   77-20683
ISBN 0-8130-0580-9 (v. 1)

CONTENTS

INTRODUCTION

Melvyn New

I

Reviewers of the first two volumes of *The Florida Edition of the Works of Laurence Sterne*, the text of *Tristram Shandy* (1978), were momentarily puzzled or amused by the appearance of the "Introduction to the Text" on page 811 of the second volume. In general, it seems to have been taken as a Shandean gesture, a compliment by way of imitation of an author whose own preface does not occur until the twentieth chapter of his third volume. Although I was not unaware of this aspect of having my introduction follow the text, my intention was rather more serious: I wanted to say something about the editor's role in the process of reading—to suggest, paradoxically enough, not the editor's unimportance but his importance. The modern stress on editorial objectivity has tended to suggest that textual introductions are neutral, nonpersuasive entities, and that their placement before a text does not raise the questions of critical mediation that have bedeviled modern literary study. It is a dangerous and deceptive suggestion.

To be sure, the historical information and arcane collations found in the textual introductions and accompanying appendixes of modern editions are not the sort of privileged information that usually calls our attention to the many problems of critical mediation; and indeed, while modern critics have seemed to hobble themselves with self-consciousness, modern editors have proceeded in blissful unconcern about where they stand (figuratively, or in the present instance, literally) in relation to their text. This unconcern has been of especial value to "scientific" editors, those who have continued to posit the possibility of objectivity in literary editing, based upon certain "rules" of procedure and

1

selection. We have in fact witnessed in recent years an interesting phenomenon: as our texts become more and more reliable, as measured by one standard, our critics, using the same standard, have felt less and less confident about interpreting them.

That standard, of course, has to do with meaning—the assertion, no longer simple, that "bear," "bare," "bar" have purposeful significations and that "bre" is an error. The stock-in-trade of the textual editor is the problematic core of modern criticism: the editor must believe that the words of a perfected text are the result of an authorial intention; and he must believe that states of the text exist in which there are "errors"—that is, deviations from that intention. Both beliefs are, critically speaking, naïve, but they are, nonetheless, the basis for all textual preparation; at one time or another, the author, the compositor, the editor, all must make choices that suggest their faith in the power of words to convey the "proper" meaning, meaning "intended" by the author. At the same time, a good reader is constantly questioning the nature and outcome of that faith, in large part through certain questions concerning textual establishment and transmission, composition and revision. Hence, a textual introduction is a particularly privileged document in that it not only explains the grounds of an editor's decisions but, when placed before a text, can predetermine the nature of the reader's questioning. While placing the introduction after the text in no way moderates the critical mediation involved in preparing it, it does allow readers to ask their own questions—and it might, as well, call attention to the premise that a textual introduction is not as neutral as Greg and Bowers might assume.

Having made my gesture to the mediation of the textual editor, what gesture can I make to excuse, much less justify, the intervention of an annotator in this age of deconstructed texts? I immediately feel compelled, for example, to make two negations on behalf of myself and my co-editors, Richard A. Davies and W. G. Day (the collective "we" of this volume): we have not completed the task of annotating *Tristram Shandy*; and we have not begun the task of interpreting it. Let me explain each statement in its turn.

In 1978, while excusing the fact that the annotations were not yet ready to be published, I wrote that "the task of fully annotating *Tristram* has proved to be even more time-consuming than we conceived." It was a careless statement, for in truth the effort to annotate "fully" any worthwhile text is an infinite rather than a time-consuming one; moreover, it is not time but one's annotations that are ultimately consumed, the incompleteness and inadequacy of any given set of notes always increasing with the passage of time. Of course we would hardly care to make this admission were we not both certain of its universality and, frankly, pleased with our efforts within the limitations I am here trying to define. George Steiner writes well about the nature of annotation: "'Looking things up' does not stop because the context pertinent to a major poem or poetic text is that of the whole ambient culture, of the whole history of and in the language of the mental sets and idiosyncrasies in contemporary sensibility. (The issue is philosophically vital: a language-act is inexhaustible to interpretation precisely because its context is the world.) . . . *In practice*, the homework of elucidation may be unending. No individual talent or life-span, no collective industry, can complete the task. But *not in theory, not formally.* . . . Theoretically, there is somewhere a lexicon, a concordance, a manual . . . which will resolve the difficulty. In the 'infinite library' . . . the necessary reference can be found."[1] I shall return in a moment to Steiner's melding of "interpretation" and "elucidation" in this passage, but for the present I want to point out that even in theory one must deny the annotator's capacity to "complete the task." Steiner concentrates on the elusiveness of answers, but just as problematic are the questions one asks of a text, which are not stable but constantly changing. The infinitude of annotation, that is, lies not only in the inexhaustibility of context but as well in the infinite variety of possible readers, both what they will and will not bring to the text.

Let me provide one illustration from the multitude of problems we confronted. It seemed unnecessary to us to annotate the word "pricks" in Sterne's sentence, "the pricks which enter'd the flesh of St. *Radagunda* in the desert, which in your road from FESSE to CLUNY, the nuns of that name will shew you for love."[2] But we did feel compelled to identify St. Radegund, and to provide translations of "Fesse" (which does not seem to have a geographical existence) and "Cluny" (which does). Our notes are, obviously, designed for scholars, but in the actual practice of annotating this passage, what manner of audience have we defined? Quite clearly, it is an audience that can be trusted to recognize a low colloquialism and bit of bawdy byplay, but not one familiar with the *Lives of the Saints,* nor one that can be expected to recognize bilingual puns. Nor is this simply to say that as the work becomes more remote in time from the annotator,

1. *On Difficulty and Other Essays* (New York: Oxford University Press, 1978), pp. 26–27.
2. *The Florida Edition of Tristram Shandy,* ed. Melvyn New and Joan New (Gainesville: University Presses of Florida, 1978), 679.14–16; hereafter cited in text.

more commentary will be required, though there is obviously some truth in that equation. Rather, the point is that questions previously of great concern to readers (e.g., is "dear, dear Jenny" *really* Catherine Fourmantel?) are no longer so, and questions upon which we have spent much effort may quite disappear from the consciousness of future readers. It is not sufficient for the annotator to deplore this or that failure of preparation in his audience; he must, if his annotations are to serve any useful purpose, address precisely those gaps between his author's and his reader's knowledge, aware always of his limited capacity to anticipate future gaps.

Needless to say, our annotations are incomplete for far less theoretical reasons. Too many notes, unfortunately, are negative statements: "we were unable to locate," "we do not know," "we cannot explain." In other instances, we shall be corrected and embellished many times over in the near future, if only because our annotations will call attention to problems for which other scholars already have explanations, drawn from their own forays into the inexhaustible context of any literary work. In addition, although we had valuable periods of study at the major collections in American and British libraries while gathering these notes, the final text was prepared at the University of Florida; and it is during the period of final editorial work that the great advantage of constant access to the British Library or the Beinecke becomes most apparent. What one wants most is the opportunity to browse amidst a multitude of works on the same subject, especially when the works already consulted just fail to parallel or elucidate a particular passage. Nonetheless, we owe especial thanks to the University of Florida, which has put considerable resources over the past decade into building a collection quite purposively directed toward the Sternean context.

Our failure to complete the annotations to *Tristram Shandy* is complemented by our failure to begin an analysis of it, or even to record the variety of analyses as a variorum edition might have done. Quite to the contrary, we have tried, with all due consciousness, to maintain a distinction between elucidation and interpretation, both in our own contributions and in what we have preserved from the abundant commentary that has drifted down the gutter of time with *Tristram*. It might be expected that the experience of annotation would have taught us the impossibility of the distinction, but quite the contrary is the case: I believe we were all healthily skeptical of the distinction before we started and are certain only now, having written our notes, that it does indeed exist, albeit with boundaries easily blurred, easily overlooked, easily forgotten. Most important, we have become convinced that it is a distinction every editor must study to preserve.

The foremost problem is that editors, quite naturally, want to respond to a text precisely as do other readers, by trying to interpret it, that is, by incorporating it into their own coherent (self-satisfying) systems of order and belief. Moreover, that system is bound to exercise a considerable influence over the questions one asks about a text, so that the process of annotation is intricately linked to the interpretative urge, which is also a series of questions and answers. I say *intricately* and not *inextricably*, however, for a strong measure of self-awareness and a consistent concern with the problem can allow the editor to untangle at least some of the linkages and to establish patterns of annotative commentary that work to keep elucidation and interpretation apart. Two brief examples of where this has not been done should suffice to illustrate the problem.

The first is Martin Battestin's Riverside textbook edition of *Joseph Andrews*.[3] I have a good deal of respect for Battestin's earlier interpretation of that work,[4] and I believe I approach his belated defense of his annotating practice, "A Rationale of Literary Annotation: The Example of Fielding's Novels,"[5] with the sympathy of a practicing annotator. Nevertheless, the substance of Arthur Sherbo's testy attack on Battestin's editing remained very much in our minds as we annotated *Tristram*, and I hope we profited from it.[6] Central to Sherbo's concern, and to my own, is that Battestin used his introduction and notes not to probe the infinite context of *Joseph Andrews*, but rather to introduce readers to the very finite context of certain sermons and sermon-writers, religious and moral ideas, that Battestin had found useful in closing the work to his own (and others') satisfaction. In marking the boundary between elucidation and inter-

3. Boston: Houghton Mifflin Company, 1961.

4. *The Moral Basis of Fielding's Art: A Study of Joseph Andrews* (Middletown, Conn.: Wesleyan University Press, 1959).

5. *SB* 34 (1981): 1–22.

6. Arthur Sherbo, "The 'Moral Basis' of *Joseph Andrews*," in *Studies in the Eighteenth Century English Novel* (East Lansing: Michigan State University Press, 1969), pp. 104–19. Battestin's introduction and notes to *Joseph Andrews* (Middletown, Conn.: Wesleyan University Press, 1967) and *Tom Jones* (Middletown, Conn.: Wesleyan University Press, 1975) are far less vulnerable to Sherbo's complaints, it should be noted; but see also John Middendorf's comments in *JNL* 35 (1975): 2.

pretation, one key distinction that proves useful is whether the commentary tries to satisfy the reader's need to close a work, or leaves the reader in a continuing state of mild irritability and unrest, because the commentary has provided the recognizable tools for multiple closures, but not the directions. Battestin's annotations try to satisfy; sometimes they will, often they will not. Our annotations, on the contrary, try to establish the groundwork for further inquiry; sometimes they will, often they will not. But where we are disappointed if the reader can find nothing to do with our commentary, no interpretation to be made based upon it, Battestin's disappointment would seem just the opposite, the feeling of failure when the reader refuses to rest with the interpretation inherent in his annotation.

A second example, closer to home, is Gardner D. Stout's edition of *A Sentimental Journey.*[7] We have here an approach seemingly quite different from Battestin's, in that Stout takes a noncommittal, "objective" stand on the issues of the work—a very "proper" annotator's stance. But Stout is far from uncommitted or objective; rather, he has closed the work in his own mind within the parameters of romantic irony, where all differences and distinctions, contrasts and conflicts, are subsumed as acceptable, compatible elements of a diversified whole. Stout's noncommittal annotations (and, as well, the annotations he does not write, most especially those required to elucidate the intricacies of Sterne's bawdy texture) work to inhibit all other readings, all the more because romantic irony is a uniquely satisfying reading for the secularist systems of the twentieth century. Stout's interpretation provides the rationale for a set of notes that are highly selective and highly interpretative; they tend, above all, to assert the innocence of the text, which, when dealing with Sterne, is a major interpretative statement.

One cannot, of course, simply declare one's annotations to be elucidatory rather than interpretative, and indeed even one's best efforts in this direction can often go astray. But certainly it helps to remain aware of the distinction and to establish certain guidelines and practices that might help to maintain it. Indeed, the first rule of annotation might well be taken from John della Casa's theory of composition, as delineated by Tristram: it is not "half so much" the annotator's Wit as his Resistance that must be exercised. For example, when research dis-

---

7. Berkeley: University of California Press, 1967.

covers that the two most pervasive texts layered into Sterne's "Abuses" sermon are sermons by Swift, one is sorely tempted to interpret; surely such a borrowing has "significance." Instead, we have simply provided the long parallel passages in the notes to elucidate the text; the interpretation must be found in the work of those who set out to explore the meanings of Sterne's interest in the language and ideas of Swift's sermons. Similarly, we have noted with diligence not only Sterne's echoes of Locke's *Essay Concerning Human Understanding* but as well some heretofore unnoted parallels to his *Some Thoughts Concerning Education;* we do not, however, trace the arguments of Traugott or Tuveson, Mac-Lean or Moglen, in their respective efforts to shape a meaning for *Tristram Shandy* around the Locke-Sterne nexus.[8] Our annotations are neither substitutes for nor summaries of previous interpretative work, nor are they interpretations in their own right. The interpretation of *Tristram Shandy* remains the work of every reader, who must, among the other tasks of intellectual quest and satisfaction, measure his efforts against those of readers before him.

II

Our annotations may be divided into four different groups, indicative of four different relationships that the text of *Tristram* has with its context: (A) its relationship to other writings by Sterne and, more broadly, to the events and experiences of his life; (B) its relationship to language, both that of the eighteenth century and of our own; (C) its relationship to authors and texts prior to and contemporary with it; and (D) its relationship to ideas, again both prior to and contemporary with Sterne's age. The distinction between (C) and (D), authors/texts and ideas, is, in all likelihood, an untenable one, but we have found it useful to distinguish between those authors/texts that Sterne certainly knew and loved, and what we might call his "index learning," his use of encyclopedias and other works of "reference," from which he borrowed not only

8. Respectively, John Traugott, *Tristram Shandy's World: Sterne's Philosophical Rhetoric* (Berkeley: University of California Press, 1954); Ernest Tuveson, "Locke and Sterne," in *Reason and the Imagination: Studies in the History of Ideas, 1600–1800,* ed. J. A. Mazzeo (New York: Columbia University Press, 1962), pp. 255–77; Kenneth MacLean, *John Locke and English Literature of the Eighteenth Century* (New Haven: Yale University Press, 1936); Helene Moglen, *The Philosophical Irony of Laurence Sterne* (Gainesville: University Presses of Florida, 1975).

ideas but as well the names of the authors who promulgated them. It is, at any rate, a distinction of convenience rather than of principle. I shall comment upon the four relationships in turn.

A. *Tristram Shandy* and Sterne.—We have considered any passage in Sterne's canon that parallels the language of a passage in *Tristram Shandy* a worthwhile elucidation of the text. Included in this category, of course, are passages in *Tristram* that echo other passages, and indeed we have tried to call attention to as many of these as possible. The serial nature of the work's publication makes such observations all the more important, and without doubt Sterne thumbed the pages of earlier volumes in 1764 and 1766, in order to create at least some appearance of continuity in his eight-year project. Our efforts to locate these parallels were greatly assisted by a machine-produced concordance for *Tristram,* prepared as a doctoral dissertation by Patricia Graves.[9] For the remainder of Sterne's canon we used Stout's edition of *Sentimental Journey,* again aided by a concordance;[10] the very fine edition of the letters by Lewis Perry Curtis;[11] the first edition of the seven volumes of sermons, published between 1760 and 1769; and the first or best edition available for his few miscellaneous pieces.[12]

More difficult, of course, is the attempt to elucidate a passage in *Tristram Shandy* by means of another passage in the canon similar in "thought." The difficulty—and the danger—of this endeavor is especially apparent in glossing a passage by means of the sermons, for doing so seems to imply a failure to distinguish between the intention and idiom of sermons and those of "literary" works. It is our belief, however, that this implication is a temporary aberration of mid-twentieth-century criticism of eighteenth-century literature, which has developed a particular tendency to locate the meaning of this literature in certain contemporary theological issues—and hence has provoked a counter-tendency to avoid sermons as of absolutely no value in the critical process. But while one

9. "A Computer-Generated Concordance to Sterne's *Tristram Shandy,*" 4 vols. (Ph.D. diss., Emory University, 1974).

10. Betty B. Pasta, David J. Pasta, and John R. Pasta, "A Short Concordance to Laurence Sterne's *A Sentimental Journey . . . ,*" 2 vols.; limited publication through the Department of Computer Science, University of Illinois at Urbana-Champaign, 1974.

11. Oxford: Clarendon Press, 1935; hereafter, *Letters.*

12. Most especially, the Scolar Press facsimile edition of *A Political Romance* (Menston, England, 1971); and the "Rabelaisian Fragment," ed. Melvyn New (*PMLA* 87 [1972]: 1083–92).

must be particularly obtuse not to acknowledge that *Tristram Shandy* is not a sermon, one must be equally obtuse to ignore the opportunity provided by Sterne's sermons (the only significant body of writings he produced prior to his great fiction), to note language and ideas anticipated in them.

Equally dangerous to the annotator is the critical (interpretative) tendency to define meaning through the establishment of connections and interlockings within a given text; in many respects modern criticism, in its formalist aspects, is precisely this, an argument for a particular way to combine selected passages of a text which are then offered as "evidences" for a reading of the entire text. The annotator must be particularly wary of this procedure; on the one hand, certain passages in a text do elucidate other passages through their proximity of language, tone, style, content; on the other hand, proximity is often created through the mediation of an interpretative perspective, one that only the variorum annotator can afford to note. We have tried to distinguish between these two occasions, not always successfully I am sure. But the effort has led to one practice that may seem rather unfortunate, namely, that we often direct attention to a verbal borrowing of three or four words, while ignoring what many readers would perceive as far more significant linkages—for example, Sterne's play with time in the Shandy parlor (vol. II, chap. 8) and in Auxerre (vol. VII, chap. 28). Hence, we may provide the full content of a note from, say, *Notes and Queries*, but we do not follow the arguments of Stedmond, New, or Swearingen[13] as we (and they) proceed through the work. Where the linking of passages would require an interpretation, a critical response, we have not linked them; where, conversely, the reason for comparison seems self-explanatory, and when a critical response can be localized or confined to a particular passage, we have made due note. We have been flexible enough to ensure that almost every major essay on *Tristram Shandy* (and a considerable number of minor ones as well) is cited at least once in the notes, often connected rather arbitrarily to the one particular passage that we felt most central to the essay's argument. But our notes are hardly a substitute for reading these essays and even less a substitute for the full-length studies that simply must be read in their entirety in order to be understood.

13. John M. Stedmond, *The Comic Art of Laurence Sterne* (Toronto: University of Toronto Press, 1967); Melvyn New, *Laurence Sterne as Satirist: A Reading of "Tristram Shandy"* (Gainesville: University of Florida Press, 1969); James Swearingen, *Reflexivity in "Tristram Shandy": An Essay in Phenomenological Criticism* (New Haven: Yale University Press, 1977).

We have also tried to elucidate *Tristram Shandy* by means of the events and experiences of Sterne's life. While every work of art invites this foolhardy enterprise, few are more inviting than *Tristram*, the author of which often signed himself "Tristram," and in the course of which not one but two characters (at least) vie for identification with him. Our work was made considerably easier because of Arthur Cash's excellent biography of the years up to 1759; his judicious suggestions of where the intersections of the text and life might profitably be explored guided us far better than the earlier biography by Wilbur Cross, in which lengthy passages from *Tristram* are often simply spliced into the biographical narrative.[14] In addition, Curtis's *Letters* and his notes to them were invaluable for this aspect of annotation. I do suspect our notes will better please those who are suspicious of the relationship between biography and the literary work than those who welcome it in all its multiple and complex possibilities. This seems, however, less the result of any predilection on our part than, once again, of the difference between elucidation and interpretation.

B. *Tristram Shandy* and language.—Our annotations in this category begin with the most basic elucidation of all, the definition of single words, never a simple task. Our first rule was to rely upon the *Oxford English Dictionary* (*OED*), supplemented on a handful of occasions by Johnson's *Dictionary* and the *English Dialect Dictionary* (*EDD*). Because of the significant frequency of citation to *Tristram*, we have tried to note every word that serves the *OED* as the initial, sole, or final illustration; we have been able to make a few corrections to the *OED*'s entries and to note several omissions, but of course any extended time spent in its pages can only produce awe. One particular set of terms, the vocabulary of eighteenth-century fortification, has been gathered in a glossary, and Chambers's *Cyclopædia*[15] rather than the *OED* has been used to supply definitions; Sterne seems to have gathered these terms from Chambers.

Our second rule, by way of defining an audience for this category of elucidation, was to define no word recorded in the *Shorter Oxford English Dictionary* (*SOED*), which we took to be the desktop dictionary of a scholarly

14. Arthur Cash, *Laurence Sterne: The Early and Middle Years* (London: Methuen & Co., 1975); Wilbur L. Cross, *The Life and Times of Laurence Sterne*, 3d ed. (New Haven: Yale University Press, 1929).

15. Ephraim Chambers, *Cyclopædia: or, an Universal Dictionary of Arts and Sciences*, 5th ed., 2 vols. (1741, 1743).

audience. Hence, while James Work and Ian Watt[16] probably define more words than we do (though both are rather inconsistent), it should be recalled that they address primarily a student audience.

Some of our scholarly audience will, I am afraid, be insulted by our effort to translate all foreign-language phrases and passages in *Tristram Shandy* and in our notes as well. Others, however, will be grateful. I take this occasion to pay particular thanks to several people who aided us in this work of translation, most particularly at the University of Florida: Richard Green, Marjorie Malvern, Albert B. Smith, and Douglas Bonneville. In the case of classical sources, we have used, wherever possible, the Loeb Classical Library texts and translations. Where a foreign phrase is not translated, one may assume that its English meaning is provided very close by in the text.

Certain combinations of words have come down to us as recorded proverbs or proverbial phrases, and we have tried to record as many of them as we could catch in *Tristram*. Our practice has been to note a record of the phrase in two collections, usually Morris Palmer Tilley's *A Dictionary of the Proverbs in England in the Sixteenth and Seventeenth Centuries* and the *Oxford Dictionary of English Proverbs*. We have also consulted Burton Stevenson's *Macmillan Book of Proverbs*.[17] There is probably no end to this sort of notation, but our work does seem to indicate a texture more than ordinarily embedded with proverbial and catch phrases and hence these notes may provide a worthwhile entrance into Sterne's style and meaning. Most particularly, we call attention to Sterne's penchant for informing the stale phrase with new potential, nowhere more humorously perhaps than in his "cock and bull" story in the very last chapter.

The most troublesome aspect of annotating Sterne's language is suggested by the observation that by "nose" Sterne rarely means simply "nose." There is throughout the work, as has often been noted, a dazzling display of the eccentric, indeed explosive orbit of the individual word and of words in contexts. For the annotator the fundamental concern is to avoid stumbling over the reader or, conversely, having the reader stumble over him. When, for example, the dig-

16. I.e., in their respective textbook editions for Odyssey Press (1940) and Houghton Mifflin's Riverside Press (1965).

17. Morris Palmer Tilley, *A Dictionary of the Proverbs in England in the Sixteenth and Seventeenth Centuries* (Ann Arbor: University of Michigan Press, 1950); *Oxford Dictionary of English Proverbs*, 3d ed. rev. by F. P. Wilson (Oxford: Clarendon Press, 1970); Burton Stevenson, *Macmillan Book of Proverbs* (New York: Macmillan, 1948).

nitaries of Strasbourg gather to consider a case of "butter'd buns," a note calling attention to a past sexual association seems obviously called for, and both Francis Grose, *A Classical Dictionary of the Vulgar Tongue* (1785), and Eric Partridge, *A Dictionary of Slang and Unconventional English* (1970), have served us well.[18] But a few pages later, when in Diego's song Sterne writes *"Her hand alone can touch the part,"* do we call attention to "part"; or do we assume a reader competent to realize the innuendo? We have, almost always, chosen the latter course, with the loss perhaps of some wit, but with the reader's concupiscent inclinations left, we hope, intact. Where the punning is particularly difficult, particularly dated, or particularly obscure, we have tried to assist the scholarly reader—that is, the reader who enters *Tristram Shandy* with the knowledge that the language is replete with sexual ambiguities and allusions. Perhaps Robert Gorham Davis, "Sterne and the Delineation of the Modern Novel," has put this aspect of Sterne most succinctly: "Sterne . . . is as insistent as the most orthodox Freudian on the fact that for some imaginations at some times every straight object, every stick, candle, wick, nose can stand for the male genital, and every hole, slit, crevice and curve, for the female . . . ."[19] In this wilderness, as Sterne himself might have warned, the annotator had best proceed with caution.

Terms from rhetoric, medicine, law, and other specialized areas are very often defined in the *SOED*. Where that is not the case, or where a definition helps to define a particular source or particular purpose, we have provided one, usually from a source that Sterne himself might have consulted.

C. *Tristram Shandy* and authors and texts.—Sterne's relationship to other authors and works, as might be expected, has been one of the primary concerns of commentators since the first two volumes appeared in December 1759. One

18. Francis Grose, *A Classical Dictionary of the Vulgar Tongue* (London, 1785; Menston, England: Scolar Press, 1968); Eric Partridge, *A Dictionary of Slang and Unconventional English*, 7th ed. (New York: Macmillan, 1970).

19. In *The Winged Skull: Papers from the Laurence Sterne Bicentenary Conference* (Kent, Ohio: Kent State University Press, 1971), p. 35. Excellent preparation for reading Sterne in this light is provided by three essays in particular: Robert Alter, *"Tristram Shandy* and the Game of Love," *ASch* 37 (1968): 316–23; Frank Brady, *"Tristram Shandy:* Sexuality, Morality, and Sensibility," *ECS* 4 (1970): 41–56; Eric Rothstein, *Systems of Order and Inquiry in Later Eighteenth-Century Fiction* (Berkeley: University of California Press, 1975), pp. 62–108. See also Robert Donovan, *The Shaping Vision: Imagination in the English Novel from Defoe to Dickens* (Ithaca, N.Y.: Cornell University Press, 1966), p. 93: "Throughout the novel . . . we are confronted by cant and jargon words and the special vocabularies of law, medicine, mathematics, rhetoric, and military science . . . .

of the first responses, for example, was that of the unsigned notice in the *London Magazine* in February 1760: "Oh rare Tristram Shandy! . . . what shall we call thee?—Rabelais, Cervantes, What?" [20] For the annotator, however, such generalized affinities must give way to the more concrete—and more treacherous—relationship variously identified as a "borrowing," a "verbal echo," or, unsympathetically, a "steal." [21] The fabric of *Tristram* is richly interwoven with the texts of other writers, on some occasions set off in a most ostentatious manner, as in the verbatim quoting of the "Memoir of the Doctors of the Sorbonne" (vol. I, chap. 20) or "Ernulphus's Curse" (vol. III, chap. 11); on other occasions the borrowings were masked, but quickly discerned by Sterne's earliest readers and the succession of commentators and annotators since; and, on more than a few occasions, they have been buried until this present edition.

The following discussion of Sterne's major sources makes no effort to analyze the significance of any particular relationship. Rather, the separation between interpretation and elucidation must begin here. Each relationship is discussed with an emphasis on primary and secondary bibliographical information. The text Sterne probably used, and the commentators who have previously discussed the debt, are the issues raised. The authors are discussed alphabetically to avoid any sense of priority. It should be noted that we have not relied on one source often invoked in discussions of this sort, namely the "catalogue" of Sterne's library, published by Todd and Sotheran of York in 1768. For several reasons, the catalogue was discounted: it contains books from other libraries

---

We feel always that Tristram, and through him Sterne, is attempting to stretch the fabric of language to its utmost extent."

20. Extract from an unsigned notice in the *London Magazine* 29 (February 1760): 111; quoted in Alan B. Howes, *Sterne: The Critical Heritage* (London: Routledge & Kegan Paul, 1974), p. 52. See also Howes, *Yorick and the Critics: Sterne's Reputation in England, 1760–1868* (New Haven: Yale University Press, 1958), pp. 13–14 and passim.

21. The first to exhibit a scholarly interest in Sterne's borrowings and, in so doing, establish to some extent his nineteenth-century reputation as a "plagiarist," was the Manchester physician Dr. John Ferriar. Beginning with an address to the Literary and Philosophical Society of Manchester in 1791 (published in the Society's *Memoirs* [1793], IV: 45–86), Ferriar pursued Sterne throughout the next twenty years, concluding with the second edition of *Illustrations of Sterne* in 1812 (the first edition was published in 1798). In the annotations we have consistently cited Ferriar from his final statement in the 1812 edition. For an account of Ferriar's findings and shifting attitude toward them, see Howes, *Yorick and the Critics*, pp. 81–88, and H. J. Jackson, "Sterne, Burton, and Ferriar: Allusions to the *Anatomy of Melancholy* in Volumes Five to Nine of *Tristram Shandy*," *PQ* 54 (1975): 457–70.

as well as Sterne's; it does not contain all his books; it does not account for the probability that Sterne had access to a library far larger than his own, namely the York Minster Library; and finally, it probably contains the 700 books Sterne bought in July 1761 but did not, in all likelihood, have time to examine.[22] Thus, we have found the evidence of parallel passages and Sterne's own comments upon his reading far more reliable indices than the "Unique Catalogue."

(1) Robert Burton (1577–1640). It was John Ferriar who first noticed the extensive borrowing by Sterne from the *Anatomy of Melancholy*, especially in Walter's funeral oration (vol. V, chap. 3). What is perhaps most noteworthy about the relationship is that Sterne never mentions Burton by name, either in *Tristram Shandy* or in his letters or other works, as opposed to the numerous references to other favorites, Cervantes, Locke, Montaigne, Rabelais. It should be pointed out, however, that the second motto to vol. V, with its allusion to Democritus (*"non Ego, sed Democritus dixit"*), is probably Sterne's own playful acknowledgment of his debt to "Democritus Junior," Burton's pseudonym; and, indeed, the two mottoes attributed to Erasmus and Horace, Sterne actually lifted from the *Anatomy*'s prefatory "Democritus to the Reader." We have used the fifth edition (1638), the last published during Burton's lifetime; it contains a passage that Sterne borrowed for his discussion of the dimensions of hell (vol. VII, chap. 14), not present in the first four editions. A check of the texts of borrowed passages in later editions did not establish any better claim than that of the fifth.

The most substantial discussion of Sterne's debt to Burton is that by H. J. Jackson in 1975.[23] In addition to recounting Ferriar's work, Jackson notes addi-

---

22. In 1930 Charles Whibley published a facsimile of the catalogue under the title *A Facsimile Reproduction of a Unique Catalogue of Laurence Sterne's Library*. W. G. Day, "Sterne's Books," *Library* 31 (1976): 245–48, establishes the fact that the catalogue does not contain the entire library. Cash, *Early and Middle Years*, pp. 203–5, discusses the Minster Library and also the 700 books: "Knowing how hard he worked during the few remaining years, how much he travelled and how often he was ill, it is difficult to imagine his reading many of them"; see *Letters*, p. 142. It has often been suggested that Sterne also had access to a large collection of books at John Hall-Stevenson's Skelton Castle; Cash, p. 194, notes that Ferriar first suggested this "good hypothesis," but also that no "documentary evidence" exists to support it.

23. Jackson, "Sterne, Burton, and Ferriar." We might note that Work also calls attention to many of the borrowings from Burton. Cf. Cross, p. 147: "The scholar that most fascinated Sterne was Robert Burton . . . ."

tional borrowings, the most significant of which is that from Burton's diatribe against war, which Sterne uses for Uncle Toby's "Apologetical Oration" (vol. VI, chap. 32). Jackson also makes the important point that Sterne's use of the *Anatomy* was at the very beginning of a revival of interest in it, so that it was a more esoteric source for Sterne than we might otherwise presume.

We have indicated several additional borrowings not previously noted; and we have used the *Anatomy* on occasion to elucidate Sterne's "science," which was often deliberately anachronistic, and best illuminated by a text from the seventeenth century rather than the eighteenth. Given the nature of the *Anatomy*, its rich layers upon layers of learning and digression, its overwhelming thoroughness and intricacy of detail, it is more than likely that further borrowings will be uncovered in time; the same can be said, of course, of the other works most important to Sterne, all of which seem to share what I have elsewhere called the "exuberance of wit." [24]

(2) Miguel de Cervantes (1547–1616). Sterne's debt to *Don Quixote* is self-avowed on numerous occasions, most dramatically perhaps near the end of *Tristram* (vol. IX, chap. 24), where he turns to Cervantes for inspiration: "GENTLE Spirit of sweetest humour, who erst didst sit upon the easy pen of my beloved CERVANTES . . ." (780.1–2). Almost always Sterne identifies a borrowing from *Quixote*, usually by specific reference to the hero, or Sancho, or, in vol. I, to Rozinante. Some borrowings are of sufficient length to establish, without reasonable doubt, that Sterne used the Motteux-Ozell translation rather than Thomas Shelton's, as Wilbur Cross believed,[25] or the more recently published translation by Charles Jarvis (1749). We have used the seventh edition, published in 1743, on the strength of an additional Ozell footnote, not in the earliest editions, that Sterne seems definitely to have appropriated; see the note to 180.25–28.

Work makes note of the most significant borrowings from Cervantes, and Gardner Stout[26] points to several more. We also have been able to add to the list. The relationship between the two authors has been mentioned by a host of

24. "Sterne, Warburton, and the Burden of Exuberant Wit," *ECS* 15 (1982): 245–74.
25. Cross, *Life*, p. 140.
26. "Some Borrowings in Sterne from Rabelais and Cervantes," *ELN* 3 (1965): 111–18. Joseph R. Jones, "Two Notes on Sterne: Spanish Sources. The Hinde Tradition," *RLC* 46 (1972): 437–44, suggests that Sterne borrowed from Fernández de Avellaneda's continuation of *Don Quixote*, but his evidence is unconvincing and we have found no further indications of influence.

commentators, but certainly Stuart Tave's discussion in *The Amiable Humorist* and Wayne Booth's in "The Self-Conscious Narrator in Comic Fiction before *Tristram Shandy*" remain the most outstanding.[27] Booth's comment in particular that "*Don Quixote* is really the first important novel using the self-conscious narrator" (p. 165) opens a large area of investigation that we have been unable to pursue as fully as one might wish. While the content of a particular Shandean intrusion might find a definite verbal echo in Cervantes, Rabelais, Fielding, or John Dunton, and hence warrant annotation, the pervasiveness of the self-conscious voice before Sterne makes it quite impossible to attribute most such passages to any one source; and indeed, more often than not, it is the tone, the attitude of voice that is the binding tie of these works, and not content at all. That is to say, Booth's comment that "every form of intrusion in *Tristram Shandy* is, I think, available in Fielding's works" (pp. 176–77), rather than allowing us to document the relationship, renders it a problem for interpretation. This is why, I might note, Cervantes does not appear as prominently as others in the annotations, even though he may well be Sterne's primary influence; and why Fielding, a similarly influential figure, is cited only rarely.

(3) John Locke (1632–1704). Without doubt, the influence of Locke's *Essay Concerning Human Understanding* (1690)[28] is the intertextual problem that has most engaged modern readers in their discussions of *Tristram Shandy*. John Traugott's *Tristram Shandy's World: Sterne's Philosophical Rhetoric* remains the most detailed attempt to work out the relationship, but one should also consult the discussions by Kenneth MacLean, Ernest Tuveson, Arthur Cash, and Helene Moglen, among others.[29]

We have approached this influence most cautiously in our annotations, limiting ourselves almost solely to definite verbal echoes of Locke's *Essay*, to most of which Sterne himself calls attention. It should be noted, whatever the significance finally assigned to Locke, that Sterne rather consistently dwells upon a few very famous and often-quoted passages from a very popular work. Hence, it is not simply fortuitous that Jean-Claude Sallé finds in the *Spectator* a

27. Respectively: Chicago: University of Chicago Press, 1960, especially chap. 7; and *PMLA* 67 (1952): 163–85. See also Anthony Close, *The Romantic Approach to "Don Quixote"* (Cambridge: Cambridge University Press, 1978), pp. 1–28.

28. We have cited the modern edition by Peter H. Nidditch (Oxford: Clarendon Press, 1975).

29. For Traugott, MacLean, Tuveson, and Moglen, see n. 8. For Cash, see "The Lockean Psychology of *Tristram Shandy*," *ELH* 22 (1955): 125–35.

source for Sterne on Lockean duration, or that I discuss the availability of the same material in Henry Baker's *The Microscope Made Easy* (1742);[30] or that many of the passages of the *Essay* to which Sterne calls attention appear verbatim in Chambers's *Cyclopædia*, under such headings as *Time, Duration, Idea*, etc. Certainly from an annotator's perspective there is little reason to support Cash's assertion—a commonplace in modern commentary—that "the book which Sterne studied most carefully, which he read and reread all of his life, the book which informed all of his work, sermons and novels, was John Locke's *Essay* . . . ."[31] Perhaps the annotator's perspective is simply too limited, but it is worth remembering that few if any literary works in the eighteenth century do not show the influence of Locke's empiricism and sensationalism, especially in fiction; and that few if any problems have more exercised modern critics than that of the relationship between philosophy and literature. That we cannot even settle the most basic problem of whether Sterne agrees or disagrees with Locke is perhaps a strong indication that the question has not yet been asked in a manner that could produce a satisfying answer.[32]

In addition to providing as extensive a record as possible of Sterne's use of the *Essay*, we have also noted similarities to *Some Thoughts Concerning Education* (1693). While we cannot be convinced that Sterne actually knew this work, its influence was widespread in the century and it does have interesting points of confluence with various statements concerning Tristram's education.[33] Finally, Sterne's use of the politics of Sir Robert Filmer in vol. I, chap. 18, and vol. V, chaps. 31–32, discussed in a brief essay by Wilfred Watson, has been considered in the annotations primarily as borrowing from Locke's response to Filmer in his *Two Treatises of Government* (1690).[34]

(4) Michel de Montaigne (1533–92). Sterne had two translations of

30. Respectively, "A Source of Sterne's Conception of Time," *RES*, n.s. 6 (1955): 180–82; and "Laurence Sterne and Henry Baker's *The Microscope Made Easy*," *SEL* 10 (1970): 591–604.

31. *Early and Middle Years*, p. 205.

32. See, for example, Mark Loveridge, *Laurence Sterne & the Argument about Design* (Totowa, N.J.: Barnes and Noble Books, 1982), pp. 129–50.

33. Lansing Van der Heyden Hammond, *Laurence Sterne's "Sermons of Mr. Yorick"* (New Haven: Yale University Press, 1948), pp. 140–41, calls attention to a "borrowing," but it is quite dubious. We have cited the modern edition of *Concerning Education* by James L. Axtell, *The Educational Writings of John Locke* (Cambridge: Cambridge University Press, 1968).

34. "The Fifth Commandment; Some Allusions to Sir Robert Filmer's Writings in *Tristram Shandy*," *MLN* 62 (1947): 234–40. We have used Peter Laslett's modern edition for the Cambridge University Press, 1966.

Montaigne's *Essais* available to him, that by John Florio in 1603 and a later one by Charles Cotton in 1685. The borrowings clearly indicate that he used Cotton's version. There were at least seven editions published before 1760,[35] but we can argue with some certainty only that Sterne used the third (1700) or a later one, since he seems to have used the "Table" added to it and subsequent editions. We have used the fifth edition of 1738, which was also "corrected and amended," according to its title-page.

The influence of Montaigne is pervasive upon Sterne, as was noticed by one of his earliest admirers, the Reverend Robert Brown, who wrote to John Hall-Stevenson in 1760: "I would lay too, that he is no stranger to Montaigne; nay that he is full as well acquainted with him, as with the book of common prayer . . . ."[36] Sterne responded to Brown soon thereafter: "You are absolutely right in most of your conjectures about me . . . . [As] 'for my conning Montaigne as much as my pray'r book'—there you are right again,—but mark, . . . I have not said I admire him as much;—tho' had he been alive, I would certainly have gone twice as far to have smoakd a pipe with him, as with Arch-Bishop Laud . . . ."[37] Sterne identifies most of his borrowings from Montaigne, and we have uncovered several additional ones. Our work was completed before the appearance of Jonathan Lamb's rambling essay "Sterne's Use of Montaigne"; its length unfortunately is not compensated by insight.[38] More valuable is Howard Anderson's earlier essay "Associationism and Wit in *Tristram Shandy*,"[39] to which Lamb seems to add little of substance.

We should note here Sterne's borrowing from Pierre Charron's *De la sagesse* (1601), translated by Samson Lennard before 1612. The debt is convincingly demonstrated by Françoise Pellan, "Laurence Sterne's Indebtedness to Charron."[40] Charron was a disciple of Montaigne and at times simply paraphrased his work; but without doubt in the concluding pages of *Tristram* (vol.

35. Based on the inconclusive inventory of the *National Union Catalogue*. Along with Ferriar, one of the first to call attention to Sterne's debt to Montaigne was William Jackson, *The Four Ages* (London, 1798), pp. 244–57.

36. *Letters*, p. 432.

37. *Letters*, pp. 121–22.

38. *CL* 32 (1980): 1–41.

39. *PQ* 48 (1969): 27–41.

40. *MLR* 67 (1972): 752–55. We have used the facsimile edition of Lennard's translation, *Of Wisdome*, in *The English Experience*, no. 315 (New York: Da Capo Press, 1971).

IX, chap. 33) and perhaps in the opening pages as well, Sterne copies from *Of Wisdom* rather than from Montaigne's "Upon Some Verses of Virgil," Charron's source. Lamb's failure to consult Pellan's essay led him to a different—and wrong—conclusion (pp. 28–29), although obviously the spirit of Montaigne hovers pervasively in Charron, and hence in Sterne, even when Sterne is borrowing verbatim from the latter.

(5) François Rabelais (c. 1494–1553). There is no author that Sterne plundered more than Rabelais, and perhaps none with whom he identified more fully. From the initial false start of *Tristram Shandy*, which survives as the "Rabelaisian Fragment," to the obvious similitude between Pantagruelism and Shandeism, to Yorick's habit of carrying *Gargantua* in his "right-hand coat pocket" (463.9), one is constantly aware of Sterne's pervasive debt to—and celebration of—the Rabelais he knew, the extraordinary translation by Thomas Urquhart and Peter Motteux, elucidated by the annotative gambols of John Ozell. We have used a "new edition" published in 1750; the first edition had been published twelve years earlier.

It was Diderot who paid Sterne the compliment "Ce livre si fou, si sage et si gai est le Rabelais des Anglois. . . . Il est impossible de vous en donner une autre idée que celle d'une satyre universelle";[41] and numerous contemporaries of Sterne echoed the idea, some in praise, others in wrath. Ferriar again led the search for particular borrowings, but perhaps the most interesting such collection is to be found in the margins of a British Library copy of *Tristram*, known as the Grenville copy. Scholars have long consulted this work, and finally in 1978 and 1980 Antony Colman published the main items in *Notes and Queries*.[42] Colman assigns the marginalia to Edmund Ferrers but does not explain why; our own assumption is that they are the work of several hands, entered throughout the century.

Huntington Brown and John M. Stedmond both provide useful comments on Sterne's debt to Rabelais; and Gardner D. Stout has a particularly

41. Denis Diderot, *Lettres à Sophie Volland*, 7th ed. (Paris: Gallimard, 1938), II: 15. Cf. Cross, p. 140: "Ozell, texts, notes, and all, Sterne had well-nigh by heart, and found them most serviceable in the act of composition. Without Rabelais, his jests, whims, anecdotes, and splendid extravagances, there would never have been a Sterne as we now know him"; and p. 262: "Never since Rabelais had 'the lumber rooms of learning' been so thoroughly overhauled and the learned blockheads dragged out and subjected to so keen a ridicule . . . ."

42. 223 (1978): 55–58 and 225 (1980): 42–45.

acute ear for catching echoes of the Rabelaisian idiom in Sterne's work.[43] The most useful essay on the subject, however, probably remains D. W. Jefferson's "*Tristram Shandy* and the Tradition of Learned Wit."[44] My edition of the "Rabelaisian Fragment," cited above, might also prove of some interest, insofar as it argues that the "Fragment" was Sterne's first effort at what evolved into *Tristram Shandy* and hence an important clue to the Rabelaisian urge in Sterne. Finally, in recognition of the importance of the relationship, we quote Henri Fluchère's interesting, though as usual verbose, comparison of the two:

> Neither of them is shaken in his faith by the confusion, the vanity or the capriciousness of the external world. One replies to them with the vehemence of his own forceful nature, which while brandishing comic insult . . . and violent satire, still leaves ample room for the positive virtues of tolerance, hope, and *joie de vivre*. The other does not enjoy such rude health, and like the age he lives in no longer possesses the spiritual passion that was still intact in the sixteenth century. Sterne is obliged to be devious, to outflank the enemy and reduce him by amusing him. . . . But it still required courage even then to adopt an attitude of intransigence towards everything that degrades, humiliates, or turns man to ridicule, and in his light-hearted but valiant fencing-match against fate Sterne shows himself a true son of Rabelais.[45]

There has been a persistent myth about Sterne's reading, begun by Ferriar, and reflecting his own interest in French imitators of Rabelais, that Sterne was heavily indebted to such authors as François Béroalde, Guillaume Bouchet, Gilles Ménage, and Bruscambille.[46] Cross is particularly enthusiastic on the subject of this debt, without offering any concrete evidence, and he has been

43. Respectively, *Rabelais in English Literature* (Cambridge: Harvard University Press, 1933); *The Comic Art of Laurence Sterne*; and "Some Borrowings."

44. *EIC* 1 (1951): 225–48. Indeed, Jefferson's essay is a good starting point for understanding Sterne's use of Burton and Montaigne, Cervantes and Swift, as well as Rabelais. See also New, "Sterne, Warburton."

45. *Laurence Sterne: From Tristram to Yorick* (Paris, 1961), trans. Barbara Bray (London: Oxford University Press, 1965), p. 176. In this passage, as throughout, Fluchère's thought is marred by a verbosity that no translator could redeem. The title of a more recent study of the relationship seemed promising: Michael Seidel's *Satiric Inheritance, Rabelais to Sterne* (Princeton, N.J.: Princeton University Press, 1979); unfortunately, the chapter on *Tristram* adds nothing to past commentary.

46. Ferriar, *Illustrations of Sterne*, 2d ed. (London, 1812), I: 40–81.

often echoed by later critics, despite the fine 1931 doctoral dissertation of C. F. Jones, "The French Sources of Sterne," which concluded that Sterne was probably not familiar with these authors in any significant way.[47] Our own view is similar. Sterne does cite Ménage once (vol. IV, chap. 21), but as we point out in our notes the single anecdote is much elaborated by Sterne, perhaps indicative of an intermediate source. Almost certainly his one citation of Bouchet and Bruscambille is taken from Ozell's notes to Rabelais, as pointed out in W. G. Day's "Sterne and Ozell."[48]

(6) Swift and the Scriblerians. One need only glance at my *Laurence Sterne as Satirist* and Michael DePorte's *Nightmares and Hobbyhorses: Swift, Sterne, and Augustan Ideas of Madness*[49] to understand the difficulty readers have had in dealing with Sterne's relationship to Swift. No resolution of that difficulty will be found here, certainly not from my hand. What I will do, first, is call attention to two very specific observations, viz., that Sterne's "Abuses of Conscience" sermon is heavily indebted in its language to two sermons Sterne believed had been written by Swift;[50] and that Sterne himself took pride in being told by old Lord Bathurst that "I have lived my life with geniuses [like Pope and Swift]; but have survived them; and, despairing ever to find their equals, it is some years since I have closed my accounts, and shut up my books, with thoughts of never opening them again: but you have kindled a desire in me of opening them once more before I die; which I now do; so go home and dine with me."[51]

Beyond this, we venture on treacherous ground. Few would deny that *Tale of a Tub*, the *Memoirs of Martinus Scriblerus*, and perhaps *Peri Bathous* as well, are in the background of *Tristram Shandy;* but the verbal echoes are rarely

47. Jones's dissertation was submitted to the University of London. Cf. Cash, *Early and Middle Years*, pp. 194–95.

48. *ES* 53 (1972): 434–36; see, however, Jeffrey R. Smitten, *"Tristram Shandy* and Spatial Form," *ArielE* 8 (1977): 45, for a suggested borrowing from Bruscambille. See also *Letters*, p. 416: "tell me the reason . . . why the Author [Béroalde] of the Moyen de parvenir (a vile,—but Witty book)—[could write] under the bondage of a poor *Canonical*"; and see Curtis's note, p. 417, n. 5.

49. San Marino, Calif.: Huntington Library, 1974.

50. "On the Testimony of Conscience" is definitely Swift's; "The Difficulty of Knowing One's Self" was published as Swift's but was questioned by the Earl of Orrery in 1752 and remains in question today. See *Irish Tracts and Sermons* (Oxford: Basil Blackwell, 1948), especially Louis Landa's "Introduction to the Sermons," pp. 103–6.

51. *Letters*, p. 305. Cf. p. 79: "I have not gone as far as Swift—He keeps due distance from Rabelais—& I from him. Swift sais 500 things, I dare not say,—unless I was Dean of Saint

sufficient to allow positive assertions, as with Burton or Rabelais. In the absence of specific borrowings, one is left with questions of tone and intent, the Scylla and Charybdis of commentary on the relationship between Sterne and his Augustan heritage. The most balanced approach was perhaps that of James Work, who very rarely cites a Scriblerian author in his annotations, but whose doctoral dissertation provides many suggestions of the possible influence of Swift and the Scriblerian tradition upon Sterne.[52] Equally balanced, and a good starting point for further investigation, is Stedmond's *The Comic Art of Laurence Sterne*. Also useful is Ronald Paulson's *Satire and the Novel in Eighteenth-Century England*.[53] Most subsequent critics, however, have been unable or unwilling to achieve a similar balance on the subject, often legitimately so since so much of one's reading of *Tristram* can turn upon one's view of the extent to which the Shandean voice is related to the Scriblerian.

For the annotator, the importance of the relationship is no less acute, and the boundary between elucidation and interpretation all the more problematic. To ignore the Scriblerians' capacity to elucidate aspects of *Tristram* would be to argue, ludicrously enough, that Sterne did not read or did not respond to his most famous immediate predecessors; but to place a passage of *Tale of a Tub* or *Peri Bathous* in juxtaposition with a passage from *Tristram* seems always to be a decidedly interpretative act. Consider, for example, these extremely well-known sentences:

> But when a Man's Fancy gets *astride* on his Reason, when Imagination is at Cuffs with the Senses, and common Understanding, as well as common Sense, is Kickt out of Doors; the first Proselyte he makes, is Himself . . . .[54]

> WHEN a man gives himself up to the government of a ruling passion, ——or, in other words, when his HOBBY-HORSE grows head-strong,—— farewell cool reason and fair discretion! (*TS*, 106.21–24)

Patricks"; and p. 132: "till I shall have the honour to be as much mal-treated as Rabelais, and Swift were, I must continue humble; for I have not filled up the measure of half their *persecutions*."

52. "The Indebtedness of *Tristram Shandy* to Certain English Authors—1670–1740" (Ph.D. diss., Yale University, 1934).

53. New Haven: Yale University Press, 1967, pp. 248–62.

54. *A Tale of a Tub*, ed. A. C. Guthkelch and D. Nichol Smith, 2d ed. (Oxford: Clarendon Press, 1958), p. 171.

It seems almost certain Sterne could not have written his sentence without re-calling Swift's, but how much of Swift's context ("A Digression on Madness") and his tone were also recalled? In this instance, not to call attention to Swift's sentence seems itself an interpretative statement, a silent comment upon the "differences" between Swift and Sterne; but, on the other hand, to suggest that juxtaposing the two passages is an act of "elucidation" quite free from "inter-pretation" is to fly in the face of contrary experience. The point is that any assertion of the influence of a Scriblerian text on *Tristram* is much more likely to be considered an interpretative act, as opposed, say, to the assertion of a parallel to Addison or Goldsmith.

And yet, of course, Swift and Pope do share the eighteenth century with Sterne and do often represent the best statements in the age of certain percep-tions and commonplaces; hence they find their way into notes far more "neutral" than one which cites *Tale of a Tub* to elucidate 106.21–24. We have tried to restrain the use of the Scriblerians simply to provide context, and at the same time have tried not to be intimidated into omitting citations because others might find them interpretative. The results, probably pleasing to no one, may be summarized by three illustrations: we cite on several occasions Swift's *Polite Conversation* to establish a context for Sterne's language, but we do not claim that Sterne read the work; we cite the passage from *Tale of a Tub* quoted above, in our note to 106.21, without further comment; and we do not suggest, although tempted to do so, that Sterne's mock dedication in vol. I, chap. 8, is in the manner of Swift's several dedications to *Tale of a Tub*, most particularly that to Sommers, and the advice therein to "peruse a hundred or two of Dedications, and transcribe an Abstract, to be applied to your Lordship . . ." (p. 23). In short, we use the Scriblerians, as we use other eighteenth-century authors, to help establish the eighteenth-century context; we quote them as well when we believe Sterne may have had a particular text in mind; and we try to avoid citing them when the parallel depends upon reading Sterne as a latter-day Scriblerian. It would be naïve for us to believe that we have preserved these categories throughout, but we hope some balance has been achieved.

In citing the Scriblerians we have used primarily modern texts, since they have been so carefully edited in recent years. It might be noted, in passing, that the very idea that *Tristram Shandy* could and should be annotated with the fullness of A. C. Guthkelch and D. Nichol Smith's *Tale of a Tub* or Charles

Kerby-Miller's *Memoirs of Martinus Scriblerus*, rather than annotated as one might *Pamela* or *Joseph Andrews*, is itself enormously suggestive. Indeed, my first rationale for editing Sterne, suggested at the Sterne Bicentenary Conference in 1968 ("Time wastes too fast"), was precisely that to do so would make evident *Tristram*'s grounding in the Augustan milieu. But just as I might once have hoped an accurate text would appeal to critics writing an essay on a topic like Sterne's "punctuation,"[55] so now I acknowledge that annotations need not (and will not) deter a critic hell-bent upon ignoring them. I shall hope only that some readers will find less useful than at present the concept of *sui generis* when they try to understand *Tristram Shandy*.

D. *Tristram Shandy and ideas.*—The final category of annotations we have provided is perhaps the most challenging for the annotator. The road to Shandy Hall is studded with the pebbles of Sterne's reading, or, more accurately perhaps, the habits of his study, none more evident than his habit of covering his intellectual tracks. It was a game he learned from several of his masters, most notably Rabelais and Burton, though one suspects that Sterne, who himself promises to supply all the "commentary, scholium, illustration, and key" (40.10–11) his work required, was a most apt pupil.

We can begin with a generalization: Sterne's "learned wit" almost always has more "wit" and less "learning" than we are led to believe. This is in no way a denigrating statement: Sterne makes no serious claim to being a scholar, as, for example, William Warburton could. Rather, the statement summarizes the conclusion of almost a dozen years of tracking the sources of Sterne's erudition, and pays tribute to the *ignis fatuus* he so artfully played. The nine volumes of *Tristram Shandy* are liberally sprinkled with the names of authors he never read, books he knew little or nothing about, and technical details (from history and science in particular) that are not the indications of a universal genius, but rather of an inveterate index-reader. At the same time, Sterne concealed (or teasingly hinted at) many of the authors and works he did consult, surely a conscious act on his part. It is no accident, for example, that Sterne several times drops the name of Albertus Rubens in his discussion of breeches (vol. VI, chap.

---

55. Obviously it did not; see Roger Moss, "Sterne's Punctuation," *ECS* 15 (1982): 179–200, published four years after an accurate text was available. Mr. Moss never does reveal the secret of what text he used.

19), and perhaps he even briefly glanced into the learned *De re Vestiaria Veterum*. The great bulk of the chapter, however, appears to have been borrowed from the equivalent of a high-school textbook on Roman costume, as our notes to the chapter make clear. The annotator who trusts Sterne is bound to be deceived.

We have already noted that Sterne nowhere overtly refers to the *Anatomy of Melancholy*, an encyclopedic work to which he had frequent recourse. Somewhat less frequently quoted, but of considerable importance to Sterne, is Ephraim Chambers's *Cyclopædia: or, an Universal Dictionary of the Arts and Sciences*, also never cited by him.[56] Its use was first noted by Sir Edward Bensly; in particular, Bensly revealed that Sterne's learned list of authorities on fortification (vol. II, chap. 3) was borrowed from this one source, the entry under *Fortification*.[57] Sterne might easily have written all that Toby tells us about the subject without consulting a single work on that list. Several decades later, Bernard Greenberg demonstrated how Sterne followed the cross-referencing system in Chambers to construct his own learned argument on the seat of the soul (vol. II, chap. 19).[58] We have considerably extended Bensly's and Greenberg's work and have in addition used the *Cyclopædia* to provide a useful eighteenth-century context for passages requiring elucidation. It is worth noting that Sterne was almost never a "passive" borrower. In instance after instance, he would add something to Chambers, an additional name on a list perhaps, or a bit of additional information culled from elsewhere. At times, indeed, one might suspect that Sterne went to Chambers's sources directly (and, after all, the *Cyclopædia* is in many respects nothing more than a huge compendium of quotations), but without doubt Chambers was his primary "reference" work.

Work makes a strong claim for the influence of Pierre Bayle's *Dictionnaire*

56. We have used the fifth edition, published in two volumes, the first dated 1741 and the second, 1743. Chambers uses a combination of typefaces and sizes for his entry headings and cross-references, all of which we have silently altered to the italic face, except, of course, when quoting the text itself. We have followed this practice for the entry headings of all the encyclopedic works consulted.

57. *TLS* (November 1, 1928), p. 806.

58. "Laurence Sterne and Chambers' *Cyclopaedia*," *MLN* 69 (1954): 560–62. Professor Greenberg was kind enough to supply us with some of his notes and advice early in our preparation of this volume, for which we are most grateful.

historique et critique (1697),[59] but we are unable to support this. Without doubt, Sterne did borrow his discussion of Luther's damnation from Bayle,[60] and perhaps as well some hints for the "Whiskers" story (vol. V, chap. 1);[61] all further claims, however, seem tenuous at best, and indeed the one essay on the subject, Francis Doherty's "Bayle and *Tristram Shandy:* 'Stage-Loads of Chymical Nostrums and Peripatetic Lumber'," presents not a single instance of borrowing convincing enough for inclusion in our notes.[62]

We do believe, however, that Sterne may have been familiar with Louis Moréri's *Le Grand Dictionnaire historique* . . . (1674), in the English translation by Jeremy Collier, 2d ed. (1701). It is true of the encyclopedic tradition in general, however, that one often finds very similar (indeed verbatim) entries transferred from one work to another, without acknowledgment, and thus one can never be absolutely certain as to precisely the entry Sterne had in hand. A study remains to be conducted into Sterne's use of the entire canon of late seventeenth- and eighteenth-century encyclopedias.

Sterne also found his information in more specialized sources. John Turnbull first noted his concealed use of Obadiah Walker's *Of Education*[63] in constructing the *Tristrapædia,* and we have added several passages to those he cites, including the entire discussion of the proper tutor for Tristram in the opening

59. "He was not . . . a learned man: nine-tenths of the 'erudition' of *Shandy* he took secondhand from compilers, notably Burton and Bayle and Chambers" (p. xxiii).

60. See the textual note to 311.23ff. in vol. II of the Florida edition, p. 853. (In the annotations, reference to the textual notes will be indicated by the abbreviation t.n., followed by the page and line numbers of the passage under consideration.) See also Melvyn New and Norman Fry, "Some Borrowings in *Tristram Shandy*: The Textual Problem," *SB* 29 (1976): 324.

61. Richard A. Davies, "'The Fragment' in *Tristram Shandy*, V, 1," *ES* 57 (1976): 522–23.

62. *Neophil* 58 (1974): 339–48.

63. "The Prototype of Walter Shandy's *Tristrapædia*," *RES* 2 (1926): 212–15. We have used the sixth edition of Walker (1699), which contains material not in the first, material that Sterne uses. An illustration of the problem of working with the encyclopedic tendency of the eighteenth century (whether manifested in a labeled "encyclopedia" or a work like Walker's) is provided by William J. Farrell's "Nature versus Art as a Comic Pattern in *Tristram Shandy*," *ELH* 30 (1963): 16–35. Farrell identifies the source of the ideal tutor for Tristram (vol. VI, chap. 5) as Quintilian, and his Renaissance treatment in John Bulwer's *Chirologia* (1644). Almost surely, Sterne had read both, but it is very clear, as I believe our notes to the passage indicate, that Sterne is here using Walker—who had undoubtedly read Quintilian and Bulwer. Particularly insofar as in the past the idea of plagiarism was less precise than in modern times, source regression becomes all the more possible; and the problem works in the other direction as well, for when we believe we have a source, it is always possible that Sterne was actually borrowing from an author who had borrowed, perhaps verbatim, from the text we have in hand.

chapters of vol. VI. Moreover, Sterne brilliantly interweaves his use of Walker in these discussions with borrowings from a work he does cite, Adrien Baillet's *Des enfans célèbres*.[64] Both Walker and Baillet discuss late-blooming geniuses and child prodigies, and Sterne borrows details from each in order to expound "learnedly" upon Julius Scaliger, Petrus Baldus, Vincent Quirino, and, of course, Justus Lipsius, among the dozen or more Renaissance scholars he glibly runs through in this part of *Tristram Shandy*. A close study of our annotations for these particular pages would perhaps serve as well as any other single group of notes to illustrate Sterne's habits in his study.

Sterne's rich details concerning childbirth were garnered primarily from John Burton's *A Letter to William Smellie, M.D.* (1753), with some additional borrowings from Chambers. As with his use of Obadiah Walker, his purpose here was twofold, to provide a texture of concrete detail and to parody his source, in this instance a Yorkshire neighbor and longtime adversary.[65] Similarly, when Sterne needed details to substantiate his whirlwind tour through France in vol. VII, he turned to Jean Aimar Piganiol de la Force's *Nouveau Voyage de France*,[66] which he both pillaged and parodied. In this latter instance, we have supplemented his borrowings from Piganiol with English sources in order to indicate the commonplace nature of Sterne's information—the stock-in-trade of travelers and travel writers of the eighteenth century, which Sterne turned to his own amusements.

The historical information surrounding the descriptions of Uncle Toby's battles was taken, as Theodore Baird noted in 1936,[67] from *The History of England, by Mr. Rapin de Thoyras. Continued . . . by N. Tindal*. Baird's purpose in his important essay was to argue that there is a carefully plotted "time-scheme" in *Tristram Shandy*, based on Tindal, and hence that Sterne is a novelist in the "great tradition." More significant, it seems to us, is the evidence Tindal

64. *Jugemens des savans sur les principaux ouvrages des auteurs. par Adrien Baillet* (Paris, 1722), vol. V, pt. 1. See New and Fry, "Some Borrowings," p. 326.

65. See Cash, *Early and Middle Years*, pp. 159–78 and passim; and Cash, "The Birth of Tristram Shandy: Sterne and Dr. Burton," in *Studies in the Eighteenth Century*, ed. R. F. Brissenden (Canberra: Australian National University Press, 1968), pp. 133–54.

66. See Van R. Baker, "Sterne and Piganiol de la Force: The Making of Volume VII of *Tristram Shandy*," *CLS* 13 (1976): 5–14.

67. "The Time-Scheme of *Tristram Shandy* and a Source," *PMLA* 51 (1936): 803–20. We have used the third edition (1743–47). Ferriar, *Memoirs* (1793), called brief attention to Tindal, but dropped the sentence from *Illustrations*.

provides, first, of Sterne's fascinating capacity to condense the essence of four folio pages into four sentences; and, second, of Sterne's full awareness of the realities of eighteenth-century warfare, inasmuch as Rapin-Thoyras is detailed and unflinching in his battlefield descriptions. We have therefore quoted at some length relevant passages from Tindal, providing a context that may prove of some use for interpretations of Toby's character and is of certain benefit for any discussion of Sterne's method of composition. We also note here, by way of apology, the lengths we take to explicate the historical context of "Slawken-bergius's Tale." Why Sterne should set his story in Strasbourg is perhaps of little interest to interpretation, but for the annotator the answer evolved into a fine exemplum of the annotative process. To come slowly but certainly to the realization that Strasbourg must have had connotations for the eighteenth century every bit as marked as, say, Munich has for the twentieth, is the equivalent, perhaps, of the interpreter's pleasure in finally solidifying his understanding of the whale's whiteness. We attempt to share some of that pleasure by a self-indulgent excess of annotation upon what we do realize is a minute aspect of the work. It is, I hope, the only such instance.

Finally, we must note that by living in the middle of the eighteenth century, Sterne creates an obvious context for the annotator to explore, but one that is nothing less than the entire literature available to the age. As we would expect, for example, Sterne knows the Bible, the *Book of Common Prayer*, Shakespeare, and—to some extent—the classics. He quotes liberally from them all.[68] But the problem here is not the works Sterne cites by title, nor the borrowings eventually identified; rather it is that we found ourselves returning to a group of texts that we came to consider as vital to our efforts quite independent of Sterne's actual familiarity with them, or the specific evidence of a borrowing. Hence, we found it convenient to establish the general nature of thought in the age by bracketing it with the *Spectator* at the beginning and Goldsmith's periodical writing at the end; we cannot doubt that Sterne read some of both, but often the point is that he need *not* have, to be writing in the same vein, since the idea we are documenting was common property. Pope is also useful in this regard, though perhaps we did not consult him as much as we could; and certainly it would be worthwhile eventually to run through the *Gentleman's Magazine* and

68. Most useful in this regard is Arthur Sherbo's "Some Not-So-Hidden Allusions in *Tristram Shandy*," in *Studies in the Eighteenth Century English Novel*, pp. 128–35.

other popular journals with an eye toward annotating *Tristram Shandy*—had we "but world enough, and time."

In much the same fashion, we had to deal with our developing awareness that Sterne had an interest in the medical theories of his day, most especially in that group of ideas discussed today under the heading *iatromechanism*. Here is an area that deserves to be far more fully explored than we were able to do, but our own purposes were well served by staying with Chambers and George Cheyne's *The English Malady* (1733) as our primary sources. What Sterne actually read in eighteenth-century science remains uncertain—and, more important, we are equally uncertain of the relationship of his reading to the problems we have identified for annotation. To be specific: Sterne seems fond of the concept of vibrations to explain sensation; we have annotated the relevant passages with Chambers and Cheyne but have not gone beyond these writers, though tempted to do so, and especially by David Hartley. Similarly, Sterne seems quite interested in the entire mechanistic tradition, but we have not pursued his interest much beyond La Mettrie's famous *L'homme machine,* a work we suspect Sterne knew (see, in particular, our note to 657.11). Of all the books that remain to be written on *Tristram Shandy,* perhaps none is more needed than one that is able to establish the meaning of Sterne's interest in eighteenth-century scientific theories.[69]

III

The notes are keyed by page and line number to the Florida edition of *Tristram Shandy*, vols. I and II. We have usually provided the first few words and the last few of the passage being annotated; where the annotation was applicable to several pages, we have indicated the opening words only. Works cited throughout by short title are listed immediately following this introduction. All other references are given in full at the first citation for any single volume of *Tristram* notes; thereafter, the work is given a readily identifiable short title for the

69. The best work on the subject up to this time is Wilfred Watson's "Sterne's Satire on Mechanism: A Study of *Tristram Shandy,*" (Ph.D. diss., University of Toronto, 1951). See also Loveridge, especially chap. 3. A good beginning on a new investigation is made by John A. Dussinger, "The Sensorium in the World of 'A Sentimental Journey'," *ArielE* 13 (1982): 3–16.

remainder of that volume, and is cited again in full at the first use for the next volume. We have minimized notes that merely cite a reference, preferring instead to provide relevant texts within the notes so that readers have readily available the particular passages that we believe are valuable in elucidating *Tristram*.

There have been several annotated textbook editions of *Tristram* prior to this scholarly edition. The best by far is that by James Aiken Work, first published in 1940. Work's annotations are primarily of a historical and pedagogical nature: he identifies historical and contemporary personages mentioned by Sterne, defines "difficult" and foreign words and phrases, and elucidates allusions that a modern student audience could not be expected to grasp. He also identifies, but almost always by citation alone, some of Sterne's major borrowings, particularly those from Rabelais, Burton, and Montaigne. So thorough is his identification of persons that we have chosen to quote his notes directly, wherever we are unable to improve on them. That we should be compelled to write "Alfonso Tostado (c. 1400–1455) was a famous theological author in Spain" to avoid Work's "an eminent Spanish theologian and author" seems an exercise in futility. Where we have a corrected set of dates or new information, we have included it in brackets within the text of the original note. Our admiration for Work's edition is great, as should be evident in the notes, so that those few occasions where we have discovered him to be in error should not be taken as anything more than the particular errors they are. Few if any eighteenth-century authors have been better served in being made available to a general reading audience than Sterne has been in James Work's edition of *Tristram Shandy*.

Ian Watt's edition for Houghton Mifflin (Riverside Press, 1965) makes some valuable additions to Work, and we have made note of them. His introduction is also of considerable value, more so than Work's, which has become somewhat dated by this time. The Norton edition (1978) is textually inaccurate and almost totally blind to the thirty-eight years of scholarship appearing since the Work edition; the annotations are primarily rewritings of Work and Watt. Insofar as the Norton Company labels its textbook editions as "Critical Editions" and "Authoritative" it has been most irresponsible in respect to *Tristram Shandy*. From Ian Campbell Ross's textbook edition for Oxford University Press (1983) we have made use of one or two suggestions, as from Graham Petrie's notes to the Penguin Books edition (1967). In their notes, these editions are fundamentally the same, Ross adding little to Petrie despite the sixteen intervening years.

We have attempted always to give credit to the first identifier of any particular borrowing, but have probably not been totally consistent. In a work that is over ten years in the making (and I date this from both my own initial collaboration with Richard Davies, which began in 1971, and W. G. Day's doctoral dissertation, "Verbal Borrowing in *Tristram Shandy*," submitted in the same year), it is often difficult to know how to allow claims of priority, especially for those sources of Sterne's borrowings that must be read and reread in order to gather as many instances as are justified. Nonetheless, we have tried very hard to honor those who have come before us, for the task of annotation has been considerably eased by the many scholars whose researches have uncovered and explained important aspects of the work. But rather than ending this introduction by paying tribute to them, it is perhaps even more appropriate to conclude with a hope for those who will follow us as students of *Tristram Shandy*, who will make use of our work, correct its errors, supply its inadequacies. We hope, then, that we have left, in Sterne's own words, "room to turn a man's self in" and "room for the controversy to go on." We strongly suspect that we have.

Gainesville, 1983

KEY TO THE NOTES

All journals are abbreviated as in the *PMLA* Bibliography. The place of publication before 1800 is understood to be London, unless otherwise indicated. Classical quotations and translations are taken from the editions of the Loeb Classical Library, Harvard University Press, unless otherwise indicated.

For *Tristram Shandy*, notes are keyed by page and line number of the Florida Edition. References to textual notes (t.n.) are also to this edition. We refer to Sterne's volume and chapter numbers as, e.g., vol. I, chap. 2.

For all other works, volume and page numbers are given as I: 2. Volume and chapter numbers are generally given as I.2; volume, chapter, and page numbers as I.2.3. We have tried to give, where applicable, both the cited author's original numbering as well as the volume/chapter/page numbers of the edition we have used, in the event the particular edition we cite is not readily available. For example, in Cervantes, I.III.2 (I: 220), the first three numbers refer to Cervantes's own divisions; the last two refer to the volume and page number of the edition we used.

SHORT TITLES

ASJ	[Sterne], *A Sentimental Journey through France and Italy by Mr. Yorick*, ed. Gardner D. Stout, Jr. (Berkeley: University of California Press, 1967).
Baird, "Time-Scheme"	Theodore Baird, "The Time-Scheme of *Tristram Shandy* and a Source," *PMLA* 51 (1936): 803–20.

Boswell, *Life of Johnson*	*Boswell's Life of Johnson*, ed. George Birkbeck Hill, rev. and enlarged by L. F. Powell, 2d ed., 6 vols. (Oxford: Clarendon Press, 1964).
Burton	Robert Burton, *The Anatomy of Melancholy*, 5th ed. (Oxford, 1638).
Cash, "Birth"	Arthur H. Cash, "The Birth of Tristram Shandy: Sterne and Dr. Burton," in *Studies in the Eighteenth Century*, ed. R. F. Brissenden (Canberra: Australian National University Press, 1968).
Cash, *Early and Middle Years*	Arthur H. Cash, *Laurence Sterne: The Early and Middle Years* (London: Methuen, 1975).
Cervantes	Miguel de Cervantes, *Don Quixote*, trans. Peter Motteux, rev. John Ozell, 7th ed., 4 vols. (1743).
Chambers	Ephraim Chambers, *Cyclopædia: or, an Universal Dictionary of Arts and Sciences*, 5th ed., 2 vols. (1741, 1743).
Chambers, *Supplement*	*A Supplement to Mr. Chambers's Cyclopædia*, ed. George Lewis Scott, 2 vols. (1753).
Cross, *Life*	Wilbur L. Cross, *The Life and Times of Laurence Sterne*, 3d ed. (New Haven: Yale University Press, 1929).
EDD	*The English Dialect Dictionary*, ed. Joseph Wright, 6 vols. (London: Henry Frowde, 1898–1905).
Ferriar	John Ferriar, M.D., *Illustrations of Sterne*, 2d ed., 2 vols. (London: Cadell and Davies, 1812).
Goldsmith, *Works*	Oliver Goldsmith, *Collected Works*, ed. Arthur Friedman, 5 vols. (Oxford: Clarendon Press, 1966).
Hammond	Lansing Van der Heyden Hammond, *Laurence Sterne's "Sermons of Mr. Yorick"* (New Haven: Yale University Press, 1948).
Handbook of English Costume	C. Willett Cunnington and Phillis Cunnington, *Handbook of English Costume in the Eighteenth Century* (Boston: Plays, 1972).
Johnson, *Dictionary*	Samuel Johnson, *A Dictionary of the English Language*, 2 vols. (1755).

Letters	[Sterne], *Letters*, ed. Lewis Perry Curtis (Oxford: Clarendon Press, 1935).
Locke, *ECHU*	John Locke, *An Essay Concerning Human Understanding*, ed. Peter H. Nidditch (Oxford: Clarendon Press, 1975).
Locke, *Some Thoughts Concerning Education*	John Locke, *The Educational Writings*, ed. James L. Axtell (Cambridge: Cambridge University Press, 1968).
Memoirs	*Memoirs of Martinus Scriblerus*, ed. Charles Kerby-Miller (New Haven: Yale University Press, 1950).
Montaigne	Michel de Montaigne, *Essays*, trans. Charles Cotton, 5th ed., 3 vols. (1738).
New, "Sterne, Warburton"	Melvyn New, "Sterne, Warburton, and the Burden of Exuberant Wit," *ECS* 15 (1982): 245–74.
OCD	*The Oxford Classical Dictionary*, ed. N. G. L. Hammond and H. H. Scullard, 2d ed. (Oxford: Clarendon Press, 1970).
ODEP	*The Oxford Dictionary of English Proverbs*, 3d ed., rev. F. P. Wilson (Oxford: Clarendon Press, 1970).
OED	*Oxford English Dictionary*.
Partridge	Eric Partridge, *A Dictionary of Slang and Unconventional English*, 7th ed. (New York: Macmillan, 1970).
Polite Conversation	*Swift's Polite Conversation*, ed. Eric Partridge (New York: Oxford University Press, 1963).
"Political Romance"	[Sterne], *A Political Romance* (York, 1759; facsimile ed., Menston, England: Scolar Press, 1971).
Pope	John Butt, gen. ed., *The Twickenham Edition of the Poems of Alexander Pope* (London: Methuen, 1939–69).
Rabelais	*The Works of Francis Rabelais, M.D.*, trans. Thomas Urquhart and Peter Motteux, with notes by John Ozell, 5 vols. (1750).
"Rabelaisian Fragment"	Melvyn New, "Sterne's Rabelaisian Fragment: A Text from the Holograph Manuscript," *PMLA* 87 (1972): 1083–92.

Sermons	[Sterne], *Sermons of Mr. Yorick* and *Sermons by the late Rev. Mr. Sterne*, 7 vols. (1760–69). In citing the *Sermons* (e.g., I.2.3), the middle number is the consecutive number of the sermon as it was reprinted in *Collected Works*, ed. Wilbur L. Cross (New York: J. F. Taylor, 1904), vols. XII, XIII.
Shakespeare	*The Riverside Shakespeare*, ed. G. Blakemore Evans, et al. (Boston: Houghton Mifflin Co., 1974).
Sherbo, *Studies*	Arthur Sherbo, "Some Not-So-Hidden Allusions in *Tristram Shandy*," in *Studies in the Eighteenth Century English Novel* (East Lansing: Michigan State University Press, 1969), pp. 128–35.
Spectator	*The Spectator*, ed. Donald F. Bond (Oxford: Clarendon Press, 1965).
Stanford Dictionary	C. A. M. Fennell, *The Stanford Dictionary of Anglicised Words and Phrases* (Cambridge: Cambridge University Press, 1964).
Stevenson	Burton Stevenson, *The Macmillan Book of Proverbs, Maxims, and Famous Phrases* (New York: Macmillan, 1948).
Stout, "Borrowings"	Gardner D. Stout, Jr., "Some Borrowings in Sterne from Rabelais and Cervantes," *ELN* 3 (1965): 111–17.
Swift, *Sermons* and *Gulliver's Travels*, in *Prose Works*	*The Prose Writings of Jonathan Swift*, ed. Herbert Davis (Oxford: Basil Blackwell, 1939–68). The *Sermons* comprise vol. IX (1948); *Gulliver's Travels*, vol. XI (1941).
Tale of a Tub	Jonathan Swift, *A Tale of a Tub*, ed. A. C. Guthkelch and D. Nichol Smith, 2d ed. (Oxford: Clarendon Press, 1958).
Tilley	Morris Palmer Tilley, *A Dictionary of the Proverbs in England in the Sixteenth and Seventeenth Centuries* (Ann Arbor: University of Michigan Press, 1950).
Tindal	Paul de Rapin-Thoyras, *The History of England*, trans. and continued by N. Tindal, 3d ed., 4 vols. in 5 (1743–47).

Watt   [Sterne], *Tristram Shandy*, ed. Ian Watt (Boston: Riverside Editions, 1965).

Winged Skull   Arthur H. Cash and John M. Stedmond, eds., *The Winged Skull: Papers from the Laurence Sterne Bicentenary Conference* (Kent, Ohio: Kent State University Press, 1971).

Work   [Sterne], *Tristram Shandy*, ed. James A. Work (New York: Odyssey Press, 1940).

NOTES TO VOLUME I

Plate (frontispiece to vol. I)] See t.n., vol. II, pp. 843–44, in this edition.

Title-page (motto)] Sterne's motto is taken from the *Enchiridion* of Epictetus (chap. 5). Montaigne uses it for the opening sentence of his essay "That the Relish of Goods and Evils, does, in a great measure, depend upon the Opinion we have of them"; it is translated by Cotton as: "MEN (says an ancient *Greek* Sentence) are tormented with the Opinions they have of Things, and not by the Things themselves" (I.40.285). Cotton does not give the original Greek, but it does appear, as was pointed out to us by J. C. Maxwell, in an edition by Pierre Coste, *Essais de Michel Seigneur de Montaigne*, 4th ed. (1739), II: 41. If Sterne did not go to the original source, it is possible that he was sufficiently interested in Montaigne to follow up the point by turning to the Coste edition.

The context of the passage in the *Enchiridion* may be of significance: "MEN are disturbed, not by Things, but by the Principles and Notions, which they form concerning Things. Death, for Instance, is not terrible, else it would have appeared so to *Socrates*. But the Terror consists in our Notion of Death, that it is terrible. When therefore we are hindered, or disturbed, or grieved, let us never impute it to others, but to ourselves; that is, to our own Principles" (trans. Elizabeth Carter, 2d ed. [1759], p. 438).

Ded. To . . . Mr. Pitt.] Sterne prepared his dedication for the second edition, published by James Dodsley on April 2, 1760; see t.n., vol. II, p. 844, in this edition. A week before, he had sent a letter to William Pitt (1708–78) forewarning the Secretary of State of his intention: "Though I

37

have no suspicion that the inclosed Dedication can offend you, yet I
thought it my duty to take some method of letting you see it, before I
presumed to beg the honour of presenting it to you next week, with the
Life and Opinions of Tristram Shandy" (*Letters*, p. 103). In his "Anecdotes of Sterne" John Croft suggests that Sterne had planned from the
beginning to dedicate the work to Pitt (in *The Whitefoord Papers*, ed.
W. A. S. Hewins [Oxford: Clarendon Press, 1898], pp. 228–29);
whether or not this is true, Sterne could not help but be aware that 1759
was a triumphant year for British foreign and military policy, and that Pitt
was being honored as the primary mover. Cf. *The Letters of Tobias Smollett*, ed. Lewis M. Knapp (Oxford: Clarendon Press, 1970), p. 87: "The
people here are in high spirits on account of our successes, and Mr. Pitt is
so popular that I may venture to say that all party is extinguished in Great-
Britain" (to John Harvie, December 10, 1759).

Ded. 2   Wight] Sterne scatters archaisms throughout *TS*; other instances include "eke" (99.25), "'yclept" (100.12), "ween" (102.7), "certes"
(174.4), "wot" (605.18, 655.15, 686.3), "whilome" (623.12), and
"yore" (596.1).

Ded. 4   bye corner of the kingdom] The first two volumes of *TS* were written
in the village of Sutton-on-the-Forest, Sterne's home after 1738. Cash,
Early and Middle Years, describes it: "The village of Sutton-on-the-
Forest, or Sutton-Galtres, as it was sometimes called, stood amid cleared
fields beyond which were bogs and patches of forest—the remains of the
great Forest of Galtres. The area was flat and damp. It bordered an ancient
Roman road running north from York which, eight miles from town,
made an un-Roman sharp turn to the right into Sutton village . . ."
(p. 67).

Ded. 5–6   fence against . . . ill health] Sterne was consumptive and seems to
have been particularly troubled by ill health during this period (Cash,
Early and Middle Years, pp. 283–84). The best study of Sterne's health in
relation to *TS* remains "Yorick Revisited," in W. B. C. Watkins, *Perilous
Balance: The Tragic Genius of Swift, Johnson, & Sterne* (1939; Cambridge:
Boar's Head Book, 1960).

Sterne seems to have liked the phrase "fence against"; cf. 25.20: "This
evil had been sufficiently fenced against . . ."; and 155.13–16: "human
laws . . . being . . . brought in to fence against the mischievous effects of

those consciences which are no law unto themselves . . . ." It occurs also in
a letter to David Garrick, April 19, 1762: "I Shandy it more than ever, and
verily do believe, that by mere Shandeism sublimated by a laughter-
loving people, I fence as much against infirmities, as I do by the benefit of
air and climate" (*Letters*, p. 163); and in *Sermons*, I.5.116 ("No doubt, she
had long fenced against this tragical event . . .") and IV.22.14 ("The evil
was well fenced against . . .").

Ded. 9   this Fragment of Life] Cf. *Letters*, p. 196: "I rest fully assured . . . of
y^r Grace's [the Archbishop of York's] indulgence to me in my endeavours
to add a few quiet years to this fragment of my life . . . ."

Elizabeth W. Harries, "Sterne's Novels: Gathering Up the Fragments," *ELH* 49 (1982): 35–49, suggests that for Sterne, "as for many of
his contemporaries, the word 'fragment' was inextricably bound up" with
Christ's command to "Gather up the fragments that remain, that nothing
be lost" (John 6: 12), and the miracle of plenty that follows (6: 13–14).
Harries finds in the concept of the "fragment" a clue (the "significance of
the apparently insignificant") to the fragmentary procedure of both *TS* and
ASJ.

1.1ff.   I Wish either, etc.] The idea that the conditions of conception determined the future of the child was a commonplace one. One repository of it
is Pierre Charron's *De la sagesse* (*Of Wisdome*), trans. Samson Lennard
(?1612), a work Sterne definitely quotes from in the last chapter of *TS* (see
n. to 806.1ff. below); it would not have been uncharacteristic of him to
have done so because he had had Charron in mind eight years before, when
he began his work. In his preface, Charron writes: "To attaine unto this
wisdome there are two meanes, the first is in the originall forming and first
temper, that is to say, in the temperature of the seed of the Parents, the
milke of the Nurse, and the first education; whereby a man is sayd to be
either well borne, or ill borne . . . . A man would little thinke of what
power and importance this beginning is, for if men did know it, there
would be more care taken, and diligence used therein than there is. . . .

"There are contrariwise two formall lets or hinderances to wisdome,
and two counter-meanes or powerfull wayes unto follie, Naturall and Acquired. The first, which is naturall, proceedeth from the originall temper
and temperature, which maketh the braine either too soft, moist, and the
parts thereof grosse and materiall, whereby the spirits remaine sottish,

feeble, lesse capable, plaine diminished, obscure, such as that is, for the most part, of the common sort of people; or too hot, ardent, and drie, which maketh the spirits foolish, audacious, vitious. These are the two extremes, *Sottishnesse* and *Follie,* Water and Fire, Lead and Mercurie . . ." (fols. a3–a4).

Late in the work Charron returns to the theme: "And *Plato* was wont to say, that he knew not in what a man should bee more carefull and diligent than to make a good sonne. . . .

"The first, which regardeth the generation, and fruit in the wombe is not accounted of and observed with such diligence as it ought, although it have as much part in the good or evill of a child (as well of their bodies as their soules) as their education and instruction after they are borne and come to some growth. . . . We men go unadvisedlie and headlong to this copulation, only provoked thereunto by pleasure, and a desire to disburthen our selves of that which tickleth and presseth us thereunto." He then provides eight points to consider before the copulatory act if a "beautifull, good, sound, wise and well composed" offspring is to be expected (pp. 458–59).

It is worth pointing out that Charron was an avid student of Montaigne and that much of his work is simply a reordering of the *Essays;* for example, the idea in Sterne's motto to vols. I and II (see above, n. to title-page), is translated by Lennard as follows: "It is not the trueth and nature of things which doth thus stirre and molest our soules, it is opinion, according to that ancient saying; Men are tormented by the opinions that they have of things, not by the things themselves." Sterne's debt to Charron was first noted by Françoise Pellan, "Laurence Sterne's Indebtedness to Charron," *MLR* 67 (1972): 752–55.

Cf. Cornelius Scriblerus, who "never had cohabitation with his spouse, but he ponder'd on the Rules of the Ancients, for the generation of Children of Wit. He ordered his diet according to the prescription of Galen, confining himself and his wife for almost the whole first year to Goat's Milk and Honey" (*Memoirs of Martinus Scriblerus,* p. 96).

For a general discussion of the relationship between *TS* and *Martinus Scriblerus,* see Ronald Paulson, *Satire and the Novel in Eighteenth-Century England* (New Haven: Yale University Press, 1967), pp. 252–54 and passim; and John M. Stedmond, *The Comic Art of Laurence Sterne*

(Toronto: University of Toronto Press, 1967), pp. 48—54 and passim.

1.7   temperature of his body] In view of Alan T. McKenzie's assertion that the
translator or printer of Charles Le Brun's *A Method To Learn to Design The
Passions* (1734) nodded in providing "the Temperature of the body" for
"temperament" (Augustan Reprint Society, 1980, nos. 200—201), it is
perhaps necessary to point out here that *temperature* was used interchangeably with *temperament* throughout the century; see, for example, 175.9
below, and *OED*, s.v. *Temperature*.

1.16   animal spirits] We may profitably turn to Burton's *Anatomy of Melancholy* for explanations of Sterne's scientific concepts and terms; e.g., "Of
the parts of the Body, there be many divisions: The most approved is that
of *Laurentius*, out of *Hippocrates:* which is, into parts *contained*, or *containing. Contained*, are either *Humours*, or *Spirits*. . . .

"Spirit is a most subtile vapour, which is expressed from the *Bloud*, and
the instrument of the soule, to performe all his actions; a common tye or
medium betwixt the body and the soule, as some will have it; or as *Para-
celsus*, a fourth soule of it selfe. *Melancthon* holds the fountaine of these
spirits to be the *Heart*, begotten there; and afterward convayed to the
Braine, they take another nature to them. Of these spirits there be three
kindes, according to the three principall parts, *Braine, Heart, Liver;
Naturall, Vitall, Animall*. The *Naturall* are begotten in the *Liver*, and
thence dispersed through the Veines, to performe those naturall actions.
The *Vitall Spirits* are made in the Heart of the *Naturall*, which by the
Arteries are transported to all the other parts: if these *Spirits* cease, then life
ceaseth, as in a *Syncope* or Swouning. The *Animal spirits* formed of the
Vitall, brought up to the Braine, and diffused by the Nerves, to the subordinate Members, give sense and motion to them all" (1.1.2.2, pp.
14—15).

A humor (see *TS*, 1.10) is defined as "a liquid or fluent part of the body,
comprehended in it, for the preservation of it; and is either innate and
borne with us, or adventitious and acquisite"; Burton goes on to outline the
ancient division of humors: blood, phlegm, choler, and melancholy.

Chambers, s.v. *Animal spirits*, takes a somewhat more scientific view:
"a fine subtile juice, or humour in animal bodies; supposed to be the great
instrument of muscular motion, sensation, *&c.*

"As it is hard to define what could never yet be brought under the judgment of our senses, all that we shall here offer concerning them, is, that they must needs be extremely subtile bodies, which escape all manner of examination by the senses, though ever so well assisted . . . ; yet are constantly moving in vast quantities, as they must of necessity be, to perform all those mighty operations which are ascribed to them.—However, the antiquity of the opinion claims some reverence."

A similar skepticism can be found in George Cheyne's *The English Malady* (1733), pp. 51–58: "The most difficult Problem in all the Animal Œconomy, is, to give any tolerable Account of *Muscular Action* or *Animal Motion*. The Similitude of a Machin put into Action and Motion by the Force of Water convey'd in Pipes, was the readiest Resemblance the *Lazy* could find to explain *Muscular Motion* by. It was easy, from this Resemblance, to forge a thin, imperceptible Fluid, passing and re-passing through the Nerves, to blow up the Muscles, and thereby to lengthen one of their Dimensions, in order to shorten the other. On such a slender and imaginary Similitude, the precarious *Hypothesis* of *Animal Spirits* seems to be built." Cheyne then goes on to dispute the idea, claiming instead that whatever the method of transmission it cannot be that of a fluid or substance resembling those that we know, but must instead be analogous to Newton's aether. He concludes: "From all which we may, I think, pretty firmly conclude, that the Notion of *animal Spirits* is of the same Leaven with the *substantial Forms* of *Aristotle* [see below, n. to 494.3], and the *cœlestial System* of *Ptolemy*."

2.2–8   the different tracks . . . off it.] Sterne seems to have Locke's analysis of the association of ideas in mind at this point, particularly the following passage: "This strong Combination of *Ideas*, not ally'd by Nature, the Mind makes in it self either voluntarily, or by chance, and hence it comes in different Men to be very different, according to their different Inclinations, Educations, Interests, *etc*. Custom settles habits of Thinking in the Understanding, as well as of Determining in the Will, and of Motions in the Body; all which seems to be but Trains of Motion in the Animal Spirits, which once set a going continue on in the same steps they have been used to, which by often treading are worn into a smooth path, and the Motion in it becomes easy and as it were Natural. As far as we can comprehend Thinking, thus *Ideas* seem to be produced in our Minds; or if they are not, this may serve to explain their following one another in an habitual train, when once they are put into that tract, as well as it does to explain such Motions of the Body" (*ECHU*, II.33.6, p. 396).

Sterne uses the Lockean concept of the "train of ideas" again, 119.20–21, 125.10, 225.1–8, 252.14, 413.10.

2.4   hey-go-mad] *OED* cites this passage as its first illustration.

2.9–14   *Pray, my dear . . . Nothing.*] Ferriar, I: 93n, suggests a possible source: "I strongly suspect, that Sterne took the incident alluded to, from the 'Description of a Country Life,' in the supplementary volume to Tom Brown's works." The passage is as follows: "Nay, to give you the last proof of their ill-breeding, in the critical minute of joy, when they ought to be all rapture and contemplation, then, even then, when they should be wrapt up in holy silence, they'll ask you a thousand foolish questions, as *mal a propos*, as if one should interrupt a popish priest at the elevation, and ask him what a clock it is" ("Description of a Country Life," in *The Works of Mr. Tom Brown*, 9th ed. [1760], IV: 263). William A. Eddy, "Tom Brown and *Tristram Shandy*," *MLN* 44 (1929): 379–81, calls attention to the same passage, with additional evidence from *ASJ* that Sterne was familiar with Brown's works.

Cf. *Sermons*, VI.37.106: "For since one principal reason, why God may be supposed to allow pleasure in this world, seems to be for the refreshment and recruit of our souls and bodies, which, like clocks, must be wound up at certain intervals . . . ."

For possible allusions in this incident to Descartes and Leibniz, see Ian Donaldson, "The Clockwork Novel: Three Notes on an Eighteenth-Century Analogy," *RES*, n.s. 21 (1970): 17–18.

2.10–12   cried my father . . . same time] Cf. Sterne's "Rabelaisian Fragment": "Good God! answer'd *Longinus Rabelaicus* (making an Exclamation, but taking Care to moderate his Voice at the same Time) . . ." (p. 1088, lines 13–15). On the relationship of the "Fragment" to *TS*, see New's introductory comments, pp. 1083–86.

2.17–20   scattered and dispersed . . . his reception.] Cf. Rabelais, III.31.207, where the physician Rondibilis advises Panurge on how to quell "carnal concupiscence" and urges certain drugs which "scatter and disperse the spirits, which ought to have gone along with and conducted

the sperm to the places destinated and appointed for its reception . . . ."
First noted by Stout, "Borrowings," p. 112.

2.19ff.   *HOMUNCULUS,* etc.] In an excellent essay, "The Shandean Homunculus: The Background of Sterne's 'Little Gentleman'," in *Restoration and Eighteenth-Century Literature: Essays in Honor of Alan Dugald McKillop* (Chicago: University of Chicago Press, 1963), pp. 49–68, Louis A. Landa has explored the scientific implications of this opening section of *TS*. Landa argues convincingly that Sterne is not really distorting contemporary views, but rather that the "account of the 'little gentleman' is based on the microscopic investigations and the speculations of such respected biologists of the late seventeenth century as Harvey, Swammerdown, Malpighi, Leeuwenhoek, de Graaf, and others whose embryological views were accepted and disseminated in the eighteenth century. These views were reflected in a theory called 'preformation' and in two schools of thought concerning human conception, the ovists and the animalculists, whose clashing ideas throw light on the opening chapters of *Tristram Shandy*" (p. 51).

Among the citations and quotations gathered by Landa to suggest how very closely Sterne was following the language of contemporary debate, the following will suffice: "But though Reason and Experience do now convince us, that all and every the most minute Part of every Animal, though ever so small, do really exist even to a single Artery, Vein, Nerve, Fibre; and all its Fluids were also in Motion, and circulated in the same, long before Generation: Yet whether this same Bud of Being, this *Minim* of Nature, this *Primordium Animalis*, this Principle of Body, this *Punctum vitae*, this *Stamen, Semen, Animalculum, Homunculus,* or *Manakin* in Miniature, was previously lodged in *Semine Masculino,* or in the *Ovum,* or Egg of the Female (for in one or the other it must needs be) is still Matter of Doubt and Dispute among Philosophers and Anatomists" (cited in Landa, p. 52, from J. C[ooke], *The New Theory of Generation, according to the Best and Latest Discoveries in Anatomy* [1762], I: 14); and: "If *in an Animalcule of the Masculine Seed of a Man, a whole Man is lock'd up,* then the several Particles previously in the *Ovum,* are no more than the first Food to this Stranger; this new arriv'd Child (who after being fatigu'd by so long a Journey, and through so many difficult and unaccessible Roads, when all those in Company with him have been so wearied, that they were

left behind and kill'd) had need of such Refreshment to rouse up his Spirits, and to make him grow up so as to become a brisk and lively Boy" (cited
in Landa, p. 59, from Patrick Blair, *Botanick Essays* [1720], p. 316).

Chambers, s.v. *Generation*, has a lengthy discussion of the animalculist
and ovulist schools. It is also worth observing that Cheyne, who is so
scornful of the theory of animal spirits (see above, n. to 1.16), is very
much an animalculist in his theory of generation (*The English Malady*, pp.
65–66).

A literary antecedent for Sterne's concerns here has been suggested by
Maurice Johnson, "A Comic Homunculus before *Tristram Shandy*," *LC*
31 (1965): 83–90; the anonymous work is entitled *The History of the Human Heart: or, The Adventures of a Young Gentleman* (1749), and does seem
to have anticipated—if not considerably outstripped—Sterne's interest in
the moment of conception: "his Conception did not take Place till twenty-
five Minutes after Twelve at Night. He had the first Perception of his
Existence, while yet in his Father's Custody; and was possessed of no other
Idea, nor sensible of Change of Place for many Days after. For though
from the first Moment of his Being he had all the Parts and Organs of a
perfect Animal, yet the several Members and component Parts were so
small, and of a Texture so infinitely delicate, that they were capable of
performing no Function sufficient to inform the Soul of the connection
between them, or furnish it with any new Ideas.

"For about fourteen Hours this Miniature of Man, whose Life is only
discoverable by the Microscope, swam in a limpid aromatic Liquid, and
at the end of that Time, when the Bride and Bridegroom were laid in Bed
. . . [and] begun the amorous Battle . . . the young *Camillo* shifted sides,
and nimbly skipped into the *Ovaria* of his Mother, where he found a
proper *Nidus* to support his little Body . . ." (cited in Johnson, pp.
84–85).

Finally, the opinion of the anonymous author of one of the first responses to Sterne, *The Clockmakers Outcry Against the Author of . . . Tristram Shandy* (1760), is worth consideration: "Most of what he says about
the *Homunculus* is false and absurd; besides (heaven forgive the poor man's
weak and obscene attempt!) *Lewenhoeck*'s system of *animalcula in semine
humano* hath long, long since been viewed in all the possible lights of
drollery and ridicule, in the schools of physic of the different universities

of Europe, by ingenious students; which subject ought to be confined
there, or to the books of their art"; we quote the facsimile reprint (New
York: Garland Publishing, 1975), pp. 15–16.

3.3–5   The minutest philosophers . . . us incontestably] Cf. George Berkeley, *Alciphron or the Minute Philosopher* (1732), Dialogue I, where Crito
and the freethinker, Alciphron, debate the definition of *minute philosopher:*
"the modern free-thinkers [says Crito] are the very same with those Cicero
called minute philosophers, which name admirably suits them, they being
a sort of sect which diminish all the most valuable things, the thoughts,
views, and hopes of men; all the knowledge, notions, and theories of the
mind they reduce to sense; human nature they contract and degrade to the
narrow low standard of animal life, and assign us only a small pittance of
time instead of immortality.

"Alciphron very gravely remarked that the gentlemen of his sect had
done no injury to man, and that, if he be a little, short-lived, contemptible
animal, it was not their saying it made him so . . . . As to what you
observe . . . it is my opinion this appellation might be derived from their
considering things minutely, and not swallowing them in the gross, as
other men are used to do. Besides, we all know the best eyes are necessary
to discern the minutest objects: it seems, therefore, that minute philosophers might have been so called from their distinguished perspicacity"
(*Works*, ed. A. A. Luce and T. E. Jessop [London: Thomas Nelson and
Sons, 1950], III: 46–47).

The reference to Cicero is to his *De Senectute*, 85 (pp. 96–97): "sin
mortuus, ut quidam minuti philosophi censent, nihil sentiam, non vereor
ne hunc errorem meum philosophi mortui irrideant"—"But if when dead
I am going to be without sensation (as some petty [minute] philosophers
think), then I have no fear that these seers, when they are dead, will have
the laugh on me!"

3.3   by the bye] A favorite, characteristic phrase; it occurs thirty-nine times in
TS, and repeatedly in Sterne's letters and other works.

3.8–11   That he consists . . . articulations] Cf. Rabelais, V.9.90: "Those
trees seem'd to us terrestrial animals, in no wise so different from brute
beasts as not to have skin, fat, flesh, veins, arteries, ligaments, nerves,
cartilages, kernels, bones, marrow, humours, matrices, brains, and articulations . . . ."

Despite the apparent verbal echo of Rabelais, Sterne is again not very far away from serious scientific writing on the subject; e.g., John Keill, *An Introduction to Natural Philosophy* (1720), p. 56: "Certainly it is not easy to conceive, how it is possible there should be contained in so narrow a compass, the Heart that is the Fountain of its Life, the Muscles necessary to its Motions, the Glands for the Secretion of its Fluids, the Stomach and Bowels to digest its Food, and other innumerable Members, without which it is impossible an Animal should subsist. But since every one of these Members is also an organical Body, they must have likewise Parts necessary to their Actions. For they consist of Fibres, Membranes, Coats, Veins, Arteries, Nerves, and an almost infinite Number of fine Tubes like to these, whose Smallness seems to exceed the very Force of the Imagination. But there are some Parts that ought to be almost infinitely less than these, as the Fluids that flow along these fine Tubes, and such are the Blood, Lymph, and Animal Spirits, whose Subtility even in large Animals is incredible."

See Melvyn New, "Laurence Sterne and Henry Baker's *The Microscope Made Easy*," *SEL* 10 (1970): 599–600.

3.13   Lord Chancellor of England] See Chambers, s.v. *Chancellor: "Lord High* CHANCELLOR *of England*, is the first person of the realm, next after the king, and princes of the blood, in all civil affairs. He is the chief administrator of justice next the sovereign; being the judge of the court of chancery."

3.13–17   He may . . . state and relation.] Work, p. 6, n. 2: "Marcus Tullius Cicero (106–43 B.C.), the Roman orator and statesman; the allusion here is to his *De Legibus*. Samuel Pufendorf (1632–1694), a German jurist, historian, and philosopher, whose chief work, alluded to here, is *De Jure Naturae et Gentium*." The allusion, however, is so general that no particular work, much less passage, can be safely assigned; Cicero's *De Officiis* also speaks much to the point of the benefits, injuries, and appeals to justice of man in society; and Sterne could as easily have had in mind Pufendorf's *De officio hominis et civis juxta legem naturalem libri duo*, where he might have read, in the standard translation, that "by the Constituting of Communities, Men were reduc'd into such an Order and Method, that they might be safe and secure from mutual Wrongs and Injuries among themselves, [and] . . . might the better enjoy those Advantages, which are to be reap'd and expected from one another . . ." (*The Whole Duty of Man According to the Law of Nature,* 2d ed. [1698], p. 246).

Cf. Locke's advice for the young student of civil law in *Some Thoughts Concerning Education,* sec. 186, pp. 294–95: "When he has pretty well digested *Tully's Offices,* and added to it *Puffendorf de Officio hominis & civis,* it may be seasonable to set him upon *Grotius de Jure Belli & Pacis,* or which perhaps is the better of the two, *Puffendorf de Jure naturali & Gentium;* wherein he will be instructed in the natural Rights of Men, and the Original and Foundations of Society, and the Duties resulting from thence."

4.1–21 To my uncle . . . him very well.] Arguing that Sterne had no precise plan when he began, R. F. Brissenden points to the characterizations of Walter and Toby in this chapter as one piece of evidence. Walter's tears and Toby's grasp of the situation (with its sexual overtones) are, Brissenden argues, quite out of character with their personalities as they eventually evolved ("'Trusting to Almighty God': Another Look at the Composition of *Tristram Shandy,*" in *Winged Skull,* pp. 264–66).

4.1 Mr. *Toby Shandy*] Cash, *Early and Middle Years,* pp. 18–19, suggests the possibility that Sterne recalled a childhood acquaintance, Colonel Thomas Palliser (his aunt Elizabeth's brother-in-law) in his portrait of Toby: "The older man was in his sixties when Laurence would have come to know him. In rough outline, he is strikingly suggestive of Uncle Toby. Perhaps Laurence even called him 'Uncle Thomas'. At least he heard him called that by his cousin, the younger Walter Palliser, with whom Sterne later attended college. Like Uncle Toby, the Colonel was a native of the North Riding of Yorkshire who had served many years as a captain of Grenadiers. He had fought in the siege of Limerick; perhaps he was the source of those realistic details about that muddy siege told in the novel . . . . Colonel Palliser had served in Flanders during the wars of both William and Anne, taking part in many battles which poor, disabled Uncle Toby could only play out on his bowling green. He was, moreover, a religious man, as one judges from his gift of a silver chalice to the Protestant church at Castletown Carne. . . . Sterne's character was not modelled upon any single historical person, but old Colonel Palliser comes closer to him than anyone else in Sterne's known life."

See also p. 19, n. 1, for Cash's effective dismissal of the theory that Toby was modeled upon Captain Robert Hinde (1720–86), famous for his miniature fortifications.

4.6–8   upon his observing . . . done it] Cf. Cornelius Scriblerus's observation of Martinus: "His disposition to the Mathematicks was discover'd very early, by his drawing parallel lines on his bread and butter, and intersecting them at equal Angles, so as to form the whole Superficies into squares" (*Memoirs of Martinus Scriblerus*, pp. 107–8).

Cf. Locke, *Some Thoughts Concerning Education*, sec. 102, pp. 206–7: "Begin therefore betimes nicely to observe your Son's *Temper;* and that, when he is under least restraint, in his Play, and as he thinks out of your sight. See what are his *Predominant Passions,* and *prevailing Inclinations* . . . . These *native Propensities,* these Prevalencies of Constitution, are not to be cured by Rules . . . though with Art they may be much mended, and turned to good purposes. But this, be sure, after all is done, the Byass will always hang on that side, that Nature first placed it . . . ."

4.15–16   tear . . . trickling down his cheeks] Sterne uses this sentimental formula again in *TS,* 33.24–25, 144.21, 161.24, 330.13–14, 746.7–8; in *ASJ,* p. 271; and in the *Sermons,* e.g., IV.22.4. The "single tear," also a sentimental formula, is used again in *TS,* 32.24, 100.26, 255.27, 265.21, 329.11, 435.7, 498.26, 511.6, 643.11, 741.13, 798.5; and also in *ASJ,* pp. 133, 214. It can also be found in the *Sermons,* e.g., I.3.69.

The use of the "single tear" after Sterne is briefly chronicled by Alfred G. Engstrom, "The Single Tear: A Stereotype of Literary Sensibility," *PQ* 42 (1963): 106–9.

5.8–9   read than the *Pilgrim's Progress*] In 1773 Johnson commented: "Few books, I believe, have had a more extensive sale" (Boswell, *Life of Johnson,* II: 238).

5.10–11   *Montaigne* dreaded . . . parlour-window] In his essay "Upon some Verses of Virgil" (III.5.71), Montaigne writes: "I am vexed that my *Essays* only serve the Ladies for a common moveable, a Book to lie in the Parlour Window; this Chapter shall prefer me to the Closet . . . ."

See 605.16–18 and n. below.

5.16   as *Horace* says, *ab Ovo.*] As Sterne—and everyone else in the eighteenth century—well knew, Horace's famous comment actually praises Homer for hurrying the reader "in medias res," as the proper way to open an epic poem: "nec reditum Diomedis ab interitu Meleagri, / nec gemino bellum

Troianum orditur ab ovo; / semper ad eventum festinat et in medias res / non secus ac notas auditorem rapit . . ." ("Nor does he begin Diomede's return from the death of Meleager, or the war of Troy from the twin eggs. Ever he hastens to the issue, and hurries his hearer into the story's midst, as if already known . . ."), *Satires, Epistles and Ars Poetica*, pp. 462–63. Cf. *TS*, 342.14–15: "write as I will, and rush as I may into the middle of things, as *Horace* advises . . . ."

5.20–22   for in writing . . . that ever lived.] Cf. Fielding's similar assertion in *Tom Jones*, book II, chap. 1: "For all which I shall not look on myself as accountable to any Court of Critical Jurisdiction whatever: For as I am, in reality, the Founder of a new Province of Writing, so I am at liberty to make what Laws I please therein" (ed. Martin Battestin and Fredson Bowers [Middletown, Conn.: Wesleyan University Press, 1975], I: 77).

5.23–26   To such . . . curious and inquisitive.] Colley Cibber, in his *Apology*, 2d ed. (1740), gives the same advice to his reader: "Now, Sir, for Amusement.—Reader, take heed! for I find a strong impulse to talk impertinently; if therefore you are not as fond of seeing, as I am of shewing myself in all my Lights, you may turn over two Leaves together, and leave what follows to those who have more Curiosity, and less to do with their Time, than you have" (p. 20). Cf. Swift, *Tale of a Tub*, p. 203: "*Curiosity* . . . affords the firmest Grasp [to hold the reader]: *Curiosity*, that Spur in the side, that Bridle in the Mouth, that Ring in the Nose, of a lazy, an impatient, and a grunting Reader. By this *Handle* it is, that an Author should seize upon his Readers . . . ."

Tristram appeals to the curious and inquisitive reader again, 74.4–11: "My way is ever to point out to the curious, different tracts of investigation . . . with the officious humility of a heart devoted to the assistance merely of the inquisitive;--to them I write,——and by them I shall be read . . ."; cf. 196.26–27 and 627.4. For the possible significance of these appeals, see Melvyn New, "The Dunce Revisited: Colley Cibber and *Tristram Shandy*," *SAQ* 72 (1973): 547–59.

6.7–8   now made public] Watt, p. 6., n. 3: "A stock journalistic phrase, used especially in titles of pamphlets on matters of public concern."

6.9–10   originally a *Turky* merchant] I.e., a member of the Turkey or Levant Company, trading in that area of the world. See Chambers, s.v. *Company:*

"*Turky* COMPANY . . . . This flourishing body had its rise under queen Elizabeth: James I. confirmed its charter in 1606 . . . .

"The places reserved for the commerce of this *Company*, are all the states of Venice, in the gulph of Venice; the state of Ragusa [in Sicily]; all the states of the grand seignior, and the ports of the Levant and [eastern] Mediterranean . . . ."

Cf. *Tom Jones*, II: 826: "She had been married young by her Relations to an old *Turkey* Merchant, who having got a great Fortune, had left off Trade."

7.1−9   from an unhappy association . . . whatsoever.] Cf. Locke, *ECHU*, II.33.9: "This wrong Connexion in our Minds of *Ideas* in themselves, loose and independent one of another, has such an influence, and is of so great force to set us awry in our Actions, as well Moral as Natural, Passions, Reasonings, and Notions themselves, that, perhaps, there is not any one thing that deserves more to be looked after" (p. 397). See also sec. 5, p. 395: "Some of our *Ideas* have a natural Correspondence and Connexion one with another . . . . Besides this there is another Connexion of *Ideas* wholly owing to Chance or Custom; *Ideas* that in themselves are not at all of kin, come to be so united in some Mens Minds, that 'tis very hard to separate them, they always keep in company, and the one no sooner at any time comes into the Understanding but its Associate appears with it; and if they are more than two which are thus united, the whole gang always inseparable shew themselves together."

7.12   *Lady-Day*] Popular name for celebration of the Feast of the Annunciation, March 25.

7.15   *Westminster* school] According to the *DNB*, s.v. *Robert Freind* (1667−1751), who served as headmaster from 1711 to 1733, Westminster during this time was "the favourite place of education for the aristocracy. Indeed the list of boys who recited the epigrams at the anniversary dinner in 1727−8 contains a far greater number of distinguished names than any other school at that period could have shown."

8.1−3   ON the fifth day . . . have expected] Cf. Montaigne, I.19.78: "I was born betwixt eleven and twelve o' Clock in the Forenoon, the last of *February, 1533* . . . ."

It was first pointed out by "HRPC" in *N&Q*, 8th ser. 7 (1895):

28–29, that this is eight rather than nine months from Tristram's March conception. John A. Hay, "Rhetoric and Historiography: Tristram Shandy's First Nine Kalendar Months," in *Studies in the Eighteenth Century II* (Toronto: University of Toronto Press, 1973), pp. 73–91, examines the possibility of Tristram's illegitimacy, citing in evidence Chambers, s.v. *Delivery:* "A *legitimate Delivery*, is that which happens at the just term, *i.e.* in the 10th lunar month. And an *illegitimate*, that which comes either sooner, or later, as in the 8th month." This point is taken up and expanded in the *Supplement* to Chambers, s.v. *Birth: "Eight months* BIRTH, *partus octimestris*, seldom if ever produces a living, or lively child. An eight month's *birth* is always weak and sickly, and scarce ever survives the fortieth day. Physicians, as well as lawyers, have doubted, whether an eight months *birth* be legitimate and vital grounded on the authority of Hippocrates, the superstitious conclusions of astrologers, the powers of numbers, and the malevolent influences of Saturn, the doctrine that the mother's labours and pains in this month are the severest, and her danger greatest." There are, to be sure, a good many hints of Tristram's illegitimacy throughout the work, some of which are gathered by Hay.

An explanation for this belief is provided by John Glaister, *Dr. William Smellie and his Contemporaries* (Glasgow: J. Maclehose, 1894), p. 191: "we find him [i.e., William Smellie] opposing the Hippocratic doctrine, which, up till this time, had been faithfully followed by almost every previous writer—we believe, by every previous writer—which was to the effect, that a foetus born at the eighth month had a less chance of survival than one born at the end of the previous month, because, it was believed, that every healthy foetus made an effort to be delivered at the end of the seventh month, and that a second effort was made at the end of the eighth, at which time the foetus, if successful, was so weakened by its former abortive attempt that it was unlikely to survive . . . ." Smellie's opposition to this theory was published in 1751 in his *Treatise on the Theory and Practice of Midwifery.*

It is almost assuredly no accident that Sterne chose November 5; see *The Book of Days: A Miscellany of Popular Antiquities in Connection with the Calendar*, ed. Robert Chambers (Philadelphia: J. B. Lippincott Company, 1862–64), II: 546: "The 5th of November marks the anniversary of two prominent events in English history—the discovery and prevention of the gunpowder treason [1605] and the inauguration of the Revolution of 1688 by the landing of William III. in Torbay." Guy Fawkes Day, as it was popularly called, was celebrated from 1606 to 1859 with a special church service and, according to Chambers, was regarded "as one of the most joyous days of the year," with masked processions and bonfires (pp. 549–50); the two events being commemorated rather insured an anti-Catholic attitude among the celebrants. Cf. Anthony Collins, *A Discourse Concerning Ridicule and Irony in Writing* (1729; Augustan Reprint Society, 1970, no. 142): "Nor do our Divines confine their *Derisions, Ridicule* and *Irony* against *Popery* to their Treatises and Discourses, but fill their *Sermons*, and especially their *Sermons* on the *Fifth* of *November*, and other political *Days*, with infinite Reflections of that Kind" (p. 32).

8.4   disasterous] Watt, p. 7, n. 1: "Sterne's spelling reminds us that disastrous comes from 'disaster,' meaning ill-starred, or born when a star or planet was in an astrologically unfavorable aspect; Sterne continues the analogy for the rest of the chapter."

8.6   *Jupiter* or *Saturn*] The most distant of the seven planets of the Ancients, and hence the coldest.

8.15–16   every man . . . gone in it] Proverbial; see Tilley, M557: "MEN speak of the fair as things went with them there"; and *ODEP*, s.v. *Speak*.

8.20–21   for an asthma . . . in *Flanders*] On Sterne's health at this time see Cash, *Early and Middle Years*, pp. 283–84, and n. to Ded. 5–6 above. Sterne returns to the phrase again, 663.13–14: "To this hour art thou not tormented with the vile asthma thou gattest in skating against the wind in Flanders?" In his letters Sterne never refers to his own illness as asthmatic, but his daughter Lydia was so afflicted: "[Lydia] is in a declining way with this vile Asthma of hers, which these last 3 winters has been growing worse & worse . . ." (to Lord Fauconberg, April 10, 1762, *Letters*, p. 160). See also *Letters*, pp. 162, 164.

8.22–9.2   She has ever . . . HERO sustained.] Sterne returns to this phrasing again in vol. VII: "For which reason I think myself inexcusable, for blaming Fortune so often as I have done, for pelting me all my life long, like an ungracious dutchess, as I call'd her, with so many small evils: surely if I have any cause to be angry with her, 'tis that she has not sent me great ones . . ." (624.19–23).

9.1   misadventures and cross accidents] Cf. *Sermons*, I.2.40 ("The House of

Feasting and the House of Mourning Described"): "Let us go into the house of mourning, made so . . . by the common cross accidents and disasters to which our condition is exposed,—where perhaps, the aged parents sit broken hearted, pierced to their souls with the folly and indiscretion of a thankless child—the child of their prayers, in whom all their hopes and expectations centred . . . ." Sterne uses a similar phrase, "failings and cross accidents," in *Sermons,* I.5.130; another, "calamities and cross accidents, to which the life of man is subject," in II.15.222; and still another, "several distresses and cross accidents," in VI.34.16. See also II.15.233, V.28.20, VI.34.5.

Cf. *TS,* 332.11–12: "the catalogue of all the cross reckonings and sorrowful *items* with which the heart of man is overcharged . . . ."

9.16   *O diem præclarum!*] A commonplace Latin tag; see Boswell, *Life of Johnson,* III: 438. The original is found in Cicero, *De Senectute,* 84, pp. 96–97: "O praeclarum diem cum in illud divinum animorum concilium coetumque proficiscar cumque ex hac turba et colluvione discedam!" ("O glorious day, when I shall set out to join the assembled hosts of souls divine and leave this world of strife and sin!").

10.4ff.   IN the same village, etc.] Sterne's description of the midwife accords well with the usual qualifications associated with the function, including her "three or four small children," childbearing being regarded as a necessary qualification. Jean Donnison, *Midwives and Medical Men* (London: Schocken Books, 1977), p. 16, quotes from Dr. William Sermon's *Ladies Companion, or, The English Midwife* (1671), on the desirable attributes of a midwife: "As concerning their Persons, they must be neither too young, nor too old, but of an indifferent age between both; well composed, not being subject to diseases, nor deformed in any part of their body; comely and neat in their Apparell, their hands small, and fingers long, not thick, but clean, their nails pared very close; they ought to be very chearfull, pleasant, and of a good discourse, strong, not idle, but accustomed to exercise, that they may be the more able (if need requires) to watch, &c.

"Touching their deportment: they must be mild, gentle, courteous, sober, chast, and patient, not quarrelsom, nor chollerick . . . .

"As concerning their minds; they must be wise, and discreet; able to flatter, and speak many fair words, to no other end, but only to deceive the apprehensive women, which is a commendable deceipt, and allowed, when it is done for the good of the person in distress."

Cf. John Maubray, M.D., *The Female Physician, Containing all the Diseases incident to that Sex . . . To which is added, the Whole Art of New Improv'd Midwifery* (1724), pp. 173–74: "She ought to be *Grave* and *Considerate*, endued with *Resolution* and *Presence* of *Mind*, in order to foresee and prevent ACCIDENTS; *Sagacious* and *Prudent* in difficult *Cases*. . . . She ought to be *Faithful* and *Silent*; always on her *Guard* to conceal those *Things*, which ought not to be spoken of." This passage was suggested to us by Professor Robert A. Erickson.

Sterne's comment that she trusted "a great deal to . . . dame nature" (lines 8–9) suggests his familiarity with the standard midwifery treatises, where this advice was always given. J. H. Aveling, *English Midwives: Their History and Prospects* (1872; New York: AMS Press, 1977), pp. 35–42, provides several examples from William Harvey, Percivall Willughby, and William Sermon, famous seventeenth-century physicians; e.g., from Willughby's *Midwife's Opusculum:* "The midwife's duty in a natural birth is no more but to attend and wait on Nature . . . . And let midwives know that they bee Nature's servants." See also in Aveling the digest of qualifications for the midwife, pp. 133–37.

11.13–19 In truth . . . fourpence] Following "An Acte concernynge the approbation of phisycyons and surgions" (*Public General Statutes of the Realm,* Henry VIII, 3, cap. 11; cited in Donnison, *Midwives,* pp. 5, 203), midwives were required to be licensed by ecclesiastical authorities and had to produce character witnesses, among whom were usually the parson and churchwardens of the parish. Though practicing without a license could result in prohibition, penance, or excommunication, by the middle of the eighteenth century the system was no longer strictly enforced (Donnison, pp. 5–6, 22). The form of oath administered to a midwife during this time is given in Aveling, *English Midwives,* pp. 90–93; a sample license (1738) is also provided (pp. 94–95): "Joseph, by Divine Permission, Bishop of Rochester, To our well-beloved in Christ Elizabeth Chapman . . . : Whereas We understand by good testimony and credible certificates that you the said Elizabeth Chapman are apt and able, cunning and expert, to use and exercise the office, business, and function of a

Midwife, We therefore by virtue of Our Power Ordinary and Episcopal, Do admit and give you power to use and exercise the said office, business, and function of a Midwife in and through our Diocese and Jurisdiction of Rochester, with the best care and diligence you may or can in this behalf, indifferently both to poor and rich, as also to perform and accomplish all things about the same, according to your oath thereupon given you upon the Holy Evangelists, as far as God will give you Grace and enable you."

11.21–22   *rights, members, and appurtenances whatsoever.*] See Cash, *Early and Middle Years*, p. 289, n. 2: "This legal phrase, which so amused Sterne, occurred in numerous legal documents—for instance, Sterne's collation to the vicarage of Sutton, BM: Add. Chart. 16159. On the face is a statement that Sterne has been invested 'with all and singular the Rights Members and Appurtenances' of his new office; *verso* a certificate of performance signed by Philip Harland, the Reverend Richard Musgrave and Ralph Robson, a church-warden, testifying that Sterne was inducted 'into yᵉ real & corporal possession of yᵉ vicarage of Sutton on yᵉ Forest with all its fruits, profits, members & appurtenances'." Sterne uses the phrase again, 45.15; and he seems to have been particularly delighted with the play of *appurtenance/purtenance* ("an appendage" / "the 'inwards' of an animal"— *OED*), substituting "purtenance" for "interior parts" in the English translation of "Ernulphus's Curse" (209.16); see vol. II, app. 8, p. 956, in this edition. See also 379.3: "the upper regions of *Phutatorius's* purtenance."

11.26   neat *Formula* of *Didius*] Cash, *Early and Middle Years*, offers a suggestion as to why *Didius* was immediately recognized as Dr. Francis Topham (1713–70), a leading York lawyer: "The clue is contained in that incident in which Didius 'coax'd many of the old licensed [midwives] in the neighbourhood, to open their faculties afresh, in order to have this whim-wham of his inserted'. The whim-wham referred to so ambiguously is only a legal phrase, in a document called a 'faculty', giving the midwife her office along with all its 'rights, members, and appurtenances whatsoever' . . . . The master of the faculties for the Northern Province of the church was Dr Francis Topham" (p. 289).

Topham plays a central role in the *Political Romance*, where he is satirized under the name Trim, well known "in all the Parish, to be . . . a little, dirty, pimping, pettifogging, ambidextrous Fellow,—who neither cared what he did or said of any, provided he could get a Penny by it" (p. 9); see Cash, pp. 262–77. Sterne later expressed regret for his pillorying Topham in the *Romance* (*Letters*, p. 147), but did not mention his more general satire here and at greater length in vols. III and IV, perhaps because Didius had become for him a generalized representative of the legal profession, and not specifically Topham.

Work, p. 12, n. 1: "In the name, Sterne may have extended an allusion to Julianus Severus Didius who in A.D. 193 purchased the Roman Empire from the praetorian guards, to the indignation of the people whose subsequent revolt forced the senate to condemn and execute him"; cf. Pope's "Epistle to Bathurst," lines 127–28: "Glorious Ambition! Peter, swell thy store, / And be what Rome's great Didius was before" (in *Epistles to Several Persons*, p. 102). Less likely, Sterne may perhaps have had in mind Titus Didius, who in 98 B.C. helped to pass the *lex Caecilia Didia*, which "established procedure for valid legislation" (*OCD*, s.v. *Didius, Titus*).

12.2   whim-wham] Seventeenth-century examples in *OED* indicate the word was in use for *penis* during that century, although this passage is cited to illustrate the definition "fantastic notion, odd fancy." Sterne may have found the word in Rabelais, I.12.188: "Will you have a whimwham? What is that, said they? It is, said he, five turds to make you a muzzle"; or IV.32.214, n. 2: "whim-whams, men's pissing tools."

12.5–9   Did not Dr. *Kunastrokius* . . . pocket?] Sterne alludes to Richard Mead (1673–1754), an eminent London physician whose private life was the subject of public comment. Walpole wrote to Horace Mann (July 25, 1750): "Dr Meade is undone, his fine collection is going to be sold; he owes above five and twenty thousand pounds. All the world thought him immensely rich; but besides the expense of his collection, he kept a table, for which alone he is said to have allowed seventy pounds a week. He was very voluptuous; and secret history says, that as his seraglio were obliged to take extraordinary pains, they too had extraordinary pay" (*Correspondence with Sir Horace Mann*, ed. W. S. Lewis et al. [New Haven: Yale University Press, 1960], IV: 165). A pamphlet entitled *The Cornutor of Seventy-Five*, which had two editions and appeared c. 1748, was rather more specific: "At last, a Thought struck the Nymph in the Head, which she hinted to the Don. She was soon understood, and the Scheme put in

Practice with as much Severity as ever Pedant flogg'd his Pupil. The Don's Posteriors were taught a Feeling, if nothing else was; but all in vain. This Night's Campaign contributed nothing to cure the Don's Itch of Blood, and several successive Nights had no better Effect; they only convinced him of the Frailty of the Flesh, and that his Part on the Stage was not to be active. From this Time he contents himself with surveying Donna Maria's naked Beauties, pressing her naked Charms, and in combing her red Locks" (p. 51).

Shortly after *TS* was published, Sterne wrote a long letter to an unknown acquaintance specifically defending this part of the work; Curtis believes that its "laboured formality . . . suggests that Sterne may have intended it as a public defence of his book, should the necessity arise" (*Letters*, p. 91). Responding first to the maxim *de mortuis nil nisi bonum*, Sterne writes: "I declare I have considered the wisdom, and foundation of it over and over again . . . and, after all, I can find nothing in it, or make more of it, than a nonsensical lullaby of some nurse, put into Latin by some pedant, to be chanted by some hypocrite to the end of the world, for the consolation of departing lechers." He then goes on to consider the reference to Mead: "I have not cut up Doctor Kunastrokius at all—I have just scratch'd him—and that scarce skin-deep.—I do him first all honour—speak of Kunastrokius as a great man—(be he who he will) and then most distantly hint at a drole foible in his character—and that not first reported (to the few who can even understand the hint) by me—but known before by every chamber-maid and footman within the bills of mortality . . . . If Kunastrokius after all is too sacred a character to be even smiled at, (which is all I have done) he has had better luck than his betters:—In the same page . . . I have said as much of a man of twice his wisdom—and that is Solomon, of whom I have made the same remark 'That they were both great men—and like all mortal men had each their ruling passion'" (pp. 88–89).

Sterne uses the formation *Kunastrokius* again, and then cancels it, in an entry in the "Journal to Eliza," May 31, 1767 (*Letters*, p. 347); its similarity to Voltaire's Cunegund, cited by Sterne a few pages later (17.1), should be noted.

12.11 HOBBY-HORSES] Work's note (p. 13, n. 3), "Hobbies," is somewhat inadequate; Watt's (p. 10, n. 5) is more useful in that it reminds us that *hobby-horse* is a child's plaything, a stick with a horse's head attached, thus making clearer Sterne's constant play on *riding* the hobby-horse. It should also be noted that the word was in use throughout the seventeenth century for "a wanton, a prostitute" (Partridge, s.v.).

Sterne may also have had in mind *Hamlet*, III.ii.135: "For O, for O, the hobby-horse is forgot," a line from a popular anti-puritanical ballad lamenting the prohibition of country games and dances, in which the hobby-horse, a participant costumed like a horse, played a large part.

Tristram was not alone in his favorable attitude toward hobby-horses. George Cheyne, for example, in his important work, *The English Malady*, advises diversion as essential to the treatment of nervous disorders: "It seems to me absolutely impossible, without such a Help, to keep the Mind easy, and prevent its wearing out the Body, as the Sword does the Scabbard; it is no matter what it is, provided it be but a *Hobby-Horse*, and an Amusement, and stop the Current of Reflexion and intense Thinking, which Persons of weak Nerves are aptest to run into" (p. 126). And in Colley Cibber's *Apology*, pp. 17–18, immediately following a passage Sterne almost certainly borrowed (see below, n. to 103.27), Cibber wrote in defense of himself: "I can no more put off my Follies, than my Skin; I have often try'd, but they stick too close to me; nor am I sure my Friends are displeased with them; for, besides that in this Light I afford them frequent matter of Mirth, they may possibly be less uneasy at their *own* Foibles, when they have so old a Precedent . . . . If *Socrates* cou'd take pleasure in playing at *Even or Odd* with his Children, or *Agesilaus* divert himself in riding the Hobby-horse with them, am I oblig'd to be as eminent as either of them before I am as frolicksome?" Cibber may have borrowed the sentiment from Dryden's "Life of Plutarch," *Works* (Berkeley: University of California Press, 1971), XVII: 275.

12.12   running horses] Cf. Grose's *Dictionary of the Vulgar Tongue* (1785): "RUNNING HORSE, or NAG, a clap, or gleet." Sterne may, of course, have had only racing horses in mind.

12.14   maggots] As Watt notes (p. 10, n. 7), *maggots* can mean "whimsical fancies." However, since Sterne is here listing specific fancies, it is quite probable that he is also punning, as does Pope in the *Dunciad*(A), I.59–60: "Maggots half-form'd, in rhyme exactly meet, / And learn to crawl upon poetic feet" (p. 67); or is alluding very specifically to the age's ever increasing scientific interest in insects and microscopic organisms. Cf. Thomas Shadwell, *The Virtuoso*, ed. Marjorie Hope Nicolson and David Stuart Rodes (Lincoln: University of Nebraska Press, 1966), III.iii.1–5: "I do assure you, gentlemen, no man upon the face of the earth is so well seen in the nature of ants, flies, humble-bees, earwigs . . . maggots, mites in a cheese, tadpoles . . . and all the noble products of the sun by equivocal generation."

12.18   *De gustibus non est disputandum*] "There is no disputing about tastes." This passage is the first example cited in the *Stanford Dictionary;* but Stevenson, p. 2282, cites the appearance of this expression in Jeremy Taylor's *Reflections upon Ridicule* (1667).

12.21–22   for happening . . . both fiddler and painter] Cf. Sterne's own "Memoirs," written for his daughter: "I remained near twenty years at Sutton, doing duty at both places—I had then very good health.—Books, painting, fiddling, and shooting were my amusements" (*Letters*, p. 4); see also pp. 122, 191.

Concerning Sterne's exercises in painting, see Cash, *Early and Middle Years*, pp. 209–14; in music, Cash, p. 208, and much more extensively, William Freedman, *Laurence Sterne and the Origins of the Musical Novel* (Athens: University of Georgia Press, 1978). Sterne's "fiddle," according to Freedman, was the viola da gamba, an instrument particularly suited for improvisation (p. 15).

An engraving of one of Sterne's artistic efforts has survived and is reproduced in Cash, plate II.

Cf. Boswell's "A Poetical Epistle to Doctor Sterne, Parson Yorick, And Tristram Shandy": "He read as humour bid him do; / If Metaphysics seem'd too dark, / Shifted to Gay from Dr. Clark[e]; / If in the least it hurt his eyes, / He instantaneously would rise, / Take up his violin and play; / His pencil next, then sketch away . . ." (*Boswell's Book of Bad Verse*, ed. Jack Werner [London: White Lion Publishers, 1974], p. 134); see also F. A. Pottle, "Bozzy and Yorick," *Blackwood's Magazine* 217 (1925): 297–313.

12.23   as the fly stings] Proverbial; variant of Tilley, M5: "When the MAGGOT bites" (i.e., when the whim takes one); and *ODEP*, s.v. *Maggot*.

Sterne may have had in mind the famous portrait of Zimri in *Absalom and Achitophel:* "A man so various, that he seem'd to be / Not one, but all

Mankinds Epitome. / Stiff in Opinions, always in the wrong; / Was every thing by starts, and nothing long: / But, in the course of one revolving Moon, / Was Chymist, Fidler, States-Man, and Buffoon: / Then all for Women, Painting, Rhiming, Drinking; / Besides ten thousand freaks that dy'd in thinking" (John Dryden, *Poems*, ed. James Kinsley [Oxford: Clarendon Press, 1958], I: 231, lines 545–52).

13.15–16   like . . . astride a mortgage] In the "Rabelaisian Fragment" Sterne had originally written "little Devil astride a Mortgage" and then changed it to "little black Devil" (p. 1089, line 68).

13.26–28   great actions . . . good ones] Cf. the dedication to vol. I, added for the second edition: "*I am, great Sir, / (and what is more to your Honour,) I am, good Sir . . . .*" The contrast between *great* and *good* is an eighteenth-century commonplace, its most famous statements perhaps being those in Fielding's novels and Gray's "Elegy Written in a Country Church-Yard." See Henry Knight Miller, *Essays on Fielding's "Miscellanies"* (Princeton: Princeton University Press, 1961), pp. 46–51.

15.2   Prince, Prelate, Pope, or Potentate] Sterne may be recalling the Oath of Supremacy required for ordination: "And I do declare, that no foreign Prince, Person, Prelate, State or Potentate, hath or ought to have any Jurisdiction . . . within this Realm" (see Richard Grey, *A System of English Ecclesiastical Law*, 4th ed. [1743], p. 49). Cf. 769.10–11.

16.1–16   My Lord . . . *tout ensemble.*] The best commentary on this paragraph is provided by R. F. Brissenden, "Sterne and Painting," in *Of Books and Humankind: Essays and Poems Presented to Bonamy Dobrée*, ed. John Butt (London: Routledge & Kegan Paul, 1964), pp. 97–98: "The painter's scale so expertly flourished here would have been instantly recognized by any of Sterne's readers with pretentions to taste. It was the invention of one of the best known authorities on painting in the seventeenth and eighteenth centuries, Roger de Piles, who had offered it to the world in 1708 in his *Cours de Peinture par Principes*. Jonathan Richardson, in his *Argument on behalf of the Science of a Connoisseur* (1719), had recommended the use of M. de Piles's scale to all gentlemen eager to learn how to judge paintings . . . ; and in 1752 Joseph Spence in his *Crito: or, a Dialogue on Beauty* suggested, rather less solemnly, that a similar scale might be used to determine the 'proportionall Excellence' of female beauty. An English translation of de Piles, *The Principles of Painting*, was published in 1743 . . . .

"De Piles is a natural Scriblerian victim for Sterne's wit. He is an unadventurous and dogmatic Platonist who tells the reader in his Preface to *The Principles of Painting* that 'the surest way to know infallibly the *true idea* of things is, to derive it from the very *basis* of their *essence and definition*.' Like Walter Shandy he is a 'systematick reasoner': and the system he constructs is notable for the crude generality of its idealistic assumptions, the rigid lack of imagination with which they are developed, and the trivial pedantry of the end product: a set of ruled columns like an examination record sheet in which various painters are awarded so many marks for their proficiency in 'the most essential parts' of their art. Design, 'the *intire thought* of a work' as de Piles calls it, was generally admitted to be the area in which it was most important for the painter to excel. Among the fifty or so artists listed in *The Principles of Painting* only Raphael scores eighteen out of twenty for design—the highest mark awarded by de Piles for anything. Tristram confidently allows himself nineteen for design, and a precise thirteen and a half for expression."

Brissenden goes on to suggest a source for the last sentence of the paragraph: "in the concluding sentence Tristram's argument depends on the compositional principle that the most important person in a history painting or a portrait should occupy the most prominent position. The rule has been enunciated by many writers; but the immediate if not the only source of Sterne's expression of it here seems to have been a passage in *The Art of Painting*, by Gérard de Lairesse [(1738), p. 35]. According to de Lairesse, 'you must place your *principal Figures* conspicuous and elevated upon the fore Ground; give them the *main Light, and the greatest Force of Colouring, in one Mass, or Group;* the *less Objects* must be somewhat lower, and their Force of Light and Colour more spread. The second Ground ought to be in *Shade,* or filled with *shady Objects.*'"

That Tristram is thinking very highly of himself when he gives his design a score of nineteen is also suggested by a synopsis of de Piles's system in James Russel's *Letters from a Young Painter Abroad to his Friends in England* (1748): "The method I have taken is this: I divide my weight into twenty parts, or degrees. The twentieth degree is the highest, and implies sovereign perfection; which no man has fully arrived at. The nineteenth is the highest degree that we know, but which no person has yet gained. And the eighteenth is, for those who, in my opinion, have come nearest to perfection; as the lower figures are for those who appear to be further from it" (p. 279).

   The parallel to Joseph Spence's *Crito* was first pointed out in *The Clockmakers Outcry*, p. 22.

16.2   daubing] "The putting a false show on anything (*obs.*); hypocritical flattery" (*OED*). Smollett's *Travels through France and Italy* (1766) is cited: "without any daubing at all, I am, very sincerely, Your affectionate humble servant" (II: 73). Cf. the primary meaning: "painting coarsely or inartistically; hence, a coarse or badly executed painting."

16.15–16   *tout ensemble*] Sterne was probably aware that the phrase had its technical meaning in the study of painting: "The *tout ensemble* of a painting, is that harmony which results from the distribution of the several objects or figures, whereof it is composed" (Chambers, s.v. *Ensemble*).

16.18   Mr. *Dodsley*] Since Robert Dodsley (1703–64) retired from his thriving Tully's Head publishing firm in March 1759, his brother James (1724–97) was most likely the Dodsley referred to here. Sterne had tried to interest Robert in *TS* in May 1759 but without success. After he had the first two volumes published in York, however, James Dodsley entered into an agreement with him for immediately publishing a second edition and vols. III and IV as well. Dodsley also published vols. I and II of the *Sermons of Mr. Yorick* in May 1760. See "Introduction to the Text," vol. II, pp. 818–25, in this edition. For an account of the Dodsleys, see Ralph Straus, *Robert Dodsley* (London: John Lane, 1910).

16.29–17.1   CANDID and Miss CUNEGUND's affairs] Sterne alludes to the hero and heroine of Voltaire's *Candide*, published in January 1759 and translated into English soon thereafter.

18.2   country-talk] *OED* cites this passage as its sole illustration.

18.7–12   brother to *Rosinante* . . . all points.] Cervantes describes Don Quixote's horse several times; Sterne may have had in mind a passage in I.I.1: "The next Moment he went to view his Horse, whose Bones stuck out like the Corners of a *Spanish* Real, being a worse Jade than *Gonela*'s, *qui tantum pellis & ossa fuit* . . . [who was but so much skin and bones]" (I: 7); or another in I.II.1: "*Rozinante* was so admirably delineated, so slim, so stiff, so lean, so jaded, with so sharp a Ridge-bone, and altogether so like one wasted with an incurable Consumption, that any one must have owned at first Sight, that no Horse ever better deserved that Name" (I: 74).

18.13–19   I know . . . of his blood.] In *Don Quixote*, I.III.1, Sancho leaves Rozinante untied, "knowing him to be a Horse of that Sobriety and Chastity, that all the Mares in the Pastures of *Cordova* could not have rais'd him to attempt an indecent thing." Nevertheless, when the Yanguesian Carriers stop with their mares in the vicinity, Rozinante "as soon as he had smelt the Mares, forsaking his natural Gravity and Reserv'dness, without asking his Master's Leave, away he trots it briskly to make 'em sensible of his little Necessities . . ." (I: 121).

The implication that Yorick's horse is not "a horse at all points," i.e., is impotent, is worth noting.

19.4   demi-peak'd] *OED*, s.v. *Demi-piqued*, cites this passage as its first illustration, with the definition "having a peak of about half the height of that of the older war-saddle."

19.7   superfine cloth] *Handbook of English Costume*, p. 420: "A superior quality of BROADCLOTH; of Spanish Merino and Saxon wool." Sterne uses the term again at 218.18; and at 542.16 (to describe Trim's montero-cap). "Plush" (19.5) is defined in the *Handbook* as "a coarse cotton with a pile like velvet" (p. 419); it is the material of Toby's red breeches, in which he courts the widow Wadman (714.10).

19.8–9   *poudrè d'or*] "Powdered with gold."

19.24   chuck-farthing and shuffle-cap] Respectively, in Johnson, *Dictionary:* "A play, at which the money falls with a chuck into the hole beneath"; and "A play at which money is shaken in a hat." Cf. John Arbuthnot, *The History of John Bull*, ed. Alan W. Bower and Robert A. Erickson (Oxford: Clarendon Press, 1976), p. 29: "He lost his Money at Chuck-Farthing, Shuffle-Cap, and All-Fours . . . ." The use of the names of these games to represent the players is unrecorded in *OED*.

20.1–2   true point of ridicule] Cf. *Letters*, p. 74, where Sterne uses this phrase in describing to Dodsley the design of *TS:* "The Plan, as you will percieve, is a most extensive one,—taking in, not only, the Weak part of the Sciences, in wch the true point of Ridicule lies—but every Thing else, which I find Laugh-at-able in my way—."

20.11–12   that they were . . . a piece] Sidney's *Arcadia* (1633), p. 115, has a very similar image for a masterful rider: "as if Centaur-like he had beene one peece with the horse."

That Sterne labels his image a "temptation of false wit" (line 13) may possibly allude to the opening lines of Horace's *Ars Poetica*, pp. 450–51: "Humano capiti cervicem pictor equinam / iungere si velit, et varias inducere plumas / undique collatis membris . . . / spectatum admissi risum teneatis, amici?" ("If a painter chose to join a human head to the neck of a horse, and to spread feathers of many a hue over limbs picked up now here now there . . . could you, my friends, if favoured with a private view, refrain from laughing?"). In his concluding *Spectator* essay on false wit, Addison uses these lines for his motto (63, I: 270).

20.22–23   *de vanitate mundi et fugâ sæculi*] "On the vanity of the world and the swift [frightful] passing of time." A commonplace; Friar John speaks of delivering a "fine long sermon, de contemptu mundi, & fuga seculi" to drowning men (Rabelais, I.42.326).

Cf. *Sermons*, VI.39.166–68 ("Eternal Advantages of Religion"): "The vanity and emptiness of worldly goods and enjoyments,—the shortness and uncertainty of life,—the unalterable event hanging over our heads . . . are meditations so obvious, and so naturally check and block up a man's way . . . that it is astonishing how it was possible, at any time, for mortal man to have his head full of any thing else?—And yet, was the same person to take a view of the state of the world,—how slight an observation would convince him, that the wonder lay, in fact, on the other side;—and that, as wisely as we all discourse, and philosophize *de contemptu mundi & fugâ sæculi;*—yet, for one who really acts in the world—consistent with his own reflections upon it,—that there are multitudes who seem to take aim at nothing higher;—and, as empty a thing as it is . . . say, *It is good to be here*."

20.24   death's head] Cf. *1 Henry IV*, III.iii.28–31: "*Bard.* Why, Sir John, my face does you no harm. *Fal.* No, I'll be sworn, I make as good use of it as many a man doth of a death's-head or a *memento mori*. I never see thy face but I think upon hell-fire . . . ." The most famous death's head, of course, is Yorick's skull.

20.29–21.1   like wit . . . incompatible movements.] Cf. "Author's Preface," vol. III, 227.14–18: "for that wit and judgment in this world never go together; inasmuch as they are two operations differing from each other as wide as east is from west.—So, says *Locke*,—so are farting and hickuping, say I." See n. to this passage below.

21.3   could compose his cough] Both Tristram and Yorick share with Sterne the common characteristic of a pulmonary ailment; see also 20.14: "going off fast in a consumption."

21.20   unkind-hearted] *OED* cites this passage as its sole example.

21.24—25   clapp'd, or spavin'd . . . broken-winded] Sterne lists several diseases of horses, common knowledge one assumes in an age when horses were the primary means of transportation.

21.29—22.1   *communibus annis*] "In average or ordinary years."

22.15   child-getting] Unrecorded in *OED*.

22.15—18   reserving nothing . . . affliction dwelt together.] Cf. Grey, *Ecclesiastical Law*, p. 50: "Is it not a Part of [the Deacon's] Office also to search for the Sick, Poor, and Impotent of the Parish, in order to their Relief?"

23.5—11   I have . . . hero of antiquity.] The identification of Yorick with Don Quixote, which begins with the comparison of his horse to Rozinante, ends with the *"cervantick* tone" with which he speaks his last words (34.25). That Sterne also identified with Cervantes's hero is suggested by a letter he wrote to William Warburton in June 1760, quoted below, n. to 34.19—22.

23.25   'twas plain . . . at noon-day] Proverbial; variant of Tilley, D56: "As clear as the DAY," and S969: "As clear as the SUN"; see also *ODEP*, s.v. *Clear*.

24.11—12   But there . . . they will] Sterne is perhaps recalling *Hamlet*, V.ii.10—11: "There's a divinity that shapes our ends, / Rough-hew them how we will . . . ."

25.1   YORICK was this parson's name] Sterne exploits with considerable brilliance the complexities of Shakespeare's jester—*memento mori* as a voice for his own work. Kenneth Monkman ("Sterne, Hamlet, and Yorick," in *Winged Skull*, pp. 112—23) notes the very early fascination Sterne seems to have had with *Hamlet* and also points out that the older pronunciation of York was Yorick. In the "Rabelaisian Fragment," written just before Sterne began *TS*, he laments for his clerical protagonist, "Alass poor *Homenas!*" (p. 1089, line 76), a sentence which may well have directed him to the idea of Yorick as an alter ego. Sterne published sermons in 1760 and again in 1766 under the name Mr. Yorick, and of course used the name for his protagonist in *ASJ*.

25.12–13   chops and changes] *OED* cites this passage as its first recorded example of the phrase used as a substantive; its meaning is primarily in *changes*, although Sterne's particular application here gives a meaning to *chops* as well.

25.24   reign of *Horwendillus*] From Theobald on, Shakespeare's eighteenth-century editors acknowledged *Hamlet*'s origins in the *Gesta Danorum* of Saxo Grammaticus (c. 1200), which was published in 1514. Book III tells the story of the murder of Amleth's father, Horwendillus (Horvendil), and of Amleth's revenge. There is no mention of Yorick anywhere in the *Gesta Danorum*, but the folk legends out of which the Amleth story grew are essentially stories of heroes who played the fool for their own safety; see Saxo's *Life of Hamlet*, trans. William F. Hansen (Lincoln: University of Nebraska Press, 1983), pp. 1–37 and passim. Since the story is not historical, Sterne's datings here (25.5) and in *ASJ* (see next paragraph) are futile, though perhaps legitimate guesses in the eighteenth century.

Cf. the fine episode in *ASJ*, where Yorick identifies himself to the Count de B**** by pointing out his name in "the grave-diggers scene in the fifth act . . . . *Me, Voici!* said I.

"Now whether the idea of poor Yorick's skull was put out of the Count's mind, by the reality of my own, or by what magic he could drop a period of seven or eight hundred years, makes nothing in this account—'tis certain the French conceive better than they combine—I wonder at nothing in this world, and the less at this; inasmuch as one of the first of our own church . . . fell into the same mistake in the very same case. — 'He could not bear, he said, to look into sermons wrote by the king of Denmark's jester.'—Good, my lord! said I—but there are two Yoricks. The Yorick your lordship thinks of, has been dead and buried eight hundred years ago; he flourish'd in Horwendillus's court—the other Yorick is myself, who have flourish'd my lord in no court . . ." (pp. 221–23). Stout notes that the disapproving clergyman was perhaps Warburton, the most influential voice in a chorus of protest.

26.3–5   That . . . of the Christian world.] Cf. Enid Welsford, *The Fool: His Social and Literary History* (London: Faber and Faber, 1935), p. 182: "In the eighteenth century the institution of the court-fool began to show signs of decadence everywhere except in the more backward countries of Europe such as Russia." Welsford notes that the last court fool in England was attached to the courts of James I and Charles I; see especially chaps. 7, 8. See also John Doran, *The History of Court Fools* (London: Richard Bentley, 1858); the two seem to be in agreement that Sterne's date for the end of court fools in Europe is somewhat too early.

26.15–20   I had . . . of this work.] Sterne never does provide this "delectable narrative," although he did seem to have some version of a continental tour in mind when he began *TS*. According to John Croft, "Sterne said that his first Plan, was to travell his Hero Tristram Shandy all over Europe and after making his remarks on the different Courts, proceed with making strictures and reflections on the different Governments of Europe and finish the work with an eulogium on the superior constitution of England and at length to return Tristram well informed and a compleat English Gentleman" (*The Whitefoord Papers*, p. 228). Croft is not always reliable, but in this instance his account gains some support from Tristram's very brief description of his own grand tour in chap. 27 of vol. VII, especially his comment that his father "saw kings and courts and silks of all colours" (617.23).

No evidence exists that Sterne himself ever served as a "governor"; on several occasions, however, between 1761 and 1765, faced with the expenses of traveling in Europe in search of better health, he did express some interest in doing so (*Letters*, pp. 140, 257).

26.15–16   Mr. *Noddy's*] "Noddy" was a generic name for a fool, a nincompoop; cf. John Hall-Stevenson's *Crazy Tales* (1762), p. 36: "'Squire NODDY coming from his travels, / By MOLLY is a captive led, / He to her Sire his mind unravels, / Her Sire consents, and MOLLY's wed." Unfortunately, all six of the Squire's children turn out to look like Molly's cousin.

26.20–27.4   I had . . . think, very right.] Robert Molesworth resided in Denmark intermittently between 1689 and 1694 and published *An Account of Denmark, as it was in the year 1692* (1694), which remained well known throughout the eighteenth century. His comments on the Danish character, while close to the spirit of Tristram's quoted remarks, are obviously not an immediate source: "It is said that Necessity is the Mother of Invention; which may be true in some degree, but I am sure too much

Necessity depresses the Spirits, and destroys it quite; neither is there any Invention here, or tolerable Imitation of what is brought in to them by Strangers. . . .

"To conclude; I never knew any Country where the Minds of the People were more of one *calibre* and pitch than here; you shall meet with none of extraordinary Parts or Qualifications, or excellent in particular Studies and Trades; you see no Enthusiasts, Mad-men, Natural Fools, or fanciful Folks, but a certain equality of Understanding reigns among them: every one keeps the ordinary beaten road of Sence, which in this Country is neither the fairest nor the foulest, without deviating to the right or left: yet I will add this one Remark to their praise, that the Common People do generally write and read" (pp. 255, 257).

Sterne may have had another source, or he may have generalized what was probably a commonplace about the northern character; see 231.12– 22, where this passage is closely echoed, and n. below.

27.5–12   With us . . . capricious] Sterne restates a commonplace of the age, that England's climate produced the wide range of whimsical and eccentric characters in which the English were beginning to take especial pride; see 71.3ff., 230.18–24ff., and nn. below.

27.13   goods and chattels] A common legal phrase; Sterne uses it again, 45.22, 151.14, 264.11, 665.9.

27.17   crasis] Johnson's definition is useful: "Temperature; constitution arising from the various properties of humours"; the illustration is from South's *Sermons:* "A man may be naturally inclined to pride, lust, and anger, as these inclinations are founded in a peculiar *crasis*, and constitution of the blood and spirits." Cf. *OED*, where this passage from *TS* provides the last example. ·

27.23   mercurial . . . a composition] Cf. "Journal to Eliza" (*Letters*, p. 332), where Sterne discusses his treatment for a venereal disorder: "am still to run thro' a Course of Van Sweetens corrosive Mercury, or rather Van Sweeten's Course of Mercury is to run thro' me—I shall be sublimated to an etherial Substance by the time my Eliza sees me—she must be sublimated and uncorporated too, to be able to see me—but I was always transparent & a Being easy to be seen thro' . . . ."

27.23–24   heteroclite . . . his declensions] William Warburton was perhaps the first to apply this metaphor of grammatical irregularity to Sterne himself. "I must not forget to thank you," he wrote to Garrick, "for the hints I received from you . . . concerning our heteroclite Parson" (June 16, 1760; quoted in *Letters*, p. 114, n. 5).

27.25   *gaité de cœur*] "Gaiety of heart, mirthfulness."

27.28–28.4   at the age . . . body's tackling] Insofar as Sterne, within a few months of his twenty-fifth birthday, was collated to the vicarage of Sutton-on-the-Forest, his home and his parish for the next twenty-one years; and insofar as at this period he began the close association with his uncle Jaques Sterne which would involve him both in politics and in a distasteful family feud; and insofar as he probably met and began courting his future wife, Elizabeth Lumley, during his twenty-sixth year, one might be tempted to draw a biographical inference from Yorick's innocence at twenty-six. See Cash, *Early and Middle Years*, chap. 4; and n. to 33.4–6 below.

28.9–10   For, to speak . . . nature to gravity] Cf. *Sermons*, I.2.45–46 ("The House of Feasting and the House of Mourning Described"): "nor can gravity, with all its studied solemnity of look and carriage, serve any end but to make one half of the world merry, and impose upon the other."

28.28–29.1   what a *French* wit . . . *mind*] Sterne has in mind maxim 257 of François de la Rochefoucauld (1613–80): "La gravité est un mystère du corps inventé pour cacher les défauts de l'esprit" (*Oeuvres Complètes* [Editions Gallimard, 1964], p. 438). In contemporary English translations (1694, 1706) it appears as "Gravity is a kind of mystical Behaviour in the Body, found out to conceal and set off the Defects of the Mind" and "Gravity is an Affectation of the Body, put on to conceal the defects of the Mind."

Shaftesbury's *Characteristicks* (1711) opens with a similar attack on gravity: "How comes it to pass then, that we appear such Cowards in reasoning, and are so afraid to stand the *Test* of Ridicule?————O! say we, the Subjects are too grave————Perhaps so: but let us see first whether they are really grave or no: for in the manner we may conceive 'em, they may peradventure be very grave and weighty in our Imagination; but very ridiculous and impertinent in their own nature. *Gravity* is of the very Essence of Imposture" (I: 11).

29.4–25   But, in plain truth . . . want of gathering.] Sterne describes a character similar to Yorick in his sermon "The Case of Hezekiah and the Messengers" (III.17.54–55): "there is scarce any character so rare, as a man of a real open and generous integrity,——who carries his heart in his hand,——who says the thing he thinks; and does the thing he pretends. Tho' no one can dislike the character,——yet, Discretion generally shakes her head,—and the world soon lets him into the reason"; and again in "St. Peter's Character" (V.31.99−100): "Peter's character . . . was possessed of such a quick sensibility and promptness of nature, which utterly unfitted him for art and premeditation;—though this particular cast of temper had its disadvantages, at the same time, as it led him to an unreserved discovery of the opinions and prejudices of his heart, which he was wont to declare, and sometimes in so open and unguarded a manner, as exposed him to the sharpness of a rebuke where he could least bear it."

29.4   unhackneyed] *OED* cites this passage as its first example; "not habituated by long practice; inexperienced." Sterne is perhaps recalling *1 Henry IV:* "Had I so lavish of my presence been, / So common-hackney'd in the eyes of men . . ." (III.ii.39−40).

29.23−24   his gibes and his jests] Cf. *Hamlet,* V.i.189: "Where be your gibes now . . . ?" asks Hamlet of Yorick's skull; see below, n. to 34.27−28.

30.3   *Jesteé*] *OED* cites this passage as its first illustration.

30.3−4   the comparison . . . all-four] Proverbial; Tilley, S460: "No SIMILITUDE (metaphor) walks (runs) upon all four (on four wheels)"; and *ODEP,* s.v. *Simile.* The origin is the Latin expression "Nullum simile quatuor pedibus currit."

Sterne uses the phrase differently at 246.12, for something moving well on all four limbs (or wheels).

30.19   book-debts] "An amount debited to a person's account in a ledger" (*OED*). Cf. 434.1.

30.20   *Eugenius's*] The name Eugenius was traditionally applied as a compliment in the eighteenth century; cf. *Spectator* 177: "*Eugenius* is a Man of an Universal Good-nature, and Generous beyond the Extent of his Fortune, but withal so prudent in the Oeconomy of his Affairs, that what goes out in Charity is made up by Good Management" (II: 198). Sterne's alleged tribute in this passage to his Cambridge and Yorkshire friend, John Hall-Stevenson (1718−85), has something of wit attached to it, as Cash notes: "Critics of eighteenth-century literature, playing the popular game of identifying fictional characters as actual people, assumed that Sterne had represented Hall as Eugenius, the faithful, prudent counsellor of *Tristram*

Shandy and *A Sentimental Journey*. If so, it was a joke: Eugenius is a stock character, the confidant, quite unlike Hall, who was never very prudent or wise. He was, however, faithful, in his odd way, and in so far as Sterne captured in the character the archetype of the friend, he may have had Hall in mind" (*Early and Middle Years*, p. 53). See also Cash's further account in chap. 9.

Perhaps more than a confidant, Eugenius here functions, as Wilbur Cross intimates (*Life*, p. 143), as an adversarius in a satiric apologia. Cross calls attention to the resemblance between the dialogue at this point and Pope's "Epistle to Dr. Arbuthnot."

Eugenius is also the companion of Tristram in the opening chapter of vol. VII, where he is portrayed, perhaps more in character, as listening to Tristram's tawdry tale and advising him to flee to France to avoid Death; see below, n. to 576.9–10.

Hall-Stevenson capitalized on the success of the first two volumes of *TS* by publishing *Two Lyric Epistles: One to My Cousin Shandy, on His Coming to Town; and the Other to the Grown Gentlewomen, the Misses of* **** (April 1760), which drew the immediate fire of Bishop Warburton. Sterne responded to the Bishop's inquiry by acknowledging Hall-Stevenson's authorship, but at the same time claiming a "nineteen years' total interruption of all correspondence with him." Sterne was almost certainly not telling the truth; or, as Lodwick Hartley suggests, he may simply have been evading it by interpreting "correspondence" to mean strictly letters. At any rate, he speaks of Hall-Stevenson in this letter as a man of "great talents . . . worth reclaiming" (*Letters*, p. 115) and in numerous letters after this indicates clearly his high regard for him.

For a full account of Hall-Stevenson's literary career, see Hartley's "Sterne's Eugenius as Indiscreet Author: The Literary Career of John Hall-Stevenson," *PMLA* 86 (1971): 428–45.

31.4   to the uttermost mite.] This phrase, which appears to be a conflation of Matthew 5: 26 ("paid the uttermost farthing") and Luke 12: 59 ("till thou hast paid the very last mite") is used again at 157.19–20 and in *Sermons*, II.11.113.

32.9ff.   REVENGE from some baneful corner, etc.] A letter that Sterne wrote in 1758 perhaps suggests very specifically the sort of harassment he here alludes to; in it he defends himself against charges that he had accused one of his parishioners of seducing the wife of another (a Mrs. Catherine Sturdy), and that he himself had cuckolded a poor farmer in his parish. He writes, he says, "as well to vindicate the Honor & Character of You & Mrs Sturdy, as my own, wch of the three, I think is most injured by the Report" (Kenneth Monkman and James Diggle, "Yorick and His Flock: A New Sterne Letter," *TLS*, March 14, 1968, p. 276). See also Cash, *Early and Middle Years*, pp. 264–65.

32.19–22 *When to gratify . . . up with.*] Sterne's probable source is Thomas Tenison, "Discourse by Way of Introduction," in *Baconiana, or Certain Genuine Remains of Sir Francis Bacon* (1679): "And when from private Appetite, it is resolv'd, that a Creature shall be sacrific'd; it is easie to pick up sticks enough, from any Thicket whither it hath straid, to make a Fire to offer it with" (p. 16); noted by Ferriar, II: 37. On *"enew"* see t.n. to 32.21, vol. II, p. 844, in this edition.

32.26 tit] Partridge, s.v., points to the variety of sexual meanings ("pudendum, penis, teat") available to Sterne, but in this instance he may have reference primarily to a small horse, a filly.

33.4–6 that when . . . fallen before him.] See *Henry VIII*, III.ii.355–58: "The third day comes a frost, a killing frost, / And when he thinks, good easy man, full surely / His greatness is a-ripening, nips his root, / And then he falls as I do." That the words are spoken by Cardinal Wolsey, an emblem of clerical vicissitudes on the highest level, provides Sterne with a rich irony in applying them to a country parson's ambitions and disappointments; noted by Watt, p. 23, n. 5.

Cf. *Letters*, p. 76, where Sterne writes to an anonymous friend concerning prudence and preferment: "Mr Fothergil, whom I regard in the Class I do you, as My best of Criticks & well wishers—preaches daily to Me Upon Your Text—'get Your Preferment first Lory! he says—& then Write & Welcome' But suppose preferment is long acoming (& for aught I know I may not be preferr'd till the Resurrection of the Just) and am all that time in labour—how must I bear my Pains?—You both fright me with after-pains (like pious Divines) or rather like able Philosophers, knowing that One Passion is only to be combated by Another." Fothergil is Marmaduke Fothergill, Esq., "one of Sterne's closest friends during the pre-Shandy days," according to Curtis (*Letters*, p. 53, n. 4). Curtis is mistaken, however, in identifying him as a surgeon; see Cash, *Early and*

Middle Years, p. 92, n. 2. The nature of Fothergill's advice indicates how possible it is that Sterne had someone other than Hall-Stevenson in mind in his portrait of Eugenius—or several other people, since his friends seem to have been agreed in advising caution and restraint.

Sterne's narrative of Yorick's career has usually been considered an idealized autobiographical account, especially of his relationship with his uncle, Jaques Sterne (1695/6–1759), and his failure to advance in the church at a rate commensurate with his ambitions. The story of Sterne's foray into local politics in the 1740s under the tutelage of his uncle, and of his subsequent disillusionment, is well told by Curtis in *The Politicks of Laurence Sterne* (Oxford: Oxford University Press, 1929). Jaques's harassment of his nephew for the next twenty years is amply explored by Sterne himself in a letter of April 5, 1751 (*Letters*, pp. 32–44), and by Cash, *Early and Middle Years*, pp. 232–40 and passim. The *Political Romance* also helps to give us some indication of the intensely competitive—and petty—world of the York ecclesiastical establishment during Sterne's day.

33.16–18   *Eugenius* stept . . . *Yorick*'s curtain] Cf. *ASJ*, p. 278: "Eugenius draws my curtain when I languish . . . ."

34.19–22   that I . . . would fit it."] Sterne alludes to Sancho's reply to the idea of his wife's being a Queen: "I doubt of it, reply'd *Sancho Pança;* for I can't help believing, that though it should rain Kingdoms down upon the Face of the Earth, not one of them would sit well upon *Mary Gutierez*'s Head . . . ." (I.I.7, I: 58). Stout ("Borrowings," p. 117), notes that Sterne often referred to his frustrated ambitions in the Church with variants of this passage; e.g., in *ASJ*, p. 200: "Gracious heaven! . . . grant me but health . . . and shower down thy mitres, if it seems good unto thy divine providence, upon those heads which are aching for them." See also *Letters* ("Journal to Eliza"), p. 386: "if a Mitre was offer'd me, I would not have it, till I could have thee too, to make it sit easy upon my brow . . ."; and p. 406: "without my Lydia, if a mitre was offered me, it would sit uneasy upon my brow."

Sterne seems to have identified the attacks on Yorick not only with his own pre-*Shandy* career, but with events following its publication as well. E.g., in March 1760 he wrote to Garrick that the rumor that he intended to make William Warburton Tristram's tutor was "one of the number of those which so unfairly brought poor Yorick to his grave" (*Letters*, p. 93); and to Warburton he echoed the present passage: "These strokes in the Dark, with the many Kicks, Cuffs & Bastinados I openly get on all sides of me, are begining to make me sick of this foolish humour of mine of sallying forth into this wide & wicked world to redress wrongs, &c. of wch I shall repent as sorely as ever Sancha Panca did of his in following his evil genius of a Don Quixote thro thick & thin . . ." (*Letters*, p. 116). For Sterne's relations with Warburton, see New, "Sterne, Warburton," pp. 245–74.

34.25   *cervantick* tone] Although we cannot confidently assert what Sterne intended by this phrase, Work's annotation—"Satirical, such as that of Cervantes in *Don Quixote*" (p. 31, n. 5)—seems rather inadequate. Some clue is provided by Sterne's phrase "*Cervantick* gravity" to describe Walter's attitude as he traps Dr. Slop into reading "Ernulphus's Curse" (200.6); and again, by his reference to the amours of Toby as containing "events . . . of so singular a nature, and so Cervantick a cast" that the telling will ensure his success (400.23–24).

Sterne uses and defines the term "Cervantic humour" in a letter written in 1759 to defend his "Minute Account" of Slop's tumble (vol. II, chap. 9): "in general I am perswaded that the happiness of the Cervantic humour arises from this very thing—of describing silly and trifling Events, with the Circumstantial Pomp of great Ones . . ." (*Letters*, p. 77). Certainly the ideas of burlesque and of irony (mock gravity) are suggested by this definition and would seem to be at work in the *TS* passages as well. See also *Letters*, pp. 120–21, where Sterne comments on his just-completed third volume: "I think there is more laughable humour,—with equal degree of Cervantik Satyr—if not more than in the last."

The complexities involved in trying to pinpoint what Sterne—or the entire century—might have in mind with a term like "*cervantick* tone" are well illustrated by Stuart Tave, *The Amiable Humorist* (Chicago: University of Chicago Press, 1960); see also below, n. to 200.6.

34.27–28   faint picture . . . in a roar!] Cf. *Hamlet*, V.i.189–91: "Where be your gibes now, your gambols, your songs, your flashes of merriment, that were wont to set the table on a roar?"

It is worth noting the report of an eighteenth-century observer of the English stage, Luigi Riccoboni, who, after commenting upon its excessive

violence, turns to *Hamlet* for illustration: "About the middle of the Play
we see the Funeral of a Princess; the Grave is dug on the Stage, out of
which are thrown Bones and Skulls: A Prince comes then and takes up a
Skull in his Hand, which the Grave-digger informs him was the Skull of
the late King's Jester; he makes a moral Dissertation upon the Skull of the
Jester, which is reckoned a Master-piece: The Audience listen with Admiration, and applaud with Transport: And it is for that Scene that the major
Part of the Spectators resort to the Play-House when *Hamlet* is performed" (*A General History of the Stage*, 2d ed. [1754; New York: AMS
Press, 1978], p. 170).

36.1−3   not a passenger . . . Y O R I C K !] Helen Sard Hughes ("A Precursor of *Tristram Shandy*," *JEGP* 17 [1918]: 227−51) suggests that Sterne
may have been influenced in this passage by the anonymous *Life and
Memoirs of Mr. Ephraim Tristram Bates* (1756), a possible source for *TS*
originally pointed out by Hester Thrale Piozzi (cited by Hughes, pp.
227−28). The *Bates* passage (p. 238; cited by Hughes, p. 244) records
the hero's death: "Thus ended the Life of a very ingenious and brave Man,
(scarce 35 Years of Age) which, tho' short, was *for his Station* full of
Honour; and rais'd for the Time as high in Rank as Merit alone carries
any Man. The Stone Mason at the Savoy tells me, he can scarce go on in his
Work, on account of the numberless Questions ask'd him; and scarce an
Hour in the Day passes, but Strangers inquire for his Tomb; and, striking
their Breasts, Cry!

Alas! poor Bates."

Hughes makes as complete an argument as can be made for the relationship between the two works; see also below, n. to 113.5−8.

The three words are, of course, Hamlet's address to Yorick's skull,
V.i.184.

37−38   (black page)] Cross, *Life*, p. 147, makes the following suggestion
concerning Sterne's black page: "Beyond a doubt Sterne saw the *Utrius
Cosmi, Maioris scilicet et Minoris Metaphysica, Physica atque Technica Historia* by Robert Flud . . . . In the first chapter, Flud described, after
Trismegistus and Moses, chaos—or the *ens primordiale infinitum, informe*,
as his Latin has it,—under the form of a very black smoke or vapor; and
for the assistance of the reader's imagination, he covered two-thirds of a

page with a black square, writing on each of its four sides *Et sic infinitum* . . . . This square became of course Sterne's page dressed in mourning for the death of 'poor Yorick'." While we cannot be as certain as Cross of this debt, Flud[d]'s work (published in 1617) does offer an example of a black page prior to Sterne. So, however, does Joshua Sylvester's *Lachrimæ Lachrimorum, or, the Distillation of Teares Shede for the untimely Death of the incomparable Prince Panaretus* (1612). The ground of the title-page is black with white letters, each verso page is also totally black (except the arms of the Prince cut in white), and the rectos are bordered in black on top and bottom and have skeletal figures along the right and left margins surrounding the text. Sylvester also published *An Elegie-&-Epistle Consolatorie, Against Immoderate Sorrow for th' immature Decease of S^r. William Sidney* (1613), in which again all the versos are black, with a small emblem cut in white on each. One suspects Sterne was aware of this tradition in elegy printing and revives it at this point in his own elegy for Yorick.

39.1   rhapsodical work] *OED* cites this passage as its last example, with the definition "Of a literary work: Consisting of a medley of narratives, etc.; fragmentary or disconnected in style." Cf. Montaigne, I.13.59: "THERE is no Subject so frivolous, that does not merit a Place in this Rhapsody"; *Spectator* 46, 144, 158; and Cibber, *Apology*, p. 425: "This Rhapsody, therefore, has been thrown in, as a Dance between the Acts, to make up for the Dullness of what would have been by itself only proper."

Cf. 536.5–7: "to rhapsodize them [Toby's campaigns], as I once intended, into the body of the work"; and 622.8–9: "where I now sit rhapsodizing all these affairs."

39.14   out-edge] *OED* records two examples (s.v. *Out-* A.3.), the first of which is this passage and the other of which is from *ASJ*, p. 228: "a couple of sparrows upon the out-edge of his window."

39.20   compound-ratio] *OED*'s first illustration of this expression is dated 1875, but with a meaning different from Sterne's, which seems to anticipate the term *inverse ratio*, as used today; cf. *OED*, s.v. *Inverse*, the example from Edmund Burke (1790): "The operation of opinion being in the inverse ratio to the number of those who abuse power."

40.5–15   But I . . . all the *world*] One persistent characteristic of the putative author of *Tale of a Tub* is his interest in the size of his volume; e.g., he talks of making "a very considerable Addition to the Bulk of the Volume, *a*

Circumstance by no means to be neglected by a skilful Writer" (p. 132). He also often alludes to the "darkness" of his writing and to the readers who will be required to interpret it; e.g.: "I desire of those whom the *Learned* among Posterity will appoint for Commentators upon this elaborate Treatise; that they will proceed with great Caution upon certain dark points, wherein all who are not *Verè adepti,* may be in Danger to form rash and hasty Conclusions, especially in some mysterious Paragraphs, where certain *Arcana* are joyned for brevity sake, which in the Operation must be divided. And, I am certain, that future Sons of Art, will return large Thanks to my Memory, for so grateful, so useful an *Innuendo*" (p. 114); and again: "'TIS true, indeed, the Republick of *dark* Authors, after they once found out this excellent Expedient of *Dying,* have been peculiarly happy in the Variety, as well as Extent of their Reputation. For, *Night* being the universal Mother of Things, wise Philosophers hold all Writings to be *fruitful* in the Proportion they are *dark* . . . .

"AND therefore in order to promote so useful a Work, I will here take Leave to glance a few *Innuendo*'s, that may be of great Assistance to those sublime Spirits, who shall be appointed to labor in a universal Comment upon this wonderful Discourse" (p. 186). See also below, n. to 66.1–12.

Like Swift, Sterne is using *innuendo* in its more technical sense, "the parenthetical explanation or specification [introduced into the text]; or the appended explanation of, or construction put upon a word, expression, or passage" rather than its more common meaning today of "an oblique hint or suggestion; an insinuation."

In his first letter to Robert Dodsley (May 23, 1759), offering for sale the first two volumes of *TS,* Sterne added as a postscript: "Some of our best Judges here w^d have had me, to have sent into the World—cum Notis Variorum—there is great Room for it—but I thought it better to send it naked into the world . . ." (*Letters,* p. 75). In a second letter (October 1759), Sterne suggests that he has done some rewriting to meet Dodsley's objections: "All locality is taken out of the book—the satire general; notes are added where wanted . . ." (*Letters,* p. 81). The last comment is puzzling, since in the first edition the only notes are those in vol. I, chap. 20, introducing the Deventer "Memoire"; vol. I, chap. 23, defining "Pentagraph"; and vol. II, chap. 19, on the identification of Lithopædus; the first and last seem integral to the text rather than explanatory annotations. See also below, n. to 268.8–10, Tristram's comment on his marbled page.

Finally, we might note that Curtis, *Politicks,* pp. 124–25, sees a satiric allusion in this passage to John Burton's publication in 1758 of *Monasticon Eboracense,* with a title-page that promised "'Copper-Plates . . . of Churches, Abbies, Ruins, &c, and other Curious Things worthy of Observation'"; Burton, Curtis notes, also promised a second volume. In actual fact, the plates are almost nonexistent and vol. II was never published. On Burton, see below, n. to 50.15–22.

41.3–4   tho' it be . . . *Tom Thumb*] These are chapbook stories. Work assumes (p. 36, n. 1) that *Jack* is a slip for *Tom;* but cf. *Tatler* 95, on a child's reading: "he had very much turned his studies . . . into the lives and adventures of Don Bellianis of Greece, Guy of Warwick, the Seven Champions, and other historians of that age. . . . He would tell you the mismanagements of John Hickathrift, find fault with the passionate temper of Bevis . . ." (ed. George A. Aitken [New York: Hadley and Matthews, 1899], II: 315–16). Sterne's reference to these folktales would appear to be commonplace among those portraying the role of a Grub-Street writer; e.g., Swift, *Tale of a Tub,* p. 68, tells us he has prepared a learned dissertation on *Tom Thumb,* "whose Author was a *Pythagorean* Philosopher. This dark Treatise contains the whole Scheme of the *Metempsychosis,* deducing the Progress of the Soul thro' all her Stages."

Cf. John Dunton, *A Voyage Round the World* (1691), I: 3: "What, thought I wi' my self very soberly, if I should oblige this World now, this ungrateful World with a *History of this strange Life of mine:*—Hang't—it dosn't deserve it . . . . Besides there may be some certain *Perquisites,* Considerations, and so forth, sometimes the World has bin *just* to things of Value, *Coriats works, Tom Thumb, seven Champions, Pilgrims Progress,*— some good, some bad, some take, some not, and mine has a chance for't."

See also Fielding's preface to *Tom Thumb. A Tragedy* (1730; reprinted in *Burlesque Plays of the Eighteenth Century,* ed. Simon Trussler [Oxford: Oxford University Press, 1969], p. 148): "It is with great Concern that I have observed several of our (the *Grubstreet*) Tragical Writers, to Celebrate in their Immortal Lines the Actions of Heroes recorded in Historians and Poets, such as *Homer* or *Virgil* . . . when the Romances, Novels, and Histories, *vulgo* call'd Story-Books, of our own People, furnish such abundant and proper Themes for their Pens, such are *Tom Tram, Hickathrift,* &c." Fielding makes the same point in his prologue (p. 151): "*Let home-bred Subjects grace the modern Muse, / And* Grub-Street *from her Self, her Heroes chuse: / Her* Story-Books *Immortalize in Fame, /* Hickathrift, Jack the Giant-Killer, *and* Tom Tram."

The story of Tom Hickathrift has been reprinted in an edition by George Laurence Gomme (London: Villon Society, 1885); Gomme notes that the tale had a chapbook or literary form from the sixteenth century on (p. xii).

41.4–5   knows no more than his heels] Sterne uses the phrase again at 399.10 and 765.11; it would appear to be a commonplace.

41.7ff.   Could a historiographer, etc.] Tristram returns to this idea in vol. VII, chaps. 42–43, where he crosses the plains of Languedoc on a mule and finds "adventures" and "human nature" in abundance; and again in *ASJ*, p. 119: "Mundungus, with an immense fortune, made the whole tour; going on from Rome to Naples—from Naples to Venice—from Venice to Vienna—to Dresden, to Berlin, without one generous connection or pleasurable anecdote to tell of; but he had travell'd straight on looking neither to his right hand or his left, lest Love or Pity should seduce him out of his road." Stout (n. to lines 51–53) cites as well *Sermons,* I.3.58: "Look into the world—how often do you behold a sordid wretch, whose straight heart is open to no man's affliction, taking shelter behind an appearance of piety . . . . Take notice with what sanctity he goes to the end of his days, in the same selfish track in which he at first set out—turning neither to the right hand nor to the left—but plods on—pores all his life long upon the ground, as if afraid to look up, lest peradventure he should see aught which might turn him one moment out of that straight line where interest is carrying him . . . ." See also 617.7–618.12, the description of Walter Shandy as a traveler.

Michael V. DePorte in *Nightmares and Hobbyhorses: Swift, Sterne, and Augustan Ideas of Madness* (San Marino: Huntington Library, 1974), p. 128, compares this passage to *Tale of a Tub,* p. 188, making the point that for both authors horseback riding is a metaphor for uncontrolled imagination, for eccentricity and madness. Swift writes: "AFTER so wide a Com-

pass as I have wandred, I do now gladly overtake, and close in with my
Subject, and shall henceforth hold on with it an even Pace to the End of my
Journey, except some beautiful Prospect appears within sight of my Way;
whereof, tho' at present I have neither Warning nor Expectation, yet upon
such an Accident, come when it will, I shall beg my Readers Favour and
Company, allowing me to conduct him thro' it along with my self. For in
Writing, it is as in *Travelling:* If a Man is in haste to be at home . . . I
advise him clearly to make the straitest and the commonest Road, be it ever
so dirty . . . .

"ON the other side, when a Traveller and his *Horse* are in Heart and
Plight, when his Purse is full, and the Day before him; he takes the Road
only where it is clean or convenient; entertains his Company there as
agreeably as he can; but upon the first Occasion, carries them along with
him to every delightful Scene in View, whether of Art, of Nature, or of
both; and if they chance to refuse out of Stupidity or Weariness; let them
jog on by themselves, and be d—n'd . . . ." DePorte ultimately argues,
however, that Sterne and Swift have widely differing attitudes.

41.9–10   from *Rome* all the way to *Loretto*] The Santa Casa, or Holy House of
Loreto, has been since the fifteenth century one of the most famous shrines
of Italy; see below, n. to 629.10. It is located on the Adriatic Sea, a few
miles south of Ancona and about 125 miles northeast of Rome.

41.16–18   He will have . . . he can fly] Cf. *Sermons*, I.2.27 ("The House of
Feasting and the House of Mourning Described"): "like travellers,
though upon business of the last and nearest concern to us, [we] may surely
be allowed to amuse ourselves with the natural or artificial beauties of the
country we are passing through, without reproach of forgetting the main
errand we are sent upon; and if we can so order it, as not to be led out of the
way, by the variety of prospects, edifices, and ruins which sollicit us, it
would be a nonsensical piece of saint errantry to shut our eyes."

42.15ff.   my mother's marriage settlement, etc.] Sterne may well have had an
actual marriage (or other) contract before him as he wrote (see, e.g., the
model marriage settlement in John Lilly, *The Practical Conveyancer*
[1719], pp. 750ff.), but the legal profession had long been subjected to
this sort of parody and he may have instead been recalling one particular
instance by Richard Steele in *The Funeral* (1701). Here the lawyer Puzzle

instructs his clerk: "What's the first Excellence in a Lawyer—Tautology? What the second? Tautology? What the third Tautology . . ."; he then has the clerk read part of a will he has drawn up: "I the said Earl of *Brumpton*, Do give, Bestow, Grant and Bequeath over and above the said Premises, all the site and Capital Messuage call'd by the name of *Oatham*, and all Outhouses, Barns, Stables and other Ædifices, and Buildings, Yards, Orchards, Gardens, Feilds, Arbors, Trees, Lands, Earths, Medows, Greens, Pastors, Feedings, Woods, Underwoods, Ways, Waters, Watercourses, Fishings, Ponds, Pools, Commons, Common of Pasture, Paths, Heath-Thickets, Profits, Commodities, and Emoluments with their, and every of their Appurtenances whatsoever . . . to the said Capital Messuage, and site belonging or in any wise appertaining, or with the same heretofore used, occupied, or enjoy'd, accepted, executed, known, or taken . . ." (I.ii, p. 36).

The possibility that Sterne was interested in Steele's play is reinforced by noting that the main characters are military men who several times use military metaphors to talk about love (e.g., II.iii, p. 53), and that the servant of the main character (Lord Hardy) is named Trim. Trim is adept both in military affairs and in affairs of the heart. Two speeches in particular suggest his character; the first, on military glory: "Now, my brave Friends and Fellow Soldiers—(*Aside.*) I must Fellow Souldier 'em just afore a Battle, like a true Officer tho' I cane 'em all the Year round beside—(*Struting about.*) Major General *Trim*, no, Pox *Trim* sounds so very short and Priggish—that my Name should be a Monosyllable! but the Foreign News will write me, I suppose, Mounsieur, or Chevalier *Trimont*, Seigneur *Trimoni*, or Count *Trimuntz*, in the *German* Army . . . . Faith, this is very pleasing this Grandeur! why after all 'tis upon the Neck of such Scoundrells as these Gentlemen, that we great Captains, build our Renown—a Million or two of these Fellows make an *Alexander* . . ." (IV.iii, p. 79); and the second, on his plan of attack to seize a coffin: "March up, march up—Now we are near the Citadel—And I halt only to give the Necessary Orders for th' Engagement . . . . I say, when you see the File in such a Posture, that half the File may Face to the House, half to the Body—You are to fall down, crying, Murder, that the Half-file fac'd to the Body, may throw it, and themselves, over you——I then march to

your Rescue—Then, *Swagger*, you, and your Party, fall in to secure my
Rear; while I march off with the Body—These are the Orders—And this,
with a little Improvement of my own, is the same Disposition *Villeroy* and
Catinat made at *Chiari*" (V.ii, p. 82).

The Funeral remained popular throughout the century and Sterne may
well have had it in mind when he conceived his own Trim; see below, n. to
57.19—58.2. All quotations are taken from the edition in *The Plays of
Richard Steele*, ed. Shirley Strum Kenny (Oxford: Clarendon Press,
1971). Its possible influence on Sterne was first suggested in *The Clockmakers Outcry*, pp. 30—31.

44.19   ingress, egress, and regress] A legal formula; Sterne uses it again,
396.13, with a bawdy implication.

45.2   *femme sole*] "A single woman."

45.28—29   In three words] A formula used several times in *TS;* see 93.14,
98.19, 803.10—11; and at least once in the *Sermons*, III.20.144. Sterne
also uses several variations; e.g., "these three words" (35.8), "not have
said three words" (47.17—18), "scarce exchanged three words" (75.15),
"the three last words" (134.7), "one single *quære* of three words"
(283.24), and "in three plain words" (786.10—11).

46.11   *toties quoties*] "Repeatedly; as often as occasion may require."

46.16—20   for my . . . mislead her judgment] C. H. G. Macafee, "The
Obstetrical Aspects of *Tristram Shandy*," *Ulster Medical Journal* 19 (1950):
15, calls this passage "a most accurate description of a well-recognised
obstetric condition, namely pseudocyesis. In this condition the patient
falsely believes herself to be pregnant, believes that she has all the subjec-
tive symptoms and produces the objective signs by abdominal distension."

Cf. Cash, "Birth," p. 139, n. 11: "There are natural great Bellies,
containing a living Child, and these we call true; and others against Na-
ture, in which instead of a Child, is engendered nothing but strange
Matter, as Wind mixed with Waters . . . they are called false Great-
Bellies"; quoted from François Mauriceau, *The Diseases of Women with
Child* (Paris, 1668), trans. Hugh Chamberlen (1752).

46.25   against the grain] Proverbial; Tilley, G404, and *ODEP*, s.v. *Against.*

47.14   wall-fruit, and green gages] Fruit trees, usually those bearing soft
fruit, benefit in England from being grown espaliered against a wall—

hence wall-fruit. This is one of the earliest recorded examples of the term *greengage*, a particular variety of plum named after Sir William Gage about 1725; *OED*'s first example is dated 1759–65.

48.5ff.   From *Stilton*, etc.] Sterne names two post stages on the road from London to Edinburgh; Stilton is fifty-nine miles north of London, and Grantham twenty-eight miles farther north. The Trent crossed the post road at Newark-on-Trent, ten miles north of Grantham. Robert Poole's *A Journey from London to France and Holland; or the traveller's useful Vade Mecum*, 2d ed. (1750) has an appendix in vol. II listing the post stages and their distances from London to Edinburgh, York being the approximate midpoint of the journey.

48.25   running divisions] The image is a musical one; *OED*, s.v. *Division:* "The execution of a rapid melodic passage, originally conceived as the dividing of each of a succession of long notes into several short ones . . . *esp*. as a variation on, or accompaniment to, a theme or 'plain song'." See a similar usage, 207.23–209.2 and n. below.

49.10   pshaw-ing and pish-ing] Cf. *Spectator* 438: "Pishes and Pshaws, or other well-bred Interjections" (IV: 40). Walter Shandy is characterized in this way again, 271.11: "My father pish'd and pugh'd"; 709.9: "would pish, and huff, and bounce, and kick"; and 756.19: "he pish'd fifty times." In 345.2–9 the interjection is analyzed and we are promised a "chapter of *pishes*"—a promise Tristram recalls in 765.6 but does not fulfill.

  OED cites this passage as its first illustration for *pshawing*.

49.14–16   nor was it . . . months after] John A. Hay, "Rhetoric and Historiography: Tristram Shandy's First Nine Kalendar Months," p. 83, points out the computational error in this sentence; it is only a little more than five months later that Tristram is conceived (the first Sunday in March 1718) and thirteen months later that he is born (November 5, 1718).

50.3–4   'Tis known . . . a bad one] Cf. Sir Thomas Browne, *Religio Medici* (1642), pt. I, sec. 25: "for obstinacy in a bad cause, is but constancy in a good" (*Works*, ed. Geoffrey Keynes [Chicago: University of Chicago Press, 1964], I: 36); behind both versions is Tacitus, *Germania*, 24: "ea est in re prava pervicacia; ipsi fidem vocant" ("such is their persistence in wrong-doing, or their good faith, as they themselves style it"), pp. 298–99. Noted in Grenville.

50.14 Dr. *Maningham*] Work, p. 44, n. 1: "Sir Richard Manningham, M.D., F.R.S. (1690–1759), the leading English man-midwife of his day; his fame was yet to be made, however, at the time of Tristram's birth." This is one of the few anachronistic slips Sterne makes; Manningham's death in 1759 probably put him in mind.

50.15–22 notwithstanding there . . . into the world] As Work points out (p. 44, n. 2), this is Sterne's first overt allusion to John Burton, M.D. (1710–71), antiquary and physician of York, and author of the *Essay towards a Complete New System of Midwifry* (1751); but see above, n. to 40.5–15, for the suggestion of a covert allusion. While Sterne certainly uses the opportunity to pillory his old adversary (see Cash, *Early and Middle Years*, pp. 91–92, 100, 103, 159–78, 290–91 and passim), he is also alluding more generally to the eighteenth-century debate between midwives and men-midwives, a debate which, coincidentally, reached a peak of sorts with Elizabeth Nihell's *Treatise on the Art of Midwifery*, published in 1759, the same year as vols. I and II of *TS*. Jean Donnison, *Midwives and Medical Men*, pp. 10–11, points out that the man-midwife became recognized throughout Europe only in the early 1600s (the first usage cited in *OED* is 1625), and describes his early career: "Men-midwives were called mainly to difficult cases, or engaged to be present in readiness for any emergency. However, many women had strong objections to male attendance even in these circumstances, and were, it was said, prepared to die rather than admit a man to the lying-in room. For this reason various stratagems—not too difficult in the half darkness in which the chamber was customarily kept—might be resorted to. . . . The man-midwife Percivall Willughby describes such an occasion in 1658. Called in by his daughter, the midwife in the case, he crept into the room on all fours in order to escape detection by the patient, the wife of a Puritan gentleman. Moreover, out of deference to the woman's modesty, the man-midwife commonly worked blind, with his hands under a sheet, a practice which sometimes led to serious error."

By the middle of the eighteenth century, says Donnison, the use of the forceps, the better education available to men, and a certain fashionable snobbery attached to the use of a man-midwife all contributed to the decline of the midwife as a medical institution. But the rise of man-midwifery did not go unchallenged, both by the midwives themselves and by some leading medical figures, and the debate continued for the next hundred years. It is in this context that we should understand the testy relationship between Dr. Slop and the midwife, keeping in mind, for example, that Queen Charlotte "at the birth of at least three of her children . . . was attended by Mrs. Draper, and Dr. William Hunter waited in an adjoining room in case he should be needed, but he was not summoned" (Donnison, p. 207, n. 37).

One argument in particular used by the midwives against their male counterparts is of particular relevance to Sterne's portrait of Dr. Slop, viz., their use of instruments. Donnison cites John Maubray's *Female Physician:* "However I know, some Chirurgeon-Practitioners are too much acquainted with the Use of *INSTRUMENTS,* to lay them aside; no, they do not (it may be) think themselves in their *Duty,* or proper *Office,* if they have not their cruel Accoutrements in Hand. And what is most unaccountable and unbecoming a Christian is that, when they have perhaps wounded the *MOTHER,* kill'd the *INFANT,* and with violent *Torture* and inexpressible *Pain,* drawn it out by Piece-meal, they think no Reward sufficient for such an extraordinary Piece of mangled Work." Donnison adds: "Similar admonitions figured in the writings of later practitioners, and the celebrated William Hunter is said to have shown his students his forceps, rusty from disuse, with the warning that 'where they may save one, they murder twenty'" (p. 31; see also pp. 32–33). For more on the "instruments of deliverance" see below, n. to 127.1–3.

The fullest account of Burton's career is by Robert Davies, "A Memoir of John Burton," *Yorkshire Archæological Journal* 2 (1873): 403–40. See also Cash, "Birth," pp. 133–54; and Curtis, *Politicks of Laurence Sterne,* passim.

50.16–17   eight miles of us] Sterne is almost certainly thinking of Shandy Hall as being in Sutton-on-the-Forest, eight miles north of York; see above, n. to Ded. 4. The move to Coxwold, where he and his friends referred to his home as Shandy Hall, was not made until the summer of 1760; Coxwold is some eighteen miles north of York.

51.6   *March* 9, 1759] According to Sterne's letter to Dodsley, he had some version of this first volume completed by May 23, 1759. A letter to his friend, John Blake, dated February 1759 by Curtis, reveals that Sterne was "very ill" at the beginning of February, when in all likelihood he started *TS* (*Letters*, pp. 73–75); cf. the statement in chap. 14: "I have been at it these six weeks" (42.2).

This is the first of four specific dates that Tristram provides for the writing of various parts of *TS*; the others are "*March* 26, 1759" (71.27); "*August* the 10th, 1761" (449.15, midway into vol. V); and "this 12th day of August, 1766" (737.3, the opening chapter of vol. IX).

51.6   dear, dear *Jenny*] Work, p. 44, n. 3: "In the earlier portions of the book, 'Jenny' represents Catherine Fourmantel, a professional singer with whom, while she appeared at the Assembly Rooms in York during the season of 1759–60, Sterne carried on an open and perhaps Platonic sentimental flirtation. . . . Later in the book 'Jenny' is probably merely a symbol for any woman beloved by any man." Work misstates his date, which should read "season of 1758–59," if indeed Jenny and Catherine are the same. Cf. Cash, *Early and Middle Years*, p. 292: "Some have assumed that she came to York in the winter of 1758–9: Tristram, in one passage, associates his 'dear *Jenny*' with a specific date—9 March 1759 . . . . But the Jenny of *Tristram Shandy* is surely not Catherine Fourmantel, tradition to the contrary, but a vague general figure of the confidante and mistress."

Four letters from Sterne to Catherine Fourmantel have been published by Curtis (*Letters*, pp. 81–84), and it is to her that he entrusted the introduction of *TS* to David Garrick (*Letters*, pp. 85–86). See also p. 82, n. 1; p. 293, n. 1; p. 339, n. 3; and p. 465 for an account of what little is known about her. It is quite probable that Sterne did have Catherine Fourmantel in mind while he was writing the first two volumes of *TS*, she being his romantic interest at the time; and equally probable that as his interest changed, so did his concept of "Jenny," becoming, as Cash says, a generalized figure. That Sterne indulged himself in this manner of relationship is indicated by the recollections of his servant (1742–45), Richard Greenwood, as recorded by the antiquary Joseph Hunter: "He used to accompany his master whenever Sterne came to York, & when there he rarely spent a night without a girl or two which Richard used to procure for him. He promised Richard to reward him for keeping these private amours of his secret . . . . Sterne too was continually after his female servants . . . .

"When any thing produced a difference between him and his wife . . . they would go together to York, where he soon lost all his [cares] in the arms of some more blooming beauty . . ." (James M. Kuist, "New Light on Sterne: An Old Man's Recollections of the Young Vicar," *PMLA* 80 [1965]: 549). Sterne's view of himself is more tolerant: "[I have] been in love with one princess or another almost all my life, and I hope I shall go on so, till I die, being firmly persuaded, that if ever I do a mean action, it must be in some interval betwixt one passion and another . . ." (*ASJ*, pp. 128–29).

It may perhaps be suggested that while Eugenius was first conceived as the generalized male friend and only later became a specific reference to John Hall-Stevenson (see above, n. to 30.20), Jenny began as a tribute to Catherine Fourmantel and, as that affair faded, became simply the generalized female friend.

51.13   could not heroine it] This example of *heroine* used as a verb is recorded by *OED* as a nonce word.

52.18ff.   He was very sensible, etc.] Louis A. Landa has traced the history of this political notion from Elizabeth through Sterne, Smollett, and Johnson in "London Observed: The Progress of a Simile," *PQ* 54 (1975): 275–88. He notes that "a Royal Proclamation issued by Queen Elizabeth in 1580 expressed concern that London was expanding at the expense of "other places abroad in the Realm, where many Houses rest uninhabited, to the decay of divers auncient good Boroughes and Townes"; and he cites a medical version of the idea in Peter Heylin's *Cosmography* (1670), p. 306: "Great Towns in the body of a State, are like the *Spleen* or *Melt* in the body natural; the monstrous growth of which impoverisheth all the rest of the Members, by drawing to it all the *animal* and *vital* spirits, which should give nourishment unto them; And in the end cracked or surcharged by its own fulness, not only sends unwholsom fumes and *vapours* unto the head, and heavy *pangs* unto the *heart*, but draws a *consumption* on it self."

Landa concludes: "It is evident that this figurative representation of London, sometimes as a dropsical head ["swollen at the expense of the nation at large"], sometimes as a wen or the spleen, often as a monstrous and overgrown head, came instantly, almost automatically to the mind of contemporaries as a conventionalized, short-hand descriptive phrase, apt and evocative for writers who . . . believed that London's massive size threatened England's welfare" (pp. 276–77).

Pope expresses the idea in "Thoughts on Various Subjects" (LXXXIII): "The people all running to the Capital city, is like a confluence of all the animal spirits to the heart; a symptom that the constitution is in danger" (*The Works of Mr. Alexander Pope, in Prose* [1741], II: 337).

The more general idea that the "body national" and "body natural" are identical is expressed by Goldsmith, *Citizen of the World*, letter 17: "It is in the politic as in the human constitution; if the limbs grow too large for the body, their size, instead of improving, will diminish the vigour of the whole" (*Works*, II: 74).

53.9   state-apoplexy] Unrecorded in *OED*.

53.13ff.   "Was I an absolute prince, etc.] Cf. John Dunton, *A Voyage Round the World*, I: 145–46: "Well, were *I a Privy-councellor, or a leading Parliament-man,* among many other excellent projects, I shou'd always be *hammering out* for the good of my *Countrey,* I wou'd certainly promote some Laws or other to prevent that *Inundation* of *Beggars* which overflow this plentiful Country . . . ."

54.3   Squirality] *OED* cites this passage as its sole example, although examples for *squiralty* are given dating from 1856.

54.6–16   Why are there . . . lives or dies."] Walter echoes the sentiments of a letter writer in *Spectator* 180 (II: 211), attacking the reign of Louis XIV (the "Sun-King"): "How should there be Industry in a Country where all Property is precarious? What Subject will sow his Land that his Prince may reap the whole Harvest? Parsimony and Frugality must be Strangers to such a People; for will any Man save to Day what he has Reason to fear will be taken from him To-morrow? . . .

"Is this then the great, the invincible *Lewis?* This the immortal Man, the *tout puissant,* or the Almighty, as his Flatterers have called him?" See also Steele's *The Englishman* 40, ed. Rae Blanchard (Oxford: Clarendon Press, 1955), pp. 161–65; and *The Christian Hero*, ed. Rae Blanchard (1932; New York: Octagon Books, 1977), p. 85: "With a Tyranny begun on his own Subjects, and Indignation that others draw their Breath Independent of his Frown or Smile, why should he not proceed to the seizure of the World . . . ."

Gibbon, at the end of the century, makes the same observation in his *Memoirs*, ed. Georges A. Bonnard (London: Nelson, 1966), p. 125: "An Englishman may hear without reluctance that in these curious and costly articles Paris is superior to London, since the opulence of the French capital arises from the defects of its government and Religion. . . . The splendour of the French nobles is confined to their town-residence: that of the English is more usefully distributed in their country-seats . . . ."

54.12   country-interest] Unrecorded in *OED*. Cf. Fielding, *Joseph Andrews*, ed. Martin C. Battestin (Middletown, Conn.: Wesleyan University Press, 1967), book II, chap. 4 (p. 112); and *Tom Jones*, book VI, chap. 2 (I: 272); and Battestin's notes to both passages. See also Curtis, *Politicks*, p. 26, where the *York Courant* (1741) is quoted: "George Fox, Esq; of Bramham-Park stands Candidate upon the COUNTRY-INTEREST." This is the party that opposed Walpole and later Pelham, and hence was identified with the Tory label. In his political activities in the 1740s, Sterne, as a Whig, was opposed to the "country-interest," though of course the Whigs and the Country Party would both have endorsed the anti-French sentiments of the passage; for a clearer understanding of the term, see W. A. Speck, *Stability and Strife: England, 1714–1760* (Cambridge: Harvard University Press, 1977), pp. 1–7 and passim.

54.21   weaker vessels] 1 Peter 3: 7: "giving honour unto the wife, as unto the weaker vessel." Cf. 344.2–3, where Susannah is called "a leaky vessel."

54.26–55.8   In this point . . . and confusion.] Although the gist of Walter's remarks is very much in accord with the general ideas of the English political writer Robert Filmer (d. 1653), there is no absolute verbal parallel with any part of his writings. Wilfred Watson, "The Fifth Commandment: Some Allusions to Sir Robert Filmer's Writings in *Tristram Shandy*," *MLN* 62 (1947): 234–40, makes the point that Sterne could well have been acquainted with Filmer's ideas through Locke's *Two Treatises of Government*, or simply because Filmer's name continued well into the eighteenth century as representative of hobby-horsical political thinking: "Locke's work tended to keep Filmer's ideas before the public eye. By 1760 there were found few to espouse the theory of the Divine Right of Kings. After nearly half a century of mixed monarchy under the first two Georges rationalizations of the Stuart regime were no longer tenable, and those who had accepted Filmer and the patriarchal theory of monarchy eagerly were anxious to forget both the theorist and his theory. But their opponents would not allow them completely to forget Filmer's *Patriarcha*. For Filmer's outmoded system was found to be useful as a means of ridicule and Filmer's name became a convenient label with which to deride a political opponent" (p. 235, n. 3). And Peter Laslett, the modern editor of Filmer, writes in his introduction: "For over two hundred years the name of Sir Robert Filmer has been a byword—a byword for obscurity" (*Patriarcha, and other Political Works* [Oxford: Basil Blackwell, 1949], p. 1). See also James Daly, *Sir Robert Filmer and English Political Thought* (Toronto: University of Toronto Press, 1979), especially his final chapter (pp. 151–71), "Filmer's Place in Political Thought."

Work, p. 47, n. 6: "Sir Robert Filmer . . . based his defence of the divine right of kings on the theory that the government of a family by its father is the true original and model of all government, and that kings rule by natural right as the supreme fathers of their people." For the possible significance of Sterne's identifying Walter as a Filmerian, see Watson, and below, nn. to chaps. 31–32, vol. V.

It should be pointed out that neither in the *Patriarcha* nor the *Anarchy of a Limited or Mixed Monarchy* (1648), nor anywhere that we could find in his writings, does Filmer admit to the desirability of mixed governments for any state, of whatever size; rather, his consistent position is that mixed governments are a "mere impossibility or contradiction" (Laslett, p. 93). He does, in *Anarchy*, note that in particular the ancient eastern monarchies were all absolute (p. 291).

55.28   both sides sung *Te Deum*] *Te deum laudamus* ("We praise thee, O God") are the first words and title of a hymn attributed to St. Ambrose and sung following a victory. The idea of both sides singing may have been suggested to Sterne by chap. 3 of *Candide*, where, after the battle between the Bulgars and the Abares, both sides sing *Te Deum*.

56.28–57.3   Surely, Madam . . . of sex.] Cf. Jean de la Bruyère, *The Characters, or the Manners of the Age* (1699), p. 81: "There may be a Friendship between persons of different Sexes, which may subsist without Enjoyment; yet a Woman will always look upon a Man as a Man, and so will a Man still look upon a Woman as a Woman." See also "Journal to Eliza" (*Letters*, p. 358): "Some Annotator . . . will take occasion, to speak of the Friendship wch Subsisted so long & faithfully betwixt Yorick & the Lady he speaks of . . . ."

57.3–7   Let me . . . is dress'd out.] More than any other author of the eighteenth century, Sterne has been credited, accurately or not, with the introduction of the word *sentimental* into the English literary consciousness. Perhaps significantly, the first two occasions of its use in *TS*, here and 327.4, are suggestive more of ironic bawdry than of sensibility, while the two remaining occurrences (710.8 and 746.6) are more in keeping with our usual notion of the word. For a very thorough discussion of the word and the concept, see R. F. Brissenden, *Virtue in Distress: Studies in the Novel of Sentiment from Richardson to Sade* (New York: Barnes and Noble, 1974), pp. 3–64.

Cf. *ASJ*, p. 257: "Nature is shy, and hates to act before spectators; but in such an unobserved corner, you sometimes see a single short scene of her's worth all the sentiments of a dozen French plays compounded together . . . ." Stout cites Sterne's evaluation of Diderot's *Fils naturel* as a gloss to this passage: "It has too much sentiment in it, (at least for me) the speeches too long, and savour too much of *preaching*— . . . 'Tis all love, love, love, throughout, without much separation in the character . . ." (*Letters*, p. 162).

See also *Letters*, p. 256: "I carry on my affairs quite in the French way, sentimentally—'*l'amour*' (say they) '*n'est rien sans sentiment*'—Now notwithstanding they make such a pother about the *word*, they have no precise idea annex'd to it . . . ."

57.8–9   I Would sooner . . . for it] Cf. *Sermons*, II.7.1: "one might as easily engage to clear up the darkest problem in geometry to an ignorant mind . . . ."

57.16–19   If mercurial . . . extravagant] Cf. *Spectator* 179 (II: 204): "I MAY cast my Readers under two general Divisions, the *Mercurial* and the *Saturnine*. The first are the gay part of my Disciples, who require Speculations of Wit and Humour; the others are those of a more solemn and sober Turn, who find no Pleasure but in Papers of Morality and sound Sense; the former call every thing that is Serious Stupid."

The terms ultimately derive from astrology, unlike *cholerick* (line 16), which derives from humors psychology.

See also *Tale of a Tub*, p. 184, where Swift distinguishes between the superficial, ignorant, and learned classes of readers.

57.19–58.2   fanciful and extravagant . . . and conduct.] Cf. below, n. to 334.13–16.

Walter's theory of Christian names provides an occasion to suggest some
of the associations that might be gathered around the names of the major
characters in the Shandy household.

First, as Kenneth Monkman has pointed out (*Winged Skull*, p. 280),
the word *shandy* appears in John Ray's *Collection of English Words not Generally Used*, 2d ed. (1691), p. 62, where it is listed as a north-country word
and defined as "wild." By 1788, it is being defined as "a little crack-
brained; somewhat crazy" (John Marshall, *The Rural Economy of Yorkshire* [1788], II: 351). Eric Rothstein (*Systems of Order and Inquiry in
Later Eighteenth-Century Fiction* [Berkeley: University of California
Press, 1975], p. 70, n. 12) takes issue with the later definition: "Joseph
Wright, *The English Dialect Dictionary*, 6 vols. (London, 1898–1905),
defines 'shandy' as, among other things, 'wild, romping, boisterous,
merry.' Cf. the 'wild and shandy' nature of Venus in James Robertson's
'Jove's Charge to Venus,' in *Poems* (2nd ed. revised, London, 1780),
p. 232; and the definition 'wild' in Francis Grose, *A Provincial Glossary*
(London, 1787), sig. G8ᵛ. The 'crack-brained' offered in *The Winged
Skull* . . . is therefore extreme."

For the name Tristram the best gloss is perhaps the opening paragraphs
of Malory's version of the Tristram legend, in which we are told the story
of Tristram's difficult birth and the words of his dying mother (Elyzabeth)
to him: "And whan she sye hym she seyde thus: 'A, my lytyll son, thou
haste murtherd thy modir! And therefore I suppose thou that arte a
murtherer so yonge, thow arte full lykly to be a manly man in thyne ayge;
and bycause I shall dye of the byrth of the, I charge my jantyllwoman that
she pray my lorde, the kynge Melyodas, that whan he is crystened let calle
hym Trystrams, that is as muche to say as a sorrowfull byrth.' . . . And
than he [Tristram's father] lette calle hym Trystrams, 'the sorrowfull-
borne chylde'" (Thomas Malory, *Works*, ed. Eugène Vinaver, 2d ed.
[Oxford: Oxford University Press, 1967], I: 371–73). Cash tells about a
"wooden statue labelled 'Old Tristram'" which stood in Sterne's youth
(and stands today) inside the church at Halifax, where he lived his adoles-
cent years. It is the "representation of a bearded beggar or poor-house
inmate presenting a box for coins . . ." (*Early and Middle Years*, p. 26).
Helen Sard Hughes ("A Precursor of *Tristram Shandy*," *JEGP* 17 [1918]:

227−51) suggests that Sterne may have been influenced by the title character in *The Life and Memoirs of Mr. Ephraim Tristram Bates* (1756). While the relationship between the two works remains problematic, there are a few parallels that argue Sterne did at least know of its existence; see nn. to 36.1–3 above, and 113.5−8 below.

Sterne may also have been familiar with the Renaissance tradition of Tristram as an amorist or libertine. See Beaumont and Fletcher, *Philaster, or Love lies a Bleeding,* IV.ii: "I think he should love venery; he is an old Sir Tristram" (in *Elizabethan Plays,* ed. Hazelton Spencer [Boston: D. C. Heath and Company, 1965], p. 821 and n. 21; cf. p. 1009, n. 62, to Middleton's *A Trick to Catch the Old One,* IV.v).

For the name Walter, Sterne perhaps knew, or could have read in Rabelais, that the equivalent of Merry Andrew in French is Merry Walter (*Bon Gaultier*) and, further, that "Gaulter (Walter) means a pleasant companion, in allusion to gaudir, to play the good-fellow (from gaudere in Latin)" (Rabelais, "Author's Prologue," vol. I, p. cxxx, n. 7); see below, n. to 58.13 (NICODEMUS'D). In view of Walter's character, the association, if intended, is obviously ironic.

The name Toby has been linked by Overton Philip James to the Apocryphal Tobias, on the basis of shared chastity; while Tobias is not used in *TS*, in *ASJ* (p. 170) there is an allusion to Captain Tobias Shandy. See *The Relation of "Tristram Shandy" to the Life of Sterne* (The Hague: Mouton & Co., 1966), p. 59. *Toby* was used during the eighteenth century for the posteriors, the buttocks (*OED*); cf. *Tickletoby* (Rabelais, IV.13, and *TS*, 267.18ff.). Much is made of this association by Max Nänny, "Similarity and Contiguity in *Tristram Shandy*," *ES* 60 (1979): 422–35.

Tristram's mother's maiden name was Elizabeth Mollineux (vol. I, chap. 15). Elizabeth, in addition to being the name of the mythical Tristram's mother, was the name of Sterne's wife as well. Rothstein has an interesting conjecture concerning Mollineux: "Tristram has his Locke from a most unlikely source, his mother, whose maiden name was Mollineux: the distinguished philosopher William Molyneux (1656–1698) was the correspondent of Locke's who posed the celebrated problem about the blind man, the cube, and the sphere. Contemporary readers would have been likely to catch the allusion, for Molyneux's correspondence with Locke was often reprinted . . ." (p. 70, n. 12).

Finally, Sterne had used the name Trim, oddly enough, for the villain
of the *Political Romance*, in which Trim represents the York ecclesiastical
lawyer Francis Topham (see n. to 11.26 above). Allegorized as the "Sexton
and Dog-Whipper," Trim is revealed as a sycophantic manipulator, out to
better his family fortunes by whatever petty means possible. Sterne certainly had in mind here the common eighteenth-century meaning for the
word *trimmer:* "one who trims between opposing parties in politics, etc.;
hence, one who inclines to each of two opposite sides as interest dictates"
(*OED*). But *trim* also has connotations more in keeping with the Corporal, particularly the idea of being fit, competent, neat, in good order—in
short, a good name for a servant or a soldier. He appears as such in
Richard Steele's *The Funeral*, where a servant named Trim, who has
served in Flanders, conducts his affairs in a hobby-horsical manner quite
anticipatory of Toby and Trim; his coffin-stealing foray is arranged in a
military manner and, after its success, Trim is declared "a perfect General" (pp. 82, 87). Trim's master in *The Funeral* is also a military man and
the play makes use of military metaphors for courtship; e.g.: "Charge her
Bravely—I wish she were a Cannon—an Eighteen Pounder for your
sake—Then I know were there occasion, you'd be in the mouth of Her"
(II.iii, p. 53); see above, n. to 42.15ff.

A final possibility for *trim* is its sexual connotation, befitting Trim's
success as a lover. Cf. "A Ballad of all the Trades," in Thomas D'Urfey's
Wit and Mirth: or Pills to Purge Melancholy (New York: Folklore Library
Publishers, 1959), IV: 61: "O the barber, the neat and nimble Barber, /
Whose Trade is ne'er the worse; / He never goes to Wash and Shave, / But
he trims, but he trims, but he trims his Maiden first."

58.3–6   The Hero of *Cervantes* . . . them] Work, p. 50, n. 1: "For the
frequent miscarriages of his enterprises, Don Quixote was wont to blame
the superior power of hostile magicians; his occasional successes were rendered the more sweet to him because they were undertaken in and glorified
by the name of his imaginary mistress, 'the empress of La Mancha, the
peerless Dulcinea del Toboso'."

58.7   TRISMEGISTUS or ARCHIMEDES] *OCD*, s.v. *Hermes Trismegistus:* "A
clumsy translation of Egyptian 'Thoth the very great', with the adj. em-
phasized by repetition . . . . When so named, Thoth is the reputed author
of the philosophico-religious treatises known collectively as *Hermetica*

. . . also of sundry works on astrology, magic, and alchemy. These are invariably late, Egyptian in the sense of being produced in Egypt by men of Greek speech, and . . . contain little or nothing of native Egyptian doctrine or custom."

Marvin K. Singleton, in two essays, has argued enthusiastically if not convincingly that a full understanding of "Sterne's novel awaits exposition of the most pervasive single source for *Tristram Shandy:* the apocryphal Greek and Latin Trismegistic (or 'Hermetic') literature" ("Trismegistic Tenor and Vehicle in Sterne's *Tristram Shandy,*" *PLL* 4 [1968]: 158). See also "Deuced Knowledge as Shandean Nub: Paracelsian Hermetic as Metaphoric Bridge in *Tristram Shandy,*" *ZAA* 16 (1968): 274–84.

"Archimedes" is the Greek mathematician and inventor (c. 287– 12 B.C.), cited at the end of vol. VI (572.7).

58.8–9   How many CÆSARS and POMPEYS] Since Sterne definitely has Shakespeare's *Julius Caesar* in mind later in this chapter (60.1), possibly he is recalling here lines in act I: "Brutus and Caesar: what should be in that 'Caesar'? / Why should that name be sounded more than yours? / Write them together, yours is as fair a name; / Sound them, it doth become the mouth as well . . ." (I.ii.142–45).

58.13   NICODEMUS'D into nothing.] Cf. Rabelais, vol. I, p. cxxx, n. 7 ("Author's Prologue"): "Certain proper names have particular ideas affix'd to them for ridiculous reasons. For instance, nothing being more common than cuckoldom and the name of John, cuckolds are therefore call'd Johns or Jans. Gaulter (Walter) means a pleasant companion, in allusion to gaudir, to play the good-fellow . . . . Nicodemus is a foolish fellow or ninny-hammer, from Nigaut and Nice, which last word has not the meaning of our word nice, but means dull."

Work (p. 50, n. 3) has a different suggestion: "Suggesting the character of Nicodemus, a Pharisee and a member of the Sanhedrin who, according to John, 3: 1–13 and 7: 45–53, in a cautious visit to Christ by night had become at heart a believer but before the Sanhedrin was afraid to avow his faith or to defend Christ; pusillanimous, weak-spirited, faint-hearted."

Cf. *Spectator* 432, the letter signed by "*Your Fool Elect,* Nicodemuncio" (IV: 20).

58.23–24   narrow prejudices of education] A term often used during the period by free-thinkers in their attacks on established religion; e.g.,

Berkeley's *Alciphron, or the Minute Philosopher,* in *Works,* III: 41 and passim. Walter uses it again in vol. V: "Prejudice of education, he would say, *is the devil,*—and the multitudes of them which we suck in with our mother's milk—*are the devil and all*" (448.6–8).

Cf. Swift, *Polite Conversation,* p. 29: "as to Blasphemy or Free-Thinking, I have known some scrupulous Persons of both Sexes, who, by a prejudiced Education, are afraid of Sprights."

59.4–5 *argumentum ad hominem*] "Argument addressed to the man." Cf. Locke, *ECHU,* IV.17.21, p. 686: "A third way [to convince others] is, to press a Man with Consequences drawn from his own Principles, or Concessions. This is already known under the Name of *Argumentum ad Hominem.*"

59.22–60.17 I never . . . fashion with 'em.] An interesting discussion of Walter's use of traditional rhetorical patterns is Graham Petrie's "Rhetoric as Fictional Technique in *Tristram Shandy,*" *PQ* 48 (1969): 479–94. Petrie argues that "with Walter, rhetoric is not just an added embellishment at which Sterne snipes maliciously from time to time; it is so integral to every aspect of his personality and his behavior that without it he could not exist. Rhetoric is not a facet of the man: it is the man himself" (p. 489).

59.23 speak of my father as he was] Sterne is perhaps recalling *Othello,* V.ii.342: "Speak of me as I am . . . ."

59.25 Θεοδίδακτος] *Theodidaktos* ("taught of God"). The word occurs in 1 Thessalonians 4: 9, translated: "But as touching brotherly love ye need not that I write unto you: for ye yourselves are taught of God to love one another."

59.25 Persuasion hung upon his lips] The idea may well have been a commonplace. See Lucian's "Demonax": "And in all this, his every word and deed was smiled on by the Graces and by Aphrodite, even; so that, to quote the comedian, 'persuasion perched upon his lips'" (*Works,* I: 149); and Robert Blair, *The Grave,* line 302: "Tho' strong Persuasion hung upon thy Lip" (1743; Augustan Reprint Society, 1973, no. 161). This last suggestion is made by Arthur Sherbo, *Studies,* p. 133.

59.28–60.1 that NATURE might . . . is eloquent."] Sterne recalls Antony's "This was the noblest Roman of them all" speech, *Julius Caesar,* V.v.73–75: "His life was gentle, and the elements / So mix'd in him that Nature might stand up / And say to all the world, 'This was a man!'"

60.4–10   *Cicero . . . Burgersdicius*] Work, p. 52, n. 7: "Cicero's treatises *De Oratore, Brutus,* and *Orator* develop a complete system of rhetorical training. Marcus Fabius Quintilianus (c. 35–c. 95) was a Roman rhetorician whose most celebrated work, the *Institutio Oratoria,* is a detailed treatise on the training of the orator. Isocrates (436–338 B.C.) was an Attic orator and distinguished teacher of eloquence. Aristotle (384–322 B.C.), the most famous and influential of Greek philosophers, was the founder of the Peripatetic school; the reference here is to his *Rhetoric,* a treatise on 'the faculty of discerning in every case the available means of persuasion.' Cassius Longinus (c. 210–273), a celebrated Greek rhetorician and philosopher surnamed 'Philologus,' is the reputed author of *On the Sublime,* a famous study of impressiveness in literary style. [This is the Longinus to whom Sterne and his age would have attributed *Peri Hupsous;* modern scholars now believe it was written some 200 years earlier, in the first century A.D. See *OCD,* s.v. *'Longinus'* and *Longinus Cassius.*] Gerhard Johann Voss (1577–1649) was a Dutch classical scholar, grammarian, and theologian of note; the reference is to his *Ars Rhetorica* and *Commentariorum Rhetoricorum Libri VI.* Caspar Schoppe (1576–1649) was a German controversialist and scholar whose chief work was his *Grammatica Philosophica.* Petrus Ramus (1515–1572) was a French logician noted for his writings against Aristotelianism. Thomas Farnaby (c. 1575–1647) was an English humanist whose *Systema Grammaticum,* written at the request of Charles I for use in the public schools, was published in 1641. Richard Crakanthorpe (1567–1624) was an eloquent Puritan divine, famous for his powers as a logician and a disputant. Francis Burgersdyk [1590–1635] was a Dutch logician famed for his *Institutionum Logicarum Libri Duo.*"

Sterne may have found his entire list in a yet undiscovered source—or, just as likely, may have put it together from his own education, since the names are standard ones. It is worth noting that such lists almost always had negative comments attached to them; see, e.g., Daniel Waterland, *Advice to a Young Student* (1730), pp. 22–24; John Clarke, *An Essay upon Study* (1731), p. 87; or Locke, *Some Thoughts Concerning Education,* sec. 94, pp. 199–200, where he attacks the failure to teach utilitarian subjects: "*Seneca* complains of the contrary Practice in his time: And yet the *Bur-*

gersdicius's and the *Scheiblers* [Christoph Scheibler, 1589–1653] did not swarm in those Days, as they do now in these. What would he have thought, if he had lived now, when the *Tutors* think it their great Business to fill the Studies and Heads of their Pupils with such Authors as these? He would have had much more reason to say, as he does, *Non Vitæ sed Scholæ discimus*, we learn not to Live, but to Dispute; and our Education fits us rather for the University, than the World."

60.10   *Dutch* logician or commentator] Cf. 763.7: "writing like a Dutch commentator to the end of the chapter . . . ." Vossius and Burgersdicius were, to be sure, Dutch, but the sentiment is a commonplace in the century, verbose and weighty scholarship being associated in the public mind with the Dutch (and Germans), from Rabelais, vol. IV, p. xviii ("Explanatory Remarks"): "I find that matter crowds upon me, and I might be more voluminous than a Dutch commentator . . ."; to Dryden, "Life of Plutarch," in *Works* (Berkeley: University of California Press, 1971), XVII: 287; to Goldsmith, *Critical Review* (September 1759): "Were such a number of original thoughts in possession of a German commentator, what folios might not be the result . . ." (*Works*, I: 210). See also *Letters*, p. 79: "tho' I have a terrible dread of writing like a dutch Commentator . . ."; and Sterne's invocation of Mynheer Vander Blonederdondergewdenstronke in vol. VI (517.12).

60.11–12   argument *ad ignorantiam*] "Argument to ignorance." In the same section of *ECHU* from which the definition of *ad hominem* is quoted (see above, n. to 59.4–5), Locke writes: "Another way that Men ordinarily use to drive others, and force them to submit their Judgments, and receive the Opinion in debate, is to require the Adversary to admit what they alledge as a Proof, or to assign a better. And this I call *Argumentum ad Ignorantiam*" (IV.17.20, p. 686).

60.14   *Jesus College*] Sterne took his A.B. degree from Jesus College, Cambridge, where he was in residence from 1733 to 1737; his M.A. degree was awarded in 1740. Jesus College was a family tradition, Sterne's greatgrandfather Archbishop Richard Sterne having been Master during the Civil War, and his grandfather Simon and his uncle Jaques having attended before him. The college, and the Sterne family's relation to it, is described at length in Cash, *Early and Middle Years*, pp. 41–62.

60.16–17   that a man . . . with 'em.] Cf. Butler, *Hudibras*, I.i.89–90: "For all a Rhetoricians Rules / Teach nothing but to name his Tools" (ed. John Wilders [Oxford: Clarendon Press, 1967], p. 4).

60.22–23   *vive la Bagatelle*] "Long live trifles!" The phrase is closely associated with Swift, who in a letter to Gay (July 10, 1732) chides the inattention of his friends to the niceties of diet and drink and then comments: "All for want of my rule Vive la bagatelle" (*Correspondence*, ed. Harold Williams [Oxford: Clarendon Press, 1965], IV: 40). Cf. Pope, Epistle I.vi.126–29: "If, after all, we must with Wilmot own, / The Cordial Drop of Life is Love alone, / And Swift cry wisely, 'Vive la Bagatelle!' / The Man that loves and laughs, must sure do well" (in *Imitations of Horace*, pp. 245–46). Sterne uses the phrase again in *ASJ*, p. 153, in La Fleur's all-purpose love letter.

61.6–7   beginning in jest, . . . downright earnest.] Possibly proverbial. See Tilley, J46: "Leave JESTING while it pleases lest it turn to earnest"; and *ODEP*, s.v. *Dogs:* "As fools and dogs use to begin in jest, and end in earnest, so did these Philistines" (quoting Joseph Hall, *Contemplations*, X.iii). See also below, n. to 389.4–5.

61.22   *Ponto* or *Cupid*] *Spectator* 499 (IV: 271) uses *Cupid* as a dog's name. We have not found another example of *Ponto* but assume it was in common use; it is most likely taken from the card game Ombre; see *OED*, s.v. *Punto*[2].

62.3–6   He knew as well . . . a step further.] Cf. W. P. W. Phillimore, *The Law and Practice of Change of Name* (London: Phillimore and Co., 1905), p. 18: "As to changes of Christian name, it is laid down very positively in the various text books that no means exist whereby a name given at baptism can be varied save, it is usual to add, at confirmation by the Bishop. This latter method, at any rate in the Anglican Church, is practically obsolete . . ."; and p. 24: "To summarize the subject of change of surnames. There are two opposing views. The advocates of the one aver that change of name without the Royal Licence or Act of Parliament is 'illegal,' and they point to an undeviating custom or practice for nearly 250 years . . . . The other view is that a man is at liberty to change his name when and as often as he pleases, that what a man's name may be is but a question of fact. Further, . . . that a practice arising within the last two or three hundred years cannot create a Common Law prerogative of the Crown, restraining and

making illegal what certainly was a common practice in ancient times."
Phillimore notes that the practice of obtaining a "Royal Licence" for the
changing of surnames began in the reign of Charles II (p. 25).

62.18–19   would not give a cherry-stone] *OED:* "as the type of a thing of
trifling value." *OED* cites this passage as its last illustration, but Sterne
obviously found the phrase useful and employs it several times again; see
220.12–13, 352.8, 569.16, 642.18–19.

62.24–27   *Andrew . . .* was the DEVIL.] Walter's dislike of *Andrew* may be
explained by its connection with *Merry Walter;* see above, n. to 57.19–
58.2. *OED* defines *Numps* as "a silly or stupid person"; its last illustration
is dated ?1730. That the Devil was referred to as *Nick* or, more commonly,
Old Nick is noted by *OED*, but the derivation is unknown.

63.3   in *rerum natura*] "In the nature or natural order of things."

63.7   EPIPHONEMA, or rather EROTESIS] See Richard A. Lanham, *A Handlist of Rhetorical Terms* (Berkeley: University of California Press, 1968),
s.v. *Epiphonema*: "Striking epigrammatic or sententious utterance to summarize and conclude a passage, poem, or speech"; and *Erotesis:* "Rhetorical question implying strong affirmation or denial."

63.7–8   raised . . . of the discourse] Sterne was fond of this musical metaphor for the "tone" of a story or discourse; cf. the elaborate discussion of
the key of Phutatorius's "Zounds," 378.4–10; and also 683.2–3: "and
having hemmed twice, to find in what key his story would best go"; and
748.19–21: "he had lost the sportable key of his voice which gave sense
and spirit to his tale."

63.15–23   What could . . . to the name.] This entire section on the "progress
and establishment" (60.27) of Walter's opinions, leading to his publication of a treatise, has some affinity to the ideas in the famous passage in sec.
IX ("A Digression on Madness") of *Tale of a Tub:* "But when a Man's
Fancy gets *astride* on his Reason, when Imagination is at Cuffs with the
Senses, and common Understanding, as well as common Sense, is Kickt
out of Doors; the first Proselyte he makes, is Himself, and when that is
once compass'd, the Difficulty is not so great in bringing over others; A
strong Delusion always operating from *without*, as vigorously as from
within" (p. 171).

Montaigne also speaks to the point: "Particular Error first makes the
Publick Error; and afterwards, in turn, the publick Error makes the

particular one; so all this vast *Fabrick* goes forming and confounding it self from hand to hand, so that the remotest Testimony is better instructed than those that are nearest, and the last inform'd better persuaded than the first. 'Tis a natural Progress: For whoever believes any Thing, thinks it a Work of Charity to persuade another into the same Opinion. Which the better to do, he will make no Difficulty of adding as much of his own Invention, as he conceives necessary to encounter the Resistance or Want of Conception he meets with in others. . . . There is nothing to which Men commonly are more inclin'd, than to give way to their own Opinions" (III.11.293 – 94).

64.9   unison] *OED* (s.v. *unison*, B.1.d.) cites this passage as its sole illustration of the usage "like-sounding; equivalent."

64.10   By his ashes!] Tristram uses a similar oath at 225.19 – 20: "By the tomb stone of *Lucian*——if it is in being,——if not, why then, by his ashes! by the ashes of my dear *Rabelais* . . . ."

65.7 – 11   'Tis to rebuke . . . with them.] Cf. Swift, *Tale of a Tub*, p. 134: "BUT, here it is good to stop the hasty Reader, ever impatient to see the End of an Adventure, before We Writers can duly prepare him for it." Sterne continues to sound like Swift throughout this chapter; see n. to 66.1–12 below.

65.13 – 15   the habitude . . . profit from it."] Work, p. 57, n. 1: "Gaius Plinius Caecilius Secundus [c. 61–c. 112], Roman author, did write 'He read nothing without making extracts, for he used to say that no book was so bad but that some part of it was useful' (*Epistolae*, 3.5); 'he,' however, was Pliny the Elder (23 – 79), the Roman naturalist, of whom his nephew was here writing."

Pliny's text: "dicere etiam solebat nullum esse librum tam malum ut non aliqua parte prodesset" (I: 176).

65.17 – 18   than the history . . . with it.] See below, n. to 555.23 – 24.

65.27ff.   *The *Romish* Rituals, etc.] The information in Sterne's note could easily have been garnered from the "Memoire" which follows, though Davies has suggested the possibility that Sterne used *The Religious Ceremonies and Customs of the Several Nations of the Known World* (1731–39); see *N&Q* 220 (1975): 14–16. The Latin quotation from Aquinas appears in Deventer following a French translation of the sentence (see 67.20–21) and may be rendered: "A child still in the womb can in no way be baptized"; for a full discussion of the "Memoire" see vol. II, app. 6, pp. 939–45, in this edition; and Melvyn New, *"Tristram Shandy* and Heinrich van Deventer's *Observations," PBSA* 69 (1974): 275–81. The relationship of the "Memoire" to the discussion of the homunculus which opens *TS* is discussed by Louis A. Landa in "The Shandean Homunculus," pp. 60–63 (see above, n. to 2.19ff.).

Sterne's purpose in the phrase "second *La chose impossible"* (66.25–26) is somewhat obscure; he may perhaps have reference to the famous statement in the *Summa Theologiæ* concerning God's omnipotence and its limits (the possible and the impossible): "Whatever does not involve a contradiction is in that realm of the possible with respect to which God is called omnipotent. Whatever involves a contradiction is not held by omnipotence, for it just cannot possibly make sense of being possible" ("Quæcumque igitur contradictionem non implicant sub illis possibilibus continentur respectu quorum dicitur Deus omnipotens. Ea vero quæcumque igitur contradictionem implicant sub divina omnipotentia non continentur, quia non possunt habere possibilium rationem"). See *Summa Theologiæ,* 1a. quaest. 25, art. 3 (New York: McGraw-Hill, 1967), V: 164–65. Sterne refers to this argument in vol. IV, where the Strasbourgers discuss the possibility of God's making a nose as big as the steeple of Strasbourg (314.5ff.).

The following translation of the "Memoire" is from Work, pp. 58–62:

Memorandum presented to the Doctors of the *Sorbonne*

An obstetrical surgeon declares to the Doctors of the *Sorbonne* that there are sometimes cases, although they are very rare, in which a mother cannot deliver her child, and in which the child is held in its mother's womb in such a way that it cannot make any part of its body appear, which latter would be a case, according to the Rituals, to baptize it, at least conditionally. The surgeon who raises the question asserts that by means of a *little injection-pipe* he can baptize the child directly, without doing any harm to the mother. He asks whether this means which he proposes is permissible and lawful, and whether it may be employed in such cases as he has described.

REPLY

The Council observes that the question proposed presents great difficulties. The Theologians assume the hypothesis that baptism, which is a spiritual birth, supposes a former birth; as they teach it, it is necessary to be born into the world to be reborn in Jesus Christ. Saint *Thomas* [Aquinas], in *part 3, question 68, article 11,* follows this doctrine as an accepted truth; one cannot, says this Holy Doctor, baptize children who are yet held in their mothers' wombs, and Saint *Thomas* bases his opinion on the fact that such children are not born and cannot be counted among other men; from this he concludes that they cannot be the object of an external action in receiving through the ministry of men the sacraments necessary to salvation: *Children remaining in maternal wombs have not yet come forth into the light that they may lead their life among other men; therefore they cannot be the objects of human action that they may receive through the ministry of men the sacraments necessary to salvation.* The rituals follow in practice what the theologians have ordained in these matters, and in a uniform manner they prohibit the baptism of infants who are retained in their mothers' wombs, if no part of their bodies appears. The agreement of the theologians and of the rituals, which are the rules of the dioceses, appears to establish an authority which settles the present question; however, the council conscientiously considering, on the one hand, that the reasoning of the theologians is founded merely upon a matter of expediency, and that the maintenance of the rituals assumes that one cannot directly baptize infants thus retained in their mothers' wombs, the which is contrary to the present supposition; and considering, on the other hand, that the same theologians teach that one may risk administering the sacraments which *Jesus Christ* has established as the easy but necessary means for the salvation of men; and deeming, furthermore, that children retained in their mothers' wombs are capable of salvation even as they are capable of damnation;—for these considerations, and in regard of the statement [Work erroneously prints *"en égard"* where Deventer and Sterne have *"eu égard"* (68.20), i.e., "and considering the statement," etc.] which affirms that a certain means has been found of baptizing children thus retained, without doing any harm to the mother, the Council deems that one may take advantage of the proposed expedient, in the faith which it has that God would never leave this sort of infants without any succour, and supposing, as is asserted, that the means under discussion is proper to procure their baptism. However, since in authorizing the proposed practice it would be proceeding to change a rule universally established, the Council believes that he who consults it ought to address himself to his bishop and to whomsoever it appertains to judge the utility and the danger of the proposed means, and since, with submission to the pleasure of the bishop, the Council deems that it would be necessary to appeal to the Pope, who has the authority to interpret the rules of the church and to derogate them in case the law cannot accommodate whatever wisdom and utility may appear in the manner of baptizing here considered, the Council cannot approve the practice without the confirmation of these two authorities. The consulter is advised at least to address himself to his bishop and to apprise him of the present decision, in order that, if the prelate agrees with the reasons upon which the undersigned doctors base their opinion, in case of necessity in which he might risk too much to wait while the permission was asked and granted, he can be authorized to employ the means which he proposes, so advantageous to the salvation of the infant. In decreeing that one may avail himself of this manner of baptism, the Council nevertheless believes that if the infants in question should come into the world, against the expectation of those who had availed themselves of this expedient, it would be necessary to baptize them *conditionally;* and in this the Council is in conformity with all the rituals which, in authorizing the baptism of an infant any portion of whose body appears, nevertheless enjoin and ordain that it be baptized *conditionally* if it comes happily into the world.

Determined in the Sorbonne, *10* April, *1733.*

66.1–12   It is . . . of the ink-horn.] Sterne's subject and tone in this paragraph are reminiscent of Swift's in the introduction to *Tale of a Tub;* e.g.: "Air being a heavy Body, and therefore . . . continually descending, must needs be more so, when loaden and press'd down by Words; which are also Bodies of much Weight and Gravity, as it is manifest from those deep *Impressions* they make and leave upon us; and therefore must be delivered from a due Altitude . . . .

"That large Portion of Wit laid out in raising Pruriences and Protuberances, is observ'd to run much upon a Line, and ever in a Circle. The whining Passions, and little starved Conceits, are gently wafted up by their own extreme Levity . . . . Bombast and Buffoonry, by Nature lofty and light, soar highest of all . . ." (pp. 60–61).

The author of the *Tale* also laments the carelessness of his readers: "BUT the greatest Maim given to that general Reception, which the Writings of our Society have formerly received, (next to the transitory State of all sublunary Things,) hath been a superficial Vein among many Readers of the present Age, who will by no means be persuaded to inspect beyond the Surface and the Rind of Things . . ." (p. 66).

66.2   Republick of Letters] Sterne uses the phrase again, 484.16. It perhaps originated with Addison; *OED* cites his *Dialogue on Medals* (1702, 1721) as its first illustration and it appears as well in *Spectator* 445 and 494, both published in 1712 (IV: 63, 252). See Goldsmith, *Citizen of the World*, letter 20 (March 20, 1760), for a commentary on the term (*Works*, II: 85–88).

66.8–10 The subtle hints . . . escapes downwards] Perhaps, as Arthur Sherbo (*Studies*, p. 128) suggests, this usage is an echo of Ecclesiastes 3: 21: "Who knoweth the spirit of man that goeth upward, and the spirit of the beast that goeth downward to the earth?"; or of *Hamlet*, III.iii.97–98: "My words fly up, my thoughts remain below: / Words without thoughts never to heaven go."

66.13 male-reader] Not recorded in *OED*; nor is "female-reader" in the next line.

70.5 *sous condition*] "Conditionally." The conclusion of the chapter may be translated thus: "by means of a little injection-pipe, and, without doing any harm to the father." For an analysis of the careful and elaborate construction of the humor of this final passage, see vol. II, app. 6, p. 943, in this edition.

70.17–71.2 I think . . . well again.] Tristram recalls his uncle "all this while . . . left knocking the ashes out of his tobacco pipe" briefly in this same chapter (72.24–25), but does not allow him to finish his sentence until vol. II, chap. 6 (114.4–8): "I think, replied my uncle *Toby*,—taking, as I told you, his pipe from his mouth, and striking the ashes out of it as he began his sentence;----I think, replied he,—it would not be amiss, brother, if we rung the bell." The Russian formalist critic Viktor Shklovsky calls attention to this and similar interrupted developments in his famous essay "A Parodying Novel: Sterne's *Tristram Shandy*," reprinted in *Laurence Sterne: A Collection of Critical Essays*, ed. John Traugott (Englewood Cliffs, N.J.: Prentice-Hall, 1968), pp. 69–71; Shklovsky concludes: "This method is for Sterne the canon." See also vol. III, chap. 1 (185.4–6): "'*I wish*, Dr. *Slop*,' quoth my uncle *Toby*, '*you had seen what prodigious armies we had in Flanders*'," a phrase which occurs first in vol. II, chap. 18 (169.14–16), and is then repeated as the opening sentence of vol. III, chap. 2 (187.1–2) and vol. III, chap. 6 (192.20).

71.3ff. Pray what was that man's name, etc.] Sterne has already referred to the influence of climate on character at 27.5–12 and will do so at length in his

"Author's Preface," 230ff.; see nn. to both passages. Of the first "observation" and its corollary—that the English climate is varied and that from
this results the variety of English characters—Work is certainly correct in
saying that they "had long been accepted as commonplaces by English
writers and natural philosophers, and Addison and Dryden were far from
being the sole patrons of the conclusion that to the variety of native characters was due the superiority of English comedy to continental" (p. 64, n.
1). Dryden does endorse English comedy over French in his "Essay of
Dramatick Poesie" (1668), though not in Sterne's climatic terms; e.g.:
"Hence the reason is perspicuous, why no *French* Playes, when translated,
have, or ever can succeed on the *English* Stage. For, if you consider the
Plots, our own are fuller of variety, if the writing ours are more quick and
fuller of spirit: and therefore 'tis a strange mistake in those who decry the
way of writing Playes in Verse, as if the *English* therein imitated the
French. We have borrow'd nothing from them; our Plots are weav'd in
English Loomes: we endeavour therein to follow the variety and greatness
of characters which are deriv'd to us from *Shakespeare* and *Fletcher* . . . .
    "But to return whence I have digress'd, I dare boldly affirm these two
things of the *English Drama:* First, That we have many Playes of ours as
regular as any of theirs; and which, besides, have more variety of Plot and
Characters: And secondly, that in most of the irregular Playes of *Shakespeare* or *Fletcher* . . . there is a more masculine fancy and greater spirit in
the writing, then there is in any of the *French*" (*Works*, XVII: 53–54).
Nothing in his other prefaces would seem to be more applicable, but it
should be noted that the "Essay" was written nowhere near the middle of
William's reign (1688–1702).
    For Addison, Work cites *Spectator* 371, which opens: "You know very
well that our Nation is more famous for that sort of Men who are called
Whims and *Humorists*, than any other Country in the World, for which
reason it is observ'd that our *English* Comedy excells that of all other
Nations in the Novelty and Variety of its Characters" (III: 396). Significantly, perhaps, in this essay Addison chides the "dull Generation of Story-
tellers," one of whom tells about the siege of Namur (p. 399); see below, n.
to 88.25.
    In *Spectator* 179 (II: 205), Addison suggests a slightly different view of
the success of English comedy, closer to that which Tristram offers as his

own: "I might likewise observe, that the Gloominess in which sometimes the Minds of the best Men are involved, very often stands in need of such little incitements to Mirth and Laughter, as are apt to disperse Melancholy, and put our Faculties in good Humour. To which some will add, that the *British* Climate, more than any other, makes Entertainments of this nature in a manner necessary." Dryden had said much the same thing in his "Essay": "we, who are a more sullen people, come to be diverted at our Playes; so they who are of an ayery and gay temper come thither to make themselves more serious: And this I conceive to be one reason why Comedy's are more pleasing to us, and Tragedies to them" (p. 48).

In Sterne's own day, Goldsmith had made much the same argument in *An Enquiry into the Present State of Polite Learning in Europe* (1759): "if we consider this, it cannot be expected, that our works of taste, which imitate our peculiar manners, can please those that are unacquainted with the originals themselves. Though our descriptions and characters are drawn from nature, yet they may appear exaggerated, or faintly copied, to those, who, unacquainted with the peculiarities of our island, have no standard by which to make the comparison.

"THE French are much more fortunate than us in this particular. An universal sameness of character appears to spread itself over the whole continent, particularly the fools and coxcombs of every country abroad seem almost cast in the same mold. . . . The Marquis of Moliere strikes all Europe. Sir John Falstaff, with all the merry men of Eastcheap, are entirely of England, and please the English alone" (*Works*, I: 292–94). Friedman's annotations to this passage trace the history of the idea back to Temple (see below, our n. to 231.12–232.4) and Addison, *Guardian* 144.

For a further account of the tradition, see J. W. Johnson, "'Of Differing Ages and Climes'," *JHI* 21 (1960): 465–80; and Franz Karl Stanzel, "*Tristram Shandy* und die Klimatheorie," *GRM*, n.s. 21 (1971): 16–28.

On Tristram's dating his time of writing (line 27), see above, n. to 51.6.

71.18   the great *Addison*] Sterne uses the same epithet for Addison in the only other overt allusion to him, 580.9.

71.29–72.1   Thus . . . before our eyes] Cf. Goldsmith, *An Enquiry into the Present State of Polite Learning:* "It is indeed a misfortune for a fine writer to be born in a period so enlightened as ours. The harvest of wit is gathered in, and little is left for him, except to glean what others have thought unworthy their bringing away" (*Works*, I: 300). Goldsmith would appear to be serious, but he is writing about the literature of France in the age of Louis XIV and in his own time.

72.5   obstetrical] *OED* dates its first illustration 1775 but does record *TS* (126.25) as its first illustration for *obstetrically*.

72.7−10   creeping upwards . . . be far off.] Cf. Swift, *Tale of a Tub*, p. 129: "For whereas every Branch of Knowledge has received such wonderful Acquirements since [Homer's] Age, especially within these last three Years, or thereabouts; it is almost impossible, he could be so very perfect in Modern Discoveries, as his Advocates pretend." Cf. *TS*, 546.20−25.
          Ακμή (*Akme*): "acme, pinnacle."

72.14   *As war begets poverty, poverty peace*] A note in the Guthkelch-Smith edition of *Tale of a Tub* suggests Sterne's probable source for this phrase. Annotating the opening of *The Battle of the Books* ("WHOEVER examines with due Circumspection into the *Annual Records* of *Time*, will find it remarked, that *War is the Child of Pride*, and *Pride the Daughter of Riches* . . .") and its marginal note ("Vid. Ephem. de *Mary Clarke*"), the editors comment: "The reference to the 'Ephem. de Mary Clarke' was thus explained by Hawkesworth [1755 ed., I: 247],—'now called *Wing's* sheet almanack, and printed by *J. Roberts* for the Company of *Stationers*'. In Swift's days the sheet almanack issued under the name of Vincent Wing was 'printed by Mary Clark, for the Company of Stationers'. It contained in columns the calendar for the year, with weather prognostications, and other entries. In the top left hand corner there was a figure showing the signs of the Zodiac, and beside it was the following rhyme: War begets Poverty, / Poverty Peace: / Peace maketh Riches flow, / (Fate ne'er doth cease:) / Riches produceth Pride, / Pride is War's ground, / War begets Poverty, &c. / (The World) goes round" (p. 217). The note cites the hoary history of the idea and refers to a *TLS* discussion between February 17 and March 30, 1916, which set forth antecedents possibly as far back as the sixth century.
          Sterne uses the phrase again in a letter dated May 7, 1763, in which he describes how his agues were treated in such a way that a fever resulted,

which brought on a loss of blood and hence agues again, "so that as *war begets poverty, poverty peace,* &c. &c.—has this miserable constitution made all its revolutions . . ." (*Letters,* p. 195).

Musical settings for the verses can be found in various songbooks throughout the century.

73.3   family-likeness] *OED*'s earliest example of this expression is dated 1824.

73.12–13   the females had no character at all] Cf. Pope, "Epistle to a Lady," lines 1–2: "NOTHING so true as what you once let fall, / 'Most Women have no Characters at all'" (*Epistles to Several Persons,* p. 46).

73.15–16   according to . . . of Christian names] Walter has in mind Dinah's defilement as related in Genesis 34: 1–31. Dinah, the daughter of Jacob, is seduced by the uncircumcised Shechem, who then asks for her in marriage. Jacob stipulates that Shechem's people must be circumcised, but after they have undergone the ritual—indeed, while they are recovering from it—Jacob and his sons slaughter them to avenge Dinah's shame.

73.29   and as afflictions . . . our good] Proverbial; variant of Tilley, A53: "AFFLICTIONS are sent us by God for our good." See also *ODEP,* s.v. *Afflictions.*

74.7–8   or in . . . and his reader] Tacitus (c. 55–c. 120 A.D.) had a reputation throughout the eighteenth century for excessive subtlety; see, for example, *Spectator* 202 (II: 291), where Steele compares himself to the historian by way of excusing himself for falling "into Observations upon [a trivial incident] which were too great for the Occasion" and ascribing it "to Causes which had nothing to do towards it." Donald F. Bond's note illuminates both the *Spectator* passage and Sterne's: "Rapin (*Reflections upon History,* chap. vii) notes that Tacitus is always seeing stratagem and policy where they do not exist. 'Policy is the Universal Motive: the Clue that unravels all Transactions. . . . In a Word, all his Characters are alike, and there is nothing of Nature in the Piece; his Reflexions seem Overstrain'd and Violent; and the Genius of the Historian, is without Variation, Impress'd on his whole Work' (*Whole Critical Works,* 1706, ii. 264–5)."

74.22–23   extream and unparallel'd modesty of nature] Cf. *Don Quixote,* II.III.44: "I am far from imposing any thing, Sir, that should urge Don *Quixote* to a Transgression in Point of Decency; for if I conjecture right,

among the many Virtues that adorn him, his Modesty is the most distinguishable" (IV: 81). Hamlet advises the Players to "Suit the action to the
word, the word to the action, with this special observance, that you o'erstep
not the modesty of nature . . ." (III.ii.17–19). Sterne uses the phrase
again to describe Toby in vol. VI (550.20–21).

Wayne Booth ("Did Sterne Complete *Tristram Shandy?*," *MP* 48
[1951]: 172–83) points specifically to this passage, along with similar
references to the story of Toby's modesty and amours (180.13–18,
244.10–12, 245.9–12, 400.22–24), to build a convincing case for the
theory that when the origin of Toby's modesty, "the choicest morsel of my
whole story" (401.8), is finally told in vol. IX, Sterne considered his work
complete: "one finds every reason to believe not only that Sterne worked
with some care to tie his major episodes together but that, with his ninth
volume, he completed the book as he had originally conceived it. Although there is no way of knowing how many volumes he originally intended to write, there can be little question that even as he wrote the first
volume he had a fairly clear idea of what his final volume—whatever its
eventual number—would contain" (pp. 173–74). For an interesting de-
murrer to Booth's argument, see R. F. Brissenden, "'Trusting to Almighty God': Another Look at the Composition of *Tristram Shandy*," in
Winged Skull, pp. 258–68; cf. above, n. to 4.1–21.

75.18   parapet . . . siege of *Namur*] For military terms, see "Glossary of
Terms of Fortification" in this volume; for an account of the siege of
Namur, see below, nn. to vol. II, chap. 1, pp. 93–94.

75.28   family-pride] Unrecorded in *OED*.

76.21–24   as the . . . after his name] Chambers, s.v. *Copernican system*,
points out that the heliocentric view was held by many ancients but forgotten "till about 250 years ago, when Copernicus revived it; from whom it
took the name of the *copernican system*." Sterne might have been parodying
the belaboring of the obvious, which is often the hallmark of the *Cyclopædia*.

Chambers mentions the retrogradation (the apparent backward or west-
ward movement) of Venus as a contributing factor of Copernicus's system,
but does so rather obscurely. If Sterne did not have another source he is
revealing a good comprehension of astronomical theory, since the observation of planetary retrogradation did play a significant role in "fortifying"

the Copernican system; see, e.g., John Keill, *Introduction to the True Astronomy*, 2d ed. (1730), pp. 26–41, 163–69 (originally published in Latin in 1718; the first English edition was published in 1721 and may well have served as the basis for the Chambers entry).

OED does not record Sterne's usage of *backslidings* as a synonym for retrogradation.

77.6–9   *Amicus Plato . . .* is my sister.] "Plato is my friend, but truth is a greater friend." Cf. *Don Quixote*, II.III.51 (IV: 159), where Quixote writes in a letter to Sancho: "*as the Saying is*, Amicus Plato, sed magis amica Veritas"; noted by Stout, "Borrowings," p. 115, n. 13.

Work (p. 68, n. 8) traces the sentiment to Plato's *Phaedo*, 91c: "And I would ask you to be thinking of the truth and not of Socrates" (*The Dialogues of Plato*, trans. B. Jowett, 4th ed. [Oxford: Clarendon Press, 1953], I: 447).

Aristotle has his own version in the *Nicomachean Ethics*, I.vi.1 (p. 17): "Both [Plato and truth] are dear to us, yet 'tis our duty to prefer the truth." And the *Stanford Dictionary*, s.v. *amicus*, recording the proverb exactly as does Sterne (with the addition, in apposition, of "amicus Socrates"), cites Reginald Scott, *The discoverie of witchcraft* (1584), p. 115.

78.3   in *Foro Scientiæ*] "In the forum of science (or knowledge)"; this would appear to be Sterne's coinage, by analogy with *in Foro Legis* (the outer forum, i.e., in the eyes of the law) and *in Foro Conscientiæ* (the inner forum, i.e., in the eyes of God, the conscience).

78.4–5   there is . . . only DEATH, brother.] The anti-militaristic idea that "he who kills one man is a murderer, while he who kills a thousand is a hero" seems to have been a commonplace, perhaps originating with St. Cyprian: "Homicidium, cum admittunt singuli, Crimen est; / Virtus vocatur cum publice geritur," which is translated "*Murder*, when *ONE* commits it, is a *Crime*, / But *Crowds* add *Sanction*, *Merit* and *Esteem*," by the anonymous translator of *St. Cyprian's Discourse to Donatus*, 2d ed. (1716), p. 13; the Latin is quoted in the preface. Edward Young uses the idea in *Love of Fame*, Satire VII: "ONE to destroy is Murder by the Law, / And Gibbets keep the lifted Hand in Awe; / To murder *Thousands* takes a specious Name, / *War's glorious Art*, and gives immortal Fame" (*Poetical Works* [1741], I: 284–85).

A famous pamphlet encouraging the murder of Oliver Cromwell appeared in England in 1657 under the title "Killing no Murder"; and indeed the phrase would appear to have been a legal commonplace: see, e.g., Giles Jacob, *A Law Grammar,* 2d ed. (1749), p. 19, where the heading of the discussion is "*Of Killing not* Murder, *but Justifiable.*" Earlier, the distinction had been explained: "It is not the bare Killing, but *Malice,* that makes the Crime of Murder . . ." (p. 14).

78.8   *Lillabullero*] The history of both the tune and the songs set to it is detailed by Claude M. Simpson, *The British Broadside Ballad and Its Music* (New Brunswick, N.J.: Rutgers University Press, 1966), pp. 449–55. Most relevant to Sterne's purposes, the song originated in Ireland in 1687 or 1688 as an anti-papist ballad, supposedly written by Thomas Wharton; its effect as a rallying point against James II and his lord deputy of Ireland, Richard Talbot, Earl of Tyrconnel, is recorded by Bishop Burnet: "A foolish ballad was made at that time, treating the papists, and chiefly the Irish, in a very ridiculous manner, which had a burden, said to be Irish words, lero, lero, lilibulero, that made an impression on the army, that cannot be well imagined by those who saw it not. The whole army, and at last all people both in city and country, were singing it perpetually. And perhaps never had so slight a thing so great an effect" (*History of His Own Time, 1724–1734* [1823], III: 319; cited by Simpson, p. 449). Cf. Anthony Collins, *A Discourse Concerning Ridicule and Irony in Writing* (1729), Augustan Reprint Society, 1970, no. 142: "I believe, it may with more Propriety be said, that King *James* II and *Popery* were *laugh'd* or *Lilli-bullero'd,* than that they were *argu'd* out of the Kingdom" (p. 35).

It is worth noting that in the very first number of the *True Patriot* (appropriately published on November 5, 1745), Fielding published an anti-Pretender song, probably his own creation, under the heading "*A Loyal Song, with a Chorus, to the Tune of Lillibullero proper to be sung at all merry Meetings.*" He had earlier (1730) written another song to the Lillibullero tune for his ballad opera, *The Author's Farce,* act III, air VIII; the opening lines seem particularly apropos to *TS:* "Let the foolish philosopher strive in his cell, / By wisdom or virtue to merit true praise, / The soldier in hardship and danger still dwell / That glory and honor may crown his last days" (ed. Charles B. Woods [Lincoln: University of Nebraska Press, 1966], p. 56).

Simpson observes that "the large number of songs and ballads set to the tune [in the first half of the eighteenth century] testifies to the vitality of this eminently singable melody," and notes that it appears in twelve ballad operas during the period, including the *Beggar's Opera*, air 44 (pp. 449, 453). He also mentions that "the tune was traditionally associated with a Sussex whistling song" (p. 455).

The plate facing is taken from William Chappell, *Old English Popular Music*, ed. H. Ellis Wooldridge, rev. ed. (London: Chappell & Co., 1893), II: 58–59.

78.18ff. *Argumentum ad Verecundiam*, etc.] Work provides the following explanations of Sterne's several types of argument, p. 71, nn. 11, 13, 14:

Argumentum ad Verecundiam: "argument addressed to modesty; an appeal to one's reverence for authority." See also *ECHU*, IV.17.19, p. 686.

Argumentum ex Absurdo: "disproof of a proposition by showing the absurdity or impossibility of one or more of its consequences."

Argumentum ex Fortiori: "with a stronger reason; hence, more conclusive."

Argumentum Fistulatorium: "literally, the argument of one who plays upon a shepherd's pipe; the argument of a whistler."

Argumentum Baculinum: "literally, the argument of a stick; an appeal to one's sense of fear."

Argumentum ad Crumenam: "an argument to the purse; an appeal to one's thrift or avarice."

Argumentum Tripodium: "argument addressed to the third leg."

Argumentum ad Rem: "argument addressed to the thing."

As Work notes, only the first three are orthodox terms of logic.

Cf. *Spectator* 239 (II: 429): "When our Universities found that there was no End of wrangling [by syllogism], they invented a kind of Argument, which is not reducible to any Mood or Figure in *Aristotle*. It was called the *Argumentum Basilinum* (others write it *Bacilinum* or *Baculinum*) which is pretty well expressed in our *English* Word Club-Law. When they were not able to confute their Antagonist, they knock'd him down . . . ."

78.24 thrown it . . . *Ars Logica*] *Art of Logic*. Cf. John Bulwer, *Chironomia; or the Art of Manual Rhetoric* (1644), ed. James W. Cleary (Carbondale: Southern Illinois University Press, 1974), p. 204, where Bulwer, having explained his reasons for adding a "new gesture" to the canon, con-

LILLIBURLERO.

The Delightful Companion, or Choice New Lessons for the Recorder or Flute (by Robert Carr), 1686 ; *Musick's Handmaid*, 1689 ; *Pills to purge Melancholy* ; and many Ballad Operas.

2. Dat we shall have a   new de-pu-tie,   Lil- li bur - le - ro,   bul-len a la, }
1. Ho ! brother Teague, dost hearde decree?   Lil- li bur - le - ro,   bul-len a la, }

[*Moderate.*]

Le - ro, le - ro, lil - li bur-le - ro, Lil-li bur-le - ro, bul-len a la,

Le - ro, le - ro, lil - li bur-le - ro, lil-li bur-le - ro, bul-len a la.

THE LATER POPULAR MUSIC.

Ho ! by my shoul it is de Talbot,
And he will cut all de English throat ;

Tho', by my shoul, de English do praat,
De law's on dare side, and Creish knows
what.

But, if dispence do come from de Pope,
We'll hang Magna Charta and demselves
in a rope.

And de good Talbot is made a lord,
And he with brave lads is coming aboard,

Who all in France have tauken a sware,
Dat dey will have no Protestant heir.

O, but why does he stay behind ?
Ho ! by my shoul, 'tis a Protestant
wind.

Now Tyrconnel is come ashore,
And we shall have commissions gillore ;

And he dat will not go to mass
Shall turn out, and look like an ass.

Now, now de hereticks all go down,
By Creish and St. Patrick, de nation's
our own.

PLATE I

cludes: "upon which ground of nature I was induced to cast in my mite into the treasury of this art."

78.26–28 And if . . . best arguments too.] Sterne's attitude toward the arguments of formal logic is paralleled by Locke's in his chapter on "Reason" (*ECHU*, IV.17), where he introduces his definitions of various terms with: "Before we quit this Subject, it may be worth our while a little to reflect on *four sorts of Arguments*, that Men in their Reasonings with others do ordinarily make use of, to prevail on their Assent; or at least so to awe them, as to silence their Opposition" (pp. 685–86).

79.14–19 THE learned . . . to commend himself] The work so carefully cited by Sterne has never been located (see W. G. Day, "*Tristram Shandy: Sterne and Bishop Hall*," *Library* 27 [1972]: 145–46); however, we have now located several editions of one of Hall's works (*Contemplations upon the principall passages of the holy history*, books III, X, XI [1624, 1628]) with a John Beale imprint, and can assume that more exist. Cf. Work, p. 72, n. 1: "Joseph Hall (1574–1656), bishop, successively, of Exeter and Norwich, satirist and polemist. Hall frequently inveighs against vanity, but I have been unable to find this particular sentence in any of his works." Day, similarly unable to find the sentence, concludes: "the most likely solution to the problem seems to be that at this point Sterne is sharing a joke with the 'learned reader'" (p. 146). Kenneth Monkman has, however, pointed out to us that there is a very similar sentiment expressed by Hall: "It is a vaine-glorious flatterie for a man to praise himselfe" (*Meditations and Vowes, Divine and Morall, The Second Century* [1624], p. 30, no. 55). A sentence close to this also appears in Abraham Cowley's "Of my Self": "It is a hard and nice Subject for a man to write of himself, it grates his own heart to say any thing of disparagement, and the Readers Ears to hear any thing of praise from him" (*Works*, 5th ed. [1678], p. 143); it appears as the opening sentence in *Spectator* 562 (IV: 519).

Sterne borrows from Hall again in *TS*, 421.13–15 and 592.16ff.; and more extensively in *ASJ* (see pp. 332–36). See also Hammond, pp. 81, 125–32, for borrowings from Hall in the *Sermons*.

See also t.n. to 79.18, vol. II, p. 845, in this edition.

80.5ff. For in this long digression, etc.] The number of eighteenth-century authors who praised digression in a manner similar to Sterne's is so large that the following citations are offered merely to indicate that Sterne's posture was something of a commonplace: Swift, "*A Digression in Praise of Digressions*," in *Tale of a Tub*, sec. VII, pp. 143–49; Dunton, *A Voyage Round the World*, I: 142: "Not but that *Digressions* are so far from being always a fault, that they are indeed often pardonable, and sometimes, a *great Beauty* to any discourse——but then they must be well turn'd and managed, they must come in naturally and easily, and seem to be almost of a piece with the main Story, tho never so far distant from it——*I love a Digression*, I must confess with all my Heart . . ."; and Fielding, *Tom Jones*, book I, chap. 2: "Reader, I think proper, before we proceed any farther together, to acquaint thee, that I intend to digress, through this whole History, as often as I see Occasion: Of which I am myself a better Judge than any pitiful Critic whatever . . ." (I: 37). Sterne's image of "good cookery" (81.19) might owe something to the opening chapter of *Tom Jones*.

For a discussion of digressiveness in eighteenth-century fiction, see especially the brilliant essay by Wayne C. Booth, "The Self-Conscious Narrator in Comic Fiction Before *Tristram Shandy*," *PMLA* 67 (1952): 163–85, and Bibliography C in *The Rhetoric of Fiction* (Chicago: University of Chicago Press, 1961), pp. 429–32. See also William Bowman Piper, "Tristram Shandy's Digressive Artistry," *SEL* 1 (1961): 65–76; and Eugene Korkowski, "*Tristram Shandy*, Digression, and the Menippean Tradition," *ScholS* 1 (1975): 3–16.

80.20   planetary system] *OED*'s earliest example is dated 1816.

81.5–11   This, Sir . . . such trifling hints.] Sterne may have been recalling the introduction to *Tale of a Tub*, in which the putative author dismisses an offer by the Royal Society to compare their books by weight and number with those of the "*Grub-street* Brotherhood": "the proposal is like that which *Archimedes* made upon a *smaller Affair, including an impossibility in the Practice"; the note reads "**Viz. About moving the Earth*" (p. 64).

See also Dryden's discussion of the use of subplots in "Essay of Dramatick Poesie": "Our Playes, besides the main design, have under plots or by-concernments, of less considerable Persons, and Intrigues, which are carried on with the motion of the main Plot: as they say the Orb of the fix'd Stars, and those of the Planets, though they have motions of their own, are whirl'd about by the motion of the *primum mobile*, in which they are contain'd: that similitude expresses much of the *English* Stage: for if contrary motions may be found in Nature to agree; if a Planet can go East and West at the same time; one way by virtue of his own motion, the other by the force of the first mover; it will not be difficult to imagine how the under Plot, which is onely different, not contrary to the great design, may naturally be conducted along with it" (*Works*, XVII: 47). Sterne, of course, images a Copernican system, Dryden a Ptolemaic one.

Sterne assuredly did not need Chambers for the "astronomy" of this passage, but the entry under *Earth* bears a close resemblance: "The terraqueous globe is now generally granted to have two motions, the one diurnal, around its own axis, in the space of 24 hours, which constitutes the natural day . . . .

"The other, annual, round the sun, in an elliptical orbit, or track, in 365 days 6 hours, constituting the year."

81.16   he steps forth like a bridegroom] Cf. Psalm 19: 5: "In them hath he set a tabernacle for the sun: which cometh forth as a bridegroom out of his chamber . . . ." We quote from the Psalter as attached to the *Book of Common Prayer* (Oxford, 1740), which differs somewhat from the King James Version. See also Joel 2: 16: "let the bridegroom go forth of his chamber."

81.17–18   brings in . . . appetite to fail.] Sterne may have been recalling *Antony and Cleopatra*, II.ii.234–37: "Age cannot wither her, nor custom stale / Her infinite variety. Other women cloy / The appetites they feed, but she makes hungry / Where most she satisfies . . . ."

82.10–12   If the fixure . . . taken place] Momus is the Greek personification of mockery and fault-finding. Sterne alludes to the story told by Lucian in *Hermotimus or Concerning the Sects:* "You have heard, I suppose, what faults Momus found in Hephaestus; if not I'll tell you. . . . Hephaestus, it seems, put together a man. . . . Momus['s] criticism of the man and his reproof of the craftsman, Hephaestus, was this: he had not made windows in his chest which could be opened to let everyone see his desires and thoughts and if he were lying or telling the truth" (*Works*, VI: 297–99).

Cf. Burton ("Democritus Junior to the Reader"): "How would *Democritus* have been moved, had he seene the secrets of their hearts? If every man had a window in his breast, which *Momus* would have had in *Vulcans* man . . ." (p. 38).

James E. Evans ("Tristram as Critic: Momus's Glass vs. Hobby-Horse," *PQ* 50 [1971]: 669–71) suggests a more contemporary source, *Chiron; or, The Mental Optician* (1758). In the preface to that work the anonymous author writes: "The very great Philosopher, who, from his heart wished that every man had a window to his heart, undoubtedly little foresaw, that in the year 1758, the improvements in perspective glasses, at present, would answer his most eager wishes. How needless his scheme would be now may appear from the following sheets, in which, thrice curious reader! we have no apprehension or fear of your dis-belief when they delineate your neighbor,—but only when they delineate yourself (I: v–vi)"; cited by Evans, p. 670. Evans goes on: "This anonymous writer accomplishes Momus's desire by having his 'mental optician,' Chiron, invent a telescope which enables him to see into every heart except, of course, his own. Each chapter of the work represents the daily observations of Chiron . . . from the tower of St. Paul's Cathedral in London."

82.11   arch-critick] Sterne uses this mode of compounding again; cf. "arch-jockey" (356.12) and "arch-wit" (385.3).

82.14   window-money] A tax on house windows was in effect in England from 1696 until the middle of the nineteenth century.

82.19   dioptrical] *OED* cites this passage as its sole example of an obsolete adjective form of *dioptric*, "capable of being seen through"; its first example, dated 1801, also is associated with beehives: "As to dioptric beehives [i.e., provided with glass windows on opposite sides] the best I have seen is of wood."

83.9   computators] *OED* cites this passage as its last illustration. Chambers, s.v. *Mercury*, depends upon the computations of Sir Isaac Newton, according to whom, "the heat and light of the sun on the surface of *Mercury*, is seven times as intense as on the surface of our earth in the middle of summer: which, as he found by experiments made for that purpose by a thermometer, is sufficient to make water boil. Such a degree of heat therefore must render *Mercury* uninhabitable to creatures of our constitution."

83.10–12   must . . . final cause] Sterne is using, facetiously we can assume, a serious distinction for Aristotle and the scholastic philosophers. Chambers defines *efficient cause* as "that which produces an effect," noting the many arguments over the term's precise meaning; and *final cause* as "the end for which any thing is done," noting as well that "*Final Causes* are of good use in ethics; but mischievous in physics, and by no means to be allowed . . . ."

If Sterne did indeed consult Chambers for this chapter (see below, n. to 85.4) he may also have glanced at the entry for *Glass:* "The chymist hold that there is no body but may be vitrified, *i.e.* converted into *glass* . . . .

". . . as *glass* is the effect, or fruit of fire, so it is the last effect: All the chymists art, and all the force of fire not being able to carry the change of any natural body beyond its vitrification."

83.13   tenements of their souls] Cf. Dryden, *Absalom and Achitophel*, lines 156−58: "A fiery Soul, which working out its way, / Fretted the Pigmy Body to decay: / And o'r inform'd the Tenement of Clay" (Kinsley ed., I: 221; cf. the note to this passage in *Works*, II: 248).

83.16−17   (bating the umbilical knot)] Sterne seems fond of this construction; cf. 275.19, 306.23, 419.24−25, 434.17, 439.9, 598.19−20.

83.24   play the fool out o'doors as in her own house.] Cf. *Hamlet*, III.i.131− 32: "Let the doors be shut upon him, that he may play the fool no where but in 's own house."

83.27   uncrystalized] *OED* cites this passage as its first illustration.

84.4−6   *Virgil* takes . . . breath of fame] In book IV of the *Aeneid*, Virgil describes the many tongues of Fame (Rumor) as she spreads the report of Dido and Aeneas: "She fills the Peoples Ears with *Dido*'s Name, / Who, lost to Honour, and the sense of Shame, / Admits into her Throne and Nuptial Bed / A wandring Guest, who from his Country fled" (trans. John Dryden [1697], lines 274−77). The full-page illustration of the passage shows Fame blowing one trumpet while holding another. Fame had long been associated with wind instruments; Chaucer, for example, makes Aeolus, an attendant on Fame, blow the clarion of laud and the clarion of slander (*House of Fame*, book III, lines 1569ff.), and in Pope's *Temple of Fame* she is armed with the trumpet of eternal praise and the trumpet of slander (lines 306−41). Butler in *Hudibras*, II.i.69−74, describes Fame's instruments with the same bawdy implications as Sterne: "Two Trumpets she does sound at once, / But both of clean contrary tones. / But whether both with the same wind, / Or one before, and one behind, / We know not; onely this can tell, / The one sounds vilely, th'other well" (p. 102).

Cf. 247.19: "the foul-mouth'd trumpet of Fame"; 521.6: "And FAME, who loves to double every thing"; and 804.15 – 16: "FAME caught the notes with her brazen trumpet and sounded them upon the house-top."

84.7 – 12   the *Italians* . . . drawing by it] Work, p. 76, n. 7: "This passage probably alludes, with purposed equivocation, to the Italian *castrati,* some of whom had been imported into England, in the face of considerable popular opposition, to aid in the presentation of operas." Cf. Goldsmith, *The Bee* 8 (November 24, 1759): "Some years ago the Italian opera was the only fashionable amusement among our nobility. The managers of the playhouses dreaded it as a mortal enemy, and our very poets listed themselves in the opposition; at present, the house seems deserted, the castrati sing to empty benches . . ." (*Works,* I: 505 – 6). See also Charles Churchill, *The Rosciad* (1761), lines 721 – 24: "But never shall a TRULY BRITISH Age / Bear a vile race of EUNUCHS on the stage. / The boasted work's call'd NATIONAL in vain, / If one ITALIAN voice pollutes the strain" (*Works,* ed. Douglas Grant [Oxford: Clarendon Press, 1956], p. 24; and see Grant's n. to the passage, pp. 470 – 71).

84.9   *forte* or *piano*] *OED* cites this passage as its first illustration of the use of the musical term *forte* ("loud and strong") as a substantive. Sterne had used *piano* ("soft and low") in a similar manner earlier, 59.4, which is the second illustration recorded by *OED;* its first illustration, dated 1730, also uses *forte* as a substantive. See also 760.3 – 4.

84.13 – 14   *ad populum*] "To the people."

84.26   *Non-Naturals*] Work's definition (p. 76, n. 8) is good: "A term formerly used by physicians to indicate the six things which because they do not enter into the composition of the body are not 'natural' yet which are essential to animal life and health and which by accident or abuse often cause disease . . . ." Cf. Burton, 1.2.2.1 (p. 65): "These six non-naturall things, are Diet, Retention [i.e., repletion] and Evacuation, which are more material than the other, because they make new matter, or else are conversant in keeping or expelling of it. The other foure are, Aire, Exercise, Sleeping, Waking, and perturbations of the mind, which only alter the matter." (It should be noted that "sleeping" and "waking" are considered together.) Sterne alludes to the non-naturals again, 354.27 – 28.

Work calls attention to a possible oblique reference to John Burton (i.e.,

Dr. Slop), who wrote *A Treatise of the Non-Naturals* (York, 1738); but Sterne alludes to that work nowhere else in *TS*, and, as Work notes, the term was in universal use.

For a further discussion of the non-naturals, see L. J. Rather, "The 'Six Things Non-Natural': A Note on the Origins and Fate of a Doctrine and a Phrase," *Clio Medica* 3 (1968): 337–47. Interestingly, Rather comments that the phrase "often excites comment" by medical historians, "because of its inapplicability to the items designated—all of which seem among the most 'natural' things in our experience. There is in fact some reason to believe that it has always seemed a not entirely suitable designation. By the end of the eighteenth century, at least, medical authors were calling it 'singular' or even 'improper'" (pp. 337–38).

The examination of waste matter, a part of diagnostic medicine from the ancients on, was always vulnerable to satire; Swift's professor in the Grand Academy of Lagado is one example: "ANOTHER Professor shewed me a large Paper of Instructions for discovering Plots and Conspiracies against the Government. He advised great Statesmen to examine into the Dyet of all suspected Persons . . . to take a strict View of their Excrements, and from the Colour, the Odour, the Taste, the Consistence, the Crudeness, or Maturity of Digestion, form a Judgment of their Thoughts and Designs: Because Men are never so serious, thoughtful, and intent, as when they are at Stool . . ." (*Gulliver's Travels*, book III, chap. 6, in *Prose Works*, XI: 174).

85.4   Pentagraphic] Sterne's definition (85.22–23) may have been derived from Chambers: "an instrument whereby designs, prints, *&c.* of any kind, may be copied in any proportion, without a person's being skilled in drawing." An illustration is provided.

OED cites this passage as its first illustration of *pantographic*.

85.10–13   Others . . . most ridiculous attitudes.] Sterne plays on *in camera*, "in a private room or chamber" (a legal term, in contrast to "in open court") and *camera obscura*, defined in Chambers as "a machine, or apparatus representing an artificial eye; whereon the images of external objects received through a double convex glass, are exhibited distinctly, and in their native colours, on a white matter placed within the machine . . . .

"By means of this instrument . . . a person unacquainted with designing, will be able to delineate objects to the last accuracy and justness . . . ."

In this paragraph and the preceding one is a hint of the advice of Leonardo da Vinci: "The Figure, and Bounds of an Object, are never seen distinctly, either in its Lights or Shadows; but 'tis in the intermediate Parts, where neither the Light, nor the Shadow are considerable, that they are the most clearly distinguish'd" (*A Treatise of Painting* [1721], pp. 176–77).

85.16   my pencil] Since the usage is now archaic, it is perhaps necessary to point out that *pencil* meant *paint-brush* to Sterne. Cf. 115.27–116.1: "How do the slight touches of the chisel, the pencil, the pen, the fiddle-stick . . . ."

85.20–21   but . . . HOBBY-HORSE] Cf. *Letters*, p. 88: "The ruleing passion *et les egarements du cœur* ["and the wanderings of the heart"], are the very things which mark, and distinguish a man's character;—in which I would as soon leave out a man's head as his hobby-horse." This is the same letter in which Sterne defended his allusion to Dr. Richard Mead as Kunastrokius; see above, n. to 12.5–9.

The relationship between Sterne's hobby-horse and the concept of the ruling passion is, of course, a problematic one. We merely note here Sterne's own possible identification of the two, and several texts which would have to be taken into account in any further discussion: e.g., Montaigne, I.37.260: "And as they say, that in our Bodies there is a Congregation of divers Humours, of which, that is the Sovereign, which according to the Complexion we are of, is commonly most predominant in us: So, tho' the Soul has in it divers Motions to give it Agitation; yet must there of Necessity be one to over-rule all the rest . . ."; and Pope, *Essay on Man*, II.131–44 (pp. 70–72): "And hence one master Passion in the breast, / Like Aaron's serpent, swallows up the rest. / As Man, perhaps, the moment of his breath, / Receives the lurking principle of death; / The young disease, that must subdue at length, / Grows with his growth, and strengthens with his strength: / So, cast and mingled with his very frame, / The Mind's disease, its ruling Passion came; / Each vital humour which should feed the whole, / Soon flows to this, in body and in soul. / Whatever warms the heart, or fills the head, / As the mind opens, and its functions spread, / Imagination plies her dang'rous art, / And pours it all upon the peccant part."

The best commentary on Pope's (and the period's) concept of the ruling passion is Maynard Mack's introduction to the Twickenham edition, as well as his notes to the relevant portions of the *Essay on Man*. See also *Sermons*, II.9.60–61 ("The Character of Herod"), where, in opposition to a view of character that suggests man is "a compound of good and evil," Sterne suggests "in all judgments of this kind, to distinguish and carry in your eye, the principle and ruling passion which leads the character—and separate that, from the other parts of it,—and then take notice, how far his other qualities, good and bad, are brought to serve and support that. For want of this distinction,—we often think ourselves inconsistent creatures, when we are the furthest from it, and all the variety of shapes and contradictory appearances we put on, are in truth but so many different attempts to gratify the same governing appetite."

86.15   HOBBY-HORSICAL] *OED*'s first recorded example is Sterne's usage in vol. III (243.2).

87.6–9   But as . . . a-cross the room] Thomas Stanley, *The History of Philosophy*, 4th ed. (1743), in his chapter on skepticism (12) gives one version of this well-known rebuttal: "one of the Cynicks, an Argument being propounded to him to take away Motion, made no Answer, but rose up and walk'd, shewing by Action and Evidence, that there is Motion" (p. 584). In his entry *Diogenes the Cynic* (7), Stanley assigns the refutation to him: "To one proving, by the *horned* Syllogism, that he had Horns, he feeling on his Forehead, *But I*, saith he, *feel none*. In like manner, another maintaining, *there was no such Thing as Motion*, he rose up and walked" (p. 302). Diogenes Laertius, VI.39, tells the same story in *Lives of Eminent Philosophers* (II: 41).

Zeno of Elea is usually considered the fountainhead of arguments denying the reality of motion (see Aristotle's *Physics*, 6.9), and indeed Ben Jonson in his preface to *The English Grammar* writes: "So *Zeno* disputing of *Quies* ["rest"], was confuted by *Diogenes*, rising up and walking" (1640; reprinted from the *Works* [Menston, Eng.: Scolar Press, 1972], p. 33).

Sterne clearly believes the two philosophers are in the same room, but it is usually assumed that Zeno lived c. 490–c. 430 B.C., Diogenes c. 400–c. 325 B.C.

88.4–6   *oss pubis . . . oss illeum*] Cf. Chambers, s.v. *Coxæ, coxendicis:* "In infants, each of these [hipbones] consists of three distinct bones, separated by cartilages; which, in adults, grow up, and constitute one firm, solid bone; whose parts, however, retain three distinct names, according to their former division, *viz.* the *os ilium, os ischium,* by some peculiarly called *os coxendicis,* and the *os pubis.*" The anatomical chart in Chambers makes it reasonably clear that Sterne selected a wound site as close as he could get without a direct hit. See below, n. to 178.23–24.

88.25   The history . . . pain of it] In *Spectator* 371, cited earlier as Sterne's probable allusion in chap. 21 (71.3ff.), Addison tells of curing those "Pests of all polite Conversation," the "dull Generation of Story-tellers," by having several of them meet together: "The first Day one of them sitting down, enter'd upon the Siege of *Namur,* which lasted till four a-Clock, their time of parting. The second Day a *North-Britain* took Possession of the Discourse, which it was impossible to get out of his Hands . . . . The third Day was engrossed, after the same manner, by a Story of the same length. They at last begun to reflect upon this barbarous way of treating one another, and by this means awaken'd out of that Lethargy with which each of them had been seized for several Years" (III: 399). Cf. *Spectator* 105 (I: 438): "I might here mention the Military Pedant, who always talks in a Camp, and is storming Towns, making Lodgments, and fighting Battels from one end of the Year to the other. Every thing he speaks smells of Gunpowder; if you take away his Artillery from him, he has not a Word to say for himself."

NOTES TO VOLUME II

93.6ff.   I must remind the reader, etc.] The attack on Namur is described at
length in Tindal, III: 289ff. He begins with a description of the fortifications and the composition of the opposing forces and concludes: "the
French and their favourers looked upon the King's enterprise [to take
Namur] as an unparalleled temerity, and doubted not but *Namur* would be
the rock, on which the Grand Confederacy should split. But all these
great, and, in appearance, invincible obstacles were not able to shake the
King's resolution; they served only to make him concert effectual measures
to surmount all difficulties, which he did to his immortal glory, the astonishment of his enemies, and the admiration of all *Europe*."

The attack on the counterscarp is described: "the general attack of the
first counterscarp, which was performed towards five o'clock that afternoon [July 27, 1695], in this manner: The *English* and *Scots* commanded
by Major-general *Ramsey* and Brigadier *Hamilton* came out of the
trenches to the right, and attacked the point of the foremost counterscarp,
which inclosed the sluice or water-stop. The enemy received them with a
furious discharge, which however did not hinder them from going on
briskly; and, notwithstanding the dreadful eruption of three or four
fougades of bombs, that lay buried in the glacis, which put them at first
into some disorder, they returned more animated to the charge, and drove
the enemy from that counterscarp. But unluckily, whilst the workmen
were making a lodgment, some sacks of wool took fire, whereby part of the
lodgment was consumed, and the *English* exposed to the shot of the
counter-guard and demi-bastion of St. *Roche,* which they sustained and
answered with incredible resolution, till the fire was extinguished and

126

some traverses cast up. On the other hand, the *Hollanders*, seeing the *English* in so hot a place, immediately went up along the *Maese* towards the breach of the counter-guard, and so vigorously attacked the enemy with their hand-granadoes, that the latter thought it safer to retreat than to defend themselves; which very much eased the *English*. The *Dutch* lodged themselves upon the counter-guard; and thus both they and the *English* preserved the foremost covered-way before *St. Nicholas*'s gate from the *Maese* to the water-stop, with part of the counter-guard. The valour and firmness of the Confederates infantry in this action is scarce to be parallelled; and it must be also acknowledged that the *French* officers behaved themselves like men of true courage, exposing themselves on the glacis of the counterscarp and on the breach of the counter-guard, with their swords in their hands, in order to encourage their soldiers" (p. 293).

Baird, "Time-Scheme," p. 807, n. 14, calls attention to the "large plan of Namur" facing p. 289 in Tindal, "in which a reader may feel pretty confident that he could stick a pin upon the exact spot of ground where Uncle Toby was standing when he received his wound." See Plate II (overleaf), a somewhat more detailed illustration from Abel Boyer, *The Draughts of the most Remarkable Fortified Towns of Europe* (1701), plate 12. Watt, pp. 499–503, also includes a map of Namur, and attempts to mark the precise spot of Toby's encounter, but both that exercise and the more general one of trying to comprehend the eighteenth century's art of fortification seem superfluous—perhaps even counter—to Sterne's purpose, which is to bewilder both Toby and the reader, while remaining quite faithful to the historical account in Tindal. The "Glossary of Terms of Fortification" provided in this volume is intended, therefore, not so much to explain the "science" as to indicate the sources of Toby's "war with words." It must be acknowledged, however, that eighteenth-century readers of the daily accounts of battles, whether in King William's wars or during the Seven Years War, were given detailed newspaper accounts of sieges and attacks, and that history books, as Tindal's account makes apparent, were equally detailed.

King William's wars began with his accession to the throne in November 1688 and ended with the Peace of Ryswick in 1697. Between 1689 and 1691, the arena was primarily Ireland, where William successfully defeated the Jacobite threat; the decisive Battle of the Boyne in July 1690

12.

NAMUR

A the Old Town
B the New Town
C the Fort of the Sambre
D the Old Castle
E Emere Gate
F Samsons Gate
G St Nicolas Gate
H the Meuse Gate
I the great Bridge
K the litle Bridge
L Chaslet Gate
M wood of Villers
N the suburb of the
        Sambre

M

E   F

A

the
Castle

B

K   G

H

Meuse

N

PLATE II

prepared the way for the fall of Limerick in 1691, a campaign in which Toby and Trim participated. William then turned his attention to the continent, where France had taken the offensive in Flanders, the so-called cockpit of Europe (see below, n. to 102.14), and had taken Namur in 1692. William's recapture of the citadel in 1695 was England's major success in this nine-year war and also its turning point. Contemporary English sentiment is indicated by Prior's "An English Ballad, On the Taking of Namur by the King of Great Britain, 1695" (1695), lines 41–48: "If *Namur* be compar'd to *Troy*; / Then BRITAIN's Boys excell'd the GREEKS: / Their Siege did ten long Years employ: / We've done our Bus'ness in ten Weeks. / What Godhead does so fast advance, / With dreadful Pow'r those Hills to gain? / 'Tis little WILL, the Scourge of *France*; / No Godhead, but the first of Men" (*Literary Works*, ed. H. Bunker Wright and Monroe K. Spears, 2d ed. [Oxford: Clarendon Press, 1971], I: 143).

94.2–4   the army . . . each other's operations] Cf. Tindal, III: 289: "The *Sambre* and the *Maese* did naturally divide the army into three general quarters. . . . For the communication of these quarters three bridges were immediately laid . . ."; and p. 290: "This castle, the principal strength of *Namur*, was built upon an hill, in an angle formed by the confluence of the *Sambre* and the *Maese* . . . ."

94.13   Writers . . . confound these terms] For example, see "Glossary of Terms of Fortification" in this volume, s.v. *Counterscarp:* "COUNTERSCARP is also used for the covert-way, and the glacis"; or *Ravelin:* "What the engineers call a *ravelin*, the soldiers generally call a *demi-lune*, or half-moon." Both entries are from Chambers.

94.19–20   or my . . . best explanatory moods] Cf. 225.11–12: "My father in one of his best explanatory moods . . . ."

94.26   cross-cut] *OED*'s first example is dated 1789.

95.16–21   and these . . . upon the digestion] In his *History of Health, and the Art of Preserving It* (Edinburgh, 1758), James Mackenzie pays tribute to Hippocrates as "*the father of physic*" (p. 80) and discusses his theories of diet and exercise (pp. 90–116), which are summarized in these sentences: "EVERY excess is an enemy to nature"; "in labour, meat, drink, sleep, and commerce with the sex, a just mediocrity and moderation should be observed . . ." (pp. 115–16). Mackenzie's own view is given on pp. 388–89, the section entitled "Of the PASSIONS and AFFECTIONS of the mind": "HE who seriously resolves to preserve his health, must previously learn to conquer his passions, and keep them in absolute subjection to reason; for let a man be ever so temperate in his diet, and regular in his exercise, yet still some unhappy passions, if indulged to excess, will prevail over all his regularity, and prevent the good effects of his temperance; it is necessary therefore that he should be upon his guard against an influence so destructive."

Sterne quotes extensively from Mackenzie in vol. V, chap. 34 (see pp. 472–73), and probably at 394.13–15 as well.

Work, p. 83, nn. 3, 4: "Hippocrates (c. 460–c. 377 B.C.), a Greek philosopher and writer, surnamed 'The Father of Medicine.' . . . Dr. James Mackenzie (1680?–1761), noted Scottish physician and author . . . ."

95.21   digestion . . . of a dinner?)] Sterne puns on *digestion*'s obsolete meaning, "the process of maturing an ulcer or wound"; the last illustration cited by *OED* is dated 1830: "By the digestion of a wound or ulcer, the old Surgeons meant bringing it into a state, in which it formed healthy pus."

96.20   an entertainment of this kind] Cf. the opening sentence of *Tom Jones*, book I, chap. 1: "AN Author ought to consider himself, not as a Gentleman who gives a private or eleemosynary Treat, but rather as one who keeps a public Ordinary, at which all Persons are welcome for their Money" (ed. Martin C. Battestin and Fredson Bowers [Middletown, Conn.: Wesleyan University Press, 1975], I: 31).

97.21   muddle-headed] *OED* cites this passage as its first illustration. Cf. *Letters*, p. 93: "Are we so run out of stock, that there is no one lumber-headed, muddle-headed, mortar-headed, pudding-headed *chap* amongst our doctors?"

97.23   unurbane] *OED* cites this passage as its sole illustration. Cf. *Letters*, p. 250: "I am sure it is not . . . my intentions to say anything that is inurbane of such a man as he is . . . ."

97.26   the reply valiant] Cf. *As You Like It*, V.iv. 68–82, where Touchstone gives his own theory of argumentation, which includes the "Retort Courteous," the "Quip Modest," the "Reply Churlish," and the "Reproof Valiant."

And cf. also the *Political Romance*, p. 44, where the meaning of the "romance" is debated by members of a political club: "they were all five rising up together from their Chairs, with full Intent of Heart, as it was thought, to return the *Reproof Valiant* . . . ."

98.27ff.   Now if you will venture, etc.] Cf. Locke, *ECHU,* II.29.3: "The *cause of Obscurity* in simple *Ideas,* seems to be either dull Organs; or very slight and transient Impressions made by the Objects; or else a weakness in the Memory, not able to retain them as received. For to return again to visible Objects, to help us to apprehend this matter. If the Organs, or Faculties of Perception, like Wax over-hardned with Cold, will not receive the Impression of the Seal, from the usual impulse wont to imprint it; or, like Wax of a temper too soft, will not hold it well, when well imprinted; or else supposing the Wax of a temper fit, but the Seal not applied with a sufficient force, to make a clear Impression: In any of these cases, the print left by the Seal, will be *obscure*. This, I suppose, needs no application to make it plainer" (pp. 363–64).

Sec. 6 of this chapter, *"Of Clear and Obscure, Distinct and Confused* Ideas," is also apropos to Sterne's discussion: "To remove this difficulty, and to help us to conceive aright, what it is, that makes the *confusion, Ideas* are at any time chargeable with, we must consider, that Things ranked under distinct Names, are supposed different enough to be distinguished, that so each sort, by its peculiar Name, may be marked, and discoursed of apart, upon any occasion: And there is nothing more evident, than that the greatest part of different Names, are supposed to stand for different Things. Now every *Idea* a Man has, being visibly what it is, and distinct from all other *Ideas* but it self, that which makes it *confused* is, when it is such, that it may as well be called by another Name, as that which it is expressed by, the difference which keeps the Things (to be ranked under those two different Names) distinct, and makes some of them belong rather to the one, and some of them to the other of those Names, being left out; and so the distinction, which was intended to be kept up by those different Names, is quite lost" (pp. 364–65). Cf. Toby's attempt to distinguish between a ravelin and a half-moon, 128.28ff.

99.10   *Malbranch*] Sterne's invocation of Nicolas Malebranche (1638–1715) is perhaps an allusion to his most famous work, *De la recherche de la vérité* (1674–75), which was translated by T. Taylor in 1694 as *Father Malebranche's treatise concerning the search after truth*. The first book is entitled

"Concerning the Errors of the Senses" and argues that "our Senses therefore are not Corrupted as is imagin'd, but 'tis that which is more Inward and Essential to the Soul, 'tis our Liberty which is corrupted. They are not our Senses that deceive us, but the Will by its rash and precipitate Judgments, leads us into Error" (p. 13).

Locke answered one of Malebranche's most famous arguments in his posthumous "An Examination of P. Malebranche's Opinion of Seeing all Things in God" (*Works* [1727], III: 429–50).

99.25   eke] See above, n. to Ded. 2.

99.28   brass-jack] Not recorded in *OED*. Cf. *OED*'s *brass-farthing:* "an emphatic equivalent of *farthing* in depreciatory expressions"; and *jack:* "19. *slang* a. A farthing. *?Obs.* b. A counter made to resemble a sovereign . . . ." Sterne's analogy would seem to involve "b" more than "a."

100.10   It is ten to one, (at *Arthur*'s)] White's Chocolate-house, converted to an exclusive club about 1730, was often mentioned in the eighteenth century as the center of London's wagering; see, e.g., Pope's "Epistle to Bathurst," lines 55–56: "His Grace will game: to White's a Bull be led, / With spurning heels and with a butting head" (in *Epistles to Several Persons*, p. 91). The "Master of the House" at White's was John Arthur, later succeeded by his son, Robert. William B. Boulton, *The Amusements of Old London* (London: J. C. Nimmo, 1901), II: 205, notes that when White's moved its premises in 1755, it is probable that "a coffee-house continued at the old premises under the style of 'Arthur's'." Possibly, White's was also called Arthur's after its Master's name; or, on the other hand, perhaps the new Arthur's retained the wagering reputation of White's.

100.12   'yclept logomachies] See above, n. to Ded. 2.

100.16   Gentle critick! etc.] Cf. *ECHU*, III.5.16: "When it is considered, what a pudder is made about *Essences*, and how much all sorts of Knowledge, Discourse, and Conversation, are pester'd and disorder'd by the careless, and confused Use and Application of Words, it will, perhaps, be thought worth while th[o]roughly to lay [the subject] open" (p. 438).

See also III.3.9: "To conclude, this whole *mystery* of *Genera* and *Species*, which make such a noise in the Schools . . . is nothing else but abstract *Ideas*, more or less comprehensive, with names annexed to them" (p. 412).

Francis Doherty suggests yet another passage (III.10.2) from *ECHU*, which, conflated with those already cited, suggests the manner in which Sterne produced his own climactic passage on the abuse and imperfection of words: "One may observe, in all Languages, certain Words, that . . . will be found, in their first Original, and their appropriated Use, not to stand for any clear and distinct *Ideas*. These, for the most part, the several *Sects* of Philosophy and Religion have introduced. . . . For having . . . had no determinate Collection of *Ideas* annexed to them, when they were first invented . . . 'tis no wonder if afterwards . . . they remain empty Sounds, with little or no signification, amongst those who think it enough to have them often in their Mouths, as the distinguishing Characters of their Church, or School, without much troubling their Heads to examine, what are the precise *Ideas* they stand for. . . . the great Mint-Masters of these kind of Terms [are] the Schoolmen and Metaphysicians . . ." (pp. 490–91); see "Sterne and Hume: A Bicentenary Essay," *E&S*, n.s. 22 (1969): 71–72.

Sterne's Greek may be translated interchangeably as "essence" or "substance"; Chambers, s.v. *Form*, provides a very useful gloss to this passage: "Aristotle calls *Form* λογος της ουσιας [*logos tes ousias*], the reason, or manner of the essence, or being of a thing: but as ουσια [*ousia*] denotes substance, as well [as] essence, a mighty controversy has arose in the schools, in which sense the word is here to be used; and whether *Forms* are to be accounted substantial, or only essential; *i.e.* whether the *Forms* of bodies be real substances, and have an existence distinct from that of matter, or not?"

101.13–14   marginal documents . . . of the elephant] Work, p. 88, n. 1: "Possibly elephant-paper, drawing paper 28 x 23 inches on which maps were printed; it is more likely, however, that the cartouche of my uncle Toby's map included among its decorations the figure of an elephant." Work's second suggestion was first offered by W. E. Buckley in *N&Q*, 6th ser. 5 (1882): 11–12: " 'The elephant' refers to Uncle Toby's map of the siege of Namur, the title of which was presumably engraved on a cartouch, as was common in old maps, among the ornaments of which an elephant was introduced. Near this, on the margin or vacant space, certain historical or statistical documents seem to have been engraved . . . . Sterne may have seen a map with an elephant; or if constructing an imaginary one he would adopt the prevailing fashion, and hit on the elephant by choice or chance."

101.14−16   together with . . . from the *Flemish*] *OED* cites this passage as its last example of *pyroballogy*, defined as "the study of the art of casting fire, i.e., of artillery." Cf. Chambers, s.v. *Pyrotechny:* "Some call *pyrotechny* by the name *artillery;* though that word is usually confined to the instruments used in war. . . . Others chuse to call it *pyrobology*, or rather *pyroballogy*, *q.d.* the art of missile fires . . . ."

Neither Chambers nor any of the other works we have consulted reveal the identity of *Gobesius*. Work, p. 88, n. 2 (following the suggestion of C. Deedes, *N&Q*, 10th ser. 5 [1906]: 115), suggests Leonhard Gorecius (fl. c. 1577), author of *Descriptio Belli Ivoniæ* (*Account of the War in Spain*), but there is no clear reason for doing so. Our own suggestion would be Balthasar Gobelin, who in 1571 became treasurer-general of artillery under Charles IX of France and later treasurer-extraordinary of war under Henry III; however, we can find no evidence that he wrote any treatises, much less why they would be in Flemish. Sterne may easily be having a joke here, especially since the remaining names of experts in this chapter were all available from Chambers.

101.21−23   my uncle *Toby* . . . *Salsines, &c.*] Cf. Tindal, III: 294: "the Elector of *Bavaria* . . . passed [the *Sambre*] amidst the enemy's continual fire, and possessed himself of the abbey of *Salsines*, a post of great importance, and which favoured the attack of *Vauban*'s line, that surrounded the works of the castle." It is perhaps worth noting that the fortifications of Namur were designed by Coehoorn and Vauban, for whom see below, n. to 102.21−24.

102.3−4   But the . . . acquisition of it.] Neither *ODEP* nor Tilley records the sentiment as proverbial, but Stevenson, p. 1978, cites Thomas Fuller's *Gnomologia* (1732), no. 4048: "Riches rather enlarge than satisfy Appetites."

102.7   ween] See above, n. to Ded. 2, for Vol. I.

102.8   incumbition] *OED* cites this passage as its sole illustration of figurative use, with the following definition: "the action of lying or pressing upon."

102.9−10   be-virtu'd . . . be-fiddled.] Sterne is recalling his description of hobby-horses, 12.13−14: "their fiddles, their pallets,——their maggots and their butterflies." He seems to have enjoyed this grammatical construction; cf. *"befetish'd"* (212.20) and "bewhisker'd" (413.19). All are cited in *OED* as sole or first illustrations.

Sterne is also recalling 86.6–15, where he speaks of "the manner of electrified bodies" in explaining the workings of the hobby-horse.

102.14   there was . . . *Italy* or *Flanders*] Here it is perhaps worthwhile, since so many passages in *TS* deal with the siege warfare of King William's and Queen Anne's reigns, to quote at some length from J. W. Fortescue's *A History of the British Army* (London: Macmillan and Co., 1910), concerning the nature of these battles. Fortescue points out that the campaigns in Flanders (for the most part, modern Belgium) took place essentially in an area bounded by the sea in the west, a line from Namur to Maestricht in the east, from Namur to Dunkirk for the southern boundary, and from Maestricht to Antwerp and the sea for the northern boundary. It was a quadrilateral about one hundred miles long by fifty miles broad in which, Fortescue comments, "the earth, fruitful by nature and enriched by art, bears food for man and beast; the waterways provide transport for stores and ammunition. It was a country where men could kill each other without being starved, and hence for centuries the cockpit of Europe" (I: 356). Within this area can be found the major battle sites mentioned by Toby: Namur, Landen, Dendermond, Steinkirk.

Fortescue continues: "A glance at any old map of Flanders shows how thickly studded was this country with walled towns of less or greater strength, and explains why a war in Flanders should generally have been a war of sieges. Every one of these little towns, of course, had its garrison; and the manœuvres of contending forces were governed very greatly by the effort, on one side, to release these garrisons for active service in the field, and, on the other, to keep them confined within their walls for as long as possible. . . .

"A second cause contributed not a little to increase the taste for a war of sieges, namely, the example of France, then the first military nation in Europe. The Court of Versailles was particularly fond of a siege, since it could attend the ceremony in state and take nominal charge of the operations with much glory and little discomfort or danger. The French passion for rule and formula also found a happy outlet in the conduct of a siege . . ." (pp. 356–57).

In view of Toby's and Trim's admiration for King William, it is perhaps worth noting that Fortescue ranks his military genius rather low, concluding him to have been "a very clever amateur" (p. 359).

102.21—24   In the . . . Mons. *Blondel*] Sir Edward Bensly, "A Debt of Sterne's," *TLS* (November 1, 1928), p. 806, suggests Chambers, s.v. *Fortification*, as the source for Toby's authorities: "The first authors who have wrote of *Fortification*, considered as a particular formed art, are Ramelli, and Cataneo, Italians. After them Errard, engineer to Henry the great of France; Stevinus, engineer to the prince of Orange, Marolois, the chevalier de Ville, Lorini, Coehorn, the count de Pagan, and the marshal de Vauban . . . ." Sheeter (spelled Scheiter by Chambers) and Blondel are mentioned later in the article.

Work, p. 88, n. 3: "Agostino Ramelli (1531?—1590?), Italian engineer, author of *Le Diverse ed artificiose machine;* Girolamo Cataneo, author of *Opera nuova di fortificare, offendere et difendere* (1564) and many other works on military science; Simon Stevinus (1548—1620), Dutch mathematician, author of *Nieuwe Maniere van Sterctebou door Spilshuysen;* Samuel Marolois (fl. early 17th C.), French mathematician, author of *Fortification, ou architecture militaire;* Antoine de Ville (1596—c. 1656), a French engineer and mathematician, author of *Les Fortifications;* Buonajute Lorini (c. 1540—c. 1611), Italian engineer highly reputed for his knowledge of fortifications, author of *Delle fortificationi;* Baron Menno van Coehoorn (1641—1704), Dutch soldier and military engineer, author of *Nieuwe Vestingbouw;* Johann Bernhard von Scheither [Sheeter] (fl. 17th C.), author of *Novissima Praxis Militaris* and other military books; Count Blaise-François de Pagan (1604—1665), soldier and author of the great *Traité des fortifications;* Sébastien le Prestre de Vauban (1633—1707), marshal of France and the most celebrated of military engineers, author of numerous treatises on all phases of the attack on and defence of fortifications; François Blondel (1617—1686), mathematician and architect, author of several works on military science, including *L'Art de jetter les bombes* and *Nouvelle manière de fortifier les places.*"

Since Tindal and Chambers seem to have provided almost all the information Sterne offers about fortification and sieges, it is quite possible that Sterne consulted none of the "authorities" listed.

Coehoorn was the engineer in charge of the siege of Namur.

102.24–27   with almost . . . invaded his library.] See *Don Quixote*, I.I.6: "THE Knight was yet asleep, when the Curate came attended by the Barber, and desir'd his Niece to let him have the Key of the Room where her Uncle kept his Books, the Authors of his Woes: She readily consented; and so in they went, and the House-keeper with 'em. There they found above a hundred large Volumes neatly bound, and a good Number of small ones . . ." (I: 42).

103.1–2   Towards . . . *August,* ninety-nine] Since Toby was wounded in late July 1695, August 1699 would be the beginning of the fifth year, unless, as Baird points out ("Time-Scheme," p. 808), we assume it took Toby two years to reach London from Namur. More likely, Sterne is simply inconsistent, since at a later point he appears to date Toby's arrival in the country in late 1699 or early 1700; in vol. VI (499.9–13), we are told that the siege of Dendermond (1706) was about seven years "after the time, that my uncle *Toby* and *Trim* had privately decamped . . . ." Two possible chronologies seem to have become confused in Sterne's mind: (1) working backward from 1701, the first year of a bowling-green campaign (538.1–4), Toby and Trim left London in the spring of 1701 (110.19–20: "As summer is coming on, continued *Trim*"), in the middle of the fourth year of a confinement that started in August 1697, and immediately began to imitate the campaigns of that summer; or (2) again working backward from 1701, the two left London in the spring of 1700, the middle of the fifth year of a confinement that started in August 1695, and spent the entire year readying the bowling green for the 1701 campaign. To be sure, there is absolutely no need to reconcile the text with either time-scheme or to believe that Sterne sought chronological exactness.

Cf. below, n. to 668.10–11.

103.2–21   to understand . . . the semi-parameter] Cf. Chambers, s.v. *Projectile:* "Two hundred years ago, the philosophers took the line described by a body *projected* horrizontally, *e. gr.* a bullet out of a cannon, while the force of the powder exceeded the weight of the bullet considerably, to be a right line; after which it became a curve.

"N. Tartaglia was the first who perceived the mistake, and maintained the path of the bullet to be a crooked line, throughout its whole extent; but it was Galileo who first determined the precise curve the bullet described; and shewed the path of the bullet, *projected* horizontally from an eminence, to be a parabola . . . .

"Sir Isaac Newton shews, in his *principia*, that the line a *projectile* describes, approaches nearer to an hyperbola than a parabola."

Sterne may also have found in this article the fact that the *parameter* is also called the *latus rectum* ("straight line"). Under Chambers's *Gunnery* entry, the following passages are relevant to Sterne's discussion: "The line or path in which the bullet flies . . . is found to be . . . a parabola.

"Maltus, an English engineer, is mentioned as the person who first taught any regular use of mortars, in the year 1634; . . . there are certain rules, founded on geometry, for all these things: most of which we owe to Gallileo . . . and his disciple Torricellius."

To gain some idea of the complexities that baffle Toby, consider the following observations from the *Projectile* entry: "The quantity or amplitude of the path AB, *i.e.* the range of the *projectile*, is to the parameter of the diameter AS, as the sine of the angle of elevation RAB to its secant.

"Hence, 1. The semiparameter is to the amplitude of the path AB, as the whole sine to the sine of double the angle of elevation." The angle of elevation is defined under *Elevation* as "the angle ARB . . . comprehended between the line of direction of a projectile AR, and the horizontal line AB"; while the elevation of a cannon is defined as "the angle, which the chase of the piece, or the axis of the hollow cylinder, makes with the plane of the horizon."

Cf. Work, p. 89, n. 6: "Niccolò Tartaglia (c, 1499–1557), Italian mathematician who treats problems of artillery in his *Questi et inventioni diverse*, and who claimed the invention of the gunner's quadrant"; and p. 90, n. 7: "François Malthus (d. 1658), '*commissaire ordinaire de l'artillerie*' in France, whose most important work was *Pratique de la guerre;* Galileo Galilei (1564–1642), the Italian astronomer and experimental scientist, who demonstrated in the fourth of his dialogues on mechanics that the path described by a projectile is, save for the resistance of the air, a parabola; Evangelista Torricelli (1608–1647), Italian physicist and mathematician, whose treatise *De Motu* reports his discoveries concerning the path of projectiles." Although Francis Malthus wrote his works in French, Chambers appears to be correct in labeling him an "English engineer"; see his preface to *A treatise of artificial fire-works . . . with divers pleasant geometricall observations, fortifications, and arithmeticall examples . . . Newly written in French, and Englished by the Authour . . .* (1629).

For a rich discussion of the art of gunnery during this period, see A. R. Hall, *Ballistics in the Seventeenth Century* (Cambridge: Cambridge University Press, 1952).

103.24   mases] I.e., mazes.

103.27   fly . . . from a serpent.] Cf. Ecclesiasticus 21: 2: "Flee from sin as from the face of a serpent . . . ."

103.27–104.6   Is it fit . . . old age.] This passage occurs in the holograph of the "Rabelaisian Fragment," where it is lined out; see New's edition, pp. 1085, 1089–90. Originally, it was Homenas's lament over the anticipated discovery of his plagiaries and the ruining of his reputation; when this happens, he says, "I may sit up whole Winter Nights baking my Blood with hectic Watchings and write as solid as a *Father* of the Church——or, I may sit down whole summer Days evaporating my Spirits into the finest Thoughts, and write as florid as a *Mother* of it, & in either Case, impair my Health, waste my animal Strength, dry up my radical Moisture, bring myself into a most costive Habit of Body, & hasten all the Infirmities of my old age,—In a Word, I may compose myself off my Legs, & preach till I burst,—and when I've done, 'twil be worse, than if not done at all."

Cf. Cibber's *Apology*, 2d ed. (1740), p. 17: "Can it be worth my while to waste my Spirits, to bake my Blood, with serious Contemplations, and perhaps impair my Health, in the fruitless Study of advancing myself . . . ." And also cf. *Don Quixote*, I.I.1: "In fine, he gave himself up so wholly to the reading of Romances, that a-Nights he would pore on 'till 'twas Day, and a-Days he would read on 'till 'twas Night; and thus by sleeping little, and reading much, the Moisture of his Brain was exhausted to that Degree, that at last he lost the Use of his Reason. A world of disorderly Notions, pick'd out of his Books, crouded into his Imagination; and now his Head was full of nothing but Inchantments, Quarrels, Battles, Challenges, Wounds, Complaints, Amours, Torments, and abundance of Stuff and Impossibilities . . ." (I: 4–5).

Cf. *TS*, 719.15–17: "I would oblige thee, provided it would not impair thy strength—or dry up thy radical moisture too fast . . . ."

104.4   radical moisture] Cf. Chambers, s.v. *Radical:* "The schools talk much of a *radical moisture* inherent in the seeds of all animals, which nourishes and preserves the vital heat or flame, as oil does a lamp; and which when exhausted, life is extinguished.

"Dr. Quincy [John Quincy (d. 1722), author of the *Lexicon Physico-Medicum* (1719), which went through many editions in the century] observes that this *radical moisture* is a mere chimera; unless we thereby mean the mass of blood which is the promptuary whence all the other juices and humours are derived . . . ."

104.7   I Would not give a groat] Proverbial; Tilley, G458, and *ODEP*, s.v. *Groat*. The groat was a fourpenny piece, not coined after 1662, although the term remained in use throughout the eighteenth century, especially to signify a very small sum; Sterne seems to have liked the phrase, using it (or a variant) at 238.11, 428.23, 755.1–2. In vol. IX (804.13) and in the *Political Romance* (p. 6), however, he uses *groat* as if it were an actual coin: "the cook sold it with some kitchen-fat to the postillion for a groat" and "he had come, with a Groat in his Hand, to search the Parish Register for his Age."

104.13–16   Writers . . . truth, than beauty.] This was perhaps a commonplace; cf. C. A. Du Fresnoy's *The Art of Painting*, trans. John Dryden, 2d ed. (1716), p. 9: "Because it is not sufficient to imitate Nature in every Circumstance, dully, and as it were literally, and minutely; but it becomes a Painter to take what is most beautiful, as being the Sovereign Judge of his own Art; 'what is less beautiful or is faulty, he shall freely correct by the Dint of his own Genius,' and permit no transient Beauties to escape his Observation." It is worth observing that Dryden's preface concerns itself with the relationship between poetry and painting.

Tristram interrupts himself in a more elaborate fashion in vol. IV, where he again compares writing to painting and omits a chapter and ten pages in order to keep "the just proportions and harmony" among the chapters of his work (pp. 372ff., especially 374.17–24).

104.17   *cum grano salis*] "With a grain of salt."

105.5–6   began to break . . . clean shirt] Cf. *Letters*, p. 90: "I thank God tho' I don't abound—that I have enough for a clean shirt every day . . . ." Curtis notes that this was considered a sign of respectability and cites Hester Thrale Piozzi, *Observations and Reflections* (1789): "it was however entertaining enough to hear a travelled gentleman [in Milan] . . . telling his auditors how all the men in London, *that were noble*, put on a clean shirt every day . . ." (ed. Herbert Barrows [Ann Arbor: University of Michigan Press, 1967], p. 54).

    Cf. 780.12–14, where Tristram admits to traveling with six shirts, and n. below.

106.5   Monsieur *Ronjat*] Cf. Tindal, III: 505, where King William's fatal fall from his horse is described: "Upon this accident, he was carried to *Hampton-Court*, where the bone was set by Monsieur *Ronjat*, Serjeant-surgeon to the King . . . ." The reference is to Étienne Ronjat, first surgeon to William III and author of *Lettre de Mr. Ronjat, Premier Chirurgien de feu Sa Majesté Britanique Guillaume III. Ecrite de Londres à un Medicin de ses amis en Hollande* (1703).

106.7–9   The desire . . . passion to it] The idea is certainly a commonplace; e.g., the opening sentence of Robert Molesworth's preface to his *An Account of Denmark* (1694): "*Health* and *Liberty* are without dispute the greatest natural Blessings Mankind is capable of enjoying; I say natural, because the contrary states are purely accidental, and arise from Nature debauched, depraved or enforced."

106.11–13   but . . . the common way] Cf. 73.26–27: "But nothing ever wrought with our family after the ordinary way."

106.19–20   the parlour . . . of his sentence.] See above, n. to 70.17–71.2.

106.21–24   WHEN a man . . . fair discretion!] Cf. *Tale of a Tub*, p. 171: "But when a Man's Fancy gets *astride* on his Reason, when Imagination is at Cuffs with the Senses, and common Understanding, as well as common Sense, is Kickt out of Doors; the first Proselyte he makes, is Himself . . . ." On Sterne's identification of the hobby-horse with the ruling passion, see above, n. to 85.20–21.

107.3   incarnate] *OED* cites this passage as its last illustration of the meaning "to cause flesh to grow upon or in (a wound or sore); to heal over."

107.5–8   The sound . . . was now rapid] Sterne touches here upon the Lockean concepts of duration and the succession of ideas, which he discusses more completely in vol. III, chap. 18 (pp. 222–25). Arthur Cash, "The Lockean Psychology of *Tristram Shandy*," *ELH* 22 (1955): 125–35, connects the phrase "succession of his ideas" to similar expressions in *TS* (e.g., 119.19–21, 125.10, 252.14, 408.25, 413.10, 435.23), as part of his argument that it is not the association of ideas that organizes the work but rather Locke's principle of a continuous, incessant train (or chain or succession) of ideas passing through the mind (see especially *ECHU*, II.14).

107.15   would be upon 'Change.] The Royal Exchange that Walter visits, London's trading center, was built in 1669. A fine contemporary appreciation of it is in *Spectator* 69: "THERE is no Place in the Town which I so much love to frequent as the *Royal-Exchange*. It gives me a secret Satisfaction, and, in some measure, gratifies my Vanity, as I am an *Englishman*, to see so rich an Assembly of Country-men and Foreigners consulting together upon the private Business of Mankind, and making this Metropolis a kind of *Emporium* for the whole Earth" (I: 292–93). Walter Shandy was, it should be recalled, a "*Turky* merchant" (6.9–10).

107.21   demigration] Migration; *OED* cites this passage as its last illustration.

108.16   manage this matter to a T] Stevenson, p. 2267, gives examples from 1699 on.

108.19–20   *James Butler*] See below, n. to 360.8–9.

108.24–25   at the . . . of *Namur*] The battle of Landen took place on July 29, 1693. For a brief account, see vol. VIII, chap. 19 (694.4–695.4, and n. below).

109.11   body-servant] *OED* cites this passage as its sole illustration.

109.12   *Non Hobby-Horsical per se*] "Not Hobby-Horsical in himself."

109.16–17   I have . . . line in it.] This construction, with its reference to drawing or painting, is a favorite with Sterne for introducing characters. Cf. 121.6–10: "Such were the out-lines of Dr. *Slop*'s figure, which . . . you must know, may as certainly be caracatur'd, and convey'd to the mind by three strokes as three hundred"; 131.25–26: "I could not give the reader this stroke in my uncle *Toby*'s picture . . ."; and *ASJ*, p. 72: "The rest of his outline may be given in a few strokes . . . ."

109.26–27   broke no squares] Proverbial; Tilley, I54: "An INCH breaks no square" (i.e., makes no difference); and *ODEP*, s.v. *Inch*. Cf. *Letters*, p. 231: "be so kind as to honour her draught upon You; but I believe I shall have paid the Money I purpose into Beckets hands by the time She will want—but if otherwise a week or fortnight, I know, will break no squares with a good & worthy friend."

109.28–110.1   looked upon . . . a humble friend] In "A Version of Pastoral: Class and Society in *Tristram Shandy*," *SEL* 7 (1967): 516–18, Howard P. Anderson calls attention to the similarity between the Toby-Trim relationship and that of Sir John Bevil and his servant Humphrey in Steele's *The Conscious Lovers* (1723); e.g.: "Sir *John Bevil*. Well, *Humphrey*, you know I have been a kind Master to you; I have us'd you, for the ingenuous Nature I observ'd in you from the beginning, more like an humble Friend than a Servant" (*The Plays of Richard Steele*, ed. Shirley Strum Kenny [Oxford: Clarendon Press, 1971], I.i, p. 307).

110.7   not hanging his ears] Proverbial; Tilley, E22.

110.21   nography——(call it ichnography, quoth my uncle)] In the *Political Romance* one solution offered to the "allegory," by a "Gentleman, who was by much the best Geographer in the whole Club" is that the "*Breeches* meant *Gibraltar;* for . . . the Ichnography and Plan of that Town and Fortress . . . exactly resembles a Pair of Trunk-Hose . . . ." But another member of the club protests that "frankly, he did not understand what *Ichnography* meant . . . ." (p. 37). *Ichnography* evidently struck Sterne as a difficult—or humorous—word; cf. the play on *chronology* and *geography* in vol. VIII (688.5−6).

110.22−23   pleased to sit down before] Trim puns on the military usage of *sit* to mean "to encamp *before* a town, etc., in order to besiege it; to begin *to* a siege"—*OED*, s.v. *Sit*, 21.c.(*b*).

110.26   could but mark me the polygon] Cf. *The New Method of Fortification, as Practised by Monsieur de Vauban*, trans. Abel Swall (1691), p. 33: "it is impossible to work on a Regular Fortification on Paper, without knowing before-hand how to inscribe Regular Figures in a Circle . . ."; or John Muller, *A Treatise Containing the Elementary Part of Fortification* (1746), p. 24, where the first step in planning a fortification is to "inscribe in a circle a polygon of as many sides as the fortification is designed to have fronts . . . ." Indeed all the books on fortification of the period spend a good many pages on basic geometrical problems, always including this particular one.

Cf. *TS*, 518.7−8: "As soon as my uncle *Toby* had laid a foundation, and taught him [Le Fever] to inscribe a regular polygon in a circle . . ."; and 539.5−6: "yet there was no town at that time within the polygon . . . ."

111.3   campaign] See below, n. to 583.23.

111.5−16   I would face . . . over it.] Sterne's information at this point goes beyond Chambers and Tindal, but we have not discovered his source, if any. Chambers does define *gazons* (see "Glossary of Terms of Fortification" in this volume), but does not indicate any relationship with *sods* (see, however, "Glossary," s.v. *Bastion*); Tindal nowhere discusses the filling of the fossé at St. Nicolas's Gate, nor does any other account of Namur we have examined. That Sterne is correct about the problem of a brick or stone facing is perhaps suggested by *The New Method*, p. 72: "If you would line the Parapet, it must be allowed a little sloaping, that the Soldiers may have the better footing. The best Lining of Parapets is with Turf. As for the Earth or Mould which you are to make use of in erecting a Parapet, it is very requisite to mix it with Withy Twigs, or Brambles, and to sow it with any Weeds that take a deep root, to bind the Earth together, so that the Cannon may not easily crumble it down." See also Chambers, the article on the *fausse-braye:* "an elevation of earth, two or three fathoms broad, round the foot of the rampart on the outside, defended by a parapet which parts it from the berme, and the edge of the ditch . . . .

"It is of little use where ramparts are faced with wall, because of the rubbish which the cannon beats down into it. For this reason, engineers will have none before the faces of the bastions, where the breach is commonly made; because the ruins falling, the *Fausse-braye* makes the ascent to the breach the easier . . . ."

111.22   something like a tansy] *OED* cites this passage as its last illustration of the phrase, with the definition "properly, fittingly, perfectly; perfect." It occurs in Rabelais, IV.22.179, and Swift, *Polite Conversation*, p. 106. *Tansy* is the name of a plant and, by extension, of a pudding or omelet flavored with juice of tansy; the precise origin of the phrase is, however, unknown.

111.25   red as scarlet] This comparison occurs in the Commination service in the *Book of Common Prayer:* "For tho' our sins be as red as scarlet, they shall be made white as snow" (cf. Isaiah 1: 18); the simile may well be a commonplace, but it is unrecorded as such.

112.11   breeches-pocket] *OED*'s sole entry is dated 1783.

113.5−8   at the bottom . . . wished for] Cf. "So great was Bates's zeal for the service that we find him by moonlight practicing the use of his firelock in a 'Bowling-green . . . so surrounded with a Hedge-row that no one suspected any People there at that Time'" (Helen Sard Hughes, "A Precursor of *Tristram Shandy*," *JEGP* 17 [1918]: 233). Hughes is quoting from

The Life and Memoirs of Mr. Ephraim Tristram Bates (1756). See above, n. to 36.1–3.

113.12   retina] *OED* cites this passage as its first illustration of a figurative usage.

113.15–17   Never did lover . . . in private] Sterne uses a similar comparison for Walter's relationship with Bruscambille: "he solaced himself with *Bruscambille* after the manner, in which, 'tis ten to one, your worship solaced yourself with your first mistress,——that is, from morning even unto night . . ." (266.19–22).

114.1–2   may make . . . of this drama.] Cf. Chambers, s.v. *Epitasis:* "the second part, or division of a dramatic poem; wherein the plot, or action . . . was carried on, heightened, warmed, and worked up, till it arrived at its state, or height, called the *catastasis* . . . ." See 316.23–317.3 and n. below.

114.5–7   taking . . . began his sentence] See above, n. to 70.17.

114.12–14   and where's *Susannah* . . . ravish her.] As Arthur Sherbo points out (*Studies*, p. 130), there is probably an allusion here to the apocryphal story of Susanna, who bathes in her garden while two elders spy upon her and later attempt her virtue.

115.10   A pudding's end] Cf. 293.7, where the trumpeter's wife (with admiration, one suspects) calls Don Diego's nose a "pudding's end." J. S. Farmer and W. E. Henley, *Slang and Its Analogues* (1890–1904), s.v. *Pudding,* provide an example of usage synonymous with *penis,* but neither they nor Partridge has an entry for *pudding's end.* G. L. Apperson, *English Proverbs and Proverbial Phrases* (London: J. M. Dent, 1929), cites James Howell's *Proverbs* (1659): "A pudding hath two ends, but a fool hath none." *EDD* cites *end-pudding* as a West Yorkshire expression for *rectum.*

John Hall-Stevenson develops an elaborate simile concerning the pudding's end in his "Epistle to the Grown Gentlewomen, the Misses of ****" (1760): "Do but contemplate a Pudding's end, / There is a String goes round about / Her Snout. / The String is very much the Pudding's friend, / He keeps her within bounds, or else she would be spoil'd, / And by his means she gets well boil'd. / . . . / I take the Marriage-noose, or Wedding-ring, / If you are prudent in your Carriage / To be a Pudding-string" (pp. 19–20).

Whatever Walter has in mind with his exclamation, it would seem that

Watt's suggestion (p. 76, n. 1) falls short: "The (unattractive) knotted end of a sausage; hence of little importance."

115.15–16 My sister . . . near her ****.] A very real problem for men-midwives; see above, n. to 50.15–22. Cf. *Man-Midwifery Analysed: And the Tendency of that Practice Detected and Exposed* (1764): "I desire every woman who loves her husband . . . seriously to consider whether she be strictly entitled to the appellation of being called a modest woman, after she has admitted a male operator thus to insult her person" (p. 21).

115.23–24 that ornamental figure . . . the *Aposiopesis*.] Sterne seems to have been especially interested in this rhetorical figure, commenting upon it in the "Rabelaisian Fragment" and again in vol. IV (383.1–2); and of course *ASJ* ends with one of the most famous aposiopestic breaks in English literature: "So that when I stretch'd out my hand, I caught hold of the Fille de Chambre's" (p. 291 and t.n.). Rabelais's use of the figure is discussed by Ozell early in vol. I, where the note defines it as "when a person, through anger and earnestness, leaves out some word or part of the sentence, and yet may be understood . . ." (I.5.151, n. 10). Cf. Pope's definition in *Peri Bathous*, ed. Edna Leake Steeves (New York: King's Crown Press, 1952), p. 46: "An excellent Figure for the Ignorant, as, *What shall I say?* when one has nothing to say; or *I can no more*, when one really can no more: Expressions which the gentle Reader is so good, as never to take in earnest." See also Richard A. Lanham, *A Handlist of Rhetorical Terms* (Berkeley: University of California Press, 1968), s.v.: "1. Stopping suddenly in midcourse—leaving a statement unfinished . . . 2. An idea, though unexpressed, is clearly perceived . . . ."

Goldsmith may have had Sterne in mind when he criticized "strokes" of modern wit in *Citizen of the World*, letter 51: "*Do you call these dashes of the pen strokes, reply'd I, for I must confess I can see no other?* And pray Sir, returned he, what do you call them? Do you see any thing good now a-days that is not filled with strokes—and dashes?—Sir, a well placed dash makes half the wit of our writers of modern humour" (*Works*, II: 215). One week later (letter 53), Goldsmith wrote very specifically against *TS*.

William J. Farrell has noted ("Nature versus Art as a Comic Pattern in *Tristram Shandy*," *ELH* 30 [1963]: 16–17) that the aposiopesis was "invariably associated with an orator so overwrought with emotion that he could not continue his speech" and hence that Sterne has misapplied the word for his own purposes. Pope's definition, however, suggests that the range of meaning associated with aposiopesis was somewhat broader in the eighteenth century than Farrell suggests.

115.24–27   Just heaven! . . . in the statue!] R. F. Brissenden suggests that Sterne is here recalling "two distinct though related passages" from William Hogarth's *The Analysis of Beauty* (1753): "And if the reader will follow in his imagination the most exquisite turns of the chissel in the hands of a master, when he is putting the finishing touches to a statue; he will soon be led to understand what it is the real judges expect from the hand of such a master, which the Italians call, the little more, Il poco piu, and which in reality distinguishes the original master-pieces at Rome from even the best copies of them. . . (pp. 61–62).

And the second passage: "Now whoever can conceive lines thus constantly flowing, and delicately varying over every part of the body even to the fingers ends, and will call to his remembrance what led us to this last description of what the Italians call, Il poco piu (*the little more* that is expected from the hand of a master) will, in my mind, want very little more than what his own observation on the works of art and nature will lead him to, to acquire a true idea of the word *Taste*, when applied to form; however inexplicable this word may hitherto have been imagined" (p. 66). The fact that Sterne includes *poco meno* ("little less"), where Hogarth does not, perhaps indicates his familiarity with the original use of the terms in musical notation. See also *ASJ*, pp. 121–23, the discussion of the French phrases *tant pis* ("so much the worse") and *tant mieux* ("so much the better").

Brissenden notes as well the allusion to Hogarth in the phrase "precise line of beauty"; see "Sterne and Painting," in *Of Books and Humankind: Essays and Poems Presented to Bonamy Dobrée*, ed. John Butt (London: Routledge & Kegan Paul, 1964) pp. 104–5. Sterne refers to Hogarth twice again in vol. II; see 121.6–10 and 141.7ff. For a discussion of Hogarth's two illustrations for *TS*, see vol. II of this edition, pp. 843–44 and 849–50, t.n. Plate.

116.1   the pen, the fiddle-stick, *et cætera*] Cf. 607.3–6: "a novice . . . troubled with a whitloe in her middle finger, by sticking it constantly into the abbess's cast poultices, *&c.*"; and *Letters*, p. 379 ("Journal to Eliza"): "O my dear Lady, cried I, did you but know the Original—but what is she to

you, Tristram—nothing; but that I am in Love with her—et ceetera—
—said She—no I have given over dashes—replied I . . . ."

Sterne's usage of *et cætera* in these instances is not innocent. Cf. *OED*,
s.v. 2.b.: "as substitute for a suppressed substantive, generally a coarse or
indelicate one"; *Romeo and Juliet*, II.i.37–38 (first quarto), is cited.
Fielding's *Shamela* provides several instances as well. Parson Tickletext
writes to Parson Oliver: "It has stretched out this diminutive mere Grain
of Mustard-seed (a poor Girl's little, *&c.*) . . ."; and Oliver responds:
"naked in Bed, with his Hand on her Breasts, *&c.* . . ." (*An Apology for
the Life of Mrs. Shamela Andrews*, ed. Sheridan W. Baker, Jr. [Berkeley:
University of California Press, 1953], pp. 11, 16; see also p. 75).

116.1–2   give the true swell . . . true pleasure!] In addition to Sterne's obvious bawdiness, he may have had in mind a sentence from Charles Avison, *An Essay on Musical Expression*, 2d ed. (1753), pp. 59–60: "And this
would pass with a great Part of Mankind for Musical Expression, instead
of that noble Mixture of solemn Airs and various Harmony, which *indeed*
elevates our Thoughts, and gives that exquisite Pleasure, which none but
true lovers of Harmony can feel."

For Avison, see below, nn. to 192.8–10, 331.9–12.

116.17   THO' my father . . . natural philosopher] Cf. 4.2–3: "my father,
who was an excellent natural philosopher . . . ." The term is denotatively
equivalent to *scientist* or *physicist* today, but its connotation, in unsympathe-
tic hands, might have suggested a virtuoso (in Shadwell's usage) or an
amateur. See also 305.16–17: "demonstrators in natural philosophy."

117.7   would try the patience of a *Job*] A proverbial expression; Tilley, J59,
and *ODEP*, s.v. *Patient*. Cf. *2 Henry IV*, I.ii.126–27: "*Fal.* I am as poor
as Job, my lord, but not so patient." See also *TS*, 196.7–8, where Dr. Slop
must have "three fifths of *Job*'s patience at least" to untie Obadiah's knots.

117.8–9   Why?. . . Wherefore?] Cf. 98.20–21: "It is a history.—A history!
of who? what? where? when?"

117.14–15   the shock . . . widow *Wadman*] The Treaty of Utrecht (1713),
which ended the Wars of the Spanish Succession, called for the demolition
of the French fortifications at Dunkirk (Tindal, IV: 314). Sterne uses the
same formula in vol. III (245.9–11): "THO' the shock my uncle *Toby*
received the year after the demolition of *Dunkirk*, in his affair with widow

Wadman." The demolition is described in chap. 34 of vol. VI (pp. 558ff.)
and the "shock" in chap. 31 of vol. IX (pp. 801ff.).

117.22–25   It is said in *Aristotle's Master-Piece . . . heavens.*] Not in *Aristotle's Master-Piece,* but in another pseudo-Aristotle, often published with
it, *Aristotle's Book of Problems:* "*Q. Why doth a Man lift up his Head towards the Heavens when he doth imagine? A.* Because the Imagination is in
the fore part of the Head, or Brain; and therefore it lifteth up itself, that
the Creeks or Cells of the Imagination may be opened, and that the Spirits
which help the Imagination, and are fit for that purpose, having their
concourse thither, may help the Imagination.

  "*Q. Why doth a Man when he museth, or thinketh on things past, look down
towards the Earth? A.* Because the Cell or Creek which is behind, is the
Creek or Chamber of Memory, and therefore that looketh towards
Heaven when the head is bowed down; and so that Cell is opened, to
the end that the Spirits which perfect the Memory should enter in"
(pp. 9–10).

  We quote from a 1755 edition bound with a 1759 edition of the *Master-
Piece;* the title-page may indicate that Sterne in this instance was not purposefully misleading: *Aristotle's Compleat Master Piece. In Three Parts . . .
To Which is added, A Treasure of Health; or, The Family Physician . . . the
twenty-seventh edition . . . 1759.* Bound into the volume, but paged separately, is *Aristotle's Book of Problems, with other Astronomers, Astrologers,
Physicians, and Philosophers . . . the twenty-fifth edition.* Together, the various parts of the *Master-Piece* make up an eighteenth-century version of a
sex manual, midwife's guide, book of home remedies, and compendium
of folk science; judging from its popularity, it seems to have been a book
no home could do without. See Work, p. 102, n. 1; and Paul-Gabriel
Boucé, "Some Sexual Beliefs and Myths in Eighteenth-Century Britain,"
in *Sexuality in Eighteenth-Century Britain,* ed. Boucé (Manchester: Manchester University Press, 1982), pp. 28–31 and passim. Boucé observes
the occurrence in *Aristotle's Masterpiece* of some discussion of the size of
the nose as an indicator of the size of the phallus, a long-standing sexual
myth that Sterne will use in vols. III and IV, most especially in "Slawkenbergius's Tale."

  Cf. John Wesley, *Directions concerning Pronunciation and Gesture* (Bristol, 1749), p. 11: "If you speak of Heaven or Things above, lift up your Eyes: If of Things beneath, cast them down . . . ."

118.5−6   I know . . . in the moon] Proverbial; Tilley, M240, and *ODEP*, s.v. *Man*.

118.11−13   Every thing . . . has two handles] Proverbial; cf. Tilley, T193, and *ODEP*, s.v. *Most*. Cf. Burton, 2.3.3 (p. 332): "Every thing saith *Epictetus* hath two handles, the one to be held by, the other not . . ." (referring to *Encheiridion*, 43, II: 527). The context in Epictetus might be worth noting; we quote from the Loeb edition: "If your brother wrongs you, do not lay hold of the matter by the handle of the wrong that he is doing . . . but rather by the other handle—that he is your brother, and that you were brought up together, and then you will be laying hold of the matter by the handle by which it ought to be carried."

See also *Letters*, p. 411, where Sterne thanks Dr. John Eustace for his gift of a walking stick: "Your walking stick is in no sense more *shandaic* than in that of its having *more handles than one*—The parallel breaks only in this, that in using the stick, every one will take the handle which suits his convenience. In *Tristram Shandy*, the handle is taken which suits their passions, their ignorance or sensibility."

118.15−16   sit down coolly, and consider within himself] Sterne uses this formula on several occasions, e.g., 273.27−274.1: "and was able to sit down coolly, and consider within himself . . ."; and 587.19−20: "but I take the matter coolly before me, and consider . . . ." See also 238.4, 445.4, 689.13.

Cf. *Sermons*, VI.34.24: "yet whoever cooly sits down and reflects upon the many accidents . . . which have befallen him . . . ."

118.17   com-at-ability] *OED* cites this passage as its sole illustration. Cf. *Letters*, p. 74: "every Thing else, which I find Laugh-at-able in my way . . . ."

118.21−22   ANALOGY . . . which different] Cf. Chambers, s.v. *Analogy:* "a certain relation, proportion, or agreement, which several things, in other respects different, bear to each other."

119.3−4   whether I . . . volume or not.] Tristram never does find a place for it.

119.5−23   IT is . . . pendulums whatever.] As Barbara Hardy points out ("A Mistake in *Tristram Shandy*," *N&Q* 207 [1962]: 261), "Sterne is wrong in telling us that the account of Uncle Toby's history has come between the ringing of the bell and the rapping at the door. This long flashback interrupts Uncle Toby at an earlier point in time, before he has finished the sentence which suggests ringing for Obadiah. He finishes this in Volume 2, Chapter 6, but he begins it in Volume 1, Chapter 21, and the flashback comes then, not when Sterne suggests. All that comes between the ringing and the rapping is a two-chapter conversation exposing Uncle Toby's ignorance of women and toying with an ambiguous sentence."

The point had been made earlier by H. K. Russell, "*Tristram Shandy* and the Technique of the Novel," *SP* 42 (1945): 589, n. 19.

119.13–17   If the hypercritick . . . and three fifths] Cf. 213.12–14, where the connoisseur measures Garrick's suspensions as being "three seconds and three fifths by a stop-watch, my Lord, each time."

119.15   the ringing . . . at the door] Barbara Lounsberry suggests that Slop is introduced as a harbinger of death and that this ringing of the bell is "a pointed allusion" to Macduff's famous speech in *Macbeth:* "Ring the alarum-bell! Murther and treason! / . . . Shake off this downy sleep, death's counterfeit, / And look on death itself!" (II.iii.74–77); see "Sermons and Satire: Anti-Catholicism in Sterne," *PQ* 55 (1976): 411. The argument would be more convincing perhaps if the ringing were of a doorbell rather than of the servant's bell.

119.19–21   the idea . . . of our ideas] Sterne again anticipates (see 107.5–8) his larger discussion of duration in vol. III, chap. 18. The issue is treated in *ECHU* in a chapter entitled "*Of Duration, and its simple Modes*" (II.14); see below, nn. to pp. 222–24, where the relevant passages are quoted.

Many critics have probed with considerable effort Sterne's interest both in Locke (for whom, see comments in the introduction to this volume, pp. 16–17) and in the problems of narrative time. As a balance to those critics, see Duke Maskell, "Locke and Sterne, or Can Philosophy Influence Literature?," *EIC* 23 (1973): 22–40; on this passage specifically, Maskell comments: "In fact the passage . . . has nothing to do with theories of time or space or anything else . . . . This passage shows the pleasure Tristram takes in talking witty, puzzling nonsense, knowingly. Tristram's puzzle is the completely illegitimate analogy he draws between two different kinds of representation, the theatre with its stage and actors located in time and space, and books, whose words are located in neither" (pp. 34–35).

120.11 a dance . . . between the acts.] Emmett L. Avery notes that by 1720 the practice of a full evening of entertainment, with *entr'acte* performances, was well established on the London stage (*The London Stage: 1660–1800, Part 2: 1700–1729* [Carbondale: Southern Illinois University Press, 1962], pp. cxvi–cxx; see also pp. cxxxvi–cxli). Cf. George Winchester Stone, Jr., *The London Stage, Part 4: 1747–76:* "The total impact of an evening in the theatre was derived from a varied 'whole show,' consisting of a *Prologue*, a full five-act *Mainpiece*, an *Epilogue*, some form of *theatrical dance* (usually narrative and comic), a two-act *Afterpiece*, a good deal of popular *music*, and during the benefit season, a number of *specialty acts*. In the midst of this Neo-Classical age a manager would hardly have dared present unrelieved by dance, song, or farce, the purest Greek or Graeco-French tragedy" (p. xxiv); see also pp. xxv–xxvi and cxxx–cxxxiii.

120.16 biographically] *OED* cites this passage as its first example.

121.1–5 IMagine . . . the Horse-Guards.] Cash, *Early and Middle Years*, p. 180, cites a quite different contemporary description of John Burton: "a tall Well sett Gentlem[n] in a light Colored Coat in Boots with a Whip under his Arm . . . who he says was called D[r] Burton of York." Moreover, although much was made of Burton's Jacobite sympathies during the '45 (see Cash's elaborate account, pp. 151–80), the fact is that Burton was "the son of an Anglican clergyman, he regularly attended services, and he never failed of his obligations to the established church" (p. 180); Sterne's caricature is thus quite imaginary in its most salient details.

Cf. the opening paragraph of *The Adventures of Gil Blas*, trans. Tobias Smollett (London: J. C. Nimmo and Bain, n.d.), I: 13: "Figure to yourself a little fellow, three feet and a half high, as fat as you can conceive, with a head sunk deep between his shoulders, and you have my uncle to the life."

121.3 sesquipedality] *OED* cites this passage as its first illustration. The original idea of lengthiness was associated with polysyllabic words, after Horace's "sesquipedalia verba" (*Ars Poetica*, line 97); applied to people, it would imply shortness ("a foot and a half"), as in *Martinus Scriblerus*, p. 145: "hast thou ever measur'd the gigantick Ethiopian, whose stature is

above eight cubits high, or the sesquipedalian Pigmey?" Sterne is thus able
to bring into play the shortness and stoutness of Dr. Slop with one word.

121.6–10 Such were . . . as three hundred.] Cf. Hogarth's *Analysis of
Beauty*, p. 135: "The general idea of an action, as well as of an attitude,
may be given with a pencil in very few lines. . . . two or three lines at first
are sufficient to shew the intention of an attitude . . . ." See above, n. to
115.24–27, and below, n. to 140.7ff.

Cf. *Work*, p. 104, n. 3: "A graceful compliment to William Hogarth
(1697–1764), English painter and engraver, whose style in caricaturing
Sterne had imitated. His *Analysis of Beauty*, a treatise written 'to fix the
fluctuating ideas of Taste,' had appeared in 1753." For another opinion—
that Sterne was more an opponent than an admirer of Hogarth and his
theories—see William V. Holtz, *Image and Immortality* (Providence,
R.I.: Brown University Press, 1970), pp. 21–38 and passim.

Sterne's evocation of Hogarth in relation to character-drawing is something of a commonplace among mid-century writers. See, e.g., *Joseph
Andrews*, book I, chap. 8: "from none of these, nor from *Phidias*, or
Praxiteles, if they should return to Life—no, not from the inimitable
Pencil of my Friend *Hogarth*, could you receive such an Idea of Surprize
. . ." (ed. Martin C. Battestin [Middletown, Conn.: Wesleyan University Press, 1967], pp. 40–41); *Tom Jones*, book X, chap. 8: "O, *Shake-
spear*, had I thy Pen! O, *Hogarth*, had I thy Pencil! then would I draw the
Picture of the poor Serving-Man . . ." (II: 555; see also Battestin's n., I:
66); *Roderick Random*, chap. 47: "It would require the pencil of Hogarth
to express the astonishment and concern of Strap, on hearing this piece of
news . . ." (ed. W. E. Henley [Westminster: Archibald Constable and
Co., 1899], II: 94); and *Peregrine Pickle*, chap. 14: "It would be a difficult
task for the inimitable Hogarth himself to exhibit the ludicrous expression
of the Commodore's countenance, while he read this letter" (ed. W. E.
Henley, I: 90–91). All four examples are cited in Holtz, p. 43.

121.11ff.   Imagine such a one, etc.] The collision between Slop and Obadiah
may have been suggested to Sterne by an episode in Montaigne, describing
a similar accident which had happened to him: "I had taken a Horse that
went very easy upon his Pace, but was not very strong. Being upon my
Return Home, a sudden Occasion falling out to make use of this Horse in

a Kind of Service that he was not acquainted with; one of my Train, a lusty proper Fellow, mounted upon a strong *German* Horse . . . to play the *Bravo*, and appear a better Man than his Fellows, comes thundering full Speed in the very Track where I was, rushing like a *Colossus* upon the little Man, and the little Horse, with such a Career of Strength and Weight, that he turn'd us both over and over topsy-turvy, with our Heels in the Air: So that there lay the Horse overthrown and stun'd with the Fall, and I ten or twelve Paces from him stretcht out at Length, with my Face all batter'd and broken . . ." (II.6.47). First suggested by William Jackson, "On Literary Thievery," in *The Four Ages* (1798), pp. 246–48.

Perhaps, as well, the passage owes something to the detailed account of Ragotin's fall from his horse in book I, chap. 19, of Scarron's *Comical Romance* (1700), trans. Tom Brown (New York: Benjamin Blom, 1968). Scarron calls attention to the minuteness of the description, saying it "has cost me more pains, than all the book besides, and yet I am not well satisfied with it neither" (p. 143). Sterne mentions Paul Scarron (1610–60), the French poet, dramatist, and novelist, and first husband of the future Madame de Maintenon, in vol. VIII, along with Rabelais and Cervantes, all of whom he suggests must be kept away from the widow Wadman, since all excite laughter, and "there is no passion so serious, as lust" (727.5–12). Cf. a letter Sterne wrote to the Marquis of Rockingham in December 1759, just after the York publication of vols. I and II: "There is an Anecdote relating to this ludicrous Satyr, which I must tell your Lord^P—& it is this, 'that it was every word of it wrote in affliction; & under a constant uneasiness of mind.' Cervantes wrote his humorous Satyr in a Prison——& Scarron his, in pain & Anguish——Such Philosophers as will account for every thing, may explain this for me." Professor Arthur H. Cash kindly provided us with a typescript of this unpublished letter, the original of which is in the Robert H. Taylor Collection, Princeton University Library. Cf. *Letters*, p. 416.

Writing to an anonymous friend who had suggested that he retrench his exuberant wit, Sterne specifically cites the incident of this chapter: "I will reconsider Slops fall & my too Minute Account of it—but in general I am perswaded that the happiness of the Cervantic humour arises from this very thing—of describing silly and trifling Events, with the Circumstantial Pomp of great Ones—perhaps this is Overloaded—& I can soon ease it . . ." (*Letters*, p. 77). A second version from Sterne's *Letter-Book* reads: "As for Slop's fall—'tis most circumstantialy related, & the affair most trifling—& perhaps you may be right in saying 'tis overloaded—but not dear S^r because of the slightness of the incident—that very thing should constitute the humour, which consists in treating the most insignificant Things with such *Ornamenta ambitiosa*, as would make one sick in another place" (*Letters*, p. 79).

121.15   under such a fardel] Sterne is perhaps thinking of *Hamlet* (III.i.75–76: "who would fardels bear, / To grunt and sweat under a weary life . . ."), since he definitely has the play in mind in the description of Slop's entrance into the parlor. See below, n. to 124.1–2.

121.23   thro' thick and thin] Proverbial; cf. Tilley, T101, and *ODEP*, s.v. *Thick*.

122.3–4   have been . . . *Whiston*'s comets?] Cf. Chambers, s.v. *Comet*, where it is pointed out that Halley's comet of 1680 approached close to the earth: "what might have been the consequence of so near an appulse, a contact, or lastly, a shock of the celestial bodies?—A deluge Mr. Whiston says!" In the *Deluge* entry, Whiston's viewpoint is elaborated: "The inquisitive Mr. Whiston, in his *New Theory of the Earth* [1696], has a very ingenious hypothesis [for the Deluge], perfectly new. He shews . . . that a comet . . . would raise a prodigious, vast and strong tide . . . ." Whiston later elaborated his theory in an appendix attached to the 1714 edition of *New Theory*, entitled "The Cause of the Deluge, Demonstrated."

The fear that some comets (and in particular Halley's, which had just reappeared, as predicted, in early 1759) might destroy the earth with a deluge or conflagration, was particularly (and humorously) associated with William Whiston (1667–1752) by the Scriblerians (see David Charles Leonard, "Swift, Whiston, and the Comet," *ELN* 17 [1979]: 284–87). Interestingly, although comets were being intensely discussed in 1759 because of the return of Halley's comet, Whiston seems to have been by and large forgotten, though his fears were still alive; see, e.g., *Gentleman's Magazine* 29 (1759): 207: "The path of the *Newtonian* Comet [i.e., Halley's], in its descent to the sun, lies directly in the way of the earth; and if, in some of its future returns, we suppose it to pass very near the earth, or to strike it, the consequence may prove, its being turned entirely out of its present orbit, or its being changed into a comet and approaching so near the sun as to be set on fire." The *GM* for 1759 has an additional discussion of comets on pp. 521–24.

122.5   NUCLEUS] *OED* cites this passage as its sole example of figurative use.

122.9   hydrophobia] *OED* cites this passage as the first illustration of usage in the etymological sense, i.e., "dread or horror of water," as opposed to the actual disease associated with rabies.

122.17   imprompt] *OED* cites this passage as its sole illustration, with the definition "Not ready or prepared; unready."

122.22–28   for in crossing . . . of mind.] Cf. the similar train of consequences that accompany Toby's accident with his books and maps, 107.23–108.5.

123.16   beluted] Covered with mud or dirt. *OED* cites this passage as its first example.

124.1–2   led him . . . blotches on him.] See *Hamlet*, I.v.74–79: "*Ghost.* Thus was I . . . / Cut off even in the blossoms of my sin, / Unhous'led, disappointed, unanel'd, / No reck'ning made, but sent to my account / With all my imperfections on my head." The ghost stands "motionless and speechless" in I.i.41–49 and I.iv.38–57. The clever alteration of "disappointed" to "unappointed" takes into account the fact that the midwife, and not Dr. Slop, has been given the position of trust with regard to Mrs. Shandy's imminent delivery.

124.5   with all the majesty of mud.] Sterne recalls the mud-diving contest in the *Dunciad*(A), II.302, p. 139: "Lo Smedley rose, in majesty of mud!" First noted by Gwin J. Kolb, "A Note on *Tristram Shandy:* Some New Sources," *N&Q* 196 (1951): 226–27.

124.9   mental reservation] As Work notes (p. 107, n. 3), Sterne alludes again to Slop's papistry, and the use of the doctrine of "mental reservation" by "Jacobites and Romish sympathizers of swearing to support the government and church of England, but 'with mental reservations.'" He cites the Catholic version of the doctrine: "All Catholic writers were, and are, agreed that when there is good reason, [equivocations with mental reservations] may be made use of, and that they are not lies. Those who hear them may understand them in a sense which is not true, but their self-deception may be permitted by the speaker for a good reason" (*The Catholic Encyclopedia* [New York, 1911], s.v. *Mental Reservation*).

The eighteenth-century Protestant version of "mental reservation" can

be found in Chambers, s.v. *Reservation:* "*Mental* RESERVATION is a proposition, which strictly taken, and according to the natural import of the
terms, is false; but if qualified with something *reserved* or concealed in the
mind, becomes true.

"Mental *reservations* are the great refuge of religious hypocrites; who
use them to accommodate their consciences with their interests: the Jesuites
are zealous advocates for mental *reservations;* yet are they real lyes, as
including an intention to deceive."

Sterne alludes to the doctrine again in his attack on Catholicism in the
"Abuses of Conscience" sermon: "his priest had got the keeping of his
conscience;—and all he would let him know of it, was, That he must
believe in the Pope;—go to Mass; . . . What;—if he perjures!—
Why;—he had a mental reservation in it" (152.14–19).

124.13   in that pickle] Proverbial; cf. Tilley, P276: "To be in a sad (sweet)
PICKLE"; and Stevenson, p. 1789.

124.16   *Argumentum ad hominem*] See above, n. to 59.4–5.

125.9   sensorium] *OED* cites this passage as its first example of playful usage:
"in non-technical writing (sometimes for 'brain' or 'mind')." It is a favorite word for Sterne; see 174.22, 178.21, 273.10, 793.21. See also the
famous passage in *ASJ,* p. 278, where God is addressed as the "great
SENSORIUM of the world" (and see Stout's n., pp. 353–54).

125.11   *Stevinus,* the great engineer] Mentioned by Sterne in his list of authors
on fortification; see above, n. to 102.21–24.

125.15–16   WRiting . . . different name for conversation] Of the many attempts to analyze Sterne's style as "conversational," the most significant are
Ian Watt, "The Comic Syntax of *Tristram Shandy,*" in *Studies in Criticism
and Aesthetics, 1660–1800: Essays in Honor of Samuel Holt Monk,* ed.
Howard Anderson and John S. Shea (Minneapolis: University of Min-
nesota Press, 1967), pp. 315–31; and Leland E. Warren, "The Constant
Speaker: Aspects of Conversation in *Tristram Shandy,*" *UTQ* 46 (1976):
51–66.

126.17   pumps] *Handbook of English Costume,* p. 80: "These were shoes with
thin pliable soles and low heels. . . . Owing to their pliability pumps
were worn by acrobats and running footmen, but were also worn for ele-
gance . . . ."

126.19   stay thy obstetrick hand] Another allusion (see above, n. to 124.5) to

Pope's *Dunciad*(B), IV.393–94: "There all the Learn'd shall at the labour stand, / And Douglas lend his soft, obstetric hand" (p. 380). First noted by Frank Brady, "*Tristram Shandy:* Sexuality, Morality, and Sensibility," *ECS* 4 (1970): 43, n. 11.

126.25   *Lucina*] One of the facets of the goddess Juno, that which makes the child see the light of day; see *OCD*, s.v. *Juno*.

126.25   obstetrically] *OED* cites this passage as its first illustration.

126.26   great son of *Pilumnus!*] "By Roman custom, when a woman was delivered, three persons kept off Silvanus ["Roman god of uncultivated land beyond the boundaries of the tillage"] from her by chopping, sweeping, and pounding with a pestle; the deities Intercidona, Deverra, and Pilumnus were supposed to preside over these actions (Varro in Aug. *De civ. D.* 6.9)" (*OCD*, s.v. *Pilumnus*).

127.1–3   thy *tire-tête* . . . behind thee.] See above, n. to 50.15–22, especially the comments on obstetrical instruments. Cash, "Birth," makes clear that Sterne's "salvation and deliverance" are replete with irony, since the primary function of the *tire-tête* and the *crotchet* was to extract a fetus by crushing or attaching its skull (pp. 146–47). As for the *forceps*, it was Burton's opinion that his own invention was "better than any yet contrived"; however, as Cash notes, "the historians, who treasure this instrument as the most odd, impractical, whimsical device ever suggested for insinuation into womankind, usually quote the words of Sir Alexander Simpson: 'an ingenious but very unserviceable forceps, working like a lobster's claws'" (p. 136). Lengthy extracts from Burton's description of his forceps (from his *New System of Midwifry* [1751], "Postscript") are provided by Alban Doran, "Burton ('Dr. Slop'): His Forceps and his Foes," *Journal of Obstetrics and Gynæcology of the British Empire* 23 (1913): 5–9. Doran concludes: "It seems a clumsy instrument. Is it not possible that it really damaged the face of some infant, or its breech or genitals . . ." (p. 8). Both Cash and Doran supply illustrations.

Cash also addresses himself (p. 143) to the bad reputation of obstetrical instruments during the century, citing an English translation of Deventer's *Manuel des Accouchemens* (see vol. II, app. 6, p. 939, in this edition): "a Man in Liquor, almost void of the use of his Senses, both void of Pity and Compassion, furnished with a Knife, a Hook, an Iron Forceps, and other Instruments horrible to Sight . . . come to the Assistance of one in

Agony . . . commonly first begins, with rash Oaths to hurt the Mother, then kill the living Infant, then with a great deal of Pain to draw it out in Pieces . . ." (p. 143; cited from *The Art of Midwifery Improv'd* [1746], p. 14).

As for the "*squirt*," Sterne is alluding to the "*petite canulle*" used by the doctors of the Sorbonne for intrauterine baptism, hence for "salvation" only from the Roman Catholic viewpoint; see vol. I, pp. 66–70.

127.4   bays] *Handbook of English Costume*, p. 416: "BAYS or BAIZE. A coarse open woollen stuff with a long nap; sometimes friezed."

127.4   thy two pistols] Doran, "Burton," p. 69, sees an allusion here to Burton's description of himself as one who "carried pistols" in *British Liberty Endanger'd* (1749), Burton's defense of his role in the '45.

127.15–16   argument *Ad Crumenam*] "Argument to the purse"; see above, n. to 78.18ff.

128.9–13   *Dennis* the critick . . . no difference.] John Dennis (1657–1734) revealed his attitude toward punning in his *Remarks on Rape of the Lock* (1728) and, earlier, in a letter to Wycherley upon receipt of the latter's *Panegyrick upon Puns* (?1695), which was published with his works in 1718. In the *Remarks*, Dennis comments: "*Puns* bear the same Proportion to *Thought*, that *Bubbles* hold to *Bodies*, and may justly be compared to those gaudy Bladders which Children make with Soap; which, tho' they please their weak Capacities with a momentary Glittering, yet are but just beheld, and vanish into Air." The letter offers an even sharper attack: "Nay, it is a more Damnable sign of Stupidity in an Englishman, to make Wit of a Quibble, than it was in the Ægyptians, to make a God of their Garlick. . . . If there be any Diversion in Quibbling, it is a Diversion of which a Fool and a Porter is as capable as is the best of you. . . . There is as much difference between the silly Satisfaction which we have from a Quibble, and the ravishing Pleasure which we receive from a Beautiful Thought, as there is betwixt a Faint Salute and Fruition" (*The Critical Works*, ed. E. N. Hooker [Baltimore: Johns Hopkins Press, 1943], II: 347, 383–84).

Dennis's antipathy to puns appears to have been generally known throughout the eighteenth century; see, e.g., the *Gentleman's Magazine* 51 (1781): 324n: "This reminds us of a pun of Garth to Rowe, who making repeated use of his snuff-box, the Doctor at last sent it to him with the two

Greek letters written in the lid, φρ (*Phi Ro*). At this the sour Dennis was
so provoked as to declare that 'a man who could make so vile a pun would
not scruple to pick a pocket.'" Cf. Pope's *Dunciad*(A) I.61n, p. 67.

128.14–24   Sir . . . so well *flanked*] Sterne borrows from Chambers, s.v.
Curtin: "CURTAIN, or COURTINE, in fortification that part of a wall, or
rampart, which is between two bastions; or which joins the flanks thereof
. . . .

"Du Cange derives the word from the Latin *cortina, quasi minor cortis*, a
little country court, inclosed with walls: he says, it was in imitation hereof,
that they gave this name to the walls and parapets of cities, which inclose
them like courts: he adds, that the *curtains* of beds take their name from the
same origin; that *cortis* was the name of the generals, or prince's tent; and
that those who guarded it were called *cortinarii* and *curtisani*.

"Besiegers seldom carry on their attacks against the *curtin;* because it is
the best flanked of any part." Noted by Bensly, "A Debt," p. 806; see
above, n. to 102.21–24.

Work, p. 111, n. 3: "Charles du Fresne du Cange (1610–1688), a
learned French philologist and historian . . . . Sterne paraphrased from
. . . Chambers's *Cyclopædia* . . . ."

128.26–129.14   we generally . . . than a ravelin.] Sterne moves from Chambers's *Curtin* entry to that under *Ravelin:* "It's use before a curtin, is to
cover the opposite flanks of the two next bastions. It is used also to cover a
bridge or a gate; and is always placed without the moat [i.e., the "fosse" or
"ditch"; see "Glossary of Terms of Fortification" in this volume] . . . .
What the engineers call a *ravelin*, the soldiers generally call a *demi-lune*, or
half-moon."

Sterne then went to Chambers's entry under *Half-Moon*, to complete
the confusion: "*Half moons* are sometimes raised before the curtin, when
the ditch is wider than it ought to be; in which case it is much the same with
a ravelin; only that the gorge of an *half-moon* is made bending in like a
bow, or crescent, and is chiefly used to cover the point of the bastion;
whereas ravelins are always placed before the curtin.—But they are both
defective, as being ill flanked."

The distinction between ravelins and half-moons seems to have eluded
many writers. Abel Boyer observes the confusion in *The Draughts of the*

most Remarkable Fortified Towns of Europe (1701), p. 4. William Horneck, *Remarks on the Modern Fortification* (1738), p. 102, is also baffled: "The Moderns generally call the same Work a Ravelin or *Half-Moon*, promiscuously; and I have scarce found any Person who could give a Reason for their distinction . . . ."

129.16−28   As for . . . double tenaille] Although the French term is common enough in the fortification manuals of the period, it is not found in Chambers; the information seems to be derived, however, from the entry under *Horn-work:* "a sort of out-work, advancing toward the field, to cover and defend a curtin, bastion, or other place suspected to be weaker than the rest.

"It consists of two demi-bastions . . . ." To crown a horn-work means to join it to a second horn-work; but Sterne (or Toby) seems confused in his final comment, since Chambers, s.v. *Tenaille,* says that tenailles "take up too much room," and are not used except when "there wants time to form a horn-work."

130.6   *Accoucheur*] *OED* cites this passage as the earliest occurrence of this French term for a man-midwife. However, John Glaister, *Dr. William Smellie and his Contemporaries* (Glasgow: James Maclehose & Sons, 1894), p. 77, cites a pamphlet written in 1748, which attacks men-midwives for "lugging about with them a Bag of *Lumber,* a more proper Badge of the *Farrier* than the *Accoucheur*" (from William Douglas, *A Letter to Dr. Smellie*). Douglas had just defined that "Lumber" as "*Crotchets, Teartets,* and *Hooks* innumerable . . ." (p. 76). Glaister's study remains an excellent source for information about the state of eighteenth-century obstetrics.

John Burton, *Letter to William Smellie, M.D.* (1753), uses *accoucheur* on numerous occasions, e.g., pp. 37, 59, 109, 135. For Sterne's familiarity with this work, see below, n. to 176.1.

130.11−13   saps, mines, blinds . . . such trumpery] Sterne repeats variations of this listing on several occasions; see 279.26 ("saps, mines, blinds, curtins"); 562.1−2 ("saps, and mines, and blinds, and gabions, and palisadoes"); and 758.9−10 ("all its trumpery of saps, mines, blinds, gabions, fausse-brays and cuvetts").

130.15   My uncle *Toby* . . . patient of injuries] Cf. Sterne's description of his

own father in the "Memoirs": "most patient of fatigue and disappointments" (*Letters*, p. 3).

130.16–17   I have told you . . . courage] Actually it is in the second chapter
that we are informed that Toby "wanted no courage" (98.4); "fifth chapter" may be a vestige of chapters later deleted. See t.n. to this sentence,
vol. II, p. 847, in this edition.

130.24–25   had scarce . . . upon a fly.] J. Homer Caskey, "Two Notes on
Uncle Toby," *MLN* 42 (1927): 322, notes that Edward Moore in *The
Gamester* (1753) has the servant Jarvis say of his master, Beverley: "O he
was a brave little Boy! And yet so merciful he'd not have kill'd the Gnat
that stung him" (I.i.5). The description, however, is almost certainly a
commonplace.

131.8–11   but whether it . . . pleasurable sensation] As Stout points out (*ASJ*,
p. 274), this is a favorite image in Sterne's writings. It is used again in *TS*,
326.18–19: "I could perceive an attempt towards a vibration in the
strings, about the region of the heart"; 415.18–20: "Poor creature! said
my uncle *Toby*, vibrating the note back again, like a string in unison";
562.10–11: "Softer visions,—gentler vibrations stole sweetly in upon his
slumbers"; and 781.19–20: "I was in the most perfect state of bounty and
good will; and felt the kindliest harmony vibrating within me . . . ." See
also *TS*, 609.3–4, 648.8–10; and *ASJ*, pp. 274, 278; and *Letters*,
pp. 138, 236, 310, 411.

Sterne was not alone in drawing an analogy between the senses and
music; George Cheyne, for example, provides a very elaborate scheme in
The English Malady (1733): "I have formerly suggested, that the best
Similitude I can form of the Nature and Actions of this *Principle* upon the
Organs of its Machin, is that of a skilful *Musician* playing on a well-tun'd
Instrument. . . .

". . . material Objects can act no otherwise upon animal Organs, but
either immediately by communicating their Action and Motion to these
Organs, and putting their constituent Parts into particular Vibrations,
intestine Action and Reaction upon one another . . . . We may conclude,
that *Smelling*, for Example, is nothing but the Action of an odorous Body
. . . giving a determin'd Impulse to the Nerves or Fibres of the Nostrils,
which, by their *Mechanism*, propagate this Vibration and Impulse, thro'

their Length to the intelligent or *sentient Principle* in the Brain (which I resemble to the *Musician*). . . .

"May not the *sentient Principle* have its Seat in some Place in the Brain, where the Nerves terminate, like the *Musician* shut up in his Organ-Room? May not the infinite Windings, Convulsions, and Complications of the Beginning of the Nerves which constitute the Brain, serve to determine their particular *Tone, Tension,* and consequently the Intestine Vibrations of their Parts?" (pp. 48–49, 61).

Cf. Chambers, s.v. *Vibration:* "Sensation is supposed to be performed, by means of the *vibratory* motion of the nerves, begun by external objects, and propagated to the brain." See also Jonathan Lamb, "Language and Hartleian Associationism in *A Sentimental Journey,*" *ECS* 13 (1980): 299–301; Lamb attempts to link Sterne and Hartley as a source for this image (among others), but admits the lack of "direct evidence" for any connection. Far more convincing is the discussion by John A. Dussinger, "The Sensorium in the World of 'A Sentimental Journey'," *ArielE* 13 (1982): 5–6. Dussinger calls attention to the Cheyne passage.

131.18   *Literæ humaniores*] "The humanities"; Chambers, s.v. *Humanities,* defines this term more specifically as "the study of the Greek and Latin tongues, grammar, rhetoric, poetry, and the ancient poets, orators, and historians."

131.22   one half of my philanthropy] Cf. Sterne's preface to vols. I and II of *Sermons* (1760), I, pp. viii–ix: "the sermons turn chiefly upon philanthropy, and those kindred virtues to it, upon which hang all the law and the prophets . . . ." The third sermon in vol. I is entitled "Philantropy [*sic*] Recommended," and takes for its text Luke 10: 36, 37.

131.23–24   This is to serve . . . subject.] Cf. Locke, *Some Thoughts Concerning Education,* sec. 82, p. 182: "But of all the Ways whereby Children are to be instructed, and their Manners formed, the plainest, easiest, and most efficacious, is, to set before their Eyes the *Examples* of those Things you would have them do, or avoid. Which, when they are pointed out to them, in the Practice of Persons within their Knowledge, with some Reflections on their Beauty or Unbecomingness, are of more force to draw or deterr their Imitation, than any Discourses which can be made to them. . . . And the Beauty or Uncomeliness of many Things, in good and ill Breeding, will be better learnt, and make deeper Impressions on them, in the *Examples* of others, than from any Rules or Instructions can be given about them. . . .

"Nothing sinking so gently, and so deep, into Men's Minds, as *Example*."

132.7   drollish] *OED* cites this passage as its last illustration; the word recurs in vol. VIII (709.7).

132.10   subacid] See below, n. to 709.6−7.

133.7−8   forgive . . . mother gave me.] Cf. *Julius Caesar*, IV.iii.119−21: "*Cas.* Have not you love enough to bear with me, / When that rash humor which my mother gave me / Makes me forgetful?" See 134.4−6 and n. below.

134.2   In a family-way] *OED* defines *in a family-way* as "in a domestic manner; with the freedom of members of the same family; without ceremony." Closely related is *in the family-way:* "pregnant." Slop may have both meanings in mind.

134.4−6   At the end . . . their accounts.] See above, n. to 133.7−8; Cassius's remark on his "rash humor" is directed to Brutus and concludes their reconciliation after they have quarreled for the first 100 lines of the scene.

134.15ff.   Your sudden appearance, etc.] Sterne borrowed his discussion of Stevinus and the sailing chariot from John Wilkins, *Mathematical Magick* (1680), pp. 155−56, 161: "But above all other experiments to this purpose, that sailing Chariot at *Sceveling* in *Holland*, is more eminently remarkable. It was made by the direction of *Stephinus*, & is celebrated by many Authors. *Walchius* affirms it to be of so great a swiftness for its motion, and yet of so great a capacity for its burden. *Ut in medio freto secundis ventis commissas naves, velocitate multis parasangis post se relinquat, & paucarum horarum spatio, viginti aut triginta milliaria Germanica continuo cursu emetiatur, concreditosq; sibi plus minus vectores sex aut decem, in petitum locum transferat, facillimo illius ad clavum qui sedet nutu, quaquæ versum minimo labore velis commissum, mirabile hoc continenti currus navigium dirigentis.* That it did far exceed the speed of any ship, though we should suppose it to be carried in the open sea with never so prosperous wind: and that in some few hours space it would convey 6 or 10 persons 20 or 30 German miles, and all this with very little labour of him that sitteth at the Stern, who may easily guide the course of it as he pleaseth.

"That eminent inquisitive man *Peireskius*, having travelled to *Sceveling* for the sight and experience of this Chariot, would frequently after with much wonder mention the extreme swiftness of its motion. *Commemorare solebat stuporem quo correptus fuerat cum vento translatus citatissimo non persentiscere tamen, nempe tam citus erat quam ventus.* Though the wind were in it self more swift and strong, yet to passengers in this Chariot it would not be at all discernable, because they did go with an equal swiftness to the wind it self. . . .

"I have often wondred, why none of our Gentry who live near great Plains, and smooth Champions, have attempted any thing to this purpose. The experiments of this kind being very pleasant, and not costly: what could be more delightful or better husbandry, than to make use of the *wind* (which costs nothing, and eats nothing) instead of *horses?*" This borrowing was first noted by Kolb, "A Note on *Tristram Shandy*." Wilkins nowhere mentions Prince Maurice of Orange, but Chambers does note that Stevinus was his engineer (see above, n. to 102.21–24); as does Horneck, *Remarks on the Modern Fortification*, p. vii: "*Simon Stevin*, for his excellent Parts and Learning sirnamed *The Wise*, was famous in his Time, and in great Esteem by Prince *Maurice* of *Orange* . . . . He seems to have been a better Mathematician than Engineer."

Of Peireskius, Charles Kerby-Miller (*Memoirs of Martinus Scriblerus*, p. 191) writes: "For generations after his death, the name of Nicholas Fabrici de Peiresc (1580–1637) was mentioned with reverence by collectors, antiquarians, and scientists. Bayle said of him 'that no man was ever more useful to the Republic of Letters than our Peiresc.' . . . Even in 1698 his name had a certain magic in it: Lister in his *Journey to Paris* says, 'But nothing pleased me more than to have seen the remains of the cabinet of the noble Peiresc, the greatest and heartiest Maecenas, to his power, of learned men of any of this age.' John Pinkerton, *A General Collection of Voyages and Travels* (1809–14), IV, 39." Cornelius Scriblerus hopes to "become . . . a second *Peireskius*" through his several antiquarian collections and "curious discoveries" (*Memoirs*, p. 97). Dr. Burton was also deeply involved in antiquarian studies; see below, n. to 143.22.

135.8   in my return . . . the *Hague*] Cf. Cash, "Birth," p. 133: "Dr Burton was excellently trained in his art. He completed the M.B. degree at St John's College, Cambridge, studied with the great Boerhaave at Leyden

. . . . He received his M.D. degree from the university at Rheims and settled in York about 1736 . . . ."

136.26–137.7   For that . . . use of them.] Cf. Warburton, *The Divine Legation of Moses*, 4th ed. (1755), book I, sec. 6, where in answering Mandeville on luxury, he points out that "it is not *luxury*, but the *consumption* of the products of arts and nature, which is of so high benefit to society" (I: 86).

See also Berkeley, "An Essay Towards Preventing the Ruin of Great Britain," in *Works*, ed. A. A. Luce and T. E. Jessop (London: Thomas Nelson, 1953), VI: 73: "There is still room for invention or improvement in most trades and manufactures, and it is probable that premiums given on that account to ingenious artists would soon be repaid a hundredfold to the public." For Sterne's possible familiarity with this work, see below, n. to 171.6–21.

139.7–10   He can read . . . misfortune.] Cf. Goldsmith, *Citizen of the World*, letter 119: "I . . . verily believe, that if I could read or write, our captain would have given me promotion, and made me a corporal" (*Works*, II: 463); the need to read and write was obviously prerequisite to advancement in the military during the century. *OED*, s.v. *Halberd*, 1.b.: "denoting the rank of a sergeant."

140.7ff.   But before the Corporal begins, etc.] R. F. Brissenden ("Sterne and Painting," pp. 99–100) provides an excellent commentary upon Trim's "attitude" and the accompanying Hogarth illustration: "Sterne has obviously amused himself by composing [the scene] as if it were a painting. Trim, the most important figure, is placed in the centre: in 'the middle of the room, where he could best see, and best be seen by, his audience' . . . . But Trim's importance is accidental and comical: he is socially the 'lowest' person in the company, he is not the author of the sermon, and he understands it only in a superficial way—he continually steps out of his oratorical role, and is far more distressed by what he is reading than are his auditors. The illustration of this scene which, at Sterne's request, was drawn by Hogarth, is completely in keeping with this spirit of comic inversion: Trim is shown standing in the classic pose of the orator, but with his back to the viewer of the picture, and not his front or his profile, as the conventions of history painting would demand.

"A striking feature of this scene is the detail with which Trim's attitude is analysed. 'Attitude', in the sense of a meaningful, expressive pose is, in the field of painting, a thoroughly technical term. 'The *Attitude* of a Figure', wrote Leonardo da Vinci in his *Treatise of Painting* [1721, p. 117], 'must be so conducted in all its parts, as that the intention of the Mind, may be seen in every Member'. . . .

"In his description of Trim, Sterne seems to have drawn mainly on Leonardo's *Treatise*, though he obviously had Hogarth's *Analysis of Beauty*, which had appeared in 1753, very much in mind also. . . .

"Leonardo's *Treatise* was not published during the author's lifetime, but was assembled from various unorganized manuscripts left behind after his death. As a result, his arguments often seem rambling and repetitive; and Sterne is perhaps parodying this, and pointing also to the perils of stating the obvious, in the excessively detailed account he gives of Trim's oratorical stance. But he is clearly in agreement with Leonardo's general thesis— namely that the painter and the sculptor must pay attention to the facts of anatomy and the law of gravity. 'A Man in bearing a Burthen', Leonardo remarks, 'has always the loaden Shoulder higher than the empty one . . . did not the Weight of the Body, and of the Burthen . . . thus make an *Equilibrium*, the Man of necessity must tumble to the Ground' [p. 112]." See also above, nn. to 16.1–16, 115.24–27, 121.6–10.

The importance of "attitudes" of painting for dramatic representation during the eighteenth century is amply indicated by a series of quotations in Holtz's *Image and Immortality*, pp. 12–13; e.g., "When you speak of yourself, the *Right* not the *Left* Hand must be apply'd to the Bosom, declaring your own Faculties, and Passions . . . . But this Action, generally speaking, should be only apply'd or express'd by laying the Hand gently on the Breast, and not by thumping it as some People do. The Gesture must pass from the *Left* to the *Right*, and there end with Gentleness and Moderation, at least not stretch to the Extremity of Violence"; quoting Thomas Betterton, *The History of the English Stage* (1741), pp. 100–101. See also Holtz's analysis of this passage and of the Hogarth illustration, pp. 26–28 and passim.

One might also approach Trim's posture through various eighteenth-century manuals of pulpit oratory, one of the most interesting of which is the short essay by the most successful preacher of the age, John Wesley. Wesley writes: "As to the Motion of the Body, it ought not to change its

Place or Posture every Moment. Neither on the other Hand, to stand like a Stock, in one fixt and immoveable Posture: But to move, in a natural and graceful Manner, as various Circumstances may require . . . . You should adapt all [the face's] Movements to the Subject you treat of, the Passions you would raise, and the Persons to whom you speak. Let Love or Joy spread a Chearfulness over your face; Hatred, Sorrow, or Fear a Gloominess . . . . Use the Right-Hand most, and when you use the Left, let it be only to accompany the other . . . (*Directions concerning Pronunciation and Gesture*, pp. 10–11).

140.9–12   in an uneasy . . . look determined] Cf. Hogarth, *Analysis of Beauty*, pp. 139–40: "what can be more conducive to that freedom and necessary courage which make acquired grace seem easy and natural, than the being able to demonstrate *when* we are actually just and proper in the least movement we perform; whereas, for want of such certainty in the mind, if one of the most finish'd gentlemen at court was to appear as an actor on the public stage, he would find himself at a loss how to move properly, and be stiff, narrow, and aukward in representing even his own character: the uncertainty of being right would naturally give him some of that restraint which the uneducated common people generally have when they appear before their betters."

141.8–9   cyclopædia of arts and sciences] Sterne's several hints that he is writing a book of universal knowledge seem to point to Swift, especially *Tale of a Tub*; e.g.: "I have been prevailed on . . . to travel in a compleat and laborious Dissertation upon the prime Productions of our Society, which . . . have darkly and deeply couched under them, the most finished and refined Systems of all Sciences and Arts . . ." (pp. 66–67). The idea that this complete system lies hidden behind an allegorical veil is perhaps borrowed from Rabelais; see below, n. to 268.8–10. The reference may also be to Ephraim Chambers's *Cyclopædia: or, an Universal Dictionary of Arts and Sciences*.

For "instrumental parts," see below, n. to 159.20–21.

141.9–11   eloquence of the senate . . . fire-side] This passage provides an interesting example of Sterne's technique of elaboration. The phrase "the senate, the pulpit, the bar" would appear to be a stock phrase of the age; see, e.g., *Critical Review* (November 1758), p. 387: "Were we concerned in educating youth for the senate, the pulpit, or the bar . . ."; or Thomas

Sheridan, *A Discourse . . . Introductory to His Course of Lectures on Elocution* (1759), p. 4: "oratorial performances, displayed in the pulpit, the senate-house, or at the bar." The remainder is Sterne's inventiveness.

141.19   line of beauty] Cf. 115.24–27 and n. above. Hogarth defines the "line of beauty," one of the central concepts of his *Analysis,* in chap. 7, much of which seems relevant to *TS:* "It is to be observed, that straight lines vary only in length, and therefore are least ornamental.

"That curved lines as they can be varied in their degrees of curvature as well as in their lengths, begin on that account to be ornamental.

"That straight and curv'd lines join'd, being a compound line, vary more than curves alone, and so become somewhat more ornamental.

"That the waving line, or line of beauty, varying still more, being composed of two curves contrasted, becomes still more ornamental and pleasing, insomuch that the hand takes a lively movement in making it with pen or pencil.

"And that the serpentine line, by its waving and winding at the same time different ways, leads the eye in a pleasing manner along the continuity of its variety, if I may be allowed the expression; and which by its twisting so many different ways, may be said to inclose (tho' but a single line) varied contents; and therefore all its variety cannot be express'd on paper by one continued line, without the assistance of the imagination, or the help of a figure . . . which will hereafter be call'd the precise serpentine line, or *line of grace* . . . represented by a fine wire, properly twisted round the elegant and varied figure of a cone" (pp. 38–39).

In addition to Brissenden and Holtz, cited earlier, see also Ronald Paulson, *Hogarth: His Life, Art and Times* (New Haven: Yale University Press, 1971), II: 302–6.

142.1–7   So much . . . stood in need.] William J. Farrell, "Nature versus Art as a Comic Pattern in *Tristram Shandy,*" pp. 27–28, argues that everything Tristram applauds in this description of Trim is "condemned" in Quintilian's *Institutes.* In particular, Trim's forward lean, his distribution of weight, and his palm turned outward instead of inward all reveal, Farrell believes, "his ignorance of rhetoric."

On the other hand, cf. John Walker, *Elements of Elocution* (1781; Menston, England: Scolar Press, 1969), pp. 266–67: "When we read to a few persons only in private, it may not be useless to observe, that we should accustom ourselves to read standing; that the book should be held in the left hand . . . . When any thing sublime, lofty, or heavenly is expressed, the eye and the right hand may be very properly elevated; and when any thing low, inferior, or grovelling is referred to, the eye and hand may be directed downwards . . . and when conscious virtue, or any heart-felt emotion, or tender sentiment occurs, we may as naturally clap the hand on the breast."

142.21ff.   The SERMON] See vol. II, app. 7, pp. 946–51, in this edition. The sermon has often been discussed by critics, most particularly by Arthur Cash, "The Sermon in *Tristram Shandy*," *ELH* 31 (1964): 395–417; Melvyn New, "Swift and Sterne: Sermons and Satire," *MLQ* 30 (1969): 198–211; J. Paul Hunter, "Response as Reformation: *Tristram Shandy* and the Art of Interruption," *Novel* 4 (1971): 132–46; Byron Petrakis, "Jester in the Pulpit: Sterne and Pulpit Eloquence," *PQ* 51 (1972): 430–47; and Michael Rosenblum, "The Sermon, the King of Bohemia, and the Art of Interpolation in *Tristram Shandy*," *SP* 75 (1978): 472–91. For a more general account of Sterne as a sermon writer, see James Downey, *The Eighteenth Century Pulpit* (Oxford: Clarendon Press, 1969), pp. 115–54; Hammond; and Downey, "The Sermons of Mr Yorick: A Reassessment of Hammond," *ESC* 4 (1978): 193–211.

143.8–11   for the writer . . . abuse him] Sterne seems to be commenting humorously upon his practice of beginning a sermon by disagreeing with his text; the most dramatic instance of this is in "The House of Feasting and the House of Mourning Described," the text of which is Ecclesiastes 7: 2–3: "It is better to go to the house of mourning, than to the house of feasting." Sterne begins: "THAT I deny—but let us hear the wise man's reasoning upon it—*for that* is *the end of all men, and the living* will *lay it to* his *heart: sorrow is better than laughter*—for a crack'd-brain'd order of Carthusian monks, I grant, but not for men of the world . . ." (I.2.24). It should be pointed out that Sterne does this far less frequently than one might imagine; the great majority of his sermons begin and end without such flourishes, though obviously the dramatic ones have attracted most attention.

143.9   snappish] *OED*'s first example is dated 1836.

143.15–16   he durst . . . his beard] Proverbial; variant of Tilley, B131: "You dare as well take a BEAR by the tooth." See also *ODEP*, s.v. *Take*.

143.20   he would . . . over his head.] Proverbial; Tilley, H756: "He pulls an
old HOUSE on his head" (i.e., acts rashly, gets into trouble); and *ODEP*,
s.v. *Pulls*.

143.22   I know nothing of architecture] Perhaps, as Doran notes ("Burton,"
p. 74), an allusion to Burton's antiquarian interests, manifested in his
Monasticon Eboracense (York, 1758). Among other things promised in the
lengthy title are "the Ichnographies of some of their Churches, Abbies,
Ruins, &c."; see above, n. to 110.21.

144.5–6   I never heard . . . *Toby*, hastily] Sterne appears to make a rare slip
here, since Trim tells Toby the entire story of his brother in 1713 (vol. IX,
chaps. 4–7, pp. 742–52), five years before this scene. Considering the
serial nature of publication, it is surprising how rare such errors are in *TS*.

145.13–17   "If a man . . . of his life."] Cf. "Self Knowledge" (*Sermons*,
I.4.80): "If a man thinks at all, he cannot be a stranger to what passes there
[in his heart]—he must be conscious of his own thoughts and desires, he
must remember his past pursuits, and the true springs and motives which
in general have directed the actions of his life." In addition to this passage
there are several others in "Self Knowledge" which reappear with little or
no alteration in "Abuses of Conscience." Quite probably it was written first
and served as a basis for "Abuses," although we have not been able to
establish a date of composition. It is perhaps worth noting that these two
sermons are the only ones in which Sterne borrows from Swift's sermons
(see Hammond, pp. 151–54). However, "The Difficulty of Knowing
One's Self," published with Swift's sermons in 1744 or 1745, is today
considered of questionable authorship (see Swift, *Prose Works*, IX:
103–6, 349–62). Further similarities between "Self Knowledge" and
"Abuses," and the borrowings from Swift's "Difficulty" and "On the Testimony of Conscience," are noted as they occur; but the three sermons
should be read in their entirety as important glosses upon the sermon in
TS.

145.20–22   as the Wise Man . . . *are before us*.] Ecclesiastes 8: 16–17:
"When I applied mine heart to know wisdom, and to see the business that
is done upon the earth: . . . then I beheld all the work of God, that a man
cannot find out the work that is done under the sun: because though a man
labor to seek it out, yet he shall not find it . . . ."

146.7–17   "Now,—as conscience . . . good also."] Cf. Swift's "On the Testimony of Conscience": "The Word *Conscience* properly signifies, that Knowledge which a Man hath within himself of his own Thoughts and Actions. And, because, if a Man judgeth fairly of his own Actions by comparing them with the Law of God, his Mind will either approve or condemn him according as he hath done Good or Evil; therefore this Knowledge or Conscience may properly be called both an Accuser and a Judge. So that whenever our Conscience accuseth us, we are certainly guilty; but we are not always innocent when it doth not accuse us . . ." (*Prose Works*, IX: 150).

Swift and Sterne may be echoing 1 John 3: 20–22: "For if our heart condemn us, God is greater than our heart, and knoweth all things. Beloved, if our heart condemn us not, then have we confidence toward God. And whatsoever we ask, we receive of him, because we keep his commandments, and do those things that are pleasing in his sight." Cf. 154.21–23.

146.24   liberty of the press] *OED*'s earliest example of this expression is dated 1769, s.v. *Liberty*, 2.b., but its use was certainly commonplace before then; for example, see *Peri Bathous*, p. 74, where a *"Rhetorical Chest of Drawers"* is proposed, which would contain *"perfectly new"* arguments for *"Peace* or *War"* or *"the Liberty* of the *Press."*

147.2–11   "At first sight . . . the judgment] Cf. "Self Knowledge" (*Sermons*, I.4.82): "We are deceived in judging of ourselves, just as we are in judging of other things, when our passions and inclinations are called in as counsellors, and we suffer ourselves to see and reason just so far and no farther than they give us leave. How hard do we find it to pass an equitable and sound judgment in a matter where our interest is deeply concerned?— and even where there is the remotest considerations of self, connected with the point before us, what a strange bias does it hang upon our minds, and how difficult is it to disengage our judgments entirely from it?"

Cf. *Spectator* 399: "We should likewise be very apprehensive of those Actions which proceed from natural Constitution, favourite Passions, particular Education, or whatever promotes our worldly Interest or Advantage. In these and the like cases, a Man's Judgment is easily perverted, and a wrong Biass hung upon his Mind. These are the Inlets of Prejudice, the unguarded Avenues of the Mind, by which a thousand Errors and secret Faults find Admission, without being observed or taken Notice of. A wise Man will suspect those Actions to which he is directed by something besides Reason, and always apprehend some concealed Evil in every Resolution that is of a disputable Nature, when it is conformable to his particular Temper, his Age, or way of Life, or when it favours his Pleasure or his Profit" (III: 495). This essay, by Addison, concerns self-deception.

Cf. also Sterne's description of the hobby-horse (86.11–15), which functions "by means of the heated parts of the rider, which come immediately into contact with the back of the HOBBY-HORSE.—By long journies and much friction, it so happens that the body of the rider is at length fill'd as full of HOBBY-HORSICAL matter as it can hold . . . ."

147.6   (as the scripture assures it may)] Cf. Proverbs 28: 14: "Happy is the man that feareth alway: but he that hardeneth his heart shall fall into mischief," and Hebrews 3: 13: "But exhort one another daily, while it is called To day; lest any of you be hardened through the deceitfulness of sin."

147.11–14   or that . . . thick darkness] Cf. Swift, "On the Difficulty of Knowing One's Self," *Prose Works*, IX: 358, 360: "For, as soon as the Appetite is alarmed, and seizeth upon the Heart, a little Cloud gathereth about the Head, and spreadeth a kind of Darkness over the Face of the Soul, whereby it is hindered from takeing a clear and distinct View of Things . . . . For, could his Enemy but look into the dark and hidden Recesses of the Heart, he considereth what a Number of impure Thoughts he might there see brooding and hovering like a dark Cloud upon the Face of the Soul . . . ." See 225.13–15 and n. below.

Sterne may also have had in mind Swift's theory of vapors from sec. IX of *Tale of a Tub*, p. 163: "For the *upper Region* of Man, is furnished like the *middle Region* of the Air; The Materials are formed from Causes of the widest Difference, yet produce at last the same Substance and Effect. Mists arise from the Earth, Steams from Dunghils, Exhalations from the Sea, and Smoak from Fire; yet all Clouds are the same in Composition, as well as Consequences: and the Fumes issuing from a Jakes, will furnish as comely and useful a Vapor, as Incense from an Altar. . . . so Human Understanding, seated in the Brain, must be troubled and overspread by Vapours, ascending from the lower Faculties, to water the Invention, and render it fruitful."

149.4–6   as *Elijah* reproached . . . *be awoke.*] See 1 Kings 18: 27: "And it came to pass at noon, that Elijah mocked them, and said, Cry aloud: for he is a god; either he is talking, or he is pursuing, or he is in a journey, or peradventure he sleepeth, and must be awaked." Sterne used the passage in "The Case of Elijah and the Widow of Zerephath, consider'd: A Charity Sermon," which he first preached and published in 1747 and later published in the first volume of his *Sermons* (see I.5.126).

Raymond A. Anselment notes that for both the "sixteenth and seventeenth centuries the prophet Elijah's retort . . . epitomizes a divinely approved use of jest" and was the "most documented illustration of divinely sanctioned ridicule" (*"Betwixt Jest and Earnest": Marprelate, Milton, Marvell, Swift & The Decorum of Religious Ridicule* [Toronto: University of Toronto Press, 1979], pp. 16, 66–67). See 389.4–5 and n. below.

149.7–9   "Perhaps HE . . . of his lust] Cf. Swift, "On the Testimony of Conscience," in *Prose Works*, IX: 153: "if he hath any of these Virtues, they were never learned in the Catechism of Honour; which contains but two Precepts, the punctual Payment of Debts contracted at Play, and the right understanding the several Degrees of an Affront, in order to revenge it by the Death of an Adversary."

149.9–13   Perhaps CONSCIENCE . . . of committing] Cf. "Self Knowledge" (*Sermons*, I.4.98): "Talk to him the moment after upon the nature of another vice to which he is not addicted, and from which perhaps his age, his temper, or rank in life secure him—take notice, how well he reasons—with what equity he determines—what an honest indignation and sharpness he expresses against it, and how insensibly his anger kindles against the man who hath done this thing."

149.25–150.3   Pray how many . . . he expected.] Article XXV of the Thirty-Nine Articles makes clear the difference between the Anglican and Roman positions: "There are two Sacraments ordained of Christ our Lord in the Gospel, that is to say, Baptism and the Supper of the Lord.

"Those five commonly called Sacraments, that is to say, Confirmation, Penance, Orders, Matrimony, and Extreme Unction, are not to be counted for Sacraments of the Gospel, being such as have grown, partly of the corrupt following of the Apostles, partly are states of life allowed by the Scriptures: but yet have not like nature of Sacraments with Baptism and the Lords Supper, for that they have not any visible Sign or Ceremony ordained of God."

150.7–12   Why, Sir . . . Seven plagues?] The seven golden candlesticks are mentioned in Revelation 1: 12, 20, and 2: 1. In the Ptolemaic system, seven planets were identified (Moon, Mercury, Venus, Sun, Mars, Jupiter, and Saturn), each with its own heaven, hence seven heavens. The seven plagues are discussed in Revelation 15–16.

Cf. Sir Thomas Browne, *Pseudodoxia Epidemica,* book IV, chap. 12, where Browne discredits the notion of the Grand Climacterical year of 63 (i.e., 7 × 9) by listing some of the many things that occur in sevens: "from the 7 Wonders of the World, from the 7 Gates of Thebes: in that 7 Cities contended for Homer, in that there are 7 Stars in *Ursa minor,* and 7 in Charles' wayn . . . . 7 heads of Nyle . . . . 7 Wise men of Greece . . . . 7 Planets . . . . That the Heavens are encompassed with 7 Circles . . ." (*Works,* ed. Geoffrey Keynes [Chicago: University of Chicago Press, 1964], II: 308–10).

150.16   strait-hearted] *OED* cites this passage as its sole illustration. Cf. "Journal to Eliza" (*Letters,* p. 351): "We must leave all all to that Being— who is infinitely removed above all Straitness of heart . . . ." Cf. *OED* entries for *straightheartedness* (1646) and *straight heart,* for which a Sterne sermon (I.3.58) is cited: "how often do you behold a sordid wretch, whose straight heart is open to no man's affliction, taking shelter behind an appearance of piety . . . ."

150.22–28   "Shall not conscience . . . *before me.*] Sterne alludes to the parable of the Pharisee and the publican, Luke 18: 10–12: "GOD, I thank thee, that I am not as other men are, extortioners, unjust, adulterers, or even as this publican." In his sermon on this text he had represented the Pharisee as praying: "GOD! I thank thee that thou hast formed me of different materials from the rest of my species, whom thou hast created frail and vain by nature, but by choice and disposition utterly corrupt and wicked.

"Me, thou hast fashioned in a different mould, and hast infused so large a portion of thy spirit into me, lo! I am raised above the temptations and desires to which flesh and blood are subject—I thank thee that thou hast made me thus—not a frail vessel of clay, like that of other men—or even this publican, but that I stand here a chosen and sanctified vessel unto thee" (*Sermons,* I.6.162).

151.17–18   Conscience . . . Letter of the Law] Cf. Romans 7: 6: "But now we are delivered from the law, that being dead wherein we were held; that we should serve in newness of spirit, and not in the oldness of the letter"; and

2 Corinthians 3: 6: "Who also hath made us able ministers of the new testament; not of the letter, but of the spirit: for the letter killeth, but the spirit giveth life."

Cf. also *Spectator* 456: "He is ever extremely partial to himself in all his Actions, and has no Sense of Iniquity but from the Punishment which shall attend it. The Law of the Land is his Gospel, and all his Cases of Conscience are determined by his Attorney" (IV: 109). This essay is Steele's; see also Addison's *Spectator* 459 (IV: 118–20), on morality vs. religion.

152.1–2   three times . . . go to confession.] The Fourth Lateran Council (1215) called for a minimum of one confession a year; why Slop says "three times" eludes us, unless Sterne was having a joke at his expense.

152.5   'tis a very short one] Hammond, p. 100, n. 5, demonstrates that Sterne's average sermon is quite brief compared to what might be considered the normal sermon length during the century.

152.15–18   That he must . . . to heaven.] Cf. *Sermons*, I.6.172–73 ("Pharisee and Publican"): "'Tis easier, for instance, for a zealous papist to cross himself and tell his beads, than for an humble protestant to subdue the lusts of anger, intemperance, cruelty and revenge, to appear before his maker with that preparation of mind which becomes him."

Cf. above, 122.19–20, where Dr. Slop crosses himself rather than holding on to his horse ("but the Doctor, Sir, was a Papist").

152.19   mental reservation] See above, n. to 124.9.

152.23   the wound digests there] See above, n. to 95.21.

152.26–28   thro' which . . . above all things] Cf. Jeremiah 17: 9: "The heart is deceitful above all things, and desperately wicked . . ."; and *Sermons*, I.4.79–80 ("Self Knowledge"): "a more remarkable instance of the deceitfulness of the heart of man to itself . . . . Scripture tells us, and gives us many historical proofs of it, besides this to which the text refers—that the heart of man is treacherous to itself and *deceitful above all things* . . ."; and VII.44.124 ("The Ways of Providence Justified to Man"): "For who can search the heart of man?—it is treacherous even to ourselves, and much more likely to impose upon others."

153.5–6   for a man . . . bubble to himself] Sterne seems to have liked this expression. See 28.20–21: "well-meaning people were bubbled out of their goods"; 237.24–26: "the great *Locke* . . . was nevertheless bubbled here"; and *Sermons*, II.7.3: "a man is altogether a bubble to himself"; and IV.26.137: "THERE is no one project to which the whole race of mankind is so universally a bubble, as to that of being thought Wise . . . ." Popular in the eighteenth century, this word for a deceptive or fraudulent scheme, or for the dupe or victim of that scheme, is obsolete today.

153.6–17   I must refer . . . and dishonour.] Cf. "Self Knowledge" (*Sermons*, I.4.95–96): "To conceive this, let any man look into his own heart, and observe in how different a degree of detestation, numbers of actions stand there, though equally bad and vicious in themselves: he will soon find that such of them, as strong inclination or custom has prompted him to commit, are generally dressed out, and painted with all the false beauties which a soft and flattering hand can give them; and that the others, to which he feels no propensity, appear at once naked and deformed, surrounded with all the true circumstances of their folly and dishonour." Swift's "Difficulty of Knowing One's Self" is almost certainly Sterne's source: "let any Man look into his own Heart, and observe in how different a Light, and under what different Complexions any two Sins of equal Turpitude and Malignity do appear to him, if he hath but a strong Inclination to the one, and none at all to the other. That which he hath an Inclination to, is always dressed up in all the false Beauty that a fond and busy Imagination can give it; the other appeareth naked and deformed, and in all the true Circumstances of Folly and Dishonour" (*Prose Works*, IX: 358).

153.18–154.2   "When *David* . . . he had done.] See 1 Samuel 24: 4–5 and 2 Samuel 11: 2–12: 14. Sterne returns to the same illustration, in the same words, as part of his demonstration of the failure of self-examination in "Self Knowledge" (*Sermons*, I.4.96): "When David surprized Saul sleeping in the cave, and cut off the skirt of his robe, we read, his heart smote him for what he had done—strange! it smote him not in the matter of Uriah, where it had so much stronger reason to take the alarm.—A whole year had almost passed from the first commission of that injustice, to the time the prophet was sent to reprove him—and we read not once of any remorse or compunction of heart for what he had done . . . ." Uriah is later called "a faithful and a valiant servant, whom he ought in justice to have loved and honoured" (p. 97), a description Sterne works into this paragraph. See also II.12.145 ("Joseph's History Considered"): "we read not once of any sorrow or compunction of heart, which they [Joseph's brothers] had felt during all that time, for what they had done."

Hammond, p. 110, suggests a parallel to a passage in Joseph Butler's sermon "Upon Self-Deceit": "Near a year must have passed, between the time of the commission of his crimes, and the time of the Prophet's coming to him; and it does not appear from the story, that he had in all this while the least remorse or contrition."

154.12–16   "So that . . . to your God] Cf. Swift, "On the Testimony of Conscience" (*Sermons*, in *Prose Works*, IX: 158): "It plainly appears, that unless Men are guided by the Advice and Judgment of a Conscience founded on Religion, they can give no Security that they will be either good Subjects, faithful Servants of the Publick, or honest in their mutual Dealings; since there is no other Tie thro' which the Pride, or Lust, or Avarice, or Ambition of Mankind will not certainly break one Time or other." See also Sterne's *Sermons* ("Thirtieth of January"), V.32.143–44: "a wicked man is the worst enemy the state has;—and for the contrary, it will always be found, that a virtuous man is the best patriot, and the best subject the king has. —And though an individual may say, what will my righteousness profit a nation of men?—I answer,—if it fail of a blessing here (which is not likely), it will have one advantage,—it will save thy own soul, and give thee that peace at the last, which this world cannot take away." See also *Sermons*, III.21.191–92 ("National Mercies considered"); and I.6.176 ("Pharisee and Publican"): "the great end of all religion . . . [is] to make us wiser and better men—better neighbours—better citizens—and better servants to GOD."

Cf. *Spectator* 399: "There is nothing of greater Importance to us, than thus diligently to sift our Thoughts, and examine all these dark Recesses of the Mind, if we would establish our Souls in such a solid and substantial Virtue, as will turn to account in that great Day, when it must stand the Test of infinite Wisdom and Justice" (III: 495–96).

154.17–19   What is written . . . say they?] Sterne alludes to Luke 10: 25–27: "And, behold, a certain lawyer stood up, and tempted him, saying, Master, what shall I do to inherit eternal life? He said unto him, What is written in the law? how readest thou? And he answering said, Thou shalt love the Lord thy God with all thy heart, and with all thy soul, and with all

thy strength, and with all thy mind; and thy neighbour as thyself." The
passage is again particularly apropos for an Assize sermon; Sterne again
discusses it in "Philantropy [*sic*] Recommended," *Sermons*, I.3.50−51.

154.21−23   if thy heart . . . *towards God*] See 1 John 3: 21: "Beloved, if our
heart condemn us not, then have we confidence toward God." See above,
n. to 146.7−17.

155.1−8   *"Blessed is . . . tower on high.*] Sterne conflates and paraphrases from
Ecclesiasticus 14: 1−2, 13: 24−26, and 37: 14: "Blessed is the man that
hath not slipped with his mouth, and is not pricked with the multitude of
sins. Blessed is he whose conscience hath not condemned him, and who is
not fallen from his hope in the Lord.

"Riches are good unto him that hath no sin, and poverty is evil in the
mouth of the ungodly. The heart of a man changeth his countenance,
whether it be for good or evil: and a merry heart maketh a cheerful countenance. A cheerful countenance is a token of a heart that is in prosperity
. . . .

"For a man's mind is sometime wont to tell him more than seven watch-
men, that sit above in an high tower."

155.15   fence against] See above, n. to Ded. 5−6.

155.21−23   I see . . . at some Assize.] The sermon was indeed preached by
Sterne in York Minster at the close of the summer assizes, July 29, 1750;
see vol. II, app. 7, p. 946, in this edition. Cash, *Early and Middle Years*,
p. 234, comments: "The sermon of a clergyman who is also a justice of the
peace, it is written for an assembly of judges, yet it comments upon the
inadequacy of human laws and the obligations to obey the higher, unwrit-
ten laws of reason and religion. . . . The Honourable Mr Baron Clive,
the Honourable Mr Baron Smythe, Sir William Pennyman, Bart (the
high sheriff) and the members of the Grand Jury were not displeased.
They unanimously requested that the sermon be sent to the press—or so
the dedication says."

Work, p. 133, n. 10: "The Temple Church, in London, where many
barristers connected with the Inns of Court attended divine services."

156.12   *Corps de Garde*] See Chambers, s.v.: "A post in an army, sometimes
under covert, sometimes in the open air, to receive a body of soldiery, who
are relieved from time to time, and are to watch in their turns, for the
security of a quarter, a camp, station, &c.

"The word is also used for the men who watch therein."

Chambers, s.v. *Corporal*, also makes clear the duty of the rank vis-à-vis the *Corps de Garde:* "an inferior officer in a company of foot, who has charge over one of the divisions, places and relieves centinels, and keeps good order in the *corps de garde;* receiving, withal, the word, of the inferior rounds that pass by his *corps de garde.*"

156.24   *Coup de main*] "A sudden and resolute assault." The *Stanford Dictionary's* first example is a complaint about its use from the *Annual Register* (1758), p. 373: "*Coup de main* and *Manoeuvre* might be excusable in Marshal Saxe as he was in the service of France, but we cannot see what apology can be made for our officers lugging them in by head and shoulders . . ." (quoted from *Stanford Dictionary*). Cf. below, n. to 242.18.

157.11   two *tables*] An allusion to the stone tablets on which the Ten Commandments were inscribed; the first and second tables refer to the two divisions of the decalogue, relating to religious and moral duties respectively; see Exodus 32: 15ff.

157.14ff.   "I said the attempt, etc.] Cf. Swift's "On the Testimony of Conscience": "The first of these false Principles is, what the World usually calleth *Moral Honesty.* There are some People, who appear very indifferent as to Religion, and yet have the Repute of being just and fair in their Dealings; and these are generally known by the Character of good Moral Men. But now, if you look into the Grounds and Motives of such a Man's Actions, you shall find them to be no other than his own Ease and Interest. For Example: You trust a moral Man with your Money in the Way of Trade; you trust another with the Defence of your Cause at Law, and perhaps they both deal justly with you. Why? Not from any Regard they have for Justice, but because their Fortune depends upon their Credit, and a Stain of open publick Dishonesty must be to their Disadvantage. But let it consist with such a Man's Interest and Safety to wrong you, and then it will be impossible you can have any Hold upon him; because there is nothing left to give him a Check, or to put in the Balance against his Profit. For, if he hath nothing to govern himself by, but the Opinion of the World, as long as he can conceal his Injustice from the World, he thinks he is safe" (*Sermons,* in *Prose Works,* IX: 152). Probably because of his audience of attorneys, Sterne diplomatically substituted a banker and a physician for Swift's tradesman and lawyer.

In "Advice to an Author," in *Characteristicks* (1711), I: 172, Shaftesbury dramatizes a quite similar view of human relations: "For thus, after some struggle, we may suppose [a man] to accost himself. 'Tell me now, my honest Heart! Am I really *honest*, and of some worth? or do I only make a fair shew, and am *intrinsecally* no better than *a Rascal?* As good a Friend, a Country-man, or a Relation, as I appear outwardly to the World, or as I wou'd willingly perhaps think my-self to be; shou'd I not in reality be glad they were hang'd, or broke their Necks, whoever they were, that stood between Me and the least portion of an Estate? Why not? since 'tis *my Interest*. Shou'd I not be glad therefore to help this matter forwards, and promote *my Interest*, if it lay fairly in my Power? No doubt; provided I were sure not to be punish'd for it'." Indeed, one may gain some idea of just how traditional Sterne's sermon is by noting that another section of the *Characteristicks*, "An Inquiry Concerning Virtue or Merit," opens with precisely the same issues that Sterne raises fifty years later: "RELIGION and VIRTUE appear in many respects so nearly related, that they are generally presum'd inseparable Companions. And so willing we are to believe well of their *Union*, that we hardly allow it just to speak, or even think of 'em a-part. It may however be question'd, whether the Practice of the World, in this respect, be answerable to our Speculation. . . . We have known People, who having the Appearance of great Zeal in *Religion*, have yet wanted even the common Affections of *Humanity*, and shewn themselves extremely degenerate and corrupt. Others, again, who have paid little regard to Religion, and been look'd upon as mere ATHEISTS, have yet been observ'd to practise the Rules of *Morality* . . . .

"This has given occasion to enquire, 'What *Honesty* or VIRTUE is, consider'd by it-self; and in what manner it is influenc'd by Religion: How far *Religion* necessarily implies *Virtue;* and whether it be a true Saying, *That it is impossible for an Atheist to be Virtuous, or share any real degree of Honesty, or* MERIT'" (II: 5–7). Shaftesbury, of course, answers these questions quite differently than Sterne; in fact, the sermon might well be considered a response to Shaftesbury's answers.

Cf. *Table Talk of John Selden*, ed. Frederick Pollock (London: Quaritch, 1927), p. 83: "They that cry downe morall honestye cry downe that wch. is a great part of Religion, my duty towards man: for Religion consists in these two, my duty towards God & my duty towards man. What care I to see a man runn after a sermon if hee cousen & cheats me as soone as hee comes home? On the other side Morallity must not bee without Religion, for if soe it may change as I see convenience, Religion must governe it, Hee that has not Religion to governe his Morallity is not a Dramme better then my Mastiff dog. so long as you stroke him & please him & doe not pinch him, hee will play with you as finely as may bee, hee's a very good morall Mastiff, but if you hurt him hee will fly in your face & tare out yor throate." See Hammond, p. 36, n. 7, for further examples from Stillingfleet, Swift, and Locke; and p. 162 for the similar idea in Tillotson.

See also Sterne's sermon "Advantages of Christianity to the world" (IV.26.158–59): "That the necessities of society, and the impossibilities of its subsisting otherwise, would point out the convenience, or if you will,——the duty of social virtues, is unquestionable:—but I firmly deny, that therefore religion and morality are independent of each other: they appear so far from it, that I cannot conceive how the one, in the true and meritorious sense of the duty, can act without the influence of the other . . . ."

157.21–25 "When there . . . of his motive.] Cf. *Sermons,* I.6.159–60 ("Pharisee and Publican"): "The pharisee was one of that sect, who, in our SAVIOUR's time, what by the austerity of their lives . . . had gradually wrought themselves into much credit and reputation with the people . . . .

"It is painful to suspect the appearance of so much good . . . ."

159.17 wanting in points of common honesty] Cf. *Sermons,* IV.26.139: "proving he has been wanting in a point of common honesty . . . ." See also vol. II, app. 7, p. 947, in this edition.

159.20–21 instrumental parts of religion] Cf. *Sermons,* I.6.174–76 ("Pharisee and Publican"), where Sterne preaches against being "caught by the pomp of such external parts of religion" and warns "that though the instrumental duties are duties of unquestionable obligation to us——yet they are still but INSTRUMENTAL DUTIES, conducive to the great end of all religion—which is to purify our hearts . . . ." Sterne altered the 1750 reading in "Abuses of Conscience" from "instrumental Duties" to "instrumental parts" (see vol. II, app. 7, p. 950, in this edition). He uses the

phrase again in *TS*, 715.18–19; see also 141.9. And see *ASJ*, p. 101: "I
guard this box, as I would the instrumental parts of my religion . . . ."

160.1   *"This likewise . . . under the sun*] See Ecclesiastes 5: 13: "There is a sore
evil which I have seen under the sun . . . ."

160.3ff.   For a general proof of this, etc.] This account of the Inquisition is
repeated more concisely in Sterne's sermon on Job (II.10): "To conceive
this, look into the history of the Romish church and her tyrants, (or rather
executioners) who seem to have taken pleasure in the pangs and convulsions of their fellow-creatures.——Examine the prisons of the inquisition, hear the melancholy notes sounded in every cell.——Consider the
anguish of mock-trials, and the exquisite tortures consequent thereupon,
mercilessly inflicted upon the unfortunate, where the racked and weary
soul has so often wished to take its leave,——but cruelly not suffered to
depart.——Consider how many of these helpless wretches have been
haled from thence in all periods of this tyrannic usurpation, to undergo the
massacres and flames to which a false and a bloody religion has condemned
them" (pp. 99–100).

Sterne may have relied upon Richard Bentley's "A Sermon Upon Popery" or William Wollaston's *The Religion of Nature, Delineated* in drawing
his picture of the Inquisition. Bentley writes: "What Bribes were hereby
procured? what false Legacies extorted? what Malice and Reveng executed? . . . Hither are haled poor Creatures . . . without any Accuser,
without allegation of any Fault. They must inform against themselves, and
make confession of something Heretical; or else undergo the discipline of
the various Tortures: a regular System of ingenious Cruelty, compos'd by
the united skill and long successive experience of the best Engineers and
Artificers of Torment . . . . The force, the effect of every Rack, every
Agony, are exactly understood: this Stretch, that Strangulation is the
utmost Nature can bear; the least addition will overpower it: this Posture
keeps the weary Soul hanging upon the Lip; ready to leave the Carcase,
and yet not suffer'd to take it's Wing: this extends and prolongs the very
moment of Expiration; continues the pangs of Dying without the ease and
benefit of Death. O pious and proper methods for the propagation of
Faith! O true and genuine Vicar of Christ, the God of Mercy, and the
Lord of Peace" (Cambridge, 1715), pp. 23–24. Wollaston writes: "Look

into the history of the *Christian Church*, and her martyrologies: examine the prisons of the *inquisition*, the *groans* of which those walls are conscious, and upon what *slight* occasions men are racked and tortured by the tormentors there: and, to finish this detail (hideous indeed, but too true) as fast as I can, consider the many massacres, persecutions, and miseries consequent upon them, which *false religion* has caused, authorized, sanctified. Indeed the *history* of mankind is little else but the history of uncomfortable, dreadful passages: and a great part of it . . . is scarcely to be red by a *good-natured* man without amazement, horror, tears" (7th ed. [1750], p. 382). See Hammond, pp. 105, 181–82. As with Trim's reading, Bentley's sermon was delivered on November 5, Guy Fawkes Day; for the anti-Catholic sentiment marking that day, see above, n. to 8.1–3.

William Warburton also wrote a sermon on the subject, which he preached during the 1745 rebellion, when anti-Catholic feeling was very high: "I shall stop a moment to hold you out a picture of *Virtue* unattended with that *Knowledge*; copied from no obscure or disgraced originals; but from such whose lives are preached up for examples, and their deaths commemorated with divine honours; . . . in one word, POPISH SAINTS. To understand this matter truly, We must consider, that *Virtue* consists in acting agreeably to those relations, in which we stand to our common Humanity, our Fellow-creatures, and our Creator [cf. *TS*, 154.12–19] . . . . But (holy Jesus!) should I relate the tricks, the treacheries, the frauds, the rapines, the delays, the horrors of imprisonment, the tortures of the rack, the bloodshed, the murders practised there, murders committed with so exquisite a malice, that *body*, *soul*, and *reputation*, are intended to fall a sacrifice at once—should I but represent, I say, these things to you in their native colours, your just indignation would endanger that heaven-born Charity, which it is my aim to recommend" ("The Edification of Gospel Righteousness," in *Works*, ed. Richard Hurd [London, 1811], IX: 169–70, 183).

Early in 1759, Adam Smith published his *Theory of Moral Sentiments*, which in its opening pages significantly echoes Sterne's portrait of Trim at this point: "As we have no immediate experience of what other men feel, we can form no idea of the manner in which they are affected, but by conceiving what we ourselves should feel in the like situation. Though our brother is upon the rack, as long as we ourselves are at our ease, our senses will never inform us of what he suffers. They never did, and never can, carry us beyond our own person, and it is by the imagination only that we can form any conception of what are his sensations . . . . By the imagination we place ourselves in his situation, we conceive ourselves enduring all the same torments, we enter as it were into his body, and become in some measure the same person with him, and thence form some idea of his sensations, and even feel something which, though weaker in degree, is not altogether unlike them. His agonies, when they are thus brought home to ourselves, when we have thus adopted and made them our own, begin at last to affect us, and we then tremble and shudder at the thought of what he feels" (ed. D. D. Raphael and A. L. Macfie [Oxford: Clarendon Press, 1976], p. 9). For a suggestive study of the relationship between Smith and Sterne, see Kenneth MacLean, "Imagination and Sympathy: Sterne and Adam Smith," *JHI* 10 (1949): 399–410. MacLean believes the idea of imaginative sympathy is apparent only in *ASJ*, but an argument could well be made that in *TS* as well Sterne examined a view of sympathy as "an experience of the imagination" lacking in moral content (p. 409).

160.9–12   Here *Trim* . . . the paragraph.] Sterne may have had in mind a formal rhetoric of gesture, but his description and those found in such rhetorics are difficult to compare; thus, Trim's motions may be those favorably described by John Bulwer in his *Chironomia: or the Art of Manual Rhetorique* (1644): "*Canon XX* The hand propellent to the left-ward, the left shoulder brought forward, the head inclined to the south-ward of the body, is an action accommodated to *aversation, excration,* and *negation.*" Just as possibly, however, Trim's gestures may coincide with those treated unfavorably: "To stretch out the hands in length to a racked extent, or to erect them upward to their utmost elevation, or by a repeated gesture beyond the left shoulder, so to throw back the hands that it is scarce safe for any man to remain behind them, to thrust out the arm, so that the side is openly discovered, or to draw sinister circles, or rashly to fling the hand up and down to endanger the offending of those that are nigh, are all prevarications in rhetoric noted and condemned by Quintilian" (ed. James W. Cleary [Carbondale: Southern Illinois University Press, 1974], pp. 181, 217–18).

160.14   saint-errant] Sterne uses the phrase in "The House of Feasting and the House of Mourning Described" (*Sermons,* I.2.26–27): "we are travellers, and . . . like travellers, though upon business of the last and nearest concern to us, may surely be allowed to amuse ourselves with the natural or artificial beauties of the country we are passing through . . . it would be a nonsensical piece of saint errantry to shut our eyes"; in "Penances" (VI.37.88): "as so many saint-errants, in quest of adventures full of sorrow and affliction"; and, if we accept Curtis's attribution (*The Politicks of Laurence Sterne* [Oxford: Oxford University Press, 1929], p. 98), in a letter published in the *York Gazetteer* in 1741: "we may impute it to the . . . *Officious* Saint-Errantry of his Religion . . . ." The attack in the last instance is directed toward Catholicism.

    OED defines *saint-errant:* "*ironical. ?Obs.* [Modelled on KNIGHT-ERRANT.] A saint who travelled in quest of spiritual adventures." The illustrations seem to make clear the ironic use of the term—a connotation of misguided religious zeal.

    Cf. Shaftesbury, *Characteristicks*, I: 20 ("A Letter Concerning Enthusiasm"): "The Crusades . . . are in less request than formerly: But if something of this militant Religion, something of this Soul-rescuing Spirit, and Saint-Errantry prevails still, we need not wonder . . . ."

160.22   tricker] I.e., trigger.

161.22–23   as pale as ashes] A proverbial comparison; Tilley, A339, and *ODEP*, s.v. *pale*. Sterne uses it again at 179.9, 545.16, 636.5. Cf. *Spectator* 12 (I: 53): "Stories of Ghosts as pale as Ashes . . . ."

162.1–2   as red as blood] Also a proverbial comparison; Tilley, B455, and *ODEP*, s.v. *Red*.

162.3   his body . . . sorrow and confinement] Cf. *ASJ*, p. 202: "I beheld his body half wasted away with long expectation and confinement . . . ."

162.19   I hope 'tis not in *Portugal*.] Sterne's reason for locating Tom's imprisonment in Lisbon, Portugal, is perhaps that country's particular contemporary reputation for excessive cruelty; see, e.g., Goldsmith, *Citizen of the World*, letter 5, February 7, 1760, in *Works*, II: 32, 34.

163.23–24   *By their fruits ye shall know them.*] Matthew 7: 18–20: "A good tree cannot bring forth evil fruit, neither can a corrupt tree bring forth good fruit. Every tree that bringeth not forth good fruit is hewn down, and cast into the fire. Wherefore by their fruits ye shall know them."

164.19   *Asiatick* Cadi] Johnson, *Dictionary:* "A magistrate among the Turks, whose office seems to answer to that of a justice of peace."

164.19–20   ebbs and flows . . . own passions] Cf. Sterne, *Sermons*, I.4.95
("Self Knowledge"): "according to their age and complexion, and the various ebbs and flows of their passions and desires." Swift has similar language in "The Difficulty of Knowing One's Self" (*Prose Works*, IX: 358):
"Nay, it is easy to observe very different Thoughts in a Man, of the Sin
that he is most fond of, according to the different Ebbs and Flows of his
Inclination to it."

See also *TS*, 669.16–17: "the passions in these tides ebb and flow ten
times in a minute"; *Letters*, p. 402: "we are all born with passions which
ebb and flow"; *Letters* ("Journal to Eliza"), p. 323: "the tide of my passions . . . flow, Eliza to thee—& ebb from every other Object in this
world . . ."; and *ASJ*, p. 70: "there is no regular reasoning upon the ebbs
and flows of our humours . . . ."

165.3–9   and if . . . the whole world] Cf. "Rabelaisian Fragment," pp.
1088–89, lines 37–45: "That if all the scatter'd Rules of the KERUKO-
PÆDIA, could be but once carefully collected . . . and then put into the
Hands of every Licenced Preacher in great Britain & Ireland just before
He began to compose, I maintain it————I deny it flatly, quoth *Pan-
urge*." Walter's discussion of the sermon would appear to be a vestige of
Sterne's original intention in the "Fragment," to write a humorous "Art of
Sermon-writing," perhaps in the manner of Pope's *Peri Bathous;* see New's
introduction to the "Fragment," p. 1083.

Some indication of Sterne's own preferences in sermon oratory can be
garnered from this passage and from an additional discussion in vol. IV,
where Yorick summarizes his views by stating he "had rather direct five
words point blank to the heart" (376.23–377.10; see n. below).

See also *Letters*, pp. 154–55, where Sterne describes his visit to the
Abbé Denis-Xavier Clément (1706–71): "most excellent indeed! his matter solid, and to the purpose; his manner, more than theatrical, and
greater, both in his action and delivery, than Madame Clairon, who, you
must know, is the Garrick of the stage here; he has infinite variety, and
keeps up the attention by it wonderfully; his pulpit . . . [is] a stage, and
the variety of his tones would make you imagine there were no less than
five or six actors on it together." See Curtis's note to the passage, p. 156,
n. 4.

Sterne's own pulpit delivery is analyzed by Arthur Cash in "Voices

Sonorous and Cracked: Sterne's Pulpit Oratory," in *Quick Springs of Sense: Studies in the Eighteenth Century,* ed. Larry S. Champion (Athens: University of Georgia Press, 1974), pp. 197–209. A primary piece of evidence is the contemporary remembrance of one of Sterne's own parishioners, Richard Greenwood, as reported to the antiquarian Joseph Hunter: "he never preached at Sutton but half the [congregation] were in tears— The Minster was crowded whenever it was known that he was to preach— he used often to preach nearly extempore. He had engaged to preach at [Farlington] . . . & when there found he had forgot his sermon—he only [asked] for a bible, & composed a most excellent sermon which he delivered from a scrap of paper no bigger than his hand" (James M. Kuist, "New Light on Sterne: An Old Man's Recollections of the Young Vicar," *PMLA* 80 [1965]: 549–50). See also Joel J. Gold, "Tristram Shandy at the Ambassador's Chapel," *PQ* 48 (1969): 421–24; and Downey, *Eighteenth Century Pulpit,* pp. 148–54.

   That Sterne's attitude is hardly unique in the century is suggested by John Mason's *An Essay on Elocution, or, Pronunciation* (1748; Menston, England: Scolar Press, 1968); e.g., "The great Design and End of a good Pronunciation is, to make the Ideas seem to come from the Heart; and then they will not fail to excite the Attention and Affections of them that hear us . . ." (p. 5); and again: "If you would acquire a just Pronunciation in Reading you must not only take in the full Sense, but enter into the Spirit of your Author: For you can never convey the Force and Fulness of his Ideas to another till you feel them yourself. No Man can read an Author he does not perfectly understand and taste" (p. 28). Mason then quotes Bishop Burnet's *Pastoral Care* (1692) to the same effect: "He that is inwardly perswaded of the Truth of what he says, and that hath a Concern about it in his Mind, will pronounce with a natural Vehemence that is far more lovely than all the Strains that Art can lead him to. An Orator must endeavour to feel what he says, and then he will speak so as to make others feel it" (pp. 28–29). The same idea is, of course, to be found in Aristotle's *Poetics* and Horace's *Ars Poetica.*

165.10–12   like *French* politicians . . . in the field.] This appears to have been a mid-eighteenth-century commonplace; cf. Fielding's *Jacobite's Journal,* ed. W. B. Coley (Middletown, Conn.: Wesleyan University Press, 1975), p. 422: "How unworthy are we to be called the Posterity of those glorious *Frenchmen*, who have so often made Fools and Bubbles of these *English*? And who have so often repaired in the Cabinet, the adverse Fortune which we have met with in the Field." That the dichotomy appealed to Sterne may be indicated by his repeated use: "my father, who was infinitely the better politician, and took the lead as far of my uncle *Toby* in the cabinet, as my uncle *Toby* took it of him in the field . . ." (250.11–14); and: "Then he has been as great, said my uncle, in the field, as in the cabinet . . ." (619.14–15).

166.4–6 *a priori . . . a posteriori*] I.e., an argument from cause to effect, or deductive reasoning; as opposed to *a posteriori*, an argument from effect to cause, or inductive reasoning. See Sterne's play on the terms in his dedication to vol. IX (733.1–7).

166.24–167.2 Can the reader . . . *Yorick*'s death.] See vol. II, app. 7, pp. 946–51, in this edition. The sermon was preached at the close of the summer assizes in York, July 29, 1750, and published less than two weeks later in York.

167.15–16 *Yorick*'s ghost . . . *still walks*.] Sterne's italics suggest an allusion, perhaps to *Hamlet*, I.v.9–10: "*Ghost*. I am thy father's spirit, / Doom'd for a certain term to walk the night . . . ."

167.17–22 The second reason . . . do it.] In May 1760, Sterne published two volumes of sermons with the title *Sermons of Mr. Yorick*; in the preface he wrote: "THE sermon which gave rise to the publication of these, having been offer'd to the world as a sermon of *Yorick*'s, I hope the most serious reader will find nothing to offend him, in my continuing these two volumes under the same title: lest it should be otherwise, I have added a second title page with the real name of the author . . . .

"I suppose it is needless to inform the publick, that the reason of printing these sermons, arises altogether from the favourable reception, which the sermon given as a sample of them in TRISTRAM SHANDY, met with from the world . . ." (I.[v]–vii).

Despite the ploy of two title-pages, the *Monthly Review* 22 (May 1760) was extraordinarily severe: "BEFORE we proceed to the matter of these Sermons, we think it becomes us to make some animadversions on the manner of their publication, which we consider as the greatest outrage against Sense and Decency, that has been offered since the first establishment of Christianity—an outrage which would scarce have been tolerated even in the days of paganism" (p. 422). To be sure, the reviewer (Owen Ruffhead) concluded that the sermons themselves abounded "with moral and religious precepts, clearly and forcibly expressed: though we here and there meet with an affectation of archness, which is unsuitable to Discourses of this nature" (pp. 424–25). And the *Critical Review* 9 (1760) was laudatory throughout: "IT is with pleasure we behold this son of Comus descending from the chair of mirth and frolick, to inspire sentiments of piety, and read lectures in morality, to that very audience whose hearts he has captivated with good-natured wit, and facetious humour. Let the narrow-minded bigot persuade himself that religion consists in a grave forbidding exterior and austere conversation; . . . we, for our parts, will laugh and sing, and lighten the unavoidable cares of life by every harmless recreation . . ." (p. 405).

Cf. 190.18 and n. below.

168.19   *en Soveraines*] "As sovereigns."

169.19–22   What I have . . . than elsewhere.] Cf. Swift, *Tale of a Tub*, p. 135: "I ought in Method, to have informed the Reader about fifty Pages ago, of a Fancy *Lord Peter* took . . . . Now, this material Circumstance, having been forgot in due Place; as good Fortune hath ordered, comes in very properly here . . . ."

170.10–13   In truth . . . second childishness] Sterne is thinking of Jaques's famous speech in *As You Like It*, II.vii.139ff., and especially lines 157–66: "The sixt age shifts / Into the lean and slipper'd pantaloon, / With spectacles on nose, and pouch on side, / . . . Last scene of all, / That ends this strange eventful history, / Is second childishness, and mere oblivion, / Sans teeth, sans eyes, sans taste, sans every thing."

170.21–28   To come . . . the whole world.] Walter's approach is diametrically opposed to that of Pope in his "Design" prefixed to the *Essay on Man:* "There are not *many certain truths* in this world. It is therefore in the Anatomy of the Mind as in that of the Body; more good will accrue to mankind by attending to the large, open, and perceptible parts, than by studying too much such finer nerves and vessels, the conformations and uses of which will for ever escape our observation" (p. 7).

170.22   steel-yard] Because of the concluding remark, Chambers, s.v. *Steel-yard*, is worth noting: "in mechanics, a kind of balance . . . by means whereof, the gravity of different bodies are found by the use of one single weight. . . . But the instrument being very liable to deceit, is therefore not to be countenanced in commerce."

170.26   *in infinitum*] "To infinity." Chambers, s.v. *Divisibility,* discusses the difference between the divisibility of physical and mathematical quantities, and notes: "We are not here contending for the possibility of an actual division *in infinitum,* we only assert, that however small a body is, it may be still farther divided; which we imagine may be called a division *in infinitum,* because what has no limits, is called *infinite."*

171.2−3   truth . . . bottom of her well] A proverbial expression traced to Democritus; see Diogenes Laertius, IX.72: "Of a truth we know nothing, for truth is in a well." The Loeb translator makes the point that "in a well" is inadequate for the Greek, which is better rendered "in an abyss" (II: 485). Rabelais speaks of "that dark pit, in the lowermost bottom whereof the truth was hid, according to the saying of Heraclitus" (III.36.240). Ozell's note suggests that the citation of Heraclitus is one of "Rabelais's affected negligences, so familiar to him. He very well knew that this sentence was ascribed to Democritus." Recorded in Tilley, T582, and *ODEP,* s.v. *Truth.*

Cf. 306.1−2: "getting down to the bottom of the well, where TRUTH keeps her little court . . . ."

171.6−21   He would often . . . of themselves.] Walter seems to echo Bishop Berkeley's "Essay Towards Preventing the Ruin of Great Britain," first published in 1721 and reprinted in his *Miscellany* in 1752; e.g.: "WHETHER the prosperity that preceded, or the calamities that succeed, the South Sea project have most contributed to our undoing is not so clear a point as it is that we are actually undone, and lost to all sense of our true interest. Nothing less than this could render it pardonable to have recourse to those old-fashioned trite maxims concerning religion, industry, frugality, and public spirit . . ."; and again: "But we are doomed to be undone. Neither the plain reason of the thing, nor the experience of past ages, nor the examples we have before our eyes, can restrain us from imitating, not to say surpassing, the most corrupt and ruined people, in those very points of luxury that ruined them. Our gaming, our operas, our masquerades, are, in spite of our debts and poverty, become the wonder of our neighbours." Berkeley even has his own "sorites": "Whether it be in the order of things that civil States should have, like natural products, their several periods of growth, perfection, and decay; or whether it be an effect, as seems more probable, of human folly that, as industry produces wealth, so wealth should produce vice, and vice ruin" (*Works*, VI: 69, 77, 85). Perhaps significantly, Walter does conclude with an "old-fashioned trite" maxim (see below, n. to 171.19−21).

Cf. n. to 136.26−137.4 above.

171.9   out of joint] Proverbial; Tilley, J75. Cf. *Hamlet*, I.v.188: "The time is out of joint . . . ."

171.13−15   making use . . . belonged to them.] Cf. Chambers, s.v. *Sorites:* "a kind of argument, wherein a number of propositions are gradually, and minutely laid together; and something inferred from the whole. . . . This method of disputing prevailed much among the stoicks; especially with Zeno, and Chrysippus. But it is very captious, and sophistical."

William J. Farrell ("Nature versus Art as a Comic Pattern in *Tristram Shandy*," p. 19) notes that Quintilian restricts the use of the sorites "for fear of appearing overly artful" and finds in the juxtaposition of Walter's "natural" talents and "artful" devices "an important technique for character creation" in *TS* (see 63.6−7, where Walter is said to "sometimes break off in a sudden and spirited EPIPHONEMA, or rather EROTESIS"; and 806.12−13, where he avails himself "of the *Prolepsis*").

Work, p. 146, n. 2: "Zeno of Citium [335−263 B.C.] was the founder of the Stoic school of philosophers; Chrysippus (c. 280−c. 206 B.C.), possibly a student of Zeno and next to him the most eminent member of the sect, was famous for his dialectic and logical skill." See below, n. to 190.3−7.

171.17−18   our poverty . . . our wills, consent.] Cf. *Romeo and Juliet*, V.i.75: "*Apothecary*. My poverty, but not my will, consents." We are indebted to Mrs. Muriel Passey for pointing out this allusion.

171.19−21   From the neglect . . . of themselves.] *ODEP*, s.v. *Take*, and Stevenson, p. 1772, record as proverbial the saying of William Lowndes, Secretary to the Treasury in the reigns of King William, Queen Anne, and King George I, as repeated by Lord Chesterfield in 1750: "Take care of the pence, and the pounds will take care of themselves." The idea has had many proverbial expressions (see, e.g., Tilley, P201, 202, 207, 213), but Sterne seems to have been familiar with Lowndes's particular formulation.

173.1–2   That an ounce . . . other people's] Sterne plays on the proverbial
expression that "an ounce of wit (discretion) is worth a pound of learning
(wit, clergy, folly)"; see Tilley, O87, and *ODEP*, s.v. *Ounce.*

173.6–13   Now . . . the identical place.] Walter rushes in where Locke
feared to tread: "Now that there is such a difference between Men, in
respect of their Understandings, I think no body, who has had any Conversation with his Neighbours, will question . . . . Which great difference in Men's Intellectuals, whether it rises from any defect in the Organs
of the Body, particularly adapted to Thinking; or in the dulness or untract-
ableness of those Faculties, for want of use; or, as some think, in the
natural differences of Men's Souls themselves; or some, or all of these
together, it matters not here to examine . . ." (*ECHU*, IV.20.5, p. 709).

The Cartesians were less cautious; see, e.g., Antoine Le Grand, *An
Entire Body of Philosophy According to . . . Des Cartes* (1694), p. 331: "the
Variety of *Wits* . . . can by no means or possibility be imputed to the
diversity of *Souls;* for in regard all *Souls* are *Intellectual* and *Incorporeal,*
and own no *Author* but GOD alone, they seem, according to Nature, to be
altogether equal . . . and then all the inequality which is deprehended in
them, must proceed from the variety of the *Organs,* and especially of the
Brain . . . .

". . . the Celerity of *Thinking,* depends much upon the disposition of
the *Body,* and . . . the inequality of the *Operations* proceeds from the
inequality of the *Organs.*"

Cf. *Sermons,* VI.38.129–30 ("On Enthusiasm"), quoted below, n. to
228.19–20. See also Walter Charleton, *A Brief Discourse Concerning the
Different Wits of Men* (1669).

But perhaps Walter has most in common on this point with the
eighteenth-century mechanists, especially the most famous, Julien Offray
de La Mettrie, who makes much the same point in *L'homme machine*
(1747; we quote from the English translation, 2d ed., 1750): "But since all
the faculties of the soul depend so much upon the proper organization of
the brain, and of the whole body, that they appear evidently to be nothing
but this organization itself; we may well call it an enlighten'd machine.
For in short, tho' man alone had receiv'd the law of nature, would he, for
this reason, be less a machine? . . .

"The soul then, is nothing but an empty term, of which we have no idea, and which a man of a right understanding ought to make use of, only to express that part which thinks in us. . . .

"Is there any further occasion, to prove that man is but an animal, made up of a number of springs, which are all put in motion by each other; and yet we cannot tell to which part of the human structure nature first set her hand. If these springs differ amongst themselves, this arises from their particular situation, from their different degrees of strength, and not from their nature; consequently the soul is only the first principle of motion, or a sensible material part of the brain, which we may certainly look upon as the original spring of the whole machine, which influences the rest, and appears to have been first form'd, so that all the other springs seem to derive their motions from thence, as we may easily perceive from some observations I shall make and which have been made upon many different embrios" (pp. 54–55, 66). For further possible allusions to La Mettrie see below, nn. to 630.19–25 and 657.11.

173.14ff.   Now, from the best accounts, etc.] Sterne's discussion of the nature of the soul is taken from Chambers and offers a good example of his mode of "learned" borrowing. Starting with the entry under *Soul,* Sterne found: "The philosophers are not at all agreed, as to the manner wherein the *soul* resides in the body. Some hold it equally diffused throughout every part thereof. Others say it influences, and acts on every part of the body, though it has its principal residence in some particular part, called the *sensory.* See SENSORY.

"This principal part, Des Cartes maintains, is the pineal gland of the brain, where all the nerves terminate *&c.*" This entry then refers the reader to PINEAL *gland,* which in turn refers to CONARIUM, where Sterne found: "a small gland, about the bigness of a pea . . . ."

From these entries he would have been directed to *Brain,* where he could find a lengthy discussion about living without one: "The *brain* does not appear absolutely necessary to animal life. We have several instances in authors of children brought forth alive, and surviving their birth for some time, without any *brain* . . . ." We are then told of the experiments of M. du Verney and M. Chirac, "the first of whom took out the *brain* and cerebellum of a pigeon; notwithstanding which it lived, sought food, had sense, and performed the common functions of life: the latter took out the

brain from a dog, yet it lived; upon taking out the cerebellum it died
. . . . To which may be added, many instances given by Mr. Boyle . . . of
animals living a long time after the separation of the head from the body
. . . ."

Sterne then returned to *Soul:* "Borri, a milanese physician, in a letter to
Bartholine, *de ortu cerebri & usu medico,* asserts, that in the brain is found a
certain, very subtile, fragrant juice, which is the principal seat or residence of the reasonable *soul;* and adds, that the subtilty and fineness of the
soul, depends on the temperature of this liquor, rather than on the structure of the brain, to which it is usually ascribed. This liquor, we conceive,
must be the same with what is usually called the *nervous juice,* or *animal
spirits.* The constitution whereof, is, doubtless, of great importance, with
regard to the faculties of the *soul.*" Finally the entry leads him to *Sensory:*
"SENSORIUM *commune,* the seat of the common sense; or that part or place
where the sensible soul is supposed more immediately to reside . . . .

"The *sensory* is supposed to be that part of the brain wherein the nerves
from all the organs of sense, terminate: which is generally allowed to be
about the beginning of the medulla oblongata . . . ."

See B. L. Greenberg, "Laurence Sterne and Chambers' *Cyclopædia,*"
MLN 69 (1954): 560–62.

In Francis Coventry's *History of Pompey the Little* (1751), ed. Robert
Adams Day (London: Oxford University Press, 1974), p. 38, Doctor
Killdarby argues with Lady Sophister about the immortality of the soul
and quotes the same passage from Chambers concerning Descartes and
Borri. The work was popular, reaching a fourth edition by 1761, but there
is no other indication that Sterne might have been familiar with it.

Martinus Scriblerus (*Memoirs,* chap. 12) also tries to locate the seat of
the soul, deciding, as does Walter, on the pineal gland (p. 137); later, in
"Double Mistress," we learn that he has been persuaded that "the Organ of
Generation is the true and only *Seat of the Soul*" (p. 158). Kerby-Miller
cites the relevant passage from Descartes, *Passiones Animae,* I.xxxi, in *The
Philosophical Works,* trans. Elizabeth S. Haldane and G. R. T. Ross
(Cambridge: Cambridge University Press, 1911), I: 345–46; he then
notes: "Like most of Descartes' theories, this one was regarded with a good
deal of skepticism and scorn in England during the early eighteenth century. The prevailing attitude is indicated by Elijah Fenton in *The Fair Nun*

(1717): 'We sage Cartesians, who profess / Ourselves sworn foes to emptiness, / Assert that souls a tip-toe stand / On what we call the pineal gland; /
As weather-cocks on spires are plac'd, / To turn the quicker with each
blast.' ll. 1–6" (*Memoirs*, pp. 286–87). Kerby-Miller also notes (p. 286)
that Prior ridiculed the search for the seat of the soul in *Alma;* see especially canto I, lines 30–79.

173.23   *Walloon* Officer . . . of *Landen*] July 29, 1693; see below, n. to
694.4–695.4. Tindal makes no mention of Walloons at Landen.

174.1–2   If death . . . from the body] Cf. Chambers, s.v. *Death,* quoted at
309.1–5, where a similar definition and a contrasting one are given.

174.4   Q.E.D.] *Quod erat demonstrandum:* "which was to be proved"; often
used for, but not limited to, mathematical demonstrations. John Burton
uses the term in his *Letter* (p. 87), after a particularly tedious contradiction
of Smellie; see below, n. to 176.1, for a full discussion of Sterne's satire of
Burton at this point.

For "certes" see above, n. to Ded. 2.

174.6–7   *Coglionissimo Borri* . . . letter to *Bartholine*] Work, p. 148, n. 5:
"Joseph Francis Borri (1627–1695), a famous chemist, empiric, and heretic. The letter referred to is *De Ortu Cerebri et Usu Medico,* written to
Thomas Bartholine (1616–1680), an eminent Danish physician. *'Coglionissimo'* is Sterne's formation on *coglione,* meaning, with an obscene implication, 'greatest dolt,' 'complete fool.'"

Coglione: "testicle."

If Sterne had read deeply in military manuals, he might have come
across the name of the famous Bartolommeo Coglioni (1400–1475), who,
according to Robert Norton (*The Gunner: Shewing the Whole Practise of
Artillerie* [1628], p. 40), introduced ordnance into the wars of Florence;
see below, n. to 689.24ff. Indeed, the name seems to have been something
of a joke among the Demoniacks; see Hall-Stevenson's facetious epigraph
to "An Epistle to the Grown Gentlewomen, the Misses of ****," where he
mentions one Bartolomeo Cogliane (p. [9]).

174.10–13   for, you must know . . . the *Anima*] Philosophy and theology had
long considered the possibility of two (or three) souls, primarily in order
to explain the difference between "life" and "mind" or "spirit." Johnson,
Dictionary, s.v. *Soul,* for example, provides as its first two definitions:

"1. The immaterial and immortal spirit of man. 2. Vital principle." In the eighteenth century, the idea of the two souls played a particularly important role in helping the natural philosophers (scientists) pursue their analysis of the physical world, while steering clear of man's relationship with God. A clear statement of the doctrine was made in 1751 by Robert Whytt, Professor of the Institutes of Medicine at Edinburgh; we quote from the second edition of *An Essay on the Vital and other Involuntary Motions of Animals* (Edinburgh, 1763), pp. 307–12: "MANY Philosophers have supposed two distinct principles in man; one of which has been called the *anima*, or soul; the other, the *animus*, or mind; by the former, they understood the principle of life and sense influencing the vital motions; and by the latter, the seat of reason or intelligence. According to them, we have the *anima*, or vital and sentient soul, in common with the brutes; but the *animus* or *mens*, which is of a more exalted nature, is proper to rational creatures alone.

"SOME modern Materialists have imagined the *anima* to be no other than a more subtile kind of matter lodged, chiefly, in the brain and nerves, and circulating with the grosser fluids. But such spirits, or subtile matter, can no more be acknowledged the vital principle or source of animal life, than the blood from which they are derived; and still with less reason can this material *anima* be supposed endued with sense, since matter, of itself, and unactuated by any higher principle, is equally as incapable of sense or perception, pleasure or pain, as it is of self-motion. Indeed, a few authors have run such lengths, as to suppose even the *animus*, or rational soul itself, material . . . .

"UPON the whole, as I cannot agree with those, who, in ascribing all our powers to mere matter, seem willing to deprive us wholly of mind; so neither, at the same time, do I see any reason for multiplying principles of this kind in man: and, therefore, I am inclined to think the *anima* and *animus*, as they have been termed, or the sentient and rational soul, to be only one and the same principle acting in different capacities." Whytt's conclusion seems to be Sterne's as well, although the issue is a most complicated one. John A. Dussinger's essay, "The Sensorium in the World of 'A Sentimental Journey'," pp. 3–16, which includes reference to Whytt but in a different context, is an excellent starting point. So is the very rich analysis of the doctrine of two souls by Lester S. King, *The Philosophy of Medicine: The Early Eighteenth Century* (Cambridge, Mass.: Harvard University Press, 1978), pp. 125–51.

Sterne's attribution of the doctrine to *"Metheglingius"* is a puzzle. Metheglin is a type of mead, made by fermenting honey and water, and Work suggests (p. 148, n. 6) an intimation that "such a theory must have been conceived when the philosopher was in his cups." Professor Eric Rothstein has suggested to us a punning allusion to Dr. Richard Mead (see above, n. to 12.5–9), whose medical writings were allied with many who held to the two-soul doctrine; see Robert E. Schofield, *Mechanism and Materialism* (Princeton, N.J.: Princeton University Press, 1970), pp. 50–51. We have not, however, found any reference to the *anima / animus* in his writings.

Jeffrey Smitten, in a note to be published in *N&Q*, suggests an allusion to Peter Browne, Bishop of Cork and Ross from 1710 until his death in 1735. Browne was an important popularizer of Locke's *Essay Concerning Human Understanding*, and in his own *Procedure, Extent, and Limits of Human Understanding* (1728) he makes a distinction between *anima* and *animus* (p. 148) in his discussion of the nature of the soul. Smitten believes that *"Metheglingius"* alludes to a well-known quarrel Browne had with the practice of drinking healths.

174.22   head-quarters] *OED* records no meaning other than military before 1851; Sterne's wordplay should be noted. For "sensorium," see above, n. to 125.9.

174.26   *Dutch* anatomists] Sterne may be offering a well-earned compliment to the Dutch medical establishment of the first half of the eighteenth century when, in particular, Hermann Boerhaave (1668–1738) turned Leyden into the medical center of Europe. Many of the great works of anatomy were indeed written by the Dutch during this period, including Thomas Bartholin and his son, Caspar, Philippe Verheyen, Frederik Ruysch, and perhaps most important, Bernhard Siegfried Albinus; see Leslie T. Morton, *A Medical Bibliography*, 3d ed. (Philadelphia: J. B. Lippincott Co., 1970), pp. 60–62.

On the other hand, Sterne may merely have had the connotations of "Dutch logician or commentator" in mind; see above, n. to 60.10.

174.27–175.1   seven senses] Cf. Ecclesiasticus 17: 5 (considered an interpolation): "They received the use of the five operations of the Lord, and in the
sixth place he imparted them understanding, and in the seventh, speech,
an interpreter of the cogitations thereof." While the passage may be considered the ultimate authority for Sterne's "seven senses" (and he repeats
the phrase at 432.3), it is very unusual to find anyone referring to more
than five senses, either in the Renaissance or the eighteenth century; e.g.,
Burton, *Anatomy*, 1.1.2.6 (p. 22): "the five Senses, of *Touching, Hearing,
Seeing, Smelling, Tasting;* to which you may adde *Scaligers* sixt sense of
Titillation, if you please; or that of *Speech*, which is the sixt eternall sense,
according to *Lullius*." Cf. *ECHU*, II.2.3 (p. 120): "This is the Reason
why, though we cannot believe it impossible to God, to make a Creature
with other Organs, and more ways to convey into the Understanding the
notice of Corporeal things, than those five, as they are usually counted,
which he has given to Man: Yet I think, it is *not possible*, for any one *to
imagine* any other *Qualities* in Bodies, howsoever constituted, whereby
they can be taken notice of, besides Sounds, Tastes, Smells, visible and
tangible Qualities. And had Mankind been made with but four Senses, the
Qualities then, which are the Object of the Fifth Sense, had been as far
from our Notice, Imagination, and Conception, as now any *belonging to a
Sixth, Seventh, or Eighth Sense*, can possibly be . . . ."
      But cf. Rabelais, IV.13.139: "The filly was soon scar'd out of her seven
senses . . . ."

175.9   temperature] See above, n. to 1.7.

175.15–17   wit, memory, fancy . . . natural parts] See 228.19–20 and n.
below.

175.20   *Causa sine quâ non*] An indispensable cause or condition, a cause or
condition without which a certain effect or result is impossible.

176.1   *Lithopædus Senonesis de Partu difficuli**] In 1751 John Burton published
his *Essay towards a Complete New System of Midwifry*, only to be upstaged
by William Smellie's far better received *Treatise on the Theory and Practice
of Midwifery* one year later. Smarting both at Smellie's failure to acknowledge his work, and at the favorable reception accorded Smellie, in 1753
Burton struck back in the 250-page *Letter to William Smellie, M.D. Containing Critical and Practical Remarks upon his Treatise . . . .* Sterne almost

assuredly had looked into the *Complete New System*, but at this point in *TS* he seems to be borrowing exclusively from the *Letter*, as was first pointed out by Ferriar, I: 130; and independently by "Jaydee" in *N&Q* 5 (1864): 414–15.

In particular, Sterne's footnote here alludes to Burton's having caught Smellie in the rather unfortunate error of mistaking the title of an illustration for the title of a book: "The seventeenth Author [listed by Smellie] . . . is *Lithopedus Senonensis*, . . . which instead of being an Author, is only the Drawing of a petrefied Child, when taken from its Mother, after she was opened; and this is evident from the Title, *Lithopædii Senonensis Icon*, which, with the Explanation, is contained in one single Page only. The Account of it, as published by *Albosius*, in 1582 [note Sterne's miscopied 1580], in Octavo, may be seen at the End of *Cordæus*'s Works in *Spachius*, . . . whence again, I think, it is evident you must have taken your Extracts from some bad Copier" (*Letter*, p. 21). It should be noted that Burton is unmerciful in his handling of this slip by his rival, commenting upon it on p. 1 ("if any Thing can be added to shock human Faith, or prejudice your Character as an Historian or Translator, it is your having converted *Lithopædii Senonensis Icon* . . . into an Author . . .") and at frequent intervals thereafter; his main point is that Smellie did not read the many authorities he cites but simply copied them—or even worse, had them copied for him—from Israel Spachius's *Gynæciorum sive de mulierum tum communibus* . . . (1597). Thus Burton also mentions that Smellie was misled into mistaking Albertus Battonus for Albertinus Bottonus by an error in Spachius's list; and in a note (p. 20), he adds that Smellie's attempt to correct his error by changing Albertus to Albertinus but failing to change Battonus to Bottonus confirms all his suspicions; Sterne's play with *Lithopædus* and *Trinecavellius* would seem to allude to this. For Sterne, whose penchant for index learning is nowhere more apparent than in this chapter of *TS*, a parody of Burton's irate attacks must have seemed particularly appropriate.

Maurice Cordaeus and Joannes Albosius were both sixteenth-century French physicians. Victor Trincavellius was an Italian physician of the same period, mentioned by Burton, p. 20.

See Doran, "Burton," pp. 16–21, and Cash, "Birth," pp. 140–42.

176.2   *Adrianus Smelvogt*] See t.n., vol. II, p. 849, in this volume.

176.2−4 That the lax . . . at that time] Cf. Burton, *Letter*, p. 122: "In my
Essay on Midwifery . . . I mentioned, 'that the lax and pliable Texture of
the Parts of the Child's Head, at Birth, greatly contributed to an easy
Delivery, because the Bones of the Cranium have little or no Sutures at that
Time, but are so thin and soft at the Edges, that they may slip over each
other . . . .'"

176.6 470 pounds averdupoise] Not in Burton; C. H. G. Macafee ("The
Obstetrical Aspects of *Tristram Shandy*," *Ulster Medical Journal* 19 [1950]:
17) avers that "The force . . . is grossly exaggerated . . . . At the most,
the force is somewhere between thirty-two to fifty pounds."

176.7−10 it so happened . . . pye of.] Cf. Burton, *Letter*, p. 90: "when the
Head is large, and has been any Time in passing betwixt the Sacrum and
Pubes, which, in general, are about four Inches ¼ distant, that then the
Head is moulded in an oblong Form, as . . . I observed. And you [i.e.,
Smellie] say . . . in all 'laborious Cases, the Vertex comes down, and is
lengthened in Form of a Sugar Loaf, nine and forty Times in fifty In-
stances;' which compressed Form, I must observe . . . is only about four
Inches Distance . . . ."

176.16−177.14 But how great . . . escapes uncrushed?] Cf. Burton, *Letter*,
p. 91, where Burton notes that Smellie uses the term "Vertex or Crown of
the Head" for that which others call "the Apex"; and pp. 122−24, where
he points out that "the Cerebellum is guarded from being too much compressed, or otherwise Convulsions or immediate Death, must ensue." Indeed, "the more the Head is squeezed, or resisted by the Bones of the
Pelvis, the more the Brain is forced towards the Cerebellum, and consequently, the Mischiefs abovementioned will ensue. Hence it is evident,
that the more Liberty there is for the Brain to be squeezed from (instead of
towards) the Cerebellum, the less this Danger is. . . . But all these Incon-
veniences are in a great Measure avoided, by turning and extracting the
Child by the Feet; because, in that Case . . . the Cerebrum is pressed
towards [the front of the brain] . . . and consequently does less Injury to
the Cerebellum than when the Apex comes first . . . . And Providence
seems to have intended this Method should be taken, whenever great
Force was to be used, by making the Bones of the lower Part of the Cranium so strong as to defend the Cerebellum from Injuries . . . ." In
fairness to Burton, it should be noted that he advocated podalic version

(feet-first delivery) only in difficult births, and discusses its dangers, pp. 117–20. In fairness to Sterne, however, it should also be noted that Burton argues against Smellie's position that one should wait for nature to take its course: "it is very evident, that whatever Method of Delivery either increases the Compressure, or prolongs the Time of it, must be the most prejudicial, and therefore ought to be avoided, if possible . . . . turning the Child must *always*, cæteris paribus, be preferable, because then the Head cannot be so long compressed; and the Injury to the Mother is at the same time less . . ." (p. 121).

176.21   Angels and Ministers . . . defend us!] The phrase occurs in *Hamlet*, I.iv.39. Sterne uses it again, 230.24.

177.20–178.7   When my father . . . as they] In the defense of himself that Sterne prepared in January 1760 (see above, n. to 12.5–9), he specifically refers to the page on which this passage first appeared, although for reasons not immediately evident: "the best judges . . . . all affirm (you say) that my book cannot be put into the hands of any woman of *character*. (I hope you except widows, doctor—for they are not *all* so squeamish—but I am told they are all really of my party in return for some good offices done their interests in the 176th page of my second volume) . . ." (*Letters*, p. 90). Even if we extend the reference to the end of the paragraph (p. 177), Sterne's intent remains obscure. Are we to assume that widows have grown as pliant as women in "warmer climates" and hence equally equipped to give easy births? No other passage in vols. I or II is any more applicable to Sterne's reference, which, we therefore assume, is not a miscitation.

177.27–178.16   It wonderfully . . . as she liked.] See above, n. to 71.3ff., and below, n. to 231.12ff., for Sterne's interest in climate-theory. Cf. Burton, 3.2.2.1 (p. 445): "Your hot and Southern countries are prone to lust, and farre more incontinent than those that live in the North . . . ."

178.17–179.12   When my father . . . to propose.] Sterne appears to have returned to Chambers, s.v. *Cæsarian Section*, for the substance of these two paragraphs: "It appears from experience, that wounds in the muscles of the epigastrium, or peritonæum, and those in the matrix, are not mortal; so that the belly of the mother may be sometimes opened to give passage for the child: but then it is not without great danger; on which account, this operation is very rarely practised, except on women newly dead. Those brought into the world in this manner, are called *Cæsares*, and *Cæsones*, *à cæso matris utero;* as were C. Julius Cæsar, Scipio Africanus, Manlius, and our Edward 6."

Work (p. 152, n. 10), believing Pliny (*Natural History*, 7.9) to have been Sterne's source, notes that it was *Manilius* Manius (who invaded Carthage in 149 B.C.) who supposedly was born by caesarean section, and not *Manlius* Torquatus. The error is actually Chambers's, compounded by Sterne, who obviously tried to display his learning by identifying the *Manlius* referred to; he probably had in mind the third-century (B.C.) consul (see *OCD*, s.v. *Torquatus* [1]).

Chambers, *Supplement*, s.v. *Section*, casts additional light on why Mrs. Shandy pales at Walter's suggestion: "Many have exclaimed against the cruelty of this operation, and certainly it is too terrible to be used on any, but the most emergent occasions; but there seem three cases in which it is justifiable, nay absolutely necessary. The first is when the mother is dead . . . . The second is when the mother is living, and the fœtus dead, and incapable of being extracted by the common passages by any help of the midwife. And the last, when the mother and child are both living, and there is found an utter impossibility of delivery any other way." Cf. John Glaister, *Dr. William Smellie and his Contemporaries*, p. 263: "Excepting [Sir Fielding] Ould in 1742, and Burton in 1751, no writer during Smellie's time even mentions the operation; so we may reasonably conclude that it was not an operation that met with much favour. Ould speaks of the operation as an 'unparalleled Piece of Barbarity,' and as 'this detestable, barbarous, illegal Piece of Inhumanity'; and he adversely criticized those who argued in favour of it. He believed that its revival at the beginning of the seventeenth century, and its more favourable consideration in France and Germany, were attributable to a theological doctrine laid down by the divines of the Roman Catholic Church, that as the soul of every child that is not baptized is annihilated, and that as the existence of the mother is already established, and as the rites of the Church were available for her, it was better for the child, whose spiritual existence was in jeopardy, to be saved, than the mother whose spiritual safety could be assured."

Finally, it might be noted that the first recorded successful caesarean operation in England, i.e., with the mother recovering, took place in 1793; see Morton, *Medical Bibliography*, p. 720, entry 6236.1.

Having discovered no reference to the birth of Hermes Trismegistus by caesarean section, we must assume that Sterne was simply preparing for the mis-naming of Tristram in vol. IV, and the part "Trismegistus" plays in it.

178.23–24   *oss coxcygis*] Sterne's unorthodox spelling for *coccygis*, the last four bones at the end of the spinal column. Burton, pp. 90ff., spends a considerable amount of energy refuting Smellie's assertion that the *coccygis* yields slightly during childbirth. It is perhaps worth noting that vol. I ends with an attempt to locate Toby's wound between the *os pubis* and the *coxendix* (see above, n. to 88.4–6), and vol. II with a similar anatomical description of the female, the pudenda being between the *os pubis* in front and the *os coccygis* behind.

179.9   pale as ashes] See above, n. to 161.22–23.

180.25–28   for not the sage *Alquife* . . . truth.] Sterne borrows directly from a footnote to *Don Quixote*, I.I.5: "*She means* Alquife, *a famous Enchanter in* Amadis de Gaul *and* Don Belianis *of* Greece, *Husband to the no less famous* Urganda *the Sorceress*" (I: 40n.). *Don Belianis of Greece* is a sixteenth-century Spanish romance; its endurance is attested to by British Library Catalogue entries for English chapbook versions dated ?1760 and ?1780.

NOTES TO VOLUME III

Plate   (frontispiece to vol. III)] See t.n., vol. II, p. 849, in this edition.

Title-page   (motto)] Sterne borrowed his motto, in all probability, from Motteux's preface to Rabelais, I, p. cxviii: "A learned and pious Englishman,
who was a bishop in France in the old times, and wrote almost as freely as
Rabelais, says, multitudinis imperitæ non formido judicia, meis tamen
rogo parcant opusculis——in quibus fuit propositi semper à nugis ad
bona transire seria." Motteux cites "Joan. Saresberiensis, in Policratico de
nugis curial"; the dash actually separates fragments of two sentences which
occur at the very end of *Policraticus*, book 8, chap. 25 (II: 425); noted by
Huntington Brown, *Rabelais in English Literature* (Cambridge: Harvard
University Press, 1933), p. 192, n. 1. Sterne's sentence, which Work
renders "I do not fear the opinions of the ignorant crowd; nevertheless I
pray that they spare my little work, in which it has ever been my purpose to
pass from the gay to the serious and from the serious again to the gay," is
his reworking of the original ". . . in which it has ever been my purpose to
pass from jests to worthy seriousness." It should be noted that John of
Salisbury (c. 1115–80) was the Bishop of Chartres, rather than of Leyden
(or Lyons) as Sterne's "*Lugdun.*" suggests. The origin of the error is unknown, though perhaps Sterne was confused by the fact that many of John
of Salisbury's works were published at Leyden—Bayle's *Dictionary*, for
example, used a Leyden edition in preparing its entry, s.v. *Sarisberi,
John of.*

185.1   "*I Wish*, Dr. *Slop*] Vol. I also begins with the words "I wish" and with
the intrusion of an "inappropriate" remark upon an ongoing activity.

186.7−8   chapter of wishes.] Sterne never wrote this chapter.

187.5   *India* handkerchief] I.e., from cloth made in India; as "thin persian" (190.1−2) refers to a particular kind of silk, attributed to Persia.

187.9−13   Matters of . . . upon their heads.] Irvin Ehrenpreis notes the prevalence of the doctrine of *maxima e minimus* in Temple and Swift, and suggests that "it was also a commonplace of historians well into the era of Bolingbroke and Voltaire" (*Swift: The Man, His Works, and the Age* [Cambridge: Harvard University Press, 1962], I: 123). Swift's "Ode to Sir William Temple" renders the idea poetically: "Great God! (said I) what have I seen! / On what poor Engines move / The Thoughts of Monarchs, and Designs of States, / What petty Motives rule their Fates!" (*The Poems of Jonathan Swift*, ed. Harold Williams, 2d ed. [Oxford: Clarendon Press, 1958], I: 29−30). Cf. Ehrenpreis, *The Personality of Jonathan Swift* (London: Methuen, 1958), pp. 64−65.

See also Montaigne, II.12.162: "The Weight and Importance of the Actions of Princes consider'd, we persuade ourselves, that they must be produc'd by some as weighty and important Causes: But we are deceiv'd, for they are push'd on, and pull'd back in their Motions, by the same Springs that we are in our little Undertakings. The same Reason that makes us wrangle with a Neighbour, causes a War betwixt Princes . . . ."

188.9−11   his whole attitude . . . he sat.] Sterne sat for Sir Joshua Reynolds (1723−92) in March and April 1760. Thomas Gray alluded to the portrait in a letter to Thomas Wharton, April 22, 1760: "Tristram Shandy is still a greater object of admiration, the Man as well as the Book. one is invited to dinner, where he dines, a fortnight beforehand. his portrait is done by Reynolds, & now engraving" (*Correspondence of Thomas Gray*, ed. Paget Toynbee and Leonard Whibley, corr. ed. [Oxford: Clarendon Press, 1971], II: 670). See Cash, *Early and Middle Years*, pp. 300−301, 315−16. William Holtz, *Image and Immortality: A Study of "Tristram Shandy"* (Providence, R.I.: Brown University Press, 1970), p. 29, calls attention to this passage as a possible allusion to Hogarth as well, the first of several in which Hogarth and Reynolds are possibly juxtaposed. See below, n. to 214.2−3; see also the discussion of Trim's "attitude" when reading the sermon, 140.7ff. and n.

The phrase "great and gracefully" echoes a standard dichotomy in the art criticism of the day, a distinction often made between Michelangelo and Raphael; e.g., see Jonathan Richardson, "Essay on the Theory of Painting" (1715), in *Works* (1773; Hildescheim, West Germany: Georg Olms Verlag, 1969), especially the section entitled "Grace and Greatness," pp. 93–123. And cf. *TS*, 215.15–16: "as in *Michael Angelo*, a want of *grace*,——but then there is such a greatness of *gusto*!—"

188.15–16   "*Coat pockets . . . in the skirt.*"] A good illustration of the fashion appears in one of the engravings included in the fifth edition (1710) of Swift's *Tale of a Tub* (facing p. 136); while Jack tears his coat to pieces, Martin gently picks at the sleeve of his own coat, which features a pocket "*cut very low down in the skirt.*" See also *Handbook of English Costume*, p. 52: "Early pockets were placed somewhat low but rose to just below waist level from about 1720"; and see the illustrations on pp. 48–49.
   Cf. *TS*, 666.3–4.

188.17–18   had he been hammering at it a month] Possibly proverbial; cf. *Two Gentlemen of Verona*, I.iii.17–18: "Nor need'st thou much importune me to that / Whereon this month I have been hammering."

189.4–10   transverse zig-zaggery . . . of that attack] Cf. 96.9–11: "my uncle *Toby*'s wound was got in one of the traverses, about thirty toises from the returning angle of the trench . . . ." *OED* cites this passage as its first illustration of *zig-zaggery; zigzag* is a term in fortification for an approach or trench carried on toward the besieged place in short turns or "zigzags," so as not to be enfiladed by the defenders.

189.18–20   A Man's body . . . jerkin's lining] Cf. Swift, *Tale of a Tub*, p. 78: "what is Man himself but a *Micro-Coat*, or rather a compleat Suit of Cloaths with all its Trimmings? As to his Body, there can be no dispute; but examine even the Acquirements of his Mind, you will find them all contribute in their Order, towards furnishing out an exact Dress . . . ."

190.1   gum-taffeta] Gum-taffeta (gummed taffeta, or taffeta stiffened with gum) was known to quickly rub or wear itself out. Hence the expression "to fret like gum-taffeta" became proverbial; Tilley, T8, points to numerous examples, including Swift, *Polite Conversation:* "Smoak Miss, you have made her fret like Gum taffety" (p. 151). Shakespeare uses velvet instead of taffeta: "I have remov'd Falstaff's horse, and he frets like a gumm'd velvet" (*1 Henry IV*, II.ii.1–2). *OED*, s.v. *Gum*, cites the present passage as its last illustration.

190.1   body-lining] *OED* cites this passage as its sole illustration.

190.3–7 *Zeno . . .* the Christians] Cf. Chambers, s.v. *Stoicks:* "a sect of
ancient philosophers, the followers of *Zeno . . . .* One of his chief followers was Cleanthes, who was succeeded by Chrysippus, and he by Diogenes Babylonius, Antipater, Panætius, and Possidonius among the
Greeks; and by Cato, Varro, Cicero, Seneca, the emperor Antoninus, *&c.*
among the Romans; and by Pantenus, and Clemens Alexandrinus, among
the Christians." Noted by Sir Edward Bensly, "A Debt of Sterne's," *TLS*
(November 1, 1928), p. 806.

If Chambers was indeed the source, Sterne's alterations are, as usual, of
interest. Three of the "Stoics" listed by Chambers are omitted from
Sterne's list—Chrysippus, Cicero, and Antoninus. Sterne had already
mentioned Chrysippus in relation to Zeno and the sorites (171.14) and
mentions him again as an orator (305.7); Diogenes Laertius writes of him:
"But for Chrysippus, there had been no Porch" (II: 293). Why Sterne
omits him here—and Cicero and Antoninus—remains a mystery.

Sterne's addition of Dyonisius Heracleotes and Montaigne is equally
puzzling. The former is perhaps a learned witticism on Sterne's part;
Diogenes Laertius tells of Dyonisius's falling away from the Stoic doctrine
because of a pain in his eyes: "Dionysius, the Renegade, declared that
pleasure was the end of action; this under the trying circumstance of an
attack of ophthalmia. For so violent was his suffering that he could not
bring himself to call pain a thing indifferent.

"When he fell away from Zeno, he went over to the Cyrenaics, and used
to frequent houses of ill fame and indulge in all other excesses without
disguise. After living till he was nearly eighty years of age, he committed
suicide by starving himself" (II: 271).

Cicero condemns him in *De Finibus*, V.94: "We think it was scandalous
of Dionysius of Heraclea to secede from the Stoics because of a malady of
the eyes" (p. 499). Montaigne treats him in such a manner as to suggest his
defection may have been proverbial to the learned: "And *Dyonisius Heracleotes*, afflicted with a vehement Smarting in his Eyes, was reduc'd, and
made to quit these Stoical Resolutions," he says in the midst of an argument
against the Stoic pride in "Apology for Raimond de Sebonde" (II.12.180).
See also Thomas Stanley, *The History of Philosophy*, 4th ed. (1743),
p. 320.

The inclusion of Montaigne as a Stoic is problematic at best; for any one passage in which he plays the Stoic another can be found in which he condemns "Stoic pride." But perhaps Sterne, like so many readers of Montaigne, remembered best his vivid essay "Of Experience," where Montaigne insists that whatever the "stone" does to his body, it never meddles with his soul; Sterne quotes from this essay in vol. IV, chap. 16.

Work, p. 160, n. 1: "Zeno [see above, n. to 171.13–15] founded, about 308 B.C., the sect of Stoics, who maintain that men should be free from passion, unmoved by joy or grief, and resigned without complaint to unavoidable necessity. Cleanthes [331– 232 B.C.] was a Stoic whose power of patient endurance earned him the epithet 'the Ass,' but who was so greatly esteemed for his high moral qualities that on the death of Zeno he became the leader of the school. Diogenes the Babylonian [c. 240–152 B.C.], a philosopher of great reputation, was at one time head of the Stoic school in Seleucia; Seneca relates (*De Ira*, 3.38) that when, while he was discoursing on anger, an insolent young fellow spat in his face, he bore the affront patiently, saying, 'I am not angry; but yet I doubt whether I ought not to be angry.' Dionysius of Heraclea [c. 328–248 B.C.] was a Stoic, praised for his moderation, until the pains of disease led him to join the Eleatics. Antipater of Tarsus (fl. 2nd C., B.C.) was the successor of Diogenes the Babylonian as leader of the Stoics. Panætius (c. 185–c. 110 B.C.), who had studied under Diogenes the Babylonian, became head of the Stoic school in Athens and wrote important works on ethics. Posidonius of Apamea (c. 130–50 B.C.), a Stoic philosopher, studied under Panætius and became the most learned man of his time. Marcus Porcius Cato Uticensis (95–46 B.C.), the Roman patriot, was a Stoic philosopher. Marcus Terentius Varro (116–27 B.C.), a learned Roman scholar and man of letters, was a 'stoicizing Platonist,' erroneously supposed to have been a professed Stoic [see below, n. to 211.6–18]. Lucius Annæus Seneca (c. 3 B.C.–65 A.D.) was a celebrated Roman Stoic and statesman. Pantænus (fl. 200), head of the catechetical school at Alexandria, was originally a Stoic. Clemens Alexandrinus (fl. 200), Greek Father of the Church, was an eclectic philosopher who adopted the moral doctrine of the Stoics and regarded Christianity as the revelation of perfect philosophical truth."

190.17   tickled off] Cf. 229.3–4: "how should I tickle it off!" Stout, "Some Borrowings," p. 113, notes that the phrase is used in Rabelais, prologue to book IV (p. lxxxii); and it occurs also in Dunton, *A Voyage Round the World* (1691), II: 100: "there's one . . . will tickle you off . . . ." Sterne also uses the phrase in his "Rabelaisian Fragment," p. 1089, line 79.

190.18   these last nine months together] On June 9, 1760, Sterne wrote to Warburton: "I am just sitting down to go on with Tristram . . ." (*Letters*, p. 112). On August 3, 1760, he wrote to Mrs. Fenton: "I have just finished one volume of Shandy . . ." (*Letters*, p. 120). Nine months previous to this, then, would be the fall of 1759, when Sterne was preparing vols. I and II of *TS*—and perhaps he is glancing at the many imitations which almost immediately began to plague him: " 'God forgive me' " (he wrote to Mary Macartney) " 'for the Volumes of Ribaldry I've been the cause of'—now I say, god forgive them—and tis the pray'r I constantly put up for those who use me most unhandsomely . . ." (*Letters*, p. 118). What Sterne most likely had in mind, however, may be revealed by his allusion in the next paragraph to the "monthly Reviewers" (line 26) and in the one that follows to "last MAY" (191.7). In May 1760, Sterne published his two-volume *Sermons of Mr. Yorick*; see above, n. to 167.17−22, for the violent reactions of the *Monthly Review*. Sterne began vol. III only a week or so after this review appeared, so we can assume either that this passage is a later interpolation or that Sterne kept a very clear focus on when his readers would have vol. III in hand.

For a full discussion of the reception of *TS* and the *Sermons*, see Alan B. Howes, *Yorick and the Critics* (New Haven: Yale University Press, 1958); Howes reorganized the materials in this volume in *Sterne: The Critical Heritage* (London: Routledge & Kegan Paul, 1974).

190.20−22   pell mell, helter skelter . . . long way] Cf. 454.29−31 and 724.22. Rabelais uses *ding dong* in this manner in V.22.150 and V.31.193. Cervantes has a similar passage (II.III.19): "Then *Corchuelo* flew at him like a Fury, helter skelter, cut and thrust, backstroke and forestroke, single and double, and laid on like any Lion" (III: 171). Sterne had combined the phrases in the "Rabelaisian Fragment": "a Flood of Tears which falling down helter skelter, ding dong . . ." (p. 1090, lines 91−93). See Stout, "Some Borrowings," p. 114.

191.11−15   than my uncle . . . and me."] Cf. 131.3−7.

191.19−21   he must . . . natural colour] In chap. 14 of *The Analysis of Beauty* (1753), pp. 113−17, Hogarth sets forth a system of coloring on a scale of 1 to 7; if Sterne is again alluding to Hogarth (see above, n. to 188.9–11), he is describing a very red face indeed, one half a tint from the darkest possible red.

OED cites this passage as its sole illustration of a burlesque nonce word formed by blending *scientifically* and *tint*.

192.6–7 he would . . . the same pitch] Sterne uses this musical metaphor again, 379.22–25: "he . . . had gradually skrewed up every nerve and muscle in his face, to the utmost pitch the instrument would bear"; see also "Rabelaisian Fragment," pp. 1090–91, lines 119–24.

192.8–10 like the sixth . . . *con strepito*] Work, p. 163, n. 1: "The reference is to the second movement of the sixth concerto in the collection of *Twelve Concerto's in Seven Parts for Four Violins, One Alto Viola, a Violincello, and a Thorough Bass, Done from Two Books of Lessons for the Harpsichord Composed by Sig. Domenico Scarlatti . . . by C[harles] Avison* (London, 1744). Scarlatti (1685–1757) was an Italian harpsichord player and composer of great excellence; Avison (c. 1710–1770) was an English composer and writer on music with whose best-known work, *An Essay on Musical Expression*, Sterne was probably familiar." See above, n. to 116.1–2; and below, n. to 331.9–12.

Con furia: "with fury"; *con strepito:* "with noise, noisily."

193.18 cornish] I.e., cornice.

193.19 buccinatory] *OED* cites this passage as its first example; the *buccinator* is the "chief muscle employed in the act of blowing."

194.23 *tire-tête, forceps* and *squirt*] See above, n. to 127.1–3.

194.24 *Hymen*] Cf. William King, *An Historical Account of the Heathen Gods and Heroes* (1710): "Hymenæus, the God presiding over Marriage, and the Protector of Virgins, was the Son of Bacchus and Venus Urania, born in Attica, where he used to rescue Virgins carried away by Thieves, and restore them to their Parents" (Carbondale: Southern Illinois University Press, 1965), p. 139. Cf. *OCD*'s far less imaginative account.

195.5 patriots] As Stout (*ASJ*, p. 227, n. to lines 44–45) points out, "After the 'patriots' led by Pulteney, Carteret, the elder Pitt, et al. came to power in 1742, after Walpole's resignation, their conduct brought professions of 'patriotism' into disrepute, and 'patriot' was widely used as an ironic term for 'a factious disturber of the government' (Johnson, *Dictionary*, 4th ed. [London, 1773]; see also his *Patriot* [London, 1774])."

Cf. Fielding, *True Patriot* 2 (November 12, 1745): "this Word *Patriot* hath of late Years been very scandalously abused by some Persons . . . . Ambition, Avarice, Revenge, Envy, Malice, every bad Passion in the Mind of Man, have cloaked themselves under this amiable Character, and have misrepresented Persons and Things in unjust Colours to the Public."

Cf. also *TS*, 415.23ff., where Walter instructs Obadiah to saddle "PA-TRIOT," only to be informed that "PATRIOT is sold."

195.17   *scrip*-tical,—squirtical] Nonce words, the first unrecorded in *OED* and the latter its sole illustration. Cf. 72.2–6.

195.19   caball-istical] A play on *cabalistic* and *caballus* (Latin for "a pack horse, a nag"). In "Life of Rabelais," which prefaces the Ozell edition, the story is told of how Rabelais had his horse (or mule) admitted to the degree of doctor of physic by the faculty of Orange (or Orleans) under the name Johannes Caballus (I, p. xiv).

196.3   cross-tied] *OED*, s.v. *cross-* 6, cites this passage as its sole example.

196.5   round-abouts] Unrecorded in *OED* for this usage.

196.7   three fifths of *Job*'s patience] Cf. 117.7 and n. above.

196.17–18   Sport of small accidents] Cf. 8.21ff.

197.1   GREAT wits jump] I.e., great wits agree or coincide. Cf. Cervantes, II.III.37 (IV: 29): "Good Wits jump"; cited by Stout, "Borrowings," p. 114. But see also Swift, *Polite Conversation*, p. 102, and Dunton, *A Voyage*, I: 122 and II: 107; the term was indeed a commonplace and appears in Tilley, W578, and *ODEP*, s.v. *Good*. Cf. 219.9–12: "the sentence and the argument in that case jumping closely in one point, so like the two lines which form the salient angle of a raveline . . ."; and 461.8–9: "the trine and sextil aspects have jumped awry . . . ."

197.8–14   the thought floated . . . one side.] The image is a commonplace one for the eighteenth century, receiving its best statement, perhaps, in Pope's famous lines: "The rising tempest puts in act the soul, / Parts it may ravage, but preserves the whole. / On life's vast ocean diversely we sail, / Reason the card, but Passion is the gale . . ." (*Essay on Man*, II.105–8, pp. 67–68; see also Mack's extensive nn. on the passage). Locke has some relevant passages in *ECHU:* "These, and a Million of other such Propositions, as many at least, as we have distinct *Ideas*, every Man in his Wits . . . must necessarily assent to (I.2.18, p. 57); "And so [without pleasure and pain] we should neither stir our Bodies, nor employ our Minds; but let our Thoughts (if I may so call it) run a drift, without any direction or design; and suffer the *Ideas* of our Minds, like unregarded shadows, to make their appearances there, as it happen'd, without attending to them" (II.7.3, p. 129); "When *Ideas* float in our mind, without any reflection or regard of the Understanding, it is that, which the French call *Reverie;* our Language has scarce a name for it . . . (II.19.1, p. 227). Sir William Temple ("Of Poetry," in *Works* [1720], I: 249), offers a similar image: "for the Mind of Man is like the Sea, which is neither agreeable to the Beholder nor the Voyager in a Calm or in a Storm, but is so to both when a little agitated by gentle Gales; and so the Mind, when moved by soft and easy Passions and Affections."

Finally, cf. Montaigne, II.12.275 ("Apology for Raimond de Sebonde"): "The Shocks and Justles, that the Soul receives from the Body's Passions can do much in it, but its own can do a great deal more: To which it is so subjected, that perhaps it is to be made good, that it has no other Pace and Motion, but from the Breath of those Winds, without the Agitation of which, it would be becalm'd and without Action, like a Ship in the middle of the Sea, to which the Winds have deny'd their Assistance . . . ."

198.2–4   Mr. *Hammond Shandy* . . . affair] James Scott, Duke of Monmouth (1649–85), bastard son of Charles II, returned from exile in the late spring of 1685 to claim the throne from James II. The attempt ended in disaster and he was executed.

John Tutchin's *A New Martyrology; or The Bloody Assizes* (1689) and his *Impartial History of the Life and Death of George Lord Jeffreys* (1689) contain no mention of a Hammond, though the latter lists 239 people executed by Jeffreys in "*Monmouth*'s affair." There were several staunchly Protestant Hammonds who might have been in Sterne's mind. The most famous, Henry H., author of the well-known *Practical Catechism* [1644], died in 1660; and Samuel H., a nonconformist divine said to have been a "butcher's son of York," died in 1665; for these and others, see *DNB*. None seems an especially likely candidate for Hammond Shandy, however; perhaps O. P. James is correct in suggesting an allusion to the hanging of Haman in the Book of Esther 7: 9–10 (*The Relation of "Tristram Shandy" to the Life of Sterne* [Hague: Mouton, 1966], p. 43).

Cf. Rabelais, III.16.110: "a certain Sydonian merchant of a low stature, but high fancy."

198.13   *implication*] Latin *implico:* "enfold, embrace, join," with the idea of an intimate connection; that Sterne is perhaps punning has been suggested by Richard A. Lanham, *"Tristram Shandy" and the Games of Pleasure* (Berkeley: University of California Press, 1973), p. 63, n. 19.

198.16–19   In the case . . . through them.] Sterne's elaborate emphasis on knots and knives at this point is readily apparent, although its precise meaning is elusive. In part, the image is that of the Gordian knot; cf. 332.22–23: "That is cutting the knot, said my father, instead of untying it." In part, it may allude to the marriage (love) knot, and to a folk-superstition about knives; cf. 664.18ff.: "A daughter of Eve . . . had better be fifty leagues off—or in her warm bed—or playing with a case-knife—or any thing you please—than make a man the object of her attention, when the house and all the furniture is her own." Swift, *Polite Conversation*, p. 71, perhaps glosses both passages: "*Miss.* Pray, Colonel, make me a Present of that pretty Knife. . . . *Col.* Not for the World, dear Miss, it will cut Love." Partridge calls the exchange "an allusion to the very old superstition that one should never give anything sharp to one's beloved—at least, before marriage." See also W. Carew Hazlitt, *Faiths and Folklore of the British Isles* (1905; New York: Benjamin Blom, 1965), II: 358.

In addition, Sterne may be glancing at *knot:* "to copulate"; J. S. Farmer and W. E. Henley, *Slang and Its Analogues* (1890–1904), cite *Othello*, IV.ii.61–62: "keep it as a cestern for foul toads / To knot and gender in!" Certainly his pun on *implico* (line 13) suggests this possibility, in which case-*knife* may simply be yet one more phallus-shaped object.

Finally, Sterne would seem to have some awareness of the mythical association of knots and childbirth. See J. G. Frazer, *The Golden Bough*, 3d ed. (London: Macmillan, 1911), pt. 2, pp. 294–300; and *Funk and Wagnalls Standard Dictionary of Folklore* (New York, 1949), s.v. *Knots:* "In medieval Europe whoever tied a knot during a wedding ceremony thus prevented the young couple from ever having children. . . . In Scotland as late as the eighteenth century this was the principal popular belief in regard to knots: the obstruction of the consummation of a marriage.

"It is a common world practice to untie all knots during childbirth to facilitate the birth. This was done in ancient Persia, was a practice of ancient Semitic peoples, is still widely observed all over rural Europe today . . . . Every knot in the house is untied during a birth, including those in the garments of inmates . . . ." Robert Gorham Davis, "Sterne and the Delineation of the Modern Novel," in *Winged Skull*, p. 38, alludes to this possible association. See also Leigh A. Ehlers, "Mrs. Shandy's 'Lint and Basilicon': The Importance of Women in *Tristram Shandy*," *SAR* 46 (1981): 71–72, for an interesting argument concerning the use of knots throughout the work.

198.22–23   his favourite instrument] Cf. 127.1–3 and n. above. Much of John Burton's complaint in his *Letter to William Smellie, M.D.* (1753) is that Smellie was too eager to use forceps, which Burton considered dangerous; see, e.g., p. 205: "I can't proceed without observing, that you still are for using your beloved Forceps upon all possible Occasions, whether it be the properest Method or not." But Burton seems to have been equally committed to the forceps he invented, as noted above.

198.26–27   alas! the nails . . . were cut close.] See above, n. to 10.4ff., William Sermon's list of desirable attributes for a midwife, which includes "their nails pared very close." Obviously this was intended to avoid injury to the mother and infant during delivery.

199.3–6   Lord! . . . undone for this bout] Cf. Swift, *Polite Conversation*, pp. 66–67: "*Col.* Ods so, I have cut my Thumb with this cursed Knife. *Lady Answ.* Ay, that was your Mother's Fault; because she only warned you not to cut your Fingers. *Lady Sm.* No, no; 'tis only Fools cut their Fingers, but Wise Folks cut their Thumbs." Partridge comments: "this late 17th–20th century proverb (rare in the 20th) has variant 'wise men'. Sense: 'the follies of the wise are prodigious' . . . ."

That Slop says he is "undone for this bout" is perhaps explained by Burton's description of the operation of the forceps in both his *New System of Midwifry* (1751), pp. 387–89, and *Letter to Smellie*, p. 142; we quote from the latter, where he describes placing the blades of the forceps around the infant's head and then adds: "I fix the great Skrew with my right Thumb, which holds the Instrument, so that pulling as strongly as I will, the Head can be no more squeezed thereby, neither can the Instrument so easily slip . . . ." However, it should be noted that Slop later asserts that were it not for his forceps, his cut thumb might well prove disastrous for the Shandy family (217.11–16); and only after a trial demonstration does he admit to being a "little aukward" because of the cut (220.9–10 and n. below).

200.4–5 *"Injuries come only from the heart"*] Sterne's italics and quotation marks indicate a direct quotation, but the closest we have come is *Henry V*, IV.viii.46: "All offenses, my lord, come from the heart." In *Sermons*, II.12.161 ("Forgiveness of Injuries"), there is a passage quoted from Ecclesiasticus 19: 16, which has much the same meaning: "There is one that slippeth in his speech, but not from his heart; and who is he that hath not offended with his tongue?"

200.6 *Cervantick* gravity] Cf. n. to 34.25 above (*"cervantick* tone"). Pope, in the *Dunciad*(A), I.19–20, perhaps best captures the age's perception of the pose of Cervantes, attributing it to Swift: "Whether thou chuse Cervantes' serious air, / Or laugh and shake in Rab'lais' easy Chair" (p. 62). Swift, the eighteenth century's exemplum of the cervantic stance, reflects upon his own method in "Verses on the Death of Dr. Swift": "His Vein, ironically grave, / Expos'd the Fool, and lash'd the Knave" (*Poems*, II: 565, lines 315–16). Others too recognized "gravity" as the particular disguise of Cervantes: "the author should never be seen to laugh, but constantly wear that grave irony which *Cervantes* only has inviolably preserv'd" (Richard Owen Cambridge, "Preface to the Scribleriad" [1751], quoted in Norman Knox, *The Word Irony and Its Context: 1500–1755* [Durham, N.C.: Duke University Press, 1961], p. 170); and "the burlesque . . . of Cervantes arises from the solemn and important air with which the most idle and ridiculous actions are related . . ." (*The Adventurer* 133, February 12, 1754). See Knox, pp. 162–73.

200.23ff. a form of excommunication, etc.] See vol. II, app. 8, pp. 952–57, in this edition.

204.9 *vel* os] Watt, p. 128, nn. 2–3: "*vel*, 'or'; os, a plural ending, like the superscribed 'i,' 's,' and 'n' letters below. All these are standard directions or rubrics allowing for a Bishop to adapt the curse to the singular or the plural; in this case 'this thief' or 'these thieves.' Sterne merely translates this as 'he,' so that Dr. Slop can make the curse apply to Obadiah.

"N.N. is an abbreviation for *Nomen, Nomina,* 'Name, Names' (to be supplied; which Slop does.)"

205.14   *Dathan* and *Abiram*] See Numbers 16: 1–35 and Psalm 106: 17.

207.23–209.2   Here . . . all the way.] Arthur Sherbo (*Studies,* p. 135) points out the several puns operating in this sentence: "Professor Work explains in a note that a 'minum' is 'a half-note' and is silent about 'running bass' which most readers would recognize as another musical term. But there is a pun in 'division,' which not only means the act of dividing something but also, from the *Oxford English Dictionary,* 'the execution of a rapid melodic passage, originally conceived as the dividing of each of a succession of long notes into several short ones.' The little interruption is all of a piece in its musical terminology, with 'division' serving as a bridge to the concluding 'running bass.'"

William Freedman, *Laurence Sterne and the Origins of the Musical Novel* (Athens: University of Georgia Press, 1978), pp. 65–66, offers an elaborate musical explanation of the passage.

209.10–11   in his vertex . . . my father] Cf. vol. II, app. 8, p. 955, in this edition; and n. to 176.16–177.14 above.

209.16   purtenance] Cf. vol. II, app. 8, p. 956, in this edition; and n. to 11.21–22 above.

211.6–18   By the golden . . . together then] Cf. Sterne's "Advantages of Christianity," (*Sermons,* IV.26.157): "——for what with celestial gods, and gods aerial, terrestrial and infernal, with the goddesses, their wives and mistresses, upon the lowest computation, the heathen world acknowledged no less than thirty thousand deities, all which claimed the rites and ceremonies of religious worship." Sterne's source was probably Burton, 3.4.1.3 (pp. 664–65): "The *Romans* borrowed from all, besides their own gods, which were *majorum* and *minorum gentium,* as *Varro* holds, certaine and uncertaine; some cœlestial select and great ones, others *Indigites* and *Semi dei* . . . : gods of all sorts, for all functions; some for the Land, some for Sea; some for Heaven, some for Hel; some for passions, diseases, some for birth, some for weddings, husbandry, woods, waters, gardens, orchards, &c. . . . And not good men only do they thus adore, but tyrants, monsters, divels, . . . beastly women, and arrant whores amongst the rest. . . . male and female gods, of all ages, sexes, and dimensions, with beards, without beards, married, unmarried, begot, not borne at all, but as *Minerva* start out of *Jupiters* head. *Hesiodus* reckons up at least 30000 gods, *Varro* 300 *Jupiters*."

Work, p. 179, n. 4: "Marcus Terentius Varro [see above, n. to 190.3−7] was the most learned scholar and author among the Romans; the reference would appear to be to his *Antiquitates Rerum Divinarum*, but actually Sterne has miscopied it from *The Anatomy* . . . ."

Cf. *Spectator* 331: "The Beard, conformable to the Notion of my Friend, Sir ROGER, was for many Ages looked upon as the Type of Wisdom. *Lucian* more than once rallies the Philosophers of his Time who endeavoured to rival one another in Beard; and represents a learned Man who stood for a Professorship in Philosophy as unqualified for it by the Shortness of his Beard" (III: 221). Cf. Sterne's use of long beards (and great wigs) to represent gravity and judgment (as opposed to wit), 238.18−19 and 263.15−16.

See also *The Works of Petronius Arbiter*, trans. Joseph Addison (1736; New York: AMS, 1975), p. 115: "I shall make thee leave this Buffoonry, tho' thou hadst a Beard of Gold"; and the annotation: "The Heathens, when they would shew a particular Devotion to any Deity, adorn'd his Statue with a golden Beard."

211.18−21   I vow . . . *Cid Hamet* offered his] Cid Hamet Benengeli, the reputed chronicler of many of Don Quixote's adventures, swears at one point that "by *Mahomet*, he would have given the best Coat of two that he had, only to have seen the Knight and the Matron walk thus Hand in Hand from the Chamber-Door to the Bed-side" (II.III.48, IV: 120). Sterne used the same phrase in a letter to Elizabeth Vesey (June 20, ?1761): "of the two bad cassocs, fair Lady which I am worth in the world, I would this moment freely give the better of 'em to find out by what irresistable force of magic it is, that I am influenced to write a Letter to you upon so short an Acquaintance . . ." (*Letters*, p. 137); and to Lydia (August 24, 1767): "I would have given not my gown and cassock (for I have but one) but my topaz ring to have seen the *petits maitres et maitresses* go to mass, after having spent the night in dancing" (*Letters*, p. 391).

In the present passage Sterne seems to have forgotten momentarily that Tristram is not a clergyman; but see also William C. Dowling, "Tristram Shandy's Phantom Audience," *Novel* 13 (1980): 291−92, for the possible

significance of the inconsistency. And cf. *TS*, 599.9–10: "That a man with
pale face, and clad in black . . . ."

212.3   So am not I] Cf. 430.12–13: "He is dead! said *Obadiah*,—he is certainly dead!—So am not I, said the foolish scullion."

212.4–6   But he is cursed . . . uncle *Toby*.] See Revelation 20: 10: "And the
devil that deceived them was cast into the lake of fire and brimstone, where
the beast and the false prophet are, and shall be tormented day and night
for ever and ever." Cf. [Daniel Defoe,] *The Political History of the Devil*
(1726), p. 406: "It must be Atheistical to the last Degree to suggest, that
whereas the *Devil* has been heaping up and amassing Guilt ever since the
Creation of Man, encreasing in hatred of God and Rebellion against him
. . . that yet Heaven had not prepar'd, or could not prepare a just Penalty
for him . . . . Heaven could not be just to its own Glory, if he should not
avenge himself upon this Rebel, for all his superlative Wickedness . . . ."

212.19–213.1   the whole set . . . coast of *Guinea*] *OED* (Be- 7.) records this
passage as its sole example of *befetish;* cf. above, n. to 102.9–10.

Sterne may have read about fetishes in Willem Bosman's *A New and
Accurate Description of the Coast of Guinea* (1705): "The Gold which is
brought us by the *Dinkirans* is very pure, except only that 'tis too much
mixed with *Fetiche's,* which are a sort of Artificial Gold composed of several Ingredients; among which some of them are very oddly shaped: . . .
There are also *Fetiche's* cast of unalloyed Mountain Gold; which very seldom come to our Hands, because they keep them to adorn themselves
. . . ." (pp. 73–74).

213.6–18   And how did *Garrick* . . . observer!] Concerning Sterne's friendship with David Garrick (1717–79) and Garrick's role in the publication
of the first two volumes of *TS*, see "Introduction to the Text," II: 821, in
this edition; *Letters*, pp. 85–87, 92–94; and Cash, *Early and Middle
Years*, pp. 294–96. Sterne refers to Garrick again in *TS* (246.3ff.,
333.13–16, 549.20), always in a highly complimentary fashion. His
view of Garrick's ability is indicated in his letters by such comments as "O
God! they have nothing here [in Paris], which gives the nerves so smart a
blow, as those great characters [Richard III] in the hands of G[arrick]!"
(p. 157); and again: "O! how I congratulate you for the Anxiety the world
has & continues to be under, for y^r return . . . to the few who love you and
the thousands who admire You—The moment you set y^r foot upon y^r

Stage—Mark! I tell it You—by some magick, irresisted power, every Fibre ab^t y^r heart will vibrate afresh & as strong & feelingly as ever: Nature with Glory at her back, will . . . light up the torch within you—& There is enough of it left, to heat and enlighten the World these many many, many Years" (p. 236).

Sterne in the present passage catches the tone of some contemporary criticism of Garrick, as evidenced in Thomas Fitzpatrick's *An Enquiry into the Real Merit of a Certain Popular Performer* . . . (1760), in which "it was agreed that we should go to the tragedy of Hamlet this evening, and each man, furnished with a printed play and a pencil, mark such improprieties, in respect of speaking, as Mr. G—— might possibly fall into" (pp. 20–21). This is followed by a list of twenty "improprieties"; and the pamphlet cites a poem to Garrick toward its conclusion: "For them, in vain the pleasing measure flows, / Whose recitation runs it all to prose; / Repeating what the poet sets not down; / THE VERB DISJOINTING FROM ITS FRIENDLY NOUN" (p. 38).

Garrick's defense of his *Macbeth* in 1762 suggests that Sterne did not put a halt to the grammarians: "tho it might appear that I stop'd at Every word in ye Line, more than Usual, yet my intention, was far from dividing the Substantive from its adjective, but to paint ye horror of Macbeth's Mind, & keep ye voice suspended a little . . ." (*Letters,* ed. David M. Little and George M. Kahrl [Cambridge: Harvard University Press, 1963], I: 350).

For a further discussion of the Sterne-Garrick relationship, see Ronald Hafter, "Garrick and *Tristram Shandy,*" *SEL* 7 (1967): 475–89. See also the chapter entitled "Acting" in Cecil Price, *Theatre in the Age of Garrick* (Oxford: Basil Blackwell, 1973), pp. 6–42.

213.14   Admirable grammarian!] Cf. Chambers, s.v. *Grammarian:* "The denomination . . . is, like that of critic, now frequently used as a term of reproach; a mere *grammarian;* a dry, plodding *grammarian, &c.*—The *grammarian* is conceived as a person wholly attentive to the minutiæ of language; industriously employed about words, and phrases; incapable of perceiving the beauties, the delicacy, finesse, extent, *&c.* of a sentiment."

See below, 358.6, for perhaps a more literal use.

Cf. Thomas Edwards, *Canons of Criticism,* 7th ed. (1765; New York: Augustus M. Kelley, 1970), p. 162, where Edwards facetiously exclaims after a particularly deplorable Warburtonian emendation, "Excellent Grammar! . . . Excellent Sense!" See below, n. to 271.19–20, for an additional indication of Sterne's probable awareness of this work.

213.19–23   And what . . . Excellent critic!] Sterne probably does have some contemporary criticism of *TS* in mind, though the most famous statement along these lines would be made by Johnson some fifteen years later: "Nothing odd will do long. 'Tristram Shandy' did not last" (Boswell, *Life of Johnson*, II: 449).

213.26   an exact scale of *Bossu's*] René Le Bossu's *Traité du poëme épique* (1675) was translated into English as *Treatise of the Epick Poem* in 1695, and long proved influential; Voltaire's *Essay . . . Upon the Epick Poetry of the European Nations From Homer down to Milton* (1727) speaks of the critic who will "not be tyranniz'd by *Aristotle, Castelvetro, Dacier, Le Bossu;* but he will extract his own Rules from the various Examples he shall have before his Eyes . . . ." (p. 47). Both treatises are reprinted by Stuart Curran (Gainesville, Fla.: Scholars' Facsimiles and Reprints, 1970); see Curran's introduction, pp. x–xi. Pope also attacked the rigidity of Le Bossu in both the prefatory matter to the *Dunciad* ("Martinus Scriblerus, of the Poem") and in chap. 15 of *Peri Bathous.* For a discussion of Le Bossu's reputation in eighteenth-century England, see A. F. B. Clark, *Boileau and the French Classical Critics in England* (Paris, 1925), pp. 243ff.; and Loyd Douglas, "A Severe Animadversion on Bossu," *PMLA* 62 (1947): 690–706. Clark comments: "this man, who represents that literary *regime* [neoclassicism] at its woodenest, is the most quoted in England of all the French critics . . . . Le Bossu's . . . at once superseded all other handbooks dealing with the heroic poem . . . ."

214.2   daub] *OED* cites this passage as its first illustration, with the definition "A coarsely executed, inartistic painting." Cf. above, n. to 16.2, "daubing."

214.2–3   not one . . . in any one group!] Sterne's connoisseur of painting is indebted to Joshua Reynolds, *Idler* 76 (September 29, 1759): "'Here,' says he, 'are twelve upright figures; what a pity it is that Raffaelle was not acquainted with the pyramidal principle; he would then have contrived the figures in the middle to have been on higher ground, or the figures at the extremities stooping or lying, which would not only have formed the group into the shape of a pyramid, but likewise contrasted the standing figures'" (ed. W. J. Bate, et al. [New Haven: Yale University Press, 1963], pp. 237–38). Sterne's earlier comment that "their heads, Sir, are stuck so full of rules and compasses, and have that eternal propensity to apply them upon all occasions" (213.1–2) may also be indebted to this *Idler* essay, p. 236: "for these rules being always uppermost, give them such a propensity to criticize . . . ."

Sterne's debt to Reynolds has been discussed by R. F. Brissenden, "Sterne and Painting," in *Of Books and Humankind*, ed. John Butt (London: Routledge & Kegan Paul, 1964), pp. 93–108; and Holtz, *Image and Immortality*, pp. 21–38 (see above, n. to 188.9–11). Both make the point that Reynolds and Sterne are directing their comments against Hogarth's *Analysis of Beauty;* but cf. Ronald Paulson's review of Holtz, *PQ 50* (1971): 484–85. It is noteworthy that the *Idler* had not yet been reprinted; therefore, unless Sterne was among the few reading the *Universal Chronicle* in which the *Idler* first appeared, quite possibly Reynolds gave his essay to Sterne when painting his portrait in March and April of 1760.

214.4–8   colouring of *Titian . . . of Angelo.*] Cf. Reynolds, *Idler* 76: "With a gentleman of this cast [i.e., a connoisseur], I visited last week the cartoons at Hampton-court; he was just returned from Italy, a connoisseur of course, and of course his mouth full of nothing but the grace of Raffaelle, the purity of Domenichino, the learning of Poussin, the air of Guido, the greatness of taste of the Charaches, and the sublimity and grand contorno of Michael Angelo; with all the rest of the cant of criticism, which he emitted with that volubility which generally those orators have who annex no ideas to their words" (p. 237). In addition to some slight changes in wording, Sterne supplements Reynolds's catalogue with "the colouring of *Titian,*" "the expression of *Rubens,*" and "the *corregiescity* of *Corregio.*" The three painters are often considered together in the works of the day, particularly as great colorists; see Hogarth, *Analysis of Beauty:* "a common sign-painter that lays his colours smooth, instantly becomes, in point of colouring, a Rubens, a Titian, or a Corregio" (p. 122). Cf. Jonathan Richardson, *Works*, pp. 88, 166, and 198, where the three are always listed together (the essays were originally published between 1715 and 1719); and Daniel Webb, *An Inquiry into the Beauties of Painting*, 2d ed. (1761), p. 94. Webb considers Titian the "greatest master" of coloring

(p. 86), and Roger du Piles in *The Principles of Painting* (1743) gives him "18" for "colouring," the highest grade awarded. Piles rates Raphael "18" for "expression," with Rubens and Domenichino just behind with "17." Finally, Webb (p. 14) notes that "among us any action that is singularly graceful, is termed Correggiesque" and later, in a footnote (p. 56), he speaks of "that correggiesque Grace, which it has so much puzzled our writers to explain." Sterne may have seen the first quotation in a review of the first edition of Webb immediately following a review of vols. I and II of *TS* in *Annual Register* 3 (1760): 249–53.

Obviously, Reynolds's and Sterne's point that these observations are the cant of critics argues their widespread appearance, so that a specific source is difficult to ascertain; Pope, for example, includes some of the clichés in his "Epistle to Mr. Jervas, With *Dryden*'s Translation of *Fresnoy*'s *Art* of *Painting*" (1716): "Each heav'nly piece unweary'd we compare, / Match *Raphael*'s grace, with thy lov'd *Guido*'s air, / *Caracci*'s strength, *Correggio*'s softer line, / *Paulo*'s free stroke, and *Titian*'s warmth divine" (*Minor Poems*, p. 157, lines 35–38).

For another example, the following details about each painter are garnered from Richard Graham's *A Short Account of the Most Eminent Painters*, 2d ed. (1716):

Titian (1488–1576): "the most universal *Genius* of all the *Lombard School*, the best *Colourist* of all the *Moderns*, and the most eminent for *Histories, Landscapes, and Portraits* . . ." (p. 285).

Peter Paul Rubens (1577–1640): "the *Prince* of all the *Flemish Masters* . . . perhaps none of his *Predecessors* can boast a more *beautiful Colouring*, a *nobler Invention*, or a more *luxurious Fancy* . . ." (p. 346).

Raphael (1483–1520): "acknowledged to have been the PRINCE of the MODERN PAINTERS; and is oftentimes styl'd the DIVINE RAPHAEL, for the inimitable Graces of his *Pencil* . . ." (p. 288).

Domenico Zampieri or Domenichino (1581–1641): "His *Talent* lay principally in the *Correctness* of his *Style*, and in expressing the *Passions* and *Affections* of the *Mind*" (pp. 350–51).

Antonio Allegri of Correggio (1494–1534): "he had a *Genius* so sublime, and was Master of a *Pencil*, so wonderfully soft, tender, beautiful, and charming . . ." (p. 296).

Nicolas Poussin (1594–1665): "the *French* Raphael . . . [whose] *Genius* appear'd in his *nice* and *judicious Observation* of the *Decorum* in his *Compositions* . . ." (pp. 358–59).

Guido Reni (1575–1642): "we may believe what Cavalier *Gioseppino* told the Pope, when he ask'd his Opinion of *Guido's Performances* . . . '*Our Pictures* (said he) *are the Work of Mens Hands; but these are made by Hands Divine*'" (pp. 343–44).

Lodovico Carracci (1555–1619): "He assisted his *Cousins* in *Founding*, and *Settling* the famous *Academy of Design*, at *Bologna* . . ." (p. 331).

Michelangelo (1475–1564): "He has the Name of the greatest *Designer* that has ever been . . ." (p. 283).

Graham's *Account* was published as part of Du Fresnoy's *The Art of Painting* in Dryden's translation.

214.6   *corregiescity*] *OED* cites this passage as its first illustration; cf. Webb's "correggiesque" in passage cited above, n. to 214.4–8.

214.12   I would go fifty miles on foot] Cf. the letter from the Reverend Robert Brown to John Hall-Stevenson (July 25, 1760) included in *Letters*, p. 432: "I'd ride fifty miles to smoak a pipe with him [i.e., Sterne]." Sterne reported to Mrs. Fenton on August 3 (*Letters*, p. 120) that he had "just finished" vol. III; in September he replied to Brown's letter, which Hall-Stevenson had shown him, and repeated the phrase: "I would certainly have gone twice as far to have smoakd a pipe with him [Montaigne], as with Arch-Bishop Laud . . ." (*Letters*, p. 122). Also cf. *TS*, 23.8–11: "the peerless knight of *La Mancha*, whom . . . I love more, and would actually have gone further to have paid a visit to, than the greatest hero of antiquity."

214.13–16   that man whose . . . care not wherefore.] Cf. Reynolds, *Idler* 76: "for these rules being always uppermost, give them such a propensity to criticize, that instead of giving up the reins of their imagination into their author's hands, their frigid minds are employed in examining whether the performance be according to the rules of art" (p. 236).

Cf. *Spectator* 411 (III: 538): "We are struck [by the pleasures of the imagination], we know not how, with the Symmetry of any thing we see, and immediately assent to the Beauty of an Object, without enquiring into the particular Causes and Occasions of it."

214.17–21   Great *Apollo!* . . . no matter.] Cf. 590.7–8, where Reynolds is
called "that son of *Apollo*." The allusion is, of course, to Apollo as the god
of learning in general, of poetry and music in particular, as opposed to
Mercury, the god of science and commerce. The "spark of thy own fire"
may be glossed by Sir William Temple's exploration of the nature of poetry: "The more true and natural Source of Poetry may be discovered, by
observing to what God this Inspiration was ascribed by the Ancients,
which was *Apollo*, or the Sun . . . . The Mystery of this Fable, means, I
suppose, that a certain Noble and Vital Heat of Temper, but especially of
the Brain, is the true Spring of [Poetry]: This was that Cœlestial Fire,
which gave such a pleasing Motion and Agitation to the Minds of those
Men, that have been so much admired in the World . . ." ("Of Poetry," in
Works, I: 236).

214.25–26   St. *Paul's thumb* . . . oaths monarchical] Work, p. 182, n. 4:
"Sterne may be thinking of Richard III, who frequently swore by St.
Paul, and Charles II, who swore by ''Od's fish.' 'God's fish' is presumably
a euphemism for 'God's flesh.' To swear by some part of the body of the
deity or of a saint was formerly, of course, very common." See below, n. to
358.27.

   We have been unable to locate Sterne's source, if any, for his awareness
of monarchical oaths (see also 216.2–4 and n. below). Shakespeare seems
to have known about King Richard's predilection, since he has him swear
by St. Paul on five different occasions in *Richard III*.

215.8   orientality] *OED:* "Eastern style or character"; this passage is cited as
first illustration. "Richness" or "exoticness" seems to be implied.

215.11–13   such a thorough . . . and articulations] See vol. II, app. 8,
p. 955, in this edition, for a discussion of how Sterne's editing of the
Gentleman's Magazine's version of "Ernulphus's Curse" brought about the
text of 209.21–22: "May he be cursed in all the joints and articulations of
his members . . . ."

215.15–16   *Michael Angelo* . . . of *gusto!*] See above, n. to 188.9–11.
Hogarth speaks of the "grandeur of gusto" of Michelangelo (*Analysis of
Beauty*, p. v), and Richardson, of Michelangelo's "sort of Greatness in the
utmost degree, which sometimes ran into the extream of terrible; though
in many instances he has a fine seasoning of Grace" (*Works*, p. 112).

215.17–18   My father . . . from all mankind] Cf. 170.17–19: "my father, Sir, would see nothing in the light in which others placed it;—he placed things in his own light . . . ."

215.24–26   that *Justinian* . . . code or digest] Cf. Chambers, s.v. *Civil Law:* "Lastly, Justinian, finding the authority of the Roman law almost abolished in the west, by the declension of the empire; resolved to make a general collection, of the whole Roman jurisprudence; and committed the care thereof to his chancellor Tribonianus.

"That minister executed his commission with a great deal of diligence, not to say precipitation: a new code was finished in 529, and a digest in 533. See DIGEST, and CODE.

"The same year he published an abridgment thereof . . . under the title of *institutes.* See INSTITUTES."

Sterne could have found much the same information under *Code,* an article he borrows from in vol. III, chap. 34 (263.19–21); see W. G. Day, "A Note on Sterne: 'Des Eaux'," *N&Q* 215 (1970): 303.

Cf. "Rabelaisian Fragment," p. 1088, lines 38–42 (where the scattered Rules of the KERUKOPÆDIA are to be "carefully collected into one Code . . . by way of a regular Institute"), and *TS,* 274.24–26: "so that *Slawkenbergius* his book may properly be considered . . . a thorough-stitch'd DIGEST and regular institute of *noses* . . . ." See also 285.18–19 and 445.5–9. Sterne may well be remembering Pope's *Peri Bathous:* "THEREFORE to supply our former Defect, I purpose to collect the scatter'd Rules of our Art into regular Institutes . . ." (ed. Edna Leake Steeves [New York: King's Crown Press, 1952], p. 7).

Work, p. 183, n. 5: "Flavius Anicius Justinianus (483–565), surnamed the Great, the most famous of the emperors of the Eastern Roman Empire, directed a commission, headed by Tribonian, in consolidating and annotating the body of Roman law in his great *Corpus Juris Civilis,* the most important of all monuments of jurisprudence."

216.2–4   from the great . . . *your eyes*)] Cf. Tindal, I: 165: "During this War, as [William] was besieging *Alençon,* some of the Inhabitants came upon the Walls with Skins in their hands, by way of Reproach, for his Mother being a Skinner's Daughter. He was so provoked at this Insult, that he swore by the *Splendor of God,* his usual Oath, he would be reveng'd. Some time after, becoming master of the Town, he accomplish'd his Oath by putting out the Eyes, and cutting off the Hands and Feet of two and twenty of the insolent Burghers." Sterne almost certainly knew about this oath without the help of Rapin-Thoyras, but the "putting out the Eyes" may have attracted his attention, in view of the scavenger's *"Damn your eyes."*

While the Latin version of "Ernulphus's Curse" does curse the eyes (208.9–11: "Maledictus sit in . . . oculis"), Sterne omits "eyes" from his translation, as did his probable source, the *Gentleman's Magazine;* see vol. II, app. 8, p. 956, in this edition. "Damn your eyes" appears as part of the refrain of the very popular folksong "Sam Hall," possibly based on earlier eighteenth-century broadside songs about low criminal types like Captain Kidd and Jack Hall. We have not been able to determine whether this refrain existed in one of these earlier versions, but clearly it was an oath associated with particularly low characters. See G. Malcolm Laws, Jr., *American Balladry from British Broadsides* (Philadelphia: American Folklore Society, 1957), L5.

216.12   julap] Johnson, *Dictionary: "Julap* is an extemporaneous form of medicine, made of simple and compound water sweetened, and serves for a vehicle to other forms not so convenient to take alone." The illustration, from Richard Wiseman's *Surgery,* is of particular relevance: "If any part of the after-birth be left, endeavour the bringing that away; and by good sudorificks and cordials expel the venom, and contemperate the heat and acrimony by *julaps* and emulsions."

216.14   the child is where it was] Cash, "Birth," pp. 151–52, argues that the fact that Mrs. Shandy's pains have stopped and the "child is where it was" are clues to a difficult birth: "Her labour has been short, stopping two hours and ten minutes after it began. It was a critical labour from the first, as evidenced by Susannah's sudden, fearful flight for the old midwife. The short, violent labour indicates that Mrs Shandy's waters had suddenly broken. Consequently, the baby has moved well down towards the pelvis. The head presents, as the midwife well knows, for she has been attempting some sort of manual extraction and has had a grip, which did not hold, upon the head. The difficulty is clear: Tristram's head is too large for the opening. . . . The possibilities have been narrowed to two: Tristram *must* be delivered by the forceps or by the *tire tête."*

C. H. G. Macafee, "The Obstetrical Aspects of *Tristram Shandy," Ul-*

ster Medical Journal 19 (1950): 20–21, reaches the same conclusion, but from a rather different route: "If one is to judge from the time that Obadiah was dispatched for the doctor and Susannah ran for the midwife, Mrs. Shandy cannot have been in labour for more than about three hours, and yet Dr. Slop proceeded upstairs with the evident intention of delivering the patient.

"Even at a second confinement three hours in most cases would be a very short labour, and for such a patient not to be delivered at the end of this time could not be regarded delay in labour. Neither could it justify any meddlesome midwifery such as Dr. Slop evidently intended. . . .

"We can conclude that the delivery was difficult—it was almost certain to be if carried out prematurely, and we can also conclude that the child did suffer, because it is recorded that it had a fit early the next morning" (see 343.6–11 and n. below).

216.16   as black as your hat] Cf. 343.7–9, where Susannah gropes to finish her simile: "There is not a moment's time to dress you, Sir, cried *Susannah*—the child is as black in the face as my—As your, what? said my father . . . ." Susannah settles for her shoe (344.1).

217.4–6   after the reduction of *Lisle* . . . in the year Ten.] Work, p. 184, n. 2: "A confused reference. Lille surrendered in December, 1708, and during the severe winter of 1709–1710 people in many provinces perished of famine and revolts broke out in every direction, but neither Lille nor Ghent was particularly concerned in the campaign of 1710."

Insofar as the siege of Lille was "one of the most celebrated sieges of modern history" (David Chandler, *Marlborough as Military Commander* [New York: Charles Scribner's Sons, 1973], p. 226), and since in vol. VI (541.1–3) Sterne correctly dates it, it is difficult to understand his confusion at this point. Robert Parker, *Memoirs of the Most Remarkable Military Transactions* (1747) does make note of a mutiny at Ghent in 1712, after the English had withdrawn from Quesnoy preparatory to the Treaty of Utrecht (see below, n. to 686.5–17): "The Soldiers, almost to a man, were highly dissatisfied, from the time that the Duke of *Ormond* had declared he was not to act against *France* . . . . To make the matter worse, they had another real cause of complaint, which was, the extream badness of their bread. This prepared them to mutiny . . ." (p. 221).

217.21   *in petto*] "In the breast"; in secret, in private.

217.23   a pink'd-doublet] *OED*'s first example is dated 1849; but see also, s.v. *Pink* (2.c.), the example from Swift (1724): "I'll pink his doublet."

218.3–4   as long as *Tully*'s second *Philippick*] Cf. Thomas Bowles, *Aristarchus* (Oxford, 1748), pp. 202–3: "His second Philippic, so called in Imitation of Demosthenes [i.e., his diatribes against King Philip of Macedon], is a most bitter Invective on the whole Life of Antony, describing it as a perpetual Scene of Lewdness, Faction, Violence, and Rapine, heightened with all the Colours of Wit and Eloquence." It is also Cicero's longest oration.

   Conyers Middleton, *History of the Life of Marcus Tullius Cicero* (Dublin, 1741), recounts one example of Cicero's use of his mantle, viz., that when Catiline threatened his life, Cicero "doubled his guard, and called some troops into the city; and . . . that he might imprint a sense of his own and of the public danger the more strongly, he took care *to throw back his gown in the view of the people, and discovered a shining breast-plate*, which he wore under it" (I: 167–68). The most memorable rendering of the device is, of course, in *Julius Caesar*, III.ii.169ff., where Antony produces first Caesar's "pink'd" mantle and then his will.

218.9   BAMBINO] *OED* cites this passage as its first illustration. It occurs, however, in Joseph Spence, *Polymetis* (1747), p. 72; in the list of subscribers is a "Reverend Mr. Sterne."

218.11   came in by head and shoulders] Proverbial; Tilley, H274, and Stevenson, p. 1098. Tilley cites *A New Dictionary . . . of the Canting Crew* (c. 1700), s.v. *Fetch:* "A meer Fetch, that is far fetched, or brought in by Head and Shoulders." The phrase is obviously apropos at this point.

   Cf. above, n. to 156.24, the quotation from the *Annual Register* (1758).

218.24   *trunk-hose*] *OED* makes clear Sterne's humor: "Full bag-like breeches covering the hips and upper thighs, and sometimes stuffed with wool or the like, worn in the 16th and early 17th c."; hence the advantage of trunk-hose over the breeches of the eighteenth century, which, according to the *Handbook of English Costume* (p. 211), "became increasingly closer fitting" as the century wore on. Cf. 726.21–23 and 775.1.

219.6   new invented *forceps*] Cf. 127.1, 198.22, and nn. above.

219.9–12   the sentence . . . a raveline] See "Glossary of Terms of Fortification" in this volume; see also above, n. to 197.1 ("GREAT wits jump").

219.16   evil (for they . . . this life)] Proverbial; Tilley, M1012 ("MISFOR-
TUNE (Evil) never (seldom) comes alone"); and *ODEP*, s.v. *Misfortunes*.

220.1–4   you have tore . . . to a jelly.] Cash, "Birth," pp. 149–50, offers an
amusing gloss to this passage; writing about the Burton forceps, he comments: "So great is the magnification of force between the screw handle and
the claw-like blades, that the operator has no sense of the pressure being
exerted by the blades. The discovery was made, to my sorrow, upon the
bones of my hands, which, like those of Uncle Toby's, were nearly broken" as the handle was turned.

220.9–10   the cut on my thumb . . . aukward] In Burton's *New System of
Midwifry*, the importance of the thumb in operating the forceps is made
clear in a set of instructions accompanying the illustration: "On the other
Hand, when the Wings . . . are to be brought together again . . . then the
Operator may thrust the End of his Thumb against the great Screw . . .
and if he would fix the Wings . . . at any certain Distance from each other,
it is done by turning the great Screw . . . with the Thumb of the Hand
that is without the *Vagina*" (p. 387). After the wings are in place on the
head the great screw is locked with the thumb, by which means "the Head
can be no more compressed, neither can the Instrument easily slip off"
(p. 389).
    See above, n. to 199.3–6.

220.13   a cherry stone the worse] Cf. 62.18–19 and n. above.

220.17–19   a child's head . . . feet after.] See above, nn. to 176.2–4,
176.16–177.14.

221.1–6   will you take . . . difficult to know] Cf. Burton, *Letter to Smellie*,
p. 97: "how is it possible that you can tell the Head of the Child from its
Breech or Knees . . . . It is an Observation of the best Operators, that
even when the Os Uteri begins to dilate, the Knees greatly resemble the
Head, and are not easily distinguishable from it, till the Orifice be more
dilated, especially while the Waters are in the Amnios."

221.17   *Obadiah*'s pumps] Cf. 126.17 and n. above.

222.6   pantoufles] I.e., pantofles, slippers; cf. 531.12.

222.14   *duration and its simple modes*] Chap. 14 of book II of *ECHU* is entitled
"Of Duration, and its simple Modes." Sterne's entire chap. 18 of vol. III

represents his most extensive borrowing from Locke in *TS;* see also above, nn. to 107.5–8, 119.19–21.

222.16–18   rapid succession . . . to another] Jean-Claude Sallé ("A Source of Sterne's Conception of Time," *RES,* n.s. 6 [1955]: 180–82) points out that Locke nowhere introduces the idea "that the amount of duration perceived by the mind depends on the speed of its train of ideas" and suggests Addison's *Spectator* 94 (June 18, 1711) as a possible source for the error: "for if our Notion of Time is produced by our reflecting on the Succession of Ideas in our Mind, and this Succession may be infinitely accelerated or retarded, it will follow, that different Beings may have different Notions of the same Parts of Duration, according as their Ideas, which we suppose are equally distinct in each of them, follow one another in a greater or less Degree of Rapidity" (I: 399). The error was a common misinterpretation of Locke, however, and could have been derived from elsewhere; an alternative source and a consideration of the relationship between this passage in *TS* and Sterne's "Fragment Inédit" is offered in Melvyn New's "Laurence Sterne and Henry Baker's *The Microscope Made Easy,*" *SEL* 10 (1970): 593–95.

Locke's position is stated in II.14.3: "'Tis evident to any one who will but observe what passes in his own Mind, that there is a train of *Ideas,* which constantly succeed one another in his Understanding, as long as he is awake. *Reflection* on these appearances of several *Ideas* one after another in our Minds, is that which furnishes us with the *Idea* of *Succession:* And the distance between any parts of that Succession, or between the appearance of any two *Ideas* in our Minds, is that we call *Duration"* (*ECHU,* p. 182). Cf. II.14.4: "Men derive their *Ideas* of Duration, from their *Reflection on the train of the* Ideas, they observe to succeed one another in their own Understandings, without which Observation they can have no Notion of *Duration,* whatever may happen in the World" (pp. 182–83).

223.8–12   the ideas of time . . . into breeches] The ideas that do not concern Toby are precisely those that are of most interest to Locke and perhaps summarize the major concerns of *ECHU.* One of Locke's most famous images is directly to the point: "Let us then suppose the Mind to be, as we say, white Paper, void of all Characters, without any *Ideas;* How comes it to be furnished? Whence comes it by that vast store, which the busy and boundless Fancy of Man has painted on it, with an almost endless variety? Whence has it all the materials of Reason and Knowledge?" (II.1.2, p. 104). Cf. II.1.6, p. 106: "He that attentively considers the state of a *Child*, at his first coming into the World, will have little reason to think him stored with plenty of *Ideas*, that are to be the matter of his future Knowledge. 'Tis by degrees he comes to be furnished with them . . . ."

223.13–14   INFINITY, PRESCIENCE, LIBERTY, NECESSITY] While all these are topics discussed in *ECHU*, Chambers, s.v. *Prescience*, offers an interesting parallel: "in theology, *prevision, or fore-knowledge* . . . . See LIBERTY, and NECESSITY." In his article s.v. *Duration*, Chambers paraphrases the same passage from Locke quoted verbatim by Sterne, but Sterne obviously went to the original in this instance.

224.4–18   To understand . . . *preconceived*] Cf. *ECHU*, II.14.3: "To understand *Time* and *Eternity* aright, we ought with attention to consider what *Idea* it is we have of *Duration*, and how we came by it. . . . For whilst we are thinking, or whilst we receive successively several *Ideas* in our Minds, we know that we do exist; and so we call the Existence, or the Continuation of the Existence of our selves, or any thing else, Commensurate to the succession of any *Ideas* in our Minds, the *Duration* of our selves, or any such other thing co-existing with our Thinking" (pp. 181–82). Sterne invented the phrase "*and so according to that preconceived*" to create a sense of interruption; he had actually completed the passage from Locke.

224.20–26   'Tis owing . . . to us at all.] Cf. *ECHU*, II.14.19: "For Men in the *measuring of the length of time*, having been accustomed to the *Ideas* of Minutes, Hours, Days, Months, Years, *etc.* which they found themselves upon any mention of Time or Duration presently to think on, all which Portions of Time, were measured out by the motion of those heavenly Bodies, they were apt to confound time and motion . . ." (p. 188).

224.22–23   (I wish . . . in the kingdom)] Work, p. 190, n. 2, suggests an allusion to one of the many imitations of *TS* to appear in 1760, *The Clockmakers Outcry Against the Author of the Life and Opinions of Tristram Shandy. Dedicated to the Most Humble of Christian Prelates* . . . . One passage reads: "The directions I had for making several clocks for the country are countermanded; because no modest lady now dares to mention a word about *winding-up a clock*, without exposing herself to the sly leers and jokes of the family, to her frequent confusion. Nay; the common expression of street-walkers is, 'Sir, will you have your clock wound-up?'" (p. 42). The "Prelate" referred to is Warburton.

The wish may simply be another indication of Walter's aversion to sexual intercourse, though it does appear to be Tristram's interpolation.

225.2–8   regular succession . . . heat of a candle.] Cf. *ECHU*, II.14.9: "Hence I leave it to others to judge, whether it be not probable that our *Ideas* do, whilst we are awake, succeed one another in our Minds at certain distances, not much unlike the Images in the inside of a Lanthorn, turned round by the Heat of a Candle" (p. 184).

Cf. *The Works of Mr. Alexander Pope, In Prose* (1741), II: 337: "Some men's Wit is like a dark lanthorn, which serves their own turn and guides their own way: but is never known (according to the Scripture Phrase) either to shine forth before Men, or to glorify their Father in heaven" ("Thoughts on Various Subjects," LXXXI).

225.9   smoak-jack] "An apparatus for turning a roasting-spit, fixed in a chimney and set in motion by the current of air passing up this" (*OED*). Sterne obviously liked the simile and repeats it in chaps. 19 and 20, leading the *OED* to credit him with establishing a new, figurative meaning for the word: "The head, as the seat of confused ideas."

225.11–12   My father . . . best explanatory moods] Cf. 94.19–20: "my uncle *Toby* was in one of his best explanatory moods . . . ."

225.13–15   where clouds . . . encompassed it about] Cf. 147.11–14: "or that the little interests below, could rise up and perplex the faculties of our upper regions, and encompass them about with clouds and thick darkness . . . ." Sterne may have been remembering Dryden's "To Oldham": "Thy Brows with Ivy, and with Laurels bound; / But Fate and gloomy Night encompass thee around" (*Poems*, ed. James Kinsley [Oxford: Clarendon Press, 1958], I: 389); or Dryden's source, the *Aeneid*, book VI: "sed nox atra caput tristri circumvolat umbra" (trans. Dryden, III: 1232, lines 1198–99): "But hov'ring Mists around his Brows are spread, / And Night, with sable Shades, involves his Head."

225.18   obfuscated and darkened over with fuliginous matter] Cf. Swift, "A Discourse Concerning the Mechanical Operation of the Spirit": "Remark your commonest Pretender to a Light *within*, how dark, and dirty, and gloomy he is *without;* As Lanthorns, which the more Light they bear in their Bodies, cast out so much the more Soot, and Smoak, and fuliginous Matter to adhere to the Sides" (*Tale of a Tub*, p. 282).

225.19–21   *Lucian* . . . dearer *Cervantes*] Cf. Fielding, *Tom Jones*, book XIII, chap. 1: "Come thou, that hast inspired thy *Aristophanes*, thy *Lucian*, thy *Cervantes*, thy *Rabelais* . . ." In his note, Battestin cites Fielding's several invocations of these satirists, including one in his obituary for Swift (*True Patriot*, November 5, 1745): "He possessed the Talents of a *Lucian*, a *Rabelais*, and a *Cervantes*, and in his Works exceeded them all" (Middletown, Conn.: Wesleyan University Press, 1975), II: 686, n. 1. See also the dedication to George Alexander Stevens's *Distress upon Distress* (1752): "Come ye Sons of sterling Humour, *Lucian, Rablais* [*sic*], *Cervantes*, and THOU, the most witty, most worthy of all, immortal *SWIFT* . . ." (in *Burlesque Plays of the Eighteenth Century*, ed. Simon Trussler [Oxford: Oxford University Press, 1969], p. 265). The grouping would appear to be a traditional one.

Cf. *TS*, 727.9–11: "suffer her not to look into Rabelais, or Scarron, or Don Quixote——

"——They are all books which excite laughter . . . ."

In invoking "Dulness" and "Gravity" as his muses for book II of *The Ghost*, Charles Churchill pays a handsome compliment to Sterne (*The Poetical Works*, ed. Douglas Grant [Oxford: Clarendon Press, 1956], p. 84, lines 161–74):

> But come not with that easy mien,
> By which you won the *lively* DEAN,
> Nor yet assume that Strumpet air,
> Which RABELAIS taught Thee first to wear,
> Nor yet that arch ambiguous face,
> Which with CERVANTES gave thee grace,
> But come in sacred vesture clad,
> Solemnly dull, and truly sad!
>
> Far from thy seemly Matron train
> Be Idiot MIRTH, and LAUGHTER vain!
> For WIT and HUMOUR, which pretend
> At once to please us and amend,

They are not for my present turn,
Let them remain in *France* with STERNE.

225.22–23   discourse devoutly to be wished for!] Cf. *Hamlet*, III.i.62–63:
"'tis a consummation / Devoutly to be wish'd."

225.24   *Ontologic*] *OED* cites this passage as its first illustration.

226.21–22   siege of *Messina* next summer] Cf. 241.20–21: "they are two
mortar-pieces for a siege next summer"; and 242.20: "with twenty other
preparations for the siege of *Messina* . . . ." Baird, "Time-Scheme,"
p. 816, dates the siege September 29, 1718, which is, of course, almost six
weeks *before* Tristram's birth. But Baird's date (taken from Tindal,
IV: 571) is that on which Messina fell to the Spanish; its surrender was,
according to Tindal, "a point of great consequence, as it made the *Span-
iards* masters of all *Sicily* . . . ." England declared war against Spain in
December 1718 (Tindal, IV: 581) and spent the rest of the winter debating
with its allies of the Quadruple Alliance (France, Germany, Holland) just
how Sicily was to be regained. Tindal describes at length the gathering of a
land and naval force, the debate over where to land, and the subsequent
indecision about whether to attack Messina or Franca Villa (IV: 590–93).
The latter was chosen and the Allies were defeated. It was only at this
point, in the summer of 1719, on the advice of Admiral Byng, that a siege
of Messina was undertaken. It began on July 20, 1719 (IV: 595); the city
surrendered on August 8, and the citadel on October 18 (IV: 596–98).

That this sentence comes on the heels of a discussion of duration may
suggest that Sterne is still playing with the malleability of time, the assumption of the passage being that Toby and Trim share the author's
knowledge that Messina will be besieged in July 1719, eight months after
the time of the present scene. It is also possible, however, that Sterne later
realized his chronological "error," for in chap. 25 he reduces the prescience to an intelligent guess: "for cardinal *Alberoni*'s intrigues at that time
being discovered, and my uncle *Toby* rightly foreseeing that a flame would
inevitably break out betwixt *Spain* and the Empire, and that the operations
of the ensuing campaign must in all likelihood be either in *Naples* or
Sicily,——he determined upon an *Italian* bridge,—(my uncle *Toby*, by
the bye, was not far out in his conjectures) . . ." (250.5–11). This conjecture, we are informed, was made about "six or seven weeks" (247.9)

before Tristram's birth-day, i.e., in the last two weeks of September, when the battle between Spain and the Empire for Messina was already underway, if not decided. Having, then, extricated himself from his chronological problem, Tristram plunges back in by reporting that Walter, the "better politician," convinces Toby that the campaign will be in Flanders, so that an Italian bridge would be useless. On the day of Tristram's birth, we must conclude, Toby is planning a Dutch bridge for a campaign in Flanders and a train of artillery for the siege of Messina.

This passage does make clear that Toby and Trim returned to their "games," despite the momentary renunciation that followed the Treaty of Utrecht; see vol. VI, chaps. 34–35.

226.22–23   boring the touch holes . . . hot poker.] The definition of "touch hole" in Chambers, *Supplement,* would have amused Sterne: "the small hole at the end of the cylinder of a gun or musquet, by which the fire is conveyed to the powder in the chamber. In a firelock, carabine, or pistol, it is called the *Touch-hole,* but in a piece of cannon it is more properly called the vent." Sterne puns again on "poker" at 727.3–4. See also below, n. to 355.9–11.

226.25   I'll make use of it, and write my preface.] In *Tale of a Tub,* Swift comments on the fact that the matter of his "Digression in the Modern Kind" (sec. V) would have been better suited for a preface; but, he goes on, "I here think fit to lay hold on that great and honourable Privilege of being the *Last Writer;* I claim an absolute Authority in Right, as the *freshest Modern,* which gives me a Despotick Power over all Authors before me. In the Strength of which Title, I do utterly disapprove and declare against that pernicious Custom, of making the Preface a Bill of Fare to the Book" (pp. 130–31).

227.11   *Agelastes*] The name, derived from the Greek ἀγέλαστος (*agelastos*), means "one who never laughs" and occurs in Rabelais, "Epistle Dedicatory to Book IV" (IV, p. lvii, n. 3). Work's suggestion (pp. 193, n. 1, and 194, n. 5) that this and other names in the preface refer to locally recognizable figures has not been substantiated. Agelastes reappears at the Visitation dinner, 384.26.

227.13   *Triptolemus* and *Phutatorius*] Triptolemus was a Greek hero and demigod, supposedly taught the arts of agriculture by Ceres. Plato and Tully name him as a judge of the dead. Why Sterne would introduce him among

primarily invented names remains unknown. He is mentioned in *Spectator* 146 (II: 76) as one of the judges of the dead; and in *Divine Legation of
Moses*, 4th ed. (1755–58), I: 202, 206, and II: 4, etc., where Warburton
argues that Triptolemus is simply another name for Osiris. He reappears
in *TS* at the Visitation dinner in vol. IV, chap. 27.

Phutatorius (Latin *fututor:* "copulator") speaks for itself; it is he who
receives the hot chestnut in his lap at the Visitation dinner.

227.14–18   for that . . . say I.] Sterne's refusal to separate wit and judgment
is reminiscent of Pope's similar refusal in *An Essay on Criticism*, lines
82–83: "For *Wit* and *Judgment* often are at strife, / Tho' meant each other's
Aid, like *Man* and *Wife*" (p. 248). The context of Pope's couplet is amply
outlined by the editors in their introduction to the poem, including the
contrasting tradition, from Ramus and Hobbes to Locke: "The important
consequence of such speculation about the nature and function of Wit was
the tendency (re-enforced by the efforts of the Royal Society to achieve a
severely scientific way of speech) to associate wit, which for La Rochefoucauld had pierced 'into the very *Bottom* of *Things*', with the merely pleasing, ornamental, fanciful, impetuous, and insubstantial. To this tendency
Locke lent his authority in his *Essay . . .*" (p. 216). The passage from
ECHU most often cited for the separation of wit and judgment is from
book II: "And hence, perhaps, may be given some Reason of that common
Observation, That Men who have a great deal of Wit, and prompt Memories, have not always the clearest Judgment, or deepest Reason. For *Wit*
lying most in the assemblage of *Ideas*, and putting those together with
quickness and variety, wherein can be found any resemblance or con-
gruity, thereby to make up pleasant Pictures, and agreeable Visions in the
Fancy: *Judgment*, on the contrary, lies quite on the other side, in separating
carefully, one from another, *Ideas*, wherein can be found the least difference, thereby to avoid being misled by Similitude, and by affinity to take
one thing for another" (II.11.2, p. 156).

Another significant passage from the *Essay*, cited in part by Audra and
Williams and by John Traugott (*Tristram Shandy's World: Sterne's Philo-
sophical Rhetoric* [Berkeley: University of California Press, 1954], p. 65),
is from book III, where Locke attacks wit as the ornament of rhetoric:
"Since Wit and Fancy finds easier entertainment in the World, than dry
Truth and real Knowledge, *figurative Speeches*, and allusion in Language,

will hardly be admitted, as *an* imperfection or *abuse* of it. I confess, in Discourses, where we seek rather Pleasure and Delight, than Information and Improvement, such Ornaments as are borrowed from them, can scarce pass for Faults. But yet, if we would speak of Things as they are, we must allow, that all the Art of Rhetorick, besides Order and Clearness, all the artificial and figurative application of Words Eloquence hath invented, are for nothing else but to insinuate wrong *Ideas,* move the Passions, and thereby mislead the Judgment; and so indeed are perfect cheat . . ." (III.10.34, p. 508). For Locke's definition of *judgment,* see IV.14. Sterne's view of wit and judgment in his preface is analyzed by Traugott, pp. 62–75.

An interesting gloss on the preface is provided by Owen Ruffhead's review of vols. III and IV in the *Monthly Review* 24 (1761), where a long passage from Hobbes (*Leviathan,* chap. 8) concerning the difference between wit and judgment is quoted as part of a lesson in discretion; Ruffhead concludes: "We shall make no apology for the length of this quotation, because, tho' written in the last century, it is as applicable to *Tristram* and his works, as if it had been penned yesterday, purposely to rebuke this Author. . . . *Fancy without Judgment,* is *not Wit*" (p. 103). Sterne's publication of his sermons (see above, n. to 167.17–22) was in large measure behind this attack, but as early as the summer of 1759, Sterne responded to criticism of his manuscript by showing an awareness that "wit" from a cleric might be criticized: "I have rec^d y^r Letter of Counsil which contrary to my natural humour, has set me half a day upon looking a little gravely and upon thinking a little gravely too. sometimes I concluded you had not spoke out, but had stronger grounds for some discouraging Hints upon Tristram Shandy, than what your good nature knew well how to tell me—particularly with regard to the point of prudence as a Divine &c. . . .

"I know not whether I am entirely free from the fault Ovid is so justly censured for—of being *Nimium ingenij sui amator* . . . . in general I have ever endeavour'd to avoid it, by leaving off as soon as possible whenever a point of humour or Wit was started, for fear of saying too much; and tother day a gentleman found fault with me upon that very score—but yours and my friend Fothergils Judgment upon this head, I hold to be more truely nice and critical—and on that side, it is the safest to err"

(*Letters*, pp. 78–79). And in a letter to Warburton, ten days after he announced he had begun vol. III, Sterne returned to the same distinction: "Be assured, my lord, that willingly and knowingly I will give no offence to any mortal by anything which I think can look like the least violation either of decency or good manners; and yet, with all the caution of a heart void of offence or intention of giving it, I may find it very hard, in writing such a book as 'Tristram Shandy', to mutilate everything in it down to the prudish humour of every particular. I will, however, do my best; though laugh, my lord, I will, and as loud as I can too" (*Letters*, p. 115).

Cf. Fielding's similar refusal to separate wit and judgment in *Tom Jones*, book IX, chap. 1.

227.19   *de fartandi et illustrandi fallaciis*] "Concerning the deceptions of fart-ing and illustrating" would be the literal translation, though by straining the syntax one might accept Work's *"Of farting, and the explaining of decep-tions"* (p. 193, n. 3). Sterne may have had in mind Rabelais, II.7.48, where item 17 of the Catalogue of the Library of St Victor is "Ars honeste fartandi [petandi] in societate, per M. Ortuinum." For Didius, see above, n. to 11.26.

227.20   That an illustration is no argument] Sterne may have been recalling a sentence in Chambers, s.v. *Analogy,* an entry he had referred to earlier (118.21–22). "Reasonings by *analogy,*" Chambers asserts, "may serve to explain and illustrate, but not to prove any thing; yet is a great deal of our philosophizing no better founded."

228.3   opacular] *OED* cites this passage as its sole illustration; the definition provided, "somewhat opaque," is perhaps too fine, since Sterne seems simply to mean "opaque."

228.5   Now, my dear . . . thrice able critics] Sterne used this formula in his "Rabelaisian Fragment": "My dear and thrice-Reverend Brethren . . ." (p. 1088, line 4). It is borrowed from Rabelais's prologues to books I, II, III, and V; e.g.: "Most noble and illustrious drinkers, and you thrice precious pockified blades; (for to you, and none else do I dedicate my writings) . . ." (I, p. cxxiii).

Cf. 72.18: "thrice happy Times!"; and 568.4: "Thrice happy book!"

228.8–11   *Monopolus,* my politician . . . repose of it] Work, p. 194, n. 5: "'A monopolist'; probably locally recognizable satire. *Kysarcius:* a portmanteau-word, probably Sterne's translation of *Baise-cul,* a 'great

lord' in Rabelais, 2.10–13 ["Kissbreech" in the Urquhart-Motteux translation, pp. 104ff.]. *Gastripheres:* another portmanteau-word, 'Paunch-
carrier,' or 'Big-belly' [Greek γαστήρ (*gaster:* "belly") and φέρω (*phero:*
"carry")]. *Somnolentius:* one who sleeps . . . [Latin *somnolentus:*
"sleepy"]."

Kysarcius, Gastripheres, and Somnolentius all reappear at the Visitation dinner, vol. IV, chap. 27.

228.19–20   memory, fancy, genius, eloquence, quick parts] Cf. 175.14–17:
"this incomprehensible contexture in which wit, memory, fancy, eloquence, and what is usually meant by the name of good natural parts, do
consist . . ."; and Sterne's sermon "On Enthusiasm": "the spiritual gifts
spoken of in Scripture, are to be understood by way of accommodation, to
signify the natural or acquired gifts of a man's mind; such as memory,
fancy, wit and eloquence; which, in a strict and philosophical sense, may
be called spiritual;—because they transcend the mechanical powers of
matter,—and proceed more or less from the rational soul, which is a
spiritual substance.

". . . these spiritual gifts . . . such as memory, fancy and wit, and other
endowments of the mind, which are known by the name of natural parts,
belong merely to us as men; and whether the different degrees, by which
we excel each other in them, arise from a natural difference of our souls,—
or a happier disposition of the organical parts of us.—They are such,
however, as God originally bestows upon us, and with which, in a great
measure, we are sent into the world" (*Sermons,* VI.38.129–30). Cf.
ECHU, II.10.8: "'Tis the business therefore of the Memory to furnish to
the Mind those dormant *Ideas,* which it has present occasion for, and in the
having them ready at hand on all occasions, consists that which we call
Invention, Fancy, and quickness of Parts" (p. 153).

Sterne links the terms again, 354.21: "memory, fancy, and quick
parts"; 382.4–5: "imagination, judgment . . . ratiocination, memory,
fancy"; and 719.17: "thy memory or fancy."

228.23–25   into the several . . . of our brains] Cf. Rabelais, III.31.210: "the
more promptly, dexterously, and copiously to suppeditate, furnish, and
supply him with store of spirits, sufficient to replenish, and fill up the
ventricles, seats, tunnels, mansions, receptacles, and celluls of the common sense . . . ."

229.3–29   Bless us! . . . done well enough.] There is some similarity in this paragraph and the one following, to Rabelais, III.3–4, where Panurge praises the debtors and borrowers; e.g., a world without lending "will be no better than a dog-kennel, a place of contention and wrangling, more unruly and irregular than that of the rector of Paris . . . . Men will not then salute one another . . . . [There will] be introduced defiance, disdain and rancour, with the most execrable troop of all evils, all imprecations and all miseries" (pp. 36–37). On the other hand, a world of generous lending produces the following response: "O how great will that harmony be . . . . I lose myself in this high contemplation.

"Then will among the race of mankind peace, love, benevolence, fidelity . . . be found . . . . Good God! Will not this be the golden age in the reign of Saturn? . . .

"O happy world! O people of that world most happy! . . .

"Cops body, I sink, I drown, I perish, I wander astray, and quite fly out of myself, when I enter into the consideration of the profound abyss of this world, thus lending, thus owing" (pp. 39, 43). Cf. also Rabelais, II.3.23: "the weather is dangerous; I am sick; I faint away."

Burton, *Anatomy*, 2.2.3 (p. 258), has a similar passage: "But hoo? I am now gone quite out of sight, I am almost giddy with roving about . . . ."

229.4   tickle it off] Cf. 190.17 and n. above.

229.14–21   there would be . . . living for us.] Sterne borrowed this passage in composing a whimsical letter to a female admirer, probably in 1765: "You are a Wit Y^{r}self, and tho' there might be abundance of peace so long as the *Moon* endured—Yet when that luscious period was run out, I fear we sh^d never agree one day to an end; there would be such Satyre & sarcasm—scoffing & flouting—rallying & reparteeing of it,—thrusting & parrying in one dark corner or another, There w^d be nothing but mischief——but then—as we sh^d be two people of excellent Sense, we sh^d make up matters as fast as they went wrong—What tender reconciliations!—O by heaven! it would be a Land of promise—milk & Honey!" (*Letters*, p. 241).

In his sermon "The Levite and his Concubine," Sterne makes some strictures on men of "wit and parts" who make "shrewd and sarcastick reflections upon whatever is done in the world . . . . it has helped to give wit a bad name, as if the main essence of it was satire: certainly there is a difference between *Bitterness* and *Saltness*,—that is,——between the malignity and the festivity of wit,——the one is a mere quickness of apprehension, void of humanity,—and is a talent of the devil; the other comes down from the Father of Spirits, so pure and abstracted from persons, that willingly it hurts no man . . ." (*Sermons*, III.18.91–93).

229.15   raillying and reparteeing] *OED* cites this passage as its sole example of the rare usage *raillying*, and its last example of *reparteeing*.

229.26–27   milk and honey] A biblical commonplace; see, for example, Exodus 3: 8: "a land flowing with milk and honey"; the "land of promise" is found in Hebrews 11: 9: "By faith he sojourned in the land of promise." In "The Levite and his Concubine" Sterne concludes with a vision of brotherly harmony similar to that he is here describing: "O my GOD! write it not down in thy book, that thou madest us merciful, after thy own image;——that thou hast given us a religion so courteous,——so good temper'd,——that every precept of it carries a balm along with it to heal the soreness of our natures, and sweeten our spirits, that we might live with such kind intercourse in this world, as will fit us to exist together in a better" (*Sermons*, III.18.95–96).

230.16–18   where the whole . . . of his cave] Thomas Salmon, *Modern History, or, The Present State of all Nations*, 3d ed. (1744), points out that in the northernmost latitudes, the winter is nine months long (I: 652 and passim); of Nova Zembla he writes: "hither the Ostiacks and Samoieds frequently venture . . . to hunt elks and rain-deer, carefully observing the wind; . . . for if the north wind sets in, there is no enduring the open country; if they cannot escape to some cave and shelter themselves till it is over, they certainly perish; from whence we may very well conclude there are no constant inhabitants there, though some pretend to have seen them" (I: 402).

230.18–24   where the spirits . . . spark is given] Cf. 27.5–12, 71.3ff., and nn. above. Sir William Temple expresses a similar view in "An Essay upon the Original and Nature of Government": "It may be said further, That in the more intemperate Climates, the Spirits, either exhal'd by Heat, or compress'd by Cold, are rendred faint and sluggish; and by that reason the Men grow tamer, and fitter for Servitude" (*Works*, I: 97).

That this idea was still quite prevalent in Sterne's day is suggested by Goldsmith's essay "The Effect which Climates have upon Men, and other

Animals," *British Magazine* (May 1760): "From hence we see the reason why the ancient Scythians were so much superior to the modern Siberian Tartars. The Scythians, tho' they lived in the same country, probably enjoyed a milder climate, and were therefore brave, well-shaped, and enterprising: the modern Siberians, on the contrary, are dwarfish, cowardly, and insolent to the last degree: extreme cold producing the same inconveniencies with extremity of heat. . . .

"Let us then be contented in accounting for the variety of the human species, to attribute it to the diversity of climate alone. It is this which may truly be said to place the distinction between the tall German and the inhabitant of Greenland but four feet high. It is climate alone which tinctures the negroes skin; that makes the Italians effeminate, and the Briton brave" (*Works*, III: 112–14). In his annotation Friedman attributes both ideas to Buffon, *Histoire naturelle* (1749), III: 527, 519–20. Cf. Goldsmith, "A Comparative View of Races and Nations" (in *Works*, III: 66–86), which first appeared in the *Royal Magazine* (June–September 1760), especially the following: "If we compare the bodies of the inhabitants of the temperate climates with those which lie to the north or south, we shall find the pores of the skin much larger than in any other part of the globe . . . . Excessive heat or cold contract the pores of the skin; and those who have been long accustomed to either, are found no way subject to those profuse sweats, which in every part of Europe are the consequences of labour . . ." (p. 82).

230.24   Angels and ministers of grace defend us!] *Hamlet*, I.iv.39; the same phrase is used earlier in *TS*, at 176.21. The phrase "*plentiful a lack* of wit" (230.28) is also from *Hamlet*, II.ii.196–200: "the satirical rogue says here that old men have grey beards . . . and that they have a plentiful lack of wit, together with most weak hams . . . ."

230.26   or run a match] Cf. John Ashton, *Social Life in the Reign of Queen Anne*, rev. ed. (New York: Scribner and Welford, 1883): "Perhaps the earliest sporting paper is 'News from *New Market:* or An Account of the Horses Match'd to Run there in *March, April,* and *May* 1704 . . .'" (p. 230). Thomas Wright, *England Under the House of Hanover*, 2d ed. (1848) quotes the following song: "To run a horse, to make a match, / To revel deep, to roar a catch; / To knock a tottering watchman down, / To sweat a woman of the town" (I: 355).

See also below, n. to 616.18, the citation from James Russel's *Letters from a Young Painter Abroad to his Friends in England* (1748), p. 6, where the phrase "a hunting match" occurs.

231.1–11   southwards into *Norway* . . . *Asiatick Tartary.*] Sterne almost certainly composed this passage while looking at a map, but we have been unable to locate the precise one. From his starting point in Russia's Novaya Zemlya islands ("*Nova Zembla,*" 230.13–14), lying between the Kara and Barents seas, he moved southwest across the northernmost regions of Scandinavia and Finland (i.e., "*North Lapland,*" 230.14). Now, having reached Norway, he turns nearly 180 degrees and moves east, but below the Arctic Circle, crossing Sweden through the northern district of Angermania to the Gulf of Bothnia, situated between Sweden and Finland. West Bothnia is that area of the Gulf belonging to Sweden; East Bothnia, to Finland. Still moving east, he enters Russia just north of the Gulf of Finland, the easternmost point of which is St. Petersburg (Leningrad). Carelia is the area north of St. Petersburg and Ingria the area south. Sterne then continues his eastward movement into Russia.

231.12–232.4   Now throughout . . . cause to complain.] In this and the next paragraph, Sterne parallels his earlier discussion of the Danish character, 26.22–27.8: "'That nature was neither very lavish, nor was she very stingy in her gifts of genius and capacity to its [Denmark's] inhabitants;-- but, like a discreet parent, was moderately kind to them all; observing such an equal tenor in the distribution of her favours, as to bring them, in those points, pretty near to a level with each other; so that you will meet with few instances in that kingdom of refin'd parts; but a great deal of good plain houshold understanding amongst all ranks of people, of which every body has a share;' . . .

"With us, you see, the case is quite different;—we are all ups and downs in this matter;—you are a great genius;--or 'tis fifty to one, Sir, you are a great dunce and a blockhead;---not that there is a total want of intermediate steps . . . ." See above, n. to this passage.

Cf. Sir William Temple's version of the commonplace in his essay "Of Poetry": "But as of most general Customs in a Country there is usually some Ground, from the Nature of the People or Climate, so there may be amongst us, for this Vein of our Stage [humor], and a greater Variety of Humour in the Picture, because there is a greater Variety in the Life. This may proceed from the native Plenty of our Soil, the Unequalness of our Climate, as well as the Ease of our Government, and the Liberty of professing Opinions and Factions . . . . Plenty begets Wantonness and Pride, Wantonness is apt to invent, and Pride scorns to imitate; Liberty begets Stomach or Heart, and Stomach will not be constrained. Thus we come to have more Originals, and more that appear what they are; we have more Humour, because every Man follows his own, and takes a Pleasure, perhaps a Pride, to shew it . . . .

"Besides all this, there is another sort of Variety amongst us which arises from our Climate, and the Dispositions it naturally produces. We are not only more unlike one another than any Nation I know, but we are more unlike our selves too at several times, and owe to our very Air some ill Qualities, as well as many good. We may allow some Distempers incident to our Climate, since so much Health, Vigour, and Length of Life have been generally ascribed to it . . . . For my own part, who have conversed much with Men of other Nations, and such as have been both in great Imployments and Esteem, I can say very impartially, that I have not observed among any so much true Genius as among the *English;* no where more Sharpness of Wit, more Pleasantness of Humour, more Range of Fancy, more Penetration of Thought or Depth of Reflection among the better sort; no where more Goodness of Nature and of Meaning, nor more Plainness of Sense and of Life, than among the common sort of Country People; nor more blunt Courage and Honesty than among our Sea-Men.

"But with all this, our Country must be confest to be what a great foreign Physician called it, the Region of Spleen; which may arise a good deal from the great Uncertainty and many sudden Changes of our Weather in all Seasons of the Year. . . . This makes us unequal in our Humours, inconstant in our Passions, uncertain in our Ends, and even in our Desires. Besides, our different Opinions in Religion, and the Factions they have raised or animated for fifty Years past, have had an ill Effect upon our Manners and Customs, inducing more Avarice, Ambition, Disguise . . . than were before in our Constitution" (*Works,* I: 247–48).

231.28–232.2 *height* of our wit . . . our necessities] Cf. *Tale of a Tub,* p. 166: "For, what Man in the natural State, or Course of Thinking, did ever conceive it in his Power, to reduce the Notions of all Mankind, exactly to the same Length, and Breadth, and Height of his own?" The sufficiency of our faculties to our needs is seriously discussed by Locke, *ECHU*, II.23.12, a section Pope paraphrases in the *Essay on Man*, I.193–206.

See also *ECHU*, IV.14.2: "Therefore as God has set some Things in broad day-light; as he has given us some certain Knowledge, though limited to a few Things in comparison, probably, as a Taste of what intellectual Creatures are capable of, to excite in us a Desire and Endeavour after a better State: So in the greatest part of our Concernment, he has afforded us only the twilight, as I may so say, of *Probability*, suitable, I presume, to that State of Mediocrity and Probationership, he has been pleased to place us in here; wherein to check our over-confidence and presumption, we might by every day's Experience be made sensible of our short-sightedness and liableness to Error; the Sense whereof might be a constant Admonition to us, to spend the days of this our Pilgrimage with Industry and Care, in the search, and following of that way, which might lead us to a State of greater Perfection" (p. 652). This chapter is on Locke's concept of judgment.

232.16–17   which *Suidas* calls *dialectick induction*] Cf. Chambers, s.v. *Induction:* "Suidas reckons three kinds of *induction;* that just mentioned, which concludes or gathers some general proposition from an enumeration of all the particulars of a kind, he calls the *dialectic induction.*" Suidas, the reputed author of an encyclopedic Greek *Lexicon*, was thought to have lived at the end of the tenth century; in reality, *Suidas* is now known to have been the name of the lexicon and not of the author (see *OCD*, s.v. *Suda*).

Cf. 306.2–5: "the learned in their way [were] as busy in pumping [TRUTH] up thro' the conduits of dialect induction—they concerned themselves not with facts—they reasoned— . . . ."

232.23–24   reverences and worships] Sterne uses this mode of address, embracing clergy and nobility, on numerous occasions; e.g., 271.23–24, 350.18–19, 401.13–14, etc.

232.27   *How d'ye*] Earlier in the century servants called on their master's or mistress's acquaintances to ask, with their compliments, "How do ye?"—equivalent, says John Ashton, to "sending in a card" (*Social Life in the Reign of Queen Anne*, p. 60). Ashton cites *Spectator* 143; see also *Tatler* 109 and Swift, "Verses on the Death of Dr. Swift," lines 123–24: "(When daily Howd'y's come of Course, / And Servants answer; *Worse and Worse*)" (*Poems*, II: 557).

Cf. *Letters*, p. 353: "but I would not write to enquire after her . . . for even how-d'yes to invalids, or those that have lately been so, either call to mind what is past or what may return . . . ."

233.3–9   I tremble . . . tails into kennels.] Cf. *Tale of a Tub*, p. 192: "HE would shut his Eyes as he walked along the Streets, and if he happened to bounce his Head against a Post, or fall into the Kennel (as he seldom missed either to do one or both) . . . ." A similar passage occurs in *Gulliver's Travels*, book III, chap. 2, where the Laputian is described as "so wrapped up in Cogitation, that he is in manifest Danger of falling down every Precipice, and bouncing his Head against every Post; and in the Streets, of jostling others, or being jostled himself into the Kennel" (*Prose Works*, XI: 144).

See also Isaiah 59: 9–10: "Therefore is judgment far from us, neither doth justice overtake us: we wait for light, but behold obscurity; for brightness, but we walk in darkness. We grope for the wall like the blind, and we grope as if we had no eyes: we stumble at noonday as in the night; we are in desolate places as dead men"; and Job 5: 14: "They meet with darkness in the daytime, and grope in the noonday as in the night." Cf. Luke 6: 39 and John 3: 19–20. Prior offers a poetic version in *Solomon*, book I, lines 721–23: "O wretched Impotence of human Mind! / We erring still Excuse for Error find; / And darkling grope, not knowing We are blind" (*Works*, ed. H. Bunker Wright and Monroe K. Spears, 2d ed. [Oxford: Clarendon Press, 1971], I: 331).

233.10–12   full butt . . . like hogs.] *OED*, s.v. *butt:* "often with the intensifying adv. *full*, implying 'point-blank' meeting or violent collision"; *EDD*, s.v. *butt*, sb. 13.2, considers "full butt" as Yorkshire dialect.

See also *Dunciad*(B), IV.525–26: "The vulgar herd turn off to roll with Hogs, / To run with Horses, or to hunt with Dogs . . ." (p. 394).

233.15–18   fiddlers and painters . . . a quadrant.] Cf. vol. III, chap. 12 (vol. I, pp. 212–14, in this edition).

233.22–27   In this corner . . . taking one.] A. L. Humphreys (*N&Q*, 11th ser. 11 [1915]: 192–94) suggests that Sterne had in mind a particular physician, William Coward (1656/7–1725), who created a stir in 1702 with a book attacking the immortality of the soul. The witticism at the profession's expense seems to be more general, however, and is found in much satiric literature of the period; e.g., *Gulliver's Travels*, book IV, chap. 6: "ONE great Excellency in this Tribe is their Skill at *Prognosticks*, wherein they seldom fail; their Predictions in real Diseases, when they rise to any Degree of Malignity, generally portending *Death*, which is always in their Power, when Recovery is not: And therefore, upon any unexpected Signs of Amendment, after they have pronounced their Sentence, rather than be accused as false Prophets, they know how to approve their Sagacity to the World by a seasonable Dose" (*Prose Works*, XI: 238). Fielding uses the same idea in *Tom Jones* (book VII, chap. 13); when the surgeon is asked whether Tom's wound is "likely to prove mortal," he replies, " 'Sir, . . . to say whether a Wound will prove mortal or not at first Dressing, would be very weak and foolish Presumption: We are all mortal, and Symptoms often occur in a Cure which the greatest of our Profession could never foresee.'—'But do you think him in Danger?' says the other. 'In Danger! ay, surely,' cries the Doctor, 'who is there among us, who in the most perfect Health can be said not to be in Danger?'" (I: 381). Cf. *Joseph Andrews*, book I, chaps. 13–15.

The relationship between doctors, fees, and apothecaries was also a traditional target of satire; one of Sancho's proverbs is "A Doctor gives his Advice by the Pulse of your Pocket" (*Don Quixote*, II.III.20, III: 181–82). See also Pope, *An Essay on Criticism*, lines 108–9: "So modern *Pothecaries*, taught the Art / By *Doctor's Bills* to play the *Doctor's Part* . . ." (p. 251); and Tom Brown, *Works* (1760), III: 88–92 (*Amusements Serious and Comical*, Amusement XI).

One of the most interesting parallels is found in a poor imitation of vols. I and II of *TS*, entitled *The Life and Opinions of Jeremiah Kunastrokius, Doctor of Physic, &c. &c. &c.* (1760): "my Father . . . knew the different Treatments necessary for the Maladies of the Nobility and the Vulgar; felt the Pulses, both of their Bodies and their Purses, knew when to *prescribe*, and when to *unprescribe*; in short, he knew to a *Scruple* how much Physick they could take, and how much Money they could pay: By this Means he made their Health and their Pockets keep Time to the Tune of his Prescriptions" (pp. 21–22).

Finally, attention should be called to Sterne's bitter attack on the medical profession in *Sermons*, VI.35.54–56: "There is another species of this crime [murder] which is seldom taken notice of in discourses upon the subject,—and yet can be reduced to no other class:—And that is, where the life of our neighbour is shortened,—and often taken away as directly as by a weapon, by the empirical sale of nostrums and quack medicines,—which ignorance and avarice blend . . . .

"So great are the difficulties of tracing out the hidden causes of the evils to which this frame of ours is subject,—that the most candid of the profession have ever allowed and lamented how unavoidably they are in the dark.—So that the best medicines, administered with the wisest heads,—shall often do the mischief they were intended to prevent.—These are misfortunes to which we are subject in this state of darkness;—but when men without skill,—without education,—without knowledge either of the distemper, or even of what they sell,—make merchandize of the miserable,—and from a dishonest principle—trifle with the pains of the unfortunate,—too often with their lives,—and from the mere motive of a dishonest gain,—every such instance of a person bereft of life by the hand of ignorance, can be considered . . . murder in the true sense . . . ." Much of this sermon is borrowed from one by Samuel Clarke, but for the present passage in *TS* Sterne built upon the slightest of hints; see Hammond, p. 121.

Aesculapius, son of Apollo and the nymph Coronis, was for both Greeks and Romans the god of medicine; of him, William King writes: "he was skilful in Divination, as well as Medicine; it being necessary for a Physician, not only to consider the former Estate of his Patient's Body, but to consult the Preservation of his Health for the future. The Knottiness of his Staff shews the Intricacy of Medicine . . ." (*An Historical Account of the Heathen Gods and Heroes* [1710; Carbondale: Southern Illinois University Press, 1965], p. 111).

233.28–234.20 In that spacious HALL . . . the profession.] *Gown* as a reference to lawyers occurs frequently in eighteenth-century literature; for example, Richard Steele's *The Funeral*, in the preface and, again, I.ii.183 (*The Plays*, ed. Shirley Strum Kenny [Oxford: Clarendon Press, 1971], pp. 20, 35). The "spacious HALL" is Westminster-Hall, of which Thomas Brown writes in his *Amusements:* "A Magnificent building, which is open to all the world, and yet in a manner is shut up, by the prodigious concourse of people, who croud and sweat to get in or out . . . . While our traveller is making his observations . . . he's frighted at the terrible approaches of a multitude of men in black gowns and round caps, that make betwixt 'em a most hideous and dreadful monster call'd *Petty-fogging . . ."* (*Works*, III: 39–40).

Sterne's satire of the legal profession here is so traditional as to defy the identification of any one possible source, if indeed any were necessary. *Gulliver's Travels*, book IV, chap. 5, does make a similar point about the delays in proceedings: "IN pleading, they studiously avoid entering into the *Merits* of the Cause; but are loud, violent and tedious in dwelling upon all *Circumstances* which are not to the Purpose. For Instance, in the Case already mentioned: They never desire to know what Claim or Title my Adversary hath to my *Cow;* but whether the said *Cow* were Red or Black; her Horns long or short . . . . After which they consult *Precedents*, adjourn the Cause, from Time to Time, and in Ten, Twenty, or Thirty Years come to an Issue.

"IT is likewise to be observed, that this Society hath a peculiar Cant and Jargon of their own, that no other Mortal can understand . . . whereby they have wholly confounded the very Essence of Truth and Falshood, of Right and Wrong; so that it will take Thirty Years to decide whether the Field, left me by my Ancestors for six Generations, belong to me, or to a Stranger three Hundred Miles off" (*Prose Works*, XI: 233–34). Charles Kerby-Miller in his edition of *Martinus Scriblerus* notes the "Englishman's proverbial hatred of the complexities, trivialities, delays, worries, and costs of civil law" and enumerates the Scriblerians' share in this detestation (pp. 307–8).

Finally, it might be noted that Bridlegoose, Rabelais's archetypal attorney, pleads the case of Toucheronde before a "centumviral court" (III.39.260). See also his description of drawing out lawsuits, III.40.266ff.

234.8–9   *John o'Nokes . . . Tom o'Stiles*] *OED*, s.v. *John-a-nokes:* "A fictitious name for one of the parties in a legal action (usually coupled with JOHN-a-STILES as the name of the other) . . . ." Cf. *TS*, 388.11; and *Spectator* 577: "*The humble Petition of* John a Nokes *and* John a Stiles, *Sheweth,* 'THAT your Petitioners have had Causes depending in *Westminster-Hall* above five hundred Years, and that we despair of ever seeing them brought to an Issue' . . ." (IV: 574). See also Prior's *Alma*, canto III, lines 514–15: "Who in these Times would read my Books, / But TOM O' STILES, or JOHN O' NOKES?" (*Works*, I: 513).

234.17   strokes of generalship] Sterne uses the phrase again, 676.17; and in
          Political Romance, p. 14: "an artful Stroke of Generalship."
234.22   I'll be shot] Sterne uses this phrase again, 344.6, 590.8, and in the
          "Rabelaisian Fragment," p. 1088, line 17.
234.26   contrist] Cf. Rabelais, II.3.23: "Lord God, must I again contrist
          myself?" Sterne may have borrowed from this chapter (in which Gargan-
          tua mourns his wife's death) earlier in his "Author's Preface" (see above, n.
          to 229.3–29); and again in Walter's funeral oration (vol. V, chap. 3).
235.16–20 "for what hinderance . . . cane chair,"] Sterne quotes Rabelais,
          III.16.109: "What hindrance, hurt, or harm doth the laudable desire of
          knowledge bring to any man, were it from a sot, a pot, a fool, a stool, a
          winter-mittain [mittain: mitten], a truckle for a pully, the lid of a gold-
          smith's crucible, an oil-bottle, or old slipper?" Sterne adds, of course, the
          "cane chair" from which he creates his argument.
236.8   *to answer one another*] Cf. Hogarth, *Analysis of Beauty*, pp. 18–19: "If
          the uniformity of figures, parts, or lines were truly the chief cause of
          beauty, the more exactly uniform their appearances were kept, the more
          pleasure the eye would receive: but this is so far from being the case, that
          when the mind has been once satisfied, that the parts answer one another,
          with so exact an uniformity . . . the eye is rejoiced to see the object turn'd,
          and shifted, so as to vary these uniform appearances." See also Richardson,
          "Essay on the Theory of Painting," p. 72: "Thus in a figure, the arms and
          legs must not be placed to answer one another in parallel lines." Sterne
          probably was aware that "embellishments" answering one another were
          considered less desirable among the connoisseurs than the introduction of
          variety.
              Cf. *TS*, 395.3–5: "There was a fine water-mill on this side, and he
          would build a wind-mill on the other side of the river in full view to
          answer it . . . ."
236.15   sow with one ear] Sterne may have conflated in his own mind three
          proverbial expressions to arrive at his simile: (1) "You cannot make a silk
          purse out of a sow's ear"; (2) "To have the sow by the right [or wrong]
          ear"; and (3) "To take the right [or wrong] sow by the ear." See *ODEP*,
          s.v. *Silk* and *Sow*; and Tilley, P666, S684, and S685. Sancho Panza uses
          the last to warn Don Quixote when he attacks the army of sheep, I.III.4
          (I: 158).

236.20   lay your hands upon your hearts] Proverbial; Tilley, H83: "Lay thy HAND on thy heart and speak the truth"; and Stevenson, p. 1060.

237.1   entablature] *OED* does not record a figurative usage for this word.

237.6   a love of good fame or feeding] Cf. *Letters*, p. 90: "I enter this *protest*, first that my end was *honest*, and secondly, that I wrote not [to] be *fed*, but to be *famous.*" Sterne is quoting Colley Cibber, *A Letter from Mr. Cibber to Mr. Pope* (1742), p. 5: "I wrote more to be Fed than be Famous . . . ." He repeats the formula again in vol. V: "the encouragement of those few in [the world], who write not so much to be fed—as to be famous" (446.15 – 16).

237.15   their *gravities*] Cf. Yorick's attitude toward gravity, 28.9ff. and n. above.

237.24 – 238.8   that the great *Locke* . . . as the rest.] See above, n. to 227.14 – 18. Cf. *ECHU*, IV.16.3: "I cannot but own, that Men's *sticking to their past Judgment*, and adhering firmly to Conclusions formerly made, is often the cause of great obstinacy in Errour and Mistake. But the fault is not that they rely on their Memories, for what they have before well judged; but because they judged before they had well examined. . . . Which is indeed to think they judged right, because they never judged at all: And yet these of all Men hold their Opinions with the greatest stiffness; those being generally the most fierce and firm in their Tenets, who have least examined them" (pp. 658 – 59).

For "bubbled," see above, n. to 153.5 – 6.

238.3   lumber of a thousand vulgar errors] Thomas Browne, in his "To the Reader," prefacing the most well-known collection of vulgar (common) errors, *Pseudodoxia Epidemica* (1646), cites as forerunners James Primerose, *De vulgi erroribus in mèdicina* (1639); Girolamo Mercurio, *De gli errori popolari d'Italia* (1603); and Laurent Joubert, *Erreurs populaires et propos vulgaires, touchant la medecine* (1579). See Browne's *Works*, ed. Geoffrey Keynes (Chicago: University of Chicago Press, 1964), II: 5. Burton's *Anatomy* is, of course, another work in the tradition.

Locke, in his introductory "Epistle to the Reader," defines his purpose thus: "*'tis Ambition enough to be employed as an Under-Labourer in clearing Ground a little, and removing some of the Rubbish, that lies in the way to Knowledge . . .*" (*ECHU*, p. 10).

238.4   sitting down cooly] See above, n. to 118.15 – 16.

238.9   *Magna Charta*] Herbert M. Atherton (*Political Prints in the Age of Hogarth* [Oxford: Clarendon Press, 1974], p. 127, n. 49), citing W. H. Dunham ("Magna Carta and British Constitutionalism," in *The Great Charter* [New York, 1965], pp. 20–47), notes that the "Magna Carta ceased to be the most important source of British constitutionalism in the seventeenth century when first the Petition of Right, and then the Revolution Settlement replaced it. In popular thought and lore, however, the Charter remained a symbol of the nation's entailed inheritance of liberties."

238.11   not worth a groat] See above, n. to 104.7.

239.13–24   Inconsistent soul . . . heart for ever?] Cf. *Sermons*, IV.22.30–31: "If there is an evil in this world, 'tis sorrow and heaviness of heart.——The loss of goods,——of health,——of coronets and mitres, are only evil, as they occasion sorrow;——take that out——the rest is fancy, and dwelleth only in the head of man.

"Poor unfortunate creature that he is! as if the causes of anguish in the heart were not enow——but he must fill up the measure, with those of caprice; and not only walk in a vain shadow,——but disquiet himself in vain too."

That the idea is a commonplace is perhaps suggested by Addison's *Spectator* 7: "Upon my Return home, I fell into a profound Contemplation on the Evils that attend these superstitious Follies of Mankind; how they subject us to imaginary Afflictions, and additional Sorrows that do not properly come within our Lot. As if the natural Calamities of Life were not sufficient for it, we turn the most indifferent Circumstances into Misfortunes, and suffer as much from trifling Accidents, as from real Evils" (I: 33).

See also *Sermons*, I.3.71–72 ("Philantropy [*sic*] Recommended"): "Inconsistent creature that man is! who at that instant that he does what is wrong, is not able to withhold his testimony to what is good and praise worthy." This sermon recounts the parable of the good Samaritan from Luke 10: 33–34: "But a certain Samaritan, as he journeyed, came where he was: and when he saw him, he had compassion on him. And went to him, and bound up his wounds, pouring in oil and wine . . . ." Sterne alludes to this biblical text in *ASJ*, pp. 97 and 276.

240.14–17   Or for example . . . give up my simile)] Sterne reported to a correspondent, Mrs. Fenton, on August 3, 1760, that he had just finished a volume of *TS*, undoubtedly the third (*Letters*, p. 120). This passage, however, almost certainly refers to the sudden death of George II on October 25 (no other event is an obvious candidate), and hence was apparently interpolated by Sterne after he had completed his draft. Sterne brought vols. III and IV to London in late December and on Christmas Day wrote to Stephen Croft about the political changes in town: "I wish you was here to see what changes of looks and political reasoning, have taken place in every company, and coffee-house since last year; we shall be soon Prussians and Anti-Prussians, B[ute]'s and Anti-B[ute]s, and those distinctions will just do as well as Whig and Tory . . . . The K[ing] seems resolved to bring all things back to their original principles, and to stop the torrent of corruption and laziness . . . . how it will end we are all in the dark" (*Letters*, p. 126).

240.21   as silent as death] Proverbial; Tilley, D135, and *ODEP*, s.v. *Silent*.

241.20–21   a siege next summer] See above, n. to 226.21–22.

241.21   jack-boots] See *Handbook of English Costume*, p. 81: "These reached above the knees with slightly spreading 'bucket tops'; the toes blocked and square . . . . Heels square and massive but not very high. . . . Made of very strong leather"; it is noted on p. 103 that these were the riding boots of the gentry and the military.

Sterne may have been aware that in the political prints and ballads of the day, Lord Bute was coming more and more to be represented by a "jack-boot," punning on his name; see Atherton, *Political Prints*, pp. 208–27 and plate 104. To be sure, Sterne would be coming in near the beginning of this association, but it is one he might readily have absorbed from the atmosphere in London in 1760. With the death of George II, Bute began his rapid rise to power as George III's most trusted minister; see Basil Williams, *The Whig Supremacy, 1714–1760*, 2d ed. (Oxford: Clarendon Press, 1962), pp. 367–71, and J. Steven Watson, *The Reign of George III, 1760–1815* (Oxford: Clarendon Press, 1960), pp. 1–7. See also above, n. to 240.14–17.

241.27–28   they were *hereditary* . . . off the entail.] Sterne may have recalled a similar play on the language for the absolute conveyance of real property in *All's Well That Ends Well*, IV.iii.278–81: "Sir, for a cardecue he will sell the fee-simple of his salvation, the inheritance of it, and cut th' entail from all remainders, and a perpetual succession for it perpetually."

To "cut off the entail" is a legal expression meaning to put an end to the limitation of an inheritance to a particular line or class of heirs; cf. Giles Jacob, *A New Law Dictionary*, 9th ed. (1772), s.v. *entail:* an estate which is entailed is one which is "abridged, limited, and tied to certain conditions . . . ." See also Jacob's comment under *perpetuity:* "A perpetuity is a thing *odious in law*, and destructive to the commonwealth; it would put a stop to the commerce and prevent the circulation of the property of the kingdom."

See also Pope, Epistle II.ii.246–47: "The Laws of God, as well as of the Land, / Abhor, a *Perpetuity* should stand . . ." (*Imitations of Horace*, p. 183).

242.5–6   Sir *Roger Shandy . . . Marston-Moor.*] Marston-Moor, eight miles west of York, was the scene of the greatest battle of the Civil War (July 2, 1644). The battle was won by Cromwell's forces. Sterne's great-grand-father, Dr. Richard Sterne (1596–1683), later Archbishop of York, be-came famous during the war for his loyalist activities and suffered for them at Cromwell's hands. Sterne's own father was named Roger; for his military career, see Cash, *Early and Middle Years*, pp. 7–23.

242.15   my half-pay?] Cf. R. E. Scouller, *The Armies of Queen Anne* (Oxford: Clarendon Press, 1966), pp. 326–27: "The Royal Warrant of 23 Febru-ary 1698 placed officers on half pay, which was also allowed for their servants . . . . On the reduction after the Peace of Utrecht the Commons resolved in agreement with the Queen: 'Whereas upon the disbanding several of Our forces, We have thought fit that half pay shall be allowed to the commission officers . . . .'"

242.18   *pontoons*] Cf. the *Spectator*'s ridicule of the use of French words and phrases in newspaper accounts of warfare: "The Black Prince passed many a River without the help of Pontoons, and filled a Ditch with Faggots as successfully as the Generals of our times do it with Fascines" (165, II: 151). Cf. above, n. to 156.24.

242.20   twenty other . . . siege of *Messina*] See above, n. to 226.21–22.

243.2   hobby-horsical] *OED* cites this passage as its first illustration, but Sterne used the term earlier; see 86.15, 109.12, 131.27. Sterne is also the first illustration for *hobby-horsically;* see 109.11.

243.13−15   had I faith . . . house of mine] A retrograde planet is one that moves contrary to the succession of signs and degrees, i.e., from east to west; Saturn, Jupiter, Mars, Venus, and Mercury all have this apparent motion at various aspects of their cycles. John Partridge, *Mikropanastron; or An Astrological Vade Mecum* (1679), cites several aphorisms concerning retrograde planets, e.g.: "All the Planets in a Nativity Retrograde and under the Earth, though the Native be of Illustrious Birth, yet he is of a falling fame and fortune" (p. 278); and "Thou mayest know that when a Planet is Retrograde, he is a man infirm, stupified and sollicitous" (p. 322); and "Fortunate Planets Retrograde are unfortunate . . ." (p. 323).

244.4−5   or to drop . . . use of one] Cf. *ECHU*, III.10.34 (p. 508), cited above, n. to 227.14−18, where Locke attacks the use of figurative language as a "perfect cheat" in rational discourse. Cf. also Prior, *Alma*, canto III, lines 313−15: "In Argument, / Similies are like Songs in Love: / They much describe; they nothing prove" (*Works*, I: 508).

244.21   O ye POWERS!] Cf. *Don Quixote*, I.II.1: "Assist me ye Powers! But it is in vain . . ." (I: 76); and Sterne's invocation of Cervantes in vol. IX (780.1ff.).

245.6   guide-post] *OED*'s first illustration is dated 1774.

245.9−11   THO' the shock . . . widow *Wadman*] See above, n. to 117.14−15.

245.18   *Bridget*] In addition to the obvious play on *bridge*, Sterne may have had in mind a connection with St. Brigid (c. 451−525), patroness of Ireland, for whom Bridewell Hospital, the London house of correction for wayward women, was named; Sterne mentions her in vol. V (412.4).

245.21   tagging of points] Work, p. 208, n. 2: "Fastening metal tags to laces; i.e., trivialities." The expression has the sound of a commonplace, but we have been unable to locate any record of it; see, however, *OED*, s.v. *Tag* $v^1$1, especially the example dated 1630: "I must e'en go tag Points in a Garret."

246.3   Now, my dear friend *Garrick*] See above, n. to 213.6−18.

246.6   opificers] *OED* defines *opificer* as "one who makes or constructs a work; a maker, framer, fabricator . . ." and cites this passage as its last illustration. Cf. Johnson, *Dictionary:* "One that performs any work; artist. A word not received."

246.7–15   I care not . . . here or there.] The question of single versus multiple plots was of great importance to neoclassical critics, though Sterne's list
seems arbitrary at best. For Le Bossu, see above, n. to 213.26; it is worth
noting that chap. 16 of book I of his *Treatise of the Epick Poem* (*Traité du
poëme épique*) is entitled "*Of the Vicious Multiplication of* Fables." Luigi
Riccoboni (1676–1753) was the author of *Réflexions historiques et critiques
sur les différens théâtres de l'Europe* (1738), translated in 1741 as *An Historical and Critical Account of the Theatres of Europe* and in 1754 as *A General
History of the Stage*. Work suggests that Sterne may have had Luigi's son,
Francesco (1707–72), in mind (p. 208, n. 5); however, the senior Riccoboni comments directly to the point: "the *English* Comedies are crowded
with Incidents, insomuch that having adapted to their Stage some *French*
Plays, the Authors have doubled the Intrigue, or they have joined them
with another Plot to keep the Spectator in Breath, and not allow him Time
to wander in his Thoughts" (2d ed. [1754; New York: AMS, 1978],
p. 172).

   Why Sterne mentions the Roman tragedian Pacuvius (220–c. 130
B.C.) in this company is not clear; it is perhaps worth noting that John
Dennis invokes his name in the preface to *Iphigenia* (1700), a stout defense, as one might expect, of "rules": "I chiefly took care to form [the
plot] as regularly as possibly I could . . . : For Irregularity in the drama,
like Irregularity in Life, is downright extravagance, and extravagance
both upon the Stage, and in the World is always either Vice or Folly, and is
often both . . . . I find it is the daily practice of our Empiricks in Poetry to
turn our two Theatres into downright Mountebanks Stages, to treat *Aristotle* and *Horace* with as contemptuous arrogance, as our Medicinal
Quacks do *Galen* and the great *Hippocrates;* and to endeavour to make the
Rules, that is, Nature and Right Reason, as ridiculous and contemptible as
the Rules have made their Writings." Dennis then notes that the story of
Iphigenia was brought to the Roman stage with great success by Pacuvius.
The preceding passage is quoted from the first edition; a substantial portion of the preface is reprinted in *Critical Works*, ed. E. N. Hooker (Bal-
timore: Johns Hopkins Press, 1943), II: 389–90.

246.10–11   single-horse chair . . . *Pompadour's vis a vis*] *OED*'s first example of *single-horse* is dated 1764. The *vis à vis* is a "light carriage for two

persons sitting face-to-face"; the fact that this particular one belongs to "madam *Pompadour*" (1721–64), the elegant mistress of Louis XV, suggests its overwhelming superiority.

For a possible play on the phrase "going upon all four," see above, n. to 30.3–4.

247.11   moon-shiny] Cf. Dunton, *A Voyage*, I: 153: "twas a *Moon shiny* Night"; Pope's letter to Lady Mary Wortley Montagu: "I lye dreaming of you in Moonshiny Nights exactly in the posture of Endymion gaping for Cynthia in a Picture" (*Correspondence*, ed. George Sherburn [Oxford: Clarendon Press, 1956], I: 439); and "Journal to Eliza" (*Letters*, p. 382): "surprize me some sweet moon Shiney Night . . . ."

247.12–14   in the lane . . . and holly] Cf. 113.17–20: The bowling-green "was sheltered from the house . . . by a tall yew hedge, and was covered on the other three sides, from mortal sight, by rough holly and thickset flowering shrubs . . . ."

247.19   foul-mouth'd trumpet of Fame] See above, n. to 84.4–6.

248.19   soss] *OED* cites this passage as its sole illustration of usage as an adverb: "with a heavy fall or dull thud." Now considered dialect.

248.23–24   break his leg . . . soon broke] Cf. Partridge, s.v. *leg, break a:* "To give birth to a bastard: low coll.: from ca. 1670 . . . ." Also recorded by Francis Grose, *A Classical Dictionary of the Vulgar Tongue* (1785), s.v. *Leg*.

249.2–11   in a panegyric . . . which cast javelins.] Sterne could have found almost all the information for this paragraph in Chambers, but the difference in phrasing and the lack of information on the "VINEA" suggest that he had another source, not yet identified. Under *Military* MACHINES (s.v. *Machines*) Chambers describes three kinds: "the first serving to launch arrows, as the scorpion; javelins, as the catapulta; stones, as the balista; or fiery darts, as the pyraboli: the second serving to beat down walls, as the battering ram and terebra: and the third to shelter those who approached the enemies wall; as the tortoise or testudo, the vinea . . . ."

Under *Ballista*, Sterne would have found that it was "a military engine in use among the ancients, somewhat like our cross-bow, though much bigger and more forcible; used . . . to throw in stones, or sometimes darts and javelins . . . . Marcellinus describes the *ballista* thus . . . ."

Under *Catapulta*, he would have found that it was "used among the antients for throwing huge stones . . . . The *catapulta* is said to be the invention of the Syrians."

Cf. Work, p. 211, n. 11: "Tyre fell to Alexander the Great in 332 B.C. . . . *Ammianus Marcellinus* (c. 330–c. 395) was a Greek historian of Rome; the reference is to his *Rerum Gestarum Libri,* 23.4."

250.5–6   for cardinal *Alberoni*'s . . . being discovered] In discussing the events of 1718–19, culminating in the retaking of Messina (see above, n. to 226.21–22), Tindal notes in his margin: "*Intrigues of* Spain"; and below that, "Alberoni*'s practices discovered in* France" (IV: 582).

Work, p. 212, n. 1: "Giulio Alberoni (1664–1752), Spanish-Italian cardinal and statesman who, as prime minister of Philip V of Spain, pursued such an ambitious foreign policy that by 1718 Spain was involved in a disastrous war with England, France, Holland, and the Empire."

250.6–20   my uncle *Toby* . . . *Italian* bridge?] See above, n. to 226.21–22. Walter's prediction is accurate in part; England declared war on Spain in December 1718, and France followed suit, forming, with the Empire and Holland, the Quadruple Alliance against Spain. The "pre-engagements" would include particularly the Treaty of Utrecht (see above, n. to 117.14–15), whereby England and France were guarantors of the neutrality of Italy. See Tindal, IV: 565, the text of instructions sent to Admiral Byng in May 1718, ordering him to attack the Spanish fleet: "Whereas the Crown of *Great-Britain,* by the several treaties made at *Utrecht,* the 14th day of *March* 1713, *N.S.* with the Emperor and the late most Christian King, became obliged to see an exact observation of the armistice and neutrality then established in *Italy,* and was guarantee for the full performance of the stipulations at that time solemnly agreed to on that head: And whereas, by a treaty made between Us and our good Brother the Emperor of *Germany,* at *Westminster,* the 25th day of *May* 1716, we stand engaged to assist, maintain, and defend him in the possession of all the . . . Rights, which he then actually enjoyed in *Europe* . . . ."

Sterne seems to have been particularly interested in English-Spanish relations during this period, perhaps because they so often centered upon the English garrison at Gibraltar, where his father went in 1727 to oppose yet another Spanish siege (again, it was the Treaty of Utrecht that gave Gibraltar "for ever" to England; see Tindal, IV: 339). The year 1727 was, quite probably, the last time Sterne saw his father (see *Letters,* pp. 3 and 7,

n. 18; Cash, *Early and Middle Years*, pp. 36–39; *Political Romance*, pp. 37–39; and above, n. to 242.5–6).

250.15 went together by the ears] Proverbial; see Tilley, E23, and Stevenson, p. 654.

251.17–252.5 For a whole week . . . cycloid itself.] Cf. Chambers, s.v. *Bridge:* "*Draw*-BRIDGE, *Pons subductarius*, is such a one as is made fast only at one end, with hinges; so that the other end may be lifted up; in which case the *bridge* stands upright, to hinder the passage of a moat, or the like.

"There are others made to draw back, to hinder the passage, and to thrust over again to afford a passage. And others, which open in the middle; half of which turns away to one side, and the other to the other; being joined again at pleasure: but these have this inconvenience, that one half of them remains on the enemy's side.

"The Marquis de l'Hopital has given the construction of a curve, in which a weight will always be a counter-balance to a *draw-bridge;* which the younger Bernoulli has shewn to be no other than the cycloid.——*Vid. Act. Erud. Lips. an.* 1695. *p.* 56. *seq.*" Noted by Bensly, "A Debt," p. 806.

Work, p. 213, n. 3: "Jacques Bernouilli (1654–1705), a famous mathematician, presented his solution of the curve in [*Acta Eruditorum* (Leipzig, 1695), pp. 65–66]; but the reference . . . Sterne took from the article 'Bridge' in Chambers's *Cyclopædia*." Guillaume-François Antoine de l'Hospital (1661–1704) was a celebrated French mathematician; see *Nouvelle Biographie Générale*, s.v., for a detailed account of his discoveries and his relation with Bernouilli.

The source for the bridges at Spires and Brisac (Breisach), towns in the southwest area of the Empire, remains unidentified.

It is possible that Sterne's discussion of bridges here is capitalizing on a *cause célèbre* in London society in early 1760, a debate concerning the type of construction to be employed for the Blackfriars Bridge over the Thames. Boswell notes Johnson's involvement in the question; see *Life of Johnson*, I: 351–52.

252.6–8 My uncle *Toby* . . . cycloid] In an insightful essay, Sigurd Burckhardt suggests that Sterne's interest in these mathematical figures (see 103.14–24, for Toby's encounter with the Parabola) provides a clue to the nature of the work: "nothing seems so obvious to him—and nothing should *be* so obvious—as that, if you want to project something over a gap, your line can never be straight, but must be indirect, parabolic, hyperbolic, cycloid.

". . . the real line of communication must be the cycloid curve, indirect, similar to the projectile's parabola" ("*Tristram Shandy*'s Law of Gravity," *ELH* 28 [1961]: 80–81).

252.19   *Savoyard*'s box] Possibly, as Work suggests (p. 214, n. 1), a hurdy-gurdy. Natives of Savoy were noted for their itinerant wanderings with this instrument and a chained monkey; see *OED*, s.v. *Savoyard*. However, Sterne far more probably had in mind the "raree-shew box" also associated with Savoyards and which he uses again, 706.5; see n. below.

253.9–10   he has crush'd . . . pancake to his face] Proverbial; see Tilley, P39, and *ODEP*, s.v. *Flat*. Tilley's earliest examples are all references to a flattened nose, while the *ODEP* cites Erasmus, *Apophthegmes* (book II, "Antigonus," no. 27), for its first illustration: "his nose as flat as a cake, bruised or beaten to his face." "As flat as a [pan]cake" was generalized by the seventeenth century.

255.16   set-stitch'd] *OED* (s.v. *set, ppl. a.* 8.): "?of 'set-work' embroidery," i.e., "A kind of embroidery used in working tapestry." This passage is cited as sole illustration.

255.25–26   he could as soon hit the longitude] Various means to determine longitude at sea occupied the attention of scientific minds throughout the century, culminating in success in Sterne's own day; see below, n. to 721.7–15.

256.1   "*ALL is not . . . purse.*"] Proverbial; see Tilley, A151: "ALL is not won that is put in the purse"; and *ODEP*, s.v. *Gain*.

258.21–24   For by the word . . . or less.] That "nose" does not mean simply "nose" is obvious, but in addition to its phallic implications, Robert G. Walker ("A Sign of the Satirist's Wit: The Nose in *Tristram Shandy*," *BSUF* 19 [1978]: 52–54) has well demonstrated the classical tradition whereby the length of one's nose was equated to the extent of one's wit, a play upon "the ambiguous meaning of *nasutus:* sagacious, witty, or large-nosed." In addition to classical sources in Horace, Persius, and Martial, Walker cites the "Explanatory Remarks" of Ozell for Rabelais, IV.9: "BY the island of Ennasin . . . Rabelais at once exposes unequal matches, and the dull jests and stupidity of gross clowns: which, as the Latin hath it, have no nose, that is, no wit" (p. xviii).

Of his "chapter of noses" Sterne wrote to his friend Stephen Croft: "I am not much in pain upon what gives my kind friends . . . so much on the chapter of *Noses*—because, as the principal satire throughout that part is levelled at those learned blockheads who, in all ages, have wasted their time and much learning upon points as foolish—it shifts off the idea of what you fear, to another point . . ." (*Letters*, p. 126).

259.6–9   Now, my . . . island of ENNASIN.] In Rabelais, IV.9, Pantagruel and his company arrive at the island of Ennasin; here the "men, women, and children, have their noses shap'd like an ace of clubs. For that reason the ancient name of the country was Ennasin," i.e., as Ozell tells us, "Noseless or flat-nosed" (pp. 117–18). The Ennasinians couple metaphorically, it would seem, by identifying their mates as the necessary concomitant to themselves; hence, "hatchet" and "helve"; "crum" and "crust"; "tap" and "spiggot" (cf. *TS*, 414.16–25). Rabelais runs through several pages of such couplings, and of course Sterne has picked up the idea in such items as buttons and buttonholes.

260.5   saving the mark] Proverbial; Stevenson, p. 1529, and *ODEP*, s.v. *God*. The latter provides this headnote: "prob. originally a formula to avert an evil omen, hence used by way of apology when something horrible, etc., has been mentioned." After the initial citation of *Romeo and Juliet*, III.ii.52–53 ("I saw the wound, I saw it with mine eyes— / God save the mark!"), the present passage is cited.

260.10   *Michaelmas* and *Lady day*] Michaelmas is celebrated on September 29 and Lady-day (Feast of the Annunciation) on March 25; in England, they are two of the four quarter-days on which rents and various other fiscal responsibilities are discharged.

260.19   cawl] I.e., *caul:* "The netted substructure of a wig" (*OED*).

260.23–261.4   Defend me . . . derived from ancestors!] Sterne strikes this particular posture of moral tolerance several times in *TS* and *ASJ*. In the latter, for example, in the chapter that follows his temptation with the *fille de chambre*, he begins: "YES——and then—Ye whose clay-cold heads and luke-warm hearts can argue down or mask your passions—tell me, what trespass is it that man should have them? or how his spirit stands answerable, to the father of spirits, but for his conduct under them?" (p. 237). The second paragraph of the chapter is quoted below, n. to 435.16−17, another passage much like the present one in tone: "—Now I love you for this—and 'tis this delicious mixture within you which makes you dear creatures what you are . . . ."

Sterne's language here may echo Numbers 16: 26: "Depart, I pray you, from the tents of these wicked men, and touch nothing of theirs, lest ye be consumed in all their sins"; or Psalm 84: 10: "I had rather be a doorkeeper in the house of my God, than to dwell in the tents of wickedness."

261.9   whimsicality] *OED* cites this passage as its first example.

261.11−14   For in a great measure . . . perfection.] Cf. 448.6−8: "Prejudice of education," Walter would say, "*is the devil,*—and the multitudes of them which we suck in with our mother's milk—*are the devil and all.*" The idea is at least as old as Cicero: "nunc autem, simul atque editi in lucem et suscepti sumus, in omni continuo pravitate et in summa opinionum perversitate versamur, ut paene cum lacte nutricis errorem suxisse videamur . . ." ("as things are, however, as soon as we come into the light of day and have been acknowledged, we at once find ourselves in a world of iniquity amid a medley of wrong beliefs, so that it seems as if we drank in deception with our nurse's milk . . ."). Cicero then goes on to suggest how education amplifies and confirms our prejudices and "general tendency to error" (*Tusculan Disputations*, pp. 226−27).

261.28−262.2   It was . . . turn'd up trumps.] The metaphor is from whist, where the final card dealt is turned face up to establish the trump suit. The description of the trump card, the ace of clubs, as "vile" may be an allusion to the belief that clubs are an unlucky suit in whist or may simply refer to the devaluing of the ace as a trump as soon as it is turned up. There is a further allusion to whist at 778.19−20.

For a somewhat different conjecture, see Timothy G. A. Nelson, "*Double-Entendres* in the Card Game in Pope's *Rape of the Lock,*" *PQ* 59 (1980): 234−38. Nelson suggests an allusion to ombre, in which the strength (virility) of the ace of spades (Spadillo) is contrasted with the weakness of the ace of clubs (Basto).

The phrase "turn up trumps" appears in both Tilley, T544, and *ODEP,* s.v. *Turn;* Burton's *Anatomy* is the first citation.

262.5−6   I mean . . . in his face] Cf. Chambers, s.v. *Nose:* "the external organ of smelling; or that part in men which stands prominent, in the middle of the face."

262.13–14   old dogs,——"of not learning new tricks."] Proverbial; Tilley, D500 ("An old Dog will learn no tricks"), and *ODEP*, s.v. *Teach*.

263.3–264.4   I am aware . . . the apple is *John*'s apple.] Sterne borrows his discussion from Locke's chapter on property in *Of Civil Government*, 2.5.27–28, in *Two Treatises of Government*, ed. Peter Laslett (Cambridge: Cambridge University Press, 1966), pp. 305–6: "Though the Earth, and all inferior Creatures be common to all Men, yet every Man has a *Property* in his own *Person*. This no Body has any Right to but himself. The *Labour* of his Body, and the *Work* of his Hands, we may say, are properly his. Whatsoever then he removes out of the State that Nature hath provided, and left it in, he hath mixed his *Labour* with, and joyned to it something that is his own, and thereby makes it his *Property*. It being by him removed from the common state Nature placed it in, it hath by this *labour* something annexed to it, that excludes the common right of other Men. For this *Labour* being the unquestionable Property of the Labourer, no Man but he can have a right to what that is once joyned to, at least where there is enough, and as good left in common for others.

"He that is nourished by the Acorns he pickt up under an Oak, or the Apples he gathered from the Trees in the Wood, has certainly appropriated them to himself. No Body can deny but the nourishment is his. I ask then, When did they begin to be his? When he digested? Or when he eat? Or when he boiled? Or when he brought them home? Or when he pickt them up? And 'tis plain, if the first gathering made them not his, nothing else could. That *labour* put a distinction between them and common."

263.5   *ex confesso*] "Confessedly."

263.14   *Tribonius*] See above, n. to 215.24–26.

263.15–16   beard being . . . his beard] Cf. above, n. to 211.6–18.

263.17   he takes up the cudgels for me] Proverbial; Tilley, C898, and *ODEP*, s.v. *Take*.

263.19–21   in the fragments . . . and *Des Eaux*] Sterne borrows from Chambers, s.v. *Code:* "In 506, Alaric, king of the Goths, made a new collection of the Roman laws, taken from the three former *Codes*, the *Gregorian*, *Hermogenian*, and *Theodosian*, which he likewise published under the title of the *Theodosian Code*. . . .

"There have been various other later *Codes,* particularly of the ancient Gothic, and since of the French kings; as the *Code* of Euridic, the *Code* Michault, *Code* Louis, *Code* Neron . . . *Code* des Eaux, *&c.*"

Cf. *Work,* p. 222, n. 3: "The Gregorian Code, of which but fragments are extant, was a collection of imperial constitutions made by a certain Gregorius, who may have been a professor at the law school of Beirut, about 295 A.D. . . . Sterne intended to write *Hermogenianus,* whose Code, compiled about 324 A.D., was supplementary to the Gregorian Code. Before the time of Justinian . . . the codes of Gregorius and Hermogenianus had been regarded as the only authoritative record of constitutions during the periods they covered; from them Justinian obtained the constitutions contained in his Code for the period prior to Constantine. The codes of Louis XIV (1638–1715), which have had a considerable influence on modern law, were the latest great codes at the time Sterne wrote. *Des Eaux* appears to be a confused reference to Louis XIV's *Ordonnance des eaux et forêts* of 1669, a famous code designed to conserve and develop French forests, of which numerous erudite interpretations were written. This slip suggests that here, as in other known cases, Sterne derived his 'erudition' from marginalia rather than from the text."

Cf. Day, "A Note on Sterne: 'Des Eaux'," p. 303; and above, n. to 215.24–26.

264.12   by teeth and claws] Variant of proverbial "tooth and nail"; see Tilley, T422, and *ODEP,* s.v. *Tooth.*

265.21   for each one's service, thou hadst a tear] Cf. 255.27–28: "having a tear at every one's service." The fact that "service" became "sorrows" in the 1780 edition (see t.n., vol. II, p. 851, in this edition), and is the reading of Work, perhaps suggests an unauthorized attempt to avoid the bawdy implication of *service.* See, e.g., 807.12–14: "My father . . . was obliged to keep a Bull for the service of the Parish"; and *ASJ,* p. 95: "I felt benevolence for her; and resolved some way or other to throw in my mite of courtesy—if not of service."

266.4ff.   *Bruscambille's* prologue, etc.] Sterne probably did not read Bruscambille, but simply lifted the reference from Rabelais, I.40.320, n. 15: "Bruscambille has repeated it in his prologue on large noses. And from thence a certain pleasant she sinner, being deceiv'd, cry'd out, Nase, me decepisti: nose, thou hast deceiv'd me. (She would never judge of a cock by his comb, any more)." Similarly, two other "authorities" cited by Walter probably came to Sterne via Ozell's footnote on the page preceding: "Bouchet, in his 24th serée (which I take to mean his evenings conferences, for I never saw the book) says that friar John's answer is not altogether a joke; for that the famous surgeon, Ambrose Paræus, has maintain'd, that the hardness of a nurse's breast may make the child have a flat nose" (p. 319, n. 14). Both notes are in that chapter of Rabelais upon which Sterne builds his own discussion of noses in chap. 38; see W. G. Day, "Sterne and Ozell," *ES* 53 (1972): 434–36; and below, n. to 276.24–277.14.

On the other hand, Jeffrey R. Smitten locates a particular passage in Bruscambille's *Pensées facetieuses* (Cologne, 1709) that amplifies the proverb "voilà qui n'à pas de nez nous servira beaucoup" and that he believes "must have been a *locus classicus*" for Walter's theory: "On en poura dire autant d'un Peintre, d'un Orfévre, de l'auteur d'un pitoyable Livre, & generalement de toute sorte de choses qui ne feront pas dans le gout des Messieurs qui se qualifient du nez fin; de manière qu'à leur sentiment tout ce qui n'à point de nez est méprisable & ne mérite pas de voir le jour. Et c'est la raison pourquoi l'on cache ordinairement le cul comme étant un visage qui n'a point de nez, & au contraire la face est toujours découverte à cause qu'il y a dans le milieu un nez; un homme sans nez est rejetté des femmes. Le physionomiste Albert le grand aussibien que le savant Trismegiste disent que les femmes estiment les grands nez nobles, & de bonne race, les mediocres, de contentement, & les petits de bon appétit" (pp. 61–62); quoted from *"Tristram Shandy* and Spatial Form," *ArielE* 8 (1977): 45. Smitten provides his own translation (p. 59, n. 9): "One could as well say it of a Painter, or a Goldsmith, of the author of a paltry book, and generally of a variety of things having no relevance to the taste of Gentlemen who style themselves fine-nosed; their feeling is that anyone who has no nose at all is contemptible and does not even deserve the light of day. And that is the reason why one customarily hides one's arse as it is a face without a nose and contrariwise one always uncovers the face as it has a nose in the middle of it; a man without a nose is repellent to women. Albertus Magnus the physiognomist as well as Trismegistus the scholar says that women think of big noses as noble, and well-bred middle-sized ones as satisfying, and little ones as having good inclinations." Possibly "strong appetites" rather than "good inclinations" is more in keeping with the spirit of the passage. We continue to believe, however, that Sterne, with one exception (see below, n. to 276.16−23), never went beyond Rabelais for his theory of noses, the same conclusion reached in the most extensive study of the problem, C. F. Jones's "The French Sources of Sterne" (Ph.D. diss., University of London, 1931).

Cf. Work, p. 224, n. 1 (on Bruscambille): "The theatrical name of le Sieur Deslauriers, a comedian whose *Prologues tant sérieux que facécieux*, facetious paradoxes and harangues on a variety of topics, appeared in an authorized edition in 1610"; p. 225, n. 2: "Guillaume Bouchet [c. 1513−93], of Poitiers, commenced publishing his *Sérées*, a vivacious melange of wit, in 1584"; and p. 233, n. 6: "Ambrose Paré (1510−1590), who first served as a military surgeon in the army of Francis I, was chief surgeon to Henry II, Francis II, Charles IX, and Henry III." Sterne inadvertently calls Paré "Andrea" at this point (267.2) but later corrects himself, not only by calling him "Ambrose" (276.9, 16, 24, etc.) but by giving "Andrea" to Scroderus (275.27); or perhaps Sterne here intended "*Scroderus (Andrea), Parœus*" but was unclear in the manuscript.

We agree with Work (p. 225, n. 2) that *Prignitz* and *Scroderus* "sound suspicious (particularly for Shandaic authorities on noses)"; in his parody of a learned footnote in "Slawkenbergius's Tale" (310.20−30), Sterne cites a "J. Scrudr." who would seem to have some relationship to Scroderus, and also Rever. J. Tubal and Von Jacobum Koinshoven.

Hafen Slawkenbergius is also an invented name; Work provides the probable etymology: "'*Slawkenbergius*' (cf. German *Schlackenberg*) means 'pile of slag,' or 'offal,' or possibly 'excrement,' and '*Hafen*' is a colloquial German term for 'chamber-pot' . . ." (p. 230, n. 1). Cf. Rabelais, I.19.222, where Ozell notes a satire against scholasticism in which the central part is played by "a certain German of Nuremberg, merrily named doctor Hafen-muss (potage de marmite)"; this might be translated "pot of mush."

266.12−13   from *Piccadilly* to *Coleman*-street] Coleman Street was in the heart of London's financial district in the mid-eighteenth century (and remains so today), running north-south between Guildhall to the west and the Royal Exchange and the Bank of England (1734) to the east. In modern terms, it is located in E.C. 2, between Gresham Street and London Wall, parallel to and immediately west of Moorgate.

266.19–24 he solaced himself with *Bruscambille* . . . to by-standers] Cf. *Letters*, p. 76 (summer, 1759): "to Sport too Much with Your wit—or the Game that wit has pointed is surfeiting—like toying with a Mans Mistress—it may be a Very delightful Solacement to the Inamorato—tho little to the bystander."

Cf. *Tom Jones*, book I, chap. 11: "Not to tire the Reader, by leading him through every Scene of this Courtship, (which, tho' in the Opinion of a certain great Author, it is the pleasantest Scene of Life to the Actor, is perhaps as dull and tiresome as any whatever to the Audience) the Captain made his Advances in Form, the Citadel was defended in Form, and at length, in proper Form, surrendered at Discretion" (I: 68–69). Battestin identifies the "great Author" as Addison (*Spectator* 261), but only for the first part of the observation. The military metaphor at the end of the quotation is, of course, worth notice in relation to *TS*.

Cf. 113.15–17, Toby's decampment for Shandy Hall and the bowling-green: "Never did lover post down to a belov'd mistress with more heat and expectation, than my uncle *Toby* did, to enjoy this self-same thing in private . . . ."

266.25–26 my father's eye . . . his appetite] Cf. Tilley, E261 ("His Eyes are bigger than his belly"); and *ODEP*, s.v. *Eye*.

267.9–12 celebrated dialogue . . . long noses.] Sterne refers to "De Captandis Sacerdotiis" ("Of Benefice-Hunters") from the *Colloquia Familiaria* of Erasmus; see below, n. to 271.1–272.18.

267.15–19 like an unback'd filly . . . the dirt.] Rabelais tells the story of Francis Villon's vengeance on Friar Tickletoby: Villon and his friends ambush Tickletoby and startle his mare, the "filly of the convent (so they call a young mare that was never leap'd yet)"; the filly "was soon scar'd out of her seven senses, and began to start, to funk it, to squirt it, to trot it, to fart it, to bound it, to gallop it, to kick it, to spurn it, to calcitrate it, to wince it, to frisk it, to leap it, to curvet it, with double jirks, and bum-motions; insomuch that she threw down Tickletoby . . . ." Ironically neither the strap nor crupper is broken in Rabelais, so that Tickletoby is dragged along the road, "his cockle brains were dash'd out . . . his arms

fell to pieces. . . . Then she made a bloody havock with his puddings; and
being got to the convent, brought back only his right foot and twisted
sandal, leaving them to guess what was become of the rest" (IV.13.137–
39). In that Sterne so often borrows verbatim, it is interesting in this
passage where he sends us to his source that the borrowing is a loose paraphrase. *Tickletoby* is a cant term for "penis" or "a wanton," according to
Partridge; cf. *Toby* (i.e., "buttocks").

267.23   what year . . . war broke out.] Events in Roman history were often
dated "from the founding of the city" (*ab urbe condita*) of Rome in 753
B.C. The second Punic War began in 218 B.C., or 535 *ab urb. con.*;
Polybius and Livy are the primary sources of information concerning it.

268.1–2   Read, read, read . . . read] Cf. 337.18–20, where we are told,
with similar insistence, to read Longinus: "you must read *Longinus*—read
away—if you are not a jot the wiser by reading him the first time over—
never fear—read him again . . . ." The parallel is interesting in view of
Sterne's main character in his "Rabelaisian Fragment," Longinus Rabelaicus; see below, n. to 337.7–20.

268.2–3   saint *Paraleipomenon*] See *OED*, s.v. *Paralipomena:* "Things omitted in the body of a work, and appended as a supplement." The singular
form, rarely used, does occur in *Don Quixote*, II.III.40, where "*Sir* Para-
lipomenon, *Knight of the three Stars*" is mentioned (IV: 47); and in John
Bulwer's *Chironomia; or the Art of Manual Rhetoric* (1644), ed. James W.
Cleary (Carbondale: Southern Illinois University Press, 1978), p. 210.

268.7   motly] The obvious meaning—"diversified in colour; variegated,
parti-coloured" (*OED*)—should not make us forget the word's association with the costumes of court fools and clowns, as in *As You Like It*,
II.vii.12–13: "I met a fool i' th' forest, / A motley fool."

268.8–10   has been able . . . the black one.] Cf. *Political Romance*, p. 45:
"——Thus every Man turn'd the Story to what was swimming uppermost
in his own Brain;—so that, before all was over, there were full as many
Satyres spun out of it,—and as great a Variety of Personages, Opinions,
Transactions, and Truths, found to lay hid under the dark Veil of its
Allegory, as ever were discovered in the thrice-renowned History of the
Acts of *Gargantua* and *Pantagruel*." Sterne is recalling Motteux's preface:
"The ingenious of our age, as well as those who lived when Rabelais
composed his Gargantua and Pantagruel, have been extreamly desirous of

discovering the truths which are hid under the dark veil of allegories in that incomparable work" (Rabelais, I, p. xxxv).

The image recurs in *TS*, vol. V (448.2–5): "there was as much good meaning, truth, and knowledge, couched under the veil of *John de la Casse*'s parabolical representation,—as was to be found in any one poetic fiction, or mystick record of antiquity."

269–70 (marbled leaf)] On the preparation of the marbled leaf for the first edition, see W. G. Day, *"Tristram Shandy:* The Marbled Leaf," *Library* 27 (1972): 143–45. An earlier instance of its use is cited by Eric Rothstein, *Systems of Order and Inquiry in Later Eighteenth-Century Fiction* (Berkeley: University of California Press, 1975), p. 66: "Conceivably the marbled paper, with its mystic meanings, is a reply to Noël-Antoine Pluche, who used it as an example of meaningless color unconnected to objects. *Le Spectacle de la nature,* 9 vols. (Paris, 1732–42), 7: 68 . . . ." In the Florida edition, the marbled leaf is a photographic reproduction of an original leaf (recto and verso), as it appeared in the first edition of 1761; the original measures 116mm. x 68mm.

271.1–272.18   *"NIHIL me pœnitet* . . . in a passion.] Sterne is quoting from the dialogue between Pamphagus and Cocles noted above, 267.9–12; the lines are translated by N. Bailey (*Familiar Colloquies,* 2d ed. [1733], p. 26) as "I am not at all sorry for this Nose. No, nor have you any occasion to be sorry for [it] . . . ." Bailey misassigns the speakers, but Sterne has them as in Erasmus. The line upon which Walter sets to work is "Conducet excitando foculo, si desuerit follis" (*Colloquia* [Leyden: Elzeviriana, 1636], p. 29), which Bailey translates: "If you have no Bellows it will serve to blow the Fire" (p. 26). Work's comment seems correct: "Sterne was forced to wrench an instrument of blowing into one of stirring or poking, and to alter both the construction and the vocabulary of his original. My father's scratching could transform the original text into *ad excitandum ficum* ["to stir up (to arouse) the fig"] or into *ad excitandum locum* ["to stir up (to arouse) the place"], either of which would serve Sterne's purpose" (pp. 229–30, nn. 3, 4). Cf. Sterne's use of *figs* in vol. VII, 647.8–23, where he purchases some from an old woman: "I had figs enow for my money . . . . I could do as little with my figs, which were too ripe already, and most of 'em burst at the side." *Place* is used with obvious bawdy intention in vol. IX, 803.5–7: "whereas the groin, your honour knows, is upon the very *curtin* of the *place*."

271.9   ambidexterity] *OED* cites this passage as its first illustration of figurative use, with the definition "superior dexterity or cleverness; shiftiness or general readiness; manysidedness."

271.18–19   Learned men . . . noses for nothing.] Cf. Montaigne, II.16.348: "Men do not write Histories of Things of so little Moment . . . ." Coleridge considered Walter's remark to have in it "more humor . . . than in the whole Slawkenburghian tale that follows" (*Coleridge's Miscellaneous Criticism*, ed. Thomas Middleton Raysor [Cambridge: Harvard University Press, 1936], p. 126).

271.19–20   I'll study the mystic . . . sense] The satire here seems directed particularly toward editors (e.g., Warburton), who often measured their success by the alteration of a substantive reading to a "better" reading. Thomas Edwards's *Canons of Criticism* was perhaps the most popular satire in this mode during the middle years of the eighteenth century (first published in 1748, it had five reprintings by 1757 and another in 1765). It is an attack on Warburton's *Shakespeare* and begins with some twenty-five canons he maintains were derived from observing the editor at work; e.g.: "I. *A Professed Critic has a right to declare, that his Author wrote whatever He thinks he ought to have written . . . .* II. *He has a right to alter any passage, which He does not understand. . . .* IV. *Where he does not like an expression, and yet cannot mend it; He may abuse his Author for it*" (p. 25).

Edwards anticipates Johnson's response to Warburton in his 1765 edition of Shakespeare; e.g., in the opening pages of *As You Like It* (vol. II), Johnson responds in a typical manner to various emendations by Warburton ("discontenance" for "countenance"; "shine" for "seem"; "varlet" for "world"; "Juniper" for "Jupiter") with phrases like "There is no need of change" (p. 4); "I cannot find the absurdity of the present reading" (p. 16); "The plain meaning of the old and true reading . . ." (p. 23); "Either reading may stand. The . . . established text is not weak or obscure" (p. 24); "I see no need of changing . . ." (p. 39); "I am afraid that no reader is satisfied with Dr. *Warburton's* emendation, however vigorously enforced . . ." (p. 46); and "Surely *Jupiter* may stand" (p. 54).

See above, n. to 213.14, for another possible allusion to Edwards.

Also cf. *Tale of a Tub*, where Peter, another "emender of texts," convinces his brothers that the prohibition against "silver fringes" is really against "silver broom-sticks," the meaning of which is to be understood in "a *Mythological*, and *Allegorical* Sense"; in short, it is "a *Mystery*" (p. 88).

271.24−272.1   the many nautical uses . . . by *Erasmus*] Two nautical uses suggested in the dialogue are as a grappling-hook in a sea-fight, and more simply, as an anchor (*Familiar Colloquies*, pp. 26−27).

272.20   *Disgrázias*] *OED:* "unpleasant accidents, misfortunes, disgraces." *OED* considers this Spanish word unnaturalized and cites Cibber's *Apology* (1739) as its sole eighteenth-century example.

273.9−10   *Slawkenbergius*'s sensorium] Cf. above, nn. to 125.9 and 131.8−11. Sterne converts his fire bellows into organ bellows in order to re-create that view of the sensorium as the seat of the *"sentient Principle . . .* in some Place in the Brain, where the Nerves terminate, like the *Musician* shut up in his Organ-Room" (George Cheyne, *The English Malady* [1733], p. 61).

273.15−19   *Slawkenbergius* . . . upon it needless.] Work, p. 231, n. 3: "George Whitefield (1714−1770), one of the founders of Methodism and a moving pulpit orator, preached that without any rational thought the soul can feel whether its actions are motivated by the devil or by the spirit of God."

Sterne directs several of his sermons against Methodism and in particular against the spiritual pride of its adherents. For example, in "Humility" he writes: "However backwards the world has been in former ages in the discovery of such points as GOD never meant us to know,——we have been more successful in our own days:——thousands can trace out now the impressions of this divine intercourse in themselves, from the first moment they received it, and with such distinct intelligence of it's progress and workings, as to require no evidence of it's truth.

"It must be owned, that the present age has not altogether the honour of this discovery;—there were too many grounds given to improve on in the religious cant of the last century;—when the *in-comings, in-dwellings,* and *out-lettings* of the Spirit, were the subjects of so much edification . . . .

"So that in fact, the opinions of methodists . . . is but a republication with some alterations of the same extravagant conceits; and as enthusiasm generally speaks the same language in all ages, 'tis but too sadly verified in this; for tho' we have not yet got to the old terms . . . yet we have arrived to the first feelings of its enterance, recorded with as particular an exactness, as an act of filiation,——so that numbers will tell you the identical place,——the day of the month, and the hour of the night, when the spirit came in upon them, and took possession of their hearts" (*Sermons*, IV.25.127–30).

See also "On Enthusiasm" (*Sermons*, VI.38.141–49). In many ways "Abuses of Conscience" may also be read as an anti-Methodist treatise in its questioning of man's capacity effectively to know himself.

273.27–274.1   sit down coolly . . . within himself] Cf. above, n. to 118.15–16.

274.6   *what was what*] Proverbial; see Tilley, K178 ("to know what is what"), and Stevenson, p. 1327.

274.9   to gird up myself] Biblical phrase; e.g., Job 38: 3, 40: 7, and Jeremiah 1: 17: "Thou therefore gird up thy loins, and arise, and speak unto them all that I command thee: be not dismayed at their faces, lest I confound thee before them."

274.14   *en-nich'd*] *OED* cites this passage as its sole illustration, s.v. *en*-B.l.a.

274.24–27   so that . . . known about them.] Cf. above, n. to 215.24–26. Sterne's multiple formulations of the concept of codes, digests, and systems are certainly noteworthy.

275.6   twenty charnel houses in *Silesia*] Silesia, an area presently divided between Poland and Czechoslovakia, was in the eighteenth century disputed between Prussia and Austria, with Prussia ultimately claiming most of it. Insofar as three-quarters of Silesia's population was said to have been killed during the Thirty Years War, its charnel houses a century later might well have been singled out; we can find no other reason for Sterne's having done so.

275.9–11   except *Crim Tartary* . . . upon them] Cf. Chambers, s.v. *Nose:* "The Crim-Tartars break the *noses* of their children while young, as thinking it a great piece of folly to have their *noses* stand before their eyes"; noted by Bensly, "A Debt," p. 806.

This perhaps explains why the hero of "Slawkenbergius's Tale" is going to return to "*Crim-Tartary*" (Crimea) after his journey to Frankfort (289.9).

275.19–21   bating the case . . . tutelage of heaven)] Cf. *The Travels of the late Charles Thompson, Esq.* (Reading, 1744), II: 266: "The *Santons*, or Saints, are such as we call Naturals or Idiots, and People who are out of their Senses, or at least make a Shew of being so, which among the *Turks* are reckon'd great Signs of Sanctity; for the *Mahometans* in general have a great Veneration for Fools and Madmen, as thinking them actuated by a divine Spirit." The observation seems to have been commonplace among eighteenth-century travelers to Turkey; see also Thomas Osborne, *A Collection of Voyages and Travels* (1745), I: 546–47.

276.16–23   That this *Ambrose Parœus* . . . in hand.] As noted above (n. to 266.4ff.), Ambrose Paré served Henry II, Francis II, Charles IX, and Henry III, but not Francis IX—who, in fact, never existed, although Sterne refers to him again in vol. IV (360.3–5): "in the story of my father and his christen-names,—I had no thoughts of treading upon *Francis* the First—nor in the affair of the nose—upon *Francis* the Ninth." Cf. Work, p. 301, n. 1: "There was no Francis IX, wherein (probably) lies the jest. If Sterne meant an actual king, he likely intended Francis I, who had a very long and large nose, who was said to have died of syphilis, and whose critics insisted on the physical consequences of his shamelessly licentious life." It does seem more likely that Sterne purposely created a nonexistent monarch for the particular honor of having Paré (whose reputation was in no way based on such skills) serve as his "nose-mender."

That Sterne was aware of Paré's "slip" concerning the surgical procedure devised by Gaspare Tagliacozzi (1545–99) suggests that he knew Tagliacozzi's work firsthand, since it was he, rather than commentators, who had pointed it out. Paré had first described a nose-restoration procedure in 1575; we quote from *Works*, trans. Th. Johnson (1678), book XXIV, chap. 21, p. 551: "There was a Surgeon of *Italy* of late years which would restore or repair the portion of the Nose that was cut away after this manner. He first scarified the callous edges of the maimed Nose round about . . . . : then he made a gash or cavity in the muscle of the arm . . . as large as the greatness of the portion of the Nose which was cut away did require: and into that gash or cavity so made, he would put that part of the Nose so wounded, and bind the Patients head to his arm, as if it were to a post . . . ; and about forty days after, or at that time when he judged the flesh of the Nose was perfectly agglutinated with the flesh of the arm; he cut out as much of the flesh of the arm cleaving fast unto the nose, as was sufficient to supply the defect of that which was lost . . . ." However,

Tagliacozzi's very thorough modern biographers have pointed out that
Paré is here describing a procedure used by other doctors, as Tagliacozzi
himself pointed out on several occasions, the first of which was in 1586:
"For Vesalius, Paré, Gourmelen and others have written that there is prepared on the arm a small hole or cavity in which the mutilated nose is
buried until the flesh . . . grows onto it, and that this flesh is molded into
the shape of a nose. But, if these fine gentlemen will pardon my saying so,
this is quite different from the actual rites of the art; far from using the aid
of flesh . . . the wound, which is inflicted on the arm for building up the
nose, has a flat and level surface, and no use whatsoever is made of flesh in
this operation, and only the skin of the arm is taken for union with the nose
by the method of implanting which professors of horticulture usually call
insitio [grafting] by a scion not separated from its stock . . ." (published as
an appendix to Girolamo Mercuriale's *De decoratione* [Frankfurt, 1587]);
we quote from a translation provided by Martha Teach Gnudi and Jerome
Pierce Webster, *The Life and Times of Gaspare Tagliacozzi* (New York:
Herbert Reichner, 1950), p. 137. A similar statement can be found in
Alexander Read's *Chirurgorum comes: or, The whole practice of chirurgery*
(1687), chap. 19, a translation of Tagliacozzi's *De Curtorum Chirurgia*
(1597).

What is most noteworthy in all this is Sterne's knowledge of the exchange, since his century, as far as Gnudi and Webster have been able to
determine, still labored under Paré's misinformation, and had in fact
turned Tagliacozzi into a figure of ridicule. See, e.g., Butler, *Hudibras*,
pt. I, canto 1, lines 279–84: "So learned *Taliacotius* from / The brawny
Part of Porter's Bum, / Cut supplementall Noses, which / Would last as
long as Parent Breech: / But when the Date of *Nock* was out, / Off dropt the
Sympathetick Snout" (ed. John Wilders [Oxford: Clarendon Press,
1967], pp. 9–10); and *Tatler* 260 (December 7, 1710): "Talicotius . . .
was the first clap doctor that I meet with in history, and a greater man in his
age than our celebrated Dr. Wall. He saw his species extremely mutilated
and disfigured by this new distemper . . . and therefore, in pursuance of a
very seasonable invention, set up a manufacture of noses, having first got a
patent that none should presume to make noses besides himself . . . .
Though the doctor had the monopoly of noses in his own hands, he is said
not to have been unreasonable. Indeed, if a man had occasion for a high

Roman nose, he must go to the price of it. A carbuncle nose likewise bore an excessive rate: but for your ordinary short turned-up noses, of which there was the greatest consumption, they cost little or nothing . . ." (ed. George A. Aitken [New York: Hadley and Mathews, 1899], IV: 322–24). Thus Sterne was drawing on a well-known figure in alluding to Tagliacozzi, but in an informed manner unusual for his century.

    Cf. Ferriar, I: 160–76.

276.16   nose-mender] *OED* cites this passage as its sole example.

276.24–277.14   Now *Ambrose Paræus* . . . for ever.] Sterne elaborates here (as noted by Ferriar, I: 46–48) upon Friar John's explanation for his long nose, in Rabelais, I.40.319–20: "according to the true monastical philosophy, it is because my nurse had soft teats, by virtue whereof, whilst she gave me suck, my nose did sink in, as in so much butter. The hard breasts of nurses make children short-nosed. But hey gay, ad formam nasi cognoscitur ad te levavi" ("By his nose you shall know him—'Unto thee I lift up . . .' [the opening verse of Psalm 123]"). Paré did indeed maintain this view; see *Works*, book XXIV, chap. 21, p. 551. It is to this passage that Ozell adds the two footnotes cited above, n. to 266.4ff.

277.5   *puisne*] I.e., puny; *OED* lists examples of this spelling up to 1782.

277.9   snubb'd] Sterne's usage antedates the various examples in *OED* for *snub* as a substantive, adjective, or verb, all having to do with a foreshortened, flattened, or turned-up nose.

277.10   *ad mensuram suam legitimam*] "At its proper size."

277.14   refocillated] *OED* cites this passage as its last example, with the definition "to revive, refresh, reanimate, comfort."

278.7   ratios] I.e., rations; *OED* cites this passage as its first illustration.

278.10   *crucifix'd*] *OED*'s last illustration is dated 1635. Sterne uses the far more common *crucified* in vol. IX (804.22–23): "never man crucified TRUTH at the rate he did . . . ."

278.21   *Ponocrates* and *Grangousier*] Ponocrates is Gargantua's tutor in book I of Rabelais; Grangousier is his father. Along with Friar John, they attempt to answer Gargantua's question: "What is the cause . . . that friar John hath such a goodly nose?" Friar John's answer is given above, n. to 276.24–277.14; Grangousier's is given at 284.17–20 (see n. below). Ponocrates's solution may have inspired "Slawkenbergius's Tale": "Because, said Ponocrates, he came with the first to the fair of noses, and therefore made choice of the fairest and the greatest" (I.40.319).

279.13–14   in this whimsical theatre of ours] Cf. Sterne's letter to Garrick, January 27, 1760: "I sometimes think of a Cervantic Comedy upon these & the Materials of yᵉ 3ᵈ & 4ᵗʰ Volˢ which will be still more dramatick,— tho I as often distrust its Successe, unless at the Universities . . ." (*Letters*, p. 87). Cf. 333.13–16 and n. below.

280.17–18   and beings inferior . . . by their noses] Cf. Montaigne, II.12.147: "*Chrysippus*, tho' in all other Things as scornful a Judge of the Condition of Animals, as any other *Philosopher* whatever, considering the Motions of a *Dog*, who coming to a Place where three Ways met, either to hunt after his Master he has lost, or in pursuit of some Game that flies before him, goes snuffing first in one of the Ways, and then in another, and after having made himself sure of two, without finding the Trace of what he seeks, throws himself into the third without Examination; he is forc'd to confess, that this Consideration is in the *Dog, I have followed my Master by the Foot to this Place, he must of necessity be gone one of these three Ways, he is not gone this Way, nor that, he must then infallibly be gone this other.*"

280.24–281.6   The gift of . . . by *juxta-position.*] Sterne paraphrases *ECHU*, IV.17.18: "the principal Act of Ratiocination is the finding the Agreement, or Disagreement of two *Ideas* one with another, by the intervention of a third. As a Man, by a Yard, finds two Houses to be of the same length, which could not be brought together to measure their Equality by *juxta*-position" (p. 685).

281.3   *medius terminus*] That term in a syllogism which does not appear in the conclusion.

281.26   thread-paper] *OED* cites the passage at the end of this chapter (285.3) as its first illustration, but the word occurs in *Spectator* 324 (1712), III: 189.

283.24   *quære*] "Query"; a common Latinism.

284.17–20   There is no cause . . . my father.] Rabelais, I.40.319: "What is the cause, said Gargantua, that friar John hath such a goodly nose? Because, said Grangousier, that God would have it so, who frameth us in such form, and for such end, as is most agreeable to his divine will, even as a potter fashioneth his vessels." This occurs just before Friar John gives his own explanation; see above, n. to 276.24—277.14.

    See also 332.15—16.

285.4   seamstressy] *OED* cites this passage as its sole illustration.

285.22—23   contrited and attrited] *OED* cites this passage as its last example
of *contrited* ("Crushed, ground to pieces, worn by rubbing"); and as its
first example of *attrited* ("worn down by continued friction").

286.4—5   considering he was . . . not without fancy] A commonplace prejudice of the age was the dullness of the German people. Thomas Salmon,
Modern History, is only one of many such observers: "the world . . . have
generally agreed to charge the whole German nation with stupidity, and
want of sense . . . . The leaden temper of the Germans (say the French)
wants to be mended, by mingling the French quick-silver with it" (II:
27). Cf. below, n. to 310.10—12.

NOTES TO VOLUME IV

289.1–2   at the close . . . sultry day] Not in the Latin. For Sterne's Latin capabilities, see t.n. to 290.13 (vol. II, p. 852, in this edition) and *Letters*, pp. 124–25, 147. It seems evident that Sterne was a competent Latinist and we see no reason to believe that a source exists for his "Fabella." Indeed, it seems likely that Sterne wrote the English version and then translated it into Latin.

289.5   crimson-sattin] Unrecorded in *OED*.

289.5   *Strasburg*] Sterne almost certainly chose the setting of Strasbourg to exploit its surprise capture by the French in 1681 as the climax of "Slawkenbergius's Tale." In addition, situated as it is in Alsace, Strasbourg contains within its history not only the varying fortunes of French and German (Austrian) masters, but of Lutheran and Catholic theologians as well, a perfect focus for the scholastic argumentativeness Sterne was ridiculing. Unfortunately, we have not located the single source that Sterne probably had available for his information on Strasbourg. In its absence, we have tried where possible to cite other contemporary sources but have also relied on two modern studies, readily accessible to English readers: Miriam Usher Chrisman, *Strasbourg and the Reform: A Study in the Process of Change* (New Haven: Yale University Press, 1967), and Franklin L. Ford, *Strasbourg in Transition: 1648–1789* (Cambridge: Harvard University Press, 1958).

For Sterne's choice of Strasbourg, see particularly Ford, p. 5: "it *was* the Reformation which changed the whole face of urban life in Strasbourg and thrust the town into a position of European prominence. Lutheranism had won the citizenry with remarkable speed and ease, and the official abolition of the Mass in 1529 merely formalized the existing situation in a now overwhelmingly Protestant community. By virtue of its location, Strasbourg was an outpost for the Reformation on the borderland of Catholic power . . . ."

289.9 *Crim-Tartary*] Cf. 275.9–11 and n. above.

289.10–11 never saw . . . in his life!] The Latin may be translated more literally: "Good gods, what an oddly shaped nose!"

289.13 a black ribban] Not in the Latin.

290.11 *Crepitare*] Sterne might have been aware of an additional meaning, "to fart."

291.3 scabbard] Sterne's humor is served by the Latin *vaginam*.

291.6–7 and putting . . . as he spoke] The Latin may be translated more literally: "bowing courteously."

291.11 'Tis not worth a single stiver] The Latin may be translated more literally: "I value it at nothing." Cf. 311.9–10: "*Martin Luther* did not care one stiver about the matter . . . ."

291.16 By dunder] The Latin *Mehercule!* ("By Hercules!") was, according to Ashley Montagu's *The Anatomy of Swearing* (London: Rapp & Whiting, 1968), pp. 31–32, "a very popular" oath in Rome, reserved entirely for men.

292.3 *fistulam*] Cf. 79.3, the *Argumentum Fistulatorium*, the argument of a piper or whistler.

292.7 *Rem penitus explorabo*] The bawdy possibilities of "I'll know the bottom of it" are abetted by the association of *penitus* (as an adverb) with *penis*, and the usual play on *rem*, i.e., "thing"; cf. 79.8–9, the *Argumentum ad Rem*, and above, n. to 78.18ff.

293.5 'Tis as soft as a flute] Sterne's Latin may be translated "So far from that that it surpasses the flute in sweetness." The "soft" is hence aural rather than tactile, though Sterne perhaps intended the ambiguity. There is no Latin equivalent for "'Tis a pudding's end"; the trumpeter's wife is simply denying in Latin her husband's "'Tis brass." Cf. above, n. to 115.10.

293.15–20 No! said he . . . that conviction] Sterne's Latin omits the phrase "the one over the other in a saint-like position" and then goes on literally: "No! said he, looking up, it is not necessary for this idea of yours to be investigated."

294.8   περιζοματέ] *Perizomate*, a girdle worn round the loins; Sterne may
have known the word from the Septuagint, where various forms appear,
e.g., in the passage from Jeremiah 1: 17 quoted above, n. to 274.9.
Sterne's ending is incorrect.

295.2–4   having uncrossed . . . his left-hand] Sterne's Latin omits this entire
phrase.

St. Nicolas, Bishop of Myra in Lycia in the fourth century, was an
exceptionally popular saint, associated particularly with sailors and children; he was also the patron saint of Russia. Work notes (p. 249, n. 4) that
his patronage included "among others, wandering scholars, vagabonds,
robbed persons, and travellers in general"; this may explain his being
invoked at this point, though it is not the common association made with
St. Nicolas. Indeed, despite the name Diego, the fact that the hero is
returning to Crimea (289.9) makes it just as likely that he is invoking the
patron saint of Russia.

295.17   taken three turns upon the parade] Sterne's Latin may be translated
literally: "had entered there."

297.1   his left-hand . . . going to mount it] All that appears in the Latin of this
phrase is "his hand."

297.6   Tut! tut!] Sterne seems to be playing, since his Latin (*"Enimvero"*)
would be translated "yes indeed" or "certainly."

297.6–9   I have been at . . . single man's lot.] Cf. Ponocrates's explanation of
why Friar John has such a "goodly nose": "Because . . . he came with the
first to the fair of noses, and therefore made choice of the fairest and the
greatest" (Rabelais, I.40.319). Sterne had already borrowed from this
paragraph; see above, n. to 278.21. Sterne's Latin would be better served
perhaps by "most splendid and most excellent."

297.12   saint *Radagunda*] St. Radegund (c. 520–87), founder of the monastery of Our Lady of Poitiers in 552, was almost certainly known to Sterne
because of her role as patroness of Jesus College, Cambridge. Her story is
amply told by F. Brittain in *Saint Radegund* (Cambridge: W. Heffer &
Sons, 1928); he concludes: "it is impossible for anyone to pass three years
at Jesus College without encountering . . . reminders of her" (p. 73).
Sterne refers to St. Radegund again, with some collegiate wit perhaps, in
vol. VIII, chap. 17 (679.14–16).

Sterne's Latin may be translated "By all holy men and women."

297.20   I smell the turpentine.] Sterne was probably aware that the turpentine
of Strasbourg was the most commonly used in England. He may also have
known that turpentine was used medicinally "for clearing the urinary passages, and as such prescribed in obstructions of the reins, in gonorrheas,
&c." (Chambers).

298.3   *Minime tangetur*] "It never shall be touched" is possibly too strong;
more accurate would be "it shall be touched as little as possible."

299.2−3   Here the stranger . . . looked up] Not in the Latin.

300.15−16   there's nothing . . . pair of breeches] Cf. Yorick's traveling in
ASJ with "half a dozen shirts and a black pair of silk breeches" (p. 65).

301.16   queen *Mab*] Usually considered an invention of Shakespeare; both
queen (i.e., *quean*) and *Mab* mean "slut"; see *Romeo and Juliet*, I.iv.53−
58, 70−71: "O then I see Queen Mab hath been with you. / She is the
fairies' midwife, and she comes / In shape no bigger than an agot-stone /
On the forefinger of an alderman, / Drawn with a team of little atomi /
Over men's noses as they lie asleep. . . . / And in this state she gallops
night by night / Through lovers' brains, and then they dream of love
. . . ."

301.20−21   The abbess of *Quedlingberg*] Sterne perhaps chooses Quedlingberg (in Saxony) because the women of the famous abbey located there (all
of noble birth) were at one time governors of the city as well.

301.22   deaness] *OED* cites this passage as its first illustration.

301.24−25   placket holes] *OED:* "an opening in an outer skirt to give access
to the pocket within." *OED* cites 414.22 as the first use of this term, also
noting (3.b.) that *placket* had obscene connotations as early as 1601. Cf.
Partridge, s.v. *placket*.

301.26−27   perched . . . pineal gland of her brain] The seat of the soul,
according to Descartes; see above, n. to 173.14ff.

302.5−18   The penitentiaries . . . bed at all.] Sterne shows an interesting
knowledge of religious orders—or at least the interesting use of a source
not yet located. The "penitentiaries of the third order of saint *Francis*"
comprised a lay order of men and women, "third order" being the term
used to distinguish such orders from the first and second orders, of fully
professed men and women, respectively. Chambers, s.v. *Third*, speaks of
the order rather ironically: "The Third *order* of Franciscans was insti-
tuted by St. Francis in 1221, in favour of people of both sexes, who being

smitten with the preachings of that saint, demanded of him an easy manner of living a Christian life . . . ." Chambers also notes that such lay orders often became religious, under titles such as *"religious penitents of the third order,* &c."

The "nuns of mount *Calvary"* are a Benedictine order, founded in 1617 at Poitiers.

The Præmonstratenses, the Cluniaks (i.e., *"Clunienses"*), and the Carthusians are briefly described in Richard Grey's clerical handbook, *System of English Ecclesiastical Law . . . for the Use of Young Students in the Universities, who are designed for Holy Orders,* 4th ed. (1743), pp. 441–42; and in Chambers as well. The first group is an Augustinian order founded in 1120, the second a Benedictine order founded in 890, and the last a contemplative order founded at Chartreuse in 1084. St. Odo (879–942) was the second Abbot of Cluny (927–42) and was considered the real force behind its rapid growth; however, we have found no reason in more recent accounts of Cluny to dispute Work's reliance on the authority of Joan Evans, *Monastic Life at Cluny* (London, 1931), p. 29: "the first nunnery of the Cluniac order was founded at Marcigny in 1056" (p. 254, n. *). Where Sterne found his information is unknown.

"The nuns of saint *Ursula"* may mean either the Ursulines, founded at Brescia in 1535, or the Society of the Sisters of St. Ursula of the Blessed Virgin, founded in 1606. Both are teaching orders and take their name from their patron saint, Ursula. Sterne might well have been familiar with the legend of Ursula, who was accompanied in martyrdom by 11,000 other virgins.

Sterne's manipulation of historical fact is perhaps evident here. Strasbourg did have a very large monastic population in the Middle Ages (Chrisman, *Strasbourg and the Reform,* p. 33) and it grew again in the eighteenth century, *after* the French gained control (Ford, *Strasbourg in Transition,* pp. 107–8). But, as in England, the monasteries were emptied by the Reformation; and although there was still far more Catholic strength and activity in and around Strasbourg than in England during the seventeenth century, Sterne's amassing of nuns is clearly a comic exaggeration.

302.13   flead] I.e., flayed.

302.14–15   thought Saint *Antony* . . . with his fire] Erysipelas, marked by an inflammation of the skin, is also known as St. Anthony's fire, from the belief that his intercession was efficacious in curing the disease. St. Anthony (c. 250–356) is often considered the father of Christian monasticism; one of his symbols is the firebrand. Sterne mentions him again, 412.1–2, in company with St. Ursula; see also below, n. to 622.6–9.

302.19   capitulars] *OED* cites this passage as its last illustration for *capitular* ("a member of an ecclesiastical chapter") and also for *capitularly* ("in the form of, or as, a chapter").

302.20   domiciliars] *OED* cites this passage as its sole example, with the definition "short for *domiciliar canon,* a canon of a minor order having no voice in a chapter."

302.21   butter'd buns] A cant expression for a woman who has intercourse with several men in quick succession (Partridge, s.v.); or, more simply, a harlot (*OED*). Cf. Richard Head and Francis Kirkman, *The English Rogue* (1671), pt. 2, p. 376: "Our plot being thus laid, and my 2d. Sweetheart desiring it, I promised to come to bed to him about midnight, which I did; but my Masters brother knowing of my design, was resolved to have the first carving of me, and that he should only have a butter'd Bun . . . ."

303.11–18   there is many . . . suffice to say] Cf. *Political Romance,* p. 8: "There are many good Similies now subsisting in the World, but which I have neither Time to recollect or look for, which would give you a strong Conception of the Astonishment . . . which this unexpected Stroke . . . impress'd upon the Parson's Looks.—Let it suffice to say . . . ."

305.7   *Chrysippus* and a *Crantor*] Chrysippus was second only to Zeno in establishing the Stoic philosophy; see above, nn. to 171.13–15 and 190.3–7. The Stoics, of course, derived their name from the Greek word for *porch* or *portico,* the covered arcade in Athens where the philosophers gathered and taught.

Crantor (c. 335–c. 275 B.C.), a philosopher of the Old Academy, was the first commentator on Plato.

305.16–17   demonstrators in natural philosophy] See above, n. to 116.17.

306.1–2   getting down . . . her little court] Cf. 171.2–3 and n. above.

306.3–4   conduits of dialect induction] See above, n. to 232.16–17. Sterne's play on the conduits of intelligence (deduction) and of dialect induction might be compared to his earlier play on *a priori/a posteriori* reasoning; see 166.4–6 and n. above.

306.12–17 It was demonstrated . . . the time.] Cf. Chambers, s.v. *Fœtus*, where the fetus is described as being first "head upwards, and its face towards its mother's belly"; then, in the ninth month, "its head, which was hitherto specifically lighter than any other part, becomes specifically heavier; its bulk bearing a much smaller proportion to its substance than it did. . . .

"The consequence of this change is, that it tumbles in the liquor which contains it: its head falls down; its feet get up; and its face turns towards its mother's back."

Sterne would seem to be using *statical* with a meaning for which *OED*'s first illustration is dated 1802: "4. Of or pertaining to forces in equilibrium or the condition of rest in bodies." But cf. 3.a.; and perhaps he was simply foreshortening *hydrostatical*, the "equilibrium of liquids and the pressure exerted by liquids at rest."

306.20–24 And if a suitable . . . sustained afterwards.] Stout calls attention to a similar observation in *ASJ*, p. 175, concerning the prevalence of dwarfs in Paris: "every third man a pigmy!—some by ricketty heads and hump backs—others by bandy legs [cf. 291.1–2, the "little dwarfish bandy-leg'd drummer"]—a third set arrested by the hand of Nature in the sixth and seventh years of their growth—a fourth, in their perfect and natural state, like dwarf apple-trees; from the first rudiments and stamina of their existence, never meant to grow higher"; and again in *Sermons*, II.10 ("Job's Account of the Shortness and Troubles of Life, considered"): God seems, Sterne writes, "to have prescribed the same laws to man, as well as all living creatures, in the first rudiments of which, there are contained the specifick powers of their growth, duration and extinction . . ." (p. 89).

Cf. George Cheyne, *The English Malady* (1733), p. 66, where the animalculist theory of generation is strongly endorsed: "The original *Stamina*, the whole *System* of the Solids, the Firmness, Force, and Strength of the Muscles, of the Viscera, and great Organs, are they not owing to the *Male*? And does the *Female* contribute any more but a convenient Habitation, proper Nourishment, and an *Incubation* to the seminal Animalcul for a Time, to enable the *organised* living Creatures to bear the *Air, Sun,* and *Day* the sooner?" See also Chambers, s.v. *Stamina:* "those simple, original parts, which existed first in the embryo, or even in the seed; and by whose distinction, augmentation, and accretion by additional juices, the human body, at its utmost bulk is supposed to be formed. . . .

"All that is essential to the animal, are the *stamina*, which exist *in ovo;* the rest being foreign, additional and even accidental."

Cf. *TS*, 354.15: "nothing left to found thy stamina in, but negations . . . ."

307.1–20   This was all . . . necessarily ensue] Sterne may have again gone to Chambers for his "learned wit," especially to the articles under *Stomach* and *Sanguification*. In the first, the stomach is defined as "a hollow, membranous, organical part of an animal, destined to receive the food after deglutition, and convert it into chyle." And in the second, he might have gathered enough to believe that he was giving Walter another outmoded theory; e.g.: "The ancients were in great perplexity about the seat of *sanguification,* or the place where, and the instrument whereby it is effected: whether in the heart, or the liver, or the lungs? but, according to the doctrine of the moderns, the heart, liver, vessels, *&c.* contribute no otherwise to the changing of the chyle into blood, than the sun does to the changing of the must into wine. . . .

"In effect, it does not appear that any thing extraneous is mixed with the circulating liquor but chyle, excepting what was before separated from it for particular occasions; unless perhaps it should receive some portion of air in the lungs, which is a point long disputed, and yet scarce ascertained." It must be noted, however, that in James Mackenzie's *The History of Health, and the Art of Preserving It* (Edinburgh, 1758), a different view is presented: "THE third stage of concoction begins where the chyle mingles with the blood, and falling soon into the right ventricle of the heart, is from thence propelled into the lungs. It will appear that the lungs are the principal instrument of sanguification, or converting the chyle into blood . . ." (p. 341). Mackenzie goes on to describe the process and then concludes: "IT follows . . . that when we take in a larger quantity of aliment than our digestive faculties are able to conquer and assimilate, such a quantity can never turn to good nourishment" (pp. 345–46). Sterne had cited Mackenzie in vol. II; see 95.16–21 and n. above.

307.20   a mortification must necessarily ensue] Cf. Mackenzie, p. 358: "WHEN this circulation [of the blood] is duly performed, man continues in good health; when it grows irregular he sickens; and when it ceases he dies. Nay, if but one member should be deprived of it, that member presently corrupts and mortifies."

307.21–23   that the nose . . . from his nose.] Petronius makes a somewhat similar observation about the size of Ascyltos's sexual organ: "Habebat enim inguinum pondus tam grande, ut ipsum hominem laciniam fascini crederes. O iuvenem laboriosum" (*Works*, p. 184). The translators of the 1712 London edition of Petronius render the passage thus: "Nature had so largely qualify'd him for a Lover, that his Body seem'd less than a part that depended on it: A lusty Rogue"; William Arrowsmith, a modern translator, renders the passage in a more Shandean manner: "for that man had a pecker of such extraordinary length that you would have thought the man was appended to the pecker rather than the pecker to the man. What a Hercules!" (*Satyricon* [Ann Arbor: University of Michigan Press, 1959], p. 97). Diego's journey to the Promontory of Noses may well find its classical precedent in the quest of Encolpius ("the crotch") for sexual rejuvenation in *Satyricon*.

308.5   The more curious . . . inquirers after nature] Cf. *Sermons*, III.18: "there is one miserable inlet to . . . evil . . . derived . . . from some of our busiest enquirers after nature,—and that is, when with more zeal than knowledge, we account for phenomena, before we are sure of their existence" (p. 85).

308.13–15   that nature . . . diameter of it.] Cf. *ASJ*, p. 174: "what struck me . . . was, the unaccountable sport of nature in forming such numbers of dwarfs—No doubt, she sports at certain times in almost every corner of the world; but in Paris, there is no end to her amusements—The goddess seems almost as merry as she is wise"; and Tristram's assertion that he has been "the continual sport of what the world calls Fortune" (8.21–22).

308.18   *petitio principii*] "A begging of the question"—a fallacy in logic consisting in arguing from a premise that stands or falls with the conclusion that it is used to prove.

308.19   which one . . . ran his head against] Proverbial; Tilley, H273 ("To run one's HEAD against a stone wall"), and *ODEP*, s.v. *Run*.

309.1–5   Now death . . . said his antagonist] Sterne may have derived his definitions from Chambers, s.v. *Death:* "generally considered as the separation of the soul from the body . . . .

"Physicians usually defined death by a total stoppage of the circulation of the blood . . . ." Cf. 174.1–2: "If death, said my father, reasoning with himself, is nothing but the separation of the soul from the body . . . ."

309.8   civilians] I.e., practitioners of civil law as opposed to those in the ecclesiastical courts, the commissaries (309.24). For Sterne's own career as a commissary in the ecclesiastical court system, see the informative essay by Cash, "Sterne as a Judge in the Spiritual Courts," in *English Writers of the Eighteenth Century*, ed. John H. Middendorf (New York: Columbia University Press, 1971), pp. 17–36; much of this information is repeated in *Early and Middle Years*, pp. 243–61.

309.17   This left room . . . to go on.] Cf. 271.18–21, Walter's assertion that "Learned men, brother *Toby*, don't write dialogues upon long noses for nothing.——I'll study the mystic and the allegoric sense,——here is some room to turn a man's self in, brother."

309.19   *ex mero motu*] "Of his own accord." Chambers provides an interesting gloss: "formal words used in the king's charters, and letters patent; signifying that he does what is contained therein of his own will, and motion.

   "The effect of these words is to bar all exceptions that might be taken to the instrument, by alledging that the prince, in passing such charter, was abused by false suggestion."

310.5–7   a dispute . . . nineteen years before.] Cf. 710.11–14: "having taken a ride with my father, that very morning, to save if possible a beautiful wood, which the dean and chapter were hewing down to give to the poor* . . ."; and Sterne's note (710.26–27): "*Mr. Shandy must mean the poor *in spirit*; inasmuch as they divided the money amongst themselves." Sterne would seem to have some particular target in mind in both these comments, but we have been unable to discover the episode or episodes to which he might be alluding; Cash, *Early and Middle Years*, p. 255, notes an event parallel to the selling of the wood.

310.10–12   two universities . . . of *Austria*] There is some confusion in eighteenth-century accounts as to whether Johannes Sturmius (1507–89) or Jacobus Sturmius (1489–1553) was the "founder" of the University of Strasbourg. Bayle's *Dictionary*, 5 vols. (1734–38), notes the confusion and opts for Johannes: "[In 1538] he opened a school which became famous, and by his means obtained of his Imperial Majesty Maximilian II the title of an University in the year 1566. . . . The College of Strasburg, of which he was Rector, became the most flourishing in all Germany" (s.v. *Sturmius*). However, in Jeremy Collier's translation of Moréri's *Dictionary* (1701), the credit goes to Jacobus: "it was by his Advice the Magistrates erected an University there in 1538, whereof he was made the chief Director." Collier does note that Johannes had persuaded Jacobus to "endeavour the settling of an University in that City, which having happily brought about, this John Sturmius was made Professor and Rector of it . . . ."

Cf. Chrisman, *Strasbourg and the Reform*, pp. 270–71, where it is made clear that Jacobus was the more instrumental in founding the school, while Johannes was the reason for its success. All sources do agree that Jacobus was a leading figure in Strasbourg's *Rat* ("senate").

The *"Popish"* university is a rather different problem. There was no such institution in Strasbourg, certainly not before 1681. However, the Jesuits had established a school in neighboring Molsheim in 1580, and in 1615 Archduke Leopold, Bishop of Strasbourg and Passau, had founded another Jesuit college in Ensisheim. In 1617, the former was elevated to a university and Archduke Leopold was exalted as its benefactor. Both schools were formed because of the success of the Protestant university, in an effort to restore orthodox Catholicism in Alsace. Thus, when Louis XIV captured Strasbourg, he moved the University of Molsheim to Strasbourg as part of that effort—but not until 1701 or 1702, twenty years *after* the events of Sterne's tale. This information can be pieced together from Ford and Chrisman and from Anton Schindling, *Humanistische Hochschule und Freie Reichstadt* (Wiesbaden: Franz Steiner Verlag, 1977), and Georges Livet, "La Guerre de Trente Ans et les traites de Westphalie. La Formation de la Province d'Alsace (1618–1715)," in *Histoire de l'Alsace*, ed. Philippe Dollinger (Toulouse: Édouard Privat, 1970). We are grateful to Professors Chrisman and Ford for some illuminating correspondence on the problem. Where Sterne gathered his information remains unknown.

It is worth noting that, at least in Goldsmith's estimation, German universities were much as Sterne facetiously pictures them; see his description of them in *An Enquiry into the Present State of Polite Learning* (1759): "BUT let the Germans have their due; if they are often a little dull, no nation alive assumes a more laudable solemnity, or better understands all the little decorums of stupidity. . . . I have sometimes attended their disputes at gradation. On this occasion, they often dispense with learned gravity, and seem really all alive. The disputes are managed between the followers of Cartesius, whose exploded system they call the new philosophy, and those of Aristotle. Though both parties are wrong, they argue with an obstinacy worthy the cause of truth . . . . The disputants become warm, the moderator cannot be heard, the audience take part in the debate, till at last, the whole hall buzzes with erroneous philosophy" (*Works*, I: 279).

310.15–311.30   in determining the point of *Martin Luther*'s damnation, etc.] Sterne found the entire debate, as well perhaps as a suggestion for connecting it to Strasbourg, in Bayle's *Dictionary*, s.v. *Luther;* see t.n. to 311.23ff. (vol. II, p. 853, in this edition), and Melvyn New and Norman Fry, "Some Borrowings in *Tristram Shandy:* The Textual Problem," *SB* 29 (1976): 324; the debt was first noted by Work, p. 261. Bayle annotates one sentence ("[They] have even falsified the day of his birth, in order to frame a scheme of his nativity to his disadvantage") with his customary elaborateness: "Martin Luther was born the tenth of November, betwixt eleven and twelve of the clock at night, at Isleben [in Bayle's n. (*A*), we are told "Isleben in the county of Mansfeld"] . . . . [His mother] being examined . . . concerning the year she was brought to bed . . . answered, that she did not very well remember it; she only knew the day and the hour. It is therefore out of pure malice, that Florimond de Remond places his birth on the twenty second of October. He thought thereby to confirm the astrological predictions of Junctinus, who, by the horoscope of this day, had defamed Martin Luther, as much as he could. This Astrologer was strongly confuted by a professor of Strasburg, who shewed, that, by the rules of Astrology, Luther was to be a great man.

"Several authors say he was born the tenth of November, or St. Martin's eve, which made his parents name him Martin . . . . And, though there be some variation between . . . Astrologers, about Luther's horoscope, yet it is so small that it deserves not to be considered. For in both, the planets are situate in the same houses; the moon, in both, is in the twelfth; Jupiter, Venus, and Mars, in the third; the Sun, Saturn, and Mercury, in the fourth. . . . The variation of these . . . Astrologers, was not so great as that of some others who differ a whole year with respect to the birth-day . . . . Gauricus places Luther's birth the twenty second of October 1484, one of the clock, ten minutes in the afternoon, and he finds by this horoscope the same abominations as Cardan." Bayle then quotes the Latin passage that Sterne copied for his footnote on p. 311, including the error "religiosissimus" for "irreligiosissimus," the humor of which, if Sterne caught it, would certainly have appealed to him. Bayle translates: *"This is strange, indeed terrible, five planets being in conjunction in Scorpio, in the ninth house which the Arabians allotted to religion, made him a sacrilegious Heretic, a most bitter and most prophane enemy to the Christian faith. It appears from the horoscope directed to the conjunction of Mars, that he died without any sense of religion, his soul steeped in guilt sailed to hell, there to be lashed with the fiery whips of Alecto, Tisiphone, and Megera thro' endless ages."* Bayle also provides, in his margin, the citation to Lucas Gauricus that Sterne copies verbatim (311.29–30) to conclude his note. The title of Gauricus's work, published in 1552, may be translated *Astrological Treatise on the Past Accidents of Many Men, by Means of an Examination of their Nativities.* Cf. Work, p. 261, n. *: "Gauricus (1476–1558) was Bishop of Civitate and a celebrated mathematician and astrologer."

It is perhaps worth noting that the date Sterne finally decides upon (November 10, 1484) is the one alternative not considered by the debating astrologers; and that Tristram too is born under the sign of Scorpio (November 5).

Alecto, Tisiphone, and Megera are the Greek Erinyes (Roman Furies), responsible for avenging crimes both during life and after death.

310.20–30   Nonnuli ex . . . Vid Idea.] For the probable source for at least some of the citations in this nonsense note, see t.n. to 310.20ff. (vol. II, pp. 852–53, in this edition). It should be noted that the authorities cited seem suspect; we have indicated above (n. to 266.4ff.) the possible relation between Scroderus and J. Scrudr. We might also take note of Gargantua's tutor, Tubal Holophernes, which Ozell takes "to be a sham-name of Rabelais's own inventing" (I.14.198); Sterne's Rever. J. Tubal is equally suspicious. N. Bardy may be connected to Jerome Bardi (1600–1667), cited in the passage Sterne lifts from Adrien Baillet in chap. 10 (337.29); the name is common enough, but Sterne's "N" is unaccounted for.

311.14   the lake of hell fire] Sterne turns the image of Luther sailing to hell (see above, n. to 310.15ff.) into a more direct echo of Revelation 21: 8: "But the fearful, and unbelieving, and the abominable, and murderers, and whoremongers, and sorcerers, and idolators, and all liars, shall have their part in the lake which burneth with fire and brimstone . . . ."

312.24 *Alexandrian* library] Work, p. 262, n. 26: "The most important library of antiquity, formed at Alexandria during the reign of the Ptolemies and said to have contained at one time about half a million manuscript volumes." The library declined after the fourth century A.D. and supposedly was finally destroyed by the Saracens in 640. Sterne refers to it again, 441.16–17.

312.25–26 hit two such nails . . . one stroke.] Variant of a proverbial expression; Tilley, N16 ("He has hit the NAIL on the head"), and *ODEP*, s.v. *Hit*.

313.6 doubled the cape] See Partridge, s.v. *Double Cape Horn:* "To be made a cuckold."

313.16–17 the printers were ordered . . . their types] Technical printing term: "To remove (type that has been 'composed' or set up) from the forme, and return each letter into its proper box or compartment in the case" (*OED*).

313.18–19 'Twas a square cap . . . of it] I.e., the present-day academic mortarboard, worn before modern times by many churchmen and members of universities on a regular basis.

314.5–6 He can do nothing . . . which implies contradictions.] See Chambers, s.v. *Imply a contradiction:* "a phrase used among philosophers, in speaking of the object of divine omnipotence.

"God can do every thing that does not *imply a contradiction* proceeding from God: by which is not meant a relation of the action to the executive power of God; for to say that God by this power could do whatever does not *imply a contradiction* proceeding from this power, would only be to say, that God can do what he can do.—In that proposition therefore is meant a relation to the other attributes and simple perfections of God: Thus, God can do whatever does not *imply a contradiction* to some other of his attributes. For instance, he cannot attest a false religion by his word, or by miracle, because this is repugnant to his goodness and truth.

"But because all things that *imply a contradiction*, cannot be said to have such a respect to the attributes of God; therefore we may say more generally, that those things *imply a contradiction*, which involve a contrariety from the terms or object.—For there are two things requisite to the being of any thing; the one on the side of the agent, *viz.* a power of acting; the other on that of the patient or object, *viz.* a non-resistance.—For want of the first condition, there are a thousand things which we cannot do; and for want of the second condition, there are many things that God cannot do: for that which, when it is affirmed, is yet denied, is impossible. See IM-POSSIBLE."

Cf. Sterne's discussion of Thomas Aquinas and intrauterine baptism in vol. I (65.27ff. and n. above).

Sterne may have been parodying a specific debate, e.g., that between Samuel Clarke and Leibniz on the attributes of God—see *A Collection of Papers which passed between the late learned Mr. Leibnitz and Dr. Clarke* (1717), suggested by Wilfred Watson, "Sterne's Satire on Mechanism" (Ph.D. diss., University of Toronto, 1951); or between Catholics and Lutherans on any number of issues. However, it seems just as probable that this entire section is a more generalized satire on scholasticism, for which Chambers is as useful a supporting document as any particular theologian or philosopher. For example, under *Matter*, Chambers provides the following observation: "Hobbes, Spinosa, *&c.* maintain all the beings in the universe to be *material*. . . . Thus *Matter* extremely subtile, and in a brisk motion, they conceive, may think; and so exclude all spirits out of the world." And under *Scholastic*, he delivers this opinion: "the school began to be wholly taken up in frivolous questions. They disputed, with great heat, about mere formalities; and even raised phantoms on purpose to combat withal.

"The *school divinity* is now fallen into the last contempt; and is scarce regarded any where, but in some of the universities, where they are still obliged by their charters to teach it."

The best study of Sterne's use of scholasticism is that by D. W. Jefferson, "*Tristram Shandy* and the Tradition of Learned Wit," *EIC* 1 (1951): 225–48.

314.8   As certainly . . . sow's ear] Variant of a proverbial expression; Tilley, P666 ("You cannot make a silk PURSE out of a sow's ear"), and *ODEP*, s.v. *Silk*.

314.15–16   he can make . . . steeple of *Strasburg*.] Rabelais defends the birth of Gargantua from the left ear of Gargamelle in a similar fashion: "but tell me, if it had been the will of God, would you say that he could not do it? Grammercy; I beseech you never dumfound or embarass your heads with these idle conceits: for I tell you, nothing is impossible with God; and, if he pleased, all women henceforth should bring forth their children at the ear" (I.6.159–60).

314.19 *575 geometrical feet in length*] All contemporary accounts of Strasbourg mention the famous steeple, though we have not found one that measures it at 575 feet. Collier's translation of Moréri's *Dictionary* comes very close: "its Steeple, which is Pyramidal, and full of Windows [is] the most esteem'd for its Workmanship and Height of any other Steeple in *Christendom*, being 574 Foot high."

315.6 *served as a frigate to launch them*] In Rabelais, the narrator refuses to "launch my little skiff any further into the wide ocean of this dispute . . ." (III.32.221); the dispute concerns whether the penis is an independent animal or not.

315.13–14 *the Parchmentarians . . . the Turpentarians*] Cf. Chambers, s.v. *Lutheranism*, where some of the "thirty nine different sects, which at different times have sprung up among the Lutherans" are listed, including the Confessionists, Antinomians, Samosatenses, Inferani, Antidiaphorists, Antiswenkfeldians and Antiosiandrians.

315.15–17 *like Pantagruel . . . out of sight.*] In the "Explanatory Remarks" to the first chapter of vol. IV of Rabelais, we are told that "Pantagruel and his attendants . . . embarked for the oracle of the holy bottle" (p. xiii).

316.14 *beguines*] A sisterhood founded in the twelfth century by Lambert le Bègue, a priest of Liege. The members were free to quit the cloister and to marry. They flourished in the Low Countries, Germany, France, Switzerland, and Italy, so there does not seem to be much validity to Toby's claim (698.18–23) that they could be found only in the Spanish Netherlands and Amsterdam.

Ozell describes them in one of his learned notes to Rabelais: "In Flanders, they call'd benings and beningues . . . certain men and certain women, who, without making vows, devoting themselves in an especial manner to works of charity and mercy, took, in imitation of the said religious, a sort of hood as a badge that should prevent peoples looking upon 'em to be entirely of the secular kind. From those words it is that they have since, corruptly, been call'd beguins and beguines . . ." (IV.46.269, n. 10).

Collier's translation of Moréri's *Dictionary*, s.v. *Beguards* and *Beguines*, gives a rather hostile view: "a certain Sect of pretended Hereticks, who rose in *Germany* and in the *Low Countreys*, about the end of the Thirteenth Age. They made profession of Monastical Life, without observing Celibacy; and maintained, if we may believe the Monks, most pernicious Errors."

Trim will fall in love with a beguine in vol. VIII, chaps. 20–22.

316.23ff.   Haste we now towards the catastrophe, etc.] Sterne's divisions are traditional, though post-Aristotelian. Dryden ("An Essay of Dramatick Poesie," in *Works* [Berkeley: University of California Press, 1971], XVII: 23) defines them thus: "*Aristotle* indeed divides the integral parts of a Play into four: First, The *Protasis* or entrance, which gives light onely to the Characters of the persons, and proceeds very little into any part of the action: Secondly, The *Epitasis*, or working up of the Plot where the Play grows warmer: the design or action of it is drawing on, and you see something promising that it will come to pass: Thirdly, the *Catastasis* . . . the heighth, and full growth of the Play: we may call it properly the Counterturn, which destroys that expectation, imbroyles the action in new difficulties, and leaves you far distant from that hope in which it found you . . . . Lastly, the *Catastrophe*, which the *Grecians* called λύσις [*lusis*], the French *le dénouement*, and we the discovery or unravelling of the Plot . . . ."

Chambers, s.v. *Act*, writes: "It is true, [Greek dramatists] considered their pieces as consisting of certain parts or divisions, which they called *protasis, epitasis, catastasis*, and *catastrophe* . . . ." Under individual entries Chambers defines these divisions in language at times very close to Sterne's:

Protasis: "the first part of a comic or tragic piece; wherein the several persons of the play are shewn, their characters and manners intimated, and the action . . . entered upon."

Epitasis: "the second part . . . wherein the plot, or action . . . was carried on, heightened, warmed, and worked up, till it arrived at its state, or height, called the *catastasis* . . . . The *epitasis* might, ordinarily, take up about our second or third act."

   Catastasis: "the third part . . . wherein the intrigue, or action set on foot in the epitasis, is supported, carried on, and heightned, till it be ripe for the unravelling in the catastrophe."

   Catastrophe: "the fourth, and last part . . . immediately succeeding the catastasis." Chambers goes on to discuss peripetia as part of the catastrophe.

317.26–27   bringing the hero . . . rest and quietness.] Actually not in the *Poetics*, but part of the received commentary; see Dacier's note to that section of the *Poetics* (X) where Aristotle distinguishes between simple and complex plots: "I call a simple Fable, that, in which there is neither Change of Condition, or Remembrance, and the unravelling of which, is only a single passage of agitation and trouble, or [to?] repose and tranquility" (*Aristotle's Art of Poetry, trans. according to Mr. Theodore Goulston's Ed. Together with Mr. D'Acier's Notes* [1709], p. 160). Cf. Bossu's *Treatise of the Epick Poem* (1695; Gainesville, Fla.: Scholars' Facsimiles & Reprints, 1970), p. 103: "That which we call here the Conclusion of the *Epick Action* is the very last passage from Agitation and Trouble, to Quiet and Repose . . . ."

318.6–8   What dost thou . . . his mule.] Cf. 301.4–5.

318.9–10   without any more *ifs* or *ands*] Proverbial; Tilley, I16, and *ODEP*, s.v. *'Ifs' and 'Ands'.*

318.14–18   *Strasburg!*—the great . . . all the world!] Cf. Collier's translation of Moréri's *Dictionary:* "STRASBURG, *Argentoratum,* the Capital City of *Alsatia* in *Germany,* and one of the fairest and greatest Cities thereof. It is a Bishop's See . . . and was for many Ages a Free and Imperial City . . . ." For its garrison, see below, n. to 323.10ff.

319.23   *Valadolid*] Cf. Cervantes, I.IV.2: "for I have known several Men in my Time go by the Names of the Places where they were born, as *Pedro de Alcala, Juan de Ubeda, Diego de Valladolid* . . ." (II: 24–25). While the tone of "Slawkenbergius's Tale" is predominantly Rabelaisian, the final pages bear a closer resemblance to the interpolated tales in *Don Quixote,* e.g., Dorothea's story of her "tragical adventures" in the chapter just cited. And while we have found no direct source for Diego's "Ode," it might be compared to the songs which so often occur in these tales; e.g.:

"But that which first wrought me to his Purpose, and undermin'd my Virtue, was a cursed Copy of Verses he sung one Night under my Window, which, if I remember right, began thus. A SONG. *A Secret Fire consumes my Heart; / And, to augment my raging Pain, / The charming Foe that rais'd the Smart, / Denies me Freedom to complain.*" A second stanza follows (II.III.38, IV: 35).

321.16–18   'Tis a bitter . . . dying *un*——."] Julia's letter might be closed in several ways besides Slawkenbergius's dubious "*unconvinced*"; one good possibility is suggested by a short dialogue in vol. IX, chap. 28 (796.12–17):

"We thought, Mr. Trim, it had been more in the middle——said Mrs. Bridget——

"That would have undone us for ever—said the Corporal.

"——And left my poor mistress undone too—said Bridget.

"The Corporal made no reply to the repartee, but by giving Mrs. Bridget a kiss."

322.4   eased his mind against the wall] Partridge suggests that *easing oneself* was used euphemistically for *ejaculation*, and the text of the verse might support that usage; to be sure, the more common meaning of *defecation* (*urination?*) might also suffice (*OED*, s.v. *Ease, v.* 1.c.).

323.10ff.   As this revolution of the *Strasburgers*, etc.] Sterne is accurate in saying the fall of Strasbourg was often spoken of—always, we might add, with a mixture of awe over Louis XIV's political treachery and scorn for Strasbourg's pride and unpreparedness. An often-republished, anonymous seventeenth-century examination of the monarch's character notes, e.g., that "this city look't upon it self secure after the Treaty at *Nemegen* [1679], confirmed by the powerful Letters the King writ to them time after time . . . . The Magistracy and Citizens thus lull'd asleep by all these fair promises and protestations, dismist the *Swisses* their Guards; but they were no sooner without doors, but Mr. *Louvois* [Michel le Tellier, Marquis de Louvois (1641–91), Minister of War] with a puissant Army began to invest their City . . ." (*The Politicks of the French King . . . trans. from the French* [1689], pp. 10–11). And the traveler William Ker writes in 1693: "Being so near Strasbourg, I had the curiosity to go see what figure that Famous City now made since it had changed its Master; for I had been thrice there before, when it flourished under the Emperor's

Protection . . . . And indeed, I found it so disfigured, that had it not been for the stately Cathedral Church . . . I could scarcely have known it. In the Streets and Exchange, which formerly were thronged with sober, rich, and peaceable Merchants, you meet with none hardly now . . . . It was formerly a rich city . . . . I confess, Strasbourge is the less to be pittied, that it so tamely became a slave, and put on its Chains without any strug-ling" (*Travels Through Flanders, Holland, Germany, Sweden and Denmark* [1693], pp. 111–12).

Collier's translation of Moréri's *Dictionary* (s.v. *Strasburg*) makes many of the same points: "The Pride and Folly of this Town, together with their over-great Love of Liberty, betray'd it into the Hands of the *French*, by refusing 500 Men the Emperor offer'd them for their Security. It is al-ready sunk in its Trade, and will sink more when the Fortifications are finished. *Dietrick*, who was look'd upon as the chief Man that betray'd the Town, was the first Man that was banished conntrary to the Capitulation, because he would not change his Religion . . . ."

Finally, Voltaire observes, in his *Age of Lewis XIV* (Dublin, 1752), I: 179: "Louvois had long conceived a design to subject [Strasbourg] to his master. Money, menaces, and intrigues, by which he had opened the gates of so many towns, prepared Louvois an entrance into Strasbourg. The magistrates were corrupted; and the people were astonished to behold their ramparts at once surrounded by 20,000 French troops . . . and their burgomasters talking of a surrender."

While these sources indicate the frequency and similarity of the eighteenth-century view of the fall of Strasbourg, Sterne seems to have borrowed his own particular account from Gilbert Burnet, *Some Letters Containing an Account of . . . Travelling through Switzerland, Italy, Some Parts of Germany*, 2d ed. (Rotterdam, 1687), pp. 274–75: "I found sev-eral good people . . . acknowledge, that there was such a Corruption of Morals spread over the whole *City*, that as they had justly drawn down on their heads the Plague of the loss of their Liberty, so this having toucht them so little, they had reason to look for severer strokes: One seeth, in the ruin of this *City*, what a mischievous thing the popular pride of a *free City* is: they fancied they were able to defend themselves, and so they refused to let an *Imperial Garrison* come within their *Town:* for if they had received only five hundred *men*, as that small number would not have been able to have oppresst their Liberties, so it would have so secured the *Town*, that the *French* could not have besieged it . . . but the *Town* thought this was a Diminution of their Freedom, and so chose rather to pay a *Garrison* of three thousand *Souldiers*, which as it exausted their *Revenue*, and brought them under great *Taxes*, so it proved too weak for their defence when the *French Army* came before them. The *Town* begins to sink in its *Trade*, notwithstanding the great circulation of *Money* that the expence of the *Fortifications* hath brought to it: but when that is at an end, it will sink more sensibly; for it is impossible for a *Place of Trade*, that is to have alwayes eight or ten thousand *Souldiers* in it, to continue long in a Flourishing State."

See Ford, *Strasbourg in Transition*, pp. 28–50. Strasbourg did indeed have, though reluctantly, over five thousand imperial troops within its walls during the 1670s, but after the Treaty of Nymwegen they were withdrawn. To defend the city against the French, Strasbourg had "five hundred trained mercenaries, of whom many were ill, plus a militia shrunken by the absence of numerous citizens at the Frankfurt fair" (p. 48).

323.14–16   Every body knows . . . in the year 1664.] Although the term "Universal Monarchy" was often used in relation to Louis XIV, "every body" did not attribute the scheme to Jean-Baptiste Colbert (1619–83), his Finance Minister. One who did, however, was John Campbell, *The Present State of Europe*, 6th ed. (1761), p. 266: "he perfectly understood the King's Humour, and flattered it; he put him upon making himself absolute in the utmost Sense of the Word . . . [and to extend] the Power, or at least the Influence of [Louis XIV] all over Christendom."

Cf. Rapin-Thoyras's "Dissertation on the Whigs and Torys," appended to vol. II of his *History:* "*Lewis* XIV, as every one knows, formed the project of an universal Monarchy in *Europe*" (Tindal, p. 806); and Robert Parker, *Memoirs of the Most Remarkable Military Transactions from the Year 1683, to 1718* (1747): "It is known to every one, that both these wars were occasioned by the pride and ambition of *Lewis* the fourteenth, who aspired at nothing less than the *universal* monarchy of *Europe* . . ." (p. 1). Insofar as Colbert assumed his highest governmental position in 1665, Sterne's date of 1664 seems particularly valid; quite probably, the entire passage is taken from a source not yet located.

For a useful account of Colbert, see John C. Rule, "Louis XIV, Roi-Bureaucrate," in *Louis XIV and the Craft of Kingship* (Columbus: Ohio State University Press, 1969), pp. 24–48.

324.12   are ever upon the catch] Proverbial; Tilley, C188, and *ODEP*, s.v. *Lie*. The meaning, as Sterne uses the phrase, is perhaps best illustrated by Tilley's example from 1681: "A High-way Man lyes at catch but for a small parcel of Money."

325.7–8   but the very posture . . . described.] In vol. III, chap. 29 (pp. 254–55).

326.3   overwritten] *OED* cites this passage as its sole illustration.

326.10   exquisitiveness] *OED* cites this passage as its sole illustration.

326.15   pupilability] *OED* cites this passage as its sole example and notes the pun on the pupils of the eyes.

Cf. 34.25–26: "a stream of lambent fire lighted up for a moment in his eyes"; and 707.5–6, the description of the Widow Wadman's eye: "one lambent delicious fire, furtively shooting out from every part of it . . . ."

326.18–19   vibration in the strings] See 131.8–11 and n. above.

326.19–21   the region . . . betwixt 'em.] Cf. 376.23–377.10 and n. below, where Sterne again contrasts head and heart.

327.4–5   What is left . . . worth stooping for.] Cf. *Twelfth Night*, II.ii.14–15, where Malvolio tosses Olivia's ring at Viola's feet: "If it be worth stooping for, there it lies . . . ."

327.21–22   Now whether . . . a more pleasureable oval] Cf. William Holtz, *Image and Immortality* (Providence, R.I.: Brown University Press, 1970), p. 30: "Walter, a study in angles and lines; Toby, his face a beaming, 'pleasurable oval' above the cross of his crutch—again the two elements of Hogarth's comic theory appear. We can only wish that he had given Sterne this scene as well." Hogarth, *Analysis of Beauty* (1753), p. 23, had commended the beauty of the oval and had called the "globe and cross" a "finely varied figure."

327.24   sea of his afflictions] Cf. *Hamlet*, III.i.58: "a sea of troubles." That Sterne is again thinking of Hamlet's most famous soliloquy is perhaps suggested by Walter's question, "did ever a poor unfortunate man . . . receive so many lashes" (328.10–11); cf. Hamlet's "For who would bear the whips and scorns of time" (line 69).

328.13   *Makay's* regiment.] Hugh Mackay (?1640–92), a general in the army of William III. He was killed at the head of his regiment at Steinkirk, a battle Toby and Trim recount in vol. V, chap. 21. See below, n. to 452.17ff.

329.2   death's door.] Proverbial; Tilley, D162, and *ODEP*, s.v. *Death*.

329.27–28   I have neither wife . . . this world.] Sterne glances perhaps at several proverbial expressions, all of which are epitomized in Bacon's famous opening sentence to "Of Marriage and Single Life": "He that hath wife and children hath given hostages to fortune." Cf. Tilley, W355, 356, 379, 380; and *ODEP*, s.v. *Wife*.

331.9–12   Attitudes are nothing . . . which is all in all.] Sterne perhaps borrows an idea from Charles Avison, *An Essay on Musical Expression*, 2d ed. (1753), one that appears to undergird much of Sterne's own theory of composition, though at this point the verbal echo simply culminates the significant passage: "As the proper Mixture of Light and Shade (called by the *Italians Chiaro-Oscuro*) has a noble Effect in Painting, and is, indeed, essential to the Composition of a good Picture; so the judicious Mixture of Concords and Discords is equally essential to a musical Composition: As Shades are necessary to relieve the Eye, which is soon tired and disgusted with a level Glare of Light; so Discords are necessary to relieve the Ear, which is otherwise immediately satiated with a continued, and unvaried Strain of Harmony. We may add (for the Sake of those who are in any Degree acquainted with the Theory of Music) that the *Preparations* and *Resolutions* of Discords, resemble the soft Gradations from Light to Shade, or from Shade to Light in Painting" (p. 23).

For Avison, see above, n. to 192.8–10.

331.20–21   laying the three . . . of his left] William J. Farrell, "Nature versus Art as a Comic Pattern in *Tristram Shandy*," *ELH* 30 (1963): 21–23, observes that Walter's actions conform to those recommended in the standard seventeenth-century manual of rhetorical gestures, John Bulwer's *Chironomia* (1644), though the resemblance is not as convincing as one might hope. Bulwer describes the gesture as "the hand collected, the fingers looking downwards, then turned and resolved" and illustrates it with a picture of two fingers of the right hand pressed against the palm of the left; see James W. Cleary's edition of *Chironomia* (Carbondale: Southern Illinois University Press, 1974), pp. 177–93. Whether Sterne did indeed borrow this gesture and later ones in Walter's speech from a manual (and no exact source has been located) or whether he created them himself, it seems evident that here and elsewhere he reflects to some extent the importance attributed to the gestures of the fingers in rhetorical address from the time of Cicero and Quintilian to at least Gilbert Austin's *Chironomia; or, A Treatise on Rhetorical Delivery* (1806). It should be noted, however, that in two other instances where gestures are carefully described, the sources are works connected with painting rather than oratory; see the chapter following (p. 333) and the earlier description of Trim's sermon-reading posture (pp. 140–41).

332.1–15   WHEN I reflect . . . upon our nature.] Sterne borrows from the opening paragraph of his sermon "Trust in God" (VI.34.3–4): "WHO-EVER seriously reflects upon the state and condition of man, and looks upon that dark side of it, which represents his life as open to so many causes of trouble;—when he sees, how often he eats the bread of affliction, and that he is born to it as naturally as the sparks fly upwards;—that no rank or degrees of men are exempted from this law of our beings . . . when one sits down and looks upon this gloomy side of things, with all the sorrowful changes and chances which surround us,—at first sight,—would not one wonder,—how the spirit of a man could bear the infirmities of his nature, and what it is that supports him, as it does, under the many evil accidents which he meets with in his passage through the valley of tears?" Sterne borrowed this passage from a sermon by Walter Leightonhouse ("Twelfth Sermon," in *Twelve Sermons* [1697], pp. 429–30), as pointed out by Hammond, p. 133. Leightonhouse reads: "He that soberly sits down, and considers the State and Condition of Man; how that *he is born unto trouble, as the sparks fly upwards,* shall find his Life perpetually surrounded with so many sorrowful Changes and Vicissitudes, that 'twill be matter of the greatest Wonder, how *the Spirit of Man could bear the Infirmities of Nature,* and carry him through the Disappointments of this *Valley of Tears.* And indeed, had not the frame of our Constitution, and the contexture of our Minds been curiously contrived by the Hand of an All-wise Being; did not the Faculties of our upper Region greatly support our tottering building of Clay . . . ."

Discussing Sterne's biblical echoes in *TS*, Arthur Sherbo calls attention to the present passage as "a particularly interesting example of probably unconscious conflation" (*Studies*, p. 129). The relationship between it and

Sterne's sermon—and Leightonhouse's sermon—suggests that it may not be a particularly valid example of the texture of Sterne's fictional prose. Nonetheless, one should note: "bread of affliction" (Deuteronomy 16: 3 and 1 Kings 22: 27); "Yet man is born unto trouble, as the sparks fly upward" (Job 5: 7); "Is there yet any portion or inheritance for us in our father's house?" (Genesis 31 :14); "Why hast thou given me but one lot and one portion to inherit" (Joshua 17: 14); and "The LORD is the portion of mine inheritance and of my cup" (Psalm 16: 5).

　　See below, n. to 333.17–334.9.

332.7　　Zooks] Work, p. 277, n. 1: "Gadzooks; a minced oath, a corruption of 'God's hooks,' referring to the nails with which Christ was fixed to the cross." Cf. below, n. to 377.20 ("ZOUNDS!").

332.15–16　　'Tis by the assistance of Almighty God] Toby still maintains "Grangousier's solution"; see 284.17–20 and n. above.

332.22–23　　That is cutting . . . untying it.] Cf. Sermons, VII.45.157 ("The Ingratitude of Israel"), where the cause of earthquakes is raised: "religion [the doubter argues] had nothing to do in [it] . . . all such violent vibrations of the earth were owing to subterraneous caverns falling down of themselves, or being blown up by nitrous and sulphureous vapours rarified by heat; . . . it was idle to bring in the Deity to untie the knot, when it can be resolved easily into natural causes.—Vain unthinking mortals!—As if natural causes were any thing else in the hands of God,—but instruments which he can turn to work the purposes of his will . . ."; and VI.38.129–30 ("On Enthusiasm"): "the interpretation cuts the knot, instead of untying it . . . ."

　　Behind Sterne's usage in both instances is the proverbial cutting of the Gordian knot; see Tilley, G375, and ODEP, s.v. Gordian knot. And cf. above, n. to 198.16–19.

333.2–9　　Socrates is so finely . . . in course."] Cf. Jonathan Richardson, the younger, An Account of Some of the Statues, Bas-reliefs, Drawings and Pictures in Italy (1722), p. 212: "Even the Manner of the Reasoning of Socrates is Express'd; he holds the Fore-finger of his Left-hand between that, and the Thumb of his Right, and seems as if he was saying, You grant me This, and This . . ."; first noted by R. F. Brissenden, "Sterne and Painting," in Of Books and Humankind (London: Routledge & Kegan Paul, 1964), p. 101, n. 1. The painting is in the Vatican and was often alluded to in the eighteenth century; see, e.g., *Spectator* 407 (III: 521) and Chambers, s.v. *School*.

333.3   connoisseurship] *OED* cites this passage as its first illustration of humorous usage as a personal title; Fielding and Richardson had both used the word previously to mean "playing the role of a connoisseur." For Sterne's attitude toward connoisseurs, see vol. III, chap. 12, pp. 212–16. Possibly, the word is a playful hint at the source of Sterne's description of the "School of Athens," since Jonathan Richardson, the elder, had published *The Connoisseur: An Essay on the whole art of criticism as it relates to painting* (1719).

333.13–16   O *Garrick!* . . . own behind it.] Cf. *Letters*, p. 87 (Sterne to Garrick, January 27, 1760): "I sometimes think of a Cervantic Comedy upon these & the Materials of ye 3^d & 4th Vol^s which will be still more dramatick,—tho I as often distrust its Successe, unless at the Universities.

"Half a word of Encouragement would be enough to make me conceive, & bring forth something for the Stage . . ."; and again to Garrick in 1765 (p. 235): "I am sometimes in my friend's [Garrick's] house, but he is always in Tristram Shandy's—where my friends say he will continue (and I hope the prophecy true for my own immortality) even when he himself is no more."

See above, n. to 213.6–18, and cf. 279.13–14.

333.17–334.9   THOUGH man is . . . sense of it.] Sterne continues his borrowing from "Trust in God" (*Sermons*, VI.34.5–6): "This expectation [that we "shall . . . live to see better days"] . . . imposes upon the sense . . . and like a secret spring in a well-contrived machine, though it cannot prevent, at least it counterbalances the pressure,—and so bears up this tottering, tender frame under many a violent shock and hard justling, which otherwise would unavoidably overwhelm it." Sterne's point in this sermon is that the usual counterbalancing force is self-love, "one of the most deceitful of human passions . . . which at all times inclines us to think better of ourselves, and conditions, than there is ground for;—how great soever the relief is, which a man draws from it at present, it too often disappoints in the end, leaving him to go on his way sorrowing,—mourning . . ." (pp. 8–9). The true counterbalance is that offered by Toby, "trust in God": "however the sorrows of a man are multiplied, he bears up his head, looks towards heaven with confidence, waiting for the salvation of God:—he then builds upon a rock against which the gates of hell cannot prevail" (pp. 10–11).

Cf. *Sermons*, I.4.102 ("Self Knowledge"): "he will discover in his progress many secret turns and windings in his heart to which he was a stranger . . . ; in these labyrinths he will trace out such hidden springs and motives for many of his most applauded actions." The metaphor is a favorite with Sterne; see, e.g., 444.22–23: "puts the most hidden springs of my heart into motion"; 604.19–20: "the resources and hidden springs which sustain them"; and 781.23–24: "some secret spring either of sentiment or rapture."

333.19–20　sudden jerks and hard jostlings] Cf. *ASJ*, p. 101: "in the justlings of the world"; as Stout points out (p. 101, n. to lines 39–40), this is "a favorite expression with Sterne." Other examples are in *Sermons*, I.2.26, II.10.100, VI.37.95; and in *Letters*, p. 224: "no hard jostlings . . . must disturb either body or mind."

334.13–16　fanciful and extravagant . . . and conducts] Sterne very carefully repeats his first description of Walter's theory of names, as it appeared a year earlier in vol. I, chap. 19 (57.14–58.2): "the reader . . . will, at first sight, absolutely condemn [it] as fanciful and extravagant . . . .

"His opinion, in this matter, was, That there was a strange kind of magick bias, which good or bad names, as he called them, irresistibly impress'd upon our characters and conduct."

334.19　GEORGE or EDWARD] Work, p. 279, n. 1: "An oblique compliment to the young George III and his brother Edward, Duke of York; during Sterne's visit to London the spring before this passage was written, he had been occasionally in the Duke's company." For Sterne's acquaintance with the Duke of York (1739–67), see *Letters*, pp. 106, 110–11, 222–23; and Boswell's "Poetical Epistle to Dr. Sterne . . . ," in *Boswell's Book of Bad Verse*, ed. Jack Werner (London: White Lion Publishers, 1974), pp. 136–37. Frederick A. Pottle briefly discusses the Duke and his "company" in "Bozzy and Yorick," *Blackwoods Magazine* 217 (1925): 308–10. Cf. *Letters*, p. 132: "You made me and my friends here very merry," Sterne wrote to Stephen Croft in March 1761, "with the accounts current at York, of my being forbid the court—but they do not consider what a considerable person they make of me, when they suppose either my going, or my not going there, is a point that ever enters the K[ing]'s head—and for those about him, I have the honour either to stand so personally well known to them; or to be so well represented by those of the first rank, as to fear no accident of that kind."

See above, nn. to 240.14—17 and 241.21.

334.24   *Trismegistus*] See above, n. to 58.7.

335.20   anew] I.e., enow; see t.n. to 32.21, vol. II, pp. 844—45, in this edition.

336.19—20   A sudden impulse comes across me] Cf. *ASJ*, p. 106: "as I generally act from the first impulse . . . ."

337.5—6   is a man . . . to follow him?] A succinct account of the debate over "rules" in eighteenth-century English criticism is provided by Emerson R. Marks, *The Poetics of Reason* (New York: Random House, 1968), pp. 38—47. What is perhaps most important to note is that Tristram is hardly alone in his rebellious attitude; and that, as Marks notes (p. 41), even those who "openly scorned the rules" were not necessarily endorsing the sort of aesthetic freedom we associate with the romantic movement.

Cf. Pope, *Essay on Criticism*, p. 256, lines 146—49: "If, where the *Rules* not far enough extend, / (Since Rules were made but to promote their End) / Some Lucky LICENCE answers to the full / Th' Intent propos'd, *that Licence* is a *Rule*"; and Goldsmith, *An Enquiry into the Present State of Polite Learning in Europe:* "THEY now took upon them to teach poetry, to those who wanted genius, and the power of disputing, to those who knew nothing of the subject in debate. It was observed, how some of the most admired poets had copied nature. From these, they collected dry rules, dignified with long names, and such were obtruded upon the public for their improvement. Common sense would be apt to suggest, that the art might be studied to more advantage, rather by imitation than precept. . . . Such rules are calculated to make blockheads talk, but all the lemmata of the Lyceum are unable to give him feeling.

"IN fact, nothing can be more absurd than rules to direct the taste of one country drawn from the manners of another" (*Works*, I: 266, 296).

337.7—20   Now this, you must know . . . read him again] Sterne alludes to the discussion of bombast and puerilities in sec. III of *On the Sublime*, and specifically to a note to that section which he may have read in Zachary Pearce's Greek-Latin edition (1724) or William Smith's English translation (1739), both of which were often reprinted during the century. The annotation is to Longinus's mention of Hegesias as a writer of "empty simple Froth" and in Smith's edition appears as follows: "*Hegesias* was a *Magnesian. Cicero* in his *Orator. c.* 226. says humorously of him, 'He is faulty no less in his Thoughts than his Expressions, so that no one who has any Knowledge of him, need ever be at a Loss for a Man to call Impertinent.' One of his frigid Expressions is still remaining. *Alexander* was born the same Night that the Temple of *Diana* at *Ephesus,* the finest Edifice in the World, was by a terrible Fire reduced to Ashes. *Hegesias* in a panegyrical Declamation on *Alexander* the Great attempted thus to turn that Accident to his Honour. 'No wonder, said he, that *Diana*'s Temple was consumed by so terrible a Conflagration: The Goddess was so taken up in assisting at *Olinthia*'s Delivery of *Alexander,* that she had no leisure to extinguish the Flames which were destroying her Temple.' 'The Coldness of this Expression, says *Plutarch in Alex.* is so excessively great, that it seems sufficient of itself to have extinguished the Fire of the Temple'" (p. 113). A similar note can be found in various seventeenth-century editions, and in Chambers as well, s.v. *Style.*

It is worth noting that the main character in Sterne's "Rabelaisian Fragment" is named Longinus Rabelaicus, and that the proposed subject is to write an "Art of Sermon-writing." New suggests that although this work is never actually begun, "its author's name suggests a parody of *Peri Hupsous* . . . perhaps in the manner of Pope's *Peri Bathous*" ("Rabelaisian Fragment," p. 1083). Sterne's advice to "read" Longinus can be paralleled to his earlier advice to "read" Rabelais (*TS,* 268.1–2). See also the reference to Longinus in vol. VIII (661.13–16).

In his sermon "Search the Scriptures" (*Sermons,* VII.42.67), Sterne calls Longinus "the best critic the eastern world ever produced . . . ."

Jonathan Lamb ("The Comic Sublime and Sterne's Fiction," *ELH* 48 [1981]: 110–43) discusses a possible context for Sterne's interest in the author of *On the Sublime.*

337.12–13   a story of a roasted horse] Proverbial; Tilley, T44, and *ODEP,* s.v. *Tale.* Both cite Cotgrave's *Dictionary of the French and English tongues* (1611), s.v. *Cicogne:* "Contes de la cicogne. *Idle histories; vaine relations; tales of a tub, or, of a roasted horse.*" Cf. Thomas Fuller, *Gnomologia* (1732), no. 2833: "It amounts to no more than the Tail of a roasted Horse."

Sterne uses the phrase in the "Rabelaisian Fragment," p. 1088, lines 17–19: "I'll be shot quoth *Epistemon* if all this Story of thine of a roasted Horse is simply no more than S—— . . . ." Sancho Panza uses it in I.III.11: "running after a Madman, who, if we may light on him again, may chance to make an end of what he has begun, not of his Tale of a roasted Horse, I mean, but of belabouring you and me thoroughly . . ." (I: 250–51); and again in II.III.70: "for all these Stories of People dying for Love are meer Tales of a roasted Horse" (IV: 323).

337.13–16   that chapters relieve . . . shifting of scenes] Fielding had undertaken to explain chapter divisions in *Joseph Andrews*, book II, chap. 1, with much the same lack of success: "I will dismiss this Chapter with the following Observation: That it becomes an Author generally to divide a Book, as it doth a Butcher to joint his Meat, for such Assistance is of great Help to both the Reader and the Carver" (ed. Martin C. Battestin [Middletown, Conn.: Wesleyan University Press, 1967], pp. 89–92). Sterne does not seem to have been influenced by Fielding's chapter.

337.16   fifty other cold conceits] Cf. *ASJ*, p. 159: "I confess I do hate all cold conceptions, as I do the puny ideas which engender them; and . . . I never would make a comparison less than a mountain at least. All that can be said against the French sublime in this instance of it, is this—that the grandeur is *more* in the *word;* and *less* in the *thing*"; and *TS*, vol. IX (763.4–5), where Tristram talks of "a cold unmetaphorical vein of infamous writing."

337.21–25   *Avicenna* and *Licetus* . . . *de omni scribili*] Sterne could have read about Avicenna's bout with Aristotle in Adrien Baillet's *Des enfans célèbres*, which Sterne cites in his own note to the paragraph, but in reference to Licetus; see n. to 337.25–338.4, following. Baillet, p. 40, writes of Avicenna: "Lorsqu'il voulut étudier la Théologie, il commença par la Métaphysique d'Aristote, qu'il lût quarante fois sans l'entendre, & il la savoit toute par cœur, sans savoir néanmoins de quel usage elle pouvoit être" ("When he decided to study theology, he began with Aristotle's *Metaphysics*, which he read forty times over without comprehending, so that he knew it quite by heart without however knowing to what use it could be put"). We have found no evidence that Licetus had a similar difficulty with Aristotle.

Work, p. 282, n. 2: "Avicenna (980–1037), the most celebrated Arabian physician and philosopher, was said to have read the *Metaphysics* forty times and even to have memorized it, without understanding it, when the chance reading of Al Farabius's treatise *Concerning the Objects of Metaphysics* at once revealed Aristotle's meaning to him" (the anecdote became a commonplace among the learned); and n. 3: "Licetus (1577–1657), named Fortunio because he had survived premature birth, was a celebrated Italian scholar and physician, one of whose works, here referred to, was *De Ortu Animae Humanae*."

De omni scribili: "concerning all kinds of writing or scribbling" (*scribili* is a nonce word); Sterne plays on the Latin commonplace *de omni scibili* ("concerning all knowable things"). See Dick Hoefnagel, "Sterne and Avicenna," *N&Q* 226 (1981): 305; Hoefnagel notes Baillet's use of the commonplace on p. 61 of *Des enfans*.

337.25–338.4 and for *Licetus . . .* human soul.] Sterne's information is borrowed from Adrien Baillet's *Des enfans célèbres*, published as vol. VI of *Jugemens des Savans sur les Principaux Ouvrages des Auteurs. Par Adrien Baillet. Revûs, corrigés, & augmentés par M. De La Monnoye de l'Académie Françoise* (Paris, 1722). The last sentence of Sterne's note (338.24–25) and part of the text (338.2–4) is taken from a passage in Baillet separated from the earlier discussion by several sentences (p. 137): "Fortunio ne fut pas long-tems sans faire connoître combien il étoit déja profond dans les Sciences & particuliérement dans la Physique & dans la Médecine, & il n'avoit que *dix-neuf* ans lorsqu'il composa un traité assés important sur l'origine de l'Ame. Le Livre auroit passé tout d'une voix pour l'Ouvrage d'un Vieillard, si Fortunio pour faire voir qu'il n'étoit encore qu'un jeune garçon, n'eût voulu faire paroître un peu d'affectation dans le Titre pompeux de *Gonopsychanthropologia de origine Animæ humanæ*" ("Fortunio very soon revealed how deeply versed he already was in the Sciences, particularly physics and medicine, and he was only *nineteen* when he composed a fairly considerable treatise on the origin of the soul. The book might easily have passed for the work of an elder, had not Fortunio, in order to show that he was still only a youth, deliberately made a show of affectation by giving it the pompous title of *Gonopsychanthropologia, concerning the Origin of the Human Soul*").

Work (p. 282, n. *) provides a translation of the first three paragraphs: "The fœtus was no larger than the palm of the hand; but his father having examined it in his capacity of physician, and having found that it was something more than an embryo, had it transported, all living, to Rapallo, where he showed it to Jerome Bardi and other physicians of the place. They found that it lacked nothing essential to life, and the father, to make a trial of his experience, undertook to complete the work of nature, and to work at the formation of the infant with the same contrivance in which chickens are hatched in Egypt. He instructed a nurse in all that she had to do, and having placed his son in an oven properly arranged he succeeded in rearing him and in nurturing him to his necessary growth by the uniformity of an artificial heat measured exactly by the degrees of a thermometer or of an equivalent instrument. (See Michael Giustinian, in the *Scrittori liguri*, 223.488.)

"People would have been quite satisfied with the industry of a father experimenting similarly in the art of generation if he had been able to prolong the life of his son for but a few months or for a few years.

"But when one recalls that this infant lived nearly eighty years, and that he composed eighty different works, all fruits of long reading, it is necessary to grant that everything which is incredible is not always untrue, and that *appearance is not always on the side of truth*."

See New and Fry, "Some Borrowings," p. 326. See also *TS*, 347.21–23. Sterne borrows from Baillet again in the opening chapters of vol. VI.

338.7   as well employed, as in picking straws.] Proverbially, pointless activity. See Tilley, S925 (cf. S923, "Go peel STRAWS"); and *ODEP*, s.v. *Peel*.

340.4–5   there are . . . could have carried] Job begins with five hundred she asses (1: 3), a number multiplied to one thousand by the end of his sufferings (42: 12). See also 428.21–22: "A curious observer of nature, had he been worth the inventory of all *Job*'s stock . . . ."

340.22   chairman] I.e., one of "the two men who carried a sedan-chair" (*OED*).

340.23   *day-tall*] I.e., from *day-taler*, "a worker engaged and paid by the day" (*OED*).

341.13–15   an observation . . . but to myself] At least one "biographical writer," Montaigne, did make a similar observation, in his essay "Of Vanity," III.9.191: "Who does not see that I have taken a Road, in which, incessantly and without labour I shall proceed, so long as there shall be Ink and Paper in the World? I can give no account of my Life by my Actions; Fortune has plac'd them too low: I must do it by my Fancies."

342.14–15   rush as I may . . . *Horace* advises] See above, n. to 5.16.

342.20–21   under this propitious reign . . . to us] See above, n. to 240.14–17.

342.24–26   As for the . . . work with.] Sterne may have had in mind the figurative use of *goose* for a fool or simpleton (*OED*, first usage dated 1547), as well as a supply of quill pens.

343.6–11   THEN reach me . . . in a fit] Cf. C. H. G. Macafee, "The Obstetrical Aspects of *Tristram Shandy*," *Ulster Medical Journal* 19 (1950): 21: "This description would fit in with either the cyanotic attacks frequently seen in the twelve to twenty-four hours following delivery of a premature baby, or might be accounted for by cerebral irritation following an intracranial hæmorrhage, the result of injury"; and Cash, "Birth," p. 153: "*Fit* was a good medical term in those days, one used to describe the convulsions in the new-born, often fatal, brought on by too great and too prolonged pressures upon the cerebellum."

  See above, n. to 216.14. On the possibility that the Sternes had a male child between 1742 and 1745, who died apparently unbaptized three weeks after his birth, see James M. Kuist, "New Light on Sterne: An Old Man's Recollections of the Young Vicar," *PMLA* 80 (1965): 549–53.

344.2–3   a leaky vessel] A play perhaps on 1 Peter 3: 7: "giving honour unto the wife, as unto the weaker vessel."

344.6   I'll be shot] See above, n. to 234.22.

346.10–347.23   But for sleep . . . for sleep.] This and the next three paragraphs suggest that Sterne may have kept a commonplace book. In the first paragraph, the sentiments are so purposively "commonplace" that identifying a particular source seems unlikely. One could suggest, however, that among Sterne's entries under "Sleep" he might have had, among others, quotations from the Bible, e.g., "The sleep of a labouring man is sweet" (Ecclesiastes 5: 12); from Shakespeare, e.g., "the innocent sleep, / Sleep that knits up the ravell'd sleave of care, / The death of each day's life, sore labor's bath, / Balm of hurt minds, great nature's second course, / Chief nourisher in life's feast" (*Macbeth*, II.ii.33–37); and perhaps from Sidney, *Astrophel and Stella*, sonnet 39: "Come sleepe, ô sleepe, the certaine knot of peace, / The baiting place of wit, the balme of woe, / The

poore man's wealth, the prisoner's release, / Th'indifferent Judge be-
tweene the high and low" (*Poems*, ed. William A. Ringler, Jr. [Oxford:
Clarendon Press, 1962], p. 184).

346.12–13   I cannot . . . upon a bad matter] Proverbial; Tilley, F17: "To set
a good FACE on the matter (on a bad matter)"; and *ODEP*, s.v. *Good*.

347.1–3   "God's blessing . . . like a cloak."] See *Don Quixote*, II.III.68:
"Now Blessings light on him that first invented this same Sleep: It covers a
Man all over, Thoughts and all, like a Cloak . . ." (IV: 304).

347.7–20   Not that I . . . without my wife] Sterne combines two separate
passages from Montaigne's "Of Experience" (III.13), perhaps led to them
by the index listing under *Sleep*: "By how much the possession of living
is more short, I must make it so much deeper and more full. Others are
sensible of Contentment, and of Prosperity, I feel it too, as well as they, but
not only as it slides and passes by; and also a Man ought to study, taste, and
ruminate upon it, to render condign thanks to him that grants it to us.
They enjoy the other Pleasures as they do that of Sleep, without knowing
it; to the End, that even Sleep itself should not so stupidly escape from me,
I have formerly caus'd my self to be disturb'd in my Sleep, that I might the
better and more sensibly relish and taste it" (pp. 396–97).

The second passage occurs twenty pages earlier, and Sterne has played
with its order to produce his closing witticism: "I love to lie hard, and
alone, even without my Wife, as Kings and Princes do, but well cover'd
with Cloaths. . . . I wean my self to my Advantage, from this Propensity
to Sloth, and am evidently better for so doing. I find the Change a little
hard indeed, but in three Days 'tis over, and see but few that live with less
Sleep, when need requires . . . . My Body is capable of a firm, but not of a
violent or sudden Agitation. I evade of late all violent Exercises I
can stand a whole Day together, and am never weary of walking: but from
my Youth, I never loved to ride upon Pavements" (pp. 376–77). Sterne's
claim that he quotes "by memory" can hardly be credited.

347.21–23   but remember, "La Vraisemblance . . . Verité."] Sterne quotes
from his earlier borrowing from Adrien Baillet, 338.22–23 ("Appearance is not always on the Side of Truth").

350.3–10   Instantly I snatch'd . . . know not why] Partly on the basis of a
close echo of this passage, Kenneth Monkman attributes to Sterne an
anonymous letter in the *Protestant York Courant* (November 3, 1747): "I

do not know whether I should go on with my Picture, thus far I look tolerably well; however, I'll be so sincere as to confess to you, I have some Oddities . . . . ——However, my Friends allow them to be very pardonable, as in my most violent Moods I never go beyond the Snapping of a Pipe, or the skimming my Hat and Wig across the Room.

"As I have a warm Affection for my Country, I never hear any ill News from Abroad, but it costs me a Pipe or two, and the storming *Bergen-op-Zoom,* cost me no less than three Glasses and a China Cup, which were unluckily overturn'd by my Hat which I had tossed from me in my Wrath.

"I imagine I make a queer Figure enough, as I march and countermarch hastily across my Room, make a sudden Halt, and perhaps stand in a musing Posture for some Time . . ." ("Sterne, Hamlet, and Yorick," in *Winged Skull,* p. 118).

Cf. Walter's snapping his pipe (115.22) and his hyperactivity (282.27ff.).

350.11–19   we live amongst riddles . . . enough for us.] Cf. 100.7–9: "the unsteady uses of words which have perplexed the clearest and most exalted understandings"; and 776.1–2: "WE live in a world beset on all sides with mysteries and riddles . . . ."

Sterne borrows from his sermon "The Ways of Providence justified to Man" (VII.44.134): "Nay, have not the most obvious things that come in our way dark sides, which the quickest sight cannot penetrate into; and do not the clearest and most exalted understandings find themselves puzzled, and at a loss, in every particle of matter?" Cf. *Sermons,* III.19.118 ("Felix's Behaviour towards Paul, examined"): "That in many dark and abstracted questions of mere speculation, we should err——is not strange: we live amongst mysteries and riddles, and almost every thing which comes in our way, in one light or other, may be said to baffle our understandings . . . ."

For an argument that this view of man as surrounded by mysteries and riddles reflects Sterne's kinship with the "scepticism of Hume," see Francis Doherty, "Sterne and Hume: A Bicentenary Essay," *E &S*, n.s. 22 (1969): 77–79. Echoes of it in the sermons might suggest, however, that "mysteries and riddles" is simply a restatement of some very commonplace Christian beliefs.

350.26–27   system builders] *OED*'s first illustration of this phrase as a compound word is dated 1776, but is a reference to *TS* (though not to this specific occurrence) by William Julius Mickle in his annotations to Camöens's *Lusiad*, book VII, p. 313: "Tristram Shandy tells us, that his father was a most excellent system-builder, was sure to make his Theory look well, though no man ever crucified the truth at such an unmerciful rate" (Oxford, 1776; New York: Garland Publishing, 1979). Mickle's comment makes clear the rather pejorative connotations attached to the phrase.

351.4−5   *Pythagoras . . . nor Mahomet*] Work, p. 293, n. 1: "Pythagoras (c. 582−c. 500 B.C.) was a Greek philosopher and mathematician whose *ipse dixit* was the law of his followers and from whose teachings the ancient lawgivers of Sicily and Grecian Italy were said by Seneca (*Epistolae*, 90.6) to have derived the laws which they established. Plato (c. 427−347 B.C.), the Athenian philosopher, was motivated by a zeal for human improvement, which found its most practical expression in dialogues on legislation and statecraft such as the *Gorgias*, the *Republic*, the *Statesman*, and the *Laws*. Solon (c. 638−c. 559 B.C.) was an Athenian statesman and lawgiver. Lycurgus (fl. c. 800 B.C.) was a traditional Spartan legislator, the reputed founder of the laws and institutions of Sparta. Ancient Moslem law was based largely on the Koran, as revealed to Mahomet (c. 570−632), the founder of Islam, and on the decisions of the prophet, who, during his lifetime, was the inspired legislator and judge of his people."

The names, perhaps excepting Mahomet, might occur to any eighteenth-century writer preparing a list of legal authorities; e.g., George Dawson, *Origo Legum: or a treatise of the origin of laws* (1694), book II, chap. 9, p. 137: "In a word, All that ever hath been said or writ about Laws, by *Moses* and the *Prophets*, by *Plato* or *Pythagoras*, or *Solon*, or *Lycurgus* . . . or all the Lawgivers of the whole World, are not near of so much worth and value, as Christ's Sermon on the Mount . . . ."

352.18   *James Butler*] See below, n. to 360.8−9. We were told in vol. II (108.19−20) that Trim's name is James Butler.

353.23−354.3   either for my own . . . to play] Sterne may be echoing Exodus 20: 5: "for I the LORD thy God am a jealous God, visiting the iniquity of the fathers upon the children . . . ." Cf. Lamentations 5: 7: "Our fathers have sinned, and are not; and we have borne their iniquities."

354.5   child of wrath!] Cf. Ephesians 2: 3: "Among whom also we all had our conversation in times past in the lusts of our flesh, fulfilling the desires of the flesh and of the mind; and were by nature the children of wrath, even as others."

354.7   book of embryotic evils] *OED* cites this passage for its first recorded usage and refers for definition to *embryonic*, 2. *fig.*: "Immature, un-developed." The context, however, would point to the definition under *embryonic*, 1.: "Pertaining to, or having the character of, an embryo."

354.13   radical heat and radical moisture] For "radical moisture" see above, n. to 104.4. Chambers, s.v. *Flame (vital)*, defines "radical heat" as the "fine, warm, ignious substance, supposed by many both of the antients and moderns, to reside in the hearts of animals, as necessary to life, or rather, as that which constitutes life itself. . . .

   "Dr. Quincy can find nothing more in the notion of vital *Flame*, than the natural warmth, which is the effect of a circulating blood; and which is always as its velocity."

354.15   stamina] See above, n. to 306.20–24.

354.21   memory, fancy, and quick parts] See above, n. to 228.19–20.

354.28   non-naturals] Cf. above, n. to 84.26. Throughout this section Sterne seems purposively to echo various phrases and ideas from the opening pages of *TS*, thus creating a texture of continuity despite the serial nature of publication. Hence, cf. 354.9–10 ("or ever thou camest into the world") and 4.16–17 ("*My Tristram's misfortunes began nine months before ever he came into the world*"); 354.20 ("the few animal spirits I was worth in the world") and 1.16–17 ("I dare say [you have] heard of the animal spirits, as how they are transfused from father to son"); and 354.22 ("were all dispersed, confused, confounded, scattered") and 2.17–18 ("it scattered and dispersed the animal spirits").

355.2–4   What a teazing life . . . in town?] Walter here gives credence to a commonplace theory that Burton in the *Anatomy* expresses thus: "Some other causes [of melancholy] are given, which properly pertaine to, and proceed from the mother: If shee be over-dull, heavy, angry, peevish, discontented, and melancholy, not onely at the time of conception, but even all the while she carries the childe in her wombe . . . her sonne will be so likewise affected, and worse, as . . . if shee grieve overmuch, be disquieted, or by any casualty be affrighted and terrified by some fearefull object, heard or seene, she endangers her childe, and spoyles the temperature of it; for the strange imagination of a woman, workes effectually upon her infant . . ." (1.2.1.6, p. 64).

On the same page, however, Burton also indicates that the father may share in the blame: "they pay their debt (as *Paul* cals it) to their wives remissely, by which meanes their Children are weaklings, and many times ideots and fooles" (p. 64).

In vol. VI (558.16–17) Sterne cites a tag from this page of the *Anatomy*.

355.9–11   There she gave vent . . . looking up] Sterne plays on *vent*, which could also mean the *anus, vulva,* or *womb* during the eighteenth century; cf. 390.23–25, where the mother is referred to in legal parlance as the *venter: "Charles* Duke of *Suffolk* having issue a son by one venter, and a daughter by another venter . . . ."

355.17–21   his head exposed . . . thousand tatters.] Cf. 176.6–7: "a weight of 470 pounds averdupoise acting perpendicularly upon it"; and 177.1: "the intellectual web is so rent and tatter'd as we see it." For the background of these observations, see nn. to the passages, above.

356.5   curvetting] *OED*'s first example is dated 1784.

356.6   two up and two down] Cf. *Letters,* p. 213 (May 19, 1764): "I have been for eight weeks smitten with the tenderest passion that ever tender wight underwent. I wish, dear cosin, thou couldest concieve . . . how deliciously I canter'd away with it the first month, two up, two down, always upon my hânches along the streets from my hôtel to hers . . . till at length I was within an ace of setting up my hobby horse in her stable for good an all."

356.12   arch-jockey of jockeys] *OED* cites this passage as its sole example of *arch-jockey.* Cf. "arch-critick" (82.11), "arch-wit" (385.3), and "arch cook of cooks" (670.20). *Arch-wit* is not recorded in *OED*.

356.17–18   undertaking criticks!] *OED* cites this passage as its sole illustration, with the uncertain definition "?engaged in literary work." Cf. *Tale of a Tub,* p. 41, where the tone of "undertaking" seems to be indicated by Swift's reference to "the Undertaker" of a proposed Academy, who will "publish his Proposals with all convenient speed . . . ." See also Work, p. 298, n. 1: "Enterprising; used here in the derogatory sense of officious, over-reaching"; and *TS,* 423.13–14: "many an undertaking critick would have built two stories higher upon worse foundations."

357.4   see you've splash'd a bishop] Work, p. 298, n. 2: "An allusion to
William Warburton (1698–1779), Bishop of Gloucester. Whether
started by Sterne or not, the report had spread in London that the pompous
and pedantic Bishop was to be caricatured in *Shandy* as Tristram's tutor.
When Sterne vigorously but perhaps disingenuously denied the rumour,
Warburton, apparently in gratitude for his escape, became Sterne's patron, recommending his book 'to all the best company in town,' pushing
the subscription to his forthcoming sermons, and even presenting him
with 'a purse of guineas.' But when he proceeded to give the successful
author books to improve his style and prudish advice to regulate his personal and literary careers, Sterne declined to follow his direction, and an
increasing coolness developed between the two men."

For a full discussion of the relationship between the two men and its
importance to *TS,* see New, "Sterne, Warburton."

357.6   Mess. *Le Moyne . . . De Marcilly*] The doctors responsible for the
"Memoire" on intrauterine baptism by means of a "squirt"; see 69.21–
23.

357.15ff.   As *Francis* the first, etc.] Sterne's note cites the *Menagiana,* a collection of observations, gossip, and bon mots, by Gilles Ménage (1613–92),
first published in 1693. We quote from a "New Edition" of this popular
work, published in Paris in 1729: "On dit que François I. voulut prendre
la Répub. des Suisses pour marraine d'un des Princes ses enfans; mais il en
perdit la pensée lorsqu'il fut qu'ils le vouloient nommer, *Sidrac, Misac &*
Abdenago [*sic*]" (II: 214). Work's translation (p. 299, n. *) suffices: "It is
said that Francis I wished to take the Republic of Switzerland as the god-
mother of one of his sons; but he changed his mind when he learned that
they wished to name him Shadrach, Meshach, and Abed-nego."

If this is indeed the immediate source for Sterne's chapter, he indulges
in an elaboration of his material quite unlike his usual interest in fitting
verbatim borrowings into the texture of his own work.

Francis I (1494–1547) ruled France from 1515 until his death.

358.26   *Shadrach, Mesech,* and *Abed-nego*] The names given to the three
friends of Daniel by Nebuchadnezzar; they are later delivered from the
fiery furnace. See Book of Daniel, 1: 7, 3: 1–30.

358.27   By saint *Peter*'s girdle] In all likelihood a nonce oath, fashioned after the Rabelaisian habit; e.g., "By St. Winifrid's placket" (IV.9.119), "By St. Anthony's hog" (IV.9.120), "By St. Patrick's slipper" (IV.12.132), "By St. Joseph's wooden shoe" (IV.15.143), etc.

359.1–2   pulling up his breeches . . . the floor.] Sterne perhaps alludes to a particular habit of Louis XIV. Cf. C. D. O'Malley, "The Medical History of Louis XIV: Intimations of Mortality," in *Louis XIV and the Craft of Kingship* (Columbus: Ohio State University Press, 1969), p. 136: "Memoirs of the period contain much gossip about the inconsequent details of Louis's frequent bouts of self-induced gastric upset . . . ; it seems, too, that there was no detail of the royal physiological processes that was not discussed with amazing frankness as to function or malfunction. Such lack of delicacy should be no cause for astonishment when one considers that the king himself set this earthly tone by such practices as giving audiences from his *chaise percée* . . . ."

360.1   disport] *OED* cites this passage as its sole illustration of the definition "bearing, carriage, deportment."

360.5   *Francis* the Ninth] See above, n. to 276.16–23.

360.8–9   that I meant the duke of *Ormond*] Trim's name, James Butler (see 108.19–20 and 352.18), was the name of both the first (1610–88) and second (1665–1745) Duke of Ormonde. The latter is the grandson and more than likely the personage Sterne alludes to. He replaced Marlborough as General of the Army in 1712 and followed the orders of Anne and Bolingbroke in implementing the Treaty of Utrecht. For doing so, he was impeached when the Whigs returned to power in 1715, and spent the rest of his life in exile in France and Spain. For a sympathetic, detailed account of his career, see the anonymous *Life of James, Late Duke of Ormonde* (1747). Sterne is certainly teasing the reader at this point since the Duke, like Trim, was wounded at the Battle of Landen in 1693 and was at Namur in 1695 (see *Life*, pp. 227–28). For his role in carrying out the Treaty of Utrecht, see *TS*, 686.5–17 and n. below.

See also Matthew Prior, "Seeing the Duke of Ormond's Picture, at Sir Godfrey Kneller's," in *Works*, ed. H. Bunker Wright and Monroe K. Spears, 2d ed. (Oxford: Clarendon Press, 1971), I: 257, where Prior waxes eloquent over the Duke's wounds at Landen: "'Till weak with Wounds, and cover'd o'er with Blood, / Which from the Patriot's Breast in Torrents flow'd . . ." (lines 10–11).

See also Wolfgang Zach, "'My Uncle Toby's Apologetical Oration' und die Politische Sinndimension von 'Tristram Shandy'," *GRM* 27 (1977): 400–402.

360.11–18   'tis wrote . . . into their duodenums] Sterne's minute description of the physical mechanism of laughter would seem to be a parody of certain seventeenth- and eighteenth-century physicians and philosophers with a mechanistic bent. Richard Cumberland, for example, quotes Thomas Willis's important work, *Anatomy of the Brain* (1664), in his own account of laughter: "First, therefore, I observe from Willis . . . that, from the above-mention'd *Communication between the Plexus Nervosus peculiar to Man, and the Nervus Diaphragmaticus,* the true Cause appears, why *Risibility* is *a Property of human* Nature; which is, because the Diaphragm, as well as the Heart, is affected with the pleasing Motion of the Imagination, and is drawn upward by the Intercourse of the Nerves proceeding from this Plexus, and is excited to repeated Heavings as it were; whence, because the Pericardium is joined to it, the Heart it-self and the Lungs are likewise mov'd; then, because the same Intercostal Nerve is continued upward with the Nerves of the Jaws, when once the Laugh is begun in the Breast, the Posture of the Mouth and Countenance pathetically corresponds thereto" (*A Treatise of the Laws of Nature,* trans. John Maxwell [1727], p. 153). Cf. John Bulwer, *Pathomyotomia; or a Dissection of the significative muscles* (1649), p. 126, where the description of laughter includes this phrase: "whence comes that succussation of the Lungs and agitation of the Midriff . . . ."

See also Swift, *Tale of a Tub,* p. 185: "The *Superficial* Reader will be strangely provoked to *Laughter;* which clears the Breast and the Lungs, is Soverain against the *Spleen,* and the most innocent of all *Diureticks*"; and Sterne himself, *TS,* 401.24–28 (and n. below): "True *Shandeism,* think what you will against it, opens the heart and lungs, and like all those affections which partake of its nature, it forces the blood and other vital fluids of the body to run freely thro' its channels, and makes the wheel of life run long and chearfully round."

The idea is of course a non-scientific commonplace as well; cf. *Spectator* 387 (III: 451): "Chearfulness is, in the first place, the best Promoter of Health. Repinings, and secret Murmurs of Heart, give imperceptible Strokes to those delicate Fibres of which the Vital Parts are composed, and wear out the Machine insensibly; not to mention those violent Ferments which they stir up in the Blood, and those irregular disturbed Motions which they raise in the animal Spirits."

360.16   inimicitious] *OED* cites this passage as its last illustration, with the definition "unfriendly, hostile, adverse." Sterne used the word in a letter to Warburton in 1760: "Of all the vile things wrote against me, the Letter . . . in the female magazeen [*Royal Female Magazine*], is the most inimicitious . . ." (*Letters*, p. 115).

360.23   I hate these great dinners] On the institution of the visitation and the visitation dinner, see Cash, "Sterne as a Judge," pp. 17–36, and *Early and Middle Years*, pp. 128–32. Cf. Goldsmith, *Citizen of the World*, letter 58: "To understand this term, you must know, that it was formerly the custom here for the principal priests [i.e., bishops] to go about the country once a year, and examine upon the spot whether those of subordinate orders did their duty, or were qualified for the task; whether their temples were kept in proper repair, or the laity pleased with their administration.

". . . the custom has been long discontinued. At present, therefore, every head of the church, instead of going about to visit his priests, is satisfied if his priests come in a body once a year to visit him . . . ." (*Works*, II: 239). Goldsmith then goes on to describe an orgy of feasting as the sole purpose of the dinner (pp. 240–42).

Sterne's **** (372.18) represents York.

361.5   *Didius*] See above, n. to 11.26.

361.11   Let my old tye wig] *Handbook of English Costume*, p. 93: "The hair was drawn back and the curls bunched together to form a queue tied with black ribbon at the nape of the neck." The wig is illustrated in the *Handbook*, p. 90.

372.24–373.1   whether by performing . . . *Holbein of Basil*] Cf. Richard Graham, *A Short Account of the Most Eminent Painters*, 2d ed. (1716), s.v. *Hans Holbein* (1497–1543): "[He] was particularly remarkable for having (like *Turpilius*, the *Roman*) perform'd all his Works with his *Left Hand*" (p. 305).

Of Turpilius, Graham writes: "a *Roman Knight*, liv'd in the time of *Vespasian*, who was chosen *Emperour*, *An. Dom.* 69. And (though he painted every thing with his *left hand*) was much applauded for his admirable *Performances* . . ." (p. 266).

373.4—6   *bend dexter . . . bend sinister*] In heraldry, the bend dexter is the common diagonal band drawn across the shield from the top left-hand corner (looking at the shield), or dexter chief, to the lower right-hand corner, or sinister base; when the band is drawn in the opposite direction, i.e., from the sinister chief to the dexter base, it is called the bend sinister and is said to indicate bastardy.

373.27   blot in my escutcheon] Sterne plays with the literal and figurative meanings of the phrase, i.e., "a stain on a person's reputation" (*OED*); Dryden (1697) is the first recorded illustration.

374.4   coach-lining] Unrecorded in *OED*.

374.5   as it did *December, January*, and *February*] See 7.21—23.

375.5   make neither head or tail of it.] Proverbial; see Tilley, H258, and *ODEP*, s.v. *Head*.

375.6   I'm to preach . . . said *Homenas*] The second chapter of the "Rabelaisian Fragment" opens: "HOMENAS who had to preach next Sunday . . ." (p. 1089, line 51). Sterne borrowed the name from Rabelais's Bishop of Papimany; Ozell annotates it as "a production of that of homme. They use it in Languedoc, when they would say, a great loggerheaded booby, that has neither wit nor breeding" (IV.48.275, n. 2). Cf. Work, p. 315, n. 4: "Homenas (homilist)."

375.14—15   (as *Montaigne* complained in a parallel accident)] In "Of the Education of Children" Montaigne relates the following anecdote (I.25.156): "I was reading a *French* Book, where after I had a long Time run dreaming over a great many Words, so dull, so insipid, so void of all Wit, or common Sense, that indeed they were only Words; after a long and tedious Travel, I came at last to meet with a Piece that was lofty, rich, and elevated to the very Clouds; of which, had I found either the Declivity easy, or the Ascent accessible, there had been some Excuse; but it was so perpendicular a Precipice, and so wholly cut off from the rest of the Work, that by the first Words I found myself flying into the other World, and from thence discover'd the Vale from whence I came so deep and low, that I had never since the Heart to descend into it any more." Montaigne, it should be noted, is not speaking of the unevenness of his own composition, but of the practice of introducing quotations from ancient authors which render modern writings, by comparison, "pale, sallow, and deform'd."

376.1—2   SEE if he is . . . light their pipes!] In *Spectator* 46, Addison describes how the Spectator had misplaced his notes in Lloyd's Coffee-house (see Sterne's use of this in vol. VII, chap. 36), how a reading of them produced various comical interpretations (similar to the Club's response to the "History of a Good Warm Watch-Coat" in Sterne's *Political Romance*), and finally how he had regained possession of the paper and, feigning indifference, had "twisted it into a kind of Match, and litt my Pipe with it" (I: 195–98).

Cf. *Spectator* 367 (III: 380): "I must confess, I have lighted my Pipe with my own Works [i.e., with *Spectators*] for this Twelve-month past . . . ."

376.4   *Kysarcius* . . . low countries.] See above, n. to 228.8–11, where Kysarcius is first mentioned; the mock geographical reference here seems almost certainly an obscene underscoring of the name.

376.17   one of the two horns of my dilemma] Cross, *Life*, p. 33, suggests an allusion to Hobbes, "to that quaint title-page of the *Leviathan* whereon is depicted graphically the horns of a dilemma, upon which hang syllogisms of various sorts while masters and students stand about in their gowns." However, both *ODEP* (s.v. *Horns*) and Stevenson (p. 576) suggest that the phrase is proverbial, from the scholastic Latin: *argumentum cornutum* ("the alternatives of a dilemma").

376.23–377.10   I was delivered . . . to the heart] Cf. 165.3–9 and n. above. See also Sterne's preface to vols. I and II of his *Sermons:* "for as the sermons turn chiefly upon philanthropy, and those kindred virtues to it, upon which hang all the law and the prophets, I trust they will be no less felt, or worse received, for the evidence they bear, of proceeding more from the heart than the head" (I: viii–ix). At least one reviewer, for the *Critical Review* 9 (1760): 405–6, found Sterne's sermons precisely as Sterne would have desired: "The reverend Mr. Sterne aims at mending the heart, without paying any great regard to the instruction of the head; inculcating every moral virtue by precepts, deduced from reason and the sacred oracles. Would to God his example were more generally followed by our clergy, too many of whom delight in an ostentatious display of their own abilities, and vain unedifying pomp of theological learning."

Sterne often uses the dichotomy of head and heart, as did his century. Particularly interesting passages from the *Sermons* include this from I.3.57: "merciful GOD! that a teacher of thy religion should ever want humanity—or that a man whose head might be thought full of the one, should have a heart void of the other"; and from II.15.223: "And indeed considering what lights they [classical philosophers] had, some of them wrote extremely well; yet, as what they said proceeded more from the head, than the heart, 'twas generally more calculated to silence a man in his troubles, than to convince, and teach him how to bear them." Cf. *Letters*, p. 134: "preaching (you must know) is a theologic flap upon the heart . . ."; p. 298: "Eliza will receive my books with this—the Sermons came all hot from the heart—I wish that could give em any title, to be offer'd to Y^{rs}——the Others came from the head—I'm more indifferent ab^t their Reception"; and p. 362 ("Journal to Eliza"): "dear Lady write anything and write it any how, so it but comes from y^r heart, twil be better than the best Letter that ever came from Pope's head."

Cf. Goldsmith's several pronouncements on rhetorical delivery in the *Bee*, especially no. 7 (November 17, 1759), where he directs his remarks to preaching: "The polite of every country have several motives to induce them to a rectitude of action . . . . The vulgar have but one, the enforcements of religion; and yet those who should push this motive home to their hearts, are basely found to desert their post. They speak to the squire, the philosopher, and the pedant; but the poor, those who really want instruction, are left uninstructed. . . .

"How then are such to be addressed; not by studied periods, or cold disquisitions; not by the labours of the head, but the honest spontaneous dictates of the heart. . . .

"From eloquence, therefore, the morals of our people are to expect emendation; but how little can they be improved, by men who get into the pulpit rather to shew their parts, than convince us of the truth of what they deliver . . ." (*Works*, I: 480–82). Friedman notes that these views seem "to reflect a fairly common way of thinking at the time he was writing" (p. 480, n. 1).

Swift, in his *Letter to a Young Gentleman, Lately enter'd into Holy Orders* (1720), also warns against words "which not one of his Hearers among a Hundred, could possibly understand" and further comments: "a Divine hath nothing to say to the wisest Congregation of any Parish in this Kingdom, which he may not express in a Manner to be understood by the meanest among them" (*Works*, IX: 65–66).

377.20   ZOUNDS!] Cf. Swift, *Polite Conversation*, p. 31: "Sir *John Perrot* was
the first Man of Quality, whom I find upon Record, to have sworn by
G——'s W——. He lived in the Reign of Queen *Elizabeth*, and was
supposed to have been a natural Son of *Harry* VIII. who might also have
probably been his Instructor. This Oath, indeed, still continues, and is a
Stock-oath to this Day . . . ." Montagu, *Anatomy of Swearing*, pp.
138–39, notes that the oath was in use long before Perrot, although the
particular corruption *Zounds* may have originated in Elizabeth's court.

377.22   *Phutatorius*] See above, n. to 227.13.

378.4–10   One or two . . . make of it.] Cf. above, n. to 63.7–8. As a musical term, *concord* is a "combination of notes which is in itself satisfactory to
the ear, requiring no 'resolution' or following chord" (*OED*).

378.23   twelve-penny oath] According to the Profane Oaths Act of 1746 (19
Geo. II, c. 21) the penalties for swearing were determined by the class of
speaker rather than by the oath uttered. Twelve pence was the fine for a
day-laborer, common soldier, or sailor; everyone else beneath the degree
of a gentleman was subject to a fine of two shillings; gentlemen, to whose
class Phutatorius might reasonably have been expected to belong, were
liable for five shillings. Sterne would have been quite familiar with the
act, since it was required to be read in church on four specific Sundays each
year and neglecting to do so rendered the clergyman liable to a fine of five
pounds.

379.3   purtenance] Cf. above, n. to 11.21–22.

379.22–26   So that notwithstanding . . . over-against him] Cf. "Rabelaisian
Fragment," pp. 1090–91, lines 119–24: "And tho' his Head was full of
Matter, & he had skrew'd up every Nerve and Muscle belonging to it, till
all cryed, *crack*, again, in order to give a due projectile Force to what He
was going to let fly full in *Longinus Rabelaicus's* Teeth, who sat over against
him . . . ." See also *TS*, 192.6–7.

379.27–28   domicile of *Phutatorius*'s brain] Cf. 228.23–25: "into the several receptacles, cells, cellules, domiciles . . . of our brains."

379.28–29   lay at least a yard below.] Sterne may be punning; see *OED*, s.v.
Yard, *sb²* 11: "The virile member, penis." In Chambers, it is the word most
often used in technical explanations.

380.3   *Gastripheres*] See above, n. to 228.8–11.

380.23–24   there is no . . . all *Johnson*'s dictionary] The "chaste" words in the eighteenth century were *flap* or *fall;* Johnson does not include this definition in his entry for either word.

380.26–27   like the temple of *Janus*] Janus was the Roman god of doors, gateways, and beginnings; the closing of the temple doors signified peace, the opening of them, war. Cf. *Sermons,* VII.41.38 ("Follow Peace"): "in the days of Augustus,—when the temple of Janus was shut, and all the alarms of war were hushed and silenced . . . ."

381.6   *Acrites* or *Mythogeras*] *Acrites,* from Greek ακριτος (*akritos*): "confused, lacking in discrimination"; *Mythogeras,* from Latin *mythos* ("story") and *gero* ("carry," i.e., a tale-bearer).

381.12–13   obscene treatise *de Concubinus retinendis*] *On Keeping Concubines;* Sterne may have found inspiration for the title in a note to Rabelais in which the reader is referred to "the ch. de concubinariis cum honestate, &c. of a small volume de fide concubinarum, &c. printed in Germany in the year 1565 . . ." (II.7.59, n. 51). For another possible use of an earlier portion of this same note, see *TS,* vol. VII, chap. 34, and n. below (633.17ff.)

381.20   hiatus] *OED* cites this passage as its sole illustration of humorous usage.

381.24   undelectable] *OED* cites this passage as its last example.

382.4–5   imagination . . . fancy] See 228.19–20 and n. above.

382.16   compursions] *OED* cites this passage as its only example; humorously, "A pursing together."

382.22   *Asker*] This occurrence is the last illustration cited by *OED*; the common name, in west midlands and Yorkshire dialect, for a newt.

383.1–2   with the aposiopestick-break . . . thus] Cf. the "Rabelaisian Fragment" where Sterne had originally set up the same situation of the exclamation "Zounds—" followed by a comment upon "the aposiopesistic Break . . . markt thus———" (p. 1091, t.n. to lines 126, 135). Perhaps because he uses it here in vol. IV, Sterne emended "Zounds" to "Damn it" and deleted "aposiopesistic" in the manuscript. For the relationship of the "Fragment" to *TS,* see New's introduction, "Rabelaisian Fragment," pp. 1083–86. Cf. *TS,* 115.23–24, and n. above.

    OED cites this passage as its last illustration of *aposiopetic;* the first and only other example is cited from Thomas Urquhart's *Jewel* (1652).

383.13–14   trifles light as air] Sterne may be recalling Iago's comment as he plots to leave Desdemona's handkerchief in Cassio's lodging: "Trifles light as air / Are to the jealous confirmations strong / As proofs of holy writ . . ." (*Othello*, III.iii.322−24). Cf. *Sermons*, VII.44.126−27: "and so oddly perplexed are the accounts of both human happiness and misery in this world,—that trifles, light as air, shall be able to make the hearts of some men sing for joy . . . ."

383.15−17 that *Euclid*'s demonstrations . . . overthrow it.] See below, n. to 465.4−5.

383.22 worth stooping for] Cf. above, n. to 327.4−5.

384.26 *Somnolentus* . . . *Agelastes*] See above, nn. to 227.11 and 228.8−11.

385.3 arch-wit] Cf. above, n. to 356.12.

385.5−6 *Yorick*, no doubt . . . *man of jest*] See *Hamlet*, V.i.184−85: "Alas, poor Yorick! I knew him, Horatio, a fellow of infinite jest, of most excellent fancy."

The clear echo of *Hamlet* here strongly suggests that "dreams of philosophy" (line 5) is also a recall (I.v.166−67): "There are more things in heaven and earth, Horatio, / Than are dreamt of in your philosophy."

386.5−8 CAN you tell me . . . the fire?] Sterne plays upon the "heat" of venereal infection, as in the term *fire-ship* for a prostitute (*OED*, seventeenth−eighteenth century); and he is perhaps also aware of the archaic *burning* which, according to Chambers, s.v., "in our ancient customs, denotes an infectious disease, got in the stews, by conversing with leud women; supposed to be the same that we now call the *venereal disease*."

386.17−387.3 but if you . . . anodyne and safe.] Eugenius's prescription perhaps owes its origin to Rabelais. Cf. the "Author's Prologue" to vol. II: "There are others in the world . . . who being much troubled with the tooth-ach . . . have found no more ready remedy, than to put the said chronicles [of Gargantua] betwixt two pieces of linnen cloth made very hot, and so apply them to the place that smarteth" (p. iv); first noted by Stout, "Some Borrowings," p. 114.

Cf. Work, p. 325, n. 2: "On the early hand presses, to insure evenness of impression the paper was printed damp." We have found no evidence that printer's ink was used for the treatment of burns—or anything else—in the eighteenth century, but the idea of a compress impregnated with oil seems legitimate enough; cf. *The London Practice of Physic*, 3d ed. (1778),

p. 393: "Burns in the face should be treated [by laying] soft paper, or rags, over the face, frequently besmeared with linseed-oil fresh drawn."

387.6   That would make a very devil of it] Yorick puns on *devil*, i.e., "Printer's devil: the errand-boy in a printing office" (*OED*, s.v. *Devil*, 5a.). *OED* cites Joseph Moxon, *Mechanick Exercises* (1683): "These Boys do in a Printing-House, commonly black and Dawb themselves: whence the Workmen do Jocosely call them Devils . . . ."

387.9–10   half in half] Cf. 420.2–4: "for instance, where the pleasure of the harangue was as *ten,* and the pain of the misfortune but as *five*—my father gained half in half. . . ." *OED* (s.v. *Half,* II.7.c.) cites this latter example as its last illustration, with the definition "half (to or by half) the total amount."

387.24   *de re concubinariâ*] "On the thing of a concubine" might indicate more clearly than other possible translations Sterne's bawdy intent. Cf. 78.18ff. and n. above ("*Argumentum ad Rem*"); and 400.15–17 (the promise of a "chapter of THINGS" and a "chapter upon WHISKERS").

388.9ff.   Had a priest, etc.] Sterne would appear to have borrowed his entire discussion from a note to Rabelais, I.19.218, n. 8: "Now, according to the canonists, it sufficeth if we be understood. Ask them whether it is a baptism to say omine atris & ilii, &c. instead of nomine patris & filii, &c. they'll tell ye no, and that such a diminution hinders it from being a baptism: for, say they, the sense and meaning is remov'd and chang'd; for atris does not signify father, nor ilii son: ergò, such baptism is null. But if this diminution be at the end of the word, as if the s be taken from patris, by saying patri, or the like, such diminution does not hinder the baptism: for one and the same sense remains in the words, but then the intention of saying them aright must go along with them. Of this we have an example in a decree, de consecr. dist. 4. cap. retulerunt. A priest, ignorant in the Latin tongue, baptizeth a child thus, in nomina patria & filia & spitum sancta amen. In this decree the pope says, the child was baptiz'd: considering the priest was a very devout man, and had an intention to speak aright, and only fail'd thro' ignorance and inscience." See W. G. Day, "Sterne and Ozell," *ES* 53 (1972): 435.

If Sterne had pursued Ozell's citation to the *Corpus Juris Canonici* he would have discovered, as Work notes (p. 327, n. 2), that Pope Zachary

(741–52) and not Pope Leo III (795–816) was responsible for the decree (*Corpus juris canonici academicum in suos tomos distributum . . . auctore Christophoro Henrico Freiesleben . . .* [Pragae, 1728], Decreti Pars III De Consecratione. Dist. IV, c. 86, p. 1135–6). Work suggests that Sterne may have been confusing the decree with "an important pronouncement regarding the intention of the priest in baptism, in a decree of Innocent III," but just as probably Sterne simply cited an authority at random. Leo III was noteworthy for having crowned Charlemagne Holy Roman Emperor in 800.

388.21   *John Stradling's*] Like Tom-o'Stiles (line 11; see above, n. to 234.8–9), Stradling seems to have been a conventional fictitious name for a party in a lawsuit, though not recorded in *OED*. Cf. *Martinus Scriblerus*, p. 164: "The *Case of* Stradling *and* Stiles, *in an Action concerning certain* black *and* white Horses." The satirical "case" was published in Pope's *Works* as "A Specimen of Scriblerus's Reports. Stradling *versus* Stiles" (see, e.g., the 1756 edition, VI: 233–37).

389.4–5   a tone two parts jest and one part earnest] The fact that Sterne defines Yorick's tone in this manner, especially when added to the evidence of his mottoes in vols. III and IV ("a jocis ad seria, a seriis vicissim ad jocos transire") and in vols. V and VI, suggests that he might have been aware of the long tradition by which the clergy and others had defended the use of a tone "betwixt Jest and Earnest" in religious controversy; see, e.g., Andrew Marvell, *The Rehearsal Transpros'd: The Second Part*, ed. D. I. B. Smith (Oxford: Clarendon Press, 1971), p. 187. See also above, n. to 149.4–6. The phrase itself, however, was in common use; cf. Burton, 2.2.3.255, and *Spectator* 338 (III: 253). See also n. to 61.6–7.

389.26ff.   It has not only been a question, etc.] As Sterne's first note indicates, he has copied this entire discussion from Henry Swinburne's *A Briefe Treatise of Testaments and Last Wills*, a work he seems to have used earlier in putting together his nonsense footnote in "Slawkenbergius's Tale" (310.20–30). We quote from the London edition of 1635: "It hath not onely beene a question amongst the best Lawyers in this Land, whether the mother bee of kinne to her childe, but after much disputation, it hath bin also adjudged for the negative, *viz.* That the mother is not of kinne to her childe, as appeareth in the case, commonly knowne by the name of the Duke of *Suffolkes* case, very famous in many bookes (though more famous for the rarenesse than for soundnes) which case was this. In the reigne of King *Edward* the sixth, *Charles* Duke of *Suffolke*, having issue a sonne by one venter, and a daughter by another venter, made his last Will, wherein he devised goods to his sonne, and so died. After whose death, the sonne died also intestate, without wife, and without issue. His mother and his sister by the fathers side, (for shee was borne of the former venter) then living. The mother tooke the Administration of her sonnes goods, according to the statute, whereby it is enacted, that in case any person dye intestate, the administration of his goods shall be committed to the next of kin, &c. The administration being thus granted to the mother, the sister by the father side, doth commence suit before the ecclesiasticall Judge, pretending herself to be next of kin, and the mother not of kin at all to the party deceased, and therefore desireth the administration formerly granted to the mother to be revoked, and to be committed unto her, as next of kin to the deceased, by force of the said statute.

"Hereupon the most learned, as well in the Lawes of this Realme, as in the Civill Law, were consulted. First, whether an administration once granted, might afterwards bee revoked? whereunto they all agreed that it might. Secondly, whether the mother were next of kin to her sonne, whereunto not onely the temporall Lawyers, but also the Civillians, (as it is reported) were of this opinion, that she was not of kinne to her own sonne. Whereupon by diffinitive judgement of the Court, the former Administration granted to the mother, was revoked, and a new administration granted to the sister, albeit she were of the halfe bloud to the deceased. According to this Judgement, divers other Administrations were granted, from the mothers, to the brethren and sisters, as next of kinne to them dying intestate, for divers yeares after. The reasons which moved the temporall Lawyers to be of this minde, that the mother should not be of kinne to her owne childe, were especially these: first, because there is a ground or principle in their law, that lands cannot lineally ascend but descend; whereupon they concluded, that goods and chattels might lineally descend, but not ascend. Secondly, because howsoever children be of the bloud or seed of their parents, yet are not parents of the bloud or seed of their children, for so they write, *Liberi sunt de sanguine patris & matris; sed pater & mater, non sunt de sanguine liberorum.* Thirdly, because the father, the mother, & the childe, though they be three persons, yet are they but *una caro*, one flesh, & consequently no degree of kindred betwixt them.

"What might be the reasons, whereby the Civilians were moved, to be of the same opinion, that the mother was not of kinne to her childe; I cannot easily conceive, unlesse it were this, viz. *Mater non numeratur inter consanguineos* ["the mother is not numbered among the blood relations"], or unlesse it were, the ancient law of the twelve tables, whereby the mother was excluded from succeeding in the inheritance of her sonne, or daughter. Thus was the judgement in this case, and these were the chiefe reasons thereof, which reasons not being very strong, the judgement could not be very sound. For first, though it be a maxime, in the laws of this Realme, that lands cannot lineally ascend, from the childe to the parents, (which maxime seemeth also to savour of the law of the twelve tables, being the most ancient part of the Civill law written) whereby (as I have said) the mother was forbidden to succeed in the inheritance of her childe, yet neverthelesse, it doth not thereby follow, that Parents, be not of kinne to their children, because they cannot succeed them in the inheritance, no more than the childe, ceaseth to be of kinne to his Parents, when he is disherited or barred to succeed in the inheritance. And touching the law of those twelve tables, it was not onely thereby ordained, that the mother should not succeed, in the inheritance of her children; but likewise, that the children should not succeed, in the inheritance of their mother, which prohibition notwithstanding the kindred, still remained entire betwixt the Parents and their children" (pp. 119–21).

Sterne's learned footnotes are culled from the margins of Swinburne or, in one case (391.28), from the text and margin. It is perhaps worth noting that while Kysarcius asserts that "reason" is strongly on the side of the determination (390.14–16), Swinburne believes the opposite.

390.3   jactitation] *OED* cites this passage as its sole illustration of an obsolete usage: "discussion; bandying to and fro."

390.13   *Triptolemus*] Cf. above, n. to 227.13.

390.18–21   It is cited in *Brook* . . . said *Kysarcius*.] Work, p. 328, n. † and n. 5: "The reference, which is to Sir Robert Broke (d. 1558), *La Graunde abridgement*, occurs in Swinburne, *op. cit.* . . . . Sir Edward Coke (1552–1634), English jurist and legal writer. The reference (which Sterne found

in Swinburne) is to the account of 'Ratcliff's Case' in Part 3 of his *Reports*."
See below, n. to 393.3–8.

390.24   venter] Cf. above, n. to 355.9–11.

391.4   of the 21st of *Harry* the Eighth] Work, p. 329, n. 6: "Swinburne's note
reads: 'Sta. H.8.an.21.c.5'; *i.e.*, Statutes of the twenty-first year of the
reign of Henry VIII, Caput 5."

391.24   consistory and prerogative courts] The function of these high ecclesiastical courts is discussed briefly by Cash, "Sterne as a Judge," pp.
21–22; especially noteworthy is the fact that the prerogative court "was
confined to wills and administrations, hearing all appeals in this category
from lower courts . . ." (p. 22).

391.28   Mater non numeratur . . . signific.] Sterne takes his Latin from the
text of Swinburne (see n. to 389.26ff. above) and his citation from the
margin. See Work, p. 329, n. *: "The reference, which he miscopied
from Swinburne [p. 121: "Bald. in L. ult. C. de verb, signif."], is to
Pietro Baldi de Ubaldis [?1327–1400], Italian jurist and professor of law
at Perugia, *In Sextum Codicis Commentaria, Tit. De verborum et rerum
significatione, Lex 5, §3*."

392.14–15   *Liberi sunt . . . sanguine liberorum.*] Sterne translates this immediately above: "that the child may be of the blood . . . etc.," except that,
like Swinburne, he adds "seed" to "blood" in both instances.

392.24–25   for there is . . . levitical law] Actually, Leviticus 18: 6ff., although it prohibits numerous cohabitations, does not specifically speak of
grandparents. However, the *Book of Common Prayer* in the eighteenth
century ended with "A table of kindred and affinity, wherein whosoever
are related, are forbidden in Scripture, and our laws to marry together";
heading the list of thirty prohibitions each for a man and a woman are
grandmother and grandfather respectively.

393.3–8   But who ever thought . . . lay with yours?"] See *Table Talk of John
Selden* (1689), ed. Sir Frederick Pollock (London: Quaritch, 1927), p.
65: "The King useing the house of Comons, as hee did in M^r. Pym & his
Company, that is chargeing them with treason [because they] charged my
Lord of Canterbury & S^r. George Ratcliffe it was just with as much
Logick as the boy that would have layen with his Grandmother said to his
father, You lay with my Mother & why should I not lye with yo^{rs}."

393.9   *Argumentum commune*] Cicero discusses the *exordium commune*, an exordium "equally applicable to both sides of the case" (*De Inventione*, I.xviii.26), and perhaps Sterne had this in mind; *argumentum commune* does not appear to be a standard term, although it is readily apparent how Yorick comes to it.

393.19–20   and as the mother's is the surest side] Proverbial; Tilley, M1205, cites Hall's *Chronicles* (1548): "If the old and trite proverbe be true that the womans side is the surer side and that the childe foloweth the wombe." See also *ODEP*, s.v. *Mother's*.

394.12   let down one loop of his hat] Since the cocked hats in fashion during the century were made by turning up the brim (i.e., "cocking" it) on three sides and keeping it in place with buttons and loops, to "let down one loop" suggests a disheveled appearance; see *Handbook of English Costume*, pp. 83–85, especially the illustration, p. 84. Cf. John Gay, *Trivia: or, The Art of Walking the Streets of London*, book I, lines 189–202, where he describes the pedestrian caught in a rain shower, "with Hat unloop'd, the Fury dread / Of Spouts high-streaming . . ." (*Poetry and Prose*, ed. Vinton A. Dearing [Oxford: Clarendon Press, 1974], I: 140–41).

Cf. *TS*, 668.17–18 ("It is not like the affair of *an old hat cock'd*——and *a cock'd old hat*") and n. below.

394.13–15   and, as the hasty sparks . . . tells us] As previously (95.16–21), Sterne seems to have his Hippocrates via James Mackenzie's *History of Health, and the Art of Preserving It:* "MODERATE joy and anger, on the other hand, and those passions and affections of the mind which partake of their nature . . . invigorate the nerves, accelerate the circulating fluids, promote perspiration, and assist digestion" (p. 389); suggested by Work, p. 332, n. 2.

395.2   fore-front] *OED* cites this passage as its sole illustration of *forefront* as a transitive verb.

395.5   to answer it] Cf. 236.8 and n. above.

395.20–21   first money that returned . . . *Missisippi*-scheme] Sterne could have found a lengthy discussion of the Mississippi Company in Tindal, IV: 619–20. Organized by John Law, a native of Scotland living in France, it was a company designed to have "the sole privilege of the trade to *Louisiana*." Tindal describes the seven subscriptions that were offered, and the manner in which "the *Actions* or *Shares*" rose from 120 to 200 to

560 by the summer of 1719, and as high as 2,050 at the point of greatest prosperity, the winter of 1719–20. From that peak, the stock rapidly declined and by the end of May collapsed: "when the fall came (except a few great fortunes that were made) there was almost a general ruin through all *France*."

Although the South Sea Bubble, which ran a parallel course with the Mississippi scheme and collapsed some six months after it, was better known in England, the English did invest in Law's enterprise; see, e.g., Pope's own note to his *Epistle to Bathurst*, lines 130–34 (p. 103). Walter was certainly into the scheme early enough to make his fortune—if, of course, he sold before the collapse.

396.10   People may laugh as they will] Cf. Sterne's comments on the Grand Tour in vol. VII, chap. 13, and n. to 593.3–6.

396.17   by the feather put into his cap] Proverbial; Tilley, F157, and *ODEP*, s.v. *Feather*. The earlier meaning of "honor without profit" seems closer to Sterne's intention than the more favorable connotations of present usage.

396.18   *tantum valet . . . quantum sonat.*] "It is worth as much as it sounds." The *Stanford Dictionary* notes *quantum valeat* ("taken for what it is worth"), but not until the late nineteenth century.

396.21   unwhirl'd] *OED* cites this passage as its sole illustration.

396.26   purchase-money] *OED*'s first illustration is dated 1763.

397.27   now or never was the time.] Proverbial; Tilley, N351, and *ODEP*, s.v. *Now*.

398.23–399.6   set about calculating . . . potatoes without end] Advising a friend against farming, Sterne wrote in 1767: "I was once such a puppy myself, as to pare, and burn, and had my labour for my pains, and two hundred pounds out of pocket.—Curse on farming (said I) I will try if the pen will not succeed better than the spade.—The following up of that affair (I mean farming) made me lose my temper, and a cart load of turneps was (I thought) very dear at two hundred pounds" (*Letters*, p. 394). For a discussion of Sterne's farming experiences in the 1740s, see Cash, *Early and Middle Years*, pp. 146–50, and Cross, *Life*, pp. 57–61.

399.10   knew no more . . . what to do.] Cf. 41.4–5 and n. above.

400.24   Cervantick a cast] See above, nn. to 34.25, 200.6.

401.8   They are the choicest morsel of my whole story!] Cf. 779.3–4, where Tristram again refers to Toby's amours as "the choicest morsel of what I

had to offer to the world . . . ." See also Rabelais, III.26.177: "thy coun-
sel I hold for a choice and delicate morsel; therefore have I reserved it for
the last bit"; and below, n. to 584.14–17.

401.22–23   the thing . . . akes dismally] Rabelais, in the concluding chapter
of book II, makes a similar complaint: "My head aches a little, and I
perceive that the registers of my brain are somewhat jumbled and disordered with the septembral juice" (II.34.252).

401.24–28   True *Shandeism* . . . chearfully round.] Cf. *Letters*, p. 139
(Sterne to Hall-Stevenson, June 1761): "I have not managed my miseries
like a wise man—and if God, for my consolation under them, had not
poured forth the spirit of Shandeism into me, which will not suffer me to
think two moments upon any grave subject, I would else, just now lay
down and die—die——and yet, in half an hour's time, I'll lay a guinea, I
shall be as merry as a monkey—and as mischievous too, and forget it all
. . . ."

Sterne rather obviously formed the term Shandeism to parallel Rabelais's "Pantagruelism," but it is as difficult to define the one as the other.
Rabelais does end his second volume in a manner similar to Sterne's at this
point: "And if you desire to be good Pantagruelists, that is to say, to live in
peace, joy, health, making yourselves always merry, never trust those men
that always peep out at one hole" (II.34.255–56). Ozell explains this as a
reference to cowled monks, but perhaps Sterne saw a more metaphorical
suggestion of a mind locked into any consistent viewpoint; cf. Obadiah
Walker, *Of Education*, 6th ed. (1699), p. 191: "nor be like a Man brought
up in a *Bottle*, see all things through *one Hole*." At any rate, it is apparent
that while Rabelais most often uses "wine" to suggest the agent of a Pan-
tagruelian mind, Sterne uses "laughter" (see 360.11–18 and n. above);
this appears, however, to be a difference in metaphor, rather than substance.

402.1–4   Was I left . . . hearty laughing subjects] Cf. *Don Quixote*, I.IV.2,
where Sancho, considering the fact that if his master's "Dominions were to
be in the Land of the Negroes, and that, consequently, the People, over
whom he was to be Governor, were all to be black," decides that the only
remedy is "loading a Ship with 'em, and having 'em into *Spain*, where I
shall find Chapmen enow to take 'em off my Hands, and pay me ready
Money for 'em . . ." (II: 28).

In view of Sterne's later correspondence with Ignatius Sancho, a former slave (see 747.1ff. and n. below), it is worth noting that Sancho Panza's attitude is quite different from Tristram's.

402.9−10   as WISE as they were MERRY] Warburton discusses the possible rise of "the old proverb of 'being merry and wise'" in his "Supplement to the Translator's Preface," *Don Quixote* (1749), trans. Charles Jarvis, 5th ed. (1788), p. xxxvii. He traces it to the morality plays of the Middle Ages, in which "the Fool of the Piece, in order to shew the inevitable approaches of Death (another of the Dramatis Personae) is made to employ all his stratagems to avoid him . . . . So that a representation of these scenes would afford a great deal of good mirth and morals mixed together."

402.14−15   (unless this vile cough . . . mean time)] Although Sterne had opened *TS* with an allusion to his ill health (see dedication to vol. I and n. above, Ded. 5−6), he seems to have had something of a recovery during 1760, when he was writing vols. III and IV; he makes no mention of his health in his letters during this period. However, within the next year his health would fail to the point of sending him, in January 1762, to the south of France in pursuit of a more congenial climate; see, e.g., *Letters*, p. 150: "Indeed I am very ill, having broke a vessel in my lungs—hard writing in the summer, together with preaching, which I have not strength for, is ever fatal to me . . . ."
Cf. 575.1−4.

402.15   I'll have another pluck at your beards] Cf. *Hamlet*, II.ii.572−73: "Who calls me villain, breaks my pate across, / Plucks off my beard and blows it in my face"; and *King Lear*, III.vii.35−36: "By the kind gods, 'tis most ignobly done / To pluck me by the beard." In the Renaissance it was a gesture of contempt; Sterne's usage seems considerably softer.

NOTES TO VOLUME V

Title-page (mottoes)] The two mottoes that appear on the title-page of the first edition are borrowed from Burton's *Anatomy* and serve to alert the reader of *TS* to the frequent, unannounced presence of Burton in vols. V and VI. Burton uses his introductory "Democritus Junior to the Reader" to explore, among other subjects, the use of a satiric voice or ironic persona and the freedom it affords; in one particular paragraph of this discussion, Sterne found his mottoes: "If I have overshot my selfe in this which hath beene hitherto said, or that it is, which I am sure some will object, too phantasticall, *too light and comicall for a Divine, too satyricall for one of my profession,* I will presume to answer with *Erasmus,* in like case, 'Tis not I, but *Democritus, Democritus dixit* [Burton's marginal note here reads: "*Mor. Encom. si quis calumnietur levius esse quam decet Theologum, aut mordacius quam deceat Christianum*"]: you must consider what it is to speake in ones owne or anothers person, an assumed habit and name; a difference betwixt him that affects or acts a Princes, a Philosophers, a Magistrates, a Fooles part, and him that is so indeed; and what liberty those old Satyrists have had, it is a *Cento* collected from others, not I, but they that say it. *Dixero si quid fortè jocosius, hoc mihi juris / Cum veniâ dabis———*" (pp. 76–77). The concluding verses are from Horace, *Satires,* I.iv.104–5, and are usually printed as "dixero quid, si forte jocosius," etc., good evidence that Sterne did not resort to the original. The lines may be translated thus: "*If in my words I am too free, perchance too light, this bit of liberty you will indulgently grant me*" (pp. 56–57). The passage from Erasmus, *Praise of Folly,* is from the introductory letter to Sir Thomas More, translated by

336

W. Kennett as follows: "*And it is a Chance if there be wanting some Quarrel-some Persons that will shew their Teeth, and pretend these Fooleries are either too Buffoon-like for a grave* Divine, *or too Satyrical for a Meek* Christian" (4th ed. [1724], p. ii). The phrase "*non Ego, sed Democritus dixit*" is Burton's invention, modified by Sterne.

Sterne appears to have added a third motto to the original two, though exactly when he did so is in doubt. It appears on all copies of the second edition, published in London in 1767; see t.n., vol. II, p. 856, in this edition. However, Kenneth Monkman has discovered that a Dublin edition published in 1762 by Henry Saunders contains the third motto, and in a form perhaps more accurate than the 1767 version. The original of both versions is a sentence from the Second Council of Carthage: "Si quis clericus aut monachus verba scurrilia joculatoria, risumque moventia loquitur, acerrime corripiatur" ("If any priest or monk speak words which are scurrilous, jesting, and exciting to laughter, let him be very sharply rebuked"). The 1762 version, from the Dublin title-page, reads: "*Si quis Clericus, aut Monachus, verba joculatoria, risum moventia serat anathema esto*" ("*If any priest or monk uses jesting words, exciting laughter, let him be denounced*"). The 1767 version, as provided at this point in the text, has the obvious misprint "*visum*" for "*risum*" (see t.n.) and "*sciebat*" ("had known") for the preferable "*serat*" ("uses") of 1762. Monkman offers several suggestions to explain how this motto appeared in Dublin five years before its appearance in London, but all solutions remain conjectural; see "*Tristram* in Dublin," *TCBS* 7 (1979): 349, 364.

In summary, then, Sterne's three mottoes to vols. V and VI show three rather different attitudes toward the complaint of previous years that it was not appropriate for a clergyman to be writing *TS*. A more unified translation of all three might clarify the difference: "If I speak too lightly or freely, you will indulge this liberty"; "If any quarrelsome persons should censure my jesting as either too light for a divine or too satirical for a decent Christian—not I, but Democritus said it"; and "If any priest or monk engages in jesting words, raising laughter, let him be damned."

Ded.] Sterne's friendship with John Spencer (1734–83) is first indicated in a letter dated by Curtis February 17, 1761 (*Letters*, p. 130); as Wilbur Cross points out (*Life*, p. 266), it lasted the remainder of Sterne's life, Spencer acting "in all ways . . . as a patron should." Curtis (*Letters*, p. 259, n. 1) provides a full account of John Spencer, "only son of the Hon. John Spencer, of Althorp, Northamptonshire, and great-grandson of Captain Shandy's hero, the Duke of Marlborough . . . . He represented Warwick from 1757 until 3 Apr. 1761, when he was created Baron Spencer of Althorp and Viscount Spencer of Althorp."

Cross notes that "Sterne sent a draft of the story of Le Fever (as far as the second paragraph of the thirteenth chapter) to Lady Spencer, with comments thereon in his own hand" (pp. 282, 624). Cross believed the manuscript was sold; Curtis, that it was at Althorp. We have not been able to locate it.

Cross also calls attention (pp. 283–84) to the report by B. N. Turner of the sole meeting between Johnson and Sterne, during which, according to Johnson, "In a company where I lately was, Tristram Shandy introduced himself; and Tristram Shandy had scarcely sat down, when he informed us that he had been writing a Dedication to Lord Spencer; and *sponte suâ* he pulled it out of his pocket; and *sponte suâ*, for nobody desired him, he began to read it; and before he had read half a dozen lines, *sponte meâ*, sir, I told him it was not English, sir" ("Account of Dr. Johnson's Visit to Cambridge, in 1765," *The New Monthly Magazine and Universal Register* 10 [1818]: 389). Since these comments were made in March 1765, Cross was possibly mistaken in assigning them to this dedication. Sterne was in London during the winter of 1764–65, making it at least possible that the dedication in hand was intended for vols. VII and VIII, which appeared at the end of January—without a dedication. On the other hand, Turner's memory may well have been faulty, too much may depend upon the word "lately," and we do have in vol. V an actual rather than suppositive dedication to Spencer (which, in fact, Turner himself believed to be the one abused by Johnson).

407.2–3 *Stilton to Stamford*] Two towns, separated by twelve miles, on the post road from London to York and Edinburgh; see above, n. to 48.5ff.

408.3–6 Shall we for ever . . . same pace?] As Work (p. 342, n. 1) points out, this is a "characteristic example of Sterne's roguishness. . . . he breaks into a castigation of plagiaries in an impassioned passage which is itself cribbed from Burton!" The borrowings are from Burton's own attack on plagiary in his introduction to the *Anatomy*, p. 7: "As Apothecaries we make new mixtures everie day, poure out of one vessell into another

. . ." and "but we weave the same web still, twist the same robe again and again . . . ." "Robe" appears in the fifth and sixth editions; "rope" is the reading of the earlier editions and is clearly intended. Sterne could have made the emendation on his own, however, since the meaning of the passage would seem to call for "rope."

Noted by Ferriar, I: 94.

408.11–18 Who made MAN . . . pettifogging rate?] Sterne continues his game with Burton by echoing, in this paragraph, the opening paragraph of the *Anatomy:* "MAN, the most excellent and noble creature of the World, the *principall and mighty worke of God, wonder of* Nature, as *Zoroastes* calls him; *audacis naturæ miraculum, the marvaile of marvailes,* as *Plato; the Abridgement and Epitome of the World,* as *Pliny; Microcosmus,* a little world, a modell of the world, Soveraigne Lord of the Earth, Viceroy of the World, sole Commander and Governour of all the creatures in it: to whose Empire they are subject in particular, and yeeld obedience; far surpassing all the rest, not in body only, but in soule; *Imaginis Imago,* created to Gods owne *Image* . . ." (1.1.1.1., p. 1).

Sterne's rewriting of his source is somewhat more eccentric than usual, especially his reassignment of Plato's comment (according to Burton) to Aristotle; of course, both phrases are too general to warrant a search through either canon.

Zoroaster is the name given to several cloudy figures of the pre-Hellenistic period. Thomas Stanley, *The History of Philosophy,* 4th ed. (1743), identifies at least six (see pt. 14, on the Chaldean philosophy); and Bayle, *Dictionary,* 5 vols. (1734–38), s.v. *Zoroaster,* discusses the difficulties of identification. Bayle does note that four books were ascribed to him (in *Suidas*), one of which was titled *On Nature* (and Bayle provides the title in Greek, as does Sterne).

St. John Chrysostom (c. 347–407) was the most important figure of the Greek Orthodox Church and, in the view of the *Catholic Encyclopedia,* "the greatest preacher ever heard in a Christian pulpit." G. B. Tennyson conducted an unsuccessful search for the phrase attributed to him; see "The true Shekinah is man," *AN&Q* 3 (1964): 58–59. As Tennyson notes, Chrysostom uses the Greek εικων (*eikon*) for "image," rather than the Hebrew *Shekinah.*

For Moses, see Genesis 1: 26–27.

408.17–18   pitiful—pimping—pettifogging rate?] Cf. *Political Romance* (p. 9), where Trim is described as a "little, dirty, pimping, pettifogging, ambidextrous Fellow . . . ."

408.19   I scorn to be . . . upon the occasion] See Horace, *Epistles*, I.xix.19–20 (pp. 382–83): "o imitatores, servum pecus, ut mihi saepe / bilem, saepe iocum vestri movere tumultus!" ("O you mimics, you slavish herd! How often your pother has stirred my spleen, how often my mirth!").

408.22   farcy] *OED* cites this passage as its first example of this disease of animals, especially horses, being applied to men—the "catachresis," or misuse, that Tristram alludes to; a pun can be assumed in view of "farcical" in the next phrase.

408.23–24   *shag-rag and bob-tail*] Cf. Rabelais, IV.33.221: "It will swallow us all, ships and men, shag, rag, and bobtail"; and *Letters*, p. 214: "we have lived (shag rag and bobtail), all of us, a most jolly nonsensical life of it . . . ." *OED* (s.v. *shag-rag*) notes that the phrase is a variant of *tag, rag, and bob tail* and defines it as "a contemptuous term for a number of persons of various sorts and conditions, all and sundry, especially of the lower classes."

409.1   Tartufs] Tartuffe is the sanctimonious hypocrite in Molière's comedy of that name (1664). Sterne uses the same term in vol. VIII (657.17), where he speaks of "the errantest Tartuffe, in science—in politics—or in religion." In *ASJ*, p. 106, Yorick fears the lady at Calais will reject his offer because "she has some mother-in-law, or tartufish aunt, or nonsensical old woman, to consult upon the occasion . . ."; and in a letter (written a month before his death) to his American correspondent, Dr. John Eustace, Sterne commented upon *TS:* "It is too much to write books and find heads to understand them. The world, however, seems to come into a better temper about them, the people of genius here being, to a man, on its side . . . . A few Hypocrites and Tartufe's, whose approbation could do it nothing but dishonor, remain unconverted" (February 9, 1768; *Letters*, p. 411).

For Sterne, the most persistent Tartuffe was Warburton (see above, n. to 357.4). It is therefore of interest that in the dedication to *The Divine Legation of Moses* (1738), Warburton criticizes the freethinker's representation of the clergy in these terms: "Now they are a Set of superstitious Bigots; *Blind Leaders of the Blind;* red hot Zealots . . . : But now again, they are a *Cabal of mere Politiques; Tartufes without Religion; Atheists in Black Gowns . . .*" (4th ed. [1755], I: xx). The strongest statement in *TS* against Warburton's cautions is perhaps the final paragraph of vol. V, chap. 1: "The drift of the curate *d'Estella's* argument was not understood.—They ran the scent the wrong way.—The world bridled his ass at the tail.—And when the *extreams* of DELICACY, and the *beginnings* of CONCUPISCENCE, hold their next provincial chapter together, they may decree that bawdy also" (414.26–415.5). Of course the mottoes to vol. V also serve as an indication that Warburton was very much on Sterne's mind as he sat down to write this installment.

409.25   queen of *Navarre*] Not Margaret of Angoulême, as Work (p. 344, n. 4) and Watt (p. 260, n. 11) suggest, but Margaret of Valois (1552–1615), first wife of Henry IV, King of France and Navarre. The key to this identification was first noted by William Jackson, *The Four Ages; Together with Essays on Various Subjects* (1798), pp. 245–46; he points out that Rebours and La Fosseuse are named as members of her court in Bayle, *Dictionary*, s.v. *Navarre (Margaret de Valois Queen of)*. Cf. t.n. to 411.24, vol. II, p. 856, in this edition. Bayle also records the name Carnavalet (n. [D]), and summarizes Margaret's character with this comment: "She was a princess of infinitely more wit and beauty than virtue."

In her memoirs, published under various titles, Margaret mentions one of the Queen's gentlemen, named Boessier; see *The Grand Cabinet-Counsels Unlocked*, trans. Robert Codrington (1658), p. 138. Numerous scandalous accounts of Margaret's court were published, and it is possible that Sterne had access to one or more of them. See Richard A. Davies, "'The Fragment' in *Tristram Shandy*, V, 1," *ES* 57 (1976): 522–23; and Ferriar, II: 58–59.

409.25   knotting-ball] Unrecorded in *OED;* but cf. *OED*, s.v. *knotting*, the illustration dated 1697: "a knotting needle, and a ball of sky-colour and white knotting."

410.19–21   And as the court . . . and devotion] Cf. Bayle, *Dictionary:* "She there led a life full of variety; it was a mixture of galantry, devotion, and study."

411.1   terras] I.e., terrace.

411.8–9   *La Rebours* and . . . inseparable.] Quoting primarily from Margaret's memoirs, Bayle paints a quite different picture; e.g., "*I heard every day from Rebours, (who was a corrupt and deceitful creature . . .) that Fosseuse did me all the ill offices she could . . . ."* Both women, along with Margaret, were rivals for King Henry's affection, although at this time Fosseuse was perhaps his favorite since she was carrying his child; see also *The Grand Cabinet-Counsels,* pp. 222–23. Sterne's comment is obviously an ironic one.

412.1–4   St. *Antony* . . . had all whiskers.] For St. Antony and St. Ursula, see above, nn. to 302.5–18 and 302.14–15. St. Francis (1181–1226), St. Dominick (1170–2221), and St. Bennet, i.e., Benedict (c. 480–c. 550) were the founders of the three great monastical orders that bear their names. St. Basil (c. 330–79) established the rules by which the monasteries of the Eastern Orthodox Church were run. For St. Bridget, see above, n. to 245.18.

412.5ff.   The Lady *Baussiere* had got into a wilderness, etc.] Sterne is remembering a discussion of charity in Burton, 3.1.3.3 (p. 426): "Poore *Lazarus* lies howling at his gates for a few crummes, he only seekes chippings, offals, let him roare and howle, famish, and eat his own flesh, he respects him not. A poore decayed kinsman of his, sets upon him by the way in all his jollity, and runnes begging bareheaded by him, conjuring by those former bondes of friendship, alliance, consanguinity &c. unkle, cosen, brother, father . . . . Shew some pitty for Christs sake, pitty a sick man, an old man, &c. hee cares not, ride on: pretend sicknesse, inevitable losse of limbes, goods, plead suretiship, or shipwrack, fires, common calamities, shew thy wants and imperfections . . . . Sweare, protest, take God and all his Angells to witnesse, *quære peregrinum* ["seek out some stranger"], thou art a counterfeit cranke, a cheater, he is not touched with it, *pauper ubique jacet* ["everywhere is the poor man neglected"], ride on, he takes no notice of it. Put up a supplication to him in the name of a thousand Orphans, an Hospitall, a Spittle, a Prison as he goes by, they cry out to him for aid, ride on, *surdo narras* ["you speak to a deaf man"], hee cares not . . . . Shew him a decayed haven, a bridge, a schoole . . . ride on, good your worship, your honour, for Gods sake, your countries sake, ride on." Noted by Ferriar, I: 97.

412.9   order of mercy] Cf. *ASJ,* p. 73: "had you been of the *order of mercy,* instead of the order of St. Francis, poor as I am, continued I, pointing at my portmanteau, full chearfully should it have been open'd to you, for the ransom of the unfortunate . . . ." Stout provides some details concerning the order: "The Order of Our Lady of Mercy, founded in Spain, in 1218, to solicit funds for ransoming Christians captured by the Moors; the members were called Mercedarians (from Maria des Mercedes). A branch of the order was established for women in 1568."

414.13–14   The curate of *d'Estella* . . . against them] Work, p. 347, n. 6: "Possibly a reference to the *Rhétorique ecclésiastique, ou traité de l'art du prédicateur* of Diego d'Estella (1524?–1578), a Franciscan teacher and author of the village of Estella in the province of Navarre." We have been unable to locate that work and hence cannot verify Work's supposition. D'Estella's best-known work is his *Contempt of the World and the Vanities Thereof,* translated by George Cotton, which went through numerous editions and titles in England during the seventeenth century. Near the end is a chapter entitled *"Against idle wordes"* (pt. 3, chap. 22), parts of which may be apropos; e.g.: "Amongst men that have had civil bringing up, it hath bene taken alwaies for a foule and a shamefull thing, to use dishonest & ribauld speeches, although they be spoken but in jest. How much more ought they then to be avoided amongst the servantes of God? Be circumspect in al thy wordes, let them be wel weighed and considered, before thou utter them . . . . Much evil growes of naughty words" (3d ed. [1622], p. 439).

Sterne may have used this name as a pseudonym for himself as early as 1739–40, based on the evidence of a letter to his future wife: "You bid me tell you, my dear L. how I bore your departure for S[taffordshire], and whether the valley where D'Estella stands retains still its looks—or, if I think the roses or jessamines smell as sweet, as when you left it . . . . The hour you left D'Estella I took to my bed" (*Letters,* p. 10). Curtis cites Diego d'Estella and mentions a 1604 edition of *Contempt* in the York Minster Library. It must be noted, however, that there is considerable controversy surrounding this letter, its date, and its authorship; see Cash, *Early and Middle Years,* p. 81, n. 3, for a summary.

414.19–25   The evil indeed . . . roaring lion.] Cf. *Tale of a Tub,* p. 147, where Swift comments on "that highly celebrated Talent among the *Modern* Wits, of deducing Similitudes, Allusions, and Applications, very Surprizing, Agreeable, and Apposite, from the *Pudenda* of either Sex, together with *their proper Uses.*"

See also Pope, *Peri Bathous*, ed. Edna Leake Steeves (New York: King's Crown Press, 1952), p. 67: "BUT the principal Branch of the *Alamode* [style] is the PRURIENT . . . . Indeed its *incredible Progress* and *Conquests* may be compar'd to those of the great *Sesostris*, and are every where known by the *same Marks*, the Images of the Genital Parts of Men or Women. It consists wholly of Metaphors drawn from two·most fruitful Sources or Springs, the very *Bathos* of the human Body, that is to say *** and ********* *Hiatus Magnus lachrymabilis* . . . ."

414.22 trouse] Perhaps, as Work suggests (p. 348, n. 7), "close-fitting, short breeches"; but Sterne may rather have had in mind the long trousers worn only by soldiers, sailors, "artisans and a few eccentrics" during the century, in lieu of the much more common knee-breeches. See *Handbook of English Costume*, pp. 214, 265.

414.22 placket-holes, and pump-handles] For *placket-holes* see above, n. to 301.24–25. *OED*'s first illustration for *pump-handles* is dated 1794.

414.23 spigots and faucets] See above, n. to 259.6–9.

415.1–2 The world bridled his ass at the tail.] Tilley, H705: "You bridle the HORSE by the tail"; his sources indicate that this expression is of French origin. Cf. Montaigne's essay "That to study Philosophy, is to learn to die" (I.19.77): "The End of our Race is Death, 'tis the necessary Object of our Aim . . . . The Remedy the Vulgar use, is not to think on't: But from what brutish Stupidity, can they derive so gross a Blindness? They must bridle the Ass by the Tail." Sterne may have been led to this passage at this time by his preparation for Walter's oration on death, which immediately follows; the passage is indexed under *"Death."*

415.19 vibrating the note back again] See 131.8–11 and n. above.

415.23–416.1 PATRIOT . . . is sold] Cf. above, n. to 195.5; and Wolfgang Zach, "'My Uncle Toby's Apologetical Oration' und die Politische Sinndimension von 'Tristram Shandy'," *GRM* 27 (1977): 410–11. Zach reads the entire paragraph, quite convincingly, as political allegory, in which the "Scotch horse" of line 20 is Lord Bute and "PATRIOT" is Pitt, who had lost office as part of the political changes that surrounded the death of George II; see above, n. to 241.21.

416.11 a map of *Sanson's*] Work, p. 349, n. 1: "Nicolas Sanson (1600–1667), French cartographer, councillor of state, and geographer to the king."

416.14 *Nevers*] The pun is perhaps too obvious to warrant notice, but see

417.27–418.1: "My father stuck his compasses into *Nevers*, but so much the faster.—What contrarieties! his, indeed, was matter of calculation . . . ."

417.25–27   When *Agrippina* was told . . . her work] Cf. Burton, 2.3.5: "as *Tacitus* [reported] of *Agrippina*, not able to moderate her passions. So when she heard her sonne was slaine, she abruptly broke off her work, changed countenance and colour, tore her haire, and fell a roaring down right . . ." (p. 337).

This borrowing from Burton's chapter "*Against sorrow for death of friends or otherwise, vaine feare, &c.*" begins the sustained collection of borrowings out of which Walter creates his own oration; Burton is the dominant source, but Bacon, Joseph Hall, and Montaigne are also cited. For a discussion of Walter's oration, see Graham Petrie, "A Rhetorical Topic in *Tristram Shandy*" *MLR* 65 (1970): 261–66. Many of the borrowings were first noted by Ferriar, I: 99–107.

The reference would seem to be to Tacitus's *Annals*, 13.16 (IV: 26–29), in which the poisoning of Britannicus is described, but neither here nor elsewhere does Agrippina act quite in the manner suggested by the passage.

418.8–12   'Tis either *Plato* . . . or *Barnard*] Sterne borrows his list of authorities from Burton, 2.3.1.1 (p. 303): "I have thought fit in this following Section, a little to digresse . . . to collect and gleane a few remedies, and comfortable speeches out of our best Orators, Philosophers, Divines, and fathers of the Church, tending to this purpose [i.e., "*A Consolatorie Digression, containing the Remedies of all manner of discontents*"]. I confesse, many have copiously written of this subject, *Plato, Seneca, Plutarch, Xenophon, Epictetus, Theophrastus, Xenocrates, Crantor, Lucian, Boethius:* and some of late, *Sadoletus, Cardan, Budæus, Stella, Petrarch, Erasmus,* besides *Austin, Cyprian, Bernard,* &c."

In *Sermons,* II.15 ("Job's Expostulation with his Wife"), Sterne discusses the commonplace that Christianity's consolatory powers surpass by far those of the ancients, in terms that perhaps cast some light on Walter's oration: "The philosophic consolations in sickness, or in afflictions for the death of friends and kindred, were just as [in]efficacious,—and were rather in general to be considered as good sayings than good remedies. ——So that, if a man was bereaved of a promising child, in whom all his hopes and expectations centered—or a wife was left destitute to mourn the loss and protection of a kind and tender husband, Seneca or Epictetus would tell the pensive parent and disconsolate widow,——that tears and lamentation for the dead were fruitless and absurd;---that to die, was the necessary and unavoidable debt of nature;—and as it could admit of no remedy—'twas impious and foolish to grieve and fret themselves upon it" (pp. 225–26).

The classical names selected by Sterne from Burton's list are well known. Cardan is Jerome Cardan (1501–76), an Italian physician, the most famous of his era; his *De consolatione libri tres* was translated into English in 1573. Budæus is Guillaume Budé (1468–1540), a French classicist of immense learning and reputation. Petrarch (1304–74), the most important Italian poet after Dante, is perhaps singled out for his sonnets on the death of Laura or his posthumous *de Contemptu Mundi*. For Stella, i.e., Diego d'Estella, see above, n. to 414.13–14.

St. Austin, i.e., Augustine (354–430); St. Cyprian (d. 258), Bishop of Carthage; and St. Barnard, i.e., Bernard (1091–1153), are all major ecclesiastical figures.

418.12–16 who affirms that . . . particular channel.] Cf. Burton, 2.3.5 (pp. 338–39): "who can blame a tender mother if she weep for her children? Beside as *Plutarch* holds, tis not in our power not to lament, *Indolentia non cuivis contingit*, it takes away mercy and pitty, not to be sad, 'tis a natural passion to weep for our friends, an irresistible passion to lament, & grieve. *I know not how* (saith *Seneca*) *but sometimes 'tis good to be miserable in misery; and for the most part all grief evacuates it self by teares . . . ."*

Plutarch is quoted from the "Consolatio ad Apollonium," in *Moralia*, II.3 (pp. 110–11).

Work, p. 351, n. 2: *"Lucius Annæus Seneca* (c. 54 B.C.–39 A.D.), 'the elder,' rhetorician, and father of the statesman and philosopher. The reference is to his *Controversiæ*, 5.30, but Sterne is 'positive' on Burton's authority." The passage is numbered 10.1.6 in the Loeb edition, I: 376–77.

418.16–19 And accordingly we find . . . his death.] Cf. Burton, 1.2.4.7 (p. 163): "So did *Adrian* the Emperour bewaile his *Antinous; Hercules, Hylas; Orpheus, Euridice; David, Absolon;* (O my deare sonne *Absolon*) *Austin* his mother *Monica, Niobe* her children . . ."; and 2.3.5 (p. 339):

"When *Socrates* was dying, his friends *Apollodorus* & *Crito* with some others, were weeping by him . . . ."

Work, p. 351, n. 3: "See 2 Samuel, 18.33–19.4. Antinous was an attendant and favourite of the emperor Hadrian (76–138); at his suicide, the emperor was deeply grieved and caused extravagant respect to be paid to his memory. Niobe, in Greek mythology, wept for her slain children even after Zeus turned her to stone. The grief of Crito, Apollodorus, and the others who were with Socrates as he drank the poisoned cup, is related in Plato's *Phædo*, 117."

419.1–3   neither wept it away . . . as the *Germans*] Cf. Burton, 2.3.5: "The *Italians* most part sleep away care and grief, if [it] unseasonably seise upon them; *Danes*, *Dutchmen*, *Polanders* and *Bohemians* drink it down; our countrymen go to playes . . ." (p. 342).

419.8–16   When *Tully* was bereft . . . it made me.] Sterne again combines two separate parts of the *Anatomy* to produce his paragraph. Cf. 1.2.4.7: "all the yeare long, as *Pliny* complaines to *Romanus*, *me thinkes I see* Virginius, *I heare* Virginius, *I talke with* Virginius, &c." (p. 162); and 2.3.5: "*Tully* was much grieved for his daughter *Tulliola's* death at first, untill such time that hee had confirmed his minde with some Philosophicall precepts, *then he began to triumph over fortune and griefe, and for her reception into heaven to bee much more joyed, then before hee was troubled for her losse*" (p. 339).

The reference to Pliny is to his *Letters*, II.i (I: 82–83); to Cicero, either his *Tusculan Disputations*, IV.xxix.63 (pp. 400–401), or perhaps *Letters to Atticus*, XII.14 (III: 28–29).

420.4   half in half] See above, n. to 387.9–10.

421.2   *Attic* salt] *OED* defines *Attic salt* (Latin *sal Atticum*) as "refined, delicate, poignant wit" and cites this passage. Cf. Pope's "*Attic* wit" in "How can I PULT'NEY, CHESTERFIELD forget, / While *Roman* Spirit charms, and *Attic* Wit" ("Epilogue to the Satires," II.84–85, in *Imitations of Horace*, p. 317). See also Pliny, *Natural History*, 31.41: "Therefore, Heaven knows, a civilized life is impossible without salt, and so necessary is this basic substance that its name is applied metaphorically even to intense mental pleasures. We call them *sales* (wit); all the humour of life, its supreme joyousness, and relaxation after toil, are expressed by this word

more than by any other" (VIII: 433); and Martial, *Epigrams*, III.20
(I: 176–77): "an otiosus in schola poetarum / lepore tinctos Attico sales
narrat?" ("or does he, idling in the Poets' School, tell witty stories touched
with Attic grace?").

Cf. *Sermons*, III.18.92–93: "certainly there is a difference between
Bitterness and *Saltness*,——that is,——between the malignity and the festivity of wit,——the one is a mere quickness of apprehension, void of
humanity,—and is a talent of the devil; the other comes down from the
Father of Spirits, so pure and abstracted from persons, that willingly it
hurts no man . . . ." Cf. Walter Charleton, *A Brief Discourse Concerning
the Different Wits of Men* (1669), p. 133: "By this, *Sir,* You plainly discern
the great *Difference* betwixt *Malignity,* and *Festivity* of Wit."

See also the anecdote Sterne recounts in *Letters*, p. 258: "A sensible
friend of mine . . . met an apothecary (an acquaintance of ours)—the
latter asked him how he did? why, ill, very ill—I have been with Sterne,
who has given me such a dose of *Atticsalt* that I am in a fever—Attic salt,
Sir, Attic salt! I have Glauber salt—I have Epsom salt in my shop, &c.—
Oh! I suppose 'tis some French salt—I wonder you would trust his report
of the medicine, he cares not what he takes himself . . . ."

421.8–9   He took them as they came.] Proverbial; Tilley, T196, and *ODEP*,
s.v. *Take*.

421.10–12   'Tis an inevitable chance . . . *All must die*.] Cf. Burton, 2.3.5:
"'Tis an inevitable chance, the first statute in *Magna Charta*, an everlasting Act of Parliament, all must die" (p. 339).

421.13–15   "If my son could not . . . with us."] Sterne borrows from Joseph
Hall, *Epistles* (1624), Decad. II, Epistle IX, "*Consolations of immoderate
griefe for the death of friends,*" p. 308 (misnumbered 318): "If they could
not have dyed, it had been worthy of wonder; not at all, that they are dead
. . . . Lo, all Princes and Monarchs daunce with us in the same ring
. . . ." See W. G. Day, "A Borrowing from Bishop Hall in 'Tristram
Shandy'," *N&Q* 220 (1975): 496.

421.16   "—*To die* . . . unto nature] Cf. *Sermons*, II.15.226 ("Job's Expostulation with his Wife"): "that to die, was the necessary and unavoidable debt of nature . . . ." Cf. 585.19: "I have no debt but the debt of
NATURE . . . ."

421.17–422.28   tombs and monuments . . . art a man."] Cf. Burton, 2.3.5

(p. 340): "Tombs and monuments have the like fate, *data sunt ipsis quoque fata sepulchris* ["since even to sepulchers themselves are dooms assigned"], kingdomes, provinces, towns, and cities have their periods, and are consumed. In those flourishing times of *Troy*, *Mycenæ* was the fairest citie in *Greece*, *Græciæ cunctæ imperitabat* ["ruled all Greece"], but it alas, and that *Assyrian Ninive are quite overthrowne;* the like fate hath that *Egyptian* and *Bœotian Thebes*, *Delos*, *commune Græciæ conciliabulum*, the common councell house of *Greece*, and *Babylon* the greatest citie that ever the sun shone on, hath now nothing but walls, and rubbish left. . . . And where is *Troy* it selfe now, *Persepolis*, *Carthage*, *Cizicum*, *Sparta*, *Argos*, and all those *Grecian* cities? *Syracuse* and *Agrigentum*, the fairest townes in *Sicily*, which had sometimes 700000 inhabitants, are now decayed, the names of *Hieron*, *Empedocles*, *&c.* of those mighty numbers of people, only left. One *Anacharsis* is remembred amongst the *Scythians*, the world it self must have an end. And as to a traveller great mountains seem plains afar off, at last are not discerned at all, cities, men, monuments decay,

————*nec solidis prodest sua machina terris* ["nor can its fabrick preserve the solid globe"],

the names are only left, those at length forgotten, and are involved in perpetuall night.

"*Returning out of Asia, when I sailed from Ægina towards Megara, I began* (saith *Servius Sulspitius* in a consolatory epistle of his to *Tully*) *to view the country round about.* Ægina *was behind mee*, Megara *before*, Pyræus *on the right hand*, Corinth *on the left*, *what flourishing townes heretofore, now prostrate and overwhelmed before mine eyes? I began to thinke with my selfe, Alas, why are we men so much disquieted with the departure of a friend, whose life is much shorter? When so many goodly cities lye buried before us. Remember O* Servius *thou art a man . . . .*"

Sterne almost certainly knew that the last paragraph was specifically cited by Warburton in the "Dedication to Free Thinkers" in his *Divine Legation of Moses;* Warburton, discussing Shaftesbury's theory of ridicule as the test of truth, makes the point that the most "natural and humane Reflexion" could be turned to ridicule and uses as an example Scarron's parody of Sulpicius's letter (4th ed. [1755], pp. xiv–xv). If Sterne had forgotten Warburton's use of the passage, his own use of it here was at best unfortunate; if he indeed did remember it, *defiant* would be the proper term. See New, "Sterne, Warburton," p. 258; above, n. to 357.4; and below, n. to 440.9. Swift also wrote a parody of Sulpicius's letter ("Shall I repine," in *The Poems of Jonathan Swift*, ed. Harold Williams, 2d ed. [Oxford: Clarendon Press, 1958], II: 419), a fact pointed out to us by Professor Arthur Scouten.

    Work, p. 354, n. 6: "Servius Sulpicius Rufus (105–43 B.C.), Roman orator and jurist. The passage is taken from Cicero's *Epistolæ ad Familiores*, 4.5, *via* Burton, 2.3.5."

422.2   laying down his pipe at the word *evolutions*] Chambers, s.v. *Evolution*, makes clear Toby's sudden attention: "in the art of war . . . a term applied to the diverse figures, turns, and motions, made by a body of soldiers, either in ranging themselves in form of battle, or in changing their form . . . ."

422.14   *Mitylenæ*] Typical of his practice as a borrower, Sterne adds one city to Burton's roll call; Mytilene (according to *OCD*, the "official" spelling) was the chief city of Lesbos and the home of Sappho.

423.7–9   *Zant . . . Archipelago* into *Asia*] Zant, an island in the Ionian Sea off the coast of Greece; in Walter's day it was in the possession of Venice and an important outpost for trade with Turkey and the East. "Archipelago" had specific reference in the eighteenth century to the Aegean Sea.

423.13–14   many an undertaking critick . . . worse foundations.] See above, n. to 356.17–18. Cf. *Sermons*, I.5.123, where Sterne comments on the Widow of Zerephath's possible dreams for herself and child: "Many a parent would build high, upon a worse foundation."

423.22   the wandering *Jew*] The Jew who, according to legend, taunted Christ on his way to Calvary and was condemned to wander over the earth until Judgment Day.

424.6   "My son is dead!] Throughout Walter's oration Sterne may have had in mind Gargantua's lament over his wife Badebec's death (Rabelais, II.3.21–24). See, e.g., p. 23: "My wife is dead, well, by G---- (da jurandi) I shall not raise her again by my crying: she is well; she is in paradise at least, if she be no higher: she prayeth to God for us; she is happy; she is above the sense of our miseries, nor can our calamities reach her. What tho' she be dead, must not we also die? The same debt, which she hath paid, hangs over our heads; nature will require it of us [an obvious commonplace, but see *TS*, 421.16], and we must all of us, some day, taste of the same sauce . . ." (see 424.4).

424.6–7   'tis a shame . . . one anchor."] Cf. Burton, 2.3.5 (p. 340): "Thou maist be ashamed, I say with *Seneca*, to confesse it, *in such a tempest as this to have but one anchor . . . .*" Burton identifies the source as Seneca's *De remediis fortuitorum* (in *Opera*, ed. Friedrich Haase [Leipzig, 1898–1907], III: 456).

424.8–14   He is got . . . of the world] Cf. Burton, 2.3.5 (pp. 341–42): "*he had risen*, saith *Plutarch*, *from the midst of a feast*, before he was drunk . . . . *Why dost thou lament my death . . . ? what misfortune is befalne me? Is it because I am not bald, crooked, old, rotten, as thou art?* . . . The *Thracians* wept still when a child was born, feasted and made mirth when any man was buried . . . ."

Plutarch is quoted from the "Consolatio," in *Moralia*, 34 (pp. 202–13); the passage "*Why dost . . . thou art?*" is from Lucian, "On Funerals," in *Works*, IV: 123. Herodotus, *Persian Wars*, V.4 (III: 4–5), comments on this practice of the Thracians.

424.15–16   Death opens the gate . . . after it] Cf. Francis Bacon, "Of Death," *The Essayes* (1625), p. 9: "*Death* hath this also; That it openeth the Gate, to good Fame, and extinguisheth Envie . . ."; first noted by Gwin J. Kolb, "A Note on 'Tristram Shandy': Some New Sources," *N&Q* 196 (1951): 226–27.

424.18–19   "Shew me the man . . . his liberty."] Cf. Hall, *Epistles*, Decad. III, Epistle II: "Shew mee ever any man that knew what life was, and was loth to leave it. I will shew you a prisoner that would dwell in his Goale, a slave that likes to be chained to his Galley" (p. 317).

See also Montaigne, I.19.82: "The Premeditation of Death, is the Premeditation of Liberty; who has learnt to die, has forgot to serve."

424.20–425.1   Is it not better . . . and melancholy] Cf. Burton, 2.3.5 (pp. 341–42): "*Is it not much better not to hunger at all then to eat: not to thirst then to drink to satisfie thirst: not to be cold then to put on clothes to drive away cold? You had more neede rejoyce that I am freed from diseases, agues, cares, anxieties, livor, love . . . .*"

The borrowing is from Lucian, "On Funerals," in *Works*, IV: 123.

425.1–3   than like a galled . . . journey afresh?] Cf. Burton, 2.3.5 (p. 340): "thou dost him great injury to desire his longer life. *Wilt thou have him crased & sickly still,* like a tired traveller that comes wearie to his Inne, beginne his journey afresh . . . ." Burton again cites *De remediis fortuitorum* (see above, n. to 424.6−7) but we have been unable to locate the sentiment in that work; Seneca, to be sure, often expresses a similar idea in his *Moral Epistles,* e.g., XCIX, "On Consolation to the Bereaved," III: 129−49, especially pp. 136−37.

425.4−10　There is no terror . . . mechanic aids] Cf. Bacon, "Of Death," in *Essayes,* p. 7: "Groanes and Convulsions, and a discoloured Face, and Friends weeping, and Blackes, and Obsequies, and the like, shew *Death* Terrible"; noted by Ferriar, I: 108. For a similar sentiment, see vol. VII, chap. 12 (pp. 591−92), and n. below.

425.7−8　'Tis better in battle than in bed] Cf. Montaigne, "Of Experience" (III.13.378): "Death is more abject, more languishing and painful in *Bed* than in Battle"; indexed as *"Death is more glorious in a Battle than in a Bed."* Cf. Trim's similar sentiment, 436.10−25.

425.9　its mutes] "A professional attendant at a funeral; a hired mourner" (*OED*). Walpole's *Anecdotes of Painting in England* (1762−80) provides *OED* with its first illustration: "It is remarkable that forty gentlemen of good families submitted to wait as mutes with their backs against the wall of the chamber where the body laid in state" (3d ed. [1782], II: 219−20).

　　Cf. Walpole to Richard West (April 21, 1739): "A long procession of flambeaux and friars; no plumes, trophies, banners, led horses, scutcheons, or open chariots . . ." (*Correspondence,* ed. W. S. Lewis et al. [New Haven: Yale University Press, 1948], XIII: 163); and John Gay, *Trivia,* book III, lines 231−32: "Why is the Herse with 'Scutcheons blazon'd round, / And with the nodding Plume of Ostrich crown'd?" (*Poetry and Prose,* ed. Vinton A. Dearing [Oxford: Clarendon Press, 1974], I: 167).

425.13−14　when we *are* . . . we are *not.*] Cf. Burton, 2.3.5 (p. 337): *"When we are, death is not, but when death is, then we are not . . . ."* Burton cites Seneca and provides the Latin (*"quum nos sumus mors non adest, cum vero mors adest, tum nos non sumus"*), but we have not been able to locate the precise source. A similar idea occurs in *Moral Epistles,* XCIX (see above, n. to 425.1−3): "Illud potius admone, nullum mali sensum ad eum, qui periit, pervenire; nam si pervenit, non periit. . . . quis enim nullius sensus est? Nec ex eo, quod est; effugit enim maximum mortis incommodum, non esse" ("This is what you should preferably advise: that no sensation of

evil can reach one who is dead; for if it can reach him, he is not dead. . . .
for what feeling can belong to one who does not exist?—nor from the fact
that he exists; for he has escaped the greatest disadvantage that death has in
it—namely, non-existence"), pp. 146–49.

425.18–23   For this reason . . . in a compliment.] Cf. Bacon, "Of Death,"
in *Essayes*, p. 8: "It is no less worthy to observe, how little Alteration, in
good Spirits, the Approaches of *Death* make; For they appeare, to be the
same Men, till the last Instant. *Augustus Caesar* died in a Complement;
Livia, conjugij nostri memor, vive & vale. Tiberius in dissimulation; As
Tacitus saith of him; *Jam Tiberium Vires, & Corpus, non dissimulatio, de-
serebant. Vespasian* in a Jest; Sitting upon the stoole; *Ut puto Deus fio. Galba*
with a sentence; *Feri, si ex re sit populi Romani;* Holding forth his Necke.
Septimius Severus in dispatch; *Adeste, si quid mihi restat agendum.* And the
like."

Work, p. 356, n. 8: "Titus Flavius Vespasianus (9–79), Roman emperor, died after cynically observing, 'Methinks I am becoming a god.'
Servius Sulpicius Galba (5 B.C.–69 A.D.), Roman emperor, addressed
his assassins: 'Strike, if it be for the good of the Roman people.' Septimius
Severus (146–211), Roman emperor, died after admonishing his attendants: 'Make haste, if there is anything more for me to do'; in 'conveying'
this paragraph from Bacon's essay . . . Sterne confusingly miscopied
Bacon's 'in dispatch.' Tiberius Claudius Nero (42 B.C.–37 A.D.), Roman emperor, vainly attempted to conceal his approaching death by maintaining a pretence of strength and debauchery. Augustus Cæsar (63
B.C.–14 A.D.), Roman emperor, died in his wife's arms, saying, 'Fare-
well Livia; live and forget not the days of our marriage.'"

Cf. *Letters*, p. 416 (written a few weeks before Sterne's death): "But I
brave evils.—et quand Je serai mort, on mettra mon nom dans le liste de
ces Heros, qui sont Morts en plaisantant" ("and when I shall have died,
my name will be placed in the list of those heroes who have died in jest").

425.25   'Twas to his wife,—said my father.] Cf. *Letters*, p. 398: "My girl has
return'd [from France] an elegant accomplish'd little slut—my wife—but
I hate to praise my wife—'tis as much as decency will allow to praise my
daughter."

426.5–10   'Tis of *Cornelius Gallus* . . . my father.] Cf. Montaigne, I.19.79:
"And betwixt the very Thighs of Women, *Cornelius Gallus,* the *Prætor*

. . ."; this is Montaigne's terse description of the untimely incident, chronicled by Pliny, *Natural History*, 7.53 (II: 628).

    Cf. 507.23ff., where Le Fever tells of his wife's death in his arms and Toby remembers a "circumstance his modesty omitted" (508.11).

427.1   the listening slave] Almost certainly an allusion to the well-known classical statue *Arrotino* ("Whetter") in the Uffizi Gallery in Florence. Edward Wright's description (*Some Observations Made in Travelling Through France, Italy, &c.* [1730], 2d ed. [1764], II: 411) makes clear how it came to be known as the "listening slave" and may even suggest that Sterne had a similar description in mind: "Others . . . pretend it was the slave that overheard and revealed the conspiracy of Catiline . . . . It seems . . . much more probable, that it was the slave who revealed the plot of Brutus's sons to bring Tarquin back again . . . ; he suspected there was some mischief in hand, because all the servants were sent out of the house; . . . he therefore stay'd at the door, and thro' a chink of it saw them . . . . The sculptor . . . represents the slave as whetting his knife . . . ." Cf. Smollett, *Travels through France and Italy* (1766), pp. 65–67.

    Sterne's "intaglio" of this figure accompanied by the "Goddess of Silence" is either his own composition or a variation upon *Arrotino* that has escaped our notice.

427.4–5   (as *Rapin* does those of the church)] Work, p. 358, n. 1: "It was the practice of Paul de Rapin [de Rapin-Thoyras] (1661–1725), French historian, in his great *L'Histoire d' Angleterre*, at the end of nearly every book to bring up to date the affairs of the church in a special section." This is one of only two overt allusions in *TS* to Rapin-Thoyras's *History of England*, the continuation of which by Nicholas Tindal (1687–1774) plays so important a role in organizing and describing Toby's campaigns. Because Theodore Baird called attention to Sterne's debt in 1936 ("Time-Scheme"), it is surprising that Work made no use of Tindal in his annotations; see also 584.12–13, the second allusion to Rapin-Thoyras.

    As an example of Rapin-Thoyras's practice, in vol. I, p. 212, he begins a section entitled "State of the Church, during the Reigns of William I. William II. Henry I. and Stephen"; and on p. 348, he begins a similar description of the Church between the reigns of Henry II and Henry III. We have used the 1743–47 four-volume edition cited as Tindal throughout these notes.

427.6–14 THOUGH in one sense . . . *Dutch* silk-mill.] Cf. Shaftesbury's "Essay on the Freedom of Wit and Humour," in *Characteristicks* (1711), pt. 3, sec. iii: "YOU have heard it (my Friend!) as a common Saying, that *Interest governs the World*. But, I believe, whoever looks narrowly into the Affairs of it, will find, that *Passion, Humour, Caprice, Zeal, Faction*, and a thousand other Springs, which are counter to *Self-Interest*, have as considerable a part in the Movements of this Machine. There are more Wheels and *Counter-Poises* in this Engine than are easily imagin'd" (I: 115). In view of the response of the kitchen to Bobby's death, this entire section of the *Characteristicks* may serve as a useful gloss; see the discussion by Alan Dugald McKillop in *The Early Masters of English Fiction* (Lawrence: University of Kansas Press, 1956), pp. 201–3.

Cf. Sterne's letter to his patron Lord Fauconberg in April 1762: "I beg pardon, my Lord, for troubling you with this long & particular acc^t about myself & my affairs; but I thought it my duty to tell you my Situation— my family, my Lord, is a very small machine; but it has many wheels in it; & I am forced too often to turn them about,—not as I would—but as I can" (*Letters*, p. 160).

428.5–6 upon the tapis] An absorption of the French idiom *sur le tapis* ("on the table[cloth]," i.e., under discussion); in use from 1690, according to the *Stanford Dictionary*.

428.21–22 had he been . . . *Job*'s stock] Job's stock is enumerated in Job 1: 3 and again, much increased, in 42: 12. See 340.4–5 and n. above.

428.23 *worth a groat*] Cf. above, n. to 104.7.

429.17–18 Well might *Locke* . . . imperfection of words.] As indeed Locke did, *ECHU*, III.9.

430.6–7 bone-laced caps] *OED* cites this passage as its sole illustration, with the definition "Trimmed with bone-lace."

430.7 bed-gowns] *OED* cites this passage as its earliest example.

430.13 So am not I . . . scullion.] Cf. 212.2–4: "He is the father of curses, replied Dr. *Slop.*——So am not I, replied my uncle"; and Swift, *Polite Conversation*, p. 74: "*Col.* But is he really dead? *Lady Answ.* Yes, Colonel, as sure as you're alive."

431.17–22 Now as I perceive plainly . . . corporal's eloquence] Cf. Thomas Sheridan, *A Discourse . . . Introductory to His Course of Lectures on Elocution* (1759), p. 4: "These neglects [of the art of oratory] are the more astonishing, because, upon examination, it will appear, that there neither is, nor ever was a nation upon earth, to the flourishing state of whose constitution and government, such studies were so absolutely necessary. Since it must be obvious to the slightest enquirer, that the support of our establishments, both ecclesiastical and civil, in their due vigour, must in a great measure depend upon the powers of elocution in public debates, or other oratorial performances, displayed in the pulpit, the senate-house, or at the bar." Sheridan repeats the idea in his *Course of Lectures on Elocution*, published three years later: "we shall in vain hope, for the many excellent effects, which might be produced by good elocution, in a country, where there is such an absolute necessity for it, to the support of our constitution, both in church, and state" (p. 5).

Sterne's readers may well have found the present passage an obvious allusion to Sheridan, who had been lecturing on oratory throughout Great Britain since 1757, and whose claims for the art were famous and, if we can trust Johnson, infamous: "Sheridan will not succeed at Bath with his oratory. Ridicule has gone down before him, and, I doubt, Derrick [Bath's Master of the Ceremonies, Samuel Derrick] is his enemy" (Boswell, *Life of Johnson*, I: 394). For an account of Sheridan's career, see Wilbur Samuel Howell, *Eighteenth-Century British Logic and Rhetoric* (Princeton: Princeton University Press, 1971): 214–43.

431.26–432.1   I said . . . by our imaginations] Cf. *Sermons*, VII.43.93–94: "in the present state we are in, we find such a strong sympathy and union between our souls and bodies, that the one cannot be touched or sensibly affected, without producing some corresponding emotion in the other.— Nature has assigned a different look, tone of voice, and gesture, peculiar to every passion and affection we are subject to; and, therefore, to argue against this strict correspondence which is held between our souls and bodies,—is disputing against the frame and mechanism of human nature.—We are not angels, but men cloathed with bodies, and, in some measure, governed by our imaginations, that we have need of all these external helps which nature has made the interpreters of our thoughts."

As *OED* (s.v. *stock*, 1.c.) makes clear, "stocks" here means the trunk of a tree, figuratively "the type of what is lifeless, motionless, or void of sensation. Hence, a senseless or stupid person"; in this sense the word *stocks* was often associated with *stones*, though neither Tilley nor *ODEP* recognizes it as proverbial.

432.3   seven senses] See above, n. to 174.27−175.1.

432.5−7   that of all . . . with the soul] In the various hierarchical orderings of the senses that philosophy has discussed down through the ages, the primacy has almost always been awarded to either sight or touch. A correspondent to the *Spectator* takes the more popular view in supporting sight: "RUMINATING lately on your admirable Discourses on the *Pleasures of the Imagination*, I began to consider to which of our Senses we are obliged for the greatest and most important Share of those Pleasures; and I soon concluded that it was to the *Sight:* That is the Sovereign of the Senses, and Mother of all the Arts and Sciences . . ." (472, IV: 170).

On the other hand, touch was always given primacy by the atomists, as indicated by Lucretius: "For TOUCH, that best, that chiefest Sense is made, / When Strokes, from THINGS WITHOUT, the Nerves invade" (*Of the Nature of Things*, trans. Thomas Creech [1714], II.416−17, I: 129). Seventeenth-century followers of atomism were rather hard pressed to choose one over the other; Walter Charleton, for example, calls sight "the noblest of Senses" on p. 136 of *Physiologia* (1654; New York: Johnson Reprint Co., 1966) and on p. 249 calls touch "that . . . constant friend, that conserves us in our first life . . . and never forsakes us, till Death hath translated us into an Eternal one." Thomas Willis has the same ambivalence: "If there be any strife for Dignity among the Senses, the Palm is given, almost by the consent of all, to Seeing, as the most noble Power . . ." (*Two Discourses Concerning the Soul of Brutes* [1683; Gainesville, Fla.: Scholars' Facsimiles and Reprints, 1971], p. 75); but cf. p. 60: "The Touch or Feeling . . . in some respect . . . is more excellent by far than the rest; because this Sense beyond all others, receives and knows the Impressions of many sensible things . . . and so obtains a most large, and as it were a general Province."

432.6   *Barbati*] "Bearded ones"; i.e., philosophers. The word occurs in Persius and Juvenal but does not appear to have entered the English language; neither *OED* nor *Stanford Dictionary* records it. Cf. Persius, *Satires*, IV.1−2 (pp. 358−59): "barbatum haec crede magistrum / dicere, sorbitio tollit quem dira cicutae" ("Imagine these to be the words of the bearded sage who was carried off by that deadly draught of hemlock"); and Juvenal, *Satires*, XIV.12–13 (pp. 264–65): "barbatos licet admoveas mille inde magistros" ("though you put a thousand bearded preceptors on his right hand").

434.1   book-debts] See 30.19 and n. above; Sterne is perhaps punning here.

434.2–4   I own myself . . . of my work] Sterne first mentions these chapters at 345.7–9 and again at 401.19. He returns to them in vol. IX (765.5).

434.11   *green-gowns, and old hats*] Partridge notes that "to give a green-gown" meant to "tumble a woman on the grass," from the sixteenth century onward. Cf. Robert Herrick's famous lines: "Many a green-gown has been given; / Many a kisse, both odde and even" ("*Corinna's* going a Maying," in *Poetical Works*, ed. L. C. Martin [Oxford: Clarendon Press, 1963], p. 67, lines 51–52).

Partridge also has an entry for *old hat:* "The female pudend: low: 1754, Fielding; Grose, 'Because frequently felt'." Cf. *TS*, 668.17–18: "It is not like the affair of *an old hat cock'd*——and *a cock'd old hat* . . . ."

435.6–9   are we not . . . flesh grass?] Sterne has Trim echo the Order for the Burial of the Dead from the *Book of Common Prayer*, which itself is made up of several biblical passages—e.g., Psalm 90: 5–6: "in the morning they are like grass which groweth up. In the morning it flourisheth, and groweth up; in the evening it is cut down, and withereth"; and Job 14: 1–2: "Man that is born of a woman is of few days, and full of trouble. He cometh forth like a flower, and is cut down . . . ." In his sermon "Job's Account of the Shortness and Troubles of Life, considered" (II.10.73–105) Sterne calls this text a "just and beautiful" reflection on the sudden revolutions of life and explicates it at some length (pp. 85–91). See also Isaiah 40: 6–8: "The voice said, Cry. And he said, What shall I cry? All flesh is grass, and all the goodliness thereof is as the flower of the field: The grass withereth, the flower fadeth: because the spirit of the LORD bloweth upon it: surely the people is grass. The grass withereth, the flower fadeth: but the word of our God shall stand for ever." This is repeated in part in 1 Peter 1: 24; see also Psalm 103: 14–15 and James 1: 10. For a discussion of Trim's funeral oration, see Byron Petrakis, "Jester in the Pulpit: Sterne and Pulpit Eloquence," *PQ* 51 (1972): 441–45.

435.12–15   What is the finest face . . . but corruption?] Trim may again be recalling the burial ritual from the *Book of Common Prayer*, which repeats

1 Corinthians 15; see especially 15: 42, 50: "So also is the resurrection of the dead. It is sown in corruption, it is raised in incorruption . . . . Now this I say, brethren, that flesh and blood cannot inherit the kingdom of God; neither doth corruption inherit incorruption."

435.16–17   —Now I love you . . . what you are] In the ambiguously named chapter "The Conquest," in *ASJ*, Yorick comments upon the aposiopesis with which the preceding chapter had ended:

> . . . it unavoidably threw the fair *fille de chambre* off her center—and then—
>
> ### THE CONQUEST.
>
> YES——and then—Ye whose clay-cold heads and luke-warm hearts can argue down or mask your passions—tell me, what trespass is it that man should have them? or how his spirit stands answerable, to the father of spirits, but for his conduct under them?
>
> If nature has so wove her web of kindness, that some threads of love and desire are entangled with the piece—must the whole web be rent in drawing them out? (*ASJ*, pp. 236–37)

435.19–20   That he has . . . be found so.] The man who is impervious to the attractions of love, according to Burton, "is not a man but a block, a very stone . . . he hath a gourd for his head, a pepon for his heart . . . ." (3.2.1.2, p. 438). Noted by Ferriar, I: 111.

436.13   In battle, I value death not this] Cf. Montaigne, I.19.94: "I have often consider'd with myself whence it should proceed, that in War, the Image of Death, whether we look upon it as to our own particular Danger, or that of another, should without Comparison appear less dreadful than at Home, in our own Houses . . . ." Cf. 425.7–8 and n. above.

Sterne may also owe something to Don Quixote's advice to the Page: "for, suppose you should be cut off at the very first Engagement by a Cannon Ball, or the spring of a Mine; what matters it? 'Tis all but Dying, and there's an end of the Business. As *Terence* says, a Soldier makes a better Figure Dead in the Field of Battle, than Alive and safe in Flight" (II.III.24; III: 218).

436.19–20   in hot pursuit . . . is not felt] Cf. Bacon, "On Death": "He that dies in an earnest Pursuit, is like one that is wounded in hot Bloud; who, for the time, scarce feeles the Hurt . . ." (*Essayes*, p. 8). Noted by Ferriar, I: 108–9.

436.28–437.1   And could I escape . . . a knapsack] Cf. Montaigne, I.19.80: "For my Part, I am of this Mind, that if a Man could by any Means avoid it, tho' by creeping under a Calf's Skin, I am one that should not be ashamed of the Shift . . . ."

437.20   kindly-hearted] *OED*'s earliest example is dated 1859.

438.16–18   I Am a *Turk* . . . without one.] Sterne may be recalling Antony's speech in act V of Dryden's *All for Love* (1678), V.i.153–56, p. 68: "Th' original Villain sure no God created; / He was a Bastard of the Sun, by *Nile*, / Ap'd into Man; with all his Mother's Mud / Crusted about his Soul."

For an account of the tradition, cf. Pope, *Essay on Criticism*, lines 40–41: "Those half-learn'd Witlings, num'rous in our Isle, / As half-form'd Insects on the Banks of *Nile*" (p. 243); and J. W. Johnson, "'Of Differing Ages and Climes'," *JHI* 21 (1960): 465–80.

Cf. also John Dunton, *A Voyage Round the World* (1691), I: 117: "—*Well*—*this 'tis to read* Seneca—one Notion begets another, and so to the end o' the Chapter, while my *poor Father's forgot* all this while as much as if he never Begot me . . . ."

439.1–15   For my own part . . . or t'other.] Cf. *Letters*, p. 157: "The devil take (as he will) these transports of enthusiasm! . . . It is a tragical nuisance in all companies as it is, and was it not for some sudden starts and dashes—of Shandeism, which now and then either breaks the thread, or entangles it so, that the devil himself would be puzzled in winding it off—I should die a martyr—this by the way I never will" (Sterne to Garrick, March 19, 1762).

Sterne expresses much the same sentiment in vol. VIII, chap. 2 (657.11–20).

439.21–22   her curiosity] Cf. 729.16–18: "I could like, said my mother, to look through the key-hole out of *curiosity*——Call it by it's right name, my dear, quoth my father . . ."; and also 735.4–7.

440.6–18   *Socrates*, and was . . . without disturbance] Sterne almost assuredly did not go to Plato's *Apology* in writing this paragraph, but rather to Montaigne's version in "Of Physiognomy" (III.12), which Cotton translates: "*I have both Friends and Kindred not being (as* Homer *says)*

begotten of a Block or of a Stone, no more than others . . . and I have three
desolate Children with which to move you to Compassion . . ." (p. 325). On
the page facing this Sterne's eye could have caught both *"Transmigration"*
and *"Annihilation"* within five lines, the latter in this passage: *"If it be an*
Annihilation of our Being, 'tis yet a Bettering of one's Condition, to enter into a
long and peaceable Night. We find nothing more sweet in Life than a quiet
Repose, and a profound Sleep without Dreams" (p. 324). The passage is
indexed under *"Death look'd upon by* Socrat. *as an indifferent Accident."*

See also *Hamlet*, III.i.55ff., the "To be, or not to be" soliloquy, especially "To sleep, perchance to dream" (line 64) and "The undiscover'd
country, from whose bourn / No traveller returns . . ." (lines 78–79).

440.9   Life of *Socrates*] John Gilbert Cooper's scholarly *Life of Socrates* (1749)
was written primarily to prove that Socrates *"invariably taught and believed*
the Immortality of the Soul, and a future Retribution of Rewards and Punish-
ments" (p. vi); that is, against a major contention of Warburton's *Divine*
Legation. Moreover, on p. 57, n. 16, Cooper quotes at length Warburton's
attack on Scarron's parody of Sulpicius (see above, n. to 421.17–422.28)
and then attacks the Bishop for his failure to distinguish between true
ridicule and the abuse of ridicule. Warburton responded by abusing
Cooper, quite gratuitously, in his edition of Pope (*Works* [1751], I: 151, n.
to *Essay on Criticism*, line 98); and Cooper riposted in *Cursory Remarks on*
Mr. Warburton's New Edition of Mr. Pope's Works (1751). Tristram refers
again to his father's *Life of Socrates*, 709.27; it seems at least probable that
the title is yet another allusion to Warburton.

440.19–25   *That we and our children . . .* sentiment also] Sterne's reference to
Josephus in this passage is slightly misleading. A comparison with the
most popular translation of the period, that of William Whiston, suggests
that Sterne's source is a secondary one. Whiston translates: "for we were
born to die, as well as those were whom we have begotten: nor is it in the
power of the most happy to avoid it. But for abuses, and slavery, and the
sight of our wives led away after an ignominious manner, with their children, these are not such evils as are natural and necessary among men"
(Flavius Josephus, *The Great Roman-Jewish War*, trans. William Whiston
[1737], ed. D. S. Margoliouth [New York: Harper and Bros., 1960], p.
271). Sterne in fact appears to have taken over a passage from Donne's
Biathanatos, merely altering the sentence order: "By *Eleazars* Oration

recorded in (d) *Josephus*, we may see how small perswasions moved men to this. [*Hee onely told them, that the Philosophers among the Indians did so. And that we and our children were borne to dy, but neither borne to serve.*] d *De bell. Judai. 1.7.c.28*" (John Donne, *Biathanatos* [1646; New York: Facsimile Text Society, 1930], p. 54). In the course of borrowing this section from Donne, Sterne misread the reference to the Indian philosophers, thereby attributing to them, on behalf of Eleazar, a sentiment which is not to be found in Josephus. See W. G. Day, "Sterne, Josephus and Donne," *N&Q* 215 (1970): 94.

441.1–2   (for we all know . . . at *Babylon*)] Alexander's death in 323 B.C. is recorded at length by Plutarch; it did occur at Babylon, where he returned despite the many ill omens presaging his death. See *Lives*, VII: 427ff.

441.3–5   from *Greece* . . . things come round.] Work, p. 368, n. 2: "Sterne burlesques serious attempts (such as that of Sir William Temple in his *Reflections upon Ancient and Modern Learning*, 1692) to trace the progress of the arts and sciences from their presumed origin in the East, to western Europe." Cf. Temple, "An Essay upon the Ancient and Modern Learning," in *Works* (1720), I: 159–60: "Science and Arts have run their Circles, and had their Periods in the several Parts of the World: They are generally agreed, to have held their course from *East* to *West*, to have begun in *Chaldea* and *Ægypt*, to have been Transplanted from thence to *Greece*, from *Greece* to *Rome;* to have sunk there, and after many Ages, to have revived from those Ashes and to have sprung up again, both in *Italy* and other more *Western* Provinces of *Europe.*"

441.7–19   By water . . . in those days!] Cf. Sterne's previous geographical excursion, 231.1–11. This journey begins where the Ganges empties into the Bay of Bengal, proceeds south around the tip of India into the Indian Ocean and then northwest into the Red Sea and the Gulf of Suez at its northern end; Tor is at the southern end of the Gulf and Suez at the northern. Joddah (Jidda) is the port city of Mecca, on the eastern shore of the Red Sea; Coptos, an ancient city on the Nile, is described by Pliny, *Natural History*, 5.11 (pp. 264–65), as "the market near the Nile for Indian and Arabian merchandise." In that Tor and Suez are considerably north of Coptos, Sterne's geography is confusing; perhaps he means that one common route was from Joddah to Coptos to Alexandria, while another was from Joddah to Tor to Suez to Alexandria.

For the Alexandrian library, see above, n. to 312.24.

441.13   karrawans] I.e., caravans.

441.20–442.5   Now my father . . . be done by] New, "Sterne, Warburton,"
p. 259, suggests that Sterne is deliberately baiting Warburton, since a
primary argument of the *Divine Legation* is that the Book of Job was
written after the patriarchs (by Ezra), and was an *allegory* of the Captivity,
an argument countered by Bishop Robert Lowth and other "answerers,"
all of whom believed Job to be among the oldest of Hebrew writings, and
historical rather than allegorical. Lowth had reopened the debate in 1753.
For Sterne's original plan to "run up" an allegory on the "Writers on the
Book of Job," see "Sterne, Warburton," p. 249, and "Introduction to the
Text," in *TS*, vol. II, pp. 818–19, in this edition. For other allusions to
Warburton in vol. V, see above, nn. to 409.1 and 421.17–422.28, and
below, nn. to 446.7–11 and 453.5–6.

442.23–24   "I have . . . says *Socrates*.] See above, n. to 440.6–18.

443.9ff.   HAD this volume been a farce, etc.] Neil D. Isaacs ("The Auto-
erotic Metaphor in Joyce, Sterne, Lawrence, Stevens, and Whitman,"
L&P 15 [1965]: 92–106) suggests that this entire chapter should be understood in masturbatory terms; among other hints, he points to "diddle"
as having slang reference to copulation, masturbation, and the penis. William Freedman, *Laurence Sterne and the Origins of the Musical Novel*
(Athens: University of Georgia Press, 1978), pp. 143–44, treats it
briefly.

443.9–10   unless every one's life . . . as a farce] In the "Life of Rabelais"
prefixed to Ozell's edition, several stories are told of Rabelais's death. In
one he is quoted as saying "Let down the curtain, the farce is done"; in
another, "Draw the curtain, the farce is over." The point is then made that
"many great men have said much the same. Thus Augustus, near his
death, ask'd his friends, whether he had not very well acted the farce of
life? And Demonax . . . said to those that were near him, what the herald
used to say when the public games were ended, You may with-draw, the
show is over . . ." (I, pp. xviii–xix).

444.5   *Calliope*] The muse of heroic and epic poetry; in setting up his opposi-
tions, Sterne contrasts the lightest and freest of musical forms with the
most dignified of the muses, a contrast similar to that between a Cremona
and a Jew's trump in the next line.

444.6   *Cremona*] A town in Lombardy where the violins of Amati, Stradi-vari, and Guarneri were made. *OED* cites this passage as its first example of the name of the town being used for its most famous product. Fielding speaks of a *"Cremona* Fiddle" in *Tom Jones,* ed. Martin C. Battestin and Fredson Bowers (Middletown, Conn.: Wesleyan University Press, 1975), book IX, chap. 5 (I: 511).

The Jew's trump, or Jew's harp, is a very simple folk instrument, played with the mouth and one finger and having the same relationship to a fine violin that a child's harmonica, perhaps, would have today.

444.21–23   who inspires me . . . into motion.] Cf. 333.17–334.9 and n. above.

445.4   sit down coolly] See above, n. to 118.15–16.

445.4–5   after the example of *Xenophon* . . . for me] Xenophon (c. 428/27 B.C.–c. 354 B.C.), Greek philosopher and historian, sets out his ideas on education primarily in his *Cyropaedia* and his *Memorabilia.* For the apt-ness of the "example" of Xenophon, see Eric Rothstein, *Systems of Order and Inquiry in Later Eighteenth-Century Fiction* (Berkeley: University of California Press, 1975), p. 91, n. 24.

Cornelius Scriblerus before the birth of his son "had composed two Treatises of Education; the one he called *A Daughter's Mirrour,* and the other *A Son's Monitor"* (*Memoirs of Martinus Scriblerus,* p. 97). There is, of course, a Scriblerian instinct behind any idea to produce a digest of knowledge; see above, n. to 215.24–26, where Sterne's several references to digests and institutes are linked to *Peri Bathous.*

445.5–9   collecting first . . . and adolescence.] Cf. Sterne's description of Slawkenbergius's book as a "thorough-stitch'd DIGEST and regular insti-tute of *noses"* (274.25–26) and an "institute of all that was necessary to be known of noses, and every thing else" (285.18–19); see also 215.24–26.

Sterne may also be borrowing for the first time from Obadiah Walker's *Of Education,* 6th ed. (1699), a work from which he borrows heavily in the remainder of vol. V, especially for the theory of auxiliary verbs; see Walker's preface: "I have therefore rather chused to gather up disorderly, and bind together, such scattered Counsels and Notions, as have occurred either in Observation, or in some *Italian Writers,* not ordinary amongst us" (p. A4).

445.17   *Nicholas Tartaglia*] See above, n. to 103.2–21.

445.19   cross-twisted] Unrecorded in *OED*.

446.1   hussive] I.e., housewife: "A pocket-case for needles, pins, thread, scis-
sors, etc." (*OED*).

446.1–2   Matter grows under our hands.] Possibly Sterne is recalling a famous passage from the opening of Quintilian's *Institutio Oratoria*, book I,
proem 3 (I: 6–7): "latius se tamen aperiente materia plus quam im-
ponebatur oneris sponte suscepi" ("The subject proved more extensive
than I had first imagined").

446.7–11   *John de la Casse . . .* a *Rider*'s Almanack.] From a few facts—
Giovanni della Casa (1503–56) was the Archbishop of Benevento and did
write a famous Renaissance conduct book called the *Galateo* (after an acquaintance of della Casa), published posthumously in 1558—Sterne spins
a rather elaborate fictional web for his own purposes. In all likelihood,
Sterne never read the *Galateo,* but rather found references to della Casa in
the *Anatomy,* 3.2.1.2 (p. 437); in Ozell's "Explanatory Remarks" in
Rabelais, V, p. xvii; and in Bayle, *Dictionary,* s.v. *Francis de la Mothe le
Vayer,* n. E (noted by Rothstein, *Systems of Order,* p. 92, n. 25). In all
three sources, the Archbishop is abused for his youthful paean to sodomy.
Sterne seems to have confused this celebration with the *Galateo;* indeed, in
vol. IX (765.23) he calls it "his *nasty* Romance." In addition, a modern
editor, R. S. Pine-Coffin (Harmondsworth, England: Penguin Books,
1958), specifically notes that the *Galateo* was written between 1551 and
1555, a period of four rather than forty years (p. 14). It is, to be sure, a
thin book, but perhaps four or five times larger than any *Rider's Almanack*
we have examined.

We have found no evidence that della Casa held anything like the theory
attributed to him. For one attempt to explain Sterne's rather elaborate
game with della Casa, see New, "Sterne, Warburton," pp. 263–74.

446.16   who write not . . . to be famous.] Cf. 237.6 and n. above.

447.12   'Twas Term-time with them] The period in which the law courts are
in session. Rabelais, too, uses this expression figuratively for a period of
particular activity: "For then the devils do their best, and drive a subtle
trade, and the tribe of canting dissemblers come out of their holes. 'Tis
then term-time with your cucullated pieces of formality, that have one face
to God, and the other to the devil . . ." (V.29.183).

Cf. *Don Quixote,* II.III, "Preface" (III: v): "*For I am not Ignorant of the*

Temptations of Satan; *and of all his Imps, the Scribbling Devil is the most Irresistible. When that Demon is got into a Man's Head, he takes the Possession for Inspiration, and, full of his false Ability,* falls slap-dash *to Writing and Publishing* . . . ."

447.16–19   So that the life . . . state of *warfare*] Cf. Warburton, *Remarks on Several Occasional Reflections* (1744), in *Works,* ed. Richard Hurd (London, 1811), XI: 232: "The state of Authorship, whatever that of Nature be, is certainly a state of war: in which, especially if it be an *holy war,* every man's hand is set, not against his enemy, but his *brother.*" The idea may be derived from Pope's preface to his *Works* (1717): "The life of a Wit is a warfare upon earth; and the present spirit of the learned world is such, that to attempt to serve it (any way) one must have the constancy of a martyr, and a resolution to suffer for its sake" (in *Pastoral Poetry and An Essay on Criticism,* p. 6). This sentence from Pope may also help to gloss the passage in vol. VIII (657.11–20) cited just above, n. to 439.1–15.

448.2   retrograde] *OED* cites this passage as its last illustration of an obscure or rare usage: "backward, slow."

448.2–5   there was as . . . of antiquity.] See above, n. to 268.8–10, for the Rabelaisian echo in this passage.

448.6–8   Prejudice of education . . . *devil and all.*] See above, nn. to 58.23–24 and 261.11–14. Montaigne discusses the force of custom in a similar manner in I.22.118–21: "But the principal Effect of the Power of Custom is, so to seize and ensnare us, that it is hardly in our Power to disengage ourselves from its Gripe; or so to come to ourselves, as to consider of, and to weigh the Things it enjoins. To say the Truth, by Reason that we suck it in with our Milk, and that the Face of the World presents itself in this Posture to our first Sight, it seems as if we were born upon Condition to pursue this Practice; and the common Fancies that we find in Repute every where about us . . . appear to be most universal and genuine. . . .

"Whoever would disengage himself from this violent Prejudice of Custom, would find several things receiv'd with absolute and undoubting Opinion, that have no other Support than the hoary Head and rivell'd Face of ancient Use . . . ."

Cf. Walter's acceptance of the doctrine of noses, 261.11–14: "For in a great measure he might be said to have suck'd this in, with his mother's milk. He did his part however.——If education planted the mistake, (in case it was one) my father watered it, and ripened it to perfection."

449.7−8   drawing a sun-dial . . . under ground.] Cf. John Donne's "The Will," lines 50−51: "And all your graces no more use shall have / Then a Sun dyall in a grave . . ." (*Poems* [1633], p. 284). *ODEP*, s.v. *Sun-dial*, cites examples after Donne from 1732, 1750, and 1761, the last being Samuel Johnson's "Thoughts on the Coronation," in *Political Writings*, ed. Donald J. Greene (New Haven: Yale University Press, 1977), p. 293: "Magnificence in obscurity is equally vain with a 'sun-dial in the grave'." Ferriar (II: 36−37) suggests Donne.

449.13−14   some men rise . . . upon small wires] Proverbial; Tilley, W255, cites Thomas Fuller (1642): "The Counsell for the King, hanging as much weight on the smallest wier as it would hold, aggravated each particular." See also *ODEP*, s.v. *Great weights*.

449.15   *August* the 10th, 1761] Sterne had written to Hall-Stevenson, probably in June: "To-morrow morning, (if Heaven permit) I begin the fifth volume of Shandy—I care not a curse for the critics—I'll load my vehicle with what goods *he* sends me, and they may take 'em off my hands, or let them alone . . ." (*Letters*, p. 140). On September 21, he wrote to another acquaintance: "I am scribbling away at my Tristram. These two volumes are, I think, the best. . . . so much am I delighted with my uncle Toby's imaginary character, that I am become an enthusiast" (p. 143). It seems reasonable to assume that the date given is an accurate one for the writing of this chapter.

449.24   nothing was well hung in our family] For those who find psycho-analytical criticism of interest, the implications of this statement are explored at some length by A: Franklin Parks, "Yorick's Sympathy for the 'Little'," *L&P* 23 (1978): 119−24.

450.8   all accessaries in murder, being principals] Cf. Giles Jacob, *A New Law Dictionary*, 9th ed. (1772), s.v. *Accessary*, III: "In the highest capital offence, namely, *high treason*, there are no accessaries, neither before nor after; for all consenters, aiders, abetters, and knowing receivers and comforters of traitors are all *principals*." No such blanket law applied to murder.

451.10   paderero] I.e., pedrero; see "Glossary of Terms of Fortification" in this volume.

451.14–15   like *Lewis* . . . for spare ends, &c.] Work, p. 377, n. 2: "To finance his long and expensive campaigns, Louis XIV frequently resorted to forced loans from the clergy." It is quite possible, however, that Sterne was speaking literally here rather than figuratively, since all armies during the period razed churches, most especially confiscating the bells because of their valuable metal. See, e.g., *The Life and Adventures of Mrs. Christian Davies, the British Amazon, Commonly called Mother Ross*, 2d ed. (1741), pt. 1, p. 58: "We spared nothing, killing, burning, or otherwise destroying whatever we could carry off. The Bells of the Churches we broke to Pieces, that we might bring them away with us. I filled two Bed Ticks, after having thrown out the Feathers, with Bell Metal . . . ." Cf. 540.18–21: "In the fourth year, my uncle *Toby* thinking a town looked foolishly without a church, added a very fine one with a steeple.——*Trim* was for having bells in it;——my uncle *Toby* said, the mettle had better be cast into cannon."

See also David Chandler, *The Art of Warfare in the Age of Marlborough* (New York: Hippocrene Books, 1976), p. 153: "To revert to the French artillery, we have seen how it possessed a provincial as well as a central organization. Over all sectors presided the powerful figure of the *Grand Maître*, invariably a Prince of the Blood or very senior officer. His authority extended over every corner of the realm . . . . He was entitled to 100 rations a day . . . a salute of five salvoes 'of the great guns', and had the right to dispose of the church-bells and cannon of every captured town (or a cash sum in lieu)."

451.29   the lead went to pot too.] Proverbial; Tilley, P504, and *ODEP*, s.v. *Go to pot* ("to be cut in pieces like meat for the pot; to be ruined or destroyed").

452.5   artilleryship] *OED* cites this passage as its first recorded example, with the following definition: "the skilful management of cannon . . . ." As a construction the word may be compared with *divinityship*; see 565.14, *OED*'s only recorded example ("knowledge of or skill in divinity").

452.17ff.   My uncle *Toby* had just then, etc.] Sterne's account of the allied defeat at Steinkirk (July 24, 1692) is taken from Tindal, III: 208–9: "the Prince of *Wirtemberg*, after he had cannonaded for above two hours, began the attack with the *Danes* upon the right, which was immediately followed by the other four *English* regiments, that composed the van-guard, and seconded by *Cuts*'s, *Mackay*'s, *Angus*'s, *Graham*'s, *Lowther*'s, the Prince of *Hesse*'s, and *Leven*'s regiments. . . . The van-guard behaved themselves with so much bravery and resolution, that tho' they received the charge of several battalions of the enemy, one after another, yet they drove them beyond one of their batteries of seven pieces of cannon, of which the *Danes* and the second battalion of the regiment of *English* guards possessed them-selves . . . . All the other regiments behaved themselves with equal brav-ery, firing muzzle to muzzle through the hedges, they on the one side, and the enemy on the other.

"The King being made sensible of the difficulties, which the vanguard had to encounter . . . his Majesty dispatched away Count *Paulin* . . . with positive orders to Count *Solms*, who commanded the main body, to send more foot to the Prince's assistance. But Count *Solms* (who is said to have been always envious of the *English* and who besides had a particular jeal-ousy of the Prince of *Wirtemberg*'s commanding the attacks, an honour, which he would have had himself) instead of obeying the King's com-mands, ordered the horse to march, and the foot to halt; which proved the loss of the day. For the ground was so strait, and the enemy had such hedges, copses, and ditches to cover them, that there was nothing to do for the horse . . . . The *English* life-guards owed their preservation to the *Danish* foot-guards; and . . . Sir *Bevil Grenville*, who commanded the Earl of *Bath*'s regiment, marched up to [the Baron of Pibrack's] relief, receiving the enemies fire, before he suffered any peloton of his battalion to discharge once.

"The King, enraged at the disappointment of the vanguard for want of a timely relief, expressed his concern by often repeating these words, *O! my poor* English! *how they are abandoned!* Nor would he admit Count *Solms* to his presence for many months after."

Work, p. 378, n. 1, and p. 380, n. 2: "Heinrich Maastricht, Count Solms (1636–1693), commanded the allied main body in its luckless at-tack on the French at Steinkirk . . . . Baron John Cutts of Gowran (1661–1707) commanded a brigade of Mackay's division which was al-most destroyed at Steinkirk; Hugh Mackay (1640?–1692) with the rank of lieutenant-general commanded the British division of the allied army at Steinkirk, where he met his death; James Hamilton, Earl of Angus, a colonel of the Cameronians, was likewise killed in the battle of Steinkirk;

Sir Charles Graham commanded a regiment at Steinkirk; David Melville, third Earl of Leven (1660–1728), also commanded a regiment at Steinkirk." We are told in vol. VI (507.15–16 and 20–21) that Toby and Trim served in Leven's regiment, while Le Fever was a lieutenant under Angus.

In all, the Allies suffered 2,000 men killed and 3,000 wounded or taken prisoner during the battle.

453.5–6   made a shift . . . listened to it] Michael O. Houlahan, "William Warburton and 'Tristram Shandy': An Ironic Source," *N&Q* 217 (1972): 378–79, notes that Sterne in this passage appears to parody the advice Warburton gave him in June 1760: "You say you will continue to laugh aloud. In good time. But one who was no more than even a man of spirit would wish to laugh in good company, where priests and virgins may be present . . ." (*Letters*, p. 119).

Warburton seems to have made no secret of his advice to Sterne; see Bishop Hurd's letter to William Mason, March 30, 1761: "And he does not seem capable of following the advice which one gave him—*of laughing in such a manner, as that Virgins and Priests might laugh with him*" (*Correspondence of Richard Hurd and William Mason*, ed. Ernest Harold Pearce and Leonard Whibley [Cambridge: Cambridge University Press, 1932], p. 53).

453.8   I would be picquetted to death] *OED* (s.v. *picket, sb.* 2.) cites Edward Phillips, *The new world of English words* (1706) for its definition: "*To Stand upon the Picket*, is when a Horseman for some Offence, is sentenc'd to have one Hand ty'd up as high as it can reach, and then to stand on the Point of a Stake with the Toe of his opposite Foot; so that he can neither stand, nor hang well, nor ease himself by changing Feet."

454.18–20   he had his foot shot off . . . at *Landen.*] For a description of the Battle of Landen (July 1693), in which Trim received his wound, see below, n. to 694.4–695.4. Tindal notes that the "Confederates lost in all about seven thousand; and, among these there was scarce an officer of note, only the Count *de Solms* had his leg shot off by a cannon-ball, of which he died in a few hours" (III: 240). Trim's partial statement of the fate of Count Solms is worth observing.

454.29–455.1   fall in upon them . . . the corporal] Cf. 190.20–22 and n.

above. The word *ounds* is a further corruption of *wounds*, i.e., "God's wounds"; see above, n. to 377.20.

456.6 church-spout] Unrecorded in *OED*.

456.22–457.3 This is the true reason . . . her value?] In *Table Talk of John Selden* (1689), immediately preceding the anecdote Sterne uses at 393.3– 8, Selden expresses a similar opinion concerning disagreements: "Tis hard to make an accomodation betwixt the King & the Parliam^t. If you & I fell out about money, you said I owed you Twenty pounds, I said I ow'd you but Tenn poundes, it may bee a third partie allowing me Twenty marks might make us freinds, But if I said I ow'd you 20^{li}. of Silver, and you said I ow'd you Twenty pound of Diamondes, wch is a sume innumerable, 'tis impossible wee should ever agree . . ." (ed. Sir Frederick Pollock [London: Quaritch, 1927], p. 65).

457.5 *Confucius*] Watt, p. 289: "Presumably a parody of nonsensical allusion-hunting by political writers." Or, perhaps, a trap for allusion-hunting by annotators; we would suggest a possible allusion to Goldsmith's "Citizen of the World," the Chinese mandarin and philosopher Lien Chi Altangi, who had attacked Sterne's manner of writing in two papers, nos. 51 and 53; see above, n. to 115.23–24.

457.11 FIFTY thousand pannier loads of devils] Cf. Rabelais, "Author's Prologue," II, p. vi: "even as I give myself fairly to an hundred thousand panniers full of devils . . ."; and again, III.22.146: "his soul goeth infallibly to thirty thousand panniers full of devils."

The incident of Tristram's circumcision may owe something to Rabelais, I.11.184–85, where Gargantua's nurses amuse themselves with his "pick-lock, pioneer, bully-ruffin, smell-smock" etc.: "It belongs to me said one. It is mine said the other. What, quoth the third, shall I have no share in it? by my faith I will cut it off then: Ha! to cut it off, said the other, would be a scurvy business: madam, is it your way to cut off little childrens things? were his cut off, he would be then master-bob."

458.18 bitter *Philippick*] Cf. 709.8–11: "he . . . would pish, and huff, and bounce, and kick, and play the Devil, and write the bitterest Philippicks . . . that ever man wrote . . . ." Also, see above, n. to 218.3–4.

459.16ff. If it be but right done, etc.] Sterne's discussion is borrowed from John Spencer's *De Legibus Hebræorum Ritualibus* (*On the Ritual Laws of the*

Hebrews), published at Cambridge in 1685; we quote from the second edition (1686). One section (I.iv.3), entitled "*De sede vel subjecto Circumcisionis*" ("*On the foundation or subject of circumcision*"), provided Sterne with his first two Greek footnotes. The next section (I.iv.4), "*De Circumcisionis origine & antiquitate*" ("*On the origin and antiquity of circumcision*"), provided him with the list of practicing nations and the two last footnotes. It should be pointed out that Spencer provides Latin translations for his Greek quotations.

We have been unable to establish any relationship between this John Spencer (1630–95) and the John Spencer to whom vols. V and VI are dedicated (see above, n. to Ded. for vol. V), but one can assume that Sterne was aware that they were namesakes.

Maimonides (Moses ben Maimon, 1135–1204), the greatest Jewish scholar of the Middle Ages, is the first authority cited by Spencer in his "Prolegomena" (a)1ʳ. Warburton, in the *Divine Legation*, 4th ed. (1755), book IV, sec. 6, calls Spencer's work "a paraphrase and comment on the third part of a famous treatise called *More Nevochim* [*Guide for the Perplexed*], of the Rabbi MOSES MAIMONIDES: of whom only to say (as is his Common Encomium) *that he was the first of the Rabbins who left off trifling*, is a poor and invidious commendation" (III: 339).

460.1–2   reading the section as follows.] Sterne uses the device of the "lacuna" again, 467.22ff., 521.4ff., 524.3ff., 560.2ff., 570.2ff., 637.12ff., 772.1ff., 773.1ff., and 777.6ff., often with an ironic reference to it, as here ("nay, if it has that convenience"); or with an ironic introduction, as at 467.21–22 ("and for this plain reason . . ."). It is perhaps worth noting that the device is not used in the first four volumes at all, but six times in vols. V and VI.

Swift in *Tale of a Tub* uses the device with similar aplomb; e.g.: "The present Argument is the most abstracted that ever I engaged in, it strains my Faculties to their highest Stretch; . . . I now proceed to unravel this knotty Point.

"*THERE IS in Mankind a certain . . . [lacuna] . . . . And this I take to be a clear Solution of the Matter" (p. 170).

The device is commonplace in eighteenth-century literature.

460.9–11   and so without stopping . . . the *Jews*] Spencer discusses this question at some length in *De Legibus*, I.iv.4, where the Jewish and Egyptian

claims and rebuttals are given side by side. Cf. Warburton, *Divine Lega-*
tion, book IV, sec. 6 (III: 340), where the same question is vexed: *"That*
either the Jews borrowed from the Egyptians, or the Egyptians from the Jews."
460.17−20   if the EGYPTIANS . . . PYTHAGORAS submitted] Cf. Spencer,
   I.iv.4 (p. 27): "non tantùm Judæos, sed & Ægyptios, Colchos, Phœn-
   icas, Syros, Arabes, Æthiopes, Troglodytas, alios, Circumcisionem in
   usu habuisse." Sterne omits the Ethiopians and adds the Cappadocians, for
   a reason not readily apparent. Perhaps such a learned list of remote so-
   cieties reminded him of a biblical list in Acts 2: 9 that seems to have
   particularly amused him; see below, n. to 551.9−16, and *ASJ,* p. 257.
   Less likely, he perhaps was familiar with a passage on circumcision in
   Herodotus, 2.104 (I: 392−93), cited by Spencer, where an allusion to the
   Syrians of the valleys of the Thermodon and the Parthenius is actually a
   reference to the Cappadocians. Cappadocia is the territory north and west
   of Syria, much of present-day Turkey; Colchis is the area at the east end of
   the Black Sea, just south of the Caucasus Mountains; Troglodytes is a
   name applied to various ancient tribes (see *OCD,* s.v. *Trogodytae*).
      Sterne probably read about Pythagoras in Spencer, p. 31: "Pythagoras
   itaque, ut ad mysticam eorum philosophiam aditum haberet, Circumcisionem subiisse dicitur" ("And thus Pythagoras, in order to have access to
   their mystical philosophy, is said to have undergone circumcision"). We
   have been unable to locate a source for Solon's inclusion among the circumcised. Sterne does list Pythagoras and Solon together, among others,
   in vol. IV; see above, n. to 351.4−5.
461.8−12   the trine and sextil . . . below with us.] Cf. Burton, 3.1.1.2
   (p. 416): "The Physitians referre this [why people love] to their temperament, Astrologers to trine and sextile Aspects, or opposite of their severall
   Ascendents, Lords of their genitures, love and hatred of Planets . . . ."
      Both Burton and Sterne are parodying legitimate catch-phrases from
   the vocabulary of astrology. According to John Partridge, *Mikropanastron;*
   or An Astrological Vade Mecum (1679), "aspects" are the "Distances of the
   Stars and Planets in the Zodiack . . . of two sorts, *viz.* good or bad, either
   helping or hindring things in matters belonging to the Judgment of Astrology" (p. 22). The sextile "is an Aspect of Friendship, although imper-
   fect, being 60 deg. distant." The trine "is when two Stars are distant 120
   degrees, and is . . . an Aspect of perfect Love and Amity" (p. 23). *OED*

cites this passage as its sole illustration of the phrase *to jump awry* ("to disagree"). Cf. 197.1 and n. above.

The ascendant is that house of the zodiac which at any given moment is just rising above the eastern horizon, and from which the horoscope is drawn. According to Partridge, it is "esteemed by the Learned in this Science, the most Energetical point in the whole Scheme, and in Nativities it is the principal Significator of Life . . ." (p. 38). The opposite of the ascendant is the house 180 degrees distant and "is an Aspect of perfect hatred." The Lord of the geniture, as Partridge notes in his chapter on the subject (pp. 83–84), is often confused; he defines it as follows: "whatsoever Planet is found strongest . . . ought to be elected Lord of the Geniture [which has] a singular propriety . . . in the Judgment of almost all the Actions or Passions of Man's life; and as some Astrologers say, they are half a Nativity."

Cf. 243.13–15 (and n. above), where Walter says, "had I faith in astrology, brother, (which by the bye, my father had) I would have sworn some retrograde planet was hanging over this unfortunate house of mine . . . ."

461.16–17   *apothecaries . . . washer-women?] The first Greek quotation is taken from Spencer, *De Legibus,* I.iv.3 (p. 25); the source is identified as "Philo, *Lib. de circumcis.*," i.e., the Jewish philosopher Philo Judaeus (c. 20 B.C.–c. 40 A.D.), whose brief "Treatise on Circumcision" can be found in his *Works,* trans. C. D. Yonge (London, 1855), III: 175–77. Work, p. 386, provides a translation: "A release from a terrible disease, and hard to cure, which they call anthrax."

The second quotation is also from Philo, and is translated by Work: "Circumcised races are most prolific and most populous."

The third quotation is not from Samuel Bochart (1599–1667), author of *Geographia Sacra* (1646), but from Herodotus, 2.37 (I: 318–19); Sterne looked at the wrong margin for n. (a), Bochart being cited on p. 30 while the borrowed passage is on the facing p. 31. The phrase may be translated: "for the sake of cleanliness."

462.5–11   *ILUS . . . under *Pharoah-neco.*] Cf. Spencer, I.iv.4, pp. 28–29: "Sanchuniatho, vetustissimus rerum Phœniciarum scriptor, ritûs hujus originem à Saturno petit: [Greek] *Ilus, qui Saturnus est, pudenda circumcisus est, & commilitones suos ad idem faciendum adegit.* Quisnam ille Saturnus fuerit, haud adeo inter doctos convenit: apud omnes autem in confessum venit, Eum Abrahami tempora superare" ("Sanchuniathon, the earliest writer of Phoenician history, sought the origin of this ritual in Saturn: *Ilus, who is Saturn, was circumcised and had his fellow soldiers do the same.* But who that Saturn might have been, is even yet not agreed upon by the learned: among all, however, it is acknowledged that he predates the time of Abraham"). This argument is answered in a parallel column: "Huic uni Sanchuniathonis testimonio, in argumento tam remotæ antiquitatis, haud multum fidei tribuendum est: cùm præsertim Authores plerique Circumcisionis originem non à Saturno sed Abrahamo deducendam sentiant. Deinde, aut ego fallor, aut Sanchuniathonis verba cœlestem Circumcisionis originem, sed (Gentium more) fabulis quibusdam obscuratam, referunt" ("To this single testimony of Sanchuniathon, in an argument of such remote antiquity, not much credence should be given: especially since most authorities agree that the origin of circumcision must derive from Abraham, not Saturn. Therefore, either I am mistaken, or the words of Sanchuniathon refer to the celestial origin of circumcision, but veiled by certain fables after the custom of the pagans"). Sterne's Greek is repeated in the italicized Latin, except that he omits the reference to Saturn.

"*Sanchuniathon* is cited by Philon of Byblos [64–141] as his ancient Phoenician authority. . . . Once suspect as a forgery, his claim is now supported by the evidence of the Ugarit texts . . ." (*OCD*). Cf. Warburton, *Divine Legation*, book IV, sec. 4 (III: 205), "the venerable history of Sanchoniathon the Phenician."

The history of Pharaoh-neco (reigned 610–594 B.C.) is told in 2 Kings 23: 29 and 24: 1–7, 2 Chronicles 35: 20–27 and 36: 1–4, Jeremiah 46, and Ezekiel 29–32. His army attacked Assyria and was momentarily successful in restoring Egyptian power in the region, but in 604 it was routed by Nebuchadnezzar, King of Babylon, and Neco retreated within his borders, never to venture forth again. Sterne is perhaps remembering in particular the dramatic closing verses of Ezekiel 32, where the uncircumcised tribes are cursed one after the other, climaxing with the Egyptians: "For I have caused my terror in the land of the living: and he shall be laid in the midst of the uncircumcised with them that are slain with the sword, even Pharaoh and all his multitude, saith the Lord GOD" (32: 32).

Insofar as Ilus, if he lived at all, did so in the 14th or 13th century B.C. (the era that Sanchuniathon chronicled), it is ludicrous for Walter to suggest that he was in Neco's army.

462.17   polemic divines] One year after the publication of vols. V and VI, Warburton delivered a stinging defense of polemical divinity in the closing pages of the *Doctrine of Grace* (1763). He argues that the term had become for Deists "the whetstone of their wit, and the constant Butt of their malice," and then goes on to add that "the thing most to be lamented is, to see any well-meaning Clergyman of affected taste and real ignorance, go out of his depth, as well as out of his profession, to exert his small talents of ridicule on the same subject, merely for the sake of being in the fashion; and, free from all malice as well as wit, treat *Polemical Divinity* (which, for all the hard name, is indeed nothing but a critical examination of the doctrines of our faith) as cavalierly as ever did Collins or Tindal, Lords Shaftsbury or Bolingbroke. Yet, had these small-dealers in second-hand Ridicule but the least adverted on their doings, they must have seen the absurdity as well as mischief of so unweighed and wanton a conduct" (*Works,* VIII: 437–38). See New, "Sterne, Warburton," pp. 259–60.

462.19   practical divinity] A useful discussion of Sterne's "practical divinity," as manifested in his sermons, is that by James Downey, *The Eighteenth-Century Pulpit* (Oxford: Clarendon Press, 1969), pp. 115–54. Downey observes that "it was not Sterne's *métier* to expatiate on the profundities of life, death, and salvation. . . . He is neither a philosopher nor a polemicist. . . . Sterne stresses the social and communal aspects of religion" (pp. 128–29). That one should not find in this preference for "practical" over "polemical" divinity a necessary diminution of Christian commitment is perhaps indicated by Louis Landa's comments on Swift in his introduction to the sermons (*Prose Works,* IX: 100–108); e.g.: "Of these controversialists Swift heartily disapproved . . . . With many of his contemporaries Swift was convinced that subtle speculations, and philosophical intricacies violate common sense" (pp. 107–8).

See below, n. to 514.12–14.

463.1ff.   *Gymnast* and captain *Tripet,* etc.] Sterne borrows this passage from Rabelais (I.35.295–98) almost verbatim, with the notable exceptions of the introductory and closing sections, which Sterne perhaps found too bold—though, significantly, Yorick carries Rabelais in his "right-hand coat pocket" where a Bible might have been expected. In Rabelais, Gargantua is forced to go to war with Picrochole and this passage describes how Gymnast tricks Picrochole's army, under the command of Tripet, into believing he is mad. The passage is solely concerned with the activities of Gymnast, but Sterne, by the simple device of inserting Tripet's name into the description (464.16), turns Gymnast's feigned mad antics into a calisthenics competition, by way of illustrating the tortuous arguments of polemic divines. The entire passage from Rabelais is as follows: "WHEN they heard these words, some amongst them began to be afraid, and bless'd themselves with both hands, thinking indeed that he had been a devil disguised; insomuch, that one of them, named good John, captain of the trained bands, took his psalter out of his codpiece, and cried out aloud, Hagios ho Theos. If thou be of God speak; if thou be of the other spirit avoid hence, and get thee going. Yet he went not away. Which words being heard by all the soldiers that were there, divers of them being a little inwardly terrify'd, departed from the place. All this did Gymnast very well remark and consider, and therefore making as if he would have alighted from off his horse, as he was poising himself on the mounting side, he most nimbly (with his short sword by his thigh) shifting his feet in the stirrup, performed the stirrup-leather feat, whereby, after the inclining of his body downwards, he forthwith launch'd himself aloft in the air, and placed both his feet together on the saddle, standing upright, with his back turned towards the horse's head. Now, said he, my case goes backward. Then suddenly, in the same very posture wherein he was, he fetched a gambol upon one foot, and, turning to the left hand, failed not to carry his body perfectly round, just into his former position, without missing one jot. Ha, said Tripet, I will not do that at this time, and not without cause. Well, said Gymnast, I have failed, I will undo this leap: then, with a marvellous strength and agility, turning towards the right hand, he fetch'd another frisking gambol as before; which done, he set his right-hand thumb upon the hind bow of the saddle, raised him up, and sprung in the air, poising and upholding his whole body upon the muscle and nerve of the said thumb, and so turned and whirled himself about three times. At the fourth, reversing his body, and overturning it upside down, and foreside back, without touching any thing, he brought himself betwixt the horse's two ears, springing with all his body into the air, upon the thumb of his left hand, and in that posture, turning like a windmill, did most actively do that trick which is called the miller's pass. After this, clapping his right hand flat upon the middle of the saddle, he gave himself such a jerking swing, that he thereby seated himself upon the crupper, after the manner of gentlewomen.

"This done, he easily pass'd his right leg over the saddle, and placed himself like one that rides in croup: But, said he, it were better for me to get into the saddle. Then putting the thumbs of both hands upon the crupper before him, and thereupon leaning himself, as upon the only supporters of his body, he incontinently turned heels over head in the air, and streight found himself betwixt the bow of the saddle in a good seat: then, with a summer-sault, springing into the air again, he fell to stand with both his feet close together upon the saddle, and there made above an hundred frisks, turns, and demi-pommads, with his arms held out a cross, and in so doing, cried out aloud, I rage, I rage, devils, I am stark mad; devils, I am mad; hold me, devils, hold me; hold, devils, hold, hold."

464.17   *en croup*] *Stanford Dictionary:* "on the crupper, on a pillion"; the first illustration is dated 1820. Work's "on the rump of the horse, behind the saddle" is also accurate (p. 388, n. 1).

464.24   demi-pommadas] *OED* cites this passage as its only recorded example, but the Urquhart-Motteux Rabelais antedates it. The *pomada* is "an exercise of vaulting upon or over a horse by placing one hand on the pommel of the saddle" (*OED*); a *demi-pomada* would hence be a half-vault.

465.4–5   clear as any one proposition in *Euclid.*] Probably a commonplace formula. Cf. 597.3–4: "as demonstratively satisfied as you can be of any truth in Euclid"; and John Burton, *Letter to William Smellie, M.D.* . . . . (1753), p. 140: "This may be demonstrated as plainly as any Proposition in *Euclid.*"

Euclid (fl. c. 300 B.C.) was a Greek mathematician whose *Elements* contains the fundamentals of all geometrical demonstration.

465.18   Tom-fool-battle] *OED*'s first illustration of an attributive usage for *Tom-fool* is dated 1819.

466.1ff.   THE first thirty pages, etc.] Wilfred Watson, "The Fifth Commandment; Some Allusions to Sir Robert Filmer's Writings in *Tristram Shandy*," *MLN* 62 (1947): 234–40, argues the presence of Filmerian thought in this chapter and the next (see above, n. to 54.26−55.8), not only in the discussion of the domestic origins of government, but more specifically in the argument concerning the "natural relation between a father and his child" (467.11−12), and the debate over the meaning of the fifth commandment. Watson points out that "in the patriarchal theory of monarchy the Fifth Commandment had been given a political meaning; for, according to Filmer, this commandment especially confirmed the jurisdictional power, considered by Filmer to be the 'Foundation of Regal Authority, by Ordination of God himself,' inherent in the parent over his child" (p. 237). Locke's argument against Filmer in *Two Treatises of Government* (1698) is similar to Yorick's against Walter, namely, "I hope 'tis no Injury to call an half Quotation an half Reason, for God says, *Honour thy Father and Mother;* but our Author contents himself with half, leaves out *thy Mother* quite, as little serviceable to his purpose" (ed. Peter Laslett [Cambridge: Cambridge University Press, 1966], p. 163). Locke also questions the jurisdiction acquired by procreation: "What Father of a Thousand, when he begets a Child, thinks farther than the satisfying his present Appetite" (p. 197). His final verdict on Filmer clearly suggests the affinity with Walter: "I never, I confess, met with any Man of Parts so Dexterous as Sir *Robert* at this way of Arguing: But 'twas his Misfortune to light upon an hypothesis that could not be accommodated to the Nature of things, and Human Affairs, his principles could not be made to agree with that Constitution and Order which God had settled in the World, and therefore must needs often clash with common Sense and Experience" (pp. 259−60). It should be kept in mind that Locke's first treatise is specifically designed to detect and overthrow "the false principles and foundation of Sir Robert Filmer and his followers" (p. 153).

466.6−19   the foundation . . . his head was worth.] Politian, i.e., Angelo Poliziano (1454−94), was a noted Italian scholar and poet, tutor in the household of Lorenzo de Medici, and the translator of Herodian. While it is possible that Politian somewhere expresses this often-repeated idea of the conjugal origins of society, we rather doubt Sterne's attribution. Indeed, it seems likely that he found his source for the entire passage in the opening sections of Aristotle's *Politics*, I.i.2−5, where the quotation from Hesiod (*Works and Days*, 405, pp. 32−33) occurs: "In this subject as in others the best method of investigation is to study things in the process of development from the beginning. The first coupling together of persons then to which necessity gives rise is that between those who are unable to exist without one another, namely the union of female and male for the continuance of the species . . . and the union of natural ruler and natural subject for the sake of security . . . . From these two partnerships then is first composed the household, and Hesiod was right when he wrote: 'First and foremost a house and a wife and an ox for the ploughing'—for the ox serves instead of a servant for the poor" (pp. 4–7).

This passage is discussed by Filmer in *Patriarcha*, ed. Peter Laslett (Oxford: Basil Blackwell, 1949), pp. 76–77: "Besides Aristotle himself confesseth that among the barbarians (as he calls them that are not Grecians) 'a wife and a servant are the same, because by nature no barbarian is fit to govern. It is fit the Grecians should rule over the barbarians, for by nature a servant and a barbarian is all one. Their family consists only of an ox for a manservant and a wife for a maid, so they are fit only to rule their wives and their beasts'." See above, n. to 466.1ff.

467.1–4 For when the ground . . . of fortification.] Cf. John Muller, *A Treatise Containing the Elementary Part of Fortification* (1746; Ottawa: Museum Restoration Service, 1968), pp. 19–20: "The origin and rise of fortification, is undoubtedly owing to the degeneracy of mankind; for in the first ages of the world, men were dispersed up and down the countries in separate families . . . . These families became in time so numerous as to form large communities, which settled all together in a place; from whence villages and towns had their origin and rise: but they found it was necessary, for the common security, to surround those towns with walls and ditches, to prevent all violences *from their neighbours and sudden surprizes*." A similar introductory statement is found in many of the works on fortification published during the century.

467.21 argutely] *OED* cites this passage as its last illustration.

468.7–8 *she is not the principal agent*] Cf. Locke, *Two Treatises*, I, sec. 55, p. 198: "And it is so hard to imagine the rational Soul should presently Inhabit the yet unformed Embrio, as soon as the Father has done his part in the Act of Generation, that if it must be supposed to derive any thing from the Parents, it must certainly owe most to the Mother . . . . Our A———— [i.e., Filmer] indeed is of another mind; for he says, *We know that God at the Creation gave the Sovereignty to the Man over the Woman, as*

being the Nobler and Principal Agent in Generation . . . . I remember not
this in my Bible, and when the place is brought where God at the *Creation*
gave the Sovereignty to Man . . . because *he is the Nobler and Principal
Agent in Generation*, it will be time enough to consider and answer it
. . . ." See also sec. 62, p. 204.

468.11–13   at large . . . and the tenth section.] As Work notes (p. 392, n. 5),
Justinian supports only Walter's first statement, that the mother has no
power: "Women, also, cannot adopt; for they have not even their own
children in their power . . ." (*The Institutes*, I.xi.10, trans. and ed.
Thomas Collett Sandars, 5th ed. [Chicago: Callaghan & Co., 1876],
p. 109). For Justinian, see above, n. to 215.24–26.

468.15   *TRIM* can repeat . . . by heart] Cf. Locke, *Some Thoughts Concerning
Education*, sec. 157 (p. 260): "The Lord's Prayer, the Creeds, and Ten
Commandments, 'tis necessary he should learn perfectly by heart, but I
think, not by reading them himself in his Primer, but by somebody's
repeating them to him, even before he can read."

468.21   as to a modest Catechumen.] The form of catechism provided in the
Book of Common Prayer includes a question requiring the recitation of the
Ten Commandments. This is followed by the query "What dost thou
chiefly learn by these commandments? *Answ.* I learn two things: My duty
towards God, and my duty towards my neighbour . . . . *Quest.* What is
thy duty towards thy neighbour? *Answ.* . . . to love him as my self, and to
do to all men as I would they should do unto me. To love, honour, and
succour my father and mother." Walter's question (470.19–20) and
Trim's reply are thus very much in keeping with the catechistic ritual.

    In answer to a questionnaire sent out in 1743 by the Archbishop of
York, Thomas Herring (1693–1757), Sterne responded: "I Catechise
every Sunday in my Church during Lent, But explain our Religion to the
Children and Servants of my Parishioners in my own House every Sunday
Night during Lent, from six o'clock till nine" (*Letters*, p. 22). Canon
S. L. Ollard, who first reported on this questionnaire (*TLS*, March 18,
1926, p. 217), comments: "in all the hundreds of returns which . . . I
have examined this is unique and stands alone."

469.7ff.   that 'tis exactly the same thing, etc.] Sterne may have had the manual
of arms in his head from his childhood acquaintance with barracks life, or
he may have consulted a handbook, e.g., *The New Exercise of Firelocks and*

Bayonets . . . (1717), pp. 1–2: "*Lay your Right Hand on your Firelocks* 1 MOTION . . . *Poise your Firelocks.* 1 MOTION . . . *Join your left Hand to your Firelocks.* 2 MOTIONS . . . *Cock your Firelocks* . . . *Recover your Firelocks* . . . *Rest on your Firelocks* . . . ." In either case, Sterne seems to have the correct terminology.

470.1–3   Every thing in this world . . . it out.] Sterne may have had in mind George Herbert's "The Church-porch," lines 239–40: "All things are bigge with jest: nothing that's plain, / But may be wittie, if thou hast the vein" (*Works,* ed. F. E. Hutchinson [Oxford: Clarendon Press, 1959], p. 16); noted by Herbert Rauter, "Eine Anleihe Sternes bei George Herbert," *Anglia* 80 (1962): 290–94. Sterne may have been led to this partic-ular passage by Herbert's distinction between coarse and fine wits at the beginning of the stanza ("Pick out of mirth, like stones out of thy ground, / Profanenesse, filthinesse, abusivenesse. / These are the scumme, with which course wits abound: / The fine may spare these well, yet not go lesse"), an issue which worried Sterne throughout his career, and which he addresses in the several mottoes to vol. V.

470.7   bear-leaders] Cf. *Letters,* p. 140, where Sterne writes of his wife to Hall-Stevenson: "she hopes you will be able to strike a bargain for me before this time twelvemonth, to lead a bear round Europe . . ."; and p. 257: "As to the project of getting a bear to lead, I think I have enough to do to govern myself . . . ."

470.12–13   SCIENCES MAY BE LEARNED . . . NOT.] Sterne's apothegm seems to have been suggested by Obadiah Walker, *Of Education,* p. 115: "By the way, take notice, that these are not both the same; that to *be learned* is *not to be wise* . . . . Besides, Sciences are easily learned, being taught by rote and course; but *Wisdom* requires greater *Advertency,* and more *accurate Obser-vation;* which all are not able to *learn,* and very few to *teach.*" Sterne's use of Walker was first noted by John M. Turnbull, "The Prototype of Walter Shandy's *Tristrapaedia,*" *RES* 2 (1926): 212–15; but Turnbull specifically cites only the parallels noted below, nn. to 483.9–16, 484.11ff.

470.17–18   any one determinate idea annexed] Locke defines "determinate idea," one of the central concerns in *ECHU,* in his prefatory "Epistle to the Reader": "*some object in the Mind, and consequently* determined, *i.e. such as it is there seen and perceived to be. This I think may fitly be called a* determi-nate *or* determin'd *Idea, when such as it is at any time objectively in the Mind, and so* determined *there, it is annex'd, and without variation* determined *to a name or articulate sound, which is to be steadily the sign of that very same object of the Mind, or* determinate *Idea. . . .*

"*I know there are not Words enough in any Language to answer all the variety of Ideas, that enter into Men's discourses and reasonings. But this hinders not, but that when any one uses any term, he may have in his Mind a* determined *Idea, which he makes it the sign of, and to which he should keep it steadily annex'd during that present discourse. Where he does not, or cannot do this, he in vain pretends to* clear or distinct Ideas: '*Tis plain his are not so: and therefore there can be expected nothing but obscurity and confusion, where such terms are made use of, which have not such a precise determination*" (p. 13).

    Cf. *Letters*, p. 256: "Now notwithstanding they [the French] make such a pother about the *word* [love], they have no precise idea annex'd to it."

471.4–6   O Blessed health! . . . gold and treasure] Cf. Burton, 1.2.4.7 (p. 170): "O blessed health! *thou art above all gold and treasure.*" Burton is quoting Ecclesiasticus 30: 15; noted by Ferriar, I: 109–10.

471.16–17   radical heat and the radical moisture] See above, nn. to 104.4, 354.13.

472.19   MOONITES] *OED* cites this passage as its only recorded example.

472.20ff.   WITH two strokes, etc.] In this chapter and the next Sterne borrows from James Mackenzie, *The History of Health, and the Art of Preserving It* (Edinburgh, 1758), pp. 207–10. Mackenzie, in this part of his work, attacks those who believe life can be prolonged by "antidotes and panaceas" and singles out "from a multitude of Nostrum-mongers . . . Friar Bacon and lord Verulam, to shew how short sighted man is . . ." (p. 204). Of the latter he then writes: "THE great lord Verulam, after ridiculing the complaint of Hippocrates, that 'life was short, and the healing art tedious.' And after justly stigmatizing the vain and extravagant encomiums bestowed upon chymical secrets, and celebrated antidotes, which at first flatter and at last deceive, he himself proposes a method *to prolong life*, which, upon a fair trial, will be found equally fallacious with the boasted preparations of the chymists.

    "THE two great causes of death, says he, are first 'the internal spirit, which like a gentle flame, wastes the body: And secondly, the external air that dries and exhausts it; which two causes conspiring together, destroy our organs, and render them unfit to carry on the functions of life:' But this waste and depredation committed by the *internal Spirit,* may be repaired, first, by making the substance of it more dense, through a regular course of *opiates* taken in small doses, and at certain times; and secondly, by moderating its heat, which may be done, says he, by a proper use of nitre.

"HE owns, indeed, with a generous frankness, that 'his manner of life did not permit him to make the necessary experiments upon these medicaments,' which is much to be lamented, for without repeated experiments it will be utterly impossible to establish opinions of this nature; and he who considers that *opium* is found by experience to weaken the nerves, and that *nitre* cools to a great degree, will scarce think these drugs proper for old age, when warmth and vigour are wanted.

"OUR author treating also of *air,* which he reckons the other great cause of premature death, recommends *chalybeate baths,* and *greasy unctions,* to exclude it; but being aware that this would stop the perspiration, and occasion distempers, he orders glysters and purges, as a succedaneum, to carry off the redundant humours; which method would not answer very well in practice.

"UPON the whole, our noble author discourses here not so much like a physician, as a profound philosopher, whose universal knowledge and sublime genius prompted him to control the common appearances of nature, and to stretch, if possible, the human life beyond its usual period. But it is remarkable, that tho' this great man took three grains of his favourite *nitre* every morning for the last thirty years of his life, he died nevertheless in the sixty-sixth year of his age."

Sterne had referred to Mackenzie earlier; see 95.16–21 and n. above. The closeness of the verbal echoes here makes it almost certain that Sterne did not borrow directly from Bacon's *Historia Vitæ et Mortis* (1623) at this point; but see below, n. to 482.6.

473.2   *Ars longa,*—and *Vita brevis.*] The first and most famous of the *Aphorisms* of Hippocrates: "Art is long, and life is short." Sterne refers to Hippocrates at 95.16–21, also in conjunction with Mackenzie.

473.5   stage-loads] Unrecorded in *OED;* Sterne is alluding to the stage upon which mountebanks exhibited themselves and their medicines throughout the eighteenth century. Cf. 658.23.

475.8–22   had not the school-men . . . dropsies.] Sterne seems to have borrowed the argument of this chapter from the Duchess of Newcastle's *Life of*

William Cavendish (1667), ed. C. H. Firth, 2d ed. rev. (London: Geo. Routledge & Sons, n.d.), p. 108: "One proof more I'll add to confirm his natural understanding and judgment, which was upon some discourse I held with him one time, concerning that famous chemist Van Helmont, who in his writings is very invective against the schoolmen, and, amongst the rest, accuses them for taking the radical moisture for the fat of animal bodies. Whereupon my Lord answered, that surely the schoolmen were too wise to commit such an error; for, said he, the radical moisture is not the fat or tallow of an animal, but an oily and balsamous substance; for the fat and tallow, as also the watery parts, are cold; whereas the oily and balsamous parts have at all times a lively heat, which makes that those creatures which have much of that oil or balsam are long lived, and appear young; and not only animals, but also vegetables, which have much of that oil or balsam, as ivy, bays, laurel, holly, and the like, live long, and appear fresh and green, not only in winter, but when they are old. Then I asked my Lord's opinion concerning the radical heat: to which he answered, that the radical heat lived in the radical moisture; and when the one decayed, the other decayed also; and then was produced either an unnatural heat, which caused an unnatural dryness, or an unnatural moisture, which caused dropsies, and these, an unnatural coldness." First noted by Wilfred Watson, "Sterne's Satire on Mechanism: A Study of *Tristram Shandy*" (Ph.D. diss., University of Toronto, 1951), pp. 27–28.

Cf. Work, p. 397, n. 1: "Jean-Baptiste van Helmont (1577–1644) was a Flemish physician and chemist; the reference is to his essay, 'Humidum Radicale,' in the *Supplementum* to his chief work, the *Ortus Medicinæ* (ed. Lyons, 1655, pp. 438–441)."

475.13   balsamous] *OED* cites this passage as its last example for *balsamic*, with the notation "*?Obs.*"

475.16–17   observation . . . *coitum est* triste."] Work, p. 397, n. 2: "After coition, every creature is dejected. This apophthegm, sometimes followed by facetious exceptions to the rule, has been traditionally assigned to Aristotle. It is a paraphrase of passages found in his *Of the Generation of Animals*, 1.18 (725b), and *Problems*, 4.6 (877a), 4.12 (877b), 4.21 (879a), and 30.1 (955a)."

John Wilkes reported, perhaps maliciously, that the garden of Medmenham Abbey, when in the hands of Francis Dashwood and the "Medmenham Monks," contained "a whimsical representation of Trophonius's cave, from whence all creatures were said to come out melancholy. Among that strange, dismal group, you might however remark a *cock* crowing and a Carmelite laughing. The words *gallum gallinaceum et sacerdotem gratis* were only legible" (*The New Foundling Hospital for Wit* [1786], III: 107). The note at the bottom of the page makes clear the entire joke: "Omne animal post coitum triste est, præter gallum gallinaceum, et sacerdotem gratis fornicantem" ("After coition every creature is dejected, except a cock crowing [cocking] and a priest getting it for free"). Sterne's contact with the Medmenham circle would have been through his acquaintance with Hall-Stevenson and with Dashwood himself; and almost assuredly he had also met Wilkes by this time.

476.1–4   So that if . . . that head.] Cf. Locke's *Some Thoughts Concerning Education*, which begins with a discussion of the child's health and reaches the conclusion that "if during his Childhood, he be constantly and rigorously kept from sitting on the Ground, or drinking any cold Liquor, whilst he is hot, the Custom of Forbearing grown into Habit, will help much to preserve him . . ." (sec. 10, p. 122).

476.13ff.   the siege of *Limerick*] An account of the siege (August 1690) is given in Tindal, III: 147ff. Tindal quotes one eyewitness report in a footnote: "Nothing induced the King to quit the siege but the season of the year, and the nature of the country, which in those parts is so much subject to be overflowed, that the soldiers could no longer remain in the trenches in wet weather; and no art nor industry could remedy this mischief" (p. 149, n. 2). As Baird notes (p. 806, n. 9), Tindal makes no mention of the flux; it seems likely that Sterne had access to another, yet undiscovered, account of the siege of Limerick.

It is perhaps worth noting that although this siege was unsuccessful, it was immediately preceded by King William's great victory at the Battle of the Boyne; and that one year later Ireland surrendered to the combined Protestant forces. Similarly, Steinkirk in 1692 (see 452.17ff.) and Landen in 1693, where Trim received his wound (see 694.4–22), were also defeats for William, although they paved the way for his victory at Namur in 1695.

477.12–13   All this was as much *Arabick* . . . uncle *Toby*] Cf. 462.3–4: "Now every word of this, quoth my uncle *Toby*, is *Arabick* to me."

481.16–17   a dram of geneva . . . drive away the vapours] Cf. George
Cheyne, *The English Malady* (1733), pp. 147–48, where he discusses the
treatment of transient vapors by "drinking a good large Dose of some
scarce, active, generous, and spirituous Liquor, that may briskly rouze
and stimulate the sluggish and unactive Solids, and rarefy, warm, and
enliven the heavy and dull Fluids . . . ." Cheyne warns, however, that
although this remedy is often successful, it "has given Occasion to some
unphilosophical and unexperienced Persons to advise it as a certain and
never-failing Remedy, even in more frequent, deeper, and more habitual
Symptoms of these Disorders: and I fear has been the Cause of the common Advice to Persons of *weak Nerves* and low Spirits, *to drink a Bottle
heartily every Day*, to take frequent *Drams*, or a *Bowl of Punch* . . . ."
    See also John Pringle, *Observations on the Diseases of the Army* (1752),
where many pages are devoted to the problems of dampness and dysentery.
Pringle notes that "moisture is one of the most frequent causes of sickness," especially in the tents, "where the ground can never be thoroughly
dry" (pp. 99–101). The result, especially during the rains of late summer,
is dysentery or the (bloody) flux or bilious fever (p. 102). He advises
digging ditches round the tents to drain off water and changing the straw
in the tents frequently; and "towards the end of the season, when the tents
are cold and damp, it may be adviseable to burn spirits in the evening,
which warm and correct the air" (p. 120). Pringle also supports the drinking as well as burning of spirits: "First, as to spirits it is to be observed,
that even when drunk to excess, they tend more to weaken the constitution
than to produce any of the common camp diseases: or if some actually fall
ill upon hard drinking, it is certain a far greater number are preserved, by
taking these liquors in moderation. Let us not confound the necessary use
of spirits in a camp, with the vice of indulging them at home; but consider,
that soldiers are often to struggle with the extreams of heat and cold, with
moist and bad air, long marches, wet cloaths and scanty provisions. Now to
enable them to undergo these hardships, it is necessary they should drink
something stronger than water, or even small beer . . ." (p. 107); and
again, "A moderate use of gin or brandy is at this time necessary; but as a
soldier's pay is insufficient in the marshy countries for providing both
wholesome food and strong liquor, it would be proper, that the public
should make, at such times, an allowance of spirits to the army, as it does to

the navy: tho', perhaps, half that quantity might be sufficient" (p. 251). Cf. Trim's summary of the soldier's life, 506.4–11.

481.21–22   *Slop* had not . . . the sermon.] Slop would seem to allude to Trim's remark, five years earlier, that the "Abuses" sermon was "wrote upon neither side . . . for 'tis only upon *Conscience*, an' please your Honours" (139.20–22), a tribute to Slop's memory or a slight slip on Sterne's part.

482.6   *consubstantials . . . occludents.*] Chambers in his entry under *Life* summarizes Bacon's opinions (see above, n. to 472.20ff.), and concludes: "this mollifying of the parts without, is to be performed by consubstantials, impriments, and occludents. See LONGÆVITY." The phrase appears in Bacon's *Historia Vitæ & Mortis*, as part of canon 26: "Malacissatio fit, *per* Consubstantialia, Imprimentia, & Occludentia" (1638 ed.), p. 472. A translation of that year renders the canon thus: "*Softning is wrought by like substances, by piercing and shutting substances*" (*The History of Life and Death*, p. 314). Insofar as "hardening" is for Bacon a cause or sign of death, agents that "soften" are of particular significance in restoring health.

OED cites this passage for its sole illustration of *impriment* ("something that impresses or imprints," a definition that lacks the idea of "penetration" evident in the translation just cited); and its first illustration of *occludent*.

482.8–9   some superficial emperic discourse] Chambers, s.v. *Dogmatici* and *Empiric* helps clarify the point of Slop's comment and the several responses: "DOGMATISTS, a sect of ancient physicians . . . [who] laid down definitions, and divisions, reducing diseases to certain genera, those genera to species, and furnishing remedies for them all . . . . In which sense the *Dogmatists* stand contra-distinguished to Empirics . . . a name given by antiquity, to such physicians, as formed themselves rules, and methods, on their own practice, and experience; and not on any knowledge of natural causes, or the study of good authors . . . .

"Medicine was almost altogether in the hands of *empirics*, till the time of Hippocrates; who first introduced reason and the use of theory therein . . . .

"But the word *empiric* is now more odious than ever; being confounded with that of *charletan*, or *quack*, and applied to persons who practise physic at random, without a proper education, or understanding any thing of the principles of the art."

482.14—15   Come! chear up . . . you land] Cf. *Spectator* 582: "I have often admired a humorous Saying of *Diogenes*, who reading a dull Author to several of his Friends, when every one began to be tired, finding he was almost come to a blank Leaf at the end of it, cried, *Courage, Lads, I see Land*" (IV: 591). The anecdote is recorded, somewhat differently, by Diogenes Laertius, *Lives of Eminent Philosophers*, VI.38 (II: 40—41). Cf. *TS*, vol. VII, chap. 6 (584.14—25).

Sterne may also have had in mind the opening line of David Garrick's popular song "Heart of Oak": "Come cheer up, my lads, 'tis to glory we steer," first sung in 1759 and published the following year; see William Chappell, *Old English Popular Music* (New York: Jack Brussel, 1961), II: 189—90.

483.2   Four years in travelling . . . to *Malachi*] I.e., from learning the alphabet, which was always preceded by a cross in the horn-books, to reading the last book of the Old Testament. Cf. Locke, *Some Thoughts Concerning Education*, sec. 158, p. 261: "As for the *Bible*, which Children are usually imploy'd in, to exercise and improve their Talent *in Reading*, I think, the promiscuous reading of it through, by Chapters, as they lye in order, is so far from being of any Advantage to Children, either for the perfecting their *Reading*, or principling their Religion, that perhaps a worse could not be found. . . . I am apt to think, that this in some Men has been the very Reason, why they never had clear and distinct Thoughts of it all their Life time."

Locke describes the practice in his day of teaching writing *after* reading: "When he can read English well, it will be seasonable to enter him in *Writing:* And here the first thing should be taught him is, to *hold his Pen right;* and this he should be perfect in, before he should be suffered to put it to Paper" (p. 262). Sterne's "year and a half . . . to write his own name" seems less an exaggeration than we might have thought.

483.4   Seven long years and more τύπτω-ing] *Tupto*-ing. The Greek means "pounding, slogging away"; as Work notes (p. 403, n. 2), it was "formerly used as a paradigm of the Greek verb." Cf. Montaigne, I.24.152: "But it seems, poor *Cyrus* was whip'd for his Pains, as we are in our

Villages, for forgetting the first Aorist of τνπτῶ" (p. 152). In his next essay, the famous "Of the Education of Children," Montaigne laments in a manner similar to Sterne's the slowness of education: "half of our Age is embezzled this Way. We are kept four or five Years to learn Words only, and to tack them together into Clauses; as many more to make Exercises; and to divide a continued Discourse into so many Parts; and [an]other five Years at least to learn succinctly to mix and interweave them after a subtle and intricate Manner" (p. 185).

Cf. Locke, *Some Thoughts Concerning Education*, sec. 147, p. 254: "When I consider, what a-do is made about a little *Latin* and *Greek*, how many Years are spent in it, and what a noise and business it makes to no purpose, I can hardly forbear thinking, that the Parents of Children still live in fear of the School-master's Rod . . . . How else is it possible that a Child should be chain'd to the Oar, Seven, Eight, or Ten of the best Years of his Life, to get a Language or two . . . ."

483.6−7   the fine statue . . . marble block] Something of a commonplace; cf. *Spectator* 215: "If my Reader will give me leave to change the Allusion so soon upon him, I shall make use of the same Instance to illustrate the Force of Education, which *Aristotle* has brought to explain his Doctrine of Substantial Forms, when he tells us, that a Statue lies hid in a Block of Marble; and that the Art of the Statuary only clears away the superfluous Matter, and removes the Rubbish. The Figure is in the Stone, the Sculptor only finds it. What Sculpture is to a Block of Marble, Education is to an Human Soul" (II: 338). Bond suggests Diogenes Laertius, *Lives of Eminent Philosophers*, V.33 (I: 480−81), as a source and cites also Pope's *Dunciad*(B), IV.270: "And hew the Block off, and get out the Man." James Sutherland annotates this line with a Pope-Warburton note: "A notion of Aristotle, that there was originally in every block of marble, a Statue, which would appear on the removal of the superfluous parts." Sutherland adds: "This notion is usually credited to Michelangelo. I have failed to trace it in Aristotle" (p. 370).

483.9−16   Was not the great *Julius* . . . other world] Cf. Walker, *Of Education*, p. 111: "*Jul. Scagiler* [*sic*] began not to learn *Greek* till 40 years old, and then mastered it in a very few months . . . . *Pet. Damianus* learned not to read till Mans Estate . . . . *Baldus* entred so late upon the Law, that they told him he intended to be an Advocate in the other World."

Work, p. 403, nn. 3, 4, 5: "Julius Cæsar Scaliger (1484–1558) was a distinguished Italian humanist, philosopher, and scientist . . . . St. Pietro Damiani (c. 1007–1072), cardinal and reformer, entered a religious life after a neglected youth spent in privation and ignorance . . . . Petrus Baldus [see above, n. to 391.28] was an eminent Italian jurist . . . . But the story that he began to study law at the age of forty . . . is apocryphal; actually, he was admitted to the degree of Doctor of Civil Law at the early age of seventeen." Walker, it is worth noting, does not indicate that Damianus was Bishop of Ostia. Sterne may have found this information in Bayle or a similar dictionary; the phrase "as all the world knows" suggests the name was unfamiliar to him and required some "index-learning."

See also Adrien Baillet, *Des enfans célèbres* (Paris, 1722), where a similar discussion takes place in the concluding section, entitled "*EXEMPLES CONTRAIRES tirés des Etudes tardives*" ("*Contrasting examples taken from those who entered studies late*"), pp. 198ff. Of Baldus, Baillet writes (p. 202): "BALDE . . . donna lieu à son Maître Bartole & à ses Camarades de le railler sur ses progrès de tortuë, & de lui dire, qu'il *sauroit quelque chose dans cent ans, & qu'il pourroit bien être Avocat en l'autre siécle*" ("BALDE caused his Master Bartole and his comrades to mock his turtle pace and to tell him that he *would know something in a hundred years and that in another century he could well be an advocate*"). See also above, n. to 337.25–338.4.

And Julius Cæsar Scaliger, Baillet writes, "fut aussi fort long-tems dans le monde sans se déterminer à suivre la Profession des Lettres . . . . Il avoit pour lors 35. ans, & l'année suivante il se mit à l'étude du Grec, dont il n'avoit pas connu une seule lettre jusqu'alors. On peut dire néanmoins avec l'Auteur de sa Vie, que le véritable commencement de ses Etudes ne doit se prendre que du tems qu'il se défit de sa Charge de Capitaine, c'est-à-dire après l'âge de 40. ans" ("[he] had been such a very long time in the world without deciding to pursue the profession of letters . . . . He had reached 35 years, and the following year he set out to study Greek, of which up to then he knew not a single letter. One can nonetheless say with the author of his *Life*, that the true beginning of his studies should only have taken place when he gave up his office as captain, that is to say, after the age of 40"), pp. 206–8.

483.17–20 when *Eudamidas . . . use of it?*] Plutarch tells the story in his *Moralia* ("Sayings of Spartans"): "Eudamidas [King of Sparta, fl. c. 330 B.C.], the son of Archidamas [King of Sparta, c. 361–338 B.C.] . . . seeing Xenocrates in the Academy, already well on in years, discussing philosophy with his acquaintances, inquired who the old man was. Somebody said that he was a wise man and one of the seekers after virtue. 'And when will he use it,' said Eudamidas, 'if he is only now seeking for it?'" (III: 319–21).

Work, p. 404, n. 6: "Xenocrates (396–314 [B.C.]) was an eminent Greek philosopher and head of the Platonic Academy at Athens."

484.5–6 a North west passage to the intellectual world] "A passage for vessels along the north coast of America, formerly thought of as a possible channel for navigation between the Atlantic and the Pacific" (*OED*, which records figurative usage from 1670). Cf. Tom Brown, *Works* (1760), III: 87 ("Amusements Serious and Comical, X: *The Philosophical or* Virtuosi *Country*"): "Those that set up for finding the north-west passage into the land of *Philosophy*, would with all their hearts, if it were possible, follow these two guides [antiquity and novelty] all at once . . . ."

484.11ff. The whole entirely depends, etc.] The theory of auxiliary verbs outlined in this chapter and the next parodies Obadiah Walker's reliance upon "common-places" as a pedagogic instrument, the use of which he explains at interminable length in *Of Education*, chap. 11. The brilliance of Sterne's parody is fully evident only when Walker's chapter is read in its entirety. Here we merely cite those passages from Walker most closely paralleled by Sterne.

Walker begins by defending "common-places" in a sentence Sterne makes use of in two separate passages: "it must be acknowledged, *that* all the Ancients; *Aristotle, Cicero*, &c. made great account of this, *that* though some have great Parts, that they can without Art perform the Effects of Art, yet all Fields have not a River or a Spring in them, but some require the diligence of a Bucket [cf. *TS*, 484.8–10]; *that* those (whom they called *Sophistæ*) who governed Learning in their days, made Profession, out of these places, to teach to discourse upon any subject *pro & con*, and to say all that could be spoken concerning it: *that* many of late days have attained to Plausibility in Discourse meerly by *Lullie*'s Art, which is but a few of those *Common-places* . . ." (pp. 138–39).

Walker then makes the point that his commonplaces "are not so profit-able to them, who already understand Sciences, as to those who are igno-rant," and praises Matteo Pellegrini, "of whose *Fonti del' ingegno* I have made much use in this Chapter"; Pellegrini's student, we are told, by the use of commonplaces "arrived to such a perfection, as to be able in a short time to write, without defacing one word, many Pages concerning any the meanest Subject proposed to him; to the great admiration of as many as knew him" (p. 140). Sterne's citation of *"Lullius"* (Raymond Lull, c. 1232–1315, a Spanish theologian and philosopher and author of the Lullian method, a mechanical learning aid similar to Pellegrini's) and *"Pelegrini"* (Matteo Pellegrini, 1595–1652, an Italian humanist whose system of predication in *I Fonti dell' ingegno ridotti ad arte* [1650] did indeed form the basis of Walker's chapter) is almost surely derived from Walker, rather than from a direct reading of either.

Sterne's next paragraph is also partially derived from Walker: "In short, the height of the Invention a *single Word* is capable of, is an high *Metaphor, Catachresis,* or *Hyperbole*" (p. 141).

Walker now runs through the use of the commonplaces to discuss two words, *"Bee"* and *"Amber"*; his commonplaces are the traditional predica-ments or categories of Aristotle: substance, quantity, quality, relation, ac-tion and passivity, place and situation, motion, time, and habit or posses-sion. (See below, n. to 493.1.) He then is ready to join words into propositions or sentences, consisting of subject, copula, and predicate; Sterne begins to copy where Walker explains the copula: "The *Copula;* for so we will at present call those *Verbs Auxiliary,* by some of which all Ques-tions are made, and by which the *Predicates,* whether Verb or Noun, are joined to the Subject. These are, *am, was,* with their divers Cases and Persons, *have, had: do, did: make, made: suffer: shall, should: will, would: may, might: can, could: owe, ought: useth or is wont.* These again vary Ques-tions by the *Tenses* or times; *present, past,* or *future;* and both these a long or short while: such are these Questions, *Is it? was it? hath it been always? lately, or a long time ago? will it be? would it be? may it be? might it be?* &c. *ought it* or *behoveth it to be? useth it;* or *is it wont to be?* Again, all these are either *affirmative* or *negative. Is it not? was it not? hath it not been? They are* also varied with *If,* as, *If it be, If it were* or *were not,* what would follow? *If Alexander* had fought with *Romans? If* the *Sun* go out of the *Zodiack?*" (pp.

147–48). It is worth noting that Sterne's only addition is "and conjugated with the verb *see*," which prepares for the end of his chapter. Why he changed Alexander and the Romans to the French and English cannot be finally ascertained, though the change does demonstrate Sterne's patriotism; England was at war with France during 1761 when he was writing vol. V.

Sterne's next sentences (486.15ff.) return to Walker's introductory comments on the use of commonplaces: "*It is* also *to be noted*, that some *Subjects* are *barren* . . . . and then *these Topicks* will be useful unto them, tho perhaps not so much as to ordinary Wits; who must read, and observe much, that they may store up a Magazin of Conceptions; and practise much also, that they may readily and easily by their *Questions* pump out what is to serve their occasions" (pp. 140–41).

Walker chooses to illustrate his method with "a Battel," which Sterne must necessarily avoid if the subject is to be a "barren" one for Trim; what the white bear signifies, if anything, has escaped us. The questions are borrowed from Walker: "*v.g.* a Battel. Have I ever seen it? At least painted? Or described? Might I have seen it? Where? How long ago? How often? Had I seen it, what would it have wrought in me? I would I had seen it, for how can I imagine it? What Notion have I of it? Hath my Friend, or Stranger or Acquaintance seen it? Had he seen it, or not seen it, what would have followed? Hath he dreamed of it?" (p. 149).

484.13 Had *Yorick* trod upon *Virgil*'s snake] Almost certainly an allusion to book II of the *Aeneid* rather than to the far more obscure *Culex* cited by Work (p. 404, n. 8). Virgil uses a simile to suggest how the Greek, Androgeos, reacted when he discovered he was in the midst of Trojans: "As when some Peasant in a bushy Brake, / Has with unwary Footing press'd a Snake; / He starts aside, astonish'd, when he spies / His rising Crest, blue Neck, and rowling Eyes; / So from our Arms, surpriz'd *Androgeos* flies" (trans. John Dryden, Kinsley ed. [Oxford, 1958], III: 1105, lines 510–14).

But see also Eclogue III, lines 144–45: "Ye Boys, who pluck the Flow'rs, and spoil the Spring, / Beware the secret Snake, that shoots a sting" (trans. Dryden, Kinsley ed., II: 886).

484.16 republick of letters] See above, n. to 66.2.

484.21–22 the elder *Pelegrini*] Walker makes no mention of there being an "elder" or "younger" Pellegrini (see above, n. to 484.11ff.), nor have we been able to discover what or whom Sterne had in mind. Perhaps the reference to "Pelegrini" in Walker sent Sterne to a biographical dictionary such as Moréri, where the only entry is for Camillus Pelegrini (1598–1664), who is spoken of as "the younger" while his uncle, another Camillus, was "the elder." Sterne may have decided that one Pellegrini family deserved another; of such conjecturing, however, there is no end.

485.5–6   for which . . . not the better] Walter's dislike of metaphor probably derives from Locke; see above, nn. to 227.14–18, 244.4–5.

485.12   versability] *OED* cites this passage as its last illustration, with the definition "aptness or readiness to be changed or turned (round)." Sterne may well have found the word in that very section of Walker from which he borrows the theory of auxiliary verbs. Walker's definition, however, is different: Wit, he says, consists of "1. *Perspicacity*, which is the Consideration of all, even the minutest, Circumstances: and, 2. *Versabiliy* [*sic*], or speedy comparing them together . . ." (p. 127). Cf. p. 139, where he speaks of the "Diligence and Versability of the Understanding . . . ."

485.16–23   For my own part . . . different things.] See t.n. to 485.19–23, vol. II, p. 857, in this edition. In addition to Tindal's report that the "*Danes* [were] to the left" (III: 147), perhaps Sterne had in mind the observation that King William exposed "himself amidst the greatest dangers, which the Prince of *Denmark* shared all along with him" (p. 148). It might also be noted that in one particular action, Tindal observes, "The *French* Protestants, the *Dutch*, and the *Danes* behaved themselves very gallantly in their respective posts; and the whole action, which lasted from three till seven, was very brisk every where, and cost the besiegers six hundred men killed upon the spot, and as many mortally wounded" (p. 149).

NOTES TO VOLUME VI

491.9−14 Did you think . . . set up together!] The tradition of portraying literary critics as asses is a hoary one, if we are to believe Swift in *Tale of a Tub*, "A Digression Concerning Criticks," pp. 98ff. See also *Don Quixote*, II.III.25 (III: 220−30), the braying contest of the aldermen; and Pope, *Dunciad*(B), II.247ff.

492.6 G-sol-re-ut] Cf. Rabelais, II.31.240−41: "And the poor devil fell to crying. That is too low, said Panurge; then took him by the ear, saying, Sing higher in ge, sol, re, ut"; and IV.19.164−65: "Alas! we are now above g sol re ut. I sink, I sink, hah my father, my uncle, my all."

"G-sol-re-ut" is the way in which the fifth note of the diatonic scale of C major was designated in the hexachord system of notation invented by the eleventh-century monk Guido of Arezzo. It was the highest G available to medieval musicians and seems to have come to signify a particularly shrill sound (in the key of G major), despite the abandonment of the system by the end of the sixteenth century.

493.1 from the bare use of the ten predicaments)] Cf. Chambers, s.v. *Category:* "The ancients, after Aristotle, generally make ten *categories* [Latin *predicaments*]: under the first, all substances are comprised; and all accidents under the nine last; *viz.* quantity, quality, relation, action, passion, time, place, situation, and habit . . . . These ten *Categories* of *Aristotle*, which logicians make such mysteries of, are now almost out of doors; and, in effect, are of little use: the less, as being things purely arbitrary, without any foundation, but in the imagination of a man, who had no authority to prescribe laws for ranging the objects of other peoples ideas."

396

See also Warburton, "Introduction," *Julian: or a Discourse Concerning the Earthquake* (1750), in *Works*, ed. Richard Hurd (London, 1811), VIII: xiii–xiv: "Aristotle's invention of the *Categories* was a surprising effort of human wit. But, in practice, *logic* is more a *trick* than a *science*, formed rather to amuse than to instruct. And, in some sort, we may apply to the *art of syllogism* what a man of wit [Butler] has observed of *rhetoric*, that it only tells us how to *name* those tools, which nature had before put into our hands, and habit taught the use of."

Insofar as Obadiah Walker's theory in *Of Education*, 6th ed. (1699), is based in part on the categories (see above, n. to 484.11ff.), Sterne has been ridiculing them throughout this section. The Scriblerians had also satirized the use of the categories in their chapter titled "Rhetoric, Logic, Metaphysics" (*Memoirs of Martinus Scriblerus*, chap. 7, p. 120): "Mark (quoth Cornelius) how the fellow runs through the prædicaments. Men, *Substantia;* two, *quantitas;* fair and black, *qualitas;* Sergeant and Butcher, *relatio;* wounded the other, *actio & passio;* fighting, *situs;* Stage, *ubi;* two o'Clock, *quando;* blue and red Breeches, *habitus.*"

493.2ff.   That the famous *Vicent Quirino*, etc.] Although Sterne raided Adrien Baillet's *Des enfans célèbres* (Paris, 1722) for many of the details in this survey of prodigies (see above, nn. to 337.25–338.4 and 483.9–16), the basic idea almost certainly came from Walker's *Of Education*. In a discussion of precocious wit, Walker catalogues those who "begun betimes, have proved admirable, and lasted a long while" (p. 102). Among others, he cites "*Torquato Tasso* [who] spoke plain at Six Months old; at Three Years went to School; at Seven he understood Latin and Greek, and made Verses; before Twelve he finished his Course of Rhetorick, Poetry, Logick, and Ethicks; at Seventeen he received his Degree in Philosophy, Laws, and Divinity . . . . *Jo. Picus*, Earl of *Mirandula*, outwent his Teachers, nor could they propose any thing to him, which he did not immediately apprehend; and the 900 *Conclusions*, which he proposed to defend against all Opposers, under Twenty Years of Age, shew what he was . . . . *Jos. Scaliger* saith of himself, that all the time he lived with his Father in his Youth, he every Day *Declamed* [*sic*], and before 17 Years old made his Tragedy *Oedipus* . . . . *Grotius* at 8 Years old made Verses, and performed his publick Exercises in Philosophy; before 15. he put forth his Comment upon *Martianus Capella*. At 16. he pleaded Causes. At 17 he put forth his Comment upon *Aratus*. *Lipsius* writ his Books *Variarum Lectionum* at 18 Years old. . . . *Alph*. *Tostatus* learned all the Liberal Sciences without being taught . . . yet was he . . . Professor of Philosophy, Divinity, and Law in the University of *Salamanca*" (pp. 102–4). Walker also mentions "one *Creighton*, a Scottishman, who at Twenty One Years old . . . understood twelve Languages . . ." (pp. 105–6).

Baillet, p. 19, cites Cardinal Pietro Bembo's account of his friend Vicenzo Quirino as follows: "LE Cardinal Bembe nous a fait connoître un autre de ses Amis nommé QUIRINUS, qui n'étant encore qu'un Enfant, proposa & soutint publiquement quatre mille cinq cens Théses dans la Ville de Rome: & il prétend, qu'il ne se trouva pas un Philosophe, de quelque Secte qu'il fut, qui ne se sentit satisfait de ses réponses, & qui ne s'en retournât convaincu, que Quirinus dans un si bas âge possédoit parfaitement la Philosophie dans toute l'étenduë de ses espéces & de ses Sectes différentes" ("Cardinal Bembo informed us of another of his friends named Quirinus, who, while still but a child, proposed and defended four thousand, five hundred theses in the city of Rome; and he claims that he found not a single philosopher, to whatever school he belonged, who was not satisfied with Quirinus's responses, and who did not return convinced that despite his youth, Quirinus had perfectly mastered philosophy throughout its branches and diverse schools").

Work, p. 409, n. 2: "Vincenzo Quirino (1479–c. 1514), a noble Venetian humanist, philosopher, and diplomat, of whose precocity, as related by his friend Cardinal Pietro Bembo (1470–1547), Italian scholar and historian of Venice, in his *De Culice Virgilii*, Sterne found an account in Baillet . . ."; and p. 410, n. 3: "Alfonso Tostado (c. 1400–1455) was an eminent Spanish theologian and author of many works and commentaries who by the age of twenty-two had received his doctorate and was said to have mastered the whole circle of human knowledge."

493.13–28   What shall we say . . . said *Yorick*] For Piereskius and Stevinus, see 134.15ff. and n. above. Sterne probably found the present anecdote in Baillet, p. 109: "A l'âge de sept ans le petit de Peiresc, qui dans tout le cours de sa vie ne s'est jamais donné le moindre air de suffisance ou de présomption, se crut assés savant, assés prudent, & assés sage, pour prendre la direction d'un frere puisné qu'il avoit, & qui s'est fait connoître

depuis sous le nom du Sieur de Valavès. Il demanda à son Pere la conduite
de ce Frere qui n'avoit que deux ans moins que lui. Il ne prétendoit pas
seulement présider à ses études; mais encore veiller sur ses mœurs &
régler ses actions. Je ne puis pas vous dire comment son Pere lui accorda sa
demande; si ce fut sérieusement ou non: mais on prétend qu'il s'acquitta si
dignement de cette commission, que depuis ce temps-là il tint lieu de
Précepteur & de Pere à son Cadet" ("At the age of seven, Peiresc's son,
who throughout his life never showed the slightest arrogance or presumption, felt that his learning, prudence, and wisdom were sufficient to un-
dertake the instruction of a younger brother, who has since become well
known as the Sieur de Valavès. He asked his father to put him in charge of
this brother, who was but two years younger than he himself. Not only did
he ask to preside over his studies but he even wanted to watch over his
morals and to regulate his actions. I cannot say how his father granted his
request, whether seriously or not, but it is claimed that he carried out his
mission with such diligence that after that time he was like a tutor and a
father to his younger brother").

494.1–2   *Grotius . . . Cordouè*] Baillet, *Des enfans célèbres,* has entries on each
of these learned figures, although the last, Ferdinand de Cordouè, is not
listed in the table of contents but rather is discussed in a section entitled
"L'ANONYME de l'an 1445," where a footnote identifies him as the anonymous personage. Baillet, p. 43, provides the information on this Spanish
theologian that Sterne sets down in lines 5–8, except for the location in
Venice, which we are unable to explain: "On auroit eu quelque raison de le
soupçonner d'être quelque chose de plus qu'un homme, s'il eut été clair
qu'il savoit *parfaitement tous les Arts & toutes les Sciences à vingt ans.* Mais
ceux qui en portoient ce jugement ne faisoient pas grand honneur à leur
raison, lorsqu'ils concluoient de-là qu'il falloit que ce jeune homme fût
l'Antechrist, & qu'il n'eût point eu d'autre pere que le Diable" ("One might
have had some reason to suspect that he was something more than a man if
it had been clear that he knew *perfectly well all the arts and all the sciences at
twenty years of age.* But those who supported that judgment of him did no
great honor to their cause, since they concluded from thence that the young
man must necessarily have been *the Antichrist and that he had been born of no
other father than the Devil*").

Work, p. 410, n. 5, provides information on all these celebrities, gathered from the pages of Baillet and Walker: "Hugo Grotius (1583–1645), the Dutch statesman, jurist, theologian, and poet, founder of the science of international law, wrote good Latin verses at nine, entered the university at twelve, at fifteen edited the encyclopædic work of Martianus Capella [see above, n. to 493.2ff.], and at sixteen took the degree of doctor of law and entered on practice as an advocate. Schoppe [see above, n. to 60.4–10] was renowned for his youthful genius and learning . . . . Both Daniel Heinsius (1580–1655) and his son Nikolaes (1620–1681), Dutch classical philologists, were remarkable for their youthful attainments; this reference is probably to the father . . . who at the age of ten was renowned for a Latin elegy, and at fourteen entered the university of Leyden where at twenty he began to explicate the classics and at twenty-five he held the chair of history and politics. Angelo Poliziano [see above, n. to 466.6–19] at the age of thirteen circulated Latin letters, at sixteen translated four books of the *Iliad* into Latin hexameters, at seventeen sent forth essays in Greek versification, and at eighteen published an edition of Catullus. Blaise Pascal (1623–1662), the French religious philosopher and mathematician . . . achieved fame at the age of seventeen with his treatise on conic sections. Joseph Justus Scaliger (1540–1609), the son of Julius Cæsar Scaliger [for whom, see above, n. to 483.9–16], was famous for his precocity in Latin and Greek. Ferdinand of Cordova (1422–c. 1480), a Spanish theologian, physician, and scholar, was celebrated at an early age for his prodigious memory and wisdom."

494.3   *substantial forms*] Like the ten predicaments (see above, n. to 493.1), this was another exploded Aristotelian concept. Cf. *Memoirs of Martinus Scriblerus*, p. 124: "This brings into my mind a Project to banish Metaphysicks out of Spain, which it was suppos'd might be effectuated by this method: That nobody should use any Compound or Decompound of the Substantial Verbs but as they are read in the common conjugations; for every body will allow, that if you debar a Metaphysician from *ens, essentia, entitas, subsistentia,* &c. there is an end of him.

"Crambe regretted extremely, that *Substantial Forms*, a race of harmless beings which had lasted for many years, and afforded a comfortable subsistance to many poor Philosophers, should be now hunted down like so many Wolves, without the possibility of a retreat. He consider'd that it had gone much harder with them than with *Essences*, which had retir'd from the *Schools* into the *Apothecaries Shops* . . . . He thought there should be a retreat for poor *substantial Forms*, amongst the Gentlemen-ushers at court; and that there were indeed *substantial forms*, such as *forms of Prayer*, and *forms of Government*, without which, the things themselves could never long subsist."

Kerby-Miller notes that "no single part of Scholastic metaphysics was more sharply attacked in the seventeenth century than the doctrine of substantial forms; from Bacon to Locke (to remain within the boundaries of the century) condemnations of this doctrine increased steadily. Indeed, much of the complaint against the Schoolmen for their 'barbarous terms,' 'unintelligible distinctions,' 'mysterious jargon,' and so on referred to Scholastic disputes over the character and attributes of substantial forms" (p. 260). Locke's attack is in *ECHU*, III.6.10: "Those therefore who have been taught, that the several *Species* of Substances had their distinct internal *substantial Forms*; and that it was those *Forms*, which made the distinction of Substances into their true *Species* and *Genera*, were led yet farther out of the way, by having their Minds set upon fruitless Enquiries after *substantial Forms*, wholly unintelligible, and whereof we have scarce so much as any obscure, or confused Conception in general" (p. 445).

A very fine essay on the concept of substantial forms and its demise in the seventeenth and eighteenth centuries is provided in chap. 3 of Lester S. King's *The Philosophy of Medicine: The Early Eighteenth Century* (Cambridge: Harvard University Press, 1978), pp. 41–63.

494.11–12 commentaries upon *Servius* and *Martianus Capella*] From Walker (see above, n. to 493.2ff.) Sterne might have learned of Grotius's commentary on Martianus Capella; Baillet also makes note of it (*Des enfans célèbres*, pp. 210–12). The commentary on Servius was probably the one written by Philippe Beroaldi (1453–1505), as recorded in Baillet, p. 53: "qu'il n'étoit encore qu'un enfant fort tendre lorsqu'il fit une Critique des Commentaires de Servius sur Virgile, & qu'il censura *très-judicieusement* les fautes de cet Auteur . . ." ("that he was still only a very young child when he made a Critique of the Commentaries of Servius on Virgil, and criticized *very judiciously* the faults of that author . . .").

Work, p. 411, n. 6: "Marius Servius Honoratus (fl. 400 A.D.) was a Roman grammarian and writer of a commentary on Virgil which was itself the subject of numerous commentaries. Martianus Capella (fl. 5th C.) was a Latin writer whose *De Nuptiis Philologiæ et Mercurii et de Septem Artibus Liberalibus*, an encyclopædia of the liberal culture of his time, was highly reputed and frequently commented upon during the Middle Ages." Beroaldi was Professor of Letters at the University of Bologna.

494.13–16 But you forget . . . no more about it.] Sterne's note quotes part of Baillet's entry on Lipsius (*Des enfans célèbres*, pp. 97–101), but the opening section is perhaps equally relevant: "LES flateurs & les idolatres de JUSTE LIPSE ont eu tant d'envie de rendre son Enfance toute miraculeuse, que non contens d'avoir fait précéder sa naissance de prodiges servant de présage pour ce qu'il devoit faire un jour, ils ont encore osé avancer, qu'il s'étoit rendu Auteur & Ecrivain dès le premier jour de sa vie. Voilà deux miracles dont la solidité devroit être bien cautionnée. Le premier ne nous regarde pas, étant arrivé la nuit de devant sa naissance; & nous laissons volontiers aux Physiciens le soin d'en faire voir l'impertinence. Pour le second . . ." ("The flatterers and idolaters of Justus Lipsius have been so eager to make his childhood perfectly miraculous that, not content with having his birth preceded by omens that presaged what he was one day to become, they have even dared claim that he became a writer and author from the very day of his birth. There you have two miracles that must be approached with circumspection. The first does not concern us, happening as it did before his birth; we are happy to let the Physicians show up its impertinence. As for the second . . .").

Sterne's note picks up at this point; Work supplies a translation: "We should have some interest, says Baillet, in showing that there is nothing ridiculous, if it was true, at least in the enigmatic sense which Nicius Erythræus has attempted to give it. This author says that to understand how Lipsius may have composed a work the first day of his life it is necessary to imagine that the first day is not that of his birth in the flesh, but that on which he commenced to use his reason; he maintains that it was at the age of nine years, and he wishes to persuade us that it was at that age that Lipsius wrote a poem.——The attempt is ingenious, etc. etc." (p. 411, n. *). The final sentence, rendered only partially by Sterne, continues: "& fort commode pour ceux qui auront à faire les éloges des Savans, & qui voudront prouver que leurs Héros auront été Auteurs des le premier jour de leur vie, quand ils n'auroient en l'usage de la raison qu'à trente ans. On peut dire à l'avantage de Lipse, que Nicius Erythræus ne s'est trompé que de trois ans, & que si le Poëme dont il s'agit est le premier essai ou le premier fruit de la raison de Lipse, ce grand Homme n'a point eu l'usage de la raison avant l'âge de douze ans" ("and very convenient for those who will have to make eulogies on the learned and who will want to prove that their heroes had been authors from the first day of their life, when they would not have had the use of reason before the age of thirty. One could claim for Lipsius that Nicius Erythræus only erred by three years and if the poem in question is the first attempt or the first evidence of reason on the part of Lipsius, this great man had not demonstrated his use of reason before the age of twelve") (Baillet, p. 101).

Work, p. 411, n. 7: "Justus Lipsius (1547–1606), a Flemish philologist and critic."

495.5   then, I think I know you, madam] Sherbo, *Studies*, p. 133, points to the similarity between this dialogue and that of Falstaff and the Hostess in *1 Henry IV* (III.iii.60–66; see also lines 118–30): "*Fal.* . . . I'll be sworn my pocket was pick'd. Go to, you are a woman, go. *Host.* Who, I? No, I defy thee. God's light, I was never call'd so in mine own house before. *Fal.* Go to, I know you well enough. *Host.* No, Sir John, you do not know me, Sir John. I know you, Sir John . . . ."

495.27–496.2   I never was . . . Is it? cried *Slop*] An allusion, of course, to the damage inflicted upon the mucous membranes of the nose and mouth by the use of mercury in the treatment of venereal disease; along with the cuckold's horns, this is probably the most overworked subject in the off-color repertory of the eighteenth century.

496.6–8   as the cataplasm . . . fomentation for me] There appears to be no significant difference between a cataplasm and a fomentation, both being the application of a warming, medicinal substance to the injured part.

496.13–497.3   *Marcus Antoninus* provided . . . lives long.] Sterne would seem to have borrowed the anecdote from Walker, *Of Education*, pp. 47–48: "*M. Aurelius* provided Fourteen of the most approved Masters of the whole Empire (the learned *Julius Pollux* being one) to educate his Son *Commodus;* and within a while cashiered Five of them, because he had observed some *Levities* in their Carriage. Yet could not the other Nine rectify the froward and barbarous Humour, perhaps suck't from, and encouraged afterward, by his Mother, at the time of his Conception in love with a Gladiator."

Work, p. 413, n. 1: "Although Marcus Aurelius Antoninus (121–180), Roman emperor and Stoic philosopher, carefully educated his son, Commodus (161–192) displayed as emperor a cruel and detestable character."

Joseph R. Jones, "Two Notes on Sterne: Spanish Sources. The Hinde Tradition," *RLC* 46 (1972): 441, suggests that Sterne's source was Antonio de Guevara's *Golden Book of Marcus Aurelius* (expanded as the *Dial of Princes*); Walker seems the far more likely source.

497.4–10   Now as I . . . to himself.] Although Sterne is about to launch into a parody of Walker (see n. to 497.11ff. below), he may also have in mind the serious and lengthy discussion of the role of a tutor in Locke's *Some Thoughts Concerning Education*, sec. 88–94; e.g.: "In all the whole Business of Education, there is nothing like to be less hearkn'd to, or harder to be well observed, than what I am now going to say; and that is, that Children should from their first beginning to talk, have some *Discreet*, *Sober*, nay, *Wise* Person about, whose Care it should be to Fashion them aright, and keep them from all ill, especially the infection of bad Company. I think this Province requires great *Sobriety, Temperance, Tenderness, Diligence*, and *Discretion* . . ." (p. 187); and again: "To form a young Gentleman as he should be, 'tis fit his *Governour* should himself be well bred, understand the Ways of Carriage, and Measures of Civility in all the Variety of Persons, Times and Places; and keep his Pupil, as much as his Age requires, constantly to the Observation of them" (p. 190).

497.11ff.   There is, continued my father, etc.] Walter's description of the proper characteristics of a tutor is based on Obadiah Walker's lengthy discussion of civility, *Of Education*, pp. 220–22, which ends where Walter begins: "THERE is a certain *mien* and *motion of the Body*, and its parts, both in acting and speaking, which is very graceful and pleasing. *Greg. Nazianz.* foretold what a one *Julian* (afterwards called the *Apostate*) would prove, when he saw his hasty, discomposed, and unseemly Gestures. S. *Ambrose* discarded a Clerk, because of an undecent motion of his Head, which he said went like a Flail."

498.1   neither*] For "*Pellegrina*," see above, n. to 484.11ff. Sterne's often conscious—and comic—effort to cover his tracks is apparent in this cita-

tion, since Pellegrini has nothing at all to do with this listing of characteristics, while Walker (where Sterne found Pellegrini cited) is the actual
source of much of it.

498.10−11   nor (according to *Erasmus*) . . . making water] In the first of his
Familiar Colloquies (trans. N. Bailey, 2d ed. [1733], p. 2), Erasmus
writes: "It is a piece of Civility to salute those that come in your way; either
such as come to us, or those that we go to speak with. And in like manner
such as are about any sort of Work, either at Supper, or that yawn, or
hiccop, or sneeze, or cough. But it is the Part of a Man that is civil even to
an Extreme, to salute one that belches, or breaks Wind backward. But he
is uncivilly civil that salutes one that is making Water, or easing Nature."

498.14−21   I will have him . . . bountiful, and brave?] Cf. Walker's catalogue of the "good dispositions" of men, whom he divides into several
types (*Of Education*, pp. 80−81): "1. Subtile, sharp, piercing, ready, vig-
ilant, attentive to Business, sagacious. 2. Argute, acute, quick in giving
Answers and Repartees, resolving Doubts and Speculative Questions, in-
ventive. 3. Facetious, merry, cheerful, gay, jovial . . . . 4. Wise, prudent, judicious . . . . 5. Free, noble, generous, bountiful, meek, peaceable, quiet, moderate, magnificent. 6. Bold, resolute . . . brave, warlike,
valiant . . . ." Walter's only original contribution, significantly, is
"learned," while the other characteristics he cites are all to be found in the
first four categories; Toby's four offerings are all found in nos. 5 and 6.
Yorick's "moderate" is found in no. 5, but his "humble" and "gentle tem-
pered" and "good" are his own contributions. Walker at this point is not
describing the attributes of the tutor, but the dispositions to be found in the
student (and in all men).

499.4   without turning back to the place] Trim is about to tell the story of Le
Fever to the kitchen circle, when Tristram remembers his mother standing outside the parlour door; see pp. 437−38.

499.8   *The Story of* LE FEVER] Cash, *Early and Middle Years*, pp. 20−21,
suggests a possible namesake for Le Fever from Sterne's childhood: "During the year in Dublin barracks [1721−22], Sterne said, 'I learned to
write, &c.' Possibly John Vincicombe, the regimental chaplain, gave Laurence his first lessons. There is another, more interesting possibility: that
his first teacher was named Lefever . . . . Richard Griffith, a minor Irish
writer who spent some time with Sterne during the autumn of 1767, said

that Sterne told him as much. Sterne added, said Griffith—though the words could hardly be Sterne's—that 'it was he who imbued my soul with humanity, benevolence, and charity'. The account is so patently improbable that Sterne's previous biographers have understandably ignored it. The army lists, however, throw the matter into a new light: they record a Lieutenant Rowland Lefever in Chudleigh's regiment. True, the first listing is for 1724, a few months after Laurence was sent to school in England, but that does not necessarily indicate that Laurence could not have known him. The record was made *after* the lieutenant joined the regiment. . . . There is also a possibility that two men, a father and son, are represented in the name of Rowland Lefever, which continues on the lists for forty years—an extremely long service for one man."

In vol. IX (739.23 and 746.11) Sterne changes the spelling to Le Fevre, which became the preferred spelling in several nineteenth-century editions.

499.9–13 of that year . . . in town] Dendermond fell to Marlborough in early September 1706. Ronald Beck argues in "The Date of Walter Shandy's Arrival," *AN&Q* 8 (1970): 152–53, that this would mean the Shandys did not move into the country until 1713, the year of the Treaty of Utrecht; he questions whether that can be accurate in the face of Walter's familiarity with the widow's designs and his resolution "for at least ten years" to oil the door hinge (239.1–2). Beck seems to have forgotten that a country house might be used intermittently while maintaining a London residence, and that Walter perhaps settles in the country for the last time in 1713 rather than for the first time; it is true, however, that when Toby moves into the country—in 1700 or 1701—Shandy Hall is unfurnished (664.10–11). Cf. above, n. to 103.1–2.

500.5–6 Ask my pen . . . not it.] Sterne uses this phrase in a letter written in 1767: "Now, I take heav'n to witness, after all this *badinage* my heart is innocent—and the sporting of my pen is equal, just equal, to what I did in my boyish days, when I got astride of a stick, and gallop'd away—The truth is this—that my pen governs me—not me my pen" (*Letters*, p. 394).

500.16–17 If I could neither . . . steal it] Not recorded in Tilley or *ODEP*, but Stevenson, p. 148, cites Chaucer's "Man of Law's Tale," lines 104–5:

"Maugree thyn heed, thou most for indigence / Or stele, or begge, or
borwe thy despence!"

501.15ff.   My uncle *Toby* laid down his knife, etc.] Sterne's sermon "Philantropy [*sic*] Recommended" (I.3.55–56) may provide a useful gloss to
Toby's instant responsiveness to the landlord's account of Le Fever: "in
such calamities as a man has fallen into through mere misfortune, to be
charged upon no fault or indiscretion of himself, there is something then
so truly interesting, that at the first sight we generally make them our own,
not altogether from a reflection that they might have been or may be so, but
oftener from a certain generosity and tenderness of nature which disposes
us for compassion, abstracted from all considerations of self. So that without any observable act of the will, we suffer with the unfortunate, and feel
a weight upon our spirits we know not why, on seeing the most common
instances of their distress. But where the spectacle is uncommonly tragical,
and complicated with many circumstances of misery, the mind is then
taken captive at once, and, *were* it inclined to it, has no power to make
resistance, but surrenders itself to all the tender emotions of pity and deep
concern. So that when one considers this friendly part of our nature without looking farther, one would think it impossible for man to look upon
misery, without finding himself in some measure attached to the interest of
him who suffers it."

502.8   what with the weather] In his *Memoirs of the Most Remarkable Military
Transactions from the Year 1683, to 1718* (1747), pp. 33–34, Robert
Parker describes "a narrow escape of my life, a stone which had been
thrown from the top of the castle [at the siege of Athlone in Ireland in
1691] as I passed under it, fell on my shoulder; the effects of which I feel to
this day, on every change of weather." In view of Trim's subsequent
"failure" to go beyond his orders (510.4–7), the moral that Parker draws
from his injury seems apropos: "This indeed I deserved for being so foolhardy, as to put myself on this command when it was not my turn; but it
was a warning to me ever after. It is an old maxim in war, that he who goes as
far as he is commanded is a good man, but he that goes farther is a fool."
    Parker, we might note, was also wounded at Namur, by a shot in his
right shoulder (p. 56).

502.9   give your honour your death] I.e., "your death of cold," an equivalent for the colloquial "catch one's death (of cold)"; Sterne uses it again, 528.12: "One must not give him his death, however . . . ."

502.23–24   whether it was not . . . a crooked one] Cf. William Horneck, trans., *Remarks on the Modern Fortification* (1738), p. 36: "The streight Curtain has always been preferred to the different Designs which have ever yet been proposed, of which some have diminished the Expence, and (at the same time) the Strength of the Place; others have somewhat augmented the Strength, but greatly diminished from its Area."

504.6   death-watch] Cf. Sir Thomas Browne, *Pseudodoxia Epidemica*, II.vii, in *Works*, ed. Geoffrey Keynes (Chicago: University of Chicago Press, 1964), II: 150–51: "FEW ears have escaped the noise of the Dead-watch, that is, the little clickling sound heard often in many rooms, somewhat resembling that of a Watch; and this is conceived to be of an evil omen or prediction of some person's death: wherein notwithstanding there is nothing of rational presage or just cause of terrour unto melancholy and meticulous heads. For this noise is made by a little sheath-winged gray Insect found often in Wainscot, Benches, and Woodwork, in the Summer."

507.15–21   *Leven's* . . . *Angus's*] Both regiments served at Steinkirk; see 454.4–5 and above, n. to 452.17ff.

507.23   *Breda*] Work, p. 422, n. 3: "A town in the Netherlands frequently used for winter quarters." Work's note seems to be based on a sentence in Baird, p. 811, n. 43: "Breda was regularly used for winter quarters"; Baird's reference to Tindal, III: 562, does not establish that fact, although it does seem likely. We do know, from *The Life and Adventures of Mrs. Christian Davies, the British Amazon, Commonly called Mother Ross*, 2d ed. (1741), pt. 1, pp. 58–60, that prisoners were housed in the town; and from Parker, *Memoirs of the Most Remarkable Military Transactions*, p. 92, that he wintered there in 1703.

507.24–25   whose wife . . . in my tent.] Cf. 426.5–10, the story of Cornelius Gallus and his wife.

509.3   a natural and a positive law] Cf. Chambers, s.v. *Law: "Natural* LAW, is that which he has made known to all mankind, by that innate light, called *natural reason*.

"*Positive* LAW, is that which he has revealed by his prophets; as those *laws* delivered to the Jews, relating to the divine worship, and polity, which may be called *divino-civil laws*, as being peculiarly directed to that people."

509.10–11   though he had . . . upon the counterscarp] Chambers, s.v. *Covert Way*, notes that a "lodgment upon the counterscarp" means a lodgment upon the covered way, and that this is "one of the greatest difficulties in a siege . . . because, usually, the besieged pallisade it along the middle, and undermine it on all sides." See "Glossary of Terms of Fortification" in this volume, s.v. *counterscarp* and *covered way*. We might recall that Toby is wounded during the assault on the counterscarp before St. Nicolas's gate at Namur (93.6–18).

509.14   turned the siege of *Dendermond* into a blockade] Cf. Tindal, III: 751: "*Dendermonde* had been for some weeks under a blockade. This the Duke of *Marlborough* ordered to be turned into a formal siege." Toby's reversal of Marlborough's action is of interest. Cf. Chambers, s.v. *Blockade:* "A *blockade* is no regular siege; inasmuch as there are no trenches or attacks."

Dendermond was one of the fortified towns of the Spanish Netherlands seized by Louis XIV in 1701, when he broke the Treaty of Ryswick and the Partition Treaties, and precipitated the War of the Spanish Succession (Marlborough's War), 1701–13. By 1706, Marlborough had already turned the military tide against France, both by his march through Germany (see 688.24ff. and n. below) and his decisive victory at Ramillies, to which the taking of Dendermond was merely a footnote.

511.4–7   The ACCUSING SPIRIT . . . out for ever.] The idea of a book of deeds being kept on every person perhaps derives from Revelation 20: 12: "And I saw the dead, small and great, stand before God; and the books were opened: and another book was opened, which is the book of life: and the dead were judged out of those things which were written in the books, according to their works." Sterne uses the idea in his sermon "Description of the World" (V.30.74–75): "there is a Being about our paths and about our beds, whose omniscient eye spies out all our ways, and takes a faithful record of all the passages of our lives; . . . these volumes shall be produced and opened, and men shall be judged out of the things that are written in them . . . ."

This passage won the immediate acclaim of those who admired Sterne's sentimental vein; see, e.g., *Letters*, January 1762, p. 150: "the thought of the accusing spirit flying up [to] heaven's chancery with the oath, you are kind enough to say is sublime—my friend, Mr. Garrick, thinks so too, and I am most vain of his approbation—your ladyship's [Lady Dacre's?] opinion adds not a little to my vanity."

511.13   THE sun . . . morning after] Possibly a commonplace. Cf. Pope, *Correspondence*, ed. George Sherburn (Oxford: Clarendon Press, 1956), I: 148: "The morning after my Exit, the sun will rise as bright as ever"; and Goldsmith, *Works*, I: 416 (*The Bee*, October 1759): "The sun, after so sad an accident, might shine next morning as bright as usual . . . ."

511.16   the wheel . . . its circle] Perhaps an echo of Ecclesiastes 12: 6: "the wheel broken at the cistern." The entire twelfth chapter is about death, "because man goeth to his long home, and the mourners go about the streets."

513.19   for it was *Yorick*'s custom] See Cross, *Life*, pp. 242–43: "This was also Sterne's custom as attested by Isaac Reed, the editor of Shakespeare, who saw the manuscript of two of Sterne's sermons and copied out the whimsical remarks sprawled across them. At the end of one bearing the title 'Our Conversation in Heaven' was the endorsement: 'Made for All Saints and preach'd on that Day 1750 for the Dean.——Present: one Bellows Blower, three Singing Men, one Vicar and one Residentiary. ——Memorandum: Dined with Duke Humphrey.' At the end of the other, entitled 'The Ways of Providence Justified to Man,' Sterne wrote: 'I have borowed most of the Reflections upon the Characters from Wollaston, or at least have enlarged from his hints, though the Sermon is truly mine such as it is.'" Neither manuscript has been located.

514.6   WATER-LANDISH *knowlege*] Sterne's coinage, based on Daniel Waterland (1683–1740). Arthur Cash notes that Waterland "was a leader in the opposition to Latitudinarianism" and a "notorious pluralist" who held the chancellorship of York Cathedral in the period immediately before Sterne joined the Cathedral Chapter (*Sterne's Comedy of Moral Sentiments* [Pittsburgh: Duquesne University Press, 1966], p. 84, n. 18). See also *Early and Middle Years*, p. 51, where Cash suggests that the reference is specifically to Waterland's *Advice to a Young Student* (1706), still in use at Cambridge in Sterne's day. No evidence has been found indicating that Sterne borrowed from Waterland's sermons. One suspects, in fact, that a sermon on the "*jewish dispensation*" would more likely be based on Warburton (i.e., his *Divine Legation of Moses*) than on Waterland.

514.7   *tritically*] *OED* cites this passage as its sole illustration. Cf. Swift's "A
Tritical Essay upon the Faculties of the Mind" (*Prose Works*, I: 246–51),
which makes clear *OED*'s definition "of a trite or commonplace character;
trite, with play on *critical*."

514.12–14   *For this sermon . . . a thief.*] Cf. "Rabelaisian Fragment,"
p. 1089, lines 52–66: "HOMENAS who had to preach next Sunday . . . &
finding Himself unable to get either forwards or backwards—with any
Grace——'d——n it,' says He . . . 'Why, may not a Man lawfully call in
for Help, in this, as well as any other human Emergency?' So without any
more Argumentation, except starting up and nimming down from the Top
Shelf but one, the second Volume of Clark tho' without any felonious
Intention in so doing, He had begun to clapp me in (making a Joynt first)
Five whole Pages, nine round Paragraphs, and a Dozen and a half of good
Thoughts all of a Row . . . ."

In a more serious vein, Sterne again addresses the question of borrowings in his preface to vols. I and II of the *Sermons*, pp. ix–x: "I have
nothing to add, but that the reader, upon old and beaten subjects, must not
look for many new thoughts,—'tis well if he has new language; in three or
four passages, where he has neither the one or the other, I have quoted the
author I made free with—there are some other passages, where I suspect I
may have taken the same liberty,—but 'tis only suspicion, for I do not
remember it is so, otherwise I should have restored them to their proper
owners, so that I put it in here more as a general saving, than from a
consciousness of having much to answer for upon that score . . . ."

Sterne's indebtedness in his sermon-writing has been investigated in
some detail by Hammond. However, some of his most basic conclusions
have been convincingly challenged by James Downey, "The Sermons of
Mr. Yorick: A Reassessment of Hammond," *ESC* 4 (1978): 193–211; see
also Downey's *The Eighteenth-Century Pulpit* (Oxford: Clarendon Press,
1969), pp. 115–54, especially his comment on and citation from John
Ferriar: "Dr. John Ferriar, who took great care to establish *Tristram
Shandy*'s indebtedness to Burton, Rabelais, and others, was typical of his
time in his less censorious attitude to sermons: 'Charges of Plagiarism in
his Sermons have been brought against Sterne, which I have not been
anxious to investigate, as in that species of composition, the principal
matter must consist of repetitions'" (p. 123; quoted from Ferriar, I: 123).

See also *Spectator* 106, in which Addison describes the practice of Sir Roger's chaplain: "At his first settling with me, I made him a Present of all the good Sermons which have been printed in *English*, and only begged of him that every *Sunday* he would pronounce one of them in the Pulpit. Accordingly, he has digested them into such a Series, that they follow one another naturally, and make a continued System of practical Divinity." Addison lists South, Tillotson, Sanderson, Barrow, and Benjamin Calamy as "Authors who have published Discourses of practical Divinity" and then concludes: "I could heartily wish that more of our Country-Clergy would follow this Example; and instead of wasting their Spirits in laborious Compositions of their own, would endeavour, after a handsome Elocution and all those other Talents that are proper to enforce what has been penn'd by greater Masters. This would not only be more easy to themselves, but more edifying to the People" (I: 441–42). Cf. Yorick's praise of "practical divinity," 462.18–20.

Addison's tolerant view was not, however, universally shared; cf. the often reprinted *Art of Preaching: in Imitation of Horace's Art of Poetry* (173_?), in which the author (Robert Dodsley? George Smalridge?) seems ambivalent at best: "Young Deacons try your Strength, and strive to find / A Subject suited to your Turn of Mind; / Method and Words are easily your own, / Or should they fail you—steal from *Tillotson*"; and later in the poem: "But some with lazy Pride disgrace the Gown, / And never preach one Sermon of their own; / 'Tis easier to transcribe than to compose, / So all the Week they eat, and drink, and doze."

514.13   Paidagunes] I.e., a pedagogue; Sterne's form is feminine. The spelling "Paida-" for the Latin *Paeda-* may simply be a compositorial error, though in the creation of proper names authorial intention is almost always impossible to ascertain.

514.13–14   *Set a thief to catch a thief*] Proverbial; Tilley, T110, and *ODEP*, s.v. *Thief*.

514.17   *Altieri's Italian* dictionary] Ferdinando Altieri's dictionary, first published in 1726 (2d ed. 1750), was the standard English-Italian dictionary until Johnson's friend Giuseppe Baretti published his in 1760. Baretti attacked Altieri's work quite severely in his preface, and indeed his subtitle claims to have added over ten thousand words to Altieri; but the *Monthly Review* 23 (September 1760) defended Altieri, suggesting that "Baretti should have spoken less contemptuously . . . of the writer whose work he has thought fit to transcribe" (quoted in C. J. M. Lubbers-Van Der Brugge, *Johnson and Baretti* [Groningen, The Netherlands: J. B. Wolters, 1951], pp. 57–58). Sterne's Italian terms are all derived from his musical knowledge rather than from Altieri's dictionary, but it is interesting to note that he cites it rather than Baretti's, which was also available to him when he wrote this passage.

515.5   *Yorick's dramatic* sermons] Cf. 165.3–9, 376.23–377.10, and nn. above. Vols. III and IV of the *Sermons* were not published until 1766. Cash, *Early and Middle Years*, p. 127, points out that in the earliest advertisement for vols. I and II of the *Sermons* (*York Courant*, March 4, 1760), they were titled *The Dramatick Sermons of Mr. Yorick*.

515.9–17   What *Yorick* could mean . . . have a meaning] Work's definitions of these musical terms are satisfactory (p. 428, n. 3): "*lentamente*": slowly; "*tenutè*": sustained, held to its full value; "*grave*": slow, solemn; "*adagio*": slowly, gracefully; "*a l'octava alta*": in the high octave; "*Con strepito*": uproariously; "*Scicilliana*": slow (as for a Sicilian dance); "*Con l'arco*": with the bow (as opposed to *pizzicato*); and "*Senza l'arco*": without the bow, *pizzicato*. Work's "for a chapel" for "*Alla capella*" might better be translated "without instrumental accompaniment."

515.18   and as he was a musical man] See above, n. to 12.21–22.

515.29–516.2   a half sheet . . . of horse-drugs.] Work, p. 429, n. 4: "Probably a sly jab at the blue-covered *Critical Review,* which had given Sterne unfavorable reviews, and at its contentious editor, Tobias Smollett, M.D., who had taken up literary and journalistic work only after failing as a practicing physician." Although the *Critical Review* was mixed in its assessment of vols. III and IV, it came nowhere near the negative campaign of the *Monthly Review,* against both *TS* and the *Sermons* (see *Critical Review* 11 [April 1761]: 314–17, and above, nn. to 167.17–22 and 190.18). If this is indeed a "jab" at the *CR*, it might be suggested that Sterne is arguing not so much his own case but more so that of his friend John Hall-Stevenson (see above, n. to 30.20), whose first dismal efforts in early 1760 were roundly abused by that journal. Hall-Stevenson responded with "A Nosegay and a Simile for Reviewers," in which, we should note, he compares critical reviewers with asses (see above, n. to 491.9–14). Throughout his subsequent career he often let fly at Smollett and the *CR;* see, e.g., "Two Lyric Epistles: or, Margery the Cook-maid" (1762) and "Queries to the Critical Reviewer" (1762). For Hall-Stevenson, the quarrel was far more political than literary; as an ally of Wilkes, he was anti-Bute and hence anti-Smollett and anti-Scots. Sterne seems to have remained for the most part aloof from these quarrels, so that when he attacks Smollett more overtly in vol. IX (pp. 780–81) and again in *ASJ,* the motivation seems preponderantly social and literary.

516.13   small *Italian* hand] I.e., the form of handwriting in use in Europe and America today, as opposed to the Gothic hand; see *OED,* s.v. *Italian,* A.3.

516.23   *Yorick's* character as a modest man] Cf. *Spectator* 231: "A just and reasonable Modesty does not only recommend Eloquence, but sets off every great Talent which a Man can be possessed of. It heightens all the Vertues which it accompanies; like the Shades in Paintings, it raises and rounds every Figure, and makes the Colours more beautiful, tho' not so glaring as they would be without it.

"Modesty is not only an Ornament, but also a Guard to Vertue. It is a kind of quick and delicate *feeling* in the Soul, which makes her shrink and withdraw her self from every thing that has Danger in it. It is such an exquisite Sensibility, as warns her to shun the first appearance of every thing which is hurtful" (II: 399).

517.10   hussar-like] *OED* cites this passage as its only recorded example. The military metaphor continues in "skirmish" and "auxiliaries." For a description of the eighteenth-century hussar (light cavalry) that helps to elucidate Sterne's metaphor, see David Chandler, *The Art of Warfare in the Age of Marlborough* (New York: Hippocrene Books, 1976): 37–39.

517.12   Mynheer Vander Blonederdondergewdenstronke] A parody, obviously, of a "Dutch commentator" (see above, n. to 60.10), but Sterne would seem to be addressing in particular those critics who objected to a clergyman writing *TS* and to "Yorick" writing sermons; see above, n. to 167.17–22. Work comments about the name: "if it means anything, the suggestion of the individual elements would add up to something like 'Super-dull-dunderhead'" (p. 430, n. 6). C. J. Rawson, in "'Tristram Shandy' and 'Candide'," *N&Q* 203 (1958): 226, suggests a possible imitation of Voltaire's name-making; e.g., Mynheer Vanderdendur in chap. 19 of *Candide.*

518.7–8   As soon as . . . polygon in a circle] See above, n. to 110.26.

518.11–13   the spring . . . against the *Turks*] Work, p. 431, n. 1: "Prince
François Eugène of Savoie-Carignano (1663–1736), a celebrated Austrian general who in 1716–1718 led the forces of Charles VI . . . against
the Turks." Sterne chose a perfect campaign for Le Fever's son to participate in, since Eugene's effort against the Turks in the Balkans was seen as a
modern crusade, and attracted volunteers from all over Europe; see Derek
McKay, *Prince Eugene of Savoy* (London: Thames and Hudson, 1977):
158–68. McKay provides an excellent account of Eugene's career and is of
particular value to readers of *TS* because of his descriptions of eighteenth-
century warfare. Prince Eugene was Marlborough's major ally in the War
of the Spanish Succession and the two shared honors as the greatest generals of the age.

519.12–13   the defeat of the *Turks* before *Belgrade*] Cf. Tindal, IV: 548:
"Whilst the King was at *Hampton-Court*, Count *Volkra*, the Imperial
Minister, brought him the news of Prince *Eugene*'s victory over the *Turks*
at *Belgrade*"; the siege and decisive battle took place in August 1717.

521.6   And FAME . . . double every thing] See above, n. to 84.4–6.

523.6–14   THE ancient *Goths* . . . not want discretion.] This paragraph
might well serve as a paradigm for the many problems encountered in
trying to track Sterne to his sources. Work, p. 434, n. 1, identifies "*Cluverius*" as "Philip Cluwer (1580–1623), German geographer and historian; the reference is to his great *Germania Antiqua* . . ."; he also suggests,
however, that the "account of the double counsels" was probably paraphrased from Sir William Temple's *Observations upon the United Provinces
of the Netherlands* (1663), book I, chap. 42, p. 297, rather than from
Cluwer's account. It seems a legitimate guess that Sterne was more likely to
find his source in Temple (or for that matter in Tacitus's *Germania*, 22)
than in Cluwer, although the verbal echoes are not as convincing as one
might prefer. Temple writes: "Therefore the old *Germans* seem'd to have
some Reason in their Custom, not to execute any great Resolutions which
had not been twice debated, and agreed at two several Assemblies, one in
an Afternoon, and t'other in a Morning; because, they thought, their
Counsels might want Vigour when they were sober, as well as Caution
when they had drunk" (*Works*, [1720], I: 51).

The main drawback to accepting Temple as the source for the present
passage is his lack of any citation of Cluwer or any parallel to the first half

of the paragraph, the geographical information in which can all be found, though with difficulty, in Cluwer (pp. 645–49, 702–5). But Cluwer wrote in Latin, and there exists an English version of his geographical opinion that is almost certainly the basis for Sterne's: "The Original of these People is very much disputed, but the Learned *Cluverius* is positive, that they were first seated . . . between the *Vistula* and the *Oder; and* afterwards incorporating the *Heruli* by Conquest, the *Rugians* and some other Vandalick Clans, they were known after this Incorporation by the general name of *Goths* . . ." (Collier's translation of Moréri's *Dictionary* [1701], s.v. *Goths*). Unfortunately, Moréri says nothing about the "wise custom of debating."

We may suggest three alternatives at this point: (1) there exists an undiscovered source that combines the information from Moréri with that of the "double counsels," not necessarily derived from Temple; (2) Sterne combined Moréri with Temple or another source; or (3) despite the verbal echoes of Moréri, Sterne did indeed consult Cluwer.

In addition, we note that Sterne's "*Bugians*" and "*Herculi*" are both errors; the correct readings, as in Cluwer and Moréri, are "*Rugians*" and "*Heruli*." Did Sterne miscopy Moréri or an undiscovered source? Or did he intentionally parody this learned invocation of ancient tribes with some names of his own—almost certainly the case if Cluwer were indeed his source, since the names appear correctly dozens of times throughout that long work. Cf. the suggestion of Frank Brady, "*Tristram Shandy*: Sexuality, Morality, and Sensibility," *ECS* 4 (1970): 43—that St. Boogar (649.13) "presides over a number of events and allusions, such as those suspicious tribes, the '*Herculi*' and the '*Bugians*' . . . ." Or was it more simply a matter of errors by the compositor, who was setting words quite unfamiliar to him—and to subsequent editors of *TS*? The recovery of an indisputable source would perhaps solve these questions, but short of that we are left with as many perplexities as solutions.

524.8–9   *beds of justice*] Cf. Chambers, *Supplement*, s.v. *Bed:* "BED *of justice, lit de justice,* in the French laws, denotes a throne whereon the king is seated in parliament . . . .

"In this sense, the king is said to hold his *lit de justice,* when he goes to the parliament of Paris, and holds a solemn session, under a high canopy erected for the purpose.

"The *bed of justice* is only held on affairs relating to the state; on which occasion, all the officers of the parliament appear in red robes; at other times they wear black ones."

524.23–24   I write one half *full*,—and t'other *fasting*] Cf. Rabelais, III, "Author's Prologue," p. ix: "Stay a little, till I suck up a draught of this bottle . . . . Ennius drinking wrote, and writing drank. Æschylus . . . drank composing, and drinking composed. Homer never wrote fasting, and Cato never wrote till after he had drank"; first noted by Stout, "Borrowings," pp. 112–13. Cf. vol. VII, chap. 4 (580.5–8).

   See also Goldsmith, *Citizen of the World*, letter 93 (*Works*, II: 376): "Believe me, my friend, hunger has a most amazing faculty of sharpening the genius; and he who with a full belly can think like a hero, after a course of fasting, shall rise to the sublimity of a demi-god."

525.18   understrapping] *OED* cites this passage as its first illustration, with the following definition: "of a subordinate or inferior character or standing."

526.1ff.   We should begin, etc.] On the outfitting of children during this period, see Philippe Ariès, *Centuries of Childhood: A Social History of Family Life*, trans. Robert Baldrick (New York: Vintage, 1965), especially his comments on the "effeminization of the little boy . . . . it became impossible to distinguish a little boy from a little girl before the age of four or five . . ." (p. 58).

528.10   dimity] A fine ribbed cotton fustian, which is a material with a linen warp and cotton weft; see *Handbook of English Costume*, pp. 407–8. Insofar as dimity is a lighter material, young Tristram stands more chance of "catching his death" while wearing dimity trousers; see above, n. to 502.9.

529.16ff.   After my father, etc.] This chapter would seem to owe something in spirit to chap. 5 of the *Memoirs of Martinus Scriblerus*, in which Cornelius establishes the classical antecedents of Martinus's playthings and games. See Joseph M. Levine's very fine study of the kind of eighteenth-century antiquarianism that the Scriblerians and Sterne both seem to represent in their respective "philosophers"—*Dr. Woodward's Shield: History, Science, and Satire in Augustan England* (Berkeley: University of California Press, 1977).

529.17ff.   he consulted *Albertus Rubenius*] The inspiration for this entire chapter may have been Addison's *Dialogues upon the Usefulness of Ancient Medals* (1726; New York: Garland Publishing, 1976), wherein three friends briefly discuss Roman costume (pp. 16–18): "I know [says Cynthio] there are several supercilious Critics that will treat an author with the greatest contempt imaginable, if he fancies the old *Romans* wore a girdle, and are amazed at a man's ignorance, who believes the *Toga* had any Sleeves to it till the declension of the *Roman* Empire. Now I would fain know the great importance of this kind of learning, and why it should not be as noble a task to write upon a Bib and hanging-sleeves, as on the *Bulla* and *Prætexta* . . . . To set [these subjects] in their natural light, let us fancy, if you please, that about a thousand years hence, some profound author shall write a learned treatise . . . distinguished into the following Titles and Chapters.

> *Of the old* British *Trowser.*
> *Of the Ruff and Collar-band.*
> *The opinion of several learned men concerning the use of*
> *the Shoulder-knot.*
> *Such a one mistaken in his account of the Surtout,* &c. . . .

I have sometimes fancied [says Eugenius] it would not be an impertinent design to make a kind of an old *Roman* wardrobe, where you should see *Toga's* and *Tunica's*, the *Chlamys* and *Trabea* . . . . The design, says *Philander,* might be very useful, but after what models would you work? *Sigonius,* for example, will tell you that the *Vestis Trabeata* was of such a particular fashion, *Scaliger* is for another, and *Dacier* thinks them both in the wrong. These are, says *Cynthio,* I suppose the names of three *Roman* taylors: for is it possible men of learning can have any disputes of this nature? May not we as well believe that hereafter the whole learned world will be divided upon the make of a modern pair of breeches?"

Sterne's citation of Rubenius may not be as reliable as Work (p. 439, n. 1) seems to have believed: "Albert Rubens (1614–1657), the eldest son of the painter and Isabella Brant, was an archaeologist and writer of some note. In his *De Re Vestiaria Veterum, Præcipue de Lato Clavo* (*Of the Clothing of the Ancients, Particularly of the Latus Clavus*) [Antwerp, 1665], from which Sterne took the following lists of articles of clothing and of authorities, Rubenius devoted nearly two hundred quarto pages to pedantic speculations on the details of ancient costume and the conflicting arguments of learned men thereupon." To be sure, within the headnote to the very first chapter of *De Re Vestiaria*, Rubens cites six of Walter's ten authorities, three others within the first three pages (pp. 3–5) and the last, Lipsius, on p. 9. It is, however, somewhat misleading to say that Sterne "took the following lists" from Rubens, both because Rubens has no "lists" as such, and because the order of Sterne's roll call is not the order of citation in *De Re Vestiaria*. The same is true of Sterne's list of garments; although each garment, excepting the Ephod, is elaborately discussed by Rubens, and although each name can be found in the elaborate table of contents (there is no index), Rubens has no convenient list, nor does Sterne follow his order of discussion. And again, although several chapters of book II are devoted to the subject of footwear, there is nothing comparable to Sterne's list of shoes. In short, although Sterne may well have glanced into Rubens (especially chap. 1), we believe it likely that he used another, far less elaborate source as well.

In particular, we would suggest Lefèvre de Morsan's *The Manners and Customs of the Romans. Translated from the French* (1740), or perhaps a later, still undiscovered work which relied heavily upon it. The most apparent borrowing is 532.7–18, which, significantly, is said to be a summary of what Walter Shandy found in Rubens. Lefèvre is the far more likely source: "The most general colour of the Roman habits was white, which, except purple peculiar to the great offices, was deemed the most honourable. The citizens in public rejoicings generally appeared in white robes, to denote their joy. Plutarch tells us, they did the same on private occasions of rejoicing, and that they wore a white habit on their birth-days, which they celebrated annually . . . . Persons of quality were distinguished, as we have said before, by the fineness, neatness, and whiteness of their habits: and we find in authors of those times, that they often sent their robes to the fuller to be cleaned and whitened. The inferior people, to avoid that expence, generally wore brown cloths. Appian informs us, that from Julius Cæsar's time, distinction of habit was no longer observed at Rome; that the freedmen were confounded with the other citizens; that the slave was drest like his master; and that except the habit of Senator, the use of all the rest was indifferently allowed to all the world. In Domitian's time we find, that the Tribunes of the legions wore the robe *Latus-clavus*" (pp. 37–38).

Again on footwear, Sterne could have found in Lefèvre a discussion closer to his own list than anything in Rubens: "The usual dress for the legs both of men and women were of two kinds; the one close, the other open. The latter was a kind of sandals, composed of soles which covered the bottom of the feet [in the margin: "*The sock*"], and were fastened to ribbands, or thongs of leather, that came cross the foot in different manners, and were twisted several times round the leg above the ancle. The other, which was close, covered the foot, and came as high as the thickest part of the leg [in the margin: "*The buskin*"]: it had an opening before, which was laced. Horace and Ovid inform us, neatness and decency required, that the dress of the leg, whether sandal or buskin, should fit well and even upon it. The shoe annexed to it ended in a point that turned back a little, and for that reason was called in Latin *Calceus rostratus*. For some time the ladies wore a kind of high-heeled buskins, or *pantofles*, which made them appear taller. . . . The dress of the legs worn by officers and soldiers, and which was called military, differed in nothing from the close sort, or buskin, except in its being stronger and fitter for marching, having the sole studded with nails" (pp. 48–49).

Lefèvre omits the "calceus incisus" and does not cite Juvenal—two clues among others that Sterne had yet another source; we suggest, however, that that source is far more likely to be in the schoolboy textbook tradition of Lefèvre than in the scholarly Latin tradition of Rubens. Lefèvre's work does give interesting reinforcement to the argument of Eric Rothstein, that the name Le Fever is somehow connected to the breeches episode; see *Systems of Order and Inquiry in Later Eighteenth-Century Fiction* (Berkeley: University of California Press, 1975), pp. 97–98.

On the garments of the Romans, Lefèvre again provides the kind of brief comments (and marginal headings) that Sterne was far more likely to consult than Rubens's dense scholarship. In the headnote and margins of chap. 4, e.g., Sterne could find the Toga, Prætexta, Lacerna, Synthesis, and Paludamentum. In the text of the chapter he could discover as well that the "*Trabea*, was only a little shorter [than the Toga], and striped with purple and white, and in process of time with gold" (p. 34); that the

"*Lacerna* . . . had a hood added to it, called *Cucullus,* which was taken off
at will" (p. 34); that the "*Paludamentum* was a military robe, like that
which the Greeks called *Chlamys*" (p. 35); that there was a "kind of vest,
called *Sagum,* which the soldiers used in the army" (p. 35); and that "under these robes they usually had two tunics" (p. 36). Sterne adds to this
inventory only the Pænula (530.16) and the comment of Suetonius on the
three kinds of Trabea (530.21–22), both of which he might have found in
Rubens's table of contents, chap. 5. Sterne's inclusion of the Ephod
(530.13) is probably a joke, since it is the name of the robe of Jewish
priests and is not discussed in any of the works on Roman costume that we
examined.

We might also note that Lefèvre comments on the fact that "Linnen did
not begin to be commonly used, till toward the declension of the empire,
when Egyptians came to settle amongst them, and they made use of it in
imitation of that people" (p. 40); cf. *TS, 532.3–6.*

Finally, although the title of Rubens's work and its opening chapter
make clear the existence of a heated debate over the *Latus Clavus,* we
quote, for simplicity's sake, Lefèvre's brief account: "The Senators had
under [the Prætexta] a tunic ample enough, called *Latus-clavus,* which was
long taken literally for an habit adorned with large studs of purple like
nail-heads, but has since been discovered to signify only a stuff with large
stripes of purple, the same as that called *Augustus-clavus,* which was peculiar to the Knights to distinguish them from the Senators, and which was
also only a stuff with narrower stripes of the same colour" (pp. 33–34).
Cf. Basil Kennett, *Romæ Antiquæ Notitia: Or, the Antiquities of Rome,* 5th
ed. rev. (1713), pp. 314–15: "The whole Body of the Criticks are
strangely divided about the *Clavi.* Some fansie them to have been a kind of
Flowers interwoven in the Cloth: Others will have them to be the Buttons
or Clasps by which the *Tunic* was held together. A Third sort contend that
the *Latus clavus* was nothing else but a *Tunic,* border'd with Purple. . . .
But the most general Opinion makes them to have been Studs or Purls
something like Heads of Nails, of Purple or Gold work'd into the *Tunic.*

"All the former Conjectures are learnedly refuted by the accurate
Rubenius, who endeavours to prove, that the *Clavi* were no more than
purple Lines or Streaks coming along the middle of the Garments . . . ."

We conclude this long note by observing that while this subject seems obviously esoteric to us, these terms and distinctions were common school-boy fare throughout the century. In the note which follows, the definitions are purposely culled from both Lefèvre and Richard Turner, *An Introduction to the Knowledge of the Antiquities of Rome for the Use of Schools* (1790), in order to reinforce that point.

530.11–22   The Toga . . . three kinds.] The Toga is, of course, a robe with-out sleeves, the most basic element of the Roman wardrobe; Sterne's "a loose gown" may glance at a passage in Lefèvre, p. 37: "A person was not thought to be drest decently without [a properly tied cincture], and it was a mark of dissolute manners not to have one, or to wear it too loose. Suetonius, speaking of Julius Cæsar, whose youth was not very regular, relates, that Sylla used to advise the nobility, *ut puerum male præcinctum caverent,* to take care of the youth with the loose gown."

The Chlamys, according to both Lefèvre, p. 35, and Turner, pp. 155–56, was the same as the Paludamentum—a military robe worn over other clothes; Turner adds that it was colored scarlet and "bordered with purple, and sometimes enriched with gold, [and] was worn by the Gener-als of the Army."

The Tunica was "a kind of waistcoat worn under the Toga; it came down to the knees, and in general had no sleeves" (Turner, pp. 156–57).

The Synthesis was "another kind of very large robe or cloak, which they put on to eat in" (Lefevre, p. 35); "a festival robe, particularly worn during the time of the Saturnalia" (Turner, p. 156).

The Pænula was "a short thick woollen, or leather coat, worn in cold or rainy weather, and also when they were on a journey" (Turner, p. 156).

"Lacema" is apparently a misprint for "Lacerna," a cloak for bad weather, riding, and military use (Lefèvre, p. 34, and Turner, p. 156); the Cucullus is its hood. The reading of "rn" as "m" is a common ty-pographical error, but in Lefèvre the "rn" in three occurrences is quite clear; one would hope eventually to find an account of the Roman wardrobe where this is not the case, although quite possibly this is the error of Sterne's own compositor.

The Prætexta, "a robe so called from its being trimmed with purple . . . was . . . worn by the Magistrates and Augurs" (Turner, pp. 153–54).

The Sagum and Trabea are defined in the previous note. It might be pointed out that in a textbook written over one hundred years earlier, the author writes: "there were three several kinds" of Trabea (Thomas Godwyn, *Romanæ Historiæ Anthologia . . . An English Exposition of the Roman Antiquities . . . for the Use of Abingdon School,* 15th ed. [1689], p. 150).

Work, p. 440, n. 3: "Caius Suetonius Tranquillus (fl. first part of 2nd C., A.D.), Roman biographer and historian. The reference, to his *De Genere Vestium,* is taken from Rubenius."

531.8–9   And The military shoe . . . notice of.] The reference is to Juvenal, *Satires,* 16, lines 22–25 (pp. 302–5): "dignum erit ergo / declamatoris mulino corde Vagelli, / cum duo crura habeas, offendere tot caligas, tot / milia clavorum" ("So, as you possess a pair of legs, you must have a mulish brain worthy of the eloquent Vagellius to provoke so many jack-boots, and all those thousands of hobnails"). Cf. Kennett, p. 325: "The *Caliga* was the proper Soldiers Shooe . . . . The Sole was of Wood like our old Galoches, or the *Sabots* of the *French* Peasants, and stuck full of Nails.

". . . And hence *Juvenal* and *Suetonius* use *Caligati* for the Common Soldiers without the addition of a Substantive." Kennett refers to this passage in Juvenal.

531.11–12   patins . . . pantoufles] I.e., pattens, pantofles.

531.19   calceus incisus] We have not found "calceus incisus" (cutwork shoe) in any of the sources cited above; for "calceus rostratus," see above, n. to 529.17ff.

532.21–23   *Egnatius . . . Joseph Scaliger*] Work, p. 441, n. 8: "Baptista Egnatius (c. 1475–1553) was a humanist of Venice; Carlo Sigonio [1523–1584] was an Italian historian and antiquary; Bossius Ticinensis: probably Matthew Bossus (1428–1502), a canon of the Lateran; Lazare de Baïf (1496?–1547) was a French scholar and diplomat; Guillaume Budé [see above, n. to 418.8–12] was a French scholar and antiquarian; Claudius Salmasius (1588–1653) was a noted French classical scholar; for Lipsius, see [above, n. to 494.13–16]. Wolfgang Lazius (1514–1565) was a German antiquary and physician; Isaac Casaubon (1559–1614) was a famous classical scholar and Protestant theologian; for Scaliger, see [above, n. to 494.1–2]."

532.25–28   That the great . . . keepers.] Sterne perhaps found his citation on p. 5 of Rubens, *De Re Vestiaria:* "Quidam clavos interpretantur fibulas, aut globulos aureos & purpureos, qui vel ad pectus assuebantur, vel latera tunicæ connectebant. His accedere videtur Bayfius cap. 7. de Re vestiaria, qui tamen cap. 12. fatetur ingenue sibi non liquere" ("Some understand the clavi to be clasps, either gold balls or purple ones, which were either sewn on the breast of the tunic or on the edges. Bayfius, in chap. 7 of his work *On Clothing*, seems to agree with these writers, though in chap. 12 he frankly confesses himself to have some doubts").

533.1   My father lost . . . the saddle] A play on the proverbial expression "to win the horse or lose the saddle"; see Tilley, H639, and *ODEP*, s.v. *Win.*

533.11   *Poco-curante's*] *OED* cites this passage as its first example, with the definition "A careless or indifferent person; one who shows little interest or concern."

Cf. Voltaire's Lord Pococurante in chap. 25 of *Candide;* women, art, music, literature, science, all are dismissed by him as being of no interest or entertainment value.

534.20   the Duke of *Marlborough*] Work, p. 443, n. 1: "John Churchill (1650–1722), first Duke of Marlborough, the great English general and statesman, was commander-in-chief of the British forces under William III and Anne." Marlborough has been the subject of countless studies, but one particularly useful in providing a context for Toby's wars is David Chandler, *Marlborough as Military Commander* (New York: Charles Scribner's Sons, 1973).

535.20–22   *That the first parallel . . . the place*] Sterne's italics would seem to indicate a quotation; the closest we have found is in John Muller, *A Treatise Containing the Elementary Part of Fortification* (1746), p. 228, where, after defining "parallels," Muller adds: "there are generally three in an attack; the first is about 300 toises from the covert-way . . . ."

Cf. Chandler, *Art of Warfare*, p. 254: "By the Vauban method, the attackers began by digging a large trench *parallel* to the defences at a distance of some 600 yards (maximum cannon range)."

536.6   rhapsodize] Cf. above, n. to 39.1.

537.3   post-morning] *OED* (s.v. *post, sb²* 12e) cites this passage as its sole example, with the definition "indicating the time at which the mail leaves or arrives."

537.7   the *Gazette*] The *London Gazette* was the official government newspaper, published three times a week beginning in 1666.

537.17   Heaven! Earth! Sea!] Sterne repeats this elemental apostrophe,
638.17 and 793.5.

538.3 – 4   In the second year . . . *Ruremond*] Both towns were captured by
Marlborough in October 1702; see Tindal, III: 563. This was the opening campaign of the War of the Spanish Succession, and a generally successful one for the Allies.

538.7 – 9   At the latter end . . . better thing] See "Glossary of Terms of Fortification" in this volume, s.v. *portcullice* and *orgues*. According to Chambers, s.v. *Portcullice*, "now-a-days, the orgues are more generally used, as
being found to answer the purpose better." Work's definition (p. 446,
n. 4) of *orgues* is rather clearly not the one Sterne had in mind.

539.9 – 10   *Amberg, Bonn* . . . and *Limbourg*] These towns were all taken in
1703; the first three are in Germany, and Huy and Limburg are in the
Netherlands (see Tindal, III: 616 – 21). All were taken under Marlborough's command, except Amberg, which was captured by the Emperor Eugene's army.

540.2   grated] *OED*'s first illustration is dated 1786.

540.3 – 4   *Ghent* and *Bruges* . . . *Flanders.*] Both Ghent and Bruges are cities
in Flanders, captured by the Allies in 1708. Brabant was the name of a
central area of the Netherlands, west and north of Flanders, containing
both Brussels and Antwerp.

540.13   *Proteus*] A minor sea-god with the power to assume all manner of
shapes.

540.13 – 15   It was *Landen* . . . and *Dendermond.*] Sterne might have intended
Landen, where Trim was wounded in 1693 (see above, n. to 108.24 – 25),
but it seems much more likely that he (or the compositor) miscopied
Landau, a town in Germany taken by Marlborough in 1704; it is discussed
in Tindal, III: 661, one page before the discussion of Traerbach, which
also fell that year. In 1705, Santvliet, Drusenheim, and Hagenau were
taken. As Baird points out ("Time-Scheme," p. 810), Sterne was probably
just gathering names from Tindal's margin at this point, and copied
"Drusen," while failing to notice that in the marginal note the name had
been hyphenated "Drusen-heim" (p. 703). On p. 751, Tindal has two
marginal notes: "Ostend *and* Menin *taken*" and "Dendermonde *and* Aeth
taken"; these sieges occurred in 1706. It would appear that Sterne's list is

not random, but rather a methodical sequence of battles in 1704, 1705, and 1706, ending where this volume had begun, with the siege of Dendermond in 1706.

541.1–3   The next year . . . into our hands] I.e., 1708; see above, n. to 540.3–4, and below, n. to 543.6–9.

541.7–8   from the beginning . . . the besiegers] Here more than anywhere else, Sterne may be playing upon the early usage of "siege" for "a privy; evacuation; excrement; the anus"—all of which definitions are included in OED. The examples cited, however, are all before 1700.

542.20–21   as the word denotes.] Sterne is almost certainly referring to "montero" rather than "quartermaster," despite the grammar of his sentence. In Spanish *montero* means "hunter" or "mountaineer," from *monte* ("mount, mountain, forest"); Sterne seems to have confused this definition of *mount* with *mounted,* i.e., on horseback, although the presence of "mounted" in line 17 may suggest a conscious play.

542.24   GALA-days] OED cites this passage as its first illustration, with the following definition: "a day of festivity, finery and show."

543.6–9   The completion . . . and the river.] Sterne borrows from Tindal's description of one of several attacks made during the very costly and very bloody four-month siege of Lille: "The Confederates, thus finding it impracticable to bring the enemy to a battle, thought fit to storm the counterscarp of *Lisle* [on September 7, 1708] . . . . Eight hundred grenadiers . . . were commanded for the attack of the right, between the *Lower Deule* and the gate *St. Andrew* . . . and sixteen hundred grenadiers . . . were commanded for the attack of the left, between the river and the gate of *St. Magdalen* . . . ." Although the attack was successful, Tindal notes that "the enemy made such a terrible fire from their out-works with their cannon, mortars, and small arms, and sprung three mines in the covered way, that there were no less than one thousand men wounded and slain" (IV: 81). Mother Ross describes a similar foray two days later: "the Besiegers having push'd as far as the Glacis of the Counterscarp, four thousand Grenadiers, beside those who were employ'd in the Works, were commanded to give the Assault, which began at Night on the 9th of *September,* and a most furious one it was. The Enemy's Fire from their Outworks, which were not yet demolish'd, made a dismal Havock, and certainly this was the most bloody Action that ever was seen . . ." (*Life and Adventures of Mrs. Christian Davies*, pt. 2, p. 11).

The description of this siege by Derek McKay, *Prince Eugene of Savoy*, pp. 115–16, is useful in establishing some of the dimensions of siege warfare: "The siege of Lille went ahead. Eugene undertook the convoying of a massive siege train along the roads from Brussels to the fortress under the eyes of the French armies. The cumbersome monster of 100 great siege guns, 60 mortars and 3,000 waggons, pulled by 16,000 horses and seven miles in length, made its way safely to Lille. . . .

"The siege would certainly have been a mammoth task even without the threat from the French armies; Winston Churchill called it 'the greatest siege operation since the invention of gunpowder'. Lille was the showpiece of the French engineering genius, Vauban, the strongest link in the chain of fortresses across France's northern frontier . . . . The allies had to construct nine miles of trenches around it, employing 12,000 peasants on the work. Inside were 15,000 troops . . . ."

The Allies had 35,000 troops under Prince Eugene conducting the siege itself, while Marlborough's army of 75,000 protected the besiegers from the French army in the field; the final casualty figures were 16,000 dead and wounded on the Allies side and 7,000 on the French; see Chandler, *Art of Warfare*, p. 309.

Sterne's sister, Mary, was born in Lille the year before his own birth; see "Memoirs," in *Letters*, p. 1.

543.16   ramallie wig] *Handbook of English Costume*, p. 94: "Worn by officers of the Guards and smart young men affecting a military air.

"The queue was a long—gradually diminishing—plait of hair tied with black ribbon bows above and below, or sometimes only below."

An illustration appears in the *Handbook*, p. 90. Insofar as it was named in commemoration of Marlborough's great victory at Ramillies in 1706, it is a particularly suitable headpiece for Toby.

544.21   Weed his grave clean] Cf. *Letters*, p. 361: "and some kind hearted Swain shall come and weed our graves, as I have weeded thine . . . ." See also *ASJ*, p. 102: "I sat by his grave, and plucking up a nettle or two at the head of it . . . ."

545.9–10   *clod of the valley!*] See Job 21: 33: "The clods of the valley shall be sweet unto him." Sterne uses the phrase in "Trust in God" (*Sermons,* VI.34.7): "and how sweet, as Job says, would the *clods of the valley be to him?*"

545.16   pale as ashes] Cf. above, n. to 161.22–23.

545.22–23   When I see him cast in the rosemary] Cf. *Hamlet,* IV.v.175: "There's rosemary, that's for remembrance"; and *Romeo and Juliet,* IV.v.79–80: "Dry up your tears, and stick your rosemary / On this fair corse, and as the custom is . . . ."

545.26–28   Gracious powers! . . . speak plain] Sterne may be conflating two passages from Isaiah: "the tongue of the stammerers shall be ready to speak plainly" (32: 4) and "Then shall the lame man leap as an hart, and the tongue of the dumb sing" (35: 6). The latter is, of course, a biblical commonplace; see, e.g., Ezekiel 24: 27, 33: 22, Matthew 9: 33, 15: 31, etc. Cf. *Sermons,* II.10.76: "that being . . . who opened the lips of the dumb, and made the tongue of the infant eloquent . . . ."

546.20–25   Let no man . . . up to perfection.] Cf. 72.7–10 and n. above.

547.10   as sure as a gun.] Proverbial; Tilley, G480, and *ODEP,* s.v. *Sure.*

549.20   my dear friend *Garrick*] See above, n. to 213.6–18, for a discussion of Sterne's relationship with David Garrick.

550.11–18   there was a plainness . . . served your purpose.] In the short autobiographical sketch Sterne wrote for his daughter, he commented in a similar fashion on his father: "a kindly, sweet disposition, void of all design; and so innocent in his own intentions, that he suspected no one; so that you might have cheated him ten times in a day, if nine had not been sufficient for your purpose . . ." ("Memoirs," in *Letters,* p. 3). Sterne uses the phrases "plainness and simplicity" and "naked and defenceless" again for Toby, 778.18–20.

550.17   through his liver] Sterne alludes to the ancient tradition of the liver as the seat of the passions, especially of love; see, e.g., Jacques Ferrand, *Erotomania, or a Treatise Discoursing of the Essence, Causes . . . and Cure of Love, or Erotique Melancholy,* trans. Edmund Chilmead (Oxford, 1640): "Love, having first entred at the Eyes, which are the Faithfull spies and intelligencers of the soule, steals gently through those sluces, and so passing insensibly through the veines to the Liver, it there presently imprinteth an ardent desire of the Object, which is either really lovely, or at least appeares to be so. Now this desire, once enflamed, is the beginning and mover of all the sedition . . . . But distrusting its owne strength, and fearing it is not able to overthrow the Reason; it presently layeth siege to the Heart: of which having once fully possest it selfe, as being the strongest fort of all, it assaults so violently the Reason, and all the noble forces of the Braine, that they are suddenly forced to yeeld themselves up to its subjection" (pp. 67–68). Ferrand reiterates his point a few pages later: "I affirme that the Liver is the Hearth that holds this Fire, and the seat of Love . . . . The Heart is the seat of Wisdome, the Lungs of speech, the Gall of Anger, the Spleene of Laughter, and the Liver of Love" (pp. 70–71); he cites Proverbs 7: 23 in support of this belief (in which a youth is tempted by a harlot "till a dart strike through his liver").

See *TS*, 563.21–22: "whether the seat of [love] is in the brain or liver"; and below, n. to 563.19–564.3.

550.20–21   unparalleled modesty of nature I once told you of] See 74.22–23 and n. above.

551.5–6   the key of my study out of my draw-well] See 407.9–12, where Tristram vows to lock his study door and throw the key into the draw-well.

551.9–16   There was the great . . . the goddess] Work, p. 456, n. 2: "The following jumble of names is probably Sterne's fun . . . . Aldrovandus (Ulisse Aldrovandi [1522–1605], a noble and celebrated Italian naturalist) he probably remembered from Burton, who frequently cites his works. Capadocius, Pontus, and Asius may echo the 'Cappadocia, in Pontus, and Asia' of Acts, 2.9. Bosphorus, Babylonicus, Mediterraneus, Persicus, and Prusicus appear likewise to be based on geographical names . . . . There were many Polixeneses in mythology and history; perhaps Sterne remembered the 'good Polixenes' in *The Winter's Tale* who was no mysogynist although his friendship for Hermione was chaste. Persicus may possibly be a slip for Persius (Aulus Persius Flaccus) (34–62), the Roman satirical poet, who, according to Bayle, a favorite authority of Sterne, 'was very chaste . . . sober, as meek as a lamb, and as modest as a young virgin.' Charles XII (1682–1718), King of Sweden, however, was an authentic and famed mysogynist. He never married, and he lived so austere a life that when the Countess of Königsmark, a celebrated wit and beauty who had become the mistress of Augustus the Strong, King of Poland, was sent to him by her lover to sue for peace, neither her charms nor her artifices were able to persuade him to treat with her." We have

omitted various conjectures by Work concerning the possible identification of Bosphorus, Pontus, and Dardanus with actual persons, since they
are not convincing.

Sterne may also have known Aldrovandus from *Memoirs of Martinus
Scriblerus*, where he is said to have been related to Martin on his mother's
side (p. 96); see Kerby-Miller's note, p. 188.

For Sterne's interest in Acts 2: 9, cf. *ASJ*, p. 257: "whenever I have a
more brilliant affair upon my hands than common, as they suit a preacher
just as well as a hero, I generally make my sermon out of 'em—and for the
text—'Capadosia, Pontus and Asia, Phrygia and Pamphilia'—is as good
as any one in the Bible"; see also above, n. to 460.17–20.

Possibly, Sterne confused Polixenes with his best friend and fellow
king, Leontes, whose conduct toward his wife, Hermione, precipitates
the action of *The Winter's Tale* and would certainly qualify as misogynistic.

The story concerning Charles XII and his negotiations with Poland in
1702 is told by Voltaire, among others: "As the Affair was delicate, he
[Augustus of Poland] entrusted it wholly to the Countess of *Konismar*, a
Swedish Lady of great Birth, to whom he was then attach'd. This Lady,
who was so famous in the World for her Wit and Beauty, was more capable
than any Minister to give Success to a Negotiation . . . .

"All her Wit and Charms were lost upon such a Man as the King of
Sweden, and he constantly refused to see her . . . . So that the Countess
. . . gain'd no other Advantage from her Journey, but the Satisfaction of
believing that the King of *Sweden* feared no Body but her" (*The History of
Charles XII*, trans. from the French [1732], pp. 73–75). It should be
noted that all of Charles XII's considerable energies were absorbed by
warfare; and that by Sterne's day he had become, in Johnson's verse, a
symbol of the futility of military ambition: "He left the Name, at which
the World grew pale, / To point a Moral, or adorn a Tale" (*Vanity of
Human Wishes*, lines 221–22).

551.20   the peace of *Utrecht*] Cf. Tindal, IV: 313: "On the 28th of *April*
[1713] the ratifications of the treaties of peace and commerce were exchanged at *Utrecht* between the Ministers of *Great-Britain* and *France*;
and, being brought to *London* . . . the Queen on the 4th of *May*, the same
day of the month, on which the war had been proclaimed eleven years
before, signed a Proclamation for publishing the peace; which was per-

formed the next day with the usual ceremonies." See below, nn. to 559.20ff. and 686.5−17.

552.4   yet *Calais . . . Mary*'s heart] Cf. Tindal, II: 47, n. 10: "She [i.e., Queen Mary] was so affected with it, that she abandoned herself to Despair; and told those about her, she should die, though they were yet Strangers to the Cause of her Death; but if they would know it hereafter, they must dissect her, and they should find *Calais* at her Heart."

The town was lost early in 1558 and Mary died the following November. The anecdote is recounted in all histories of the period.

552.10   MOTIVE-MONGER] *OED* cites this passage as its earliest illustration, with the definition "One who 'traffics' in motives."

553.5−6   I told the reader . . . not eloquent] In vol. II, chap. 4: "My uncle *Toby*, by nature, was not eloquent" (105.22−23).

553.13   *Tertullus*] Sterne may have in mind either of two men. One is Tertullus, the orator in Acts 24: 1−8, who speaks against Paul (himself a soldier, we should note) and is answered by him; cf. Acts 24: 25: "And as he [Paul] reasoned of righteousness, temperance, and judgment to come, Felix [the governor] trembled." The other is Tertullian (c. 160−c. 240), the "first great writer of Latin Christianity, whose chief work, *Apologeticus adversus Gentes pro Christianis*, an expertly argued vindication of the Christian church against false accusations, was the weightiest apologia for Christianity produced during the first two centuries" (Work, p. 458, n. 2); cf. *OCD*, s.v. *Tertullian*.

Sterne had written about the first Tertullus in his sermon "Felix's Behaviour towards Paul, examined" (III.19), which perhaps makes him the more likely candidate.

554.4   *My uncle* TOBY's *apologetical oration*.] Toby's speech owes something, perhaps, to Don Quixote's defense of knight-errantry over the profession of scholar, as delivered in I.IV.10−11; e.g.: "It is then no longer to be doubted, but that this Exercise and Profession surpasses all others that have been invented by Man, and is so much the more honourable, as it is more expos'd to Dangers. . . . [The] Object and End is Peace, which is the greatest Blessing Man can wish for in this Life. . . . This Peace is the true End of War." Don Quixote then goes on to discuss the sufferings and hardships of the soldier (having forgotten, it would seem, that he began by defending knight-errantry): "he depends on his miserable Pay, which he receives but seldom, or perhaps never; or else in that he makes by Marauding, with the Hazard of his Life, and Trouble of his Conscience. Such is sometimes his want of Apparel, that a slash'd Buff-Coat is all his Holiday Raiment and Shirt . . . . But above all, when the Day shall come, wherein he is to put in practice the Exercise of his Profession . . . when the Day of Battle shall come, then, as a Mark of his Honour, shall his Head be dignified with a Cap made of Lint, to stop a Hole made by a Bullet, or be perhaps carried off maim'd, at the Expence of a Leg or an Arm. And if this do not happen, but that merciful Heaven preserve his Life and Limbs, it may fall out that he shall remain as poor as before, and must run through many Encounters and Battles, nay always come off victorious, to obtain some little Preferment . . ." (II: 146–50). See also Trim's defense of the soldier against the curate, 506.3–12.

Toby's oration is similar to Quixote's in tone, but it is from Burton's introduction to the *Anatomy* that Sterne borrows specific passages, and it may be important to remember that Burton is here delivering his famous diatribe *against* war. Cf. 556.19–557.2 with Burton's "what intolerable misery poor souldiers endure, their often wounds, hunger, thirst, &c. the lamentable cares, torments, calamities & oppressions that accompanie such proceedings . . ." ("Democritus to the Reader," p. 30); and "By means of which [the pursuit of "honor"] it comes to passe that daily so many voluntaries offer themselves, leaving their sweet wives, children, friends, for six pence (if they can get it) a day, prostitute their lives and limbs, desire to enter upon breaches, lye sentinell, perdue, give the first onset, stand in the forefront of the battell, marching bravely on with a cheerfull noise of drums and trumpets . . . so many banners streaming in the ayre . . . variety of colours, cost and magnificence . . ." (p. 32).

Yorick's comment (557.4–5) is also from Burton: "what plague, what furie brought so divellish, so brutish a thing as war first into mens minds? Who made so soft and peaceable a creature, born to love, mercie, meeknesse, so to rave, rage like beasts, and run on to their own destruction?" (p. 30).

Burton may also have suggested Toby's discussion about Troy, although he adds further details: "The siege of *Troy* lasted ten years eight months, there died 870000 *Grecians*, 670000 *Trojans*, at the taking of the City, and after were slain 276000 men, women, and children of all sorts" (p. 30). Toby's final comment that he and Trim are "answering the great ends of our creation" on the bowling green contrasts sharply with one of Burton's final comments: "Which is yet more to be lamented, they perswade them, this hellish course of life is holy . . ." (p. 33).

For an analysis of Toby's oration and its borrowing from Burton, see Wolfgang Zach, "'My Uncle Toby's Apologetical Oration' und die Politische Sinndimension von 'Tristram Shandy'," *GRM* 27 (1977): 394–98.

555.23–24   When *Guy*, Earl of *Warwick . . . England*] Work, p. 460, n. 1: "A legendary hero of English romance, whose popular exploits have been retold in many forms since the twelfth century. The school-boy's copy was probably one of the ballads or chap-books popular during the seventeenth and eighteenth centuries. The histories of Parismus, Prince of Bohemia, and of his son, Parismenos, were very popular imitations of the Spanish chivalric romances. *Valentine and Orson* was a romance of the Charlemagne cycle, popular in many languages and versions since the fifteenth century. The *Seven Champions* may be a slip for *The Seven Champions of Christendom*, the name given in many popular medieval tales to the seven national saints (George of England, Denis of France, James of Spain, Anthony of Italy, Andrew of Scotland, Patrick of Ireland, and David of Wales), whose exploits have been celebrated in countless romances, ballads, and plays." Sterne uses the title *Seven Champions of England* earlier, 65.18.

Fielding has a similar catalogue of chapbook romances in *Joseph Andrews*, ed. Martin Battestin (Middletown, Conn.: Wesleyan University Press, 1967), book I, chap. 1, p. 18: "Such are the History of *John* the Great, who, by his brave and heroic Actions against Men of large and athletic Bodies, obtained the glorious Appellation of the Giant-killer; that of an Earl of *Warwick*, whose Christian Name was *Guy;* the Lives of *Argalus* and *Parthenia*, and above all, the History of those seven worthy Personages, the Champions of Christendom." Battestin notes that the first written version of *Seven Champions* was by Richard Johnson in 1596.

556.6–7   Did any one of you shed more tears for *Hector?*] Burton, 2.3.5 (p. 337), makes the point that "*Austin* shed teares when he red the destruction of *Troy*"; actually Augustine as a youth wept over the story of Dido

("to bewail dead Dido, because she killed herself for love . . .") and be-
rated himself for having done so to the detriment of his own soul (*Confes-
sions*, I.13, pp. 38–43).

Cf. Yorick's assertion in *ASJ* that when the evils of the world press upon
him, he retreats into the story of Aeneas and Dido: "I see the injured spirit
wave her head, and turn off silent from the author of her miseries and
dishonours—I lose the feelings for myself in hers—and in those affections which were wont to make me mourn for her when I was at school"
(p. 225).

556.7–9 And when . . . without it] Both Work (p. 461, n. 3) and Watt
(p. 350, n. 4) note that Priam's mission to retrieve Hector's body was
successful (at least in Homer's account, *Iliad*, 24), but perhaps Toby's
chapbook version told a different story.

556.16 scatter cypress] The cypress has long been associated with death and
cemeteries; the Romans dedicated the cypress tree to Pluto, and along with
the Greeks laid cypress twigs in the coffins of the dead. Coffins supposedly
were made of cypress wood; see *Twelfth Night*, II.iv.51–52: "Come away,
come away, death, / And in sad cypress let me be laid." Cf. *ASJ*, p. 116: "I
would fasten [my affections] upon some sweet myrtle, or seek some melancholy cypress to connect myself to . . . ."

557.17 we were answering the great ends of our creation.] Cf. *Sermons*,
IV.23.36: "they who will not be persuaded to answer the great purposes of
their being, upon such arguments as are offered to them in scripture, will
never be persuaded to it by any other means, how extraordinary soever
. . . ."

558.16–17 *Quanto id* . . . sayeth *Cardan*.] Sterne's source, Burton, 1.2.1.6,
p. 64, reads: "we make choice of the best Rammes for our sheepe, reare the
neatest Kine, and keep the best dogges, *Quanto id diligentius in procreandis
liberis observandum?* And how carefull then should wee bee in begetting of
our children?"; noted by Ferriar, I: 93. The reference to Cardan is un-
justified and may possibly be explained by the fact that in the fifth edition
of the *Anatomy*, "*Cardan*" appears on the top line of p. 64. The correct
author, cited by Burton, is Jean Fernel, *Universa medicina* (1554; Geneva,
1679), p. 135. See t.n., vol. II, p. 859, in this edition.

For Cardan, see above, n. to 418.8–12. Jean Fernel (1497–1558) was a

French physician, surnamed the modern Galen.

Also see above, n. to 355.2–4.

559.3–4   the rest of the confederating powers.] Britain's alliance with the Dutch and the Empire received additional slight support from Savoy and Portugal.

559.7   all the days of my life] A biblical commonplace; Genesis 3: 14 and 3: 17, Deuteronomy 6: 2, Joshua 4: 14, etc. Sterne uses it again, 589.13 and 637.19–20.

559.15–16   from the month of *March* to *November*] I.e., the campaign season, since troops were kept inactive during the winter months.

559.20ff.   The *French* were so backwards all that summer, etc.] Sterne takes his account of the dismantling of Dunkirk from Tindal, IV: 327ff.: "Monsieur *Tugghe*, Deputy from the Magistrates of *Dunkirk*, presented to the Queen an address or petition, 'wherein he begged her Majesty's clemency for sparing the harbour and port of that town.' But he was told by the Lord *Bolingbroke*, 'That the Queen beheld with sorrow the damages, which the inhabitants of that town would sustain by the demolition of its ramparts and harbour: But she did not think it convenient to make any alteration in an affair agreed on by a treaty.' *Tugghe*, not discouraged by this repulse, presented a second address, wherein he suggested, 'That the preservation of the harbour of *Dunkirk*, without works and fortifications, might, in time, be equally useful, and become even absolutely necessary, both for her Majesty's political views, and the good of her subjects.' This he endeavoured to evince, by a long deduction of several particulars, and then concluded with presuming to hope, 'That her Majesty would graciously be pleased to recall part of her sentence, by causing her thunderbolts to fall only on the martial works, which might have incurred her displeasure, and by sparing only the mole and dykes, which, in their naked condition, could, for the future, be no more than an object of pity.'"

Sterne's several rows of asterisks indicating the English ministers' "private reasons" perhaps allude to the quarrel between the *Guardian* and the *Examiner* concerning the delay; Tindal (IV: 327) had written that the arguments for immediate dismantling in the *Guardian* were "not only a great mortification to *Tugghe* and the other *French* agents, but also gave no small offence to some of the *British* Ministers, as appeared by the severe

animadversions that were published by the authors of the *Examiner*."
Steele was the author of the attack on the ministers in the *Guardian* (August 7, 1713), which he followed with a pamphlet, *The Importance of Dunkirk Consider'd;* this in turn was answered by Swift in *The Importance of the Guardian Consider'd*. For an account of the debate see Irvin Ehrenpreis, *Swift: The Man, His Works, and the Age* (Cambridge: Harvard University Press, 1967), II: 689ff. There is no evidence that Sterne read any of the materials, though his version of the affair is certainly closer to Steele's than to Swift's.

Tindal's account continues with the process of dismantling: "About the beginning of *September,* the Colonels *Armstrong* and *Clayton* were appointed Commissioners to see the fortifications of *Dunkirk* demolished; and at the same time two Captains of men of war were, by the Admiralty, named to see the harbour filled up . . . . [On September 26] a dispute arose between Sir *James Abercromby*, the *British* Commandant, and Monsieur *le Blane*, the *French* Intendant of the Province, about the manner of carrying it on. The *French* intended to have made a breach in the ramparts, or main fortifications of the town; but the two *English* Commissioners having made the Commandant sensible, that, if the same was permitted, the *English* garrison was not safe, and the *French* might easily make themselves masters of the place; Sir *James* insisted, and it was at last agreed to by *le Blane*, that all the out-works, both towards the sea and the land, should be first demolished; next, the harbour ruined and filled; afterwards the main fortifications of the place razed and destroyed; and last of all, the citadel" (IV: 328).

Baird ("Time-Scheme," p. 812, n. 53) observes that Fort Louis is not mentioned in Tindal's account but is clearly marked as the most distant of the outworks on the plan of Dunkirk facing p. 328. See also Steele's *The Englishman* 31 (December 15, 1713), for a clear presentation of the strategical problems surrounding the demolition of Dunkirk (ed. Rae Blanchard [Oxford: Clarendon Press, 1955], pp. 126–28). It might be worth noting that one of the most vituperative pamphlets against Steele and the Whig position was written by the anonymous "Toby" (William Wagstaffe?); see *The Englishman* 57, pp. 233–36.

559.25–27   to spare the mole . . . of pity] For "mole," Partridge records the meaning "penis" for the nineteenth and twentieth centuries, but one suspects it was available to Sterne as well.

561.19–22 STILLNESS . . . in his arm chair.] Sterne's "poetic" effort may reflect Milton's description of evening in *Paradise Lost*, IV.598–609: "Now came still Ev'ning on, and Twilight gray / Had in her sober Livery all things clad; / Silence accompanied . . . / . . . till the Moon / Rising in clouded Majesty, at length / Apparent Queen unveil'd her peerless light, / And o'er the dark her Silver Mantle threw." We thank Professor Dustin Griffin for calling this parallel to our attention; see also *Il Penseroso*, lines 31–60.

561.23–25 No longer *Amberg* . . . *Dendermond*, the next] See 539.9–10, 540.13–15, and nn. above.

562.10–11 Softer visions . . . his slumbers] Cf. 131.8–11 and n. above. See also Edmund Burke, *A Philosophical Enquiry into the Origin of our Ideas of the Sublime and Beautiful* (1757), ed. J. T. Boulton (London: Routledge & Kegan Paul, 1958), pp. 149–51: "from this description it is almost impossible not to conclude, that beauty acts by relaxing the solids of the whole system. . . . Who is a stranger to that manner of expression so common in all times and in all countries, of being softened, relaxed, enervated, dissolved, melted away by pleasure? . . . Our position will . . . appear confirmed . . . if we can shew that such things as we have already observed to be the genuine constituents of beauty, have each of them separately taken a natural tendency to relax the fibres. . . . As a beautiful object presented to the sense, by causing a relaxation in the body, produces the passion of love in the mind; so if by any means the passion should first have its origin in the mind, a relaxation of the outward organs will as certainly ensue in a degree proportioned to the cause." Sterne may have used (or parodied) Burke on other occasions as well, to establish the nature of love; see below, nn. to 702.10–16, 708.1–16.

562.22–563.4 a description . . . upon him to pronounce] Sterne's chapter is heavily dependent upon Burton's discussion of "Love Melancholy" in the third partition of the *Anatomy*, but there are sufficient additional materials included to suggest other sources as well, not all of which have been identified. These opening comments do derive from Burton, 3.1.1.2 (p. 408): "*It is worth the labour,* saith *Plotinus,* to consider well of *Love, whether it be a God or a Divell, or passion of the minde, or partly God, partly Divell, partly passion.* Hee concludes Love to participate of all three, to arise from Desire of that which is beautifull and fayre, and defines it to be *an action of the minde, desiring that which is good. Plato* calls it the *great Divell,* for his vehemency, and soveraignty over all other passions, and defines it an appetite, *by which we desire some good to be present. Ficinus* in his Comment addes the word Faire to this definition . . . ."

Plotinus (205–69/70) and Marsilio Ficino (1433–99) are important commentators on Plato and major neoplatonic philosophers in their own right; the references are to Plato's *Symposium* (probably, as Work suggests, Plato's theory of the daemon, 202–3), Ficino's *Commentary* (6.7–8), and Plotinus's *Enneades* (III.5).

For Sterne's further borrowings from this partition of the *Anatomy,* see *TS,* vol. VIII, chap. 33.

563.7–12   the same temper . . . bouncing *Cantharidis.*] Work, p. 467, n. 4, identifies the source of this passage as Sir John Floyer and Edward Baynard, *The History of Cold-Bathing* (1702); we quote from the fifth edition (1722), pt. 2, pp. 199–200: "How many Men has intempestive and over Blistering destroy'd . . . by mixing the venomous and corrosive Effluvium's of the *Cantharides* with the Blood, accuating the *Pulse,* besides bringing *Stranguries,* and other Mischiefs on the *Bladder?* insomuch that I believe the Devil himself, old *Beelzebub,* to be nothing but a great *Cantharid,* the Prince of *Flies,* they act so according to his Nature, to plague Mankind where-ever they are applied. . . . And here I cannot omit a Story of an Apothecary's Man, in *Fleet-street,* whose Master died in a few Days Sickness of a *Fever,* which his Doctors quickly made malignant. *Quoth he,* I wonder that my Master should die so soon, for he had a Dozen *Blisters* on, and they all drew very strong: That is true, *quoth one standing by,* thou art in the right on't, for in Four Days Time (together with the help of a Team of Doctors) he was drawn out of his Bed into the Vault over the way there, pointing at St. *Dunstan*'s Church."

In Sterne's day, and long before, cantharides, a preparation of Spanish flies, was also known—as it is today—as an aphrodisiac. See, e.g., Goldsmith's attack on the first two volumes of *TS,* where bawdiness is called "a very proper succedaneum to cantharides, or an assa fœtida pill" (*Citizen of the World,* letter 53, in *Works,* II: 222).

563.13–18   I have nothing . . . *moods and passions*.] Work, p. 467, n. 5,
identifies this as St. Gregory Nazianzen's comment to his friend and correspondent Philagrius, and translates it: "Bravo! that you philosophize in
your sufferings" (*Epistola* 32). An intermediate source has not been located, although one feels fairly certain that Sterne was not quoting directly
from St. Gregory (for whom, see above, n. to 497.11ff.).

563.19–564.3   Nor is it . . . stink again.] These two paragraphs are a confusing amalgamation of Burton and at least one other source, perhaps Ferrand, *Erotomania* (see above, n. to 550.17), a work often cited by Burton.
As suggested in the Grenville copy of *TS* (VI: 399), Ferrand (p. 334) is
almost certainly the source for the opinion of Gordonius: "And of this
opinion is *Gordonius*, who would have them whipped *ad putorem usq.*, till
they stinke againe *cap*. 15. *de Amore*." Burton, 3.2.5.1 (p. 542), contains
the same information, but his language is different: "*Gordonius would have
them soundly whipped, or to coole their courage, kept in prison*, and there fed
with bread and water, till they acknowledge their errour, and become of
another minde." Work, p. 468, n. 8, identifies Gordonius as the French
physician Bernard de Gordon (fl. c. 1283–c. 1308) and the reference as
Lilium Medicinæ, 2.20.

   Neither Burton nor Ferrand links Rhasis (fl. 925), an Arabian physician, or Dioscorides (fl. 75), a Greek physician and author of a great
Materia Medica, with major schools of thought, though both are mentioned with some frequency. Ferrand does discuss the question "*Whether in
Love-Melancholy, the Heart, be the seat of the Disease, or the Braine*"
(chap. 9, pp. 77ff.), but like everyone else in the seventeenth century he
clearly identifies the initial organ affected by love as the liver (see above, n.
to 550.11–18). At a later point (p. 172), Ferrand discusses Rhasis's attempt to determine the size of the liver by the size of the fingers, because of
the "Mutuall and Reciprocall sympathy" between the two—which may
help to explain Walter's advice to Toby to avoid holding hands with the
widow Wadman (727.15–18). Burton covers similar ground, 3.2.1.2
(pp. 441–43). See also above, n. to 550.17.

   Burton and Ferrand both frequently mention the various refriger-
ants—cucumbers, water lilies, purslane, and the like. Sterne, however,
seems particularly indebted to one paragraph in Ferrand, pp. 264–65:
"THE first Medicinall remedy shall be a Clyster, composed of cooling and

moystening Ingredients: among which it will doe well to mixe Hempseed, *Agnus Castus*, and the like . . . . Sometimes also I adde hereto some few graines of Camphire: or else I temper it with water of Lettice, Purslane, or water-Lillies: and so give it him to drinke . . . ." Aëtius (a Greek physician, fl. 540) and Dioscorides are among those cited as recommending these drugs; Aëtius is not mentioned in this regard (though frequently cited elsewhere) in the *Anatomy*.

"Hanea" returns us to Burton, who writes: "Those *Athenian* women, in their solemne feasts called *Thesmopheries*, were to abstaine nine daies from the company of men, during which time . . . they laid a certain hearb named *Hanea*, in their beds, which asswaged those ardent flames of love, and freed them from the torments of that violent passion" (p. 543). What is being described, however, is the *agnus castus*, an aromatic shrub or tree, sometimes called the chaste tree, or chaste-lamb tree, supposedly able to preserve chastity; see Pliny, *Natural History*, 24.38 (VII: 47), and Ferrand, p. 256. Work, p. 468, n. 7, suggests that Burton mistransliterated the Greek ἄγνος (*agnos*), but that seems rather unlikely, although we do not have another explanation. At any rate, Burton and Sterne seem alone in their use of the word; see below, n. to 728.6–11.

Ferrand is dubious about the efficacy of precious stones (p. 272), but mentions topaz specifically as someone else's prescription on p. 317. Burton also notes its supposed quality: "Idem præstat Topatius annulo gestatus" ("Topaz is likewise recommended, worn in a ring"), p. 544 (misnumbered 534). Work, p. 468, n. 7, notes that "according to medieval lapidaries, the topaz had a tranquillizing effect on all the passions, but was particularly valuable as a cure for sensuality." Tristram puts on his own topaz ring in vol. IX, chap. 13 (763.16).

564.10   camphorated cerecloth] Both Burton and Ferrand recommend camphor. Burton, p. 544 (misnumbered 534), writes: "Huc faciunt medicamenta venerem sopientia, *ut Camphora pudendis alligata, & in brachâ gestata (quidam ait) membrum flaccidum reddit*" ("Here they make medicines to allay lust, *such as putting camphor on the parts, and carrying it in the breeches (one saith) keeps the penis flaccid*"). Burton calls camphor inimical to lust in the highest degree.

Ferrand also mentions camphor frequently; e.g.: "I would not suffer them to weare cloathes that are lined with Furres, Ermine, or Velvet

. . . . All these things I would banish . . . and instead thereof substitute *Camphire,* which by reason of it's cold quality, very much tempereth the heat of the blood" (p. 238). He also notes that if it seems too dangerous to have these "Oyntments, Cere-cloathes, or cooling Fomentations aplied," then the patient might be girded about "with a thin plate of lead" (p. 269). See also p. 272, where the opinion is cited that camphor excels all other remedies in virtue and efficacy.

Ferrand finds "Idlenesse" a very dangerous cause of love-melancholy and recommends that physicians "take care that our Patient be alwaies in some serious Imployment or other . . . whether it be in Warlike Actions, or Hunting, Study, or Husbandry" (pp. 248–49).

565.10–11   *deeply* in love . . . *over head and ears in it*] Cf. 693.21–23: "So, thou wast once in love, Trim! . . . Souse! replied the corporal—over head and ears!" See also "Journal to Eliza" (*Letters,* p. 355): "I sh^d not be astonish'd, Eliza, if you was to declare, 'You was up to the ears in Love with Me'." This expression is perhaps proverbial; see Tilley, H268, and *ODEP,* s.v. *Over.*

565.14   divinityship] *OED* cites this passage (wrongly referenced as chap. 36) as its only recorded example for the definition "knowledge of or skill in divinity"; see above, n. to 452.5, and below, n. to 669.15.

565.20   concupiscible] *OED* cites this passage as its last illustration, with the definition "Vehemently to be desired; worthy to be longed for or lusted after."

570.6–7   by the help . . . the cold seeds] Work, p. 473, n. 1: "The seeds of the cucumber, gourd, pumpkin, etc. Such a diet was thought to cool the blood and compose the passions." George Cheyne, *The English Malady* (1733), pp. 103–19 and passim, recommends as a last resort a diet of "Milk, with Seeds or Grains, and the different Kinds of Vegetable Food" for those very seriously disordered in mind or body. He makes very clear that this is an extreme prescription for extreme illness.

570.9ff.   Now, etc.] See Watt, p. 359, n. 1: "The letters 'Inv. T.S.' and 'Scul. T.S.' below the 'tolerable straight lines' are conventional abbreviations below engravings, here meaning 'Tristram Shandy created (*invenit,* "invented")' this and 'Tristram Shandy engraved (*sculpsit,* "sculpted")' this."

571.15–17   In this last volume . . . of my way.] Cervantes praises his narrator in a similar fashion rather late in the work, II.III.44 (IV: 78): "He has therefore in this second Part avoided all distinct and independent Stories, introducing only such as have the Appearance of Episodes, yet flow naturally from the Design of the Story, and these but seldom, and with as much Brevity as they can be express'd. Therefore since he has ty'd himself up to such narrow Bounds, and confin'd his Understanding and Parts, otherwise capable of the most copious Subjects, to the pure Matter of this present Undertaking, he begs it may add a Value to his Work; and that he may be commended, not so much for what he has writ, as for what he has forborn to write."

572.5   The emblem . . . says *Cicero*] Watt, p. 360, n. 2: "'*Recta via*,' or 'the right path of life,' is a phrase often used by Cicero." Many passages in Cicero's writings might be applicable to Sterne's point; e.g., *De Finibus*, book III, sec. 24: "Ut enim histrioni actio, saltatori motus non quivis sed certus quidam est datus, sic vita agenda est certo genere quodam, non quolibet; quod genus conveniens consentaneumque dicimus" ("For just as an actor or dancer has assigned to him not any but a certain particular part or dance, so life has to be conducted in a certain fixed way, and not in any way we like. This fixed way we speak of as 'conformable' and suitable" (pp. 242–43).

572.6   The *best line!* say cabbage-planters] Cf. 655.6–12: "I defy the best cabbage planter that ever existed, whether he plants backwards or forwards, it makes little difference in the account (except that he will have more to answer for in the one case than in the other)—I defy him to go on cooly, critically, and canonically, planting his cabbages one by one, in straight lines . . . ." Robert Alter points out that "'Planting' is a low colloquialism for inserting the male member, or, more generally, for sexual intercourse. 'Cabbage' is extant at least in nineteenth-century sources as an epithet for the female pudendum . . ." ("*Tristram Shandy* and the Game of Love," *ASch* 37 [1968]: 319–20). Alter also calls attention to "'case' . . . the familiar Renaissance term for the vagina," and the "parallel, auditory pun in the accented syllable of 'account'." Cf. J. S. Farmer and W. E. Henley, *Slang and Its Analogues* (London, 1890–1904), s.v. *cabbage, plant, greens*. A passage in Rabelais may be apropos here, although in its literal context Panurge is simply praising those who stay on land rather than venture out to sea: "O twice and thrice happy those that plant cabbages! O destinies, why did you not spin me for a cabbage-planter? O how

few are there to whom Jupiter have been so favourable, as to predestinate
them to plant cabbages! They have always one foot on the ground, and the
other not far from it. Dispute who will of felicity, and summum bonum,
for my part, whosoever plants cabbage, is now by my decree proclaim'd
most happy . . ." (IV.18.162).

572.6–8   the shortest line . . . to another.] The famous first assumption of
Archimedes in *On the Sphere and Cylinder:* "Of all lines which have the
same extremities the straight line is the least." See above, n. to 58.7.

572.10   birth-day suits!] *OED*, s.v. *birth-day suit*: "a dress worn on the king's
birthday." But see Keith Stewart, "'Birthday Suit', 'Birthday Clothes', and
Sterne," *N&Q* 213 (1968): 463, for indications that the definition
"nakedness" was also available to Sterne. For Sterne's use of the former
meaning, see *Letters*, p. 312: "Mrs. Draper, habited for conquest, in a
birthday suit . . . ."

NOTES TO VOLUME VII

Title-page (motto)] This sentence from Pliny the Younger has an interesting context in view of the structure—or lack of it—in *TS*. Pliny defends the long description he has given of his villa and argues that "a writer's first duty is to read his title, to keep on asking himself what he set out to say, and to realize that he will not say too much if he sticks to his theme, though he certainly will if he brings in extraneous matter.

"You know the number of lines Homer and Virgil devote to their descriptions of the arms of Achilles and Aeneas: yet neither passage seems long because both poets are carrying out their original intention. You see too how Aratus traces and tabulates the smallest stars, but because this is his main subject and not a digression ("Non enim excursus hic eius, sed opus ipsum est"), his work does not lack proportion" (*Epistles*, V.vi, I: 353–55).

575.1–4   No—I think . . . give me leave] See 402.14–15 and n. above. For Sterne's health during the three years between the publication of vols. V–VI and VII–VIII, see "Introduction to the Text," vol. II, pp. 827–30, in this edition.

575.4–9   and in another place . . . good spirits.] See 82.1–6: "[I] have so complicated and involved the digressive and progressive movements, one wheel within another, that the whole machine, in general, has been kept a-going;---and, what's more, it shall be kept a-going these forty years, if it pleases the fountain of health to bless me so long with life and good spirits." But it is at the end of vol. VI that Tristram draws his straight line with the help of "a writing-master's ruler" (pp. 571–72).

444

Sterne's alteration from "fountain of health" to "fountain of life" may
not be entirely by chance; the latter is a biblical commonplace. See especially Proverbs 13: 14: "The law of the wise is a fountain of life, to depart
from the snares of death"; and Proverbs 14: 27: "The fear of the Lord is a
fountain of life, to depart from the snares of death." See also Psalm 36: 9.

575.11–12   unless the mounting . . . fool with me] Cf. Horace, *Satires*,
II.iii.247–49 (pp. 172–73): "Aedificare casas, plostello adiungere
mures, / ludere par impar, equitare in harundine longa, / si quem delectet
barbatum, amentia verset" ("Building toy-houses, harnessing mice to a
wee cart, playing odd and even, riding a long stick—if these things delighted a bearded man, lunacy would plague him"). Erasmus uses the
image in *Moriae Encomium* ("Prefatory Epistle from Erasmus to Sir
Thomas More"): "Proinde si uidebitur, fingant isti me latrunculis interim
animi causa lusisse, aut si malint, equitasse in arundine longa"; White
Kennett translates: "So that if they please, let themselves think the Worst of
me, and fancy to themselves that I were all this while a playing at Push-
pin, or rideing Astride on a Hobby-Horse" (*Praise of Folly* [1724], p. iii).
EDD records "to have on the stick" as a West Yorkshire expression for "to
make a fool of" (s.v. *Stick*, 11.15).

576.9–10   of a nun . . . eating a muscle] Cf. Burton, 1.1.3.2 (p. 32): "as of
him that thought himselfe a shell-fish; of a Nunne, and of a desperate
Monk, that would not be perswaded but that he was damned"; suggested
by Work, p. 480, n. 2.

We are unable to supply the joke Tristram was telling, but it seems
evident that its ingredients had a long history. Burton's sentence does not
appear to be bawdy, though quite possibly he too was relying upon an
audience that would recognize certain catchphrases. John Dunton, e.g.,
tells a joke about the "eating of oysters" in *A Voyage Round the World*
(1691), I: 129. In one of his notes to *Hamlet*, Warburton comments: "the
critic only changed this for that; by a like figure, the common people say,
You *rejoice the cockles of my heart*, for *the muscles of my heart*; an unlucky
mistake of one shell-fish for another" (*Works of Shakespeare* [1747], VIII:
191); to which Thomas Edwards responded in *Canons of Criticism*, 7th ed.
(1765; New York: Augustus M. Kelley, Publishers, 1970): "In this note
. . . the reader may see the whole strength of Mr. Warburton's reasoning;
I know not which to admire most: the consistency of his argument, the

decency of his language, or the wit of his lenten jest about shell-fish, which makes so proper a conclusion" (p. 133).

See also John Hall-Stevenson, *Makarony Fables* (1768), fable II ("The Doctor and the Student"): "Lobsters ought not to think like oysters; / They were not made to be confin'd, / And spend their days like them in cloysters; / To stand when they should stir and bustle, / Gaping and studying like a muscle."

576.18–19   for by sin, we are told, he enter'd the world] Cf. Romans 5: 12: "Wherefore, as by one man sin entered into the world, and death by sin; and so death passed upon all men, for that all have sinned."

576.23–24   and as thou seest . . . by the throat] For the well-documented argument that Sterne himself lost his voice in the spring of 1762 and never recovered its full use, see Arthur Cash, "Voices Sonorous and Cracked: Sterne's Pulpit Oratory," in *Quick Springs of Sense*, ed. Larry S. Champion (Athens: University of Georgia Press, 1974), pp. 205–9.

577.5   I will lead him a dance] A conscious inversion, perhaps, of the usual order of the medieval icon, both in pictures and verse, of Death leading a variety of persons to the grave—the Danse Macabre, or Totentanz, or Dance of Death. Sterne could hardly have been unaware of the tradition, perhaps through the widely reproduced woodcuts of Hans Holbein the Younger (1497–1543).

577.9   Joppa] A port city of ancient Israel (the modern Jaffa) from which Jonah went to sea to escape God's mission (Jonah 1: 3); and where Peter received his vision that allowed him to continue to preach to the Gentiles (Acts 11: 5–17).

Eugenius takes "world's end" chronologically rather than geographically in order to turn his compliment.

577.15   *Allons!*] "Let's go!" The *Stanford Dictionary* notes several examples of anglicized usage before Sterne.

577.21–22   Rochester church . . . Canterbury] The three towns are on the road between London and Dover; the dean and chapter of Rochester gave Tristram his copy of "Ernulphus's Curse" (202.4–7). Thomas à Becket (c. 1118–70) was murdered and enshrined in the Canterbury Cathedral.

Just before his own departure for France in 1762, Sterne wrote from Chatham: "Yes—Yes, here I am—no matter why or wherefore—but what is more material, I am much mended even at Chatham!—Goodness!

What shall I be in the balsamic air of Languedoc . . . ." And from Dover, he was almost as cheerful: "I am ten, nay 15 per Cent better, only he took his Idea of me, from a pale sour face I set one morning . . . which he took to be the forerunners of my Exit not into France, but into the Vale of Jehosophat—We shall soon, by Gods blessing be in the one—& by his mercy I hope I shall not go so speedily into the other as my Phiz seems to prophesy . . ." (Arthur Cash, "Some New Sterne Letters," *TLS* [April 3, 1965], p. 284).

578.7ff.   Why, there is not time, etc.] Tristram's behavior during the cross-ing may owe something to Panurge's behavior during a storm at sea in Rabelais, IV.18.159ff.; e.g.: "Alas! alas! where is our main course? . . . our top-mast is run adrift. Alas! who shall have this wreck? . . . don't let go the main tack nor the bowlin. I hear the block crack; is it broke? . . . My heart's sunk down below my midriff. By my troth I am in a sad fright . . . . Bou, bou, bou, ou, ou, ou, bou, bou, bous. I sink, I'm drown'd, I'm gone, good people, I'm drown'd" (p. 163).

578.11   the nervous juices . . . volatile salts] Chambers, s.v. *Nervous Spirit or Juice:* "a pure, subtile, volatile humour, better known by the name of *animal spirits;* secreted from the arterious blood in the cortical part of the brain, collected in the medulla oblongata, and thence driven, by the force of the heart, into the cavities of the nerves; to be conveyed by them throughout the body, for the purposes of sensation and animal motion." Cf. above, n. to 1.16, where another Chambers entry expresses skepticism concerning the animal spirits.

In the entry for *Salt,* Chambers defines *fixed salts* as those which, "being more gross and material, resist and sustain the fire; and are not raised by it, but remain, after calcination, or distillation, in the earthy part, at the bot-tom"; *volatile salts,* on the contrary, "are those light, subtile ones, which rise easily upon distillation, or are even exhaled by the nose, and rendered sensible to the smell." *Salt* here is not common table salt but, more broadly, any solid, soluble, noninflammable substance having a taste; thus defined, it represented for many eighteenth-century chemists and physi-cians one of the five constituent elements of all bodies. For a thorough discussion, see Lester S. King, *The Philosophy of Medicine; The Early Eighteenth Century* (Cambridge: Harvard University Press, 1978), pp. 65–76.

578.16−17   hearts like stones] Proverbial comparison; Tilley, H311. Cf. *TS*, 747.9−10.

578.19−21   Madam! how is it . . . tenth time, sir] An interesting gloss upon this passage may be found in Defoe's *Roxana*, when during the storm at sea both Roxana and her servant Amy show great signs of repentance. Safely on land, Amy refuses to re-embark and, Defoe writes, "the People in the Inn laugh'd at her, and jested with her; ask'd her, if she had any Sins to confess, that she was asham'd shou'd be heard of? and that she was troubled with an evil Conscience; told her, if she came to Sea, and to be in a Storm, if she had lain with her Master, she wou'd certainly tell her Mistress of it; and that it was a common thing, for poor Maids to confess all the Young-Men they had lain with; that there was one poor Girl that went over with her Mistress, whose Husband was a ——r, in ——, in the City of *London*, who confess'd, in the Terror of a Storm, that she had lain with her Master, and all the Apprentices so often, and in such and such Places, and made the poor Mistress, when she return'd to *London*, fly at her Husband, and make such a Stir, as was indeed, the Ruin of the whole Family" (ed. Jane Jack [London: Oxford University Press, 1964], p. 130).

   For the play on "undone," see above, n. to 321.16−18; cf. 796.15.

578.23   The wind chopp'd about! s'Death!] Cf. 444.2−3: "but there's a man there—no—not him with the bundle under his arm—the grave man in black.—S'death!" It is, of course, a minced expression of the oath "God's death."

579.4−14   It is a great inconvenience . . . Beauvais.] Cf. Jean Aimar Piganiol de la Force's *Nouveau Voyage de France* (1724; Paris, 1755), II: 213, where the three routes from Calais to Paris are delineated: "*Ce Voyage se peut faire par trois routes différentes. La premiere en passant par Beauvais; la seconde en passant par Amiens; & la troisieme, qui est la plus longue, est celle de Lisle.*"

   Van R. Baker's "Sterne and Piganiol de la Force: The Making of Volume VII of *Tristram Shandy*," *CLS* 13 (1976): 5−14, is a thorough discussion of Sterne's debt. Baker notes that in the present instance the facing map would have shown Sterne that Arras was on the Lille route and Chantilly on the way to Amiens.

   Where Sterne has provided the substance of Piganiol we have not provided an additional translation.

579.15   travel-writer] *OED* cites this passage as its sole illustration.

580.5–6   by all who have *wrote and gallop'd*] Cf. 524.23–24 and n. above.

580.8–10   from the great *Addison* . . . at his a—] Sterne is probably alluding
to Addison's introductory comments to his *Remarks on Several Parts of
Italy* (1705): "*For before I enter'd on my Voyage I took care to refresh my
Memory among the* Classic *Authors, and to make such Collections out of 'em as
I might afterwards have Occasion for. I must confess it was not one of the least
Entertainments that I met with in Travelling, to examine these several De-
scriptions, as it were, upon the Spot, and to compare the Natural Face of the
Country with the Landskips that the Poets have given us of it.*" Sterne uses the
same epithet, "great," in the only other reference to Addison in *TS*, 71.18.

Cf. Walpole's letter to Henry Zouch, March 20, 1762, *Correspondence*,
ed. W. S. Lewis and Ralph M. Williams (New Haven: Yale University
Press, 1951), XVI: 52: "It is like Mr Addison's travels, of which it was so
truly said, that he might have composed them without stirring out of
England." Alan H. Vrooman, "The Origin and Development of the *Sentimental Journey* as a Work of Travel Literature and of Sensibility" (Ph.D.
diss., Princeton University, 1940), p. 48, calls attention to this passage as
an indication that Sterne's comment on Addison's travels was probably a
commonplace.

580.13–14   and have wrote . . . as well as not.] Cf. *ASJ*, p. 84: "much grief
of heart has it oft and many a time cost me, when I have observed how
many a foul step the inquisitive Traveller has measured to see sights and
look into discoveries; all which, as Sancho Pança said to Don Quixote, they
might have seen dry-shod at home." The allusion is to *Don Quixote*,
II.III.5 (III: 46), but as Stout points out in his annotation, the ultimate
source is Joseph Hall's *Quo Vadis?* (1617): "some grave and painefull Author hath collected into one view, whatsoever his country affords worthy of
marke; having measured many a fowle step for that, which we may see
dry-shod . . ." (p. 32).

See below, n. to 592.16–593.2; and above, n. to 79.14–19.

580.19   dark as pitch] A proverbial comparison; see Tilley, P357, and
ODEP, s.v. *Black as soot*. "As long as my arm" (line 24) also seems a
proverbial comparison, though it is not recorded as such. "What is what"
(lines 20–21) is proverbial; see above, n. to 274.6. Sterne may have
deliberately trivialized his diction to suit the occasion.

580.28-29   was not Democritus . . . town-clerk of *Abdera?*] Democritus
(c. 460-c. 357 B.C.) was a Greek physical philosopher, perhaps best
known to Sterne through Burton's use of the pseudonym "Democritus
Junior." In his introduction to the *Anatomy*, Burton writes: "After a
wandring life, he setled at *Abdera* a town in *Thrace*, and was sent for thither
to be their Law-maker, Recorder or Town-clerke, as some will; or as
others, he was there bred and born. Howsoever it was, there he lived at
last in a garden in the suburbs, wholly betaking himself to his studies, and
a private life, *saving that sometimes he would walk down to the haven, and
laugh heartily at such varietie of ridiculous objects, which there he saw*. Such a
one was *Democritus*" ("Democritus to the Reader," p. 2).

　　Cf. Sterne's borrowing from Burton (*"non Ego, sed Democritus dixit"*)
for a motto to vols. V and VI; and his telling a story about the town of
Abdera (via Burton) in *ASJ*, pp. 130-31.

581.1-2   town-clerk of Ephesus] Work, p. 483, n. 3: "A reference to Heraclitus (c. 540-c. 475 B.C.), a celebrated Greek philosopher who quitted
his magistracy in Ephesus, which was hereditary in his family, to apply
himself to philosophic speculation. From his lonely life, philosophic pro-
fundity, and contempt for mankind he was hyperbolically called, in contrast to Democritus, 'the weeping philosopher'."

581.6ff.   CALAIS, *Calatium*, etc.] This entire chapter is a parodic rewriting of
Piganiol's entry on Calais, *Nouveau Voyage*, II: 226-32; the relevant passages have been rearranged to parallel Sterne's development: "CALAIS,
Calesium, Calasium, Caletium, est une Ville & Port de mer qui n'étoit
autrefois qu'un Village du Comté de Guines . . . [p. 226].

　　"On y compte environ quatorze mille habitans, sans y comprendre le
Courgain, ni la Ville-basse [p. 229].

　　"La basse Ville est à l'extrémité des fortifications de la Ville de Calais.
On y compte environ quatre cens quarante maisons, ou familles [p. 231].

　　"Il n'y a dans Calais qu'une Paroisse & quatre Couvents. L'Eglise Par-
oissiale est sous l'invocation de la Vierge. Le vaisseau n'est pas de plus
grands; mais il est régulier, en forme de croix, & décoré d'onze Chapelles.
Ce qu'il y a de plus remarquable est le maitre-Autel, qui est tout construit
de marbre de Carare, & a cinquante six pieds de haut sur trente-un de
large. . . . La tour qui sert de Clocher est fort élevée, placée au milieu de

l'Eglise, & portée par quatre piliers forts délicats. Sa flêche est octogone & de pierre, & il en sort une autre qui est couverte d'ardoise [p. 228].

"Les rues de Calais sont belles & droites, & aboutissent presque toutes à la seule place qu'il y a, & qui est au milieu de la Ville. Cette place est très-mal pavée, mais d'ailleurs très-belle & très-grande, puisque sa longueur du levant au couchant est de soixante six toises, & sa largeur de cinquante-huit [p. 229].

"Il n'y a point de fontaines à Calais, & l'on ne s'y sert que de l'eau de cîterne [p. 228].

"La Maison de Ville est sur la place. Le bâtiment en est ancien & en mauvais état. . . . Il y a deux grosses cloches dans la flêche, dont l'une est pour l'horloge, & l'autre pour avertir de fermer les portes, & pour appeller les Magistrats [p. 229].

"*Le Courgain* fait partie de la Ville de Calais, & tire son nom de ce qu'anciennement il y avoit en cet endroit des pêcheurs qui gagnoient peu de chose. C'est là que résident tous les Matelots & tous les pêcheurs de Calais. Il y a huit petites rues, & les maisons en sont de brique & assez jolies. On y compte environ trois-cents quarante familles [pp. 228–29].

"Il y a dans cette Ville une autre Tour, appellée la *Tour du Guet,* parce qu'elle sert à découvrir les vaisseaux qui viennent de la mer, & à avertir de l'approche des ennemis en temps de guerre, soit par mer, soit par terre . . . [p. 230].

"La Citadelle de Calais est une des plus grandes qu'il y ait. Elle conserve son ancienne enceinte & son fossé . . . . Elle est si avantageusement située, qu'elle commande non-seulement la Ville & le Port, mais encore toute la campagne des environs. . . . Celui que l'on nomme *la tête de Gravelines* est encore mieux fortifié. Tout le circuit de cette Place est enveloppé par un bon chemin couvert, auquel on a pratiqué un avant-fossé du côté de la basse Ville [pp. 232–33].

". . . Philippe de France Comte de Boulogne la fit entourer de murailles, & S. Louis l'unit au domaine de la Couronne. Cette petite Ville étoit déja si bien fortifiée en 1448. qu'Edouard Roi d'Angleterre l'ayant assiégée, il ne put la prendre que par famine, & après un an de siege. Les habitans de Calais s'étoient défendus avec tant de valeur & de courage, qu'ils étoient réduits a la derniere extrémité lors qu'ils demanderent à capituler. Il étoit trop tard. Edouard, piqué de leur belle défense, refusa de leur pardonner, à moins qu'ils ne lui livrassent six d'entr'eux, pour être pendus. A cette proposition, *Eustache de saint Pierre*, le plus considérable de la Ville, & que d'autres nomment *Jean d'Aire*, s'offrit pour être une de ces six victimes. Sa génerosité & son amour pour ses compatriotes animerent si fort les autres, que le nombre de six fut aussitôt rempli. Ces six héros, nuds en chemise & la corde au col, s'étant présentés à Edouard, il alloit les faire pendre, si la Reine sa femme n'avoit fait auprès de lui les plus fortes instances pour obtenir leur grace, qui lui fut enfin accordée . . ." [pp. 226–27].

The following is our translation: "CALAIS . . . is a town and seaport that was formerly only a village of the County de Guines . . . .

"Above 14,000 people live there, not including either the Courgain or the lower town.

"The lower town is on the edge of the fortifications of Calais and contains about 440 [note Sterne's 420] houses or families.

"There is only one parochial church and four convents in Calais. The parochial church is protected by the Virgin Mary. The nave is not one of the largest, but it is regular, in the form of a cross, and decorated with eleven chapels. What is more remarkable is the high altar, which is made entirely of Carrara marble and is fifty-six feet high and thirty-one feet wide . . . . The tower which contains the bells is quite high, situated in the middle of the church and supported by four very delicate pillars. The steeple is octagonal and made of stone, and another spire, which is slate-covered, rises out of it.

"The streets of Calais are beautiful and narrow, and nearly all of them end at the only public square, which is in the middle of the town. This square is very poorly paved, but very beautiful and very large, since its length from east to west is sixty-six toises and its width, fifty-eight toises [the difference of eight toises is equivalent to about forty-eight feet; see *TS*, 582.17].

"There are no fountains at all in Calais and the people only use cistern water.

"The town-hall is on the square. The building is old and in bad repair. . . . There are two great bells in the steeple, one to mark the time and the other to close the gates and to call the magistrates.

"*The Courgain* is part of the town of Calais and takes its name ["small gain"] from its former inhabitants, poor fishermen who did not earn much. It is the residence of all the sailors and fishermen of Calais. There are eight small streets and the houses are of brick and quite pretty. About 340 families live there.

"There is in this town another tower, called the *Tour de Guet* ["watch-tower"], because it serves to sight vessels coming from the sea and to warn of the approach of enemies in time of war, whether by sea or by land . . . .

"The citadel of Calais is one of the largest there is. It still has its old wall and its fossé . . . . It is so advantageously situated that it dominates not only the town and the port but also all the surrounding champaign. . . . That which they call *la tête de Gravelines* is even better fortified. The entire circumference of the place is surrounded by a fine covered-way, to which has been added an advance-ditch, facing the lower town.

"Philip of France, Count of Boulogne, had the [citadel] walled in, and St. Louis united it under the domain of the crown. This little town was already so well fortified in 1448 that Edward, King of England, having besieged it, could take it only by famine and after a year of siege. The inhabitants of Calais had defended themselves with so much valor and courage that they were reduced to the last extremity when they asked to surrender. It was too late. Edward, piqued by their strong defense, re-fused to pardon them, unless they delivered to him six of themselves to be hanged. At this proposition, *Eustache de saint Pierre*, the most eminent person in the town, otherwise called *Jean d'Aire*, offered himself as one of the six victims. His generosity and his love for his compatriots so stirred the others that the number six was immediately filled. Once these six heroes, naked but for their shirts and the ropes around their necks, had presented themselves to Edward, he was going to have them hanged, but the Queen made such strong pleas to obtain their pardon that it was finally granted . . . ."

583.4—5   but as that . . . of their diet] The longstanding belief in the power of seafood to increase sexual potency appears to have some basis in Renais-sance medicine; see, e.g., Jacques Ferrand, *Erotomania* (Oxford, 1640), p. 246: "the generative vertue of Salt . . . is indeed very great. And this is the reason that Fishes are more fruitfull, and multiply faster, then [*sic*] any other living creatures whatsoever."

Tristram's comment, it should be noted, is not in Piganiol's *Nouveau Voyage*.

583.16–17   Philip of France] Philippe VI (1293–1350); he served as king from 1328 until his death.

583.23   campaign] *OED* cites this passage as its last illustration of an obsolete meaning: "A tract of open country; a plain." Cf. *Champaign*. Sterne uses the term earlier, 111.3.

583.24   after all that is *said* and *done*] Variant of the proverbial expression "easier said than done"; see Tilley, S116, 117, and Stevenson, p. 2037.

583.28–584.1   being no less . . . in ours] Cf. 552.4–5: "yet *Calais* itself left not a deeper scar in *Mary*'s heart, than *Utrecht* upon my uncle *Toby*'s"; and nn. to 552.4 above and 584.4–13 below.

584.4–13   the siege of Calais . . . own words] This is Sterne's second overt allusion to Paul Rapin-Thoyras's *L'Histoire d'Angleterre*, Tindal's translation and continuation of which we have used throughout as Sterne's source for historical events; see above, n. to 427.4–5.

Tindal is actually much briefer than fifty pages, but Sterne does seem to have borrowed a few salient phrases from his account of the siege of Calais (1346–47): "This Place [i.e., Calais], which was exceeding strong, was no less incommodious to the *English*, than *Dunkirk* has been in our days. In becoming master of it, he [Edward III] not only freed himself from a very troublesome Neighbourhood, but also opened a way into *France*
. . . .

"Mean time, the Siege, or rather Blockade of *Calais*, was still continued by Sea and Land" (I: 425–26).

Tindal then recounts Froissart's story of Eustace de St. Pierre in something less than 500 words.

584.14–17   BUT courage . . . be too much] John Dunton makes a similar denial in his *A Voyage Round the World* (I: 141), after a few learned lines on Westminster: "This Ancient and Noble City of *Westminster*, Built near a Plat of Ground formerly called *Thorney*, from the Brakes and Thorns which then cover'd it, but now *Illustrious for its Building*, Famous for its *Inhabitants*, and render'd populous and remarkable by its *Seats of Law*, and Courts of *Justice*——Now by this grave period, does the reader think I'm going to transcribe *Stow*, or some wise Fellow or other in *praise of Westminster*—That very ugly unhandsome reflection on *Kainophilus*, who is not a person that uses to Colour *Old Books,* or new Bind 'em, and then put 'em off for New, has turned his resolution, and you shan't hear one word more of its *Antiquity,* Founder, or any thing else . . . ."

Dunton had promised earlier that his description of London, "as being the *best Flower* in the Book, shall be my *Master-Piece* . . ." (I: 126); cf. Tristram's comment on Toby's amours as the "choicest morsel of my whole story" (401.8).

584.24–25   to Boulogne] Sterne takes the Beauvais route, Boulogne being the first major town along the way, and Montreuil the second.

585.1ff.   BOULOGNE, etc.] In an entertaining note on this chapter, "A Shandean Number Game," *N&Q* 216 (1971): 339, Harold Love points out that this seventh chapter of the seventh volume contains seven paragraphs, the last of which contains seven words; that the sum of "size" and "ace" is seven; that Tristram's debts are estimated at £7,000 (actually, they are estimated separately at £1,000 and £6,000); and that the expression "a jolly set of us" contains a bilingual pun.

An attempt to find this sort of number symbolism throughout *TS* can be found in Douglas Brooks, *Number and Pattern in the Eighteenth-century Novel* (London: Routledge & Kegan Paul, 1973), pp. 160–82.

585.8   size-ace!] Rabelais's description of dice makes clear Sterne's use of gamester's jargon to distinguish the short and tall observers: "He told us that twenty-one chance devils, very much fear'd in our country, dwelt there in six different stories, and that the biggest twins or braces of them were called sixes, and the smallest amb's-ace; the rest cinques, quarters, treys, and duces. When they were conjur'd up, otherwise coupled, they were call'd either sice cinque [i.e., a roll of six and five], sice quater, sice trey, sice duce, and sice ace [i.e., a roll of six and one, the highest and lowest numbers on the dice]; or cinque quater, cinque trey, and so forth" (V.10.92).

585.11   ma chere fille!] "My dear girl!"

585.19   debt of NATURE] Cf. 421.16: "—*To die,* is the great debt and tribute due unto nature . . . ."

585.23–24   death-looking, long-striding] Both compounds are unrecorded in *OED*.

585.24   scare-sinner] *OED* cites this passage as its sole example.

586.1   quoth mine Irish host] Unidentified.

586.7   By Jasus! . . . HUMANITIES] Cf. Piganiol, *Nouveau Voyage*, II: 225:
"Il y a dans Boulogne plusieurs Maisons Religieuses de l'un & de l'autre
sexe; une Maison des Prêtres de l'Oratoire qui y enseignent les Humanités
& la Philosophie . . ." ("There are several religious houses for both sexes
in Boulogne; one house belongs to the Priests of the Oratory, who teach
humanities and philosophy . . .").

586.16   *"the most haste, the worst speed"*] Proverbial; Tilley, H198, and
ODEP, s.v. *Haste*.

587.6–7   *That something . . . first setting out.*] If we may judge from Smollett's *Travels Through France and Italy* (1766), Sterne is only mildly exaggerating the fragility of eighteenth-century coaches. Smollett's solution: "I
mention this circumstance, by way of warning to other travellers, that they
may provide themselves with a hammer and nails, a spare iron-pin or two,
a large knife, and bladder of grease, to be used occasionally in case of such
misfortune" (II: 79).

In at least one of his letters from France, Sterne indeed sounds more like
Smollett than himself: "Can you conceive a worse accident than that in
such a journey, in the hottest day and hour of it, four miles from either tree
or shrub which could cast a shade of the size of one of Eve's fig leaves—
that we should break a hind wheel into ten thousand pieces, and be obliged
in consequence to sit five hours on a gravelly road, without one drop of
water or possibility of getting any—To mend the matter, my two
postillions were two dough-hearted fools, and fell a crying—Nothing was
to be done! By heaven, quoth I, pulling off my coat and waistcoat, something shall be done, for I'll thrash you both within an inch of your lives—
and then make you take each of you a horse, and ride like two devils to the
next post for a cart to carry my baggage, and a wheel to carry ourselves
. . ." (*Letters*, p. 183).

587.11   Diable!] "The devil!"

587.19–20   but I take . . . before me] Cf. 118.15–16 and n. above.

588.19   the inn-keeper's daughter] Janatone is mentioned again in *ASJ*, pp.
121–22, when Yorick arrives at the inn in Montreuil. Of her father, Stout
notes that he was "identified as Mons. Varennes, master of the Hôtel de la
Cour de France, by John Poole (1786?–1872), the dramatist, in 'Sterne at
Calais and Montreuil,' *London Magazine and Review*, Jan. 1825, pp.

38–46 . . . . Poole notes (p. 44) that Varennes' inn was 'the only one of any importance' in Montreuil at the time of Yorick's journey . . . ."

589.1   A slut!] As the *OED* notes (s.v. *Slut*, 2.b.), the word was in playful use, without serious imputation of bad qualities, throughout the eighteenth century.

589.7   *statue's thumb*] We remain uncertain about the reference here, but possibly Sterne is alluding to the classical notion of the "model statue," the *Doryphorus* (*Boy Carrying a Spear*) of Polyclitus, which supposedly established the ideal measures for the human body. Certainly Sterne's eye would have been caught by this rule concerning the thumb: "The Thumb contains a Nose" (C. A. Du Fresnoy, *The Art of Painting*, trans. John Dryden [1716], p. 129); see below, n. to 589.14. See also Pliny, *Natural History*, 34.55 (IX:169).

589.14–15   as if I . . . the wettest drapery.] As Sterne probably knew, the use of wet drapery, the practice of the ancient sculptors, was not recommended for painters; see, e.g., Du Fresnoy, *Art of Painting*, pp. 142–43: "The ancient Statuaries, made their Draperies of wet Linen, on purpose to make them sit close and streight to the Parts of their Figures . . . . Those great Genius's of Antiquity, finding that it was impossible to imitate with Marble the Fineness of Stuffs or Garments . . . thought they could not do better . . . than to make use of such Draperies, as hinder'd not from seeing through their Folds, the Delicacy of the Flesh, and the Purity of the Outlines . . . . But Painters, on the contrary, who are to deceive the Sight, quite otherwise than Statuaries, are bound to imitate the different Sorts of Garments, such as they naturally seem . . . ." Roger du Piles, *The Principles of Painting* (1743), pp. 117–18, makes much the same point.

589.18–19   the abbey of Saint Austreberte . . . Artois hither] Sterne may have found this information in Piganiol, *Nouveau Voyage*, II: 224: "L'Abbaye de Sainte Austreberte a été transférée d'Artois en cette Ville."

589.23   measure them at your leisures] Watt, p. 373, n. 2, quotes from Boswell's *Life*, III: 356, Johnson's comment that "ancient travellers guessed; modern travellers measure."

590.3–4   thou mayest go off . . . and lose thyself.] Cf. Yorick's encounter with the grisette in *ASJ*, who Yorick reports "seem'd really interested, that I should not lose myself" (p. 162).

590.6−8   painted by Reynolds . . . I'll be shot] For Reynolds, see above, n. to
188.9−11. For Apollo, see above, n. to 214.17−21; this earlier invocation
to Apollo follows immediately upon a borrowing from Reynolds, *Idler* 76,
ed. W J. Bate et al. (New Haven: Yale University Press, 1963).

For the phrase "I'll be shot," see above, n. to 234.22.

590.13   *devote*] Cf. *ASJ*, pp. 263−64: "There are three epochas in the empire
of a French-woman—She is coquette—then deist—then *devôte:* the empire during these is never lost—she only changes her subjects: when
thirty-five years and more have unpeopled her dominions of the slaves of
love, she re-peoples it with slaves of infidelity—and then with the slaves of
the Church."

Cf. Smollett, *Travels*, I: 74−75: "When I said the French people were
kept in good humour by the fopperies of their religion, I did not mean that
there were no gloomy spirits among them. There will be fanatics in religion, while there are people of a saturnine disposition, and melancholy
turn of mind. The character of a *devotee*, which is hardly known in England, is very common here. You see them walking to and from church at
all hours, in their hoods and long camblet cloaks, with a slow pace, de-
mure aspect, and downcast eye. Those who are poor become very troublesome to the monks, with their scruples and cases of conscience: you may see
them on their knees, at the confessional, every hour in the day. The rich
devotee has her favourite confessor, whom she consults and regales in private, at her own house . . . ."

OED and *Stanford Dictionary* indicate the word was in use during the
seventeenth century.

590.13−16   a terce to a nine . . . and capotted] Sterne borrows terms from
piquet; a "terce to a nine" or a *tierce minor* are the lowest three cards of a
suit, i.e., seven, eight, and nine. To hold a *tierce* is an advantage, although
a *tierce minor* is so small a one that some authorities consider it none at all.
To be "piqued" is to have one's opponent win thirty points on cards and
play before you begin to score; to be "repiqued" is to have the opponent
win thirty points on cards alone before you begin to score; and to be "capot-
ted" is to have one's opponent win all the tricks of the game. The combination here is hyperbolic, it not being possible to be piqued and repiqued in a
single hand.

590.18−20 I wish . . . card and spin] Piganiol, *Nouveau Voyage*, does not mention the carders and spinners of Abbeville, but the works there did attract the attention of other travelers; see, e.g., Edward Wright, *Some Observations Made in Travelling Through France, Italy, &c.*, 2d ed. (1764), I: 2: "the meaner people [of Abbeville] are kept from idleness and want, by means of a great woollen manufacture, which employs and supports a vast number of them." Sterne is perhaps glancing ironically at the motto on the royal arms of France: "Lilia non laborant neque nent" ("They toil not, neither do they spin"); see Thomas Nugent, *The Grand Tour*, 2d ed. (1756), IV: 9, 26.

591.1−4 *de Montreuil . . . poste] Work, p. 491, n. *: "The reference is to the *Liste générale des postes de France*, an official guide or set of tables of the post-roads of France, published annually in Paris, from 1708 to 1779, by successive members of the Jaillot family." Piganiol, *Nouveau Voyage*, also provides posts; see, e.g., II: 223, 251−52.

591.9−592.9 WAS I in a condition . . . punctual attention] R. F., in *Gentleman's Magazine* 68 (June 1798): 471, has suggested a source for this sentiment in Bishop Burnet's *History of his own Time:* "He [Archbishop Leighton] used often to say, that if he were to choose a place to die in, it should be an inn; it looking like a Pilgrim's going home, to whom this world was all as an inn, and who was weary of the noise and confusion in it. He added, that the officious tenderness and care of friends was an entanglement to a dying man, and that the unconcerned attendance of those that could be procured in such a place would give less disturbance"; we quote directly from Burnet (1724), I: 589. Ferriar (II: 43) calls attention to this suggestion in *Illustrations,* but adds: "The real source of this thought, however, is in the *Cato* of Cicero : 'Ex vita ista discedo, tanquam hospitio, non tanquam ex domo: commorandi enim natura diversorium nobis dedit, non habitandi locum'" ("I depart from life as from a lodging, rather than a real home: For nature has given us an inn to stay at, not to live in").

A sentiment quite similar to Tristram's is expressed several times by Montaigne, e.g., I.19.94−95: "I do verily believe, that it is those terrible Ceremonies and Preparations wherewith we set it [death] out, that more terrify us, than the Thing itself; a new quite contrary Way of Living, the

Cries of Mothers, Wives, and Children, the Visits of astonish'd and afflicted Friends, the Attendance of pale and blubber'd Servants, a dark
Room set round with burning Tapers, our Beds environed with Physicians and Divines; in fine, nothing but Ghostliness and Horror round
about us, render it so formidable, that a Man almost fancies himself dead
and buried already"; again, III.9.232–34: "I feel Death always twitching
me by the Throat, or by the Back: But I am of another Temper, 'tis in all
Places alike to me; yet might I have my Choice, I think I should rather
choose to die on *Horseback* than in a *Bed,* out of my own House, and far
enough from my own People. There is more Heart-breaking than Consolation in taking leave of one's *Friends;* I am willing to omit that civility, for
that of all the Offices of Friendship is the only one that is unpleasant . . . .
Your Heart is wounded with Compassion to hear the mourning of those
that are your real Friends . . . . Let us live, and be merry amongst our
Friends, let us go die, and be sullen amongst *Strangers.* A Man may find
those for his Money will shift his Pillow and rub his Feet . . ."; and again,
III.9.240: "in my Travel, I seldom come to my Inn, but that it comes into
my Mind to consider whether I could there be Sick, and dying at my Ease
. . . ."

 Cf. 425.4–10 and n. above.

592.10 the inn at Abbeville] Cf. Sacheverell Stevens, *Miscellaneous Remarks
Made on the Spot, in a Late Seven Years Tour through France, Italy, Germany
and Holland* (1756), p. 7: "the accomodations [of the inn at Abbeville]
were very indifferent and the wine worse."

592.14 by Genevieve!] St. Genevieve (c. 422–c. 500), patron saint of Paris.

592.16–593.2 "*MAKE them like* . . . of heaven.] Cf. Joseph Hall, *Quo
Vadis?,* pp. 83–84: "None of the least imprecations, which *David,* makes
against Gods enemies, is, *Make them like unto a wheele, o Lord:* Motion is
ever accompanied with unquietnesse; and both argues, and causes imperfection, whereas the happy estate of heaven is described by rest . . . ." See
above, n. to 580.13–14.

 The text is that of Psalm 83: 13: "O my God, make them like a wheel; as
the stubble before the wind"; in the *Book of Common Prayer* the text is:
"make them like unto a wheel."

 For Sterne's use of *Quo Vadis?* here and in *ASJ,* see Gardner D. Stout,

Jr., "Sterne's Borrowing from Bishop Joseph Hall's *Quo Vadis?*," *ELN* 2 (1965): 196–200.

592.19   the children of men in the latter days] Sterne conflates two biblical commonplaces.

593.3–6   Now . . . death and the devil] Cf. *Letters*, pp. 204–5: "the Thiness of the pyrenean Air brought on continual breaches of Vessels in my Lungs, & with them all the Tribe of evils insident to a pulmonary Consumption—there seem'd nothing left but gentle change of place & air;—& accordingly I put myself into motion. & with a cheary heart, having traversed the South of France so often that I ran a risk of being taken up for a Spy, I jogg'd myself out of all other dangers—& hope in 9 or 10 Weeks to bekiss y^r hands in perfect . . . health."

Sterne glances at his own thinness in the *Political Romance*, where he appears under the name "Lorry Slim." See also plate VII in Cash, *Early and Middle Years*, the painting by Thomas Patch of Sterne greeting Death; Patch's work is described in detail on pp. 310–11. We have found no evidence that Bishop Hall was particularly corpulent. His engraved portrait in *Resolutions and Decisions of Divers Practical Cases of Conscience*, 2d ed. (1650), suggests a man of average size.

In his sermon on the prodigal son (III.20.152–53), Sterne seriously defends the desire for travel: "the passion is no way bad,——but as others are,——in it's mismanagement or excess;——order it rightly the advantages are worth the pursuit; the chief of which are——·to learn the languages, the laws and customs, and understand the government and interest of other nations,——to acquire an urbanity and confidence of behaviour, and fit the mind more easily for conversation and discourse;——to take us out of the company of our aunts and grandmothers, and from the track of nursery mistakes; and by shewing us new objects, or old ones in new lights, to reform our judgments——by tasting perpetually the varieties of nature, to know what *is good*——by observing the address and arts of men, to conceive what *is sincere*,——and by seeing the difference of so many various humours and manners,——to look into ourselves and form our own."

Cf. Walter's desire to send Bobby on the Grand Tour, 396.11–24.

593.11   Ixion's wheel] See t.n., vol. II, p. 859, in this edition.

593.19–22 I love the Pythagoreans . . . *think well*."] The italicized words translate the Greek, the source of which has not been located. Pythagoras's rejection of the body was well known; Diogenes Laertius, *Lives of Eminent Philosophers*, VIII.9, recounts one particularly Shandean statement of his view: "Of sexual indulgence, too, he says, 'Keep to the winter for sexual pleasures, in summer abstain; they are less harmful in autumn and spring, but they are always harmful and not conducive to health.' Asked once when a man should consort with a woman, he replied, 'When you want to lose what strength you have'" (II: 328–29).

593.24–25 with too lax or too tense a fibre] Sterne uses a standard medical concept of the period. See, e.g., George Cheyne, *The English Malady* (1733), pp. 45–46: "That there is a certain *Tone, Consistence,* and Firmness, and a determin'd Degree of *Elasticity* and *Tension* of the Nerves or Fibres, how small soever that be . . . necessary to the perfect Performance of the *Animal Functions,* is I think, without all Question, from an Excess *over* or Defect *under* which, in some eminent Degree, Diseases of one Kind or another certainly arise. Those I am chiefly concern'd for . . . are what proceeds from the Defect, or that Degree which falls below the just Mediocrity necessary for perfect Health: That is, those Diseases that ensue upon a too lax, feeble, and *unelastick* State of the *Fibres* or *Nerves* . . . ."

594.5–6 a vow not to shave my beard] Perhaps a glance at the Nazarite vow; see Numbers 6: 5: "All the days of the vow of his separation there shall no rasor come upon his head . . . ."

594.8–23 from which *Lessius* . . . almost to nothing.] Cf. Burton, 2.2.3 (p. 246): "*Franciscus Ribera in cap.* 14. *Apocalyps.* will have Hell a materiall and locall fire in the center of the earth, 200. *Italian* miles in diameter . . . . But *Lessius lib.* 13. *de moribus divinis cap.* 24. will have this locall hell far lesse, one *Dutch* mile in Diameter, all filled with fire and brimstone: because, as hee there demonstrates, that space Cubically multiplyed, will make a Sphere able to hold eight hundred thousand millions of damned bodies (allowing each body sixe foot square) which will abundantly suffice; Cùm certum sit, inquit, factâ subductione, non futuros centies mille milliones damnandorum" ("Since it is certain, he said, that when the reckoning is made, there will not be an infinite number of the damned"). Noted by Ferriar, I: 111–13.

This passage is not in the first four editions of the *Anatomy*; Burton may have borrowed it for his fifth edition from John Wilkins, *The Discovery of A World in the Moon*, pp. 200–201, published in the same year (1638).

Work, p. 494, nn. 1, 2: "Leonardus Lessius (1554–1623), a Jesuit theologian . . . . A Dutch mile is about 4.4 English miles. Francisco Ribera (1537–1591), a Spanish Jesuit, commentator, and devotional writer; this passage . . . Sterne probably took from Burton . . . . An Italian mile is about .9 of an English mile."

595.13   Priapus at your tails] Chambers, s.v. *Priapus* and *Priapism*, provides a sufficient account: "a fabulous deity . . . who, for the extraordinary size of his parts, was exceedingly revered by the women . . . . The . . . poets and painters represent [him] with a yard always stiff and erect." It is perhaps worth noting that it is Priapus's curse (of impotency) and the attempts to overcome it that form what little plot exists in Petronius's *Satyricon*; e.g.: *"There's Hope whilst Life!——*Priapus *grant our Pray'r, / Renerve our Strength, and Steel our Arms to dare"* (*Works* [1736; New York: AMS Press, 1975], p. 273; see also pp. 39ff. and 279ff.). See below, n. to 624.6–9.

595.14   into what a delicious . . . am I rushing?] Cf. Burton, 1.3.2.4 (p. 204): "But where am I? Into what subject have I rushed? What have I to do with Nunnes, Maids, Virgins, Widows? I am a Batcheler my self, and lead a Monastick life in a Colledge . . ."; noted by Ferriar, I: 114. Actually this expression is a favorite device of Burton, often expressed in Latin. See, e.g., "Democritus to the Reader," p. 67: *"sed quo feror hospes?"* ("but where am I rushing to, a mere novice?"); and 2.2.3 (p. 258): *"quo demum ruetis sacrificuli?"* ("whither, O priests, are you rushing so fast?").

595.15   midst of my days] Cf. Psalm 102: 24: "I said, O my God, take me not away in the midst of my days"; and Jeremiah 17: 11: "he that getteth riches, and not by right, shall leave them in the midst of his days, and at his end shall be a fool."

595.22–596.1   *Ailly au clochers* . . . in the world] Although Piganiol (*Nouveau Voyage*, II: 251) mentions Ailli aux Clochers (see n. to 596.6–8 below), he says nothing about it, nor do the other travel books we have consulted. Sterne may simply have been playing on *cloche:* "bell"; *clocher:* "steeple, belfry."

596.6–8 *Ailly au clochers* . . . AMIENS] Sterne may again have consulted his book of post-roads (see above, n. to 591.1–4), or Piganiol, *Nouveau Voyage*, II: 251–52. "Hixcourt" is an error for "Flixcourt."

596.16 avance-courier] Sterne's error for an *avant-courier:* "one who runs or rides before; a herald" (*OED*).

597.3–4 was you as . . . truth in Euclid] See above, n. to 465.4–5; see also 383.15–17.

597.17–19 Then there wants . . . some odd liards] The smallest French coin, the *liard*, was worth about half a farthing, English money; four liards made a *sol* or *sou*, or about one English half-penny; the *livre* contained twenty sous, about ten pence (its smallest version was the three-livre piece). This information was available to travelers in many sources; see, e.g., Nugent (*Grand Tour*, IV: 16), who warns that "no coin of a former reign will pass in this king's time; for they call in all their coins upon the demise of their kings" (p. 17).

597.22–23 still might the flesh . . . the spirit] Cf. Galatians 5: 17: "For the flesh lusteth against the Spirit, and the Spirit against the flesh: and these are contrary the one to the other: so that ye cannot do the things that ye would."

597.28 Monsieur le Curè] Parish priest; the *Stanford Dictionary*'s first example is from Smollett's *Travels* (1766).

598.8 the stables of Chantilly] Perhaps the best comment on Chantilly was made by John Sican, when he wrote to Swift in 1735: "The roads are excellent, postchaises very commodious, and the beds the best in the world; but the face of the country in general is very wretched; of which I can't mention a more lively instance than that you meet with wooden shoes and cottages like those in *Ireland*, before you lose sight of *Versailles*. I am persuaded, Sir, you will find a particular pleasure in taking a view of the *French* noblemen's houses, arising from the similitude between the good treatment the *Houhynhnms* meet with here, and that which you have observed in your former travels. The stables that *Lewis* the Fourteenth has built are very magnificent; I should do them an injury in comparing them to the Palace of St. *James*'s: yet these seem but mean to any one who has seen that of the Duke of *Bourbon* at *Chantilly*, which lies in a straight line, and contains stalls for near a thousand horses, with large intervals between each; and might very well, at first view, be mistaken for a noble palace . . ." (Swift, *Correspondence*, ed. Harold Williams [Oxford: Clarendon

Press, 1965], IV: 424). Vrooman, "Origin and Development of the *Sentimental Journey*," p. 63, n. 1, directs our attention to this letter.

Cf. Nugent, *Grand Tour,* IV: 28: "the stables [of Chantilly] are more magnificent than can be conceived."

598.12   as plain as my nose] Proverbial comparison; Tilley, N215, and *ODEP,* s.v. *Plain.*

598.16–18   by which means . . . towards the Abby] Piganiol (*Nouveau Voyage,* II: 216) comments on the Benedictine Abbey of St. Denis and its rich treasury, with its "infinité de choses précieuses." Both he and Nugent (*Grand Tour,* IV: 30) make the point that the monks of St. Denis were very assiduous in showing and explaining their treasures to travelers. For Judas's lantern, see t.n. to 598.21, vol. II, p. 860, in this edition.

Sterne was not alone in believing the jewels to be false; cf. Smollett, *Travels,* I: 81–82: "nor shall I detain you with a detail of the *Tresors de St. Denis,* which, together with the tombs in the abbey church, afforded us some amusement while our dinner was getting ready [cf. Tristram's account of Auxerre, 618.18ff., where the Shandys visit the tombs "whilst dinner is coddling"]. All these particulars are mentioned in twenty different books of tours, travels, and directions, which you have often perused. . . . As for the treasures, which are shewn on certain days to the populace gratis, they are contained in a number of presses, or armoires, and, if the stones are genuine, they must be inestimable: but this I cannot believe. Indeed I have been told, that what they shew as diamonds are no more than composition . . . ."

598.19   stuff and nonsense!] Proverbial expression; Stevenson, p. 2232.

599.2   so this is Paris!] Sterne's attitude toward Paris seems to be steeped in traditional English prejudices. See, for example, Steele's *The Englishman* 40 (1714): "As I drew near to *Paris* . . . I wondered when I should get out of the Lanes and Alleys, for there are scarcely six Streets wider than the narrow End of St. *Martin's-lane,* so they are forced to have shallow Chariots with Crane Necks for the *Beau Monde;* which, together with the Height of the Houses and Cleanliness of the Inhabitants, they seem to want nothing but Sea-coal Fires to make it Inside and Outside the best Nose-gay in *Europe*" (ed. Rae Blanchard [Oxford: Clarendon Press, 1955], pp. 162–63). See also Goldsmith's *Citizen of the World* (1760), letter 78: "But their civility to foreigners is not half so great as their admiration of themselves. Every thing that belongs to them and their nation is great; magnificent beyond expression; quite romantic! every garden is a paradice, every hovel a palace, and every woman an angel. They shut their eyes close, throw their mouths wide open, and cry out in rapture: Sacre! What beauty; O Ciel, what taste, mort de ma vie, what grandeur . . . .

"I fancy the French would make the best cooks in the world, if they had but meat; as it is they can dress you out five different dishes from a nettle top, seven from a dock-leaf, and twice as many from a frog's haunches . . ." (*Works*, II: 321–22). Goldsmith borrowed portions of his essay from Steele.

599.6　The streets however are nasty] Cf. *The Present State of the Court of France, and City of Paris* (1712), p. 13: "Altho' it Rains not, yet one cannot help often walking in Dirt; for, all the Filth is cast into the Streets, and the Vigilance of the Magistrates suffices not to keep 'em clean . . . ." This and subsequent references to *The Present State* are intended to suggest not that Sterne borrowed from that work but rather the commonplace, perhaps even stale, nature of his observations on Paris.

599.9–10　That a man with pale face . . . black] Cf. *Letters*, p. 155, where Sterne reports to his wife after several months in Paris: "I have got a colour into my face now, though I came with no more than there is in a dishclout."

As at 211.18–19, where Tristram vows by his "two bad cassocks," Sterne again seems to conflate Tristram and Yorick. See above, n. to 211.18–21; and see 636.4: "seeing a person in black." Cf. *ASJ*, pp. 155–56: "I walked up gravely to the window in my dusty black coat, and looking through the glass saw all the world in yellow, blue, and green, running at the ring of pleasure"; see also p. 164.

599.15　and no one gives the wall!] Sterne alludes to the long tradition whereby courtesy was shown by allowing another pedestrian to pass on the side farthest from the gutter, and superiority shown by claiming that side for oneself; see *Romeo and Juliet*, I.i.12: "I will take the wall of any man or maid of Montague's." Cf. *The Present State*, p. 22: "No body is obliged in the Streets to uncover before whomsoever . . . . The Dregs of the People enjoy the same Priviledge; they give the Way to no body; they suffer not the least Affront . . . ."

Cf. Boswell's *A Tour to the Hebrides*, ed. Frederick A. Pottle and Charles H. Bennett (New York: Literary Guild, 1936), p. 192: "[Johnson] said that in the last age, when his mother lived in London, there were two sets of people, those who gave the wall and those who took it; the peaceable and the quarrelsome. When he returned to Lichfield after having been in London, his mother asked him whether he was one of those who gave the wall, or those who took it. Now it is fixed that every man keeps to the right; or, if one is taking the wall, another yields it, and it is never a dispute." See also John Gay's elaborate discussion in *Trivia: or, the Art of Walking the Streets of London* (1716), book II, lines 45–64.

600.4–5 Now I cannot . . . that lean horse?] Cf. *The Present State*, p. 7: "The Coach-men are so brutish, and have such whore-son frightful Voices, and the cracking of their Whips, augments the Noise after so horrible a manner, as if all the Furies were in motion to make a Hell of *Paris*."

600.17–19 the French love good eating . . . gentlemen] Cf. Burton, 1.2.2.2 (p. 73): "*A Cooke of old was a base knave* (as *Livy* complaines) *but now a great man in request: Cookery is become an art, a noble science, Cookes are Gentlemen; Venter Deus* ["Belly is God"]." Sterne might also have been recalling Philippians 3: 18–19, which he had quoted in his sermon "Our Conversation in Heaven" (V.29.34): "For many walk, of whom I have told you often, and now tell you even weeping, that they are the enemies of the cross of Christ: Whose end is destruction, whose God is their belly, and whose glory is in their shame, who mind earthly things."

Cf. *The Present State*, p. 11: "It is not exaggerating to say, that all *Paris* is a great Inn. Eating-houses and Taverns are seen every where; the Kitchins are smoking every Hour, because they are eating every Hour: To Breakfast, and to eat all Day is the same thing in *France*"; and p. 40: "The *Peripatetics* and *Stoics* never labour'd so much upon the *Reformation* of Manners as *French Cooks* upon the satisfaction of the Belly."

600.19–20 and forasmuch as *the periwig maketh the man*] Cf. Sterne's letter to his Paris banker, Robert Foley, October 7, 1765 (*Letters*, p. 260): "It is a terrible thing to be in Paris without a perriwig to a man's head! In seven days from the date of this, I should be in that case, unless you tell your neighbour Madame Requiere to get her *bon mari de me faire une peruque à bourse, au mieux—c'est à dire—une la plus extraordinaire—la plus jolie—*

la plus gentille— . . ." ("good husband to make me a bag wig as well as he is able—in other words—one of the most extraordinary—the prettiest—the most pleasing . . ."). See also *ASJ* ("The Wig"), p. 158 and n.

600.22   Capitouls] The magistrates of Toulouse were called "Capitouls," but Sterne's joke, if any, eludes us.

600.23   pardi!] I.e., *pardieu:* "by God!" "Heavens!"

601.9–10   *"That they . . . seen every thing,"*] Sterne's italics and quotation marks would seem to indicate a proverb, but we have not been able to locate one recorded.

601.17   the five hundred grand Hôtels] Cf. Nugent, *Grand Tour,* IV: 64, where he identifies *Hotels* as the palaces of the nobility and adds: "As there are a great number of these hotels in *Paris,* we should exceed the limits of our plan, if we entered into a detail of each . . . ."

601.20–22   are best to be . . . Lilly] Cf. William Lily and John Colet, *A Short Introduction of Grammar* (1549; Menston, England: Scolar Press, 1970); the first sentence is: "A NOUNE is the name of a thing that may be seen, felt, heard or understand [*sic*]." This work, frequently reprinted throughout the seventeenth and eighteenth centuries, became known as *Lily's Grammar.*

601.25ff.   That by the last survey, etc.] Sterne appears to have extracted his list verbatim from Germain Brice's *Description de la Ville de Paris,* 4 vols. (Paris, 1752), I: 38–39. Brice lists not only the number of streets but the number of lanterns in each district, so that Sterne's comment on the darkness of Paris is particularly perverse. The date 1716 may have been extracted from an earlier passage: "Depuis l'année 1716. le nombre des maisons est extrémement augmenté" (I: 27).

This list of Paris districts occurs in other travel books as well, but Brice's is the only one we have located that gives the number of streets; see Baker, "Sterne and Piganiol," p. 13, n. 5.

Sterne again comments on the narrowness of Paris streets in *ASJ,* pp. 175–76; Stout notes that the observation was a commonplace among eighteenth-century travelers.

602.25–30   their gates . . . as you chuse] Cf. *The Travels of the late Charles Thompson, Esq.* (Reading, 1744), I: 14: "THE Things that more particularly engage a Traveller's Attention at *Paris* are, the Palaces, the Churches and Abbeys, the University, Academies, Libraries, Hospitals, Squares,

Statues, Gates, and Bridges. Of each of which in their Order.

"THE Royal Palaces are four in Number, *viz.* The *Old Palace,* the *Louvre,* the *Tuilleries,* and the *Palace Royal.*"

Thompson had just listed the districts of Paris, as does Sterne, and he goes on to describe the inscriptions on the portico of the Louvre (p. 15); see below, n. to 603.2−6.

602.27−28   St. *Roche* and *Sulplice*] Both churches are considered outstanding examples of the French "classical" style and both were completed in the middle of the eighteenth century; see Maurice Dumolin and George Outardel, *Les Églises de France* (Paris: Librairie Letouzey et Ané, 1936), pp. 160−70. Nugent, *Grand Tour,* IV: 56, mentions them together at the very end of his tour of Paris churches.

603.2−6   you will read . . . DOWN.] That these lines were engraved on the portico of the Louvre is reported by several eighteenth-century travelers, among them John Northleigh (1702): "On the Porches you see several Inscriptions, sufficiently demonstrating that the *French* were always good at flattering their Monarchs . . . . Upon this Occasion I cannot forbear inserting three Distichs made by the *French* Poets, exceeding for their Loftiness the Structure itself . . . ." Northleigh then quotes, among the three, "*Non orbis gentem, non urbem gens habet ullam, / Urbsve Domum, Dominum nec Domus ulla parem*" (quoted from John Harris, *Navigantium atque Itinerantum Bibliotheca, or a Complete Collection of Voyages and Travels* [1748], II: 728). The same lines are used as the motto to Steele's *Englishman* 40 (see above, n. to 599.2); Blanchard translates: "The world holds no race, no race a city, or any city a house, or any house a master equal [to these]" (pp. 161, 433). See also *Travels of the late Charles Thompson,* I: 15, and above, n. to 602.25−30.

603.7−8   The French have . . . upon it.] Cf. *Spectator* 104: "The Model of this *Amazonian* Hunting-Habit for Ladies, was, as I take it, first imported from *France,* and well enough expresses the Gayety of a People who are taught to do any thing so it be with an Assurance . . ." (I: 435); and Goldsmith, *An Enquiry into the Present State of Polite Learning:* "WE have long been characteriz'd as a nation of spleen, and our rivals on the continent as a land of levity" (*Works,* I: 297). Both characterizations reflect longstanding traditions.

603.9−11   IN mentioning the word *gay* . . . the word *spleen*] Sterne may simply be thinking in terms of opposites or he may be remembering Pliny's linking of laughter and spleen, perhaps by way of the *Memoirs of Martinus Scriblerus:* "He had met with a saying, that *'Spleen, Garter,* and *Girdle* are the three impediments to the *Cursus.'* Therefore Pliny (lib. xi. cap. 37.) says, that such as excel in that exercise have their *Spleen* cauteriz'd. 'My son (quoth Cornelius) runs but heavily; therefore I will have this operation performed upon him immediately. Moreover it will cure that immoderate Laughter to which I perceive he is addicted: For laughter (as the same author hath it, ibid.) is caused by the bigness of the Spleen'" (p. 113). See Pliny, *Natural History*, 11.80 (III: 560–61).

603.15   undercraft] *OED* cites this passage as its last example, with the definition "a sly, underhand trick."

604.16–19   No;——I cannot stop . . . their finances] Sterne runs through the commonplaces of travel books; see, e.g., Nugent, *Grand Tour*, IV: 5–19, in which he covers government, parliaments, taxes, military, clergy, and, in one all-inclusive chapter, *"persons, manners, customs, learning, language, trade, coins, and manner of travelling."*

604.20   resources and hidden springs] Cf. above, n. to 333.17–334.9.

604.20–23   qualified as I . . . and reflections] Sterne's witticism was anticipated, in a more serious vein, by Goldsmith's *Citizen of the World*, letter 3: "The remarks of a man who has been but three days in the country can only be those obvious circumstances which force themselves upon the imagination . . ." (*Works*, II: 21); noted by Vrooman, "Origin and Development of the *Sentimental Journey*," p. 50.

605.4   *consideratis, considerandis*] "All things considered."

605.7   their puny horses] The small size of French horses as opposed to English appears to have been a frequent cause of comment. Cf. *ASJ*, p. 135, where Sterne annotates his "little *bidet*" as "Post horse"; and see Stout's commentary on the passage.

      See also 600.5, "that lean horse."

605.16–18   though their reverences . . . parlour] Cf. *Letters*, p. 412 (February 1768): "I will send you a set of my books—they will take with the generality—the women will read this book [i.e., *ASJ*] in the parlour, and Tristram in the bed-chamber." See also above, 5.10–11, where Tristram predicts his book will turn out to be what Montaigne dreaded, "a book for a parlour-window."

605.19   volving] *OED* cites this passage as its last example, with the definition "to turn over in the mind; to consider."

606.1   Andoüillets] In Rabelais, Pantagruel lands on the island of "Chitterlings," which Ozell informs us is the translator's version of Rabelais's "Andouilles"; Ozell goes on to define Andouilles as "a big hog's gut stuff'd with chitterlings cut small, and other entrails cut into small pieces, and season'd with pepper and salt, not forgetting sweet herbs" (IV.35.226, n. 1). Both Rabelais and Sterne play upon the bawdy possibilities of sausages; cf. Tom's courtship of the Jew's widow in *TS*, vol. IX, chaps. 5–7.

606.9   *sinovia*] I.e., *synovia*, the lubricating fluid secreted in the interior of the joints.

606.14   the thigh-bone of the man of Lystra] See Acts 14: 8: "And there sat a certain man at Lystra, impotent in his feet, being a cripple from his mother's womb, who never had walked."

606.18–24   annointing it . . . and cochlearia] Sterne would seem to be speaking from some personal experience or consulting a *Pharmacopœia* or medical handbook, but we have not located the particular source. The first five herbs listed are mild and basic emollients (softeners), although "white lillies" seem to have fallen into disuse in the eighteenth century; "the woods," usually "decoction of the woods," was the standard term for recipes including guaiacum, sassafras, and the like. We assume the prioress holds her scapulary across her lap to prevent the smoke from reaching her nostrils.

   Wild chicory, water cresses, and cochlearia (scurvy-grass) are stronger herbs and were used in the treatment of scurvy; chervil and sweet cecily were supposedly effective as diuretics and as treatments for dropsy. See William Lewis, *The New Dispensatory*, 2d ed. (1765). Sterne seems to be suggesting that the prioress's complaint was dropsical or scorbutical—perhaps both.

607.1   hot baths of Bourbon] There are at least three hot-water spas—Bourbonne-les-Bains, Bourbon-L'Archambault, or Bourbon-Lancy—that Sterne might have had in mind; the first is located in northeast and the other two in central France (L'Archambault some fifteen miles west of Moulins, and Lancy twenty miles east).

607.5   whitloe] An inflammation or swelling; cf. "white swelling," 609.22 and n. below.

607.6   cast poultices, &c.] Cf. above, n. to 116.1.

607.11   calesh] I.e., calash.

607.14   rump-ends] *OED* cites this passage as its sole illustration.

607.18   hot-wine-lees] This passage is cited as an illustration in *OED*, s.v. *Wine-lees:* "sediment deposited in a vessel containing wine." Kenneth Monkman has informed us that wine-lees were used to scour material such as felt; see *OED*, s.v. *Dress, v.* 13.g.

608.9   saint-wise] Unrecorded in *OED*.

608.17   conventical] *OED* cites this passage as its first recorded example, with the definition "Of or pertaining to a convent."

609.2–4   a little tempting bush . . . the passions] Cf. above, n. to 131.8–11; and Burton, 3.2.3.3 (p. 470), where cosmetics and fashionable clothes are labeled the "trap of lust, and sure token, as an Ivy-bush is to a Taverne."

609.22   white swelling by her devotions] Francis Grose, *Classical Dictionary of the Vulgar Tongue* (1785), s.v. *Additions and Corrections:* "a woman with child is said to have a white swelling." *OED* (s.v. *swelling, vbl. sb.* 2.) defines *white swelling* as simply a swelling without redness.

Cf. Chambers, *Supplement*, s.v. *White:* "We have several examples of successful cures of *White Swellings* of the joints, or tumors, from inspissated lymph, by a small stream of warm water falling from a height on them.

"When the water is impregnated with penetrating medicines or natural minerals, its virtues are greater."

610.17   By my fig!] Cf. chap. 43 (647.15ff.), where Tristram and the "gossip" discuss a purchase of figs and eggs. Partridge suggests *pudendum muliebre*, but not as early as the eighteenth century; Sterne's usage in both instances, however, suggests that the meaning may have been available to him. See also *OED*, s.v. *Fig, sb.*¹ 4: "a type of anything small, valueless, or contemptible"; and *sb.*², the Renaissance *fico*—a gesture of scorn, with phallic overtones, made by thrusting the thumb between the first two fingers. Far less likely, but worth mentioning, is *EDD*'s entry, s.v. *Fig, sb.*¹ 6: "the droppings of a donkey" (Northumberland).

See also 271.1–272.18 and n. above.

611.5   obstreperated] *OED* cites this passage as its sole illustration, with the definition "to make a noise or clamour."

611.12   as sure as a gun] See above, n. to 547.10.

613.21ff.   Now I see no sin, etc.] Sterne's joke is based on the indecency of *foutre* ("to fuck") and the ambiguity of *bouger* ("to stir, budge, move"), with a probable allusion to *bougre* ("bugger"); see below, n. to 649.13. Work's assertion (p. 510, n. 1) that *bouger* "was not in polite usage during the eighteenth century" is not substantiated; it is not an elegant word, but it was in use.

The inspiration for Sterne's elaborate joke may have been a far more innocent footnote in Rabelais, I.11.183n., explaining "harribourquet": "In the original it is, harri bourriquet. Bourriquet is such a title for an ass as jade is for a horse: so harri bourriquet, says Cotgrave, are words wherewith the millers, &c. in France drive forward their asses. M. du Chat says the same thing, only he confines it to Languedoc . . . ." In *The Present State*, pp. 64–65, the author tells an anecdote about a coachman whose horse would not move unless thoroughly cursed.

Sterne labels France "foutre-land" in a letter to Hall-Stevenson, *Letters*, p. 214. Cf. Boswell, *On the Grand Tour: Italy, Corsica, and France, 1765–1766*, ed. Frank Brady and Frederick A. Pottle (New York: McGraw-Hill Book Company, 1955), p. 246: "The ostlers and postillions were impertinent dogs, crying always, 'Foutre! sacré dieu!' without rhyme or reason."

614.6–7   (like fa, sol, la, re, mi, ut] The names given by Guido of Arezzo to the six notes of the hexachord system. See above, n. to 492.6

615.5–8   There's FONTAINBLEAU . . . LYONS] Sterne may have again consulted his *Book of Post-Roads*, or a map in Piganiol, *Nouveau Voyage*, vol. I, facing p. 195. Nugent, *Grand Tour*, IV: 146–75, also describes the route, including the information that Dijon is the "capital of the dutchy of *Burgundy*" (p. 169) and Macon "the capital of the district of *Maconnois* . . ." (p. 173). Cf. Smollett, *Travels*, I: 128: "There are two post roads from Paris to Lyons, one of sixty-five posts, by the way of Moulins; the other of fifty-nine, by the way of Dijon in Burgundy. This last I chose, partly to save sixty livres, and partly to see the wine harvest of Burgundy, which, I was told, was a season of mirth and jollity among all ranks of people."

615.14–21   Alas! Madam . . . better appetite from it] Cf. *Sermons* ("Our

Conversation in Heaven"), V.29.39–40: "Preach to a voluptuous epi-
cure, who knows of no other happiness in this world, but what arises from
good eating and drinking;—such a one, in the apostle's language, whose
God was his belly;—preach to him of the abstractions of the soul, tell of its
flights, and brisker motion in the pure regions of immensity;—represent
to him that saints and angels eat not,—but that the spirit of a man lives for
ever upon wisdom and holiness, and heavenly contemplations:—why, the
only effect would be, that the fat glutton would stare a while upon the
preacher, and in a few minutes fall fast asleep.—No; if you would catch
his attention . . . you must preach to him out of the Alcoran,—talk of the
raptures of sensual enjoyments . . . ;—there you touch upon a note which
awakens and sinks into the inmost recesses of his soul;—without which,
discourse as wisely and abstractedly as you will of heaven, your representations of it, however glorious and exalted, will pass like the songs of melody
over an ear incapable of discerning the distinction of sounds."

615.22–23   as I never blot any thing out] Sterne is perhaps recalling Ben
Jonson's famous comment: "*I remember,* the Players have often mentioned
it as an honour to *Shakespeare,* that in his writing, (whatsoever he penn'd)
hee never blotted out a line. My answer hath beene, would he had blotted a
thousand"; quoted from *Timber: or, Discoveries* (1641), in *Elizabethan and
Jacobean Quartos,* ed. G. B. Harrison (New York: Barnes and Noble,
1966), p. 28.

616.10–15   All you need . . . pleasure of the chase] Cf. Piganiol, *Nouveau
Voyage,* I: 196: "*Fontainebleau* est un Bourg, avec une Maison Royale, situé
dans le Gâtinois, au milieu d'une forêt . . ."; and Nugent, *Grand Tour,* IV:
137: "*Fontainebleau* is a small town of the Gatinois . . . situated in the
middle of a forest three miles from the river Seine . . . and forty-two from
Paris . . . . The *French* kings have chosen this for a hunting-seat, by
reason of its situation . . . ." Nugent then spends some four pages describing the royal palace that Tristram dismisses as "something great."

616.18   taking care only . . . out-gallop the king] Cf. James Russel's *Letters
from a Young Painter Abroad to his Friends in England* (1748), p. 7:
"Amongst the diversions at Fontainbleau, I was at . . . a hunting match
. . . where it is surprizing to see what a number of fine English hunting
horses come bounding in. As soon as his Majesty &c. arrive, the stag is
unharboured: the King, who is the best of horse-men, is always foremost

in the chace. There is something very noble and delightful in the sight of two or three hundred horse-men streaming after him along the plain: nobody is permitted to ride before him; and, if it happens to be a wet day, he takes delight in riding slow, and in having every body soaked about him."

617.4–5   As for SENS . . . *archiepiscopal see*."] Cf. Piganiol, *Nouveau Voyage*, I: 197: "SENS, *Agendicum Senonûm, Senones*, Ville Archiépiscopale . . ."; and Nugent, *Grand Tour*, IV: 167: "the seat of an archbishop."

617.6   For JOIGNY . . . the better.] We do not know the nature of Sterne's quarrel with Joigny, but Smollett seems equally disenchanted with the town: "We stopped for a refreshment at a little town called Joigne-ville, where (by the bye) I was scandalously imposed upon, and even abused by a virago of a landlady . . ." (*Travels*, I: 136).

617.11–13   except my mother . . . is common sense)] For an attempt to explain Mrs. Shandy's knitting, see Leigh A. Ehlers, "Mrs. Shandy's 'Lint and Basilicon': The Importance of Women in *Tristram Shandy*," *SAR* 46 (1981): 63–64.

617.16–18   his researches . . . fruit even in a desert] Cf. *ASJ*, p. 115: "I pity the man who can travel from *Dan* to *Beersheba*, and cry, 'Tis all barren— and so it is . . . to him who will not cultivate the fruits it offers. I declare, said I . . . that was I in a desart, I would find out wherewith in it to call forth my affections. . . ." Sterne develops this idea more fully in chap. 43 (see below, n. to 646.18–19) and in *ASJ*, pp. 114–16. In all these instances, Sterne suggests about travel what from the very beginning he has affirmed about composition (41.7ff.): "Could a historiographer drive on his history, as a muleteer drives on his mule,—straight forward;----for instance, from *Rome* all the way to *Loretto*, without ever once turning his head aside either to the right hand or to the left,—he might venture to foretell you to an hour when he should get to his journey's end;-----but the thing is, morally speaking, impossible: For, if he is a man of the least spirit, he will have fifty deviations from a straight line to make with this or that party as he goes along, which he can no ways avoid." The interplay here between subject and metaphor is worth observing.

617.23   silks] Sterne may mean the counsels of the various kings and courts, *silks* being used allusively in recognition of their silk gowns; *OED*'s first example of such usage is dated 1810, but no other meaning of *silks* seems satisfactory.

618.4　opiniatry] *OED* cites this passage as its last example. Cf. *Letters*, p. 58: "The person calld in such a Case, sh^d be *your friend*, not one who will . . . fortify them in their Opinatrè . . . ."

618.18ff.　We'll go, brother Toby, etc.] Sterne's information on Auxerre is again culled from the pages of Piganiol, *Nouveau Voyage*, I: 201–3: "L'Abbaye de S. Germain est un lieu où l'on compte jusqu'à soixante corps saints, & une quantité prodigieuse de Reliques. . . . M. Seguier Evêque d'Auxerre fit ouvrir tous les tombeaux en 1636. & fit un procès-verbal de l'état où il avoit trouvé les corps saints. L'on conduit d'abord les Curieux au tombeau de saint Héribalde, Prince de la Maison de Baviere, qui sous Charlemagne, Louis le Débonnaire, & Charles le Chauve, eut beaucoup de part au Gouvernement de l'Etat. Il fut Moine, puis Abbé de ce Monastere, & enfin Evêque d'Auxerre, & Archichapelain, c'est-à-dire, grand Aumônier de France. . . .

"Dans la Chapelle de sainte Maxime sont les corps de sainte Maxime Dame Italienne, venue en France à la suite du corps de S. Germain, lorsqu'on le transporta ici de Ravenne où ce Saint mourut; de S. Optat Evêque d'Auxerre . . . ."

The following is our translation: "The Abbey of St. Germain is a place where one can count up to sixty canonized bodies and a prodigious quantity of relics. . . . M. Seguier, Bishop of Auxerre, had all the tombs opened in 1636 and made an official report of the circumstances in which he had found the canonized bodies. They take the curious first to the tomb of St. Heribald, Prince of the House of Bavaria, who under Charlemagne, Louis the Debonair, and Charles the Bald, played a large role in the government of the state. He was a monk, then Abbot of the monastery, and finally Bishop of Auxerre, and Archchaplain, in other words, Grand Chaplain of France. . . .

"In the chapel of St. Maxima are the bodies of St. Maxima, an Italian woman come to France after the body of St. Germain, when they transported it here from Ravenna, where this saint died; [and] of St. Optat, Bishop of Auxerre . . . ."

618.20　monsieur Sequier] See t.n. to 618.20, vol. II, p. 860, in this edition.

619.8　St. Heribald] A Benedictine monk and abbot of the monastery of St. Germain and eventually Bishop of Auxerre (d. c. 857).

619.10–11   reigns of Charlemagne . . . the Bald] Charlemagne ruled in France from 768 to 814 and was succeeded by his son, Louis the Debonair, who in turn was succeeded by his son, Charles the Bald, who ruled from 840 until his death in 877.

619.19–20   when any thing hugely tickled him] Sterne recalls a phrase he had used previously for Walter, 394.6–7: "my father was hugely tickled with the subtleties of these learned discourses"; see also 447.22–23: "My father was hugely pleased with this theory of *John de la Casse*."

619.27–620.5   the bones of . . . added my father] Numerous saints have been named Maxima (including one particularly revered in France, but about whom nothing else is known) and several have been named Maximus, although Sterne almost surely had in mind merely the play on the Latin masculine and feminine forms. See *Book of Saints*, 5th ed. (New York: Thomas Y. Crowell, 1966).

620.6   Saint Germain] Bishop of Auxerre (c. 380–448). He died at Ravenna, which accounts for the origin of St. Maxima's pilgrimage; see above, n. to 618.18ff.

620.17   unless one could purchase] As Watt notes (p. 392, n. 6), "Trim is thinking of the practice of purchasing officer's commissions in the army he knows."

620.25   Saint *Optat*] Bishop of Auxerre (d. c. 530). Latin *optatus:* "longed for, desired, welcomed."

621.16ff.   Now this is the most puzzled skein of all] Tristram's multiple journeys through Auxerre comprise perhaps the single most discussed incident in *TS* among twentieth-century critics. For example, in *Winged Skull*, three of the first four essays discuss the passage, viz., Jean-Jacques Mayoux, "Variations on the Time-sense in *Tristram Shandy*," pp. 7–8; Robert Gorham Davis, "Sterne and the Delineation of the Modern Novel," pp. 32–33; and Helene Moglen, "Laurence Sterne and the Contemporary Vision," p. 71. See also A. A. Mendilow, *Time and the Novel* (London: Peter Nevill, 1952), pp. 158–99.

622.6–9   and I am moreover . . . all these affairs.] Work, p. 516, n. *: "'Antony' was the name by which Sterne's friend Hall-Stevenson [see above, n. to 30.20] was known to his intimates. Alluding probably to the saint, the name may have been chosen from certain humorous parallels and antitheses in the men's careers. St. Antony, the founder of Christian asceticism [see above, n. to 302.14–15], retired from the society of men to a ruined castle, and eventually his sanctity attracted numerous disciples; Hall-Stevenson, hardly an ascetic, retired to his castle, which from its ruinous condition he called 'Crazy Castle,' where his bibulous hospitality attracted a Rabelaisian group of men who . . . called themselves Demoniacs . . . . 'Don Pringello' was the name given by Hall-Stevenson to an architect to whom, as one of the Demoniacs, he had ascribed one of his *Crazy Tales*." See Cash's discussion of the Demoniacs in *Early and Middle Years*, pp. 185–95 and passim; and Lodwick Hartley, "Sterne's Eugenius as Indiscreet Author: The Literary Career of John Hall-Stevenson," *PMLA* 86 (1971): 428–45. In a separate note, Hartley makes an argument for identifying Don Pringello with Sir William Chambers (1726–96), whose full fame as an architect was established in the 1770s; see "The 'Don Pringello' of Sterne and Hall-Stevenson," *N&Q* 219 (1974): 260–62.

Hall-Stevenson's "scholium" to Don Pringello's tale (entitled "The Fellowship of the Holy Nuns; or the Monk's wise Judgment" and certainly not in good taste) is a tribute to his help in restoring Crazy Castle: "Don Pringello was a celebrated Spanish Architect, of unbounded generosity; at his own expence, on the other side of the Pyrenean mountains, he built many noble castles, both for private people, and for the *public*, out of his own funds; he repaired several palaces, situated upon the pleasant banks of that delightful river, the Garonne, in France, and came over on purpose to rebuild Crazy Castle; but, struck with its venerable remains, he could only be prevailed upon to add a few ornaments, suitable to the stile and taste of the age it was built in" (*Crazy Tales* [1762], p. 99). Sterne mentions Hall-Stevenson's renovations in a letter from Toulouse in October 1762 (*Letters*, pp. 184–85).

Since Sterne's actual journey ended in Toulouse, it has been assumed that "Mons. Sligniac" might be the landlord mentioned in a letter written in August 1762, and that the pavilion is part of the country-house he describes: "Well! here we are after all, my dear friend—and most deliciously placed at the extremity of the town, in an excellent house well furnish'd, and elegant . . . . Of the same landlord I have bargained to have the use of a country-house which he has two miles out of town, so that myself and all my family have nothing more to do than to take our hats and remove from the one to the other" (*Letters*, p. 183).

622.9   rhapsodizing] Cf. above, n. to 39.1.

622.15   I can go directly by water to Avignon] Both Piganiol and Nugent mention this alternative route. See *Nouveau Voyage*, I: 266: "*Ceux qui cherchent les plus courts chemins, ou qui sont pressés par leurs affaires, s'embarquent à Lyon sur le Rhône, pour aller en Provence . . .*" ("Those who look for shortcuts or who are hurried by their business embark at Lyons on the Rhone to go to Provence . . ."); see also p. 347. And see Nugent, *Grand Tour*, IV: 179: "From *Lyons* you may go down as far as *Avignon* by water; for there are boats that descend the *Rhone* almost every day, and move with great expedition on this rapid river." The "rapid Rhone" (623.5) is a standard phrase found in many travel books of the period.

Tristram's journey down the Rhone passes the area to the west known as Vivarais and the area to the east, Dauphiné, as well as the three cities mentioned. The Hermitage and Côte Rôtie were the most famous vineyards of the Rhone valley; as Watt notes (p. 394, n. 1), the Côte Rôtie would actually have been passed first. Frank Schoonmaker, in a modern description of the vineyards (*Encyclopedia of Wine*, 5th ed. [New York: Hastings House, 1973], pp. 103, 170), suggests the view from the Rhone: the Hermitage, "produced on a single steep, spectacular, terraced hillside some 50 miles south of Lyon"; and the Côte Rôtie, "some twenty miles south of Lyon. The vineyards, which overlook a great bend in the river and face almost due south, are incredibly steep, and consist really of a series of narrow terraces . . ."

Piganiol provides no parallel passage, nor does any other travel book we have examined. Nugent, IV: 181, does comment briefly on the wine of the Hermitage; and Wright, *Some Observations*, I: 12–13, comments on both wines.

623.12   whilome] See above, n. to vol. I, Ded. 2; Sterne's archaism here seems more to the purpose than in other instances.

623.13–15   the rocks, the mountains . . . about her] Cf. *ASJ*, p. 285: "Nature! in the midst of thy disorders, thou art still friendly to the scantiness thou hast created—with all thy great works about thee, little hast thou left to give, either to the scithe or to the sickle—but to that little, thou grantest safety and protection . . . ."

"Let the way-worn traveller vent his complaints upon . . . your rocks—your precipices . . . mountains impracticable—and cataracts . . . ."

624.23   chaise-undertaker] *OED* cites this passage as its only recorded example, with the definition "One who undertakes to renovate chaises, a dealer in second-hand chaises." Cf. 639.16, "chaise-vamper."

624.6−9   Do, my dear Jenny . . . of his manhood] One literary character before Tristram who publicly affirms his impotence is Encolpius, the hero of Petronius's *Satyricon;* his efforts to remove the curse of Priapus is usually considered one of the major themes of the work. See above, nn. to 307.21−23, 595.13.

624.13−14   whispering these words . . . any other man] We have been unable to substitute words for the asterisks, as can so easily be done on a similar occasion, 449.22. John Preston, *The Created Self: The Reader's Role in Eighteenth-Century Fiction* (London: Heinemann, 1970), pp. 160−61, suggests a purposeful obscurity on Sterne's part.

624.17−18   I'll go into Wales . . . goat's-whey] Cf. *Memoirs of Martinus Scriblerus,* p. 96: "For he never had cohabitation with his spouse, but he ponder'd on the Rules of the Ancients, for the generation of Children of Wit. He ordered his diet according to the prescription of Galen, confining himself and his wife for almost the whole first year to Goat's Milk and Honey"; see also Kerby-Miller's note to this passage, p. 188.

John Arbuthnot, *An Essay Concernng the Nature of Aliments* (1731), comments on the nutritious quality of milk but places goat's milk after that of women, asses, and mares. Sterne may simply be referring to the traditional linking of goats with sexual potency.

For Arbuthnot, as for many in the eighteenth century, health was disturbed by two basic conditions, fibers too relaxed or fibers too rigid (see above, n. to 593.24−25). His discussion of the latter condition is of a nature possibly to have caught Sterne's attention apropos of Tristram's problem: "too great Rigidity and Elasticity of the Fibres, which is such a Degree of Cohesion as makes them inflexible to the Causes, to which they ought to yield . . . . Too great Elasticity is that Quality by which they resist against Elongation . . . .

"Rigidity of the Organs is such a State as makes them resist that Expansion, which is necessary to carry on the Vital Functions." Milk, he goes

on, is too nourishing for the condition, "but Whey proper as an Emollient
. . ." (pp. 155–58).

    Cf. below, n. to 625.13–14, and above, n. to 1ff.

624.19–22   for blaming Fortune . . . many small evils] Sterne recalls his
phrasing from vol. I: "I have been the continual sport of what the world
calls Fortune; and though I will not wrong her by saying, She has ever
made me feel the weight of any great or signal evil;---yet with all the good
temper in the world, I affirm it of her, That in every stage of my life, and
at every turn and corner where she could get fairly at me, the ungracious
Duchess has pelted me with a set of as pitiful misadventures and cross
accidents as ever small HERO sustained" (8.21–9.2).

625.5–626.24   a day in Lyons . . . Christ was tied] Sterne again turns to
Piganiol for his information. His first remark, that Lyons is "the most
opulent and flourishing city in France," would seem to be a bit of humor at
the expense of Paris; cf. Piganiol, *Nouveau Voyage*, I: 247: "Lyon est la
seconde Ville de France, & ne cede qu'à Paris. Elle est comme au centre de
l'Europe, & par le moyen de ces deux rivieres, elle peut faire un commerce très-florissant" ("Lyons is the second city of France and second only
to Paris. It is as though it were at the center of Europe, and by means of its
two rivers is able to conduct a very flourishing commerce"). Cf. Nugent,
Grand Tour, IV: 157: "*Lyons* is the capital of the *Lyonois* in the kingdom of
France, situated at the confluence of the rivers *Rhone* and *Soane* . . . . It is a
place of great antiquity . . . . Its situation in the middle of *Europe* . . . the
greatness of its commerce and manufactures . . . renders it the second city
of this great and flourishing kingdom."

    Both Piganiol and Nugent describe the clock in the tower of the Cathe-
dral of St. John the Baptist. See Piganiol, I: 248: "On remarquera la
fameuse horloge qui est à côté du Chœur. C'est à présent un morceau bien
dérangé. Elle fur [*sic*] faite par *Nicolas Lippius*, de Bâle, l'an 1598 . . . ."
("One will note the famous clock on the side of the Choir. It is at present a
piece quite out of order. It was made by Nicolas Lippius of Basil in 1598
. . . ."); and Nugent, IV: 158: "The clock on the right side of the choir is
esteemed a most curious piece of mechanism, and was made by *Lippius*, a
mathematician of *Basil* . . . ."

    Both mention the library of the Jesuits, but only Piganiol (I: 252)
mentions the "Chinese History": "La Bibliotheque de cette Maison est une

des plus belles qu'il y ait dans le Royaume, étant composée d'environ quarante mille volumes. . . . Le P. Colonia, dans son Histoire Littéraire, dit que l'on trouve dans cette Bibliotheque un Livre unique en France . . . . C'est une *Histoire Générale de la Chine* en trente Volumes imprimés à Pekin, en beau papier, & en beaux caracteres Chinois" ("The library of this house [belonging to the Jesuits] is one of the most beautiful in the kingdom, being composed of about 40,000 volumes. . . . Father Colonia, in his *Histoire Littéraire,* says that in this library can be found a book unique in France . . . . It is a *General History of China* in thirty volumes, printed in Peking, on fine paper and in beautiful Chinese characters"). See also Nugent, IV: 160.

Both mention the ancient church of St. Ireneus and its relics, but only Piganiol provides details of the pillar: "On montre ici une partie de la Colonne que l'on dit être celle à laquelle Jesus-Christ fut attaché pendant qu'on le flagelloit . . . ." ("Here is displayed a part of the column they say is that to which Jesus Christ was tied while they lashed him . . .") (I: 250).

625.13–14   milk coffee . . . consumption] Coffee was considered medicinal in the eighteenth century; see, e.g., Chambers: "Its . . . real virtues, owned by the physicians, consist in this; that being an excellent drier, it carries off fumes and disorders of the head arising from too much moisture, dissipates megrims, and absorbs acrimonies of the stomach . . . .

"It likewise promotes circulation, but best with people of a pretty corpulent habit; being found hurtful to those who are thin, lean, dry, and of a bilious temperament . . . it is said to be prejudicial likewise . . . where there is a spitting of blood . . . ."

A clue to why coffee might have seemed efficacious to Tristram, despite the contraindications, is suggested by Chambers's final observation: "Mixing it with milk or cream renders it nourishing." Cf. Sterne's letter to Hall-Stevenson, August 12, 1762: "I am taking asses milk three times a day, and cows milk as often . . ." (*Letters,* p. 181). Earlier in the letter Sterne recounts his bleeding the "bed full" from a "breach" in his lungs.

626.22   *valet de place*] *OED*, s.v.: "A man who acts as a guide to strangers or tourists; a cicerone." Chesterfield's *Letters* (1750; *1774*) is cited as the first illustration.

626.24–26   and after that . . . at Vienne] Piganiol mentions Vienne, a beautiful city on the banks of the Rhone (*Nouveau Voyage,* I: 347–53), but nowhere mentions Pontius Pilate; Nugent, however, gives an account (*Grand Tour*, IV: 180): "a chapel called *Our Lady of Life*, which is said to have been the *Prætorium* of *Pilate*, governor of this town. Over the door there is a stone-ball with this inscription, *Hoc est pomum sceptri Pilati* ["This is the orb of the scepter of Pilate"]. They pretend likewise to shew the house where *Pontius Pilate* lived during his exile, (for he is said to have been banished hither by *Tiberius*) the tower where he was imprisoned, and the lake where he is reported to have drowned himself."

 Cf. Work, p. 520, n. 5: "In his *Recherches curieuses d'antiquité* (Lyon, 1683), p. 168, Spon explains that 'the name of an Italian, Humbert Pilati, Secretary to the last Dauphin Humbert, has given rise to all those idle dreams of calling a tower at Vienne near the Rhone the Tower of Pilate; a country-house near Saint Vallier, the House of Pilate; and the church of Notre Dame de la Vie, the Prætorium of Pilate.'" We tend to agree with the conclusion of Baker, "Sterne and Piganiol," p. 10, that Sterne probably did not see a copy of Spon but was working from other sources; see below, n. to 627.2ff. Sterne does, however, allude to Spon, not only at 628.21 but in *ASJ* as well: "and after two or three hours poring upon it [a manuscript fragment], with almost as deep attention as ever Gruter or Jacob Spon did upon a nonsensical inscription . . ." (p. 251).

627.2ff. *Tomb of the two lovers.*] Although Sterne cites Spon at one point (628.21) as a source for this episode, his account may well be derived solely from Piganiol, which contains all the information he needed: "L'an 1707, au mois de Juîn, Messieurs du Consulat de Lyon firent démolir un monument ancien & célebre, appellé le *Tombeau des deux amans*, qui étoit dans le fauxbourg de Vaise. L'origine de ce tombeau, ou petit temple, a fort exercé les Sçavans. Comme il n'y restoit point d'inscription, & qu'aucun Auteur ancien n'en a parlé, plusieurs Ecrivains ont donné l'essor à leurs conjectures. Les uns ont dit que c'étoit le tombeau de deux amans qui moururent de joie en se revoyant après une longue absence. Les autres que c'étoit le tombeau d'Herode & d'Herodias, qui furent relégués à Lyon par Caligula. D'autres croyent que ces deux amans étoient deux Chrétiens, mari & femme, qui avoient vécu ensemble en gardant la chasteté. M. Spon croyoit que c'étoit un Autel dédié à quelque divinité payenne qu'on adoroit à l'entrée de la Ville. Le P. Menestrier jugeoit que ce monument fut consacré à la mémoire de deux Prêtres du Temple d'Auguste, nommés l'un & l'autre *Amandus*, par un de leurs affranchis qu'ils avoient institué leur héritier. M. Brossette oppose quelques difficultés au sentiment de ce Jésuite, & en propose un nouveau avec beaucoup de modestie. Il conjecture que ce monument pourroit bien être le tombeau d'un *Amandus*, qui, selon une inscription rapportée par M. Spon, en érigea un à sa sœur bien aimée. Le tombeau des deux Amans est célebre dans le Roman d'Astrée, où l'on voit qu'on le faisoit servir à la religion de l'amitié. *L'amour de Periandre & de moi*, dit Hylas, *prit cependant un si grand accroissement, que d'ordinaire on nous appelloit les deux amis; & parce que nous desirions de la conserver telle, afin de l'affermir davantage, nous allâmes au sépulchre des deux Amans . . . ; là nous tenant chacun d'une main, & de l'autre l'un des coins de la tombe, nous fîmes, suivant la coutume du lieu, les sermens réciproques d'une fidelle & parfaite amitié, appellant les ames de ces deux fidelles Amans, pour témoins du serment que nous faisions*, &c. M. Brossette déplore avec raison que ce monument après avoir échappé à la fureur des peuples barbares, ait enfin péri par les mains de ceux mêmes qui devoient se faire une espece de religion de le conserver" (Piganiol, *Nouveau Voyage*, I: 264–66; a footnote identifies the reference to Spon as "Antiquités de Lyon, pag. 125"). Our translation follows.

"In the year 1707, in the month of June, the gentlemen of the Consulate of Lyons caused to be demolished an ancient and celebrated monument called the *Tomb of the two lovers*, in the suburb of Vaise. The origin of this tomb or little temple has truly challenged the learned. Since absolutely no inscription survived and since no ancient authors spoke of it, several writers gave full play to their conjectures. Some said it was the tomb of two lovers who died of joy on seeing each other again after a long absence. Others, that it was the tomb of Herod and Herodias, who were exiled to Lyons by Caligula. Others believed that these two lovers were two Christians, husband and wife, who had lived together while maintaining their chastity. M. Spon believed that it was an altar dedicated to some pagan divinity that was worshipped at the entrance to the city. Father Menestrier judged that this monument was consecrated to the memory of two priests of the Temple of Augustus, both named *Amandus*, by one of their freedmen whom they had named their heir. M. Brossette raises some objections to this Jesuit's idea and proposes a new one with much modesty. He conjectures that the monument could well be the tomb of an *Amandus*, who, according to an inscription reported by M. Spon, erected a tomb in memory of his beloved sister. The tomb of the two lovers is well known in the romance of Astrée where one sees it made to serve the religion of affection. *The love of Periandre and me,* says Hylas, *meanwhile grew so much that ordinarily we were called the two friends; and because we desired to keep it thus, in order to further strengthen it, we went to the sepulcher of the two lovers . . . . There, each of us holding the other's hand and with our free hand on a corner of the tomb, we made, following the local custom, the reciprocal oaths of a faithful and perfect friendship, calling the souls of these two loyal lovers to witness the oath that we made,* &c. M. Brossette deplores with reason that this monument, after having escaped the fury of the barbarians, finally perished by the hands of those same ones who should have made for themselves a religious observance to save it."

Although Sterne may well have taken his idea of the separated lovers from Honoré d'Urfe's *L'Astrée* (1607–27), its elements are at least as old as Xenophon's *Ephesian Tale.*

Cf. Nugent, *Grand Tour,* IV: 164: "Near the gate of Vezé, they discover'd some years ago an antient mausoleum, supported in the nature of an altar by four columns, and whose architecture seemed to be of the age of Augustus. As there was no inscription found with it, various opinions were handed about concerning this tomb; but the most probable is that of father *Menestrier, viz.* That it was a monument in form of a temple or altar, consecrated to the memory of one of *Augustus*'s priests, called *Amandus,* by two of his freed men, whom he left his heirs. . . . This antient monument, after having escaped the fury of barbarous ages, was shamefully destroyed by the magistrates of *Lyons* in 1707." See also *Travels of the late Charles Thompson,* I: 50–51: "In one of the Suburbs, call'd *Veize,* is a Tomb supported by four Pillars, supposed by some to belong to *Herod* and *Herodias,* who, according to Tradition, were starv'd to Death here: Others say, it was raised in Memory of a married Couple, who had made and kept a Vow of perpetual Continence: And others, that it was erected for two Lovers, who died of Joy upon their meeting together unexpectedly after a long Absence. Be this as it will, it is generally call'd the Tomb of the *Lovers.*"

627.8   fibrillous] This occurrence is the last illustration cited by *OED;* a fibril is a small fiber.

628.17 *pabulum*] *OED* cites this passage as its first example of figurative usage, with the definition "that which nourishes and sustains the mind or soul; food for thought."

628.17−18 *Frusts, and Crusts, and Rusts*] *OED* cites this passage for the first occurrence of *Frust,* with the definition "a fragment"; cf. Johnson, *Dictionary,* s.v. *Frustum:* "[Latin]: A piece cut off from a regular figure. A term of science." For *Rusts,* cf. *Memoirs of Martinus Scriblerus,* p. 103, and n. thereto (p. 209), which cites, among others who attacked antiquarians for their "supposed love of rust for its own sake," Pope's "Epistle to Addison," lines 35−38: "With sharpen'd sight pale Antiquaries pore, / Th' inscription value, but the rust adore; / This the blue varnish, that the green endears, / The sacred rust of twice ten hundred years!" (*Minor Poems,* p. 203).

628.21 Spon] Jacob Spon (1647−85), French antiquarian and historian; see above, nn. to 626.24−26, 627.2ff.

629.6 *Lyons-waistcoat*] This is the earliest example cited in the H-N supplement to *OED* for the attributive use of "Lyons" for "silk," an association made explicit in Chambers, *Supplement,* s.v. *Silk,* where the standard measurements are referred to as "aunes" or "ells of Lyons."

629.7−8 in my wild way of running on] Cf. 28.17: "Sometimes, in his wild way of talking, he [i.e., Yorick] would say . . . ."

629.10 Mecca . . . Santa Casa] Work, p. 521, n. 2: "The great holy city of Islam, the birthplace of Mohammed and the site of the Kaaba; the most sacred of all Mohammedan shrines. The Santa Casa, or Holy House, is a stone building in Loreto, Italy, said to have been the home of the virgin Mary in Nazareth whence it was aerially transported to Loreto by angels. It is a celebrated objective of Roman Catholic pilgrimages, and in Sterne's day its treasury contained a large number of rich and curious votive offerings."

Cf. 41.9−10 ("from *Rome* all the way to *Loretto*") and n. above.

629.14 *Videnda*] *OED* cites this passage as its first illustration, with the definition "things worth seeing or which ought to be seen."

629.14−15 tho' *last*—was not, you see, *least*] Proverbial; Tilley, L82, and *ODEP,* s.v. *Last.*

629.17 *Basse Cour*] "Lower court"; stable-yard.

629.21 Monsieur Le Blanc] Cf. Boswell, *On the Grand Tour,* p. 257 (January 2, 1766): "Finding [in Lyons] that the best places were taken for Saturday, I engaged the first place for Monday . . . [and] went to the house of Le Blanc, *baigneur* ["bath-keeper"], where I paid three livres a day, for which I had my room and wax candles, and was shaved and dressed." In *ASJ* Sterne identifies the innkeeper at Calais by name; see pp. 87, 336–38. If the two Le Blancs are indeed the same person, it suggests that Sterne did not stay in "the best places" during his stay in France.

629.24ff.   'Twas by a poor ass, etc.] Thackeray, who objected violently to Yorick's weeping over a dead ass in *ASJ*, pp. 138–41, wrote of this chapter: "A critic who refuses to see in this charming description wit, humor, pathos, a kind nature speaking, and a real sentiment, must be hard indeed to move and to please" (*English Humorists* [New York: Thomas Y. Crowell, 1902], p. 154).

630.5–6   there is a patient . . . looks and carriage] Cf. the descriptions of Toby, 105.26–29: "he had never seen any thing like it in my uncle *Toby*'s carriage;—he had never once dropp'd one fretful or discontented word;—he had been all patience,—all submission"; 130.15: "My uncle *Toby* was a man patient of injuries"; and 132.1–3: "My father, in this patient endurance of wrongs, which I mention, was very different . . . ."

See also 750.4–6, the description of Tom, "an open, cheary hearted lad, with his character wrote in his looks and carriage . . . ."

630.19–25   for parrots, jackdaws . . . for conversation] Sterne is perhaps ridiculing the century's interest in the possibility of speech in animals. Julien Offray de La Mettrie, *Man a Machine, trans. from the French*, 2d ed. (1750), is only one of many who discuss the possibility: "In a word, is it an absolute impossibility to teach this animal to speak? really I think not.

"I would take the baboon, preferably to all others, till chance leads us to the discovery of some other species more resembling ours; . . . I would chuse one, that had the most sensible face, and that answered best my expectation in a thousand pretty little tricks. . . .

"I dare not decide whether the organs of speech in a monkey, are incapable with all possible diligence, of attaining pronunciation: but an absolute impossibility of this kind would indeed surprize me . . . . Mr. *Locke* who certainly was never suspected of credulity, made no difficulty in believing the history Sir *William Temple* gives us in his memoirs, of a parrot that answered pertinently to every thing it was asked, and learnt like us to hold a conversation" (pp. 20–22). For a brief but useful investigation of the background of this passage, see Aram Vartanian's edition of La Mettrie (Princeton: Princeton University Press, 1960), pp. 214–17.

See above, n. to 173.6–13, and below, n. to 657.11, for other possible borrowings from La Mettrie.

630.26–29   I can make nothing . . . the dialogue] Cf. 569.11–14: "For these reasons a discourse seldom went on much further betwixt them, than a proposition,—a reply, and a rejoinder; at the end of which, it generally took breath for a few minutes, (as in the affair of the breeches) and then went on again."

631.1   But with an ass, I can commune for ever.] Cf. Sancho's lament over Don Quixote's "strict Injunction of Silence," I.III.11 (I: 247): "Could Beasts speak, as they did in *Æsop*'s Time, 'twould not have been half so bad with me; for then might I have communed with my Ass as I pleas'd, and have forgot my ill Fortune." First noted by Stout, "Borrowings," p. 115.

633.16   And who are you? said he.] Cf. *ASJ*, p. 221: "THERE is not a more perplexing affair in life to me, than to set about telling any one who I am . . . ."

633.17ff.   But it is an indubitable verity, etc.] Sterne may have found the basis for the joke of this chapter in Ozell's discussion of the custom of "couillage" (Rabelais, II.7.58, n. 51): "In France they called by the name of couillage a certain tribute paid before Luther by priests, for licences to keep wenches. . . . But to proceed: it was the proctors that laid this tribute of couillage, and the tradition of Metz has preserved there the memory of what passed in the 16th century between one of those gentlemen and a poor curate of the diocese of Treves. He was called upon for a crown, to which his share of that duty amounted annually, and the good man declined paying, because he said he kept no woman. No matter for that, replied the archbishop's officer, you must pay your dues; if you can do without a girl, that is nothing to thy master and mine; he has nothing to do with that. The money he must have . . . ."

634.3   *Pardonnez moi*] "Pardon me."

634.5–6   which being a post royal . . . postillion] Nugent, *Grand Tour*, IV: 17, suggests a different method of calculation: "All those posts that lead from *Paris* or *Lyons*, or from any place where the king actually resides, are called royal posts, and the charge of riding them is double the others, with regard to the horses, but not to the postilion." Smollett, *Travels*, I: 128, calls them "undoubtedly a scandalous imposition."

St. Fons is the first post south of Lyons.

634.16   The devil take . . . these people!] Cf. *ASJ*, p. 233, where Yorick compliments the French as "a loyal, a gallant, a generous, an ingenious, and good temper'd people as is under heaven," but then adds, "if they have a fault—they are too *serious*." As Stout notes, the observation runs contrary to the usual English view of the French as a "gay people" (cf. 603.7–8 and n. above: "The French have a *gay* way of treating every thing that is Great"). See *ASJ*, pp. 233n, 248n.

Swift, in *Examiner* 32, had anticipated Sterne's observation on the French character: "a People . . . who are usually so serious upon Trifles, and so trifling upon what is serious . . ." (*Prose Works*, III: 107).

635.7   Aye! for the salt] Sterne alludes to the *gabelle*, the tax on salt, one of four primary taxes in France; see Nugent, *Grand Tour*, IV: 7.

635.16–17   but I will go to ten thousand Bastiles first] Yorick delivers a similar apostrophe in *ASJ* when informed he may be put into the Bastille for lacking a passport: "'tis thou, thrice sweet and gracious goddess, addressing myself to LIBERTY, whom all in public or in private worship, whose taste is grateful, and ever wilt be so, till NATURE herself shall change . . . Gracious heaven! cried I, kneeling down upon the last step but one in my ascent . . ." (pp. 199–200). See Stout's note, p. 199.

635.18–636.2   O England! . . . my apostrophè] Cf. the closing sentence of the "Abuses of Conscience" sermon (*TS*, 164.20–21): "but like a *British* judge in this land of liberty and good sense . . ."; and 212.12–13: "the oaths we make free with in this land of liberty of ours are our own . . . ."

636.4   a person in black] Cf. above, n. to 599.9–10.

636.4–5   as pale as ashes] Cf. above, n. to 161.22–23.

636.8–9   I go by WATER . . . by OYL.] Sterne plays on the Roman Catholic practice of anointing with oil in the Sacrament of Unction of the Sick, often called Extreme Unction because it became associated with last rites; the Anglican church abandoned the custom in 1552.

637.1–3   Whereas—had you first . . . complain'd] Sterne's comment upon excessive taxes in France is repeated in *ASJ*, pp. 66, 262; Stout notes that "many English travelers attacked the . . . oppressiveness of French taxes . . ." (p. 262n).

637.10   PAR LE ROY.] "By [order of] the king."

637.19–20   all the days of his life] Cf. above, n. to 559.7.

637.24   fermiers] Tax-collectors; cf. *OED*, s.v. *Farmer*² 1.

638.4   AND SO THE PEACE WAS MADE] Watt's suggestion (p. 403, n. 3) that this is an allusion to the Peace of Paris in 1763 between England and France, ending the Seven Years War, is amplified quite convincingly by Wolfgang Zach, "'My Uncle Toby's Apologetical Oration' und die Politische Sinndimension von 'Tristram Shandy'," *GRM* 27 (1977): 405–10.

638.14   my remarks were *stolen*] Cf. *Spectator* 46, where Addison misplaces his notes containing hints for future essays (I: 195–98); and above, n. to 376.1–2.

638.17   Heaven! earth! sea! fire!] Cf. above, n. to 537.17.

639.9–10   Sancho Pança when he lost . . . more bitterly.] Sterne alludes to *Don Quixote*, I.III.9, where Sancho awakens to find his Ass missing, and "finding himself depriv'd of that dear Partner of his Fortunes, and best Comfort in his Peregrinations, he broke out into the most pitiful and sad Lamentations in the World; insomuch that he wak'd Don *Quixote* with his Moans" (I: 222). The image evidently appealed to Sterne, for he uses it again in *ASJ:* "The man seemed to lament it [the death of his ass] much; and it instantly brought into my mind Sancho's lamentation for his; but he did it with more true touches of nature" (p. 138).

639.11–14   WHEN the first . . . had cast them] Cf. Rabelais, II.34.252: "the registers of my brain are somewhat jumbled and disordered with the septembral juice." Sterne had borrowed from the same passage in vol. IV; see above, n. to 401.22–23.

Stout, "Borrowings," p. 114, notes that *OED* does not record this use of *register*.

639.16   chaise-vamper] *OED* cites this passage (incorrectly referenced as vol. VIII) as its only recorded example and provides the same definition as for *chaise-undertaker*; see above, n. to 623.23.

639.21–22   as full of wit, as an egg is full of meat] Proverbial; see *ODEP*, s.v. *Full*; and *Romeo and Juliet*, III.i.22–23: "Thy head is as full of quarrels as an egg is full of meat . . . ." Cf. Dunton, *A Voyage,* II: 14: "this Book is as full of Profit, as an Egg of Meat . . . ."

640.1 Louis d'Ors] Cf. Nugent, *Grand Tour,* IV: 17: "the *Louis d'Or* . . . is a piece of gold worth 24 *livres,* and equal to about a guinea *English* money."

640.3 Dodsley, or Becket] For Dodsley, see above, n. to 16.18. As noted in "Introduction to the Text (vol. II, pp. 825–26, in this edition), Sterne turned from Dodsley to Thomas Becket and P. A. Dehondt to publish vols. V and VI of *TS* in December 1761, and they remained his publishers to the end of his life—publishing vols. VII–IX of *TS,* vols. III–IV of the *Sermons* (1766), and *ASJ* (1768). Curtis, *Letters,* pp. 167–68, provides a detailed sketch of Thomas Becket (?1722–1813): "Formerly with Andrew Millar, he had as recently as 10 Jan. 1760 set up for himself at Tully's Head, near Surrey Street, Strand (*Public Advertiser* for that date), where in partnership with a Dutchman, P. A. Dehondt, who retired from the firm in 1772, he endeavoured to swell profits by the importation of foreign books, among which those by Rousseau and Mme Riccoboni were prominent. Sterne's patronage, which in 1780 Dehondt declared to have been 'extremely profitable', he may have secured through the efforts of his friend Garrick (Bodleian Library: MS. Add. C. 89, ff. 32–3; John Taylor, *Records of my Life,* London 1832, i. 383). . . . He retired in 1809 with the reputation of having been 'one of the most eminent booksellers in London' (Taylor, op. cit. i. 383–4) . . . ."

640.16 May-poling] Unrecorded in *OED.*

640.18 philosophating] *OED* cites this passage as its last illustration, with the definition "To reason as a philosopher; to philosophize."

640.22 *a la folie*] "Madly"; to excess.

641.15 *J'en suis bien mortifiée*] "I am simply mortified!"

641.18 unfrizled] *OED* cites this passage as its last example. Cf. *Letters,* p. 179, where Sterne comments on his daughter's stay in Paris: "[she] does nothing but look out of the window, and complain of the torment of being frizled.—I wish she may ever remain a child of nature—I hate children of art."

641.20 *Tenez*] "Here, take them!"

642.8 all out of joints] Perhaps an echo of *Hamlet,* I.v.188: "The time is out of joint."

642.23 *For all the* JESUITS *had got the cholic*] Sterne alludes to the suppression

of the Jesuit order in France, beginning with regional decrees in early
1762 that closed schools and confiscated Jesuit property, and culminating
in August 1762 with a nationwide decree against the order. Louis XV
suspended its operation for some eight months, but in the spring of 1763
the full law went into effect, with devastating results for the Jesuit establishment in France. For a Catholic view of these events, see Martin P.
Harney, S.J., *The Jesuits in History* (New York: America Press, 1941),
pp. 306–13.

Sterne was living in France during these events and commented several
times upon them; e.g., to Garrick, March 19, 1762: "the affairs of the
Jesuits, which takes up one half of our talk" (*Letters*, p. 157); and to Lord
Fauconberg, April 10, 1762: "I could never have been in France at so
critical a period, as this, when two of the greatest Concerns that ever
affected the Interest of this kingdome are upon the Anvil together—the
Affair of the Jesuists [*sic*]—& the War . . ." (*Letters*, p. 160). Sterne's
sympathies are indicated by his recommending to Fauconberg the anti-
Jesuit work *Compte rendu des Constitutions des Jésuites* (1762), by Louis-
René de Caradeuc de la Chalotais.

644.3–4   So now I am . . . Ormond resided] Work, p. 533, n. 1: " 'Nothing
to see' may be one of Sterne's characteristic slaps at Catholicism, for the
sight for which Avignon has been famous since the fourteenth century is
its great papal palace." It should be noted, however, that Piganiol,
Nouveau Voyage, I: 284–85, and Nugent, *Grand Tour*, IV: 185, both
dismiss the palace in a sentence or two. Neither author mentions the fact
that James Butler, Duke of Ormond, spent over thirty years in exile in
Avignon; see above, n. to 360.8–9. Sterne might have read a brief account of the Duke in exile in the anonymous *Life* (1747), pp. 541–44,
cited above, n. to 360.8–9.

644.17   arming himself at all points] *OED*, s.v. *point*, D.1.e.: "at all points:
in every part, in every particular or respect (Usually with *armed*)." Cf.
Hamlet, I.ii. 199–200: "a figure like your father, / Armed at point exactly, cap-a-pe . . . ." See also *TS*, 18.12, where Rosinante is described as
"undoubtedly a horse at all points."

644.25–26   and hearing . . . as a proverb] Sterne alludes to the mistral, the
northwest wind that sweeps down the Rhone valley and is especially felt by

the towns at the southern end, Avignon and Orange. We have found only
one proverb recorded concerning the wind in Avignon: "Avignon ven-
teuse, sans vent contagieuse" ("Avignon is windy, without being con-
tagious"); see M. Le Roux de Lincy, *Le Livre des Proverbes Français*, 2d
ed. (Paris, 1859), I: 310. Nugent mentions that Orange was "liable to
frequent winds" (*Grand Tour*, IV: 184), but says nothing about the winds
in Avignon.

645.13–22 I Had now . . . at this rate?] Cf. Sterne's letter to Hall-
Stevenson, October 19, 1762, after having settled in Toulouse: "The physicians here are the errantest charlatans in Europe, or the most ignorant of
all pretending fools—I withdrew what was left of me out of their hands,
and recommended my affairs entirely to Dame Nature—She (dear goddess) has saved me in fifty different pinching bouts, and I begin to have a
kind of enthusiasm now in her favour, and in my own, That one or two
more escapes will make me believe I shall leave you all at last by translation, and not by fair death. I am now stout and foolish again as a happy
man can wish to be . . ." (*Letters*, pp. 185–86).

646.4–6 I should traverse . . . foot could fall.] Piganiol may have given
Sterne his idea for this route; cf. *Nouveau Voyage*, II: 58: "CE *Voyage n'est
que de pure curiosité: car la route en est si détournée & si longue, qu'il n'y a
personne qui voyage pour affaires qui s'avise de la suivre. Les Curieux qui
voudront l'entreprendre, se serviront des Itinéraires que j'ai donnés pour aller
de Paris à Toulon: mais lorsqu'ils partiront d'Avignon, ils quitteront cette route
pour prendre celle qui suit*" ("This journey is only for pure curiosity: since
the road there is so circuitous and long no one who travels for business
would think to take it. The curious who would like to try it, will use the
itineraries I gave for going from Paris to Toulon, but when they leave
Avignon they will quit this road to take that which follows"). The itinerary
contains all the towns mentioned at 651.11–13 in *TS*; it proceeds southwest
from Avignon to Lunel and Montpellier, then skirts the Mediterranean
coast before turning northwest to Toulouse. Piganiol's map, facing p. 59,
might have helped Sterne's memory at this point, but it is worth recalling
that Sterne had lived in this area between the summer of 1762 and the
winter of 1764, residing in Toulouse the first year and then wintering in
Montpellier before turning back toward England. Cf. *Letters*, p. 207

(January 5, 1764): "I took a ride when the first part of this was wrote towards Pezenas" (i.e., Pesçnas, as in *TS*, 651.12).

646.12−13   and that nature . . . her abundance, *&c.*] Cf. *ASJ*, p. 268: "I NEVER felt what the distress of plenty was in any one shape till now—to travel it through the Bourbonnois, the sweetest part of France—in the hey-day of the vintage, when Nature is pouring her abundance into every one's lap, and every eye is lifted up—a journey through each step of which music beats time to *Labour,* and all her children are rejoicing as they carry in their clusters . . . ." Cf. *TS*, 649.20ff., the description of Nannette, "a sun-burnt daughter of Labour."

646.18−19   This is most terrible . . . my plains better.] That a traveler could turn a "*plain* into a *city*" by his own efforts of communication and association is an idea Sterne returns to at length in *ASJ*, pp. 114−15: "—What a large volume of adventures may be grasped within this little span of life by him who interests his heart in every thing, and who, having eyes to see, what time and chance are perpetually holding out to him as he journeyeth on his way, misses nothing he can *fairly* lay his hands on.—

"—If this won't turn out something—another will—no matter—'tis an assay upon human nature—I get my labour for my pains—'tis enough—the pleasure of the experiment has kept my senses, and the best part of my blood awake, and laid the gross to sleep.

"I pity the man who can travel from *Dan* to *Beersheba,* and cry, 'Tis all barren—and so it is; and so is all the world to him who will not cultivate the fruits it offers."

The idea is hardly original with Sterne; cf. Bacon's dedication in *The Historie of the Raigne of King Henry the Seventh* (1622): "And it is with *Times,* as it is with *Wayes.* Some are more *Up-hill* and *Down-hill,* and some are more *Flat* and *Plaine;* and the *One* is better for the *Liver,* and the *Other* for the *Writer.*" And see the more extensive discussion in *Idler* 97 (February 23, 1760): "The greater part of travellers tell nothing, because their method of travelling supplies them with nothing to be told. He that enters a town at night and surveys it in the morning, and then hastens away to another place, and guesses at the manners of the inhabitants by the entertainment which his inn afforded him, may please himself for a time with a hasty change of scenes . . . but let him be contented to please himself without endeavour to disturb others." Johnson then parodies a traveler who describes only the changing scene and comments: "thus he conducts his reader thro' wet and dry, over rough and smooth, without incidents, without reflection . . . .

"He that would travel for the entertainment of others, should remember that the great object of remark is human life" (pp. 298–300).

Vrooman, "Origin and Development of the *Sentimental Journey*," p. 52, calls attention to both the Bacon and the Johnson passages.

See above, nn. to 41.7ff., 617.16–18.

647.2–3   the fairs of *Baucaira* and *Tarascone*] Beaucaire and Tarascon are towns on the Rhone, just south of Avignon. Sterne mentions the famous fair at Beaucaire in a letter from Toulouse, August 14, 1762: "Our luggage weighed ten quintals—'twas the fair of Baucaire—all the world was going, or returning—we were ask'd by every soul who pass'd by us, if we were going to the fair of Baucaire—No wonder, quoth I, we have goods enough!" (*Letters*, p. 183).

647.15   I had figs enow] See above, n. to 610.17.

647.26   to form the least probable conjecture] Cf. 89.16–19: "if I thought you was able to form the least judgment or probable conjecture to yourself, of what was to come in the next page,—I would tear it out of my book."

648.8–9   set o'vibrating together] Cf. 131.8–11 and n. above.

649.4–7   the best Muscatto . . . drop of it.] As Van R. Baker observes, Sterne "had hardly arrived in Montpellier before he was looking into the cost and means of shipping some [wine] to Lord Fauconberg, in Yorkshire" ("A French Provincial City and Three English Writers: Montpellier as Seen in the 1760s by Sterne, Smollett, and Boswell," *ECLife* 2 [1976]: 55). In this instance, however, the wine was probably red rather than muscatto. Sterne resided in Montpellier for five months in 1763–64; see *Letters*, pp. 200–211.

649.10   carousal] *OED* cites this passage as its first illustration, with the definition "a fit of carousing, a drinking-feast or carouse; revelry in drinking." The word was often confused with *carousel*, which the *OED* defines as a "tournament in which knights, divided into companies . . . engaged in various plays and exercises . . . ." Johnson, deriving *carousal* from *carouse*, defines it simply as a "festival"; and Carlyle, perhaps with Sterne in mind, speaks of a carousel as "a kind of superb betailored running at the ring" (cited in *OED*). Sterne's passage suggests as much of one definition as the other, examples of which date from 1650.

649.12   running at the ring of pleasure] As Stout (*ASJ*, p. 156) points out, the term originally indicated a chivalric exercise in which a rider attempted to pass the point of his lance through a suspended ring (*OED*). Rabelais's delightful retelling of the story of Hans Carvel's "ring" (III.28) indicates the bawdy meaning available to Sterne—and indeed Rabelais makes the application specific in II.1.9–10: "Some other puffes did swell in length by the member, which they call the labourer of nature, in such sort, that it grew marvellous long, plump, jolly, lusty, stirring, and crest-risen in the antique fashion . . . : but if it happened the aforesaid member to be in good case . . . then to have seen those strouting champions, you would have taken them for men that had their lances settled on their rest, to run at the ring, or tilting quintain." In Paris, Yorick looks out from his hotel window to see all the world "in yellow, blue, and green, running at the ring of pleasure.—The old with broken lances . . ." (*ASJ*, p. 156 and n.).

649.13   By saint Boogar] Work, p. 537, n. 2: "A phonetic coinage from the French *bougre* or English *bugger*"; Sterne continues the joke with the saints "at the backside of the door of purgatory." Cf. above, n. to 613.21ff.

650.15–18   'twas a . . . TRISTESSA!] "The *rondel* or *rondeau* is so named because it was originally intended as an accompaniment to the dance called *ronde* or *rondel,* still surviving in the western provinces of France, in which the dancers joined hands and went round in a circle according to the time of the song, the soloist and chorus taking alternate parts, while a minstrel not infrequently accompanied the whole song on a kind of violin called the viole" (L. E. Kastner, *A History of French Versification* [Oxford: Clarendon Press, 1903], p. 249). Gascony is in southwestern France, but there seems to be no other basis for the attribution.

The verses may be translated thus: "Long live joy! Fie on sadness!" Work, p. 538, n. 3, notes that *fidon* = *fi-donc,* apparently the Provençal accent as Sterne heard it.

651.5–8   Just disposer . . . nut brown maid?] Cf. "The Grace," in *ASJ,* pp. 283–84, where Yorick sees "*Religion* mixing in the dance" of the peasant family; for an interesting discussion of the relationship between the two scenes, see Jeffrey L. Duncan, "The Rural Ideal in Eighteenth-Century Fiction," *SEL* 8 (1968): 527–31.

Also cf. *Sermons*, III.20.147–48: "When the affections so kindly break loose, Joy, is another name for Religion.

"We look up as we taste it: the cold Stoick without, when he hears the dancing and the musick, may ask sullenly . . . What it means; and refuse to enter: but the humane and compassionate all fly impetuously to the banquet . . . . Was it not for this that GOD gave man musick to strike upon the kindly passions; that nature taught the feet to dance to its movements . . . ."

651.6   lap of content] Cf. *Letters*, p. 234: "I shall spend every winter of my life, in the same lap of contentment, where I enjoy myself now—and wherever I go—we must bring three parts in four of the treat along with us—In short we must be happy within—and then few things without us make much difference—This is my Shandean philosophy.—You will read a comic account of my journey from Calais thro' Paris to the Garonne, in these volumes . . . ."

651.7   and dance, and sing, and say his prayers] Cf. *ASJ*, p. 248, on the French manner of spending Sundays: "Happy people! that once a week at least are sure to lay down all your cares together; and dance and sing and sport away the weights of grievance, which bow down the spirit of other nations to the earth."

651.8   nut brown maid] A phrase made commonplace by the popular old ballad "The Nut-Brown Maid." Prior's sophisticated rewriting of it, "Henry and Emma" (1708), concludes: "Thro' all her laughing Fields and verdant Groves, / Proclaim with Joy these memorable Loves. / From ev'ry annual Course let One great Day, / To celebrated Sports and Floral Play / Be set aside . . . / And everlasting Marks of Honour paid, / To *the true Lover*, and *the Nut-brown Maid*" (*Works*, ed. H. Bunker Wright and Monroe K. Spears, 2d ed. [Oxford: Clarendon Press, 1971], I: 300, lines 766–73).

651.9   insiduous] *OED* considers this an erroneous spelling of *insidious*. Cf. *Letters*, p. 64: "the worse and more insiduous appears every step of the managem^t of that affair."

651.14   Perdrillo's pavillion] Cf. 622.6–9 and n. above. See also t.n., vol. II, p. 861, in this edition.

NOTES TO VOLUME VIII

655.7   cabbage planter] See above, n. to 572.6. And cf. Montaigne, "To study Philosophy, is to learn to die," I.19.85: "I would always have a Man to be doing, and as much as in him lies, to extend and spin out the Offices of Life; and then let Death take me planting Cabbages, but without any careful Thought of him, and much less of my Garden's not being finished." Sterne had borrowed from this essay parts of Walter's and Trim's funeral orations.

655.14   *Freeze-land, Fog-land*] Nonce words; *freeze-land* is unrecorded in *OED*, and the only example of *fog-land* cited is dated 1886.

656.3–4   with all the meanders . . . her DIEGO] Sterne recalls phrasing from "Slawkenbergius's Tale": "these meanders and unsuspected tracts" (300.19–20), and "many meanders and abrupt turnings of a lover's thorny tracks" (319.25–26).

656.16–20   That of all . . . for the second.] Montaigne comments in a similar vein upon his own style of writing: "I fall to without Premeditation or Design, the first Word begets the Second, and so to the End of the Chapter" (I.39.284). See also II.10.87: "I have no other Officer to put my Writings in Rank and File but only Fortune. As Things come into my Head, I heap them one upon another, which sometimes advance in whole Bodies, sometimes in single Files: I am content that every one should see my natural and ordinary Pace, as ill as it is. I suffer myself to jog on at my own Rate and Ease."

    Sterne may also have been recalling Addison's discussion of false wit in *Spectator* 60, where Gilles Ménage is quoted: "*Monsieur* de la Chambre *has told me, that he never knew what he was going to write when he took his Pen into his Hand; but that one Sentence always produced another. For my own Part, I never knew what I should write next when I was making Verses"* (I: 257). Sterne cites the *Menagiana* in vol. IV, chap. 21 (see above, n. to 357.15ff.).

This pose of spontaneity in writing was held throughout the composition of *TS;* see Sterne's letter to Mary Macartney (?June 1760): "to me inconsiderate Soul that I am, who never yet knew what it was to speak or write one premeditated word, such an intercourse would be an abomination; & I would as soon go and commit fornication wth the Moabites, as have a hand in any thing of this kind unless written in that careless irregularity of a good and an easy heart . . ." (*Letters*, p. 117).

657.2   the devil and all his imps] Cf. Tilley, M706: "No MARVEL it is if the imps follow when the devil goes before."

657.11   Pope and his Portrait* are fools to me] Work, p. 540, n. 2, suggests that Sterne is "probably referring to one of the several allegorical engravings of Alexander Pope receiving inspiration from the classic gods, muses, and poets. In Warburton's edition of Pope, with which Sterne was familiar, *Windsor Forest* is prefaced by an engraving of Pope, laurel-crowned, with pen poised, taking dictation from Flora; the *Satires* are preceded by an engraving of the poet similarly seated, receiving inspiration from Mercury and Apollo; another engraving in the same volume graphically illustrates the lines from the *Epilogue to the Satires*, Dialogue 2, apostrophizing his pen: 'O sacred weapon! left for Truth's defence, / Sole Dread of Folly, Vice, and Insolence! / To all but Heav'n-directed hands deny'd, / The Muse may give thee, but the Gods must guide.'"

It is also possible that Sterne is referring instead (or in addition) to a passage in Julien Offray de La Mettrie's *L'homme machine* (1747), translated into English as *Man a Machine;* we quote from the second edition (1750), p. 62: "Let us view the picture of the famous Mr. Pope, whom at least we may call the *English* Voltaire. The efforts and nerves of his genius are strongly represented in his physiognomy; it seems to be all in a sort of convulsion; his eyes seem ready to start from their orbit, his eye-brows raise themselves with the muscles of his forehead. Why all this? 'tis because the source of the nerves is, as if it were in labour, and the whole body, if I may so say, feels the pangs of a painful delivery. If there is not an inward cord which thus forcibly pulls those without, how can we account for these surprizing phænomena? In order to explain all this, if we admit a soul, this in effect would be the same as if we were to call in the operation of the holy ghost." Strictly from a pictorial standpoint, the painting that most seems to fit La Mettrie's description is that by Michael Dahl; see William K. Wimsatt, *The Portraits of Alexander Pope* (New Haven: Yale University Press, 1965), pp. 90–96. Sterne's acquaintance with La Mettrie's work has been suggested elsewhere in these notes (see above, nn. to 173.6–13, 630.19–25), but this is perhaps the most convincing evidence; Sterne's final evaluation of La Mettrie's general thesis, however, is probably given in *ASJ*, p. 271: "I am positive I have a soul; nor can all the books with which materialists have pester'd the world ever convince me of the contrary."

657.13–20   but I have no . . . the next chapter] Cf. above, nn. to 439.1–15, 447.16–19. If Work is correct (see above, n. to 657.11), the allusion to Warburton's edition of Pope may be said to tie this particular passage even more closely to the Bishop; but even if Pope's portrait alludes instead to La Mettrie, Warburton does not seem very distant from Sterne's mind, as "TARTUFFE" (657.17) indicates (see above, n. to 409.1). And cf. Sterne's letter of June 9, 1767: "This nasty gout! . . . I wish it was the portion of splenetic philosophers, and Tartuffe's of all denominations,—at least I should not torment my philanthropy much about them; but when it falls upon an open cheerful hearted man . . . I grieve from my soul that such feelings should be thwarted—and would write or fight with more zeal to restore him to himself, than all the *subscriptions* or *subsidies* in the world could kindle in me, in another case . . ." (Earl R. Wasserman, "Unedited Letters by Sterne, Hume, and Rousseau," *MLN* 66 [1951]: 74).

The word *zeal*, in religious matters, carried a pejorative connotation throughout the century. In *Tale of a Tub*, Swift describes Jack's "discovery" of the word: "For, the Memory of *Lord Peter*'s Injuries, produced a Degree of Hatred and Spight, which had a much greater Share of inciting Him, than any Regards after his Father's Commands . . . . However, for this Meddly of Humor, he made a Shift to find a very plausible Name, honoring it with the Title of *Zeal*; which is, perhaps, the most significant Word that hath been ever yet produced in any Language . . ." (p. 137). Sterne's comment on "good works" is a glance at the Methodist controversy, in which the term played a central role; see *Joseph Andrews*, book I, chap. 17, especially Battestin's n. 2, p. 82 (Middletown, Conn.: Wesleyan University Press, 1967). See also above, n. to 273.15−19.

657.21−658.13   Bon jour . . . occasion for it.] Sterne is perhaps indebted here (as Ferriar, I: 48−49, first suggested) to the opening paragraph of Rabelais's prologue to book IV: "GOOD people, God save and keep you! Where are you? I can't see you: stay—I'll saddle my nose with spectacles——Oh, oh! 'twill be fair anon, I see you. Well, you have had a good vintage, they say: this is no bad news to Frank, you may swear. You have got an infallible cure against thirst: rarely perform'd of you, my friends! You, your wives, children, friends, and families are in as good case as hearts can wish; 'tis well, 'tis as I'd have it: God be praised for it, and if such be his will, may you long be so. For my part, I am thereabouts, thanks to his blessed goodness; and by the means of a little pantagruelism, (which you know is a certain jollity of mind, pickled in the scorn of fortune) you see me now hale and cheery, as sound as a bell, and ready to drink, if you will. Wou'd you know why I'm thus, good people? I'll e'en give you a positive answer—Such is the Lord's will, which I obey and revere; it being said in his word, in great derision to the physician, neglectful of his own health, Physician, heal thyself" (pp. lxi−lxii).

658.9   night-draught] This antedates the earliest example recorded in *OED* (s.v. *night* 13.b.), which is dated 1776.

658.10   periclitating] *OED* cites this passage as its last example of usage as a transitive verb, with the definition "endangering." Sterne may have found the word in Rabelais. For "pardi" see above, n. to 600.23.

658.11−12   By my . . . black velvet mask!] See Allardyce Nicoll, *A History of English Drama: 1660−1900*, 4th ed. (Cambridge: Cambridge University Press, 1952), I: 14, n. 3: "The habit of mask-wearing seems to have come in shortly after the Restoration, and, although abandoned by 'Civil Gentlewomen' by 1680, it was not suppressed entirely until the edict of Anne in 1704. It rapidly became the recognised mark of a prostitute, although even 'ladies of quality' . . . seem not to have minded being taken by their gentlemen friends as *femmes d'amour*." Nicoll also calls them "Women of doubtful character, 'vizard Masks' as they were euphemistically styled." Cf. Millamant's reaction to Mirabell's *inprimis* that she not go to plays in a mask ("Detestable *Inprimis*! I go to the Play in a Mask!"), in Congreve's *The Way of the World*, IV.i.244, in *The Complete Plays*, ed. Herbert Davis (Chicago: University of Chicago Press, 1967), p. 451.

658.21–23   we count . . . single mountebank] Cash points out that "the archbishop and aldermen were real enough" (*Early and Middle Years*, p. 3). Sterne's great-grandfather, Dr. Richard Sterne (?1596–1683), was the Archbishop of York from 1664 until his death.

The meaning of "Welch judge" has eluded us.

659.1–3   "IT is with Love . . . the matter] Sterne plays on a proverbial expression; see Tilley, C877: "The CUCKOLD is the last that knows of it"; and *ODEP*, s.v. *Cuckold*. Cf. John Arbuthnot, *The History of John Bull*, ed. Alan W. Bower and Robert A. Erickson (Oxford: Clarendon Press, 1976), pp. 12–13: "It is a true saying, *That the last Man of the Parish that knows of his Cuckoldom, is himself.*"

659.3–8   this comes . . . with my forefinger] Cf. the discussion in Prior's *Alma*, canto I, of the proper bodily location of love, especially lines 349–50: "Love's Advocates, sweet Sir, would find Him / A higher Place, than You assign'd Him" (*Works*, ed. H. Bunker Wright and Monroe K. Spears, 2d ed. [Oxford: Clarendon Press, 1971], I: 480).

659.15   pre-notification] *OED* cites this passage as its first illustration.

660.1–2   WHY weavers . . . a man with a pined leg] Cf. Montaigne, "Of Cripples," III.11.300–301. In a section of this essay, headed by the marginal note "*Lame People best at the Sport of* Venus," Montaigne comments: "'Tis a common Proverb in *Italy, That he knows not* Venus *in her perfect Sweetness, who has never lain with a Lame Mistress*. . . . and the same is said of the Men as well as of Women; for the Queen of the *Amazons* answer'd the *Scythians*, who courted her to love . . . *Lame Men perform best*. . . . I have lately learnt, that ancient *Philosophy* has it self determin'd it, which says, that the Legs and Thighs of Lame Women, not receiving, by reason of their Imperfection, their due Aliment, it falls out, that the genital Parts above, are fuller, and better supply'd, and much more vigorous. . . . the *Greeks* decry'd the Women Weavers, as being more hot than other Women, by reason of their sedentary Trade; which they do without any great Motion or Exercise of the Body [marginal note: "*Women Weavers more lustful than other Women*"]."

Ferriar, I: 123, refers to Montaigne's "essay on the subject" of this chapter as "the best commentary" on it; we assume he means "Of Crip-ples."

661.10   grinding the faces of the impotent] Sterne may possibly be echoing Isaiah 3: 15: "What mean ye that ye beat my people to pieces, and grind the faces of the poor? saith the Lord GOD of hosts." If so, it might be noted that this section of Isaiah is particularly misogynistic, the next verses reading: "Moreover the LORD saith, Because the daughters of Zion are haughty, and walk with stretched forth necks and wanton eyes . . . therefore the Lord will smite with a scab the crown of the head of the daughters of Zion, and the LORD will discover their secret parts" (3: 16–17).

661.11   be-peppering] *OED* cites this passage as its last illustration.

661.13–16   If I was you . . . both read Longinus] In *On the Sublime* Longi-nus asserts that "the greatest Thoughts are always uttered by the greatest Souls" and illustrates it with Parmenio and Alexander: "When *Parmenio* cried, 'I would accept these Proposals if I was *Alexander*,' *Alexander* made this noble Reply, 'And so would I, if I was *Parmenio*.' His Answer shew'd the Greatness of his Mind" (trans. William Smith [1739; Del-mar, N.Y.: Scholars' Facsimiles and Reprints, 1975], pt. 1, sec. 9, p. 19). See also Smith's note to the passage, p. 120, and Work, p. 544, n. 1.

662.3–4   hair off . . . pluck it off myself] Cf. Kunastrokius's "delight," 12.5–9.

663.10–12   Is it not enough . . . off thy hands.] Of the 4,000 copies printed of vols. V and VI, some 1,000 remained unsold fifteen months after pub-lication. Sterne's concern is manifested in every letter to Becket during this period; see *Letters*, pp. 191–92, 199, 203–4, 211. See also "Introduction to the Text," vol. II, p. 827, in this edition.

663.13–14   with the vile asthma . . . wind in Flanders?] Cf. 8.20–21 ("for an asthma I got in scating against the wind in *Flanders* . . .") and n. above.

663.16–17   thou brakest a vessel in thy lungs] Cf. Sterne's letter in January 1762: "Indeed I am very ill, having broke a vessel in my lungs . . ." (*Letters*, p. 150); and in August 1762: "About a week or ten days before my wife arrived at Paris [July 1762] I had the same accident I had at Cam-bridge, of breaking a vessel in my lungs. It happen'd in the night, and I bled the bed full . . ." (*Letters*, p. 180).

663.23–664.1   it will scarce bear . . . single tittle] Cf. Sterne's instructions to the printer of the *Political Romance:* "do not presume to alter or transpose one Word . . . nor so much as add or diminish one Comma or Tittle, in or to my *Romance* . . ." (p. 50).

664.14–16 (who to the character . . . upholsterer too)] This is one of several occasions on which Sterne ties his later volumes to the earlier ones by repeating descriptive phrases for his characters. In vol. II, written five years earlier, he had described Trim as attending uncle Toby as "valet, groom, barber, cook, sempster, and nurse" (109.2–3). Cf. 709.6–7, 710.3–4, and nn. below.

664.18 A daughter of Eve] Cf. *Sermons,* III.19.106–7: "It seems that Drusilla, whose curiosity, upon a double account, had led her to hear Paul,— (for she was a daughter of Abraham——as well as of Eve) . . ."; and *Letters,* p. 235: "Mrs G[arrick] . . . the best and wisest of the daughters of Eve."

665.1–2 or playing with a case-knife] Cf. above, n. to 198.16–19. A case-knife is simply a knife with a sheath, a rather obvious sexual analogy.

665.19 day-shifts] Unrecorded in *OED* in this sense.

666.11 decemberly] *OED* cites this passage as its only recorded example.

667.6 *etiquette*] The *Stanford Dictionary* cites Chesterfield, Walpole, Junius, and Smollett's *Travels* and *Humphry Clinker* as examples of usage between 1750 and 1771. The word seems to have been much in vogue and in the process of naturalization during Sterne's day.

668.10–11 a vacancy)—of almost eleven years] As Baird points out ("Time-Scheme," p. 818), this would set the date of Toby's coming into the country in 1702 or 1703, which is inconsistent with other chronological clues; see above, n. to 103.1–2.

668.12–13 the second blow . . . the fray] Proverbial; Tilley, B475, and *ODEP,* s.v. *First.*

668.17–18 It is not . . . *old hat*] See Partridge, s.v. *old hat:* "The female pudend: low . . . Grose, 'Because frequently felt'." Cf. above, n. to 394.12, on "cocked" hats.

669.13 *Terra del Fuogo*] I.e., Tierra del Fuego, the archipelago off the southern tip of South America. Whether we take the name literally ("Land of Fire") or follow Partridge's entry, s.v. *fugo* ("the rectum: C.17–18: low coll."), Sterne's usage is probably not innocent.

669.15   divinityship] An unrecorded humorous usage of the first definition in *OED:* "the status or personality of a divinity"; cf. 565.14 and *Letters*, p. 216 (to Mrs. Montagu): "Unless you are suffocated w^h Insense, Y^r Divinityship, next winter will you be so merciful as to recieve a Scruple or two from my hands . . . in the mean time . . . I must be content to worship afar off . . . ."

669.16–17   the passions . . . flow] Cf. 164.19–20 and n. above.

670.2   gashly] *OED* cites this passage to illustrate its definition of "gashly" as an obsolete form, meaning "ghastly, horrid." More probably, Sterne had in mind an adjectival form of *gash;* cf. *OED,* s.v. *Gashy.*

670.2–3   taking off my furr'd cap] Cf. *Letters,* p. 207, in which Sterne writes to his banker friend Robert Foley about the pleasures of retirement: "When you have got to your fireside, and into your arm-chair . . . and are so much a sovereign as to sit in your furr'd cap (if you like it, tho' I should not, for a man's ideas are at least the cleaner for being dress'd decently) . . . ."

670.10   I shall never have a finger in the pye] Proverbial: Tilley, F228, and *ODEP,* s.v. *Finger.* Cf. the obscure bawdy pamphlet *Rinology: or, A Description of the Nose* (Dublin, 1736), p. 14: "He had a Finger in the Pye, as sure as I'm there [at the keyhole]. And when the Child was got, he put a Nose to 't."

670.18   staragen] *OED:* "*obs.* form of TARRAGON"; this passage is cited as first example.

670.20   devil's dung] Asafoetida, a particularly foul-smelling drug, also used in cooking. It seems to have been considered an aphrodisiac; see above, n. to 563.7–12, the quotation from Goldsmith.

670.20   arch cook of cooks] Cf. 356.12 and n. above: "arch-jockey of jockeys."

671.9   LOVE is certainly, at least alphabetically speaking] Cf. Cervantes, I.IV.7: "You yielded to one who has not only the four S's* [*As if we shou'd say, sightly, sprightly, sincere, and secret], which are requir'd in every good Lover, but even the whole *Alphabet;* as for Example, he is, in my Opinion, *Agreeable, Bountiful, Constant, Dutiful, Easy . . .*" etc. (II: 100).

671.16–672.11   F utilitous . . . R idiculous] Sterne's list contains a number of nonce words:

"Futilitous": "futile" (*OED;* only example recorded).

"Galligaskinish": unrecorded in *OED;* derived from *galligaskins,* "a more or less ludicrous term for loose breeches in general" (*OED*). See *TS,* 379.21.

"Handy-dandyish": unrecorded in *OED;* probably formed with the child's game "handy-dandy" in mind: "a small object is shaken between the hands by one of the players, and, the hands being suddenly closed, the other player is required to guess in which hand the object remains" (*OED*). By extension, "handy-dandyish" could suggest the offering of a choice, or simply rapid alteration, as being aspects of love.

"Iracundulous": "inclined to anger; irascible" (*OED;* only example recorded).

"Ninnyhammering": derived from *ninnyhammer* ("fool"); may also be considered a nonce word.

673.12   Love-militancy] Unrecorded in *OED.*

673.16   wicker gate] Cf. 704.8, 705.12. Sterne may have had in mind a gate made of wicker, but it seems far more likely that his usage is a solecism for *wicket gate:* "A small door or gate made in, or placed beside, a large one, for ingress and egress when the large one is closed; also, any small gate for foot-passengers, as at the entrance of a field or other enclosure" (*OED*).

674.2–3   set on fire like a candle, at either end] Sterne plays with the proverbial expression (Tilley, C48 and G328, and *ODEP,* s.v. *Burn*) indicating prodigality or sociability, "to burn or light a candle at both ends," and makes it serve his own purposes. Cf. 675.7–8.

See also *Spectator* 265 (II: 531): "But our Female Projectors were all the last Summer so taken up with the Improvement of their Petticoats, that they had not time to attend to any thing else; but having at length sufficiently adorned their lower Parts, they now begin to turn their Thoughts upon the other Extremity, as well remembring the old Kitchin Proverb, that if you light your Fire at both Ends, the middle will shift for its self." Bond, n. 4, remarks that the "proverb" is "apparently an invention of Mr. Spectator; no other example is known."

674.17–675.4   I beseech you . . . quoth my father.] The discussion here bears comparison with those in vol. I, chap. 25, on the location of Toby's wound (88.4–6), and vol. II, chap. 19, where Walter explains the advantage of the "*Cæsarian* section" (178.17–24); cf. also the comment on Toby's ignorance concerning the right and wrong end of a woman (117.19–21). The play at this point would seem to be on the "blind gut" as a term for the *cæcum* and, more generally, for any tubular passage with one end closed. See below, n. to 679.14–16.

675.13–14   *blind* or *mantelet*] See "Glossary of Terms of Fortification" in this volume.

676.17   stroke of generalship] Cf. above, n. to 234.17.

676.27   from Dan to Beersheba] A Biblical formula: "from Dan even to Beersheba" (Judges 20: 1; 2 Samuel 24: 2). Dan marked the northern and Beersheba the southern boundary of Canaan. Sterne uses the expression in *ASJ*, p. 115.

677.2–5   For as there was . . . but smoak.] Sterne anticipates his brilliant use of pulsations in *ASJ*, pp. 97, 161–65, climaxing in Yorick's assertion, "Trust me, my dear Eugenius . . . 'there are worse occupations in this world *than feeling a woman's pulse*'" (p. 165).

677.20–21   elementary and practical part of love-making] Cf. 562.19–20, where Sterne promises "one of the most compleat systems, both of the elementary and practical part of love and love-making . . . ."

678.21   Bouchain] The siege of Bouchain in August 1711 was one of Marlborough's great triumphs, the well-fortified town surrendering in just twenty days. A large foldout map of the town and its fortifications is provided by Tindal, vol. IV, facing p. 210. An advertisement at the end of vol. IV notes that the "plans" in Tindal's *History* were available "singly, at the price of 6*d*. each."

679.2   snuffy] *OED:* "soiled with snuff"; the first example is dated 1840.

679.14–16   the pricks which enter'd . . . for love.] See above, n. to 297.12. St. Radegund was known for her mortifications, according to F. Brittain, *St. Radegund* (Cambridge: W. Heffer & Sons, 1928), p. 24: "In her private life, Radegund practised every kind of austerity to mortify the flesh. She wore a hair-shirt, slept on a bed of ashes and sackcloth, and took only the poorest and sparsest of food. She . . . practised self-laceration, burning her flesh with a red-hot iron cross, and wearing a triple iron chain until it bit into her body." Cf. Eric Rothstein, *Systems of Order and Inquiry in Later Eighteenth-Century Fiction* (Berkeley: University of California

Press, 1975), p. 84: "'Fesse' is French and 'clunis' Latin for 'buttock,' so that this spiritual voyage becomes a shifting of hams with 'pricks' *in media re*."

681.6−8   as *Servius Sulpicius* . . . and Pyreus] Cf. 421.17−422.28 and n. above.

681.14−16   I have never . . . pass'd done deeds] Cf. 535.13−15: "the good nature of my uncle *Toby* . . . chatting kindly with the corporal upon past-done deeds."

682.7−8   a man should ever . . . along with him] Sterne recalled this passage in his response to a highly complimentary letter from an American physician, Dr. John Eustace, which he received in February 1768 (*Letters*, p. 411): "I am very proud, sir, to have had a man, like you, on my side from the beginning; but it is not in the power of any one to taste humor, however he may wish it—'tis the gift of God—and besides, a true feeler always brings half the entertainment along with him. His own ideas are only call'd forth by what he reads, and the vibrations within, so entirely correspond with those excited, 'tis like reading *himself* and not the *book*." Cf. *Letters*, p. 234, quoted above, n. to 651.6.

683.2−3   and having . . . would best go] See above, n. to 63.7−8.

685.13−20   from the first creation . . . telling his story] The "science" of chronology was largely built in the seventeenth century by scholars like Archbishop Ussher (1581−1656), and was still taken quite seriously in the eighteenth century. For example, see John Blair, *Chronology and History of the World* (1754), in which dates are provided for all the major biblical events, including creation (October 23, 4004 B.C.), the beginning of the flood (December 7, 2349), the birth of Abraham (1996), and the departure of the Israelites from Egypt (May 5, 1491). In his preface, Blair praises the study of chronology as the "EYE OF HISTORY," lighting the "most dark, and complicated Revolutions of Mankind." The fact that he dedicates his work to the Lord Chancellor, and that the list of subscribers includes the Prince of Wales and the Archbishops of Canterbury and York, suggest Blair was not alone in assigning importance to this sort of activity, though we have been told earlier in *TS* (443.3) that Toby "was no chronologer" and will be told later in this chapter that it is the science a "soldier might best spare" (689.14−15).

Blair's *Chronology* dates events by several different methods, including

the Greek Olympiads; the "years of Nabonnassar" (the first recorded King
of Babylonia—perhaps alluded to in Sterne's reference to "Dynasties");
and the founding of Rome (*ab urbe condita*). Sterne's term "Urbecondita's"
(i.e., "by the founding of cities") seems to be of his own devising, and is
not recorded in *OED*; see above, n. to 267.23.

685.22–23   but as MODESTY . . . hands open] As W. G. Day has pointed out,
the allusion to Guido Reni's painting, variously called "Liberality and
Modesty" or "Generosity and Modesty," is perhaps a compliment to
Sterne's patron, John Spencer (see above, n. to Ded., vol. V), who possessed a studio version of it ("A Novel Compliment," *BSECS Newsletter* 5
[1974]: 6–7). Ferriar, I: 115–16, is the first to have noted the allusion to
Guido; Sterne mentions him in his catalogue of painters, 214.7.

686.1–2   last cast-year of the last cast-almanack] Both compounds are unrecorded in *OED;* they are constructed by analogy perhaps to cast-clothes,
i.e., something discarded.

686.5–17   seventeen hundred and twelve . . . incredible vigour] Tindal provides an account of the closing campaign of the war, noting that the Dutch
States General, whose army was under the command of Prince Eugene,
"having resolved to prosecute the operations of the war, the trenches were
opened before *Quesnoy,* and the siege carried on with all imaginable vigour under the command of General *Fagel* [a Dutch general, François Nicolas Fagel (1655–1718)]." However, the Duke of Ormond, acting under
new orders, informed Eugene and the Allies "That the *French* King had
agreed to several articles demanded by the Queen, as a foundation for a
suspension of arms; and, among others, the giving up immediately into
our possession the Town of *Dunkirk* [see above, n. to 559.20ff.]. That the
Duke therefore could no longer cover the siege of *Quesnoy,* being obliged
by his instructions to march with the Queen's troops, and those in her pay,
and to declare a cessation of arms, as soon as *Dunkirk* was delivered up
. . ." (IV: 274). Noted by Baird, "Time-Scheme," p. 813, n. 56.

The complicated story of these "orders" is told in the anonymous *Life of
James, Late Duke of Ormond* (1747); and earlier by Richard Steele in *The
Englishman* 2, nos. 10, 11, 21, ed. Rae Blanchard (Oxford: Clarendon
Press, 1955), pp. 291–99, 334–36, all written during the time of Or-
mond's impeachment trial. The gist of Toby's complaint against Ormond
is found in the third Article of Impeachment, as provided by Steele: "He,

the said Duke, in Violation of the Queen's Instructions to him, and of the Declarations he had made to the Pensionary of *Holland*, and the Confederate Generals, and of the last Orders sent him by Mr. *St. John* [Bolingbroke], and in pursuance of a wicked Promise he had made to the Mareschal *Villars*, contrary to his Allegiance, and the Laws of this Realm, did, during the War, traiterously advise, and endeavour to perswade the Confederate Generals . . . to raise the Siege of *Quesnoy*, and did further traiterously refuse to act any longer against *France*, and declared he could no longer cover the Siege, but was obliged by his Instructions to march off with the Queen's Troops, and those in her Majesty's Pay" (pp. 335–36). As Blanchard notes (p. 457), Ormond seems actually to have been acting under direct orders from Bolingbroke. See also above, n. to 360.8–9.

J. W. Fortescue, *A History of the British Army* (London: Macmillan and Co., 1910), I: 552, provides a colorful account of these events, culled primarily from Robert Parker's *Memoirs* (1747). We quote at some length to indicate the extent to which Toby's hostility toward the Peace of Utrecht was shared by the army; and because Sterne's father, Roger, was one of the soldiers affected by these events, his regiment having been disbanded by Ormond's order the year before Laurence was born (Cash, *Early and Middle Years*, p. 2): "By July [1712] the subservience of the British Ministry to Lewis the Fourteenth had been so far matured that Ormonde was directed to suspend hostilities for two months, and to withdraw his forces from Eugene. Then the troubles began. The auxiliary troops in the pay of England flatly refused to obey the order to leave Eugene, and Ormonde was compelled to march away with the British troops only. Even so the feelings of anger ran so high that a dangerous riot was only with difficulty averted. The British and the auxiliaries were not permitted to speak to each other, lest recrimination should lead either to a refusal of the British to quit their old comrades, or to a free fight on both sides. The parting was one of the most remarkable scenes ever witnessed. The British fell in, silent, shamefaced, and miserable; the auxiliaries gathered in knots opposite to them, and both parties gazed at each other mournfully without saying a word. Then the drums beat the march and regiment after regiment tramped away with full hearts and downcast eyes, till at length the whole column was under way, and the mass of scarlet grew slowly less and less till it vanished out of sight.

"At the end of the first day's march Ormonde announced the suspension of hostilities with France at the head of each regiment. He had expected the news to be received with cheers: to his infinite disgust it was greeted with one continuous storm of hisses and groans. Finally, when the men were dismissed they lost all self-control. They tore their hair and rent their clothes with impotent rage, cursing Ormonde with an energy only possible in an army that had learned to swear in the heat of fifty actions."

688.26−689.9   how Marlborough could have marched . . . Hochstet?]
Sterne brilliantly condenses four double-column folio pages from Tindal (III: 654−57), describing "*The Duke of* Marlborough'*s march into* Germany" (marginal note, p. 654) in the 1704 campaign. Relevant passages in Tindal are: "From *Maestricht* the Duke of *Marlborough* marched to *Bedburg* . . . and advanced from *Bedburg* to *Kerpenord*, the next day to *Kalsecken* . . . . He therefore continued his march with unwearied diligence, and advanced to the camp of *Neudorff* near *Coblentz* . . . . Then the Duke passed the *Neckar* near *Ladenburg*, where he rested three days. . . . [He] marched from *Ladenburg* to *Mildenheim* . . . . On the 24th [of June], the army marched from thence [Westerstet] to *Elchingen;* the next day to *Gingen*. On the 30th, the army marched from thence to *Landthaussen* on the right, and *Balmertshoffen* on the left . . . . About five o'clock in the afternoon [July 2], they came before *Schellenberg* . . . advanced to the enemy's works without once firing, threw their fascines into the ditch, and passed over with inconsiderable loss.

"On the 5th of *July,* the Duke of *Marlborough* passed the *Danube* . . . . On the 10th, the whole army passed the *Lech* . . . .

"The Confederate army . . . decamped, on the 4th of *August* from *Friburg,* and marched that night to *Kippach.*

"The next morning, they decamped from thence, and marched to *Hokenwert* . . . . The 10th, they marched to *Schonevelt* . . . . They [the enemy] were possessed of a very advantageous post, on a hill near *Hochstet*, their right flank being covered by the *Danube*, and the village of *Blenheim* . . . ."

As Baird (p. 814, n. 57) points out, Sterne alters the spelling of many of the place names; while many of the changes can be attributed to his own misreading, or the compositor's failure to read the manuscript correctly, it also seems possible that Sterne took a purposefully cavalier attitude toward the spelling of place names. Cf. 422.14–17: "The fairest towns that ever the sun rose upon, are now no more: the names only are left, and those (for many of them are wrong spelt) are falling themselves by piecemeals to decay, and in length of time will be forgotten . . . ."

David Chandler, *Marlborough as Military Commander* (New York: Charles Scribner's Sons, 1973) provides a useful map of the campaign of 1704 (pp. 134–35).

689.24–690.14   I am far from controverting . . . was born] Sterne's discussion seems to have been borrowed from Chambers, s.v. *Gunpowder* (as noted by Work, p. 565, n. 5): "The invention of *gunpowder* is ascribed, by Polydore Virgil, to a chymist . . . .

"Thevet says, the person here spoke of, was a monk of Fribourg, named Constantine Anelzen: but Belleforet and other authors, with more probability, hold it to be Bartholdus Schwartz . . . : at least it is affirmed, he first taught the use of it to the Venetians, in the year 1380, during the war with the Genoese . . . .

"But what contradicts this account, and shews *gunpowder* of an older æra, is, that Peter Mexia, in his *Various Readings,* mentions, that the Moors being besieged in 1343, by Alphonsus XI. king of Castile, discharged a sort of iron mortars upon them, which made a noise like thunder: which is seconded by what Don Pedro, bishop of Leon, relates in his chronicle of king Alphonsus, who reduced Toledo, *viz.* that in a sea combat between the king of Tunis, and the Moorish king of Seville, above four hundred years ago, those of Tunis had certain iron tuns or barrels, wherewith they threw thunder-bolts of fire.

"To say no more, it appears that our Roger Bacon knew of *gunpowder* one hundred and fifty years before Schwartz was born: that excellent fryar mentions the composition in express terms, in his treatise *de Nullitate Magiæ,* published at Oxford in 1216." (The recipe follows.)

Work, p. 565, nn. 4, 5, 6: "Berthold Schwartz, a German monk, is said to have been the inventor of fire-arms, and perhaps of gunpowder, about 1330; Wenceslaus (1361–1419) became Holy Roman Emperor in 1378.

"The chronicler Pedro, bishop of Leon, died in 1112. Sterne was led astray by misreading his source for this passage, 'Gunpowder,' in Ephraim Chambers' *Cyclopædia* . . . .

"In his *De Mirabili Potestate Artis et Naturæ*, Roger Bacon (c. 1214–c. 1294), English philosopher and scientist, revealed considerable knowledge of explosive powders."

As is so typical with Sterne, he flourishes his learning by correctly pointing out that Wenceslaus was the ruler of Germany at this time, having succeeded his father, Charles IV (1316–78); it is precisely this sort of information that a work like Blair's *Chronology* could readily supply (see above, n. to 685.13–20).

690.14–24   And that the Chinese . . . all the world] Many of the military treatises Sterne might have examined give attention to the invention of gunpowder, often repeating the information in Chambers; many add as well the claim of the Chinese. See, e.g., Robert Norton, *The Gunner: Shewing the Whole Practise of Artillerie* . . . (1628), p. 37 (misnumbered 39): "*Uffano* reporteth, that the invention and use as well of Ordnance as of Gunne-powder, was in the 85 yeere of our Lord, made knowne and practized in the great and ingenious Kingdome of *China* . . . ." See above, n. to 174.6–7.

In view of Trim's question, "How come priests and bishops . . . to trouble their heads so much about gun-powder?" (690.1–3), it is interesting to note that Warburton discussed the history of gunpowder in his *Julian, or A Discourse Concerning the Earthquake* . . . (1750), including an investigation of the Chinese claim: "It is true, that when the missionaries had opened themselves a way into China . . . we are told, amongst the other wonders of these remote regions, of fire-arms, both great and small; which had been in use for sixteen hundred years . . . .

"But this fable of the ancient use of cannon in China is not to be charged on the missionaries, but on the Chinese themselves, the proudest and vainest people upon earth . . . . They boasted, in the same manner, of the antiquity . . . of their astronomy and mathematics" (*Works*, VIII: 198, 200). Warburton then goes on to dismiss their claim, in a manner similar to Uncle Toby's, by citing their lack of knowledge of the military use of cannon; see New, "Sterne, Warburton," pp. 271–72.

692.4–5   and there *happening* . . . sea-port town whatever] Sterne seems to be using a familiar trope for a never-never-land setting. Cf. *Winter's Tale*, where the coastline of Bohemia is clearly established; and Edmund Burke, *A Philosophical Enquiry into the Origin of our Ideas of the Sublime and Beau-*

tiful (1757), ed. J. T. Boulton (London: Routledge & Kegan Paul, 1958), p. 21: "In his favourite author he is not shocked with the continual breaches of probability, the confusion of times, the offences against manners, the trampling upon geography; for he knows nothing of geography and chronology, and he has never examined the grounds of probability. He perhaps reads of a shipwreck on the coast of Bohemia; wholly taken up with so interesting an event, and only solicitous for the fate of his hero, he is not in the least troubled at this extravagant blunder. For why should he be shocked at a shipwreck on the coast of Bohemia, who does not know but that Bohemia may be an island in the Atlantic ocean?" Just possibly, Sterne was reading Burke's *Enquiry* at this time; see below, nn. to 702.10–16, 708.1–16.

692.8 It might; said Trim, if it had pleased God] Trim here offers Grangousier's solution, as Toby had done earlier, 284.17–20; see n. above. See also the dispute between the Nosarians and Antinosarians, pp. 313–15, especially 315.1–3: "This at once started a new dispute, which they pursued a great way upon the extent and limitation of the moral and natural attributes of God . . . ."

692.12–14 and having *Silesia* . . . Bavaria to the south] Sterne may have consulted a map or other geographical authority; see, for example, Collier's translation of Moréri's *Dictionary* (1701), s.v. *Bohemia:* "It has *Silesia* and *Moravia* on the East, *Lusatia* or *Lausnitz* and *Upper-Saxony* on the North, *Franconia* on the West, and *Bavaria* on the South."

693.6–9 King William . . . had it's billet."] *ODEP,* s.v. *bullet,* traces this idea to Gascoigne's *Poesies,* I.155 (1573); but we can see that the expression was specifically associated with William III from John Wesley's *Journal* (June 6, 1765): "So true is the odd saying of King William, that 'every bullet has its billet'" (ed. Nehemiah Curnock, 8 vols. [London: Charles H. Kelly, n.d.], V: 130).

693.23 over head and ears!] Proverbial; Tilley, H268, and *ODEP,* s.v. *Over.* See above, n. to 565.10–11.

694.4–695.4 Your honour remembers . . . with great prudence] The account of the Battle of Landen (July 29, 1693) is taken from Tindal, III: 238–40 (as noted by Baird, "Time-Scheme," pp. 806–7, n. 10). After some initial successes, the tide turned against the Allies and they were forced into a disorderly retreat; Sterne pieces together his description from

Tindal's: "After the *Hanover* horse had been broken, the rest of the Confederate right wing of horse . . . was soon overthrown by the enemy, who
now had the opportunity of charging them both front and flank. The
Elector of *Bavaria* did what he could to resist the numerous multitude of
the enemies horse, that charged him thus; but, finding it impossible, with
no small difficulty he retreated over the bridge, and rallied on the other
side as many of the scattered horse and foot as could get over, to favour the
retreat of those, who were ready to pass. The King did what he could to
remedy this disorder, riding to the left to bring up the *English* horse for the
relief of the right wing. . . . they were forced to charge the enemy in the
same order they rid up to them (and most of them had rid as fast as their
horses could gallop) but that did not hinder them from doing extraordinary service. The King himself charged at the head of Lord *Galway*'s
regiment, which distinguished itself very much on this occasion. Colonel
Wyndham, at the head of his regiment, charged several times through and
through the enemy's squadrons. . . . the Duke of *Ormond*, having
charged at the head of one of *Lumley*'s squadrons, received several
wounds, and had his horse shot under him . . . .

"The King, seeing the battle lost, ordered the infantry to retreat . . .
and finding, that the enemies were surrounding him on all sides, he ordered the regiments of *Wyndham*, *Lumley*, and *Galway* to cover his retreat
over the bridge at *Neerhespen*, which he gained with great difficulty. There
was now nothing but confusion and disorder in the Confederates camp; all
those, who could not get the passes for the retreat, being pressed by the
enemy, were forced to throw themselves into the river, where many were
drowned . . . . Lieutenant-General *Talmash* brought off the *English* foot
with great prudence, bravery, and success . . . .

"The King in this battle was seen every where, acting the different parts
of a General and of a private soldier. He had supported the whole action
with so much courage, and so true a judgment, that it was thought he got
more honour that day, than even when he triumphed at the *Boyne*. He
charged himself, in several places, and was in the midst of the most imminent dangers; many being shot round about him with the enemies cannon,
and himself escaping no less than three musket shots . . . a third, which
carried off the knot of his scarf, and left a small contusion on his side. . . .
And the Prince of *Conti*, in an intercepted letter to his Princess, declared,

'I saw the King exposing himself to the greatest dangers; and surely so much valour very well deserved the peaceable possession of the crown he wears.'"

General Hugh Wyndham (d. 1708) is mentioned several times in R. E. Scouller's *The Armies of Queen Anne* (Oxford: Clarendon Press, 1966); he appears to have been active primarily in the Spanish campaigns. Henry Lumley (1660–1722) was an English general who also fought at Steinkirk and Namur and participated in Marlborough's 1704 march through Germany. Henri de Ruvigny, Earl of Galway (1648–1720), was born in France but entered the English army in 1690 as a major-general of horse and received his title in 1697. François-Louis de Bourbon, Prince de Conti (1664–1709), led the French cavalry at Landen. François-Henri de Montmorency, duc de Luxembourg (1628–95), was the Marshall of France who headed the French army at Landen. Thomas Talmash, or Tollemache (?1651–94), was a lieutenant-general who fought at Limerick and Steinkirk.

Fortescue, *History of the British Army*, I: 378, reminds us that the "losses on both sides were very severe. That of the French was about eight thousand men; that of the Allies about twelve thousand, killed, wounded, and prisoners . . . ."

See above, n. to 454.18–20.

694.21–22   he deserves a crown . . . shouted Trim.] Possibly proverbial; cf. *ODEP*, s.v. *worth:* "As well worth it as a thief is worth a rope."

695.21   unpinn'd her mob] Cf. *Handbook of English Costume*, p. 158: "Always an undress head wear; worn throughout the century but becoming popular in the 1730's.

"The mob had a puffed-out crown placed high at the back of the head, with a deep flat border surrounding the face like a bonnet and side pieces carried down like short lappets. These might be left dangling or pinned under the chin . . . ."

696.5–6   cæteris paribus] "Other things being equal."

696.15   care-taking] *OED* cites this passage as its sole example of the definition "taking care *of*."

698.19–24   I dare say . . . of good-nature.] See above, n. to 316.14.

699.14–24   My fever ran very high . . . left the room] See "Journal to Eliza"

(*Letters*, p. 326): "Twas a prophetic Spirit, wch dictated the Acc^t of Corp^l Trim's uneasy night when the fair Beguin ran in his head,—for every night & almost every Slumber of mine, since the day We parted, is a repe[ti]tion of the same description . . . ."

700.14   sisserara] I.e., siserary. *OED:* "*With a siserary:* with a vengeance; suddenly, promptly."

701.6—7   there is no resisting our fate.] Proverbial; see Tilley, F83, and *ODEP,* s.v. *Flying* (i.e., "No flying from fate").

702.3—9   Let me see it . . . on the dressing.] Sterne's inspiration for Trim's story may have come in part from John Burton's account of the escape of the Pretender after the Battle of Culloden in 1745, in *A Genuine and True Journal of the most miraculous Escape of the Young Chevalier* (1749); the passage which might particularly have caught Sterne's eye occurs on p. 43: "After having got some Refreshment, the Captain desired the Maid-servant to wash his Feet; which being done, he desired her then to wash his Man's [that is, the Prince in disguise]. But she replied, 'That tho' she had washed his [the Captain's], yet she would not wash that lubberly Lown his Servant's.' But the Captain told her, 'His Servant was not well; and therefore he asked her to do it.' She then undertook it; but rubbed his Feet so hard, that she hurt him very much. On which the Pr. spoke to the Captain in *English,* to desire her not to rub so hard, nor go so far up with her Hand, he having only a Philibeg on."

For John Burton, see above, n. to 50.15—22.

702.10—16   In five or six minutes . . . I live] Cf. Burke, *A Philosophical Enquiry,* p. 151: "There can be no doubt that bodies which are rough and angular, rouse and vellicate the organs of feeling, causing a sense of pain, which consists in the violent tension or contraction of the muscular fibres. On the contrary, the application of smooth bodies relax; gentle stroking with a smooth hand allays violent pains and cramps, and relaxes the suffering parts from their unnatural tension; and it has therefore very often no mean effect in removing swellings and obstructions. The sense of feeling is highly gratified with smooth bodies." See above, nn. to 562.10—11, 692.4—5; and below, n. to 708.1—16.

702.24—703.2   I will never . . . softer than satin] Trim's repetitive tribute to the Beguine's hands is perhaps anticipated by Sir Roger De Coverley's similar tribute to his "perverse widow" in *Spectator* 113; three times he comments that "she has certainly the finest Hand of any Woman in the World" (I: 463–66).

704.3   love-romances] Unrecorded in *OED*.

704.22   the archives of Gotham] Work, p. 575, n. 1: "An allusion to the apparent simplicity, which served to conceal the real shrewdness, of the 'wise men' of Gotham." The expression "as wise as a man of Gotham" is proverbial; see Tilley, M636, and *ODEP*, s.v. *Wise*. Sterne uses "the Wise Men of Gotham" in "Journal to Eliza," *Letters*, p. 331.

706.5   raree-shew-box] John Stedmond ("Uncle Toby's 'Campaigns' and Raree-Shows," *N&Q* 201 [1956]: 28–29) points to the description of "raree shows" in Joseph Strutt's *Glig Gamena Angel Deod or The Sports and Pastimes of the People of England* (London, 1801), p. 130: "a species of scenic exhibition with moving figures, bearing some distant analogy to the puppets [which] appeared at the commencement of the last century"; Stedmond quotes at length the description of one such show in Queen Anne's reign, the moving and elaborate exhibition of the siege of Lisle, reminiscent of Toby's creation of the bowling green. Strutt also speaks of a raree show with a "combination of many different motions, and tolerably well-contrived . . . ." *Raree* is supposedly the Savoyard's attempt at *rare*, suggestive of the fact that these exhibits were often the work of the itinerant wanderers of Savoy; see above, n. to 252.19. See also the addition to Stedmond's note by George Speaight, *N&Q* 201 (1956): 133–34.

706.12   Thracian* Rodope's] Sterne borrows from a marginal note in Burton, 3.2.[2.]3 (p. 466): "*Heliodor. 1. 2. Rodophe Thracia tam inevitabili fascino instructa, tam exacte oculis intuens attraxit, ut si in illam quis incidisset, fieri non posset quin caperetur.*"

Work, p. 576, n. *: "Rhodopis of Thrace was a celebrated Greek courtesan of the sixth century, B.C. The Latin, taken from Heliodorus's *An Æthiopian History*, 2.25, via *The Anatomy* . . . , may be translated: Rhodopis of Thrace was provided with such inevitable fascination, and attracted so perfectly with her eyes when looking at anyone, that if anyone fell in with her it was impossible but that he would be captivated."

From here to the end of vol. VIII Sterne relies heavily on this section of the *Anatomy*.

706.21   Gallileo look'd for a spot in the sun.] The eighteenth century gener-
         ally credited Galileo with the discovery; see, e.g., John Keill, *An Introduc-
         tion to the True Astronomy*, 2d ed. (1730), p. 43: "The great *Italian* Phi-
         losopher *Galileus*, first discovered them with his Telescope."
707.5−6   one lambent delicious fire] Cf. above, n. to 326.15.
708.1−16   Now of all the eyes . . . cares to?"] Cf. Burke, *A Philosophical
         Enquiry*, p. 118: "I think then, that the beauty of the eye consists, first, in
         its *clearness;* what *coloured* eye shall please most, depends a good deal on
         particular fancies; but none are pleased with an eye, whose water (to use
         that term) is dull and muddy. We are pleased with the eye in this view, on
         the principle upon which we like diamonds, clear water, glass, and such
         like transparent substances. Secondly, the motion of the eye contributes to
         its beauty, by continually shifting its direction; but a slow and languid
         motion is more beautiful than a brisk one; the latter is enlivening; the
         former lovely."
            See also Jacques Ferrand, *Erotomania, or, a Treatise Discoursing of the
         Essence, Causes . . . and Cure of Love, or Erotique Melancholy*, trans. Ed-
         mund Chilmead (Oxford, 1640), p. 171: "*Aristotle* . . . will have the Eyes
         also to bee very considerable in these Predictions [of the disease of love-
         melancholy] . . . because, saith he, the Eye is the most Spermaticall part
         about the Head. And indeed the *Wiseman* knew an Adulterous Woman by
         her eyes better, and with more assurance, than any man can by the Hand
         . . . ."
            Burton also has a lengthy discussion of the power of the eye in love,
         3.2.2.2 and 3.2.2.3 (pp. 448ff.). At one point he remarks: "it is not the
         eye of it selfe that entiseth to lust, but an *adulterous eye*, as *Peter* termes it [2
         Peter 2: 14: "Having eyes full of adultery, and that cannot cease from
         sin"], a wanton, a rolling, lascivious eye . . ." (p. 466). Cf. also Burton,
         p. 466 ("'Tis not the eye, but carriage of it, as they use it, that causeth such
         effects"), with *TS*, 707.11−12 ("That it is not so much the eye . . . as it is
         the carriage of the eye . . ."). Sterne's simile, however, would seem to be
         his own.
708.9   milk of human nature] Cf. Walter's comment: "so much do'st thou
         possess, my dear Toby, of the milk of human nature . . ." (719.11−12).
         Stevenson, pp. 1574−75, suggests that "the milk of human kindness"

became proverbial after its occurrence in *Macbeth*, I.v.16–17: "Yet do I fear thy nature, / It is too full o' th' milk of human kindness . . . ."

709.1–2 for I call . . . better for it] Cf. *ASJ*, pp. 128–29: ". . . [I have] been in love with one princess or another almost all my life, and I hope I shall go on so, till I die, being firmly persuaded, that if ever I do a mean action, it must be in some interval betwixt one passion and another . . . ." Sterne makes much the same point in *Letters*, p. 256.

709.6–7 but from a little . . . drollish impatience] See above, n. to 664.14–16. One of the earlier descriptions of Walter speaks of his "acute and quick sensibility of nature, attended with a little soreness of temper; . . . in the little rubs and vexations of life, 'twas apt to shew itself in a drollish and witty kind of peevishness:—He was, however, frank and generous in his nature,——at all times open to conviction; and in the little ebullitions of this subacid humor . . ." (132.4–10). Cf. 735.10–13: "Nothing but the fermentation of that little subacid humour, which I have often spoken of, in my father's habit, could have vented such an insinuation——he was however frank and generous in his nature, and at all times open to conviction . . ."; and 757.17–20: "he broke out at once with that little subacid soreness of humour which, in certain situations, distinguished his character from that of all other men."

OED cites the present passage as the first use of *subacid* (1765), with the following definition: "2. Of character, temper, speech, etc.: Somewhat acid or tart; verging on acidity or tartness." Actually the occurrence in vol. II, 132.10 (1759), should have been cited.

709.10 bitterest Philippicks] Cf. 458.17–18 ("the *chapter upon sash-windows*, with a bitter *Philippick* at the end of it . . .") and n. above.

709.15–16 A Devil 'tis . . . Turk."*] As noted by Ferriar (I: 116–17), Burton, 3.2.4 (p. 538), quotes these verses and attributes them to "R. T.," that is, Robert Tofte (d. 1620), from whose translation of Benedetto Varchi's *Blazon of Jealousie* (1615) they are taken; see Franklin B. Williams, Jr., "Robert Tofte an Oxford Man," *RES*, n.s. 6 (1955): 178.

709.27 my father's life of Socrates] See above, n. to 440.9.

710.3–4 in the sharpest exacerbations . . . discontented word] See above, nn. to 664.14–16, 709.6–7. In vol. II, Sterne had mentioned the "sharp paroxisms and exacerbations of his [Toby's] wound . . ." (95.22–23) and a few chapters later the fact that Toby "had never once dropp'd one fretful or discontented word . . ." (105.28).

710.8   whiffing] *OED* cites this passage as its first example of usage as a transitive verb, with the definition "to utter with a whiff or puff of air."

710.12−14   to save if possible . . . to the poor*] Cf. Sterne's letter to Hall-Stevenson, November 13, 1764: "'Tis a church militant week with me, full of marches, and countermarches—and treaties about Stillington common, which we are going to inclose . . ." (*Letters*, p. 232). Whether Sterne is actually alluding to this or some other particular action by the dean and chapter of York is unknown; cf. 310.5−7. Cash, *Early and Middle Years*, p. 255, records a parallel event.

710.15−16   and of singular service . . . battle of Wynnendale] The battle occurred at the end of September 1708 as part of the effort to resupply the besiegers at Lille (see 217.4−6, 541.1−3, and nn. above). Tindal's account of the battle in vol. IV includes a map facing p. 84 which makes clear the wooded terrain; and on p. 85, Wynendale is identified in a note: "an inconsiderable place in *Spanish Flanders*, adjoining to a wood, called the wood of *Wynendale*, eleven miles South-West of *Bruges*, and twenty-eight North of *Lisle*."
     Cf. below, n. to 750.18−751.2.

710.26   the poor *in spirit*] Cf. Matthew 5: 3: "Blessed are the poor in spirit: for theirs is the kingdom of heaven."

711.5   gap'd knife] *OED* cites this passage to illustrate *Gapped*: "Having the edge notched or serrated." Possibly, Sterne meant *gaped* instead, i.e., "opened" (*OED*, s.v. *Gape*).

711.15−16   What became of that story, Trim?] For a discussion of Trim's untold story, see Michael Rosenblum, "The Sermon, The King of Bohemia, and the Art of Interpolation in *Tristram Shandy*," *SP* 75 (1978): 484−87.

712.21−22   the Devil, who never lies dead in a ditch] Proverbial; Tilley, D293, and *ODEP*, s.v. *Seldom*. Cf. *Letters*, p. 181: "tho' by the bye the D[evil] is seldom found sleeping under a hedge."

713.1−2   *te Deum*] See above, n. to 55.28.

714.1   steep] *OED:* "(*jocular*) To 'wet', initiate or celebrate by a drink"; this passage is cited as sole illustration of figurative usage.

714.5   campaign-trunk] Unrecorded in *OED;* cf. 543.17 ("campaigning trunk") and 738.5 ("campaign trunk"). *OED* does note that compounds with *campaign* often had very specific reference to the "campaigns" of Marlborough.

714.7   ramallie-wig] See above, n. to 543.16.

714.8   pipes] *OED* (s.v. *pipe* 4.j.) cites this passage as its earliest example, with the definition "Small articles made of pipe-clay used for keeping the large periwigs in curl."

715.16−21   an expression of Hilarion . . . leave off kicking."] Cf. Burton, 3.2.5.1 (p. 542): "If thine horse be too lusty, *Hierome* adviseth thee to take away some of his provender, by this meanes those *Paules, Hillaries, Antonies,* and famous Anachorites subdued the lusts of the flesh, by this meanes *Hillarion made his Asse, as he called his own body, leave kicking,* (so *Hierome* relates of him in his life) when the Divell tempted him to any such foule offence." Noted by Ferriar, I: 117.

Work, p. 583, n. 1: "Saint Hilarion (291−371), who introduced the monastic system into Palestine. The incident which follows is related in St. Jerome's *Vita S. Hilarionis Eremitæ,* 3, and is mentioned in *The Anatomy* . . . ."

715.18−19   other instrumental parts of his religion] See above, n. to 159.20−21.

716.13−17   For my hobby-horse . . . a fiddle-stick] Cf. 12.7−14; Sterne carefully recalls the specific catalogue of his first description of the hobby-horse by mentioning "a maggot, a butterfly, a picture, a fiddle-stick." And by affirming that it has "scarce one hair or lineament of the ass," he recalls rather precisely the hobby-horse of Kunastrokius.

716.15   filly-folly] *OED* cites this passage as its last example, with the definition "A foolish or ridiculous notion; a foolish hobby." The relationship to the hobby-horse, based on *filly,* should be obvious.

719.15−17   I would . . . too fast] Cf. 104.2−6 and above, nn. to 103.27−104.6 and 104.4.

719.17   memory or fancy] See above, n. to 228.19−20.

719.18   these gymnicks inordinately taken] Cf. Burton's warning against sexual excess, 2.2.2 (p. 240): "others impotent, of a cold and dry constitution cannot sustaine those gymnicks without great hurt done to their owne bodies, of which number (though they be very prone to it) are melancholy men for the most part." Burton also suggests that immoderation *"consumes the spirits, and weakneth the braine."*

719.20   *nolens, volens*] "Willing or unwilling"; "whether willing or not."

720.12ff.   I wish, Yorick, said my father, etc.] Sterne is actually reading Burton, not Plato: "[Love] may be reduced to a twofold division, according to the principall parts which are affected, the Braine and Liver: *Amor & amicitia* ["love & friendship"], which *Scaliger . . . Valesius* and *Melancthon* warrant out of *Plato . . .* from that speech of *Pausanias* belike, that makes two *Veneres* and two loves. *One Venus is ancient without a mother, and descended from heaven, whom we call cœlestiall; The younger, begotten of Jupiter and Dione, whom commonly we call Venus. Ficinus* in his comment upon this place *cap.* 8. following *Plato,* calls these two loves, two Divells, or good, and bad Angels according to us . . . . *Lucian* to the same purpose hath a division of his own, *One love . . . causeth burning lust: the other is that golden chain which was let down from heaven . . . and stirres us up to comprehend the innate and incorruptible beauty, to which we were once created"* (3.1.1.2, pp. 409—10); noted by Ferriar, I: 117—18. See above, n. to 562.22—563.4, for an earlier borrowing from this section of Burton.

Sterne seems to have garbled, perhaps intentionally, Burton's reference to "Valesius" (Francisco de Vallés [1524—92], a Spanish physician), whom Burton cites again in the opening of the next member, 3.1.2.1 (p. 413): *"Valesius lib. 3. contr.* 13. defines this love which is in men, *to bee an affection of both powers, Appetite, and Reason.* The rationall resides in the Braine, the other in the Liver . . . ." The work alluded to is *Controversiarum medicarum et philosophicarum* (1564); Ficino (for whom see above, n. to 562.22—563.4) lived a century before Valesius and hence wrote no commentary upon him. Cf. Work, p. 587, n. 3.

The image of a golden chain of love, concord, harmony, extending from heaven to earth, is longstanding. It occurs in the *Iliad,* 7 (Pope trans., lines 25—26): "Let down our golden everlasting Chain, / Whose strong Embrace hold Heav'n, and Earth, and Main . . ."; and in Plato, Boethius, Chaucer, Spenser, and, of course, Milton's *Paradise Lost,* book II, lines 1004—6, 1051—52. Sterne may have consulted Lucian as well as Burton; see "In Praise of Demosthenes," 13: "And at this point, my good friend, you could wax philosophical in your discourse about the two impulses of love that come upon men, the one that of a love like the sea . . . of

Earthly Aphrodite surging with the fevered passions of youth, the other
the pull of a heavenly cord of gold that . . . impels men to the pure and
unsullied Form of absolute beauty . . ." (*Works*, VIII: 253). See also
Ludwig Edelstein, "The Golden Chain of Homer," in *Studies in Intellectual History* (Baltimore: Johns Hopkins University Press, 1953), pp.
48–67.

720.13–14 I know there were two RELIGIONS] Cf. *Sermons* ("Advantages of
Christianity"), IV.26.156–57: "tho 'tis true, the ablest men gave no credit
to the multiplicity of gods,—(for they had a religion for themselves, and
another for the populace) . . . ." The so-called "double doctrine" played
an important part in religious polemics during the eighteenth century,
most especially perhaps in the writings of Warburton; see, e.g., *The Divine Legation of Moses*, 4th ed. (1755), II: 127: "'He [i.e., Pythagoras, the
source of the doctrine, according to Warburton] divided his disciples (says
Origen) into two classes, the one he called the ESOTERIC, the other, the
EXOTERIC. For to *Those* he intrusted the most perfect and sublime doctrines; to *These*, the more vulgar and popular.' And, indeed, he was so
eminent in this practice, that the *secret* or *esoteric doctrine of* Pythagoras
became proverbial." See book III, sec. 3 (II: 114ff.), of the *Divine Legation* for a rather full discussion of the idea.

721.7–15 I think the procreation . . . which fills paradise.] Sterne neatly
combines two passages in Burton, separated by 150 pages, in order to
create his joke. In the passage cited immediately above, 3.1.1.2 (p. 410),
Ficinus is quoted as saying that although the one love is "*base*" it is to be
respected; "*for indeed both are good in their own natures: procreation of children is as necessary as that finding out of truth* . . ."; Sterne then goes to
3.2.5.3 (p. 566) to find Slop's response: "Consider the excellency of Virgins, *Virgo cœlum meruit*, marriage replenisheth the earth, but virginity
Paradise . . . ."

Work, p. 588, n. 4: "As early as 1713 an act of Parliament had offered
rewards up to £20,000 for methods of determining the longitude at sea; at
the time Sterne was writing this volume considerable sums were being
paid to John Harrison of Foulby (1693–1776) for his chronometer, for
which he eventually received the full reward." For a detailed account of
this invention see under *Projects* in the *Annual Register* (1765), pp.
113–33.

721.9−10   To be sure . . . in the world] Cf. Burton, 3.1.1.2 (p. 412): love "keepes peace on earth, quietnesse by sea . . . ."

723.22   *affects*] *OED*, s.v. *affect*, *v*¹2a, cites this passage (misdated 1760) as its last example, with the definition "To be drawn to, have affection or liking for; to take to, be fond of, show preference for; to fancy, like, or love."

724.3−4   I would lay . . . his constant wager] See 542.27: "it was either his *oath*,—his *wager*,—or his *gift*."

725.4   fourth general division] Cf. "Rabelaisian Fragment," p. 1089, lines 52−56: "HOMENAS who had to preach next Sunday . . . having foul'd two clean Sheets of his own, and being quite stuck fast in the Enterance upon his third General *Division* . . . ."

It is impossible to tell whether Sterne had a particular system of division in mind. *OED*, s.v. *Division*, II.10, defines the word in general terms: "One of the parts into which anything is or may be divided." Johnson, *Dictionary*, s.v. *Division*, 6, is more specific: "Parts into which a discourse is distributed."

726.16   'Twere better to keep . . . her fancy.] Cf. Ferrand, *Erotomania*, p. 143: "Hairines . . . is a signe of the abundance of Excrements: And for this reason, those men that are hairy, are fuller of seed, & therefore more addicted to *Venery*, than those that are smooth. . . . A woman cannot endure a man that hath but little Beard; not so much, for that they are commonly cold and impotent, as that, so much resembling Eunuches, they are for the most part inclined to basenesse, cruelty, and deceitfulnesse." This hoary idea obviously undergirds the "Fragment" in vol. V, chap. 1, as well as Walter's advice at this point.

726.21−22   Let not . . . of our ancestors.] See 218.24 and n. above.

727.3−4   For this cause . . . tongs and poker.] Cf. 226.22−23: "[Trim] is this instant boring the touch holes with the point of a hot poker." The aural pun of "poker" is obvious; whether Sterne also plays on "tongs" is not certain, but Johnson, *Dictionary*, may provide some clue to a possibly longstanding bit of bawdry in the entire phrase: "TONG. *n.*s. [see TONGS.] The catch of a buckle. This word is usually written *tongue*, but, as its office is to hold, it has probably the same original with *tongs*, and should therefore have the same orthography."

727.10   Rabelais, or Scarron, or Don Quixote] Cf. above, n. to 225.19−21.

Sterne may have borrowed from the French humorist Paul Scarron (1610–60) on at least one occasion; see above, n. to 121.11ff.

727.15–18   And if thou . . . the temper of thine.] See above, n. to 563.19–564.3. Ferrand notes at another point that "the unequall and confused beating of the Pulse" is a symptom of love, another reason, perhaps, for Walter's advice; see *Erotomania*, p. 114.

727.22–728.2   Thou must begin . . . I believe rightly.] Cf. Burton, 3.2.5.1 (p. 544, misnumbered 534): "*Amatus Lucitanus* cured a young Jew that was almost mad for love, with the syrope of Hellebor, & such other evacuations and purges, which are usually prescribed to black choller: *Avicenna* confirmes as much if need require, and *blood-letting above the rest* . . . . Those old *Scythians* had a trick to cure all appetite of burning lust, by letting themselves blood under the eares . . ."; noted by Work, p. 592, n. 3. While neither Amatus nor Avicenna makes clear how the "syrope of Hellebor" was to be applied, Sterne appropriates two passages close by in Burton to arrive at an anointing of "the part": "Ad extinguendum coitum, ungantur membra genitalia, & renes & pecten aquâ, in qua opium Thebaicum sit dissolutum . . ." ("To extinguish coitus, anoint the genitals and belly and chest with water in which opium Thebaicum has been dissolved . . ."); and "*genitalia illinita succo Hyoscyami aut cycutæ, coitus appetitum sedant* . . ." ("the genitals smeared with juice of henbane or hemlock quiets the appetite for coitus . . .").

Amatus Lusitanus is the pseudonym of João Rodriguez, de Castello Branco (1511–68), a Portuguese physician. For Avicenna, see above, n. to 337.21–25.

Rabelais covers much the same ground as Burton in his chapter "How the physician Rondibilis counselleth Panurge" (III.31.205ff.). Many of the same cooling herbs are recommended (p. 207), as well as the Scythian "cure" for excessive appetites (pp. 212–13). This is the same chapter Sterne borrowed from in the opening pages of vol. I; see 2.17–20 and n. above.

728.2–5   But thou must eat . . . and water-hens] Sterne moves to an earlier section of the *Anatomy* for this advice; see Burton, 1.2.2.1 (pp. 66–67): "*Savanarola* discommends Goats flesh, and so doth *Bruerinus* . . . calling it a filthy beast, and rammish . . . .

"*Hart, and Red Deere hath an evill name, it yeelds grosse nutriment* . . . .

Young Foales are as commonly eaten in *Spaine* as red Deere . . . ; but such meats aske long baking, or seething, to qualifie them, and yet all will not serve. . . .

"Amongst Fowle, Peacocks and Pigeons, all fenny Fowle are forbidden, as Ducks, Geese, Swannes, Hearnes, Cranes, Coots, Didappers, Waterhens . . . ."

728.6–11   As for thy drink . . . stead of them.] Cf. Burton, 3.2.5.1 (p. 543): "Those opposite meats which ought to be used, are Cowcumbers, Mellons, Purselan, water lillies, Rue, Woodbine, Amni, Lettice, which *Lemnius* so much commends . . . . Those *Athenian* women, in their solemne feasts called *Thesmopheries*, were to abstaine nine daies from the company of men, during which time, saith *Ælian*, they laid a certain hearb named *Hanea*, in their beds, which asswaged those ardent flames of love, and freed them from the torments of that violent passion."

Burton mentions verbena several times in this chapter, but not the species vervain. Either Sterne knew the two labels were often interchanged, or he perhaps considered himself to be translating from Burton's discreet Latin (p. 544, misnumbered 534): "Verbena herba gestata libidinem extinguit . . ." ("Carrying a verbena herb extinguishes lust . . ."); and "*Da verbenam in potu & non erigetur virga sex diebus* . . ." ("Give verbena in a potion and the penis will not rise for six days . . ."). On hanea, see above, n. to 563.19–564.3.

Levinus Lemnius (1505–68), a Dutch physician whose *Touchstone of Complexions* appeared in English in 1576, is often cited by Burton. Work, p. 593, n. 5: "Claudius Ælianus (fl. c. 200) was a Roman author and teacher of rhetoric; the reference is to his *De Natura Animalium*, 9.26, *via* Burton . . . ."

NOTES TO VOLUME IX

Title-page (motto)] Sterne borrows from Burton's preface to his discussion of
"love-melancholy," 3.1.1.1 (p. 407): "as *Julius Cæsar Scaliger* besought
*Cardan (Si quid urbaniusculè lusū à nobis, per deos immortales te oro Hiero-
nyme Cardane ne me malè capias)* ["Though you should prefer a somewhat
more polite amusement, by the immortal Gods, Hieronymus Cardan,
take me not badly amiss"]. I beseech thee good Reader, not to mistake me,
or misconstrue what is here written; *Per Musas & Charites, & omnia
Poetarum numina, benigne lector, oro te, ne me malè capias* ["By the Muses
and Charites, and by the grace of all the poets, gentle reader, do not take
me ill"]." Noted by Work, p. 595.

Ded.   TO A GREAT MAN.] Work, p. 597, n. 1: "In this dedication to Pitt,
to whom the opening volumes of *Shandy* had been dedicated seven years
before, Sterne gracefully alludes to the Great Commoner's absence from
office between 1761 and 1766, and to his becoming in 1766 premier, Viscount Pitt, and Earl of Chatham."

Ded. 1–3   HAVING . . . to Lord *******.] Cf. above, n. to 166.4–6.

Ded. 5   Court-latin] Unrecorded in *OED*.

734.1–2   Nothing is so perfectly . . . of ideas] Michael V. DePorte, *Nightmares and Hobbyhorses: Swift, Sterne, and Augustan Ideas of Madness* (San
Marino, Calif.: Huntington Library, 1974) pp. 137–54, provides an
interesting context for this dedication, demonstrating the eighteenth-
century conviction that diversions were useful for the treatment of mental
illness. He cites, among others, George Cheyne, *The English Malady*
(1733), p. 126: "It is upon this Account that I would earnestly recommend

to all those afflicted with *Nervous* Distempers, always to have some innocent entertaining *Amusement* to employ themselves in . . . . It seems to me
absolutely impossible, without such a Help, to keep the Mind easy, and
prevent its wearing out the Body, as the Sword does the Scabbard; it is no
matter what it is, provided it be but a *Hobby-Horse*, and an Amusement,
and stop the Current of Reflexion and intense Thinking, which Persons of
weak Nerves are aptest to run into."

734.4   Statesmen and Patriots] Cf. above, nn. to 195.5, 415.23−416.1.

734.8−15   Whose Thoughts proud Science . . . him company.] Sterne appropriates these lines from Pope's description of the "poor Indian" in
Epistle I of the *Essay on Man*, lines 99−112 (pp. 27−28):

> Lo! the poor Indian, whose untutor'd mind
> Sees God in clouds, or hears him in the wind;
> His soul proud Science never taught to stray
> Far as the solar walk, or milky way;
> Yet simple Nature to his hope has giv'n,
> Behind the cloud-topt hill, an humbler heav'n;
> Some safer world in depth of woods embrac'd,
> Some happier island in the watry waste,
> Where slaves once more their native land behold,
> No fiends torment, no Christians thirst for gold!
> To Be, contents his natural desire,
> He asks no Angel's wing, no Seraph's fire;
> But thinks, admitted to that equal sky,
> His faithful dog shall bear him company.

735.1   time and chance] Cf. Ecclesiastes 9: 11: "time and chance happeneth to
them all." Sterne uses the phrase again in *ASJ*, p. 114: "to see, what time
and chance are perpetually holding out to him . . ."; and in several sermons, most especially II.8, the text for which is the chapter and verse just
cited.

735.4−6   my mother's *curiosity* . . . would have it] Cf. 729.16−18; and
439.21−22 and n. above.

735.10−11   Nothing but . . . often spoken of] See above, n. to 709.6−7.

736.15   least mote or speck of desire] Cf. Matthew 7: 1−3: "JUDGE not, that
ye be not judged. For with what judgment ye judge, ye shall be judged

. . . . And why beholdest thou the mote that is in thy brother's eye, but considerest not the beam that is in thine own eye?"

737.2–3 And here am I sitting . . . 1766] Cf. *Letters*, p. 284 (July 23, 1766): "at present I am in my peaceful retreat, writing the ninth volume of Tristram—I shall publish but one this year, and the next I shall begin a new work of four volumes, which when finish'd, I shall continue Tristram with fresh spirit."

737.5–7 his prediction . . . that very account."] Cf. 4.10–14: "he said his heart all along foreboded . . . That I should neither think nor act like any other man's child . . . ."

Wayne Booth's argument that Sterne definitely concluded *TS* with vol. IX (despite the assertion, cited in the previous note, that he would continue) draws support from the many echoes of and allusions to vol. I in these closing pages; see "Did Sterne Complete *Tristram Shandy?*," *MP* 48 (1951): 172–83. Booth's observations have been reinforced by some additional echoes we have noted, the most important of which is the probable use of Charron's *Of Wisdome* in vol. I, chap. 1, and vol. IX, chap. 33.

737.8–13 The mistake . . . criminal.] In his edition of *TS* (Baltimore: Penguin Books, 1967), p. 657, Graham Petrie notes that the late J. C. Maxwell suggested that this paragraph is a "ludicrous but perfectly fair application of the moral theory" of William Wollaston, *The Religion of Nature Delineated* (1726): "Therefore nothing can interfere with any proposition that is true, but it must likewise interfere with nature (the nature of the relation, and the natures of the things themselves too), and consequently be *unnatural,* or *wrong in nature*" (p. 13).

738.12–14 and where a buckle . . . the dead.] Cf. *Handbook of English Costume*, p. 245: "The side curls [of wigs], whether single or multiple, were rigid hollow rolls, lying horizontally, and frequently described as 'buckles', from the French 'boucle'.

"Hence the somewhat misleading term 'a buckled wig' which meant, not that it carried a metal buckle, but was adorned with this type of rolled curl."

738.21–22 nor worth a button] Proverbial; Tilley, B782, and *ODEP*, s.v. *Button.*

739.3–4 *had not Quantity . . . to Grace*] Cf. Hogarth, *Analysis of Beauty*

(1753), p. 30: "The grandeur of the Eastern dress, which so far surpasses the European, depends as much on quantity as on costliness.

"In a word, it is quantity which adds greatness to grace."

739.14−15   had my uncle Toby . . . in armour] Cf. James Boswell, *London Journal* (New York: McGraw-Hill, 1950), p. 227: "I went to St. James's Park, and, like Sir John Brute, picked up a whore. For the first time did I engage in armour, which I found but a dull satisfaction"; and again, p. 255. See also *ASJ*, p. 156: "the young in armour bright . . . ."

739.18   at *sixes and sevens*] Proverbial; Tilley, A208, and *ODEP*, s.v. *Sixes*. The term originated in dicing.

739.22   sallied forth in the red plush.] Cf. *Spectator* 129 (II: 14): "The Smartest of the Country Squires . . . when they go a wooing . . . generally put on a red Coat." Cf. also William Wycherley, *The Plain Dealer*, II.i.570, where Novel maintains that "red Breeches, tuck'd up Hair or Perruke, a greasie broad Belt, and now adayes a short Sword" are signs of courage; and where the widow Blackacre declares to a suitor: "Marry come up, you saucy familiar *Jack!* You think with us Widows, 'tis no more than up, and ride. Gad forgive me, now adayes, every idle, young, hectoring, roaring Companion, with a pair of turn'd red Breeches, and a broad Back, thinks to carry away any Widow, of the best degree . . ." (*Plays*, ed. Arthur Friedman [Oxford: Clarendon Press, 1979], pp. 416, 423).

741.16   simplicity of his heart] Cf. 115.13−14: "Then it can be out of nothing in the whole world, quoth my uncle *Toby*, in the simplicity of his heart . . . ."

741.17   alout] Usually spelled *allout* (i.e., all out, completely), and probably obsolescent by the eighteenth century.

744.8   un-ecclesiastically] *OED* cites this passage as its first example.

745.15   sausage-shop] *OED*'s earliest example is dated 1859.

746.1−2   He was an honest . . . blood warm'd] Cf. 144.19−20: "he [i.e., Tom] was as honest a soul, added *Trim*, (pulling out his handkerchief) as ever blood warm'd."

747.1ff.   WHEN Tom, etc.] On July 21, 1766, a former slave, Ignatius Sancho, wrote to Sterne in praise of his writings and in particular of a passage in his sermon on Job (*Sermons*, II.10.98−99): "Consider how great a part of our species in all ages down to this, have been trod under the feet of cruel and capricious tyrants, who would neither hear their cries, nor pity their distresses.—Consider slavery—what it is,—how bitter a draught, and how many millions have been made to drink of it . . . ." Sancho asks him to "give half an hours attention to slavery . . . that subject handled in your own manner, would ease the Yoke of many, perhaps occasion a reformation . . ." (*Letters*, pp. 282–83).

Within the week, Sterne responded: "There is a strange coincidence, Sancho, in the little events (as well as the great ones) of this world: for I had been writing a tender tale of the sorrows of a friendless poor negro-girl, and my eyes had scarse done smarting with it, when your Letter of recommendation in behalf of so many of her brethren and sisters, came to me——but why *her brethren?*—or your's, Sancho! any more than mine? It is by the finest tints, and most insensible gradations, that nature descends from the fairest face about St James's, to the sootiest complexion in africa: at which tint of these, is it, that the ties of blood are to cease? and how many shades must we descend lower still in the scale, 'ere Mercy is to vanish with them?—but 'tis no uncommon thing, my good Sancho, for one half of the world to use the other half of it like brutes . . . .

"If I can weave the Tale I have wrote into the Work I'm ab^t—tis at the service of the afflicted . . . ." (*Letters*, pp. 285–86).

The first chapter of vol. IX locates the author in his study on "this 12th day of *August*, 1766," but it is quite probable that Sterne did not write his chapters in sequence. We do not, of course, know whether he did weave his "tender tale" into *TS*, i.e., whether what we have here is a fragment or the entire tale.

See above, n. to 402.1–4, for another indication of Sterne's attitude toward slavery.

747.9 slut] See above, n. to 589.1.

747.9–10 heart of stone] See above, n. to 578.16–17.

748.20 sportable] *OED* cites this passage as its sole illustration. Cf. *ASJ*, p. 217: "I have something within me which cannot bear the shock of the least indecent insinuation: in the sportability of chit-chat I have often endeavoured to conquer it . . . ."

See also above, n. to 63.7–8.

750.18–751.2 It was owing . . . open field.] See above, nn. to 540.3–4,

710.15–16. Tindal provides an account of the battle, but not the precise detail of the Count de la Motte's pressing "too speedily into the wood"; see IV: 84–86. The French lost between 6,000 and 7,000 men in the two-hour battle, the Allies 912, according to Tindal.

751.3–4   Why therefore . . . made in heaven?] Sterne plays on the proverb that marriages are made in heaven; see Tilley, M688, and *ODEP*, s.v. *Marriages*.

753.4–6   and there is . . . hit the mark.] Somewhere behind Trim's humor may lurk a couplet recorded by John Ray, *A Collection of English Proverbs* (Cambridge, 1678), p. 57: "He that woes a maid must fain, lie and flatter: / But he that woes a widow, must down with his breeches and at her."

753.15–17   has no object . . . of the *many*] Cf. Sterne's sermon on the character of Herod, in which he outlines a theory of the ruling passion and derives Herod's character from ambition; the conclusion of the sermon condemns war as the outcome of ambition: "Consider what havock ambition has made—how often the same tragedy has been acted upon larger theatres—where not only the innocence of childhood——or the grey hairs of the aged, have found no protection——but whole countries without distinction have been put to the sword . . ." (*Sermons*, II.9.70).

Sterne returns to the theme in the very next sermon, "Job's Account of the Shortness and Troubles of Life, considered" (II.10.97): "Consider the dreadful succession of wars in one part or other of the earth, perpetuated from one century to another with so little intermission, that mankind have scarce had time to breathe from them, since ambition first came into the world . . . ."

Sterne's italicized "*few*" and "*many*" in the present passage may be an indication that his tone regarding Toby is ironic at this point.

754.1   coat-skirt] *OED*'s first illustration is dated 1851.

754.12–16   I say . . . along with them?] On Sterne's linking of Warburton's *Divine Legation* and Swift's *Tale of a Tub*, see New, "Sterne, Warburton," pp. 273–74. The *Tale* is dedicated to "Prince Posterity."

754.17–26   I will not argue . . . upon us both!] Several biblical echoes help give this paragraph an intensity that sets it apart from the humor surrounding it. See, e.g., Psalm 78: 39: "For he remembered that they were but flesh; a wind that passeth away, and cometh not again"; Job 7: 9: "As the cloud is consumed and vanisheth away: so he that goeth down to the grave shall come up no more"; and Proverbs 31: 10: "Who can find a virtuous woman? for her price is far above rubies."

In his sermon on Job (II.10), Sterne's text is Job 14: 1–2: "Man that is born of a woman is of few days, and full of trouble. He cometh forth like a flower, and is cut down: he fleeth also as a shadow, and continueth not." Sterne comments (p. 90): "With how quick a succession, do days, months and years pass over our heads?—how truely like a shadow that departeth do they flee away insensibly, and scarce leave an impression with us?"

Cf. Sterne's letter of September 20, 1765, as he again made preparations to "fly from death" by wintering on the continent: "Few are the minutes of life, and I do not think that I have any to throw away . . ." (*Letters*, p. 257).

755.1 Now, for what . . . that ejaculation] Cf. *ASJ*, p. 290, where Yorick breaks his oath of silence in the "Case of Delicacy" by exclaiming, "O my God! . . .

"—You have broke the treaty, Monsieur, said the lady, who had no more slept than myself.—I begg'd a thousand pardons—but insisted it was no more than an ejaculation . . . ."

See also above, n. to 104.7.

757.18–20 little subacid soreness . . . other men.] Cf. above, n. to 709.6–7.

758.8–10 I wish . . . and cuvetts] Cf. 130.8–13: "but I wish the whole science of fortification, with all its inventors, at the Devil . . . . I would not, I would not, brother *Toby*, have my brains so full of saps, mines, blinds, gabions, palisadoes . . . and such trumpery, to be proprietor of *Namur* . . . ."

758.18–20 She contented herself . . . promised for her] On behalf of a child at baptism, the godfathers and godmothers promise that they will renounce, in the words of the *Book of Common Prayer*, "the devil and all his works, the vain pomp and glory of the world, with all covetous desires of the same, and the carnal desires of the flesh, so that thou wilt not follow, nor be led by them." They also promise to have the child taught the Apostles' Creed, the Lord's Prayer, and the Ten Commandments in the vulgar tongue, "and all other things which a Christian ought to know and believe to his soul's health . . . ."

759.9   Particularly the *cuvetts;* replied my father.] Insofar as *cuvettes* are
trenches, Walter is probably repeating the joke Sterne had already used in
vol. VIII (715.10–13): "I declare, corporal I had rather march up to the
very edge of a trench——
        "—A woman is quite a different thing—said the corporal.
        "—I suppose so, quoth my uncle Toby."
    We should also note, however, the possibility that Sterne is aware that
cuvette may also mean "bedpan"; suggested by Watt, p. 471, n. 1.

760.3–4   *piano. . . . fortissimè.*] See above, n. to 84.9.

760.7–12   he instantly took out . . . his pocket.] Work, p. 614, n. 3: "Although local customs varied in Sterne's day, the sacrament was usually
administered monthly, frequently on the first Sunday of each month. Here
is probably a sly reference to Mr. Shandy's habit of taking care of 'some
other little family concernments' the first Sunday night of each month"; see
6.9–26.
    Undoubtedly Work is correct, although we might note that Sterne him-
self administered the sacrament to his congregation five times a year, according to his answers on a visitation questionnaire in 1743; see *Letters,*
pp. 21–23. Curtis suggests Palm Sunday, Easter, Whitsunday, the Sunday in the octave of Michaelmas, and Christmas Day.

761.16–20   The best way . . . for other purposes, better.] Cf. "The House of
Feasting and the House of Mourning Described" (*Sermons,* I.2.28): "a
season of affliction is in some sort a season of piety—not only because our
sufferings are apt to put us in mind of our sins, but that . . . they allow us
what the hurry and bustle of the world too often deny us,—and that is a
little time for reflection, which is all that most of us want to make us wiser
and better men . . . ." Hammond, p. 124, quotes from a sermon by James
Foster as a possible source for this phrasing: "For there are too many, to
whom a time of affliction is a season of *some sort* of piety, because, then their
sufferings put them in mind of their *sins* . . . ."

762.5–10   Then by changing . . . in the next] Sterne seems to echo a portion
of the response in the catechism to the question "What is thy duty towards
thy neighbour?": "To keep my body in temperance, soberness, and chastity . . . ."

762.14–15   that sniveling virtue of Meekness] Any Christian text would
offer a contrary view of meekness, but cf. Steele's *The Christian Hero,* ed.

Rae Blanchard (1932; New York: Octagon Books, 1977), p. 51: "how necessary is that Sublime and Heroick Virtue, Meekness, a Virtue which seems the very Characteristick of a Christian, and arises from a great, not a groveling Idea of things . . . .".

In his sermon "Humility" (IV.25.116), Sterne speaks feelingly of the virtue of meekness: "'tis he who possesses his soul in meekness, and keeps it subjected to all the issues of fortune, that is the farthest out of their reach." The sermon goes on to speak of Christ as the example of humility and meekness and is perhaps the most christological of Sterne's sermons. The temptation to compare some of its observations to Walter's character is strong; e.g.: "Christianity, when rightly explained and practised, is all meekness and candour, and love and courtesy . . ." (p. 123).

763.2   gummous] *OED* cites this passage as its only recorded example of the figurative use of the word, with the definition "Of the nature of gum, gum-like."

763.4   unmetaphorical] *OED* cites this passage as its first example.

763.6   plumb-lift] Not recorded in *OED*. Sterne seems to have in mind the same definition given under *plumb, a.* and *adv.*, B.1.: "Of motion or position: Vertically, perpendicularly; straight *down;* rarely, straight *up.*"

763.7   Dutch commentator] See above, n. to 60.10.

763.16   put my topaz ring upon my finger] Considered a sexual depressant; see above, n. to 563.19–564.3.

763.21   (there is no rule without an exception)] Proverbial; Tilley, R205, and *ODEP*, s.v. *Rule.*

764.7–8   Ludovicus Sorbonensis . . . as he calls it] This seems to be Sterne's invention, apparently with a glance at the Sorbonne. The Greek means "an external matter."

764.9   soul and body . . . they get] Stout compares this passage to one in *ASJ*, pp. 68–69, as a "characteristic expression of Sterne's belief in the interaction of benevolence and physical well-being." He cites parallels in several of the sermons, e.g., VII.43.93: "in the present state we are in, we find such a strong sympathy and union between our souls and bodies, that the one cannot be touched or sensibly affected, without producing some corresponding emotion in the other." Cf. I.5.135: "a disinclination and backwardness to do good, is often attended, if not produced, by an indisposition of the animal as well as rational part of us:—So naturally do the soul and body, as in other cases so in this, mutually befriend, or prey upon each other."

Sterne had already made a similar point in *TS*, vol. III, chap. 4: "A Man's body and his mind, with the utmost reverence to both I speak it, are exactly like a jerkin, and a jerkin's lining;—rumple the one—you rumple the other" (189.18–20; cf. n. above). Tristram then goes on to deny the analogy in his own case.

OED does not record "joint-sharers," but does include similar constructions—e.g., *joint-laborers, joint-partners*, with the comment that the usage occurs "esp. in words of legal or technical use" (s.v. *Joint, a.2.*).

764.12   genteelized] *OED* cites this passage as its first illustration of a rare usage.

765.4–8   I could write . . . done with them] In vol. IV (345.6–9), Tristram promises "to write the three following favorite chapters, that is, my chapter of *chamber-maids*—my chapter of *pishes*, and my chapter of *button-holes*." In vol. V (434.7–11) he asks the reader to give him credit for the first and last: "and . . . accept of the last chapter in lieu of it; which is nothing, an't please your reverences, but a chapter of *chamber-maids, green-gowns, and old hats*."

In vol. IV (335.20–21), Tristram mentions the promise of a "chapter of knots"; see above, n. to 198.16–19.

765.11   know no more than my heels] Cf. 41.4–5 and n. above.

765.12–13   pelting kind of *thersitical* satire] Sterne alludes to the Homeric character Thersites (line 16), described in Chapman's *Iliad* (book II, lines 181ff.) as the "filthiest fellow" of all, "squint-eyd" and "crooke-backt" (*Chapman's Homer*, ed. Allardyce Nicoll, 2d. ed. [Princeton, N.J.: Princeton University Press, 1967], I: 51–52); and in the dramatis personae of Shakespeare's *Troilus and Cressida* as "*a deformed and scurrilous Greek*." His speeches are characterized by their vicious and abusive language; he is the archetypal railer and complainer.

OED's first illustration of *thersitical* is dated 1650.

765.22–766.6   To this . . . of that *Investment*.] See above, n. to 446.7–11. We have not located Sterne's source, if any, for the story of della Casa's penance. Obadiah Walker's *Of Education*, 6th ed. (1699), does have a brief account of his falling into disfavor: "the neglect of their Pens hath ruined very many; and particularly the great Master of Civility, the Author of *Galateo*. For going to present to the *Pope* a Petition by mistake he delivered a Copy of licentious Verses writ by himself: whereby he lost the *Pope*'s Favour, his own Reputation, and all Hopes of future Advancement" (p. 234); cf. p. 118: "*Nonnus, in penance* for his *Dionysiaca*, paraphras'd the Gospel of S. *John*."

"*Investment*" is an obvious play on della Casa's being a bishop, as are the several allusions to "purple," i.e., the bishop's robes.

767.2–3 "How our pleasures . . . in this world;"] The idea is, of course, a commonplace, but perhaps Sterne was looking at his first volume of *Sermons* as he wrote this section of *TS* (see above, n. to 761.16–20). The first sermon is "Inquiry after Happiness," in which he writes: "our pleasures and enjoyments slip from under us in every stage of our life. . . . there is a plain distinction to be made betwixt pleasure and happiness. For tho' there can be no happiness without pleasure—yet the converse of the proposition will not hold true.—We are so made, that from the common gratifications of our appetites, and the impressions of a thousand objects, we snatch the one, like a transient gleam, without being suffered to taste the other . . ." (I.1.21). A few pages later, in "The House of Feasting and the House of Mourning Described," he sermonizes: "So strange and unaccountable a creature is man! he is so framed, that he cannot but pursue happiness— and yet unless he is made sometimes miserable, how apt is he to mistake the way . . ." (p. 29).

769.10–11 prince, prelate, pope, or potentate] Cf. 15.1–2 and n. above: "the above dedication was made for no one Prince, Prelate, Pope, or Potentate . . . ."

769.17–18 out-do Rousseau] Although Sterne never met Jean-Jacques Rousseau (1712–78), they had several mutual acquaintances. Cross, *Life*, p. 343, suggests that at one time (1764) Sterne had planned his travel itinerary to be able to visit him in Geneva. The idea expressed is so quintessentially Rousseau that it is impossible to identify a particular source; the simple, natural life is praised in both *La Nouvelle Héloïse* (1761) and *Émile* (1762), for example. An earlier statement occurs in the *Discours sur l'origine et les fondements de l'inégalité parmi les hommes* (1755); one passage, among many, encapsulates Rousseau's view with a quotation from Locke: "On the contrary, nothing is so gentle as man in his primitive state, when, placed by nature at an equal distance from the stupidity of brutes and the

fatal enlightenment of civil man, and limited equally by instinct and reason to protecting himself from the harm that threatens him, he is re-
strained by natural pity from needlessly harming anyone himself, even if
he has been harmed. For according to the axiom of the wise Locke, *where
there is no property, there is no injury*" (*Discourse on the Origin of Inequality*,
trans. and ed. Donald A. Cress [Indianapolis: Hackett Publishing Co.,
1983], p. 144).

769.18   bar length] *OED*, s.v. *Bar*, I.2.: "A thick rod of iron or wood used in
a trial of strength, the players contending which of them could throw or
pitch it farthest; the distance thrown was measured in lengths of the bar.
Hence in obs. fig. phrases." The example given is from *Pamela* (1742);
EDD, defining *bar-length* as "a good length or way," cites *Clarissa* (1748)
and this passage.

769.20   poor piece . . . my fire in)] Cf. William King, *An Historical Account
of the Heathen Gods and Heroes* (1710; Carbondale: Southern Illinois University Press, 1965), p. 96: "The Greeks had a perpetual Fire burning to
the Honour of Vesta . . . . Numa Pompilius restor'd the ancient Ceremonies and Rites of the Goddess Vesta [in Rome] . . . and took care to
preserve a Fire which . . . was call'd Eternal, because always to continue
Burning; . . . he ordain'd her four Priestesses, who . . . were to continue
in the Service thirty Years, during which time they were to preserve their
Virginity . . . ; it was their Duty to attend the sacred Fire . . . ." See also
OCD, s.v. *Vesta*, *Vestals*.

   Cf. *ASJ*, p. 258: "they seem'd to be two upright vestal sisters, unsapp'd
by caresses, unbroke in upon by tender salutations . . . ."

772.14–19   *"L—d! I cannot . . . look at it."*] The widow Wadman here appears to run through an exercise with auxiliary verbs concerning something which, like the white bear, has not been seen. Cf. especially Walter's
penultimate question: "Is there no sin in it?" (487.16).

773.14   This requires a second translation] In the chapter "The Translation.
Paris" in *ASJ*, pp. 170–73, Sterne explores more fully the "secret so
aiding to the progress of sociality"—that of mastering "this *short hand*,
and . . . rendering the several turns of looks and limbs, with all their
inflections and delineations, into plain words."

775.1   trunk-hose] See above, n. to 218.24.

776.1–2   WE live in a world . . . and riddles] Cf. *Sermons*, III.19.118

("Felix's Behaviour towards Paul, examined"): "we live amongst mysteries and riddles, and almost every thing which comes in our way, in one
light or other, may be said to baffle our understandings . . . ." See also
350.11—19 and n. above.

776.16   Platonic exigences] Cf. Chambers, s.v. *Platonic love:* "denotes a
pure, spiritual affection, subsisting between the different sexes, abstracted
from all carnal appetites, and regarding no other object but the mind, and
its beauties . . . .

    "The world has a long time laugh'd at Plato's notions of love and friend-
ship.—In effect, they appear arrant chimera's, contrary to the intentions
of nature, and inconsistent with the great law of self-preservation . . . ."

778.4   concessible] *OED* cites this passage as its first illustration.

778.15—16   determined to play her cards herself.] Proverbial? See *ODEP*,
s.v. *Play:* "Play one's cards well = to make good use of one's resources or
opportunities."

778.19—20   playing out . . . the *ten-ace*] In whist, to have the tenace is to
possess the first and third best cards while being the last player, which
makes possible the taking of both tricks when that suit is played. Cf.
261.28—262.2 and n. above.

779.2—4   all along been hastening . . . offer to the world] Sterne recalls his
earlier language in vol. IV (400.19—401.8): "The thing I lament is . . .
that I have not been able to get into that part of my work, towards which, I
have all the way, looked forwards, with so much earnest desire; and that is
. . . the amours of my uncle *Toby* . . . . They are the choicest morsel of
my whole story!" See n. to 401.8 above.

779.8—10   It is one comfort . . . of this chapter] Cf. *Letters*, p. 294 (January
?7—9, 1767): "I miscarried of my tenth Volume by the violence of a fever,
I have just got thro'—I have however gone on to my reckoning with the
ninth, of wch I am all this week in Labour pains . . . ."

    OED records Sterne's use of "uncritical" (line 9) under the definition
"not critical; lacking in judgement; not addicted to criticism"; it seems
probable, however, that the word is here related to the crisis or turning
point of a disease, although the precise meaning of the paragraph remains
obscure.

779.11—12   serous or globular parts of the blood] See Cheyne, *The English
Malady*, pp. 81—82: "The *Blood* . . . separates into two Parts, one of a

more glutinous and solid Texture, call'd the *Globular,* and the other of a more thin and fluid Nature, called the *Serous* Part . . . ."

780.2–3   Thou who glided'st daily through his lattice] In his preface, Cervantes talks of his work as *"the Child of Disturbance, engendered in some dismal Prison, where Wretchedness keeps its Residence, and every dismal Sound its Habitation"* (I: xi). *"Prison"* is annotated: "The Author is said to have wrote this satyrical Romance in a Prison." In the account of the author prefixed to the Motteux-Ozell edition, the following sketch of Cervantes is provided: "he had been many Years a Soldier, five a Captive, and from thence had learnt to bear Afflictions patiently; that at the Battle of *Lepanto* he lost his Left Hand by the Shot of a Harquebus . . ." (I: v). In one of his last letters, written the month of his death, Sterne asked Mrs. Montagu to "tell me the reason, why Cervantes could write so fine and humourous a Satyre, in the melancholly regions of a damp prison . . ." (*Letters,* p. 416).

Near the conclusion of *Don Quixote* (II.III.45) Cervantes invokes the Sun, "by whose assistance Man begets Man, on thee I call for help! Inspire me, I beseech thee, warm and illumine my gloomy Imagination, that my Narration may keep pace with the Great *Sancho Pança'*s Actions throughout his Government; for without thy powerful Influence, I feel my self benum'd, dispirited and confus'd——Now I proceed" (IV: 90). And a few pages earlier (II.III.44) Cid Benengeli invokes poverty: "O Poverty! Poverty! . . . fatal Indigence . . . why dost thou intrude upon Gentlemen, and affect well-born Souls . . ." (IV: 83–84).

780.12   My shirts!] Yorick also travels abroad with only "half a dozen shirts and a black pair of silk breeches . . ." (*ASJ,* p. 65). Cf. 105.5–6 and n. above.

780.14–17   a cunning gypsey . . . *out* of Italy.] Sterne's visit to Italy in 1765–66 is recounted by Cross, *Life,* pp. 398–404. On November 15, 1765, he wrote from Turin, the first stop of the tour, and he seems to have remained in Italy until May (see *Letters,* pp. 263–76).

Curtis (*Letters,* p. 278, n. 3) calls attention to the fact that this paragraph repeats an anecdote which first appeared in the *St. James Chronicle* (June 14–17, 1766) at the time of Sterne's return to England: "*To the Printer of* The S.J. Chronicle. Sir, Before the celebrated Tristram Shandy returned from France, his Laundress brought home his Shirts complete in

Number, but when he came to his Lodgings in Town, and was going to dress, the Servant putting one to the air, behold both the laps were cut off. On Examination the Whole were found deficient in the same Manner. Now, Mr. Baldwin, is it not very likely that the Laundress, being far advanced in her Pregnancy, might take it in her Head, that such soft Linen would make excellent Baby-Clothes to wrap the little dear Creature in, and by this Kind of fortunate Circumstance would inherit the same Wit and Humour as that renowned Author? Your humble Servant, Risibilis" (p. 1). By specifying "*fore*-laps," Sterne sets up his own bawdy reason for the curtailment; cf. "A Panegyrick upon Cundums," in *Works of Rochester, Roscommon and Dorset* (1731), II: 225: "For now tormented sore with scalding Heat / Of Urine, dread fore-runner of a Clap! / With Eye repentant, he surveys his Shirt / Diversify'd with Spots of yellow Hue, / Sad Symptom of ten Thousand Woes to come!"

780.15 *fore*-laps] Unrecorded in *OED*.

780.18−781.16 And yet . . . at least I did] Sterne's comments here are specifically directed toward Tobias Smollett, whose record of his own European tour, *Travels through France and Italy* (1766), is a target for Sterne's wit in *ASJ* as well, where Smollett is characterized as Smelfungus: "The learned SMELFUNGUS travelled from Boulogne to Paris—from Paris to Rome—and so on—but he set out with the spleen and jaundice, and every object he pass'd by was discoloured or distorted—He wrote an account of them, but 'twas nothing but the account of his miserable feelings" (p. 116); see also pp. 117−18 and Stout's introduction, pp. 13−15, 32−38.

Smollett was a most unhappy traveler abroad, and his complaint was quite consistent: bad accommodations at outrageous prices. For example, see I: 139: "my daily expence would have amounted to about forty-seven livres . . . . I was so provoked at this extortion, that . . . I drove to another auberge, where I now am, and pay at the rate of two-and-thirty livres a day, for which I am very badly lodged, and but very indifferently entertained"; and p. 148: "they demand . . . the exorbitant price of four livres a head for every meal . . . . I insisted, however, upon paying them with three . . ."; and p. 203: "We . . . had a very indifferent dinner; after which, I sent a loui'dore to be changed, in order to pay the reckoning. The landlord . . . deducted three livres a head for dinner, and sent in the rest of the money by my servant. Provoked more at his ill manners, than at his extortion, I ferretted him out of a bed-chamber . . . and obliged him to restore the full change . . . ."

Significantly, Smollett nonetheless comes to the same conclusion about traveling as Sterne, though obviously not with the same grace: "And here, once for all, I would advise every traveller who consults his own ease and convenience, to be liberal of his money to all that sort of people; and even to wink at the imposition of aubergistes on the road, unless it be very flagrant. So sure as you enter into disputes with them, you will be put to a great deal of trouble, and fret yourself to no manner of purpose" (I: 211).

See also Sterne's letter to Ignatius Sancho, June 30, 1767: "But I am a resign'd being, Sancho, and take health and sickness as I do light and darkness, or the vicissitudes of seasons—that is, just as it pleases God to send them . . . only taking care, whatever befalls me in this silly world— not to lose my temper at it.—This I believe . . . to be the truest philoso- phy—for this we must be indebted to ourselves, but not to our fortunes" (*Letters*, p. 370).

780.19–21   at Sienna . . . time at Capua] Capua is just north of Naples, on the road to Rome; Raddicoffini (Radicofani), the site of a famous castle, is some seventy miles north of Rome. Sienna is about forty miles farther north, on the road to Florence. Sterne traveled the road from Florence to Naples and back, and is probably recalling the names from that journey; see Cross, *Life*, pp. 401–5. Edward Wright, *Some Observations Made in Travelling Through France, Italy, &c.* . . . , 2d ed. (1764), describes each place as part of his own tour; see I: 146–48, II: 374–78. Smollett, *Travels*, II: 73–74, 77, says of Sienna: "we were indifferently lodged in a house that stunk like a privy"; and of Radicofani that the inn was "very large, very cold, and uncomfortable" and "the adjacent country . . . naked and barren." He did not go to Capua.

780.20   Pauls] *OED* cites this passage as its first illustration of the translation of *paolo*, an obsolete Italian coin.

781.20   kindliest harmony vibrating within me] See 131.8–11 and n. above; and see especially *ASJ*, pp. 273–74, where Sterne again employs the image of a vibrating sensibility in relation to Maria.

781.22–24   every thing . . . sentiment or rapture.] Cf. above, n. to 333.17– 334.9.

781.27ff.   'Tis Maria, etc.] Yorick feels compelled to visit the poor Maria, whom "my friend, Mr. Shandy, met with near Moulines." See *ASJ*, pp. 268–76. For an interesting analysis of both scenes, see Paul D. Mc-Glynn, "Sterne's Maria: Madness and Sentimentality," *ECLife* 3 (1976): 39–43; of Maria, McGlynn concludes: "she is sexually attractive, unattainable, and removed from communication—and therefore thematically central to both novels" (p. 43).

In the *Monthly Review* 36 (1767): 98–99, Ralph Griffiths, who had been rather consistently hostile toward *TS*, found this encounter with Maria almost to his liking: "What a pretty, whimsical, affecting kind of episode has he introduced, in his chapter entitled INVOCATION! and which he has, with unusual propriety, begun with a very striking *invocation* to——But our Readers shall have the chapter entire, except the abrupt transition in the two last lines, which, in our opinion, serve but to *spoil all*, by an ill-tim'd stroke of levity . . . ." For the possibility that Sterne was using the incident to "advertise" *ASJ*, see Stout, p. 16, and the discussion by Rufus Putney, "The Evolution of *A Sentimental Journey*," *PQ* 19 (1940): 364–67.

783.21–23 MARIA look'd wistfully . . . alternately] Sterne develops this sequence more fully in *ASJ*, p. 168, in his description of the beautiful Grisset, who "look'd sometimes at the gloves, then side-ways to the window, then at the gloves—and then at me. I was not disposed to break silence—I follow'd her example: so I look'd at the gloves, then to the window, then at the gloves, and then at her—and so on alternately." In the meeting with Maria in *ASJ* he returns to the structure in yet another variation: "I sat down close by her; and Maria let me wipe them [her tears] away as they fell with my handkerchief.—I then steep'd it in my own—and then in hers—and then in mine—and then I wip'd hers again—and as I did it, I felt such undescribable emotions within me, as I am sure could not be accounted for from any combinations of matter and motion" (p. 271).

784.5 the wit that ever Rabelais scatter'd] Cf. 29.22–24, where Yorick is said to have had "too many temptations in life, of scattering his wit and his humour,—his gibes and his jests about him."

784.7–12 I would set up . . . to the world.] Cf. Sterne to Mrs. Montagu, ?June 1764 (*Letters*, p. 216): "Would Apollo, or the fates, or any body else, had planted me within a League of Mrs Mountague this Summer, I could have taken my horse & gone & fetch'd Wit & Wisdome as I wanted them—as for nonsense—I am pretty well provided myself both by nature & Travel."

785.9–10   the foam of Zeuxis his horse] Work, p. 632, n. 1: "Sterne is perhaps confusing Zeuxis (fl. 400 B.C.), the celebrated Greek painter, with Nealces (fl. 245 B.C.), a Greek painter who, according to Pliny (*Naturalis Historia*, 35.36 [10]), succeeded in painting the foam at a horse's mouth by throwing his sponge at the picture."

More exactly, Pliny tells the story of Protogenes, another fourth-century Greek painter, who created foam on a dog's mouth by throwing his sponge. Pliny then adds: "It is said that Nealces also following this example of his achieved a similar success in representing a horse's foam by dashing a sponge on the picture in a similar manner . . ." (*Natural History*, IX: 339). Montaigne (I.33.246) retells the story of Protogenes as an example of the whims of Fortune; and Chambers, s.v. *Chance*, also uses it as "an eminent instance of the force of *chance* . . . ." It appears to have been a commonplace illustration.

785.14–19   And here . . . Gargantua's shepherds] In Rabelais, I.25.257, the cake bakers "did injure" the shepherds "most outrageously, calling them prating gablers, lickorous gluttons, freckled bittors, mangy rascals, shite-arsed scoundrels, drunken roysters, sly knaves, drowsy loiterers, slap-sauce fellows, slabberdegullion druggels, lubbardly louts, cousening foxes, ruffian rogues, paultry customers, sycophant varlets, drawlatch hoydons, flouting milk-sops, jeering companions, staring clowns, forlorn snakes, ninny lobcocks, scurvy sneaksbies, fondling fips, base loons, saucy coxcombs, idle lusks, scoffing braggards, noddy meacocks, blockish grutnols, doddipol joltheads, jobernol goosecaps, foolish loggerheads, slutch calf-lollies, grout-head gnatsnappers, lob-dotterels, gaping changelings, codshead loobies, woodcock slangams, ninny hammer flycatchers, noddipeak simpletons, turgy gut, shitten shepherds, and other such defamatory epithets . . . ."

OED cites the present passage in *TS* for its last illustration of *doddypole* and *jolthead*.

785.18   cake-bakers] Unrecorded in *OED*.

785.23–25   All I wish is . . . *own way*."] Tristram has asked this indulgence from the beginning: "Therefore, my dear friend and companion, if you should think me somewhat sparing of my narrative on my first setting out,—bear with me,—and let me go on, and tell my story my own way . . ." (9.18−21).

787.1 Spanish proverb] Several proverbs can be suggested, but none is quite as appropriate as one might wish. Sancho Panza offers "a buen entendedor, pocas palabras" (II.III.37), which may be translated thus: "to the good listener, few words are required"; Ozell translates it more familiarly as "a Word to the wise is enough" (IV: 29).

A similar sentiment is "en boca cerrada no entran moscas," i.e., "a shut mouth catches no flies." In England it was known as a "Spanish proverb"; see Tilley, M1247, and *ODEP*, s.v. *Close*.

See also Ian Campbell's suggestion (*Tristram Shandy* [Oxford: Oxford University Press, 1983], p. 594) of a line from Calderón: "En las venturas de amor / dice más el que más calla" ("In affairs of love, the less said the better").

787.4−8 a condemnation . . . *making it.*"] Cf. *ASJ*, pp. 110−12, where Yorick condemns the French practice of "making love by *sentiments*" and comments: "I should as soon think of making a genteel suit of cloaths out of remnants . . ." (p. 111). Sterne's association of the French with "sentiment" goes as far back as vol. I, where he recommends to Madam "the pure and sentimental parts of the best *French* Romances" (57.4−5). See also his letter, ?August 23, 1765: "I myself must ever have some dulcinea in my head—it harmonises the soul . . . but I carry on my affairs quite in the French way, sentimentally—'*l'amour*' (say they) '*n'est rien sans sentiment*' . . ." (*Letters*, p. 256); the last phrase recurs in *ASJ*, p. 153.

787.7 the REAL PRESENCE] The Roman Catholic doctrine that the body and blood, soul and divinity, of Christ are really and substantially present in the Eucharist, a doctrine held to be "repugnant to the plain words of Scripture" in article 28 of the Thirty-Nine Articles.

787.9 black-pudding] American readers may need to be informed that black-pudding is a kind of sausage made of blood and suet, sometimes with the addition of meat.

787.15 sub-blushing] *OED* (s.v. *Sub-* IV.21.) cites this passage as its sole illustration.

787.24−25 They are written . . . Book.] The Solemnization of Matrimony in the *Book of Common Prayer* lists three reasons: "First, it was ordained for the procreation of children, to be brought up in the fear and nurture of the Lord, and to the praise of his holy Name. Secondly, it was ordained for a remedy against sin, and to avoid fornication, that such persons as have not the gift of continency, might marry, and keep themselves undefiled members of Christs body. Thirdly, it was ordained for the mutual society, help, and comfort, that the one ought to have of the other, both in prosperity and adversity . . . ."

788.6−7   they are certain . . . comforts?] Proverbial; Tilley, C330 ("CHILDREN are certain cares but uncertain comforts"), and *ODEP*, s.v. *Children*.

790.3   allons] "Let's go!" Cf. 577.15 and n. above.

791.4   the Corporation] The Corporation, the self-governing body of York, received ratification in 1212, and the first mayor was installed a year later (*The Victoria History of the Counties of England: The City of York*, ed. P. M. Tillott [Oxford: Oxford University Press, 1961], pp. 32−33). Its operations in the eighteenth century are amply summarized, pp. 229−40.

791.11−14   She had accordingly . . . of it.] Cf. Chambers, s.v. *Anatomy:* "In effect, Glisson treated particularly of the liver; Wharton of the glands; Havers of the bones: Graaf of the pancreatic juice, and the parts of generation . . . .

"The best systems of the art, as it now stands, are those of Verheyen, Drake, Keil, Heister, Winslow, *&c.*"

Work, p. 636, nn. 2, 3, *: "James Drake (1667−1707), physician and political writer, was author of a popular medical treatise called *Anthropologia Nova, or a New System of Anatomy*.

"Thomas Wharton (1614−1673), a noted anatomist, discussed the nature of the brain in his *Adenographia; sive Glandularum Totius Corporis Descriptio*.

"Regnier de Graaf (1641−1673), a celebrated Dutch physician, was the author of works on each of these subjects; Mrs. Wadman probably examined his *De Virorum Organis Generationi Inservientibus*."

792.16   body-surgeon] Unrecorded in *OED*.

793.5   Heaven! Earth! Sea!] Cf. above, n. to 537.17.

793.16−20   having got his wound . . . struck him] Sterne again closely echoes his earlier language, at 96.9−14: "because my uncle *Toby*'s wound was got in one of the traverses, about thirty toises from the returning angle of the trench, opposite to the salient angle of the demi-bastion of *St. Roch;*——so that he was pretty confident he could stick a pin upon the identical spot of ground where he was standing in when the stone struck him."

793.21 sensorium] See above, n. to 125.9.

794.10 critick *in keeping*] Cf. Pope, *Correspondence*, ed. George Sherburn (Oxford: Clarendon Press, 1956), I: 2: "And though such poor Writers as I, are but Beggars, however no Beggar is so poor but he can keep a Cur, and no Author is so beggarly but he can keep a Critic."

796.1 AND here is the *Maes . . . Sambre*] Cf. above, n. to 94.2—4.

796.15 And left . . . undone too] Cf. 321.16—18 and n. above.

798.1—2 IT was like . . . laugh or cry."] Sterne may have been remembering lines from *Two Gentlemen of Verona*, I.iii.84—87: "O, how this spring of love resembleth / The uncertain glory of an April day, / Which now shows all the beauty of the sun, / And by and by a cloud takes all away."

798.8 a *quart major to a terce*] In piquet, a quart-major is the sequence of ace, king, queen, and knave, while a terce is simply any three successive cards in one suit. The phrase implies considerable superiority. Cf. above, n. to 261.28—262.2.

800.22 apotheosize] *OED* cites this passage as its first example, misdated 1760 and with incorrect volume and page references.

801.10ff. Take a full sheet, etc.] Cf. Sterne's sermon on Charity (I.5.139—40): "let any number of us here imagine ourselves at this instant engaged in drawing the most perfect and amiable character, such, as according to our conceptions of the deity, we should think most acceptable to him, and most likely to be universally admired by all mankind. —I appeal to your own thoughts, whether the first idea which offered itself to most of our imaginations, would not be that of a compassionate benefactor, stretching forth his hands to raise up the helpless orphan?"

802.7—8 the Corporal wrote down the word H U M A N I T Y] Cf. *Sermons*, I.3.70—71 ("Philantropy [*sic*] Recommended"): "I think there needs no stronger argument to prove how universally and deeply the seeds of this virtue of compassion are planted in the heart of man, than in the pleasure we take in such representations of it: and though some men have represented human nature in other colours, (though to what end I know not) that the matter of fact is so strong against them, that from the general propensity to pity the unfortunate, we express that sensation by the word *humanity,* as if it was inseparable from our nature. That it is not *insepara-ble,* I have allowed in the former part of this discourse, from some re-proachful instances of selfish tempers, which seem to take part in nothing beyond themselves; yet I am perswaded and affirm 'tis still so great and noble a part of our nature, that a man must do great violence to himself, and suffer many a painful conflict, before he has brought himself to a different disposition."

Hammond, p. 161, notes similar passages in two sermons of Tillotson: "To do good, is the most pleasant employment in the world. It is natural, and whatever is so, is delightful. We do like ourselves, whenever we relieve the wants and distresses of others. And therefore this virtue, among all other, hath peculiarly entitled itself to the name of humanity"; and again: "compassion for the sufferings of others, is a virtue so proper to our nature, that it is therefore called humanity, as if it were essential to human nature . . . ."

803.13 – 14   unravellings of a spider's web] The traditional combat between spiders and the flies caught in their webs lurks behind Sterne's simile, perhaps, although the most pithy statement of the battle was not written until 1821, by Mary Howitt: "Will you walk into my parlour? said a Spider to a Fly." See also "Battle of the Books," in *Tale of a Tub,* pp. 229–30.

804.13   kitchen-fat] Unrecorded in *OED.* For "groat," see above, n. to 104.7.

804.15   FAME caught the notes] See 84.4–6 and n. above; see also 247.19, 521.6.

806.1ff.   THAT provision, etc.] Sterne borrows from two passages in Pierre Charron, *Of Wisdome,* trans. Samson Lennard (1612): "Carnell Love is a fever and furious passion, and very dangerous unto him that suffereth himselfe to be carried by it . . . . As it is naturall, so is it violent and common to all, and therefore in the action thereof it equalleth and coupleth fooles and wise men, men and beasts together. It maketh all the wisdome, resolution, contemplation & operation of the soule beastly and brut-ish. . . .

"Philosophie speaketh freely of all things, that it may the better finde out their causes, governe and judge of them . . . . all the motion of the world resolveth and yeeldeth to this copulation of the male and female: on the other side it causeth us to accuse, to hide our selves, to blush for shame, as if it were a thing ignominious and dishonest. We call it a shamefull act, and the parts that serve thereunto our shamefull parts. But why shamefull, since naturall . . . .

"This action then in itselfe, and simply taken, is neither shamefull nor vitious, since it is naturall and corporall, no more than other the like actions are: yea, if it be well ordered, it is just, profitable, necessarie, at the least, as it is to eat and drinke" (book I, chap. 22, pp. 83, 85).

"The first point and proofe of the miserie of man is his birth; his entrance into the world is shamefull, vile, base, contemptible; his departure, his death, ruine, glorious and honorable: whereby it seemeth that he is a monster and against nature, since there is shame in making him, honor in destroying him. . . . The action of planting and making man is shamefull, and all the parts thereof, the congredients, the preparations, the instruments, and whatsoever serves thereunto is called and accounted shamefull, and there is nothing more uncleane in the whole nature of man. The action of destroying and killing him honourable, and that which serves thereunto glorious: we gild it, we inrich it, we adorne our selves with it, we carrie it by our sides, in our hands, upon our shoulders. . . . When we goe about to make a man, we hide our selves, we put out the candle, we do it by stealth. It is a glorie and a pompe to unmake a man, to kill him . . . ." (book I, chap. 39, p. 138). As Françoise Pellan points out in "Laurence Sterne's Indebtedness to Charron," *MLR* 67 (1972): 752–55, Charron is here leaning heavily upon Montaigne (III.5.72, 110–11); but a comparison of the two versions clearly shows that in this instance Sterne is using the student, not the master. In addition to the passages in III.5, Charron may also be remembering a sentence in II.12: "A *Philosopher* being taken in the very Act, and asked what he was doing, coldly reply'd, *I am planting Man;* no more blushing to be so caught, than if they had found him planting Garlick" (p. 297).

806.13   *Prolepsis*] *OED* cites this passage as its last example. Chambers, s.v. *Prolepsis:* "a figure in rhetoric, by which we anticipate, or prevent what might be objected by the adversary."

Cf. 171.13–15 and n. above.

806.15–16   Why then . . . against it?] No similar passage occurs in *Of*

Wisdome, although a few pages before Sterne's first borrowing Charron links Plato and Diogenes in their attitude toward ambition: "And to say the trueth, there is greater glory in refusing and trampling glory under foot, than in the desire and fruition thereof, as *Plato* told *Diogenes*" (I.20, p. 79). Plato is a natural enough choice, however, as a proponent of the sentiment expressed; for example, in the essay upon which Charron's comments are based, Montaigne quotes him: "The *Gods,* says *Plato,* have given us one disobedient and unruly Member, that like a furious Animal attempts by the violence of its Appetite, to subject all things to it" (III.5.87). Similar sentiments abound in Plato's writings.

Diogenes (see above, n. to 87.6–9) is a less likely choice, although several of his recorded comments might have served Walter's purpose; e.g.: "bad men obey their lusts as servants obey their masters." But perhaps Diogenes on marriage is most apropos at this point: "Being asked what was the right time to marry, Diogenes replied, 'For a young man not yet: for an old man never at all'." See Diogenes Laertius, *Lives of Eminent Philosophers,* VI.66, 54 (II: 69, 55).

Cf. Rabelais, III.31.210: "Diogenes . . . defined lechery, the occupation of folks destitute of all other occupation." Sterne quotes from this chapter at 2.17–20 (see n. above); see also n. to 727.22–728.2.

806.16   recalcitrate] *OED* cites this passage as its first illustration of the definition "to show strong objection or repugnance."

806.19   congredients] *OED:* "A component part, ingredient"; this passage is cited as sole illustration, but Sterne, as noted above, is borrowing from Samuel Lennard's translation of Charron (1612).

807.12–13   My father . . . great tythes] The "great tythes" were the church revenues derived from major produce of the soil—corn, hay, wood, and fruit. An impropriator was a layman in possession of those revenues; Sterne suggests that such possession entailed certain obligations, such as the keeping of the town-bull.

807.15   *pop-visit*] *OED* cites this passage as its first illustration, with the definition "A short, hasty, or unannounced visit, in which one 'pops in'."

808.17   It is as hairy as I am] Charles Parish, "The Shandy Bull Vindicated," *MLQ* 31 (1970): 48–52, argues that this sentence convinces Walter that Obadiah's child was sired by the bull and hence that the bull can be cleared of the charge of impotence. The implication of bestiality is tied to a similar suggestion in vol. V, chap. 3, where Obadiah is accused of siring a mule; it is reinforced by the allusion to Europa, who was carried away by Zeus after he had taken the form of a bull.

The argument is based, however, on Parish's primary assumption that the child's hairiness is a sign that it was not born early, when in fact hairiness is more often associated with pre-term birth—i.e., the lanugo covering which comes in the fifth month and usually disappears by the ninth. Walter's response, then, may only indicate his relief that Obadiah's wife had indeed "come before her time" and that the bull might yet prove potent.

808.23–25 driven into Doctors Commons . . . his life] Doctors' Commons was the name given to that area near St. Paul's where ecclesiastical courts heard various civil cases, including divorces. Sterne may be playing on the proverb "He that has lost his credit is dead to the world"; see Tilley, C817, and *ODEP*, s.v. *Lost*.

Tilley, B716, and *ODEP*, s.v. *Town*, make the point that the word *town-bull* was used figuratively for "a man" from the seventeenth century on; see also Partridge, s.v. *town-bull* (i.e., "a wencher").

809.2 A COCK and a BULL] Tilley, S910, and *ODEP*, s.v. *cock-and-bull story*, both record the phrase and cite several seventeenth-century examples, including Burton. *OED* suggests a parallel to the French *coq-à-l'âne* ("a cock on an ass") and offers several definitions, e.g.: "a long rambling, idle story"; "tedious, disconnected, or misleading talk"; and "an idle, concocted, incredible story." Cf. Booth, "Did Sterne Complete *Tristram Shandy?*," p. 181: "it was common for earlier facetious writers to call their entire books 'cock-and-bull stories' (in French, *coq-à-l'âne*). Sterne, who knew many of these works well, can hardly have failed to intend this meaning for the phrase when he wrote that final line." See also Mary Claire Randolph, "The French *Coq-à-l'âne* as a Satiric Form," *N&Q* 181 (1941): 100–102. A parallel is also often suggested to the phrase "tale of a tub."

It seems a particularly characteristic gesture that Sterne would end his work with a bawdy revivification of a proverbial expression.

APPENDIX

Glossary of Terms of Fortification

A similar glossary appears as app. 2 in Watt's edition, pp. 505–7. His explanation of eighteenth-century warfare in app. 1, pp. 499–503, is also useful, especially his effort to mark the exact spot upon which Toby was wounded. Equally useful for its clear exposition of a most complicated subject is David Chandler's *The Art of Warfare in the Age of Marlborough* (New York: Hippocrene Books, 1976); of particular interest are his estimates of casualties for the major battles and sieges between 1688 and 1745 (apps. 2, 3).

Generally the definitions are quoted directly from Chambers; in two instances we have had recourse to John Muller, *A Treatise Containing the Elementary Part of Fortification* (1746). The plate is from Chambers.

BANQUETTE "A little foot-bank, or elevation of earth forming a path which runs along the inside of a parapet; by which the musqueteers get up, to discover the counterscarp, or to fire on the enemies in the moat, or in the covert-way.

"The *banquette* is generally a foot and half high, and almost three foot broad; having two or three steps to mount it by."

BASTION "A huge massive of earth usually faced with sods, sometimes with brick, rarely with stone, standing out from a rampart, whereof it is a principal part.

"A *bastion* consists of two faces and two flanks. . . .

"The union of the two faces makes the outmost or saliant angle, called also the *angle of the bastion*. . . ." See plate, figures o and p.

BLINDS "Defences usually made of oziers, or branches interwoven and laid across, between two rows of stakes about the height of a man, and four or

553

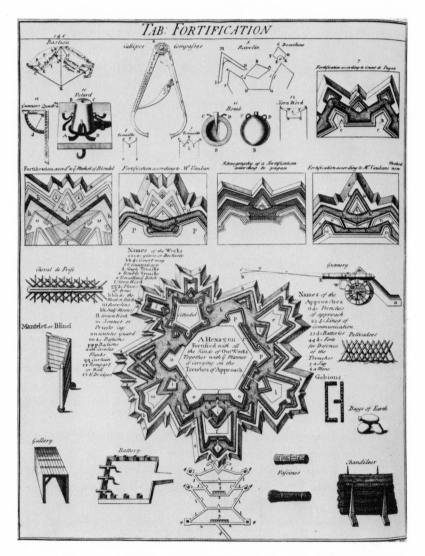

PLATE III

five foot apart; used particularly at the heads of trenches, when they are extended in front towards the glacis; serving to shelter the workmen, and prevent their being overlooked by the enemy." See plate for illustration (figure 17).

BREASTWORKS See PARAPET.

CIRCUMVALLATION "A line or trench, with a parapet, thrown up by the besiegers, encompassing all their camp, to defend it against any army that may attempt to relieve the place.

"This line is to be cannon-shot distant from the place . . . ."

COUNTERGUARD (s.v. *Envelope* in Chambers) "A mount of earth, sometimes raised in the ditch of a place, and sometimes beyond it; being either in form of a simple parapet, or of a small rampart bordered with a parapet.

"These *envelopes* are made, where weak places are only to be covered with single lines; without advancing towards the field . . . ."

COUNTERSCARP "The exterior slope, or acclivity of the ditch, looking towards the campaign.

"COUNTER-SCARP is also used for the covert-way, and the glacis.

"*To be lodged on the counter-scarp,* is to be lodged on the covert-way, or the glacis."

COVERED WAY (s.v. *Covert Way* in Chambers) "A space of ground level with the adjoining country, on the edge of the ditch, ranging quite round the half-moons, and other works without-side the ditch. . . .

"One of the greatest difficulties in a siege, is to make a lodgment on the *covert way;* because, usually, the besieged pallisade it along the middle, and undermine it on all sides." See plate, figure b.

CROSS BATTERIES (s.v. *Battery* in Chambers) "Two batteries at a considerable distance from each other, which play a-thwart one another at the same time, and upon the same point, forming right angles . . . ."

CURTIN "That part of a wall, or rampart, which is between two bastions; or which joins the flanks thereof. . . .

"The *curtin* is usually bordered with a parapet five foot high; behind which the soldiers stand to fire upon the covert way, and into the moat." See plate, figure q. See also above, n. to 128.14–24.

CUVETTE (s.v. *Cunette* in Chambers) "A deep trench, about three or four fathom wide, sunk along the middle of a dry moat, to lade out the water; or to make the passage more difficult to the enemy."

DEMI-BASTION "A kind of fortification, that has only one face, and one flank."

DEMI-CULVERIN "A piece of ordnance commonly 4½ inches bore, 10 foot long, 2700 pound weight; its charge is 7 pound 4 ounces of powder; and it carries a shot of 10 pounds 11 ounces; and shoots point blank 175 paces."

DITCH "Called also *Foss*, and *Moat*, a trench dug round the rampart, or wall of a fortified place, between the scarp, and counterscarp.

"Some *Ditches* are dry; others full of water: each whereof have their advantages." See plate, figure h.

DOUBLE TENAILLE See TENAILLE.

EPAULEMENT "A side-work hastily thrown up, to cover the cannon, or the men.

"It is made either of earth thrown up, of bags filled with sand or earth, or of gabions, fascines, *&c.* with earth . . . .

"EPAULEMENT, is also used for a demi-bastion . . . placed at the point of a horn or crown-work."

ESPLANADE See GLACIS.

FACE "FACES *of a bastion,* are the two foremost sides, reaching from the flanks to the point of the bastion, where they meet. . . .

"FACE *of a place,* denotes the interval between the points of two neighbouring bastions, containing the curtain, the two flanks, and the two *Faces* of the bastions that looked towards one another.

"This is otherwise called the *tenaille* of the place."

FAUSSE-BRAYE "An elevation of earth, two or three fathoms broad, round the foot of the rampart on the outside, defended by a parapet which parts it from the berme [i.e., the space between the ditch and the base of the parapet], and the edge of the ditch: its use is for the defence of the ditch. . . .

"It is of little use where ramparts are faced with wall, because of the rubbish which the cannon beats down into it. For this reason, engineers will have none before the faces of the bastions . . . ."

FLANK "A line, drawn from the extremity of the face, towards the inside of the work. . . .

"Or, *Flank* is that part of the bastion, which reaches from the curtin to the face, and defends the opposite face, the *Flank*, and the curtin."

FOSS(E) "A ditch, or moat."

GABIONS "Large baskets, made of osier twigs, woven of a cylindrical form, six foot high, and four wide; which being filled with earth, serve as a defence, or shelter from the enemy's fire." See plate for illustration.

GAZONS "Turfs, or pieces of fresh earth covered with grass, cut in form of a wedge, about a foot long, and half a foot thick: to line or face the outside of works made of earth, in order to keep up the same, and prevent their mouldering."

GLACIS The slope or declivity of the counterscarp; "being a sloping bank which reaches from the parapet of the counterscarp, or covert-way, to the level side of the field." See plate, figure a. Also called ESPLANADE.

GORGE "The entrance of a bastion; or of a ravelin, or other out-work . . . .

"The GORGE *of a bastion*, is what remains of the sides of the polygon of a place, after retrenching the curtins: in which case it makes an angle in the centre of the bastion. . . .

"GORGE *of a half moon*, or *ravelin*, is the space between the two ends of their faces next the place."

HALF-MOON "An outwork, consisting of two faces, forming together a salient angle, whose gorge is turned like an *half moon*. . . .

"*Half moons* are sometimes raised before the curtin, when the ditch is wider than it ought to be; in which case it is much the same with a ravelin; only that the gorge of an *half-moon* is made bending in like a bow, or crescent, and is chiefly used to cover the point of the bastion; whereas ravelins are always placed before the curtin.—But they are both defective, as being ill flanked." See plate, figures 5 (top) and k. See also above, n. to 128.26–129.14.

HORN-WORK "A sort of out-work, advancing toward the field, to cover and defend a curtin, bastion, or other place suspected to be weaker than the rest . . . .

"It consists of two demi-bastions . . . joined by a curtin." See plate, figures 9 and f.

ICHNOGRAPHY "The plan or representation of the length and breadth of a fortress, the distinct parts of which are marked out, either on the ground itself, or upon paper."

INVESTING "The opening a siege, and the incamping of an army round the place, to block up its avenues, and prevent all ingress and egress. . . . It is the cavalry that always begins to *invest* a place."

LODGMENT "A work cast up by the besiegers, during their approaches, in some dangerous post, which they have gained, and where it is absolutely necessary to secure themselves against the enemies fire; as in a covert-way, in a breach, the bottom of a moat, or any other part gained from the besieged.

"*Lodgments* are made by casting up earth, or by gabions, or palisades, . . . mantelets, or any thing capable of covering soldiers in the place they have gained, and are determined to keep."

MANTELET See BLINDS.

MINE "A subterraneous canal, or passage dug under the wall, or rampart of a fortification, intended to be blown up by gun-powder."

MOLE "A massive work formed of large stones laid in the sea by means of coffer-dams, extended either in a right line or an arch of a circle, before a port; which it serves to close; to defend the vessels in it from the impetuosity of the waves, and prevent the passage of ships without leave."

ORGUES "Thick long pieces of wood pointed and shod with iron, and hung each by a separate rope over the gateway of a city, ready on any surprize or attempt of the enemy to be let down to stop up the gate." See above, n. to 538.7–9.

OUT-WORKS "All those works made without side the ditch of a fortified place, to cover and defend it. . . .

"*Outworks*, called also *advanced* and *detached works*, are those which not only serve to cover the body of the place, but also to keep the enemy at a distance, and prevent his taking advantage of the cavities and elevations usually found in the places about the counterscarp . . . . Such are, ravelins, tenailles, hornworks . . . ."

OUVRAGE DE CORNE See HORN-WORK.

PADERERO (s.v. *Pedrero* in Chambers) "A small piece of ordnance, used on board ships for the discharging of nails, broken iron, or partridge shot on an enemy attempting to board."

PALISADO (s.v. *Palisade* in Chambers) "An inclosure of stakes, or piles driven into the ground, six or seven inches square, and eight foot long; three whereof are hid under ground. . . .

"*Palisades* are used to fortify the avenues of open forts, gorges, half-moons, the bottoms of ditches, the parapets of covert-ways; and in general all posts liable to surprize, and to which the access is easy. . . ." See plate.

PARALLELS   "Deep trenches 15 or 18 feet wide, joining the several attacks together; they serve to place the guard of the trenches in, to be at hand to support the workmen when attacked. There are generally three in an attack; the first is about 300 toises from the covert-way, the second 160, and the third near or on the glacis . . ." (Muller, pp. 227–28).

PARAPET   "A defence or skreen, on the extreme of a rampart, or other work, serving to cover the soldiers, and the cannon from the enemy's fire. . . .

"*Parapets* are raised on all works, where it is necessary to cover the men from the enemy's fire; both within and without the place, and even the approaches. . . .

"The *Parapet* of the wall is sometimes of stone.—The *Parapet* of the trenches is either made of the earth dug up; or of gabions, fascines, barrels, sacks of earth, or the like."

PETARD   "A brass pot fixed upon a strong square plank, which has an iron hook to fix it against a gate or palissades; this pot is filled with powder, which when fired, breaks every thing about it, and thereby makes an opening for an enemy to enter the place" (Muller, p. 228).

PLACE   "A general name for all kinds of fortresses, where a party may defend themselves."

PORTCULLICE   "An assemblage of several great pieces of wood laid or joined across one another, like an harrow; and each pointed at the bottom with iron. . . .

"These formerly used to be hung over the gate-ways of fortified places, to be ready to let down in case of a surprize, when the enemy should come so quick, as not to allow time to shut the gates.

"But now-a-days, the orgues are more generally used, as being found to answer the purpose better."

RAMPART   "A massy bank, or elevation of earth raised about the body of a place, to cover it from the great shot; and formed into bastions, curtins, &c." See plate, figure r.

RAVELIN   "A detached work, composed only of two faces, which make a salient angle, without any flanks; and raised before the curtin on the counterscarp of the place. . . .

"It's use before a curtin, is to cover the opposite flanks of the two next bastions. It is used also to cover a bridge or a gate; and is always placed without the moat.

"What the engineers call a *ravelin*, the soldiers generally call a *demi-lune*, or half-moon." See plate, figures 5 (top) and i.

REDANS (s.v. *Redens* in Chambers) "A kind of work indented in form of the teeth of a saw, with saliant and re-entering angles; to the end that one part may flank or defend another."

REDOUBT "A small square fort, without any defence but in front; used in trenches, lines of circumvallation, contravallation, and approach; as also for the lodging of corps de garde, and to defend passages." See plate, figure 4 (bottom).

RETURNING ANGLE (s.v. *Angle, Re-entering* in Chambers) "That whose vertex is turned inwards, towards the place."

SALIENT ANGLE (s.v. *Angle, Saillant* in Chambers) "That which advances its point toward the field."

SAP "A work carried on under ground, to gain the descent of a ditch, counterscarp, or the like." See plate, figure 5 (bottom).

SCARP "The interior slope of the ditch of a place; that is, the slope of that side of a ditch which is next to the place, and faces the campaign."

SODS See GAZONS.

TALUS "The slope or diminution allowed to [a bastion or rampart]; whether it be of earth, or stone; the better to support its weight. . . .

"The *exterior Talus* of a work, is its slope on the side towards the country . . . . The *interior Talus* of a work, is its slope on the inside, towards the place."

TENAILLE "A kind of out-work, consisting of two parallel sides, with a front, wherein is a re-entering angle. . . .

"In strictness, that angle, and the faces which compose it, are the *tenaille*. . . .

"*Double, or flanked* TENAILLE, is a large out-work consisting of two simple *tenailles*, or three salians, and two re-entering angles . . . ." See plate, figures 8, 9, e.

TERRACE (or Terras) "An earth-work usually lined, and breasted with a strong wall, in compliance with the natural inequality of the ground."

TOISE "A French measure, containing six of their feet, or a fathom."

TRAVERSE "A trench with a little parapet, sometimes two, one on each side, to serve as a cover from the enemy that might come in flank."

SELECTIVE INDEX OF
AUTHORS CITED IN THE NOTES

561